THE COMPLETE
HAMMER'S
SLAMMERS
Volume 2

Baen Books by David Drake

The RCN Series
With the Lightnings
Lt. Leary, Commanding
The Far Side of the Stars
The Way to Glory
Some Golden Harbor
When the Tide Rises
In the Stormy Red Sky

Hammer's Slammers
The Tank Lords
Caught in the Crossfire
The Butcher's Bill
The Sharp End
Paying the Piper
The Complete Hammer's
Slammers, Volume 1

Independent Novels
and Collections
The Reaches Trilogy
Seas of Venus
Foreign Legions, ed. by David
Drake
Ranks of Bronze
Cross the Stars
The Dragon Lord
Birds of Prey
Northworld Trilogy
Redliners
Starliner
All the Way to the Gallows
Grimmer Than Hell
Other Times Than Peace
Patriots

The Undesired Princess and The
Enchanted Bunny
(with L. Sprague de Camp)
Lest Darkness Fall and To Bring
the Light
(with L. Sprague de Camp)

The General Series
Warlord with S.M. Stirling
(omnibus)
Conqueror with S.M. Stirling
(omnibus)
The Chosen with S.M. Stirling
The Reformer with S.M. Stirling
The Tyrant with Eric Flint

The Belisarius Series
with Eric Flint
An Oblique Approach
In the Heart of Darkness
Belisarius I: Thunder at
Dawn (omnibus)
Destiny's Shield
Fortune's Stroke
Belisarius II: Storm at Noontide
(omnibus)
The Tide of Victory
The Dance of Time
Belisarius III: The Flames of
Sunset (omnibus)

Edited by David Drake
The World Turned Upside Down
(with Jim Baen & Eric Flint)

THE COMPLETE
HAMMER'S SLAMMERS
Volume 2

DAVID DRAKE

THE COMPLETE HAMMER'S SLAMMERS, VOL. 2

Copyright © 2009 by David Drake

"Introduction" © 2006 by David G. Hartwell

At Any Price © 1985 by David Drake
Counting the Cost © 1987 by David Drake
Rolling Hot © 1989 by David Drake
The Warrior © 1991 by David Drake
"The Day of Glory" © 2006 by David Drake
"We Happy Few" © 1997 by David Drake
"What's for Sale" © 2006 by David Drake

A Baen Book

Baen Publishing Enterprises
P.O. Box 1403
Riverdale, NY 10471
www.baen.com

ISBN: 978-1-4391-3334-7

Cover art by Kurt Miller

First Baen printing, February 2010

Distributed by Simon & Schuster
1230 Avenue of the Americas
New York, NY 10020

Library of Congress Cataloging-in-Publication Data: t/k

Printed in the United States of America

10 9 8 7 6 5 4 3 2 1

CONTENTS

**INTRODUCTION: IN DEFENSE OF DAVID DRAKE'S
HAMMER'S SLAMMERS STORIES:
BY DAVID G. HARTWELL** 1

**FOREWORD: WE HAPPY FEW
BY DAVID DRAKE** 7

AT ANY PRICE 13

COUNTING THE COST 151

ROLLING HOT 319

THE WARRIOR 527

THE DAY OF GLORY 669

AFTERWORD: WHAT'S FOR SALE 699

IN DEFENSE OF DAVID DRAKE'S HAMMER'S SLAMMERS STORIES:

AN INTRODUCTION BY DAVID G. HARTWELL

Any fiction that portrays war in SF, since the 1960s, has generally been eliminated from the leading ranks unless it is entirely dedicated to the proposition that war is, in Isaac Asimov's phrase, the last refuge of the incompetent. All military SF became suspect in the 1970s, and most of it was rejected by major portions of the serious readers of literate SF, as advocating war. This was evident at Robert A. Heinlein's famous guest of honor speech at MidAmericon in Kansas City in 1976, at which he was publicly booed for stating that war was a constant in world history, and that there was every indication that there would continue to be war in the future. At least since that time, much of the literary SF community has unfortunately failed to distinguish portrayal of war from advocacy of war, or to be interested in examining military SF. The literary community even tends to avoid the authors at convention parties. The only leading writer to overcome this has been Joe Haldeman, author of *The Forever War*, and a majority of his fiction since has not been military SF. And so those authors hang out with their own crew, usually the Baen crew, mostly at conventions in the midwestern and southeastern US, where they are not so easily marginalized.

David Drake was a well-known young horror writer and fan, who published both fantasy and SF in the magazines in the mid-1970s. I knew David fairly well then. He was a young attorney who had served in Vietnam. He was most prominent in horror circles. He was on the editorial board of Stuart David Schiff's distinguished small press horror magazine, *Whispers,* and co-proprietor, with Karl Edward Wagner and Jim Groce, of Carcosa, a leading small press founded to publish the works of Manly Wade Wellman, who was a mentor to both Wagner and Drake. He was on the first Young Writers panel at the first World Fantasy Convention in 1975. He got a great literary agent, Kirby McCauley, who gathered all the best in the horror field in the 1970s under his aegis. And he soon had a contract to write his first novel, *The Dragon Lord*, a gritty, realistic Arthurian fantasy.

Jim Baen was editing *Galaxy* in those days, struggling heroically to keep it alive, and one of the writers whose SF he was publishing was David Drake. But no matter how nobly Baen strove to keep it alive—and he was widely admired throughout the SF community for his efforts—the magazine was failing and, just before it died, Baen moved to Ace Books, under publisher Tom Doherty. Baen was and is a smart editor, and was used to making bricks without straw, and silk purses out of a variety of materials on a low budget.

I was the SF editor for Berkley Books and bought the Drake novel. But my superiors at Berkley couldn't imagine doing a short story collection by a not-yet-published first novelist, so I was not allowed to offer to buy Drake's *Hammer's Slammers*. Jim Baen bought it immediately, and published it quickly and successfully. The rest, as they say, is history. The Hammer's Slammers stories became Drake's trademark, for better or worse. And when Jim Baen moved to Tor and then founded Baen Books, David Drake became one of his trademark writers, so much so that in 1984 when Bruce Sterling, in the course of founding the cyberpunk movement in his fanzine *Cheap Truth*, attacked Baen Books, he named David Drake, Jerry Pournelle, and Vernor Vinge as symbols of Baen, and of the military/militarist right wing. At that point Drake's fiction fell out of the serious discourse in the SF and fantasy field, with very little questioning of the accuracy or merits of Sterling's attacks, or the virtues of Drake's writing. It was military and that was enough.

A loyal friend, Drake has remained a mainstay of Baen Books to this day, and stayed with Kirby McCauley, his agent through thick and thin. I am fortunate to be the editor of his fantasy series, *Lord of the Isles*, and doubly so because since I have a doctorate in medieval literature, and since David reads classical Latin writers for pleasure, I can enjoy many of the references and allusions to classical sources. Not all, I hasten to add, but it keeps me on my toes and I like that.

But this is an introduction to a volume of Hammer's Slammers stories, and so I'd like to mention a few things that might not be immediately obvious. Certainly Drake uses both his detailed knowledge of military history and his own experiences and observation from his service in Vietnam to construct what is probably the most authentic military SF fiction of this era. But it appears to me that he is often doing a great deal more and that his fiction can yield up some surprising additional benefits.

For instance, his early story,"Ranks of Bronze,"and the later novel of that title, adapts a real historical event(a lost legion of Roman soldiers, Crassus' mercenaries—see Drake's afterword to the novel) and translates it into SF. A Roman legion is snatched from Earth into space to be used as mercenaries owned and operated by superior aliens out for profit, to fight relatively low-cost, low-technology wars on alien planets against alien races, with whom they have no personal quarrel, and perhaps only dimly comprehend. No one in the legion has any choice in this. The soldiers behave in a convincingly plausible way, the way Roman soldiers would. They are a very effective fighting force and can most often win. They are moved without notice from one planet to another, fight (sometimes die). They are wretched.

This is military SF with the contemporary politics stripped off, and removed from the level of policy decisions. The soldiers go to a place. They are told who to fight. They win or die. They go to the next place. This is, it seems to me, the true experience of the ordinary fighting man or woman in a military organization throughout history, who has very limited choice. Various individuals manifest good or bad behavior, sanity or craziness, cleverness or stupidity. And luck matters. No one has the big picture, which may be known when the fighting is over and may not. The ones who do the job best tend to survive and perhaps rise in the ranks. Some of them are bad and or crazy, but not stupid, which leads to death. There is very little moral choice possible, but the characters we tend to admire are those who are sane, careful, and make moral choices as they can. And try to live with them afterward. There is no access to those who make policy in Drake's military fiction. All in all it is a fairly dark vision of human life.

By using SF as a distancing device, and by further using classical mercenaries as soldier characters, Drake constructs a fictional space in which he can investigate and portray certain kinds of human behavior, heroism, loyalty, cowardice, the strategic working out of detailed military actions and the impact on them of individuals behaving well or not, of high and low technology for killing functioning properly or not. And he can do this with something analogous to clinical detachment as the killing commences, without advocating policy.

No one who reads Drake properly can imagine him advocating war. War exists and Drake chooses or is compelled to portray it as it is, and has been, and might be close up. This military SF is not military pornography but rather a form of horror fiction (see "The Interrogation Team," for instance). It is not intended to deaden the sensibilities to the horrors of war, but to awaken them. Like Ambrose Bierce's "Chickamauga." Like Stephen Crane's "The Red Badge of Courage." Or sometimes like Tolstoy's descriptions of the advance of Napoleon's armies on Moscow in *War and Peace*. Historical parallels abound in Drake's stories, but distanced into space and the future. This is the same David Drake as the horror writer, not a different person.

There is immense sympathy for the character who has done repulsive things in battle to win, and finds it difficult to live with himself afterward. There is much evidence in Drake's personal afterwords to his books that he identifies with that position and that it relates to his own military experience (see, for instance, his essay

"How They Got That Way"). That is how we most often return to experience the horror, through personal connection with character, after our detachment has been required by all the distancing devices. If you remain detached, you are not getting it, or rather by saying to yourself, in effect undisturbed, "yes, this is the way war is," you are denying any broader literary meaning. This is the paradox of Drake's military fictions.

All of the above is evident in his early stories and in *Ranks of Bronze*, and many other novels. It is the essence of the Hammer's Slammers stories. I'd like to talk about a particular story now to extend the point about broader literary meaning.

Drake's novella, "The Warrior," is superficially about tank warfare, and about the contrast between the attitudes and behaviors of two commanders of tanks in the Slammers, Sergeant Samuel "Slick" Des Grieux and Sergeant Lucas Broglie, during two military operations nearly ten years apart. Reduced perhaps to oversimplification, Des Grieux is a warrior and Broglie is a soldier; Broglie is sane and Slick is not. They hate each other immediately. Slick Des Grieux is the central character, and his battles are observed in close detail. His tanks are both vehicles and war machines, intelligently extrapolated from the impressive and powerful tanks of today. They are big, fascinating machines, like spaceships are, and are central to the SF appeal. The story is set on two distant planets, the battles are against two different enemies, who are relatively faceless and unimportant. But the enemies have hired competent mercenary armies to defend them against the Slammers, and for the climax, Broglie is hired by a company that ends up opposed to the Slammers. And so in the end it is Broglie against Des Grieux.

This is the story of the madness of Achilles, which is horrific. It is David Drake's *Iliad* (particularly books XIX-XXIV). It is also Drake's criticism of *The Iliad*, achieved by removing the control of the gods, and the behavior to a different, and psychologically realistic, situation. While literature, as Matthew Arnold said, is the criticism of life, it is also sometimes quite acutely the criticism of other literature, in dialogue with other works. This is one of the central traditions of genre literature, a conversation among texts, but it is somewhat rarer in genre to find that conversation extending to the classics (by which I mean classical literature, not genre classics). There is probably a good master's degree essay, if not a doctoral dissertation, to be done on the classical influences on the Hammer's Slammers stories.

I think I will stop now. This is an introduction intended to compliment Drake fans and to give access to readers who are not already Drake readers, perhaps even to readers who have previously decided, without reading any, that there are no Drake stories worth their attention. Think again. Consider some of the things I have said. Now it is time to read, or reread, some stories.

David G. Hartwell
Pleasantville, NY
April 2005

FOREWORD: WE HAPPY FEW

> We few, we happy few, we band of brothers;
> For he today that sheds his blood with me
> Shall be my brother; be he ne'er so vile,
> This day shall gentle his condition.
> And gentlemen in England now abed
> Shall think themselves accursed they were not here,
> And hold their manhoods cheap whiles any speaks
> That fought with us upon Saint Crispin's day.
>
> —Shakespeare

I wouldn't have—and couldn't have—written these stories without being a Nam vet. Because of that and because I'm sometimes accused of believing things that I certainly don't believe, I've decided to state clearly what I think about Viet Nam and about war in general. I don't insist that I'm right, but this is where I stand.

The speech Shakespeare creates for Henry V to deliver on the morning of Agincourt (the Speech on St. Crispin's Day) is one of his most moving and effective. The degree to which the sentiments therein are true in any absolute sense, though—that's another matter.

My own suspicion is that most soldiers (and maybe the real Henry among them, a soldier to the core) would have agreed with the opinion put in the mouth of the Earl of Warwick earlier in the scene. Warwick, noting the odds were six to one against them, wishes that a few of the men having a holiday in England were here with the army in France. One of the leader's jobs is to encourage his troops, though. If Henry'd had a good enough speechwriter, he might have said exactly what Shakespeare claims he did.

A soldier in a combat unit may see the world, but he or she isn't likely to "meet exotic people" in the sense implied by the recruiting posters. (Mind you, one's fellow soldiers may turn out to be exotic people, and one may turn into a regrettably exotic person oneself.) I travelled through a fair chunk of Viet Nam and a corner of Cambodia. My only contact with the locals as people came on a couple Med CAPs in which a platoon with the company medics and the Civil Affairs Officer entered a village to provide minor medical help and gather intelligence.

My other contacts involved riding an armored vehicle past silent locals; searching a village whose inhabitants had fled (for good reason; the village was a staging post for the North Vietnamese just over the Cambodian border, and we burned it that afternoon); the Coke girls, hooch maids, and boom-boom girls who were really a part of the U.S. involvement, not of Viet Nam itself.

And of course there's also the chance that some unseen Vietnamese or Cambodian was downrange when I was shooting out into the darkness. That doesn't count as meeting people either.

I was in an armored unit: the 11th Armored Cavalry, the Blackhorse Regiment. Infantrymen probably saw more of the real local people, but not a lot more. The tens of thousands of U.S. personnel working out of air-conditioned buildings in Saigon, Long Binh, and other centers saw merely a large-scale version of the Coke girls, hooch maids, and boom-boom girls whom combat units met. The relative handful of advisors and Special Forces were the only American citizens actually living among the Vietnamese as opposed to being geographically within Viet Nam.

I very much doubt that things were significantly different for soldiers fighting foreign wars at any other period of history. Sensible civilians need strong economic motives to get close to groups of heavily armed foreigners, and the needs of troops in a war zone tend to be more basic than a desire to imbibe foreign culture.

Soldiers aren't any more apt to like all their fellows than members of any other interest group are. In school you were friends with some of your classmates, had no particular feelings about most of the rest, and strongly disliked one or two. The same is true of units, even quite small units, in a war zone. The stress of possible external attack makes it harder, not easier, to get along with the people with whom you're isolated.

And isolated is the key word. We changed base frequently in the field. One day we shifted an unusually long distance, over fifty miles. The tank I was riding on was part of a group that got separated from the remainder of the squadron. We had three tanks, four armored personnel carriers modified into fighting vehicles (ACAVs), an APC with added headroom and radios (a command track), and a light recovery vehicle that we called a cherrypicker though it had just a crane, not a bucket. We ran out of daylight.

By this point three ACAVs and the command track had broken down and were being towed. The remaining ACAV and one of the tanks were going to blow their engines at any moment. All the vehicles were badly overloaded with additional weapons and armor, and the need to pack all the squadron's gear for the move had exacerbated an already bad situation.

We shut down, trying by radio to raise the new base camp which *had* to be somewhere nearby. The night was pitch dark, a darkness that you can't imagine unless you've seen rural areas in a poor part of the Third World. We were hot, tired, and dizzy from twelve hours' hammering by tracked vehicles with half of the torsion bars in their suspensions broken.

And we were very much alone. So far as I could tell, nobody in the group would have described himself as happy, but we were certainly a few. Personally, I felt like a chunk of raw meat in shark waters.

The squadron commander's helicopter lifted from the new base, located our flares, and guided us in. No enemy contact, no harm done. But I'll never forget the way I felt that night, and the incident can stand as an unusually striking example of what the whole tour felt like: I was alone and an alien in an environment that might at any instant explode in violence against me.

Don't mistake what I'm saying: the environment and particularly the people of Viet Nam and Cambodia were in much greater danger from our violence than we were from theirs. I saw plenty of examples of that, and I was a part of some of them. I'm just telling you what it felt like at the time.

So Shakespeare was right about "few" and wrong about "happy." The jury (in my head) is still out about folks who missed the war counting their manhoods cheap.

I'd like to think people had better sense than that. The one thing that ought to be obvious to a civilian is that war zones are an experience to avoid. Nonetheless, I know a couple men who've moaned that they missed "Nam," the great test of manhood of our generation. They're idiots if they believe that, and twits if they were just mouthing words that had become the "in" thing for their social circles.

I haven't tested my manhood by having my leg amputated without anesthetic; I don't feel less of a man for lack of the experience. And believe me, I don't feel more of a man for anything I saw or did in Southeast Asia.

The people I served with in 1970 (the enlisted men) were almost entirely draftees. At that time nobody I knew in-country:

thought the war could be won;

thought our government was even trying to win;

thought the brutal, corrupt Saigon government was worth saving;

thought our presence was doing the least bit of good to anybody, particularly ourselves.

But you know, I'm still proud of my unit and the men I served with. They weren't exactly my brothers, but they were the folks who were alone with me. Given the remarkably high percentage of those eligible who've joined the association of war-service Blackhorse veterans, my feelings are normal for the 11th Cav.

Nobody who missed the Viet Nam War should regret the fact.

It was a waste of blood and time and treasure. It did no good of which I'm aware, and did a great deal of evil of which I'm far too aware. But having said that . . .

I rode with the Blackhorse.

Dave Drake
Chatham County, NC

AT ANY PRICE

Ferad's body scales were the greenish black of extreme old age, but his brow horns—the right one twisted into a corkscrew from birth— were still a rich gray like the iridium barrel of the powergun he held. The fingertips of his left hand touched the metal, contact that would have been distracting to most of his fellows during the preliminaries to teleportation.

Molt warriors had no universal technique, however, and Ferad had grown used to keeping physical contact with the metallic or crystalline portion of whatever it was that he intended to carry with him. He was far too old to change a successful method now, especially as he prepared for what might be the most difficult teleportation ever in the history of his species—the intelligent autochthons of the planet named Oltenia by its human settlers three centuries before.

The antechamber of the main nursery cave had a high ceiling and a circular floor eighteen meters in diameter. A dozen tunnel archways led from it. Many young Molt warriors were shimmering out of empty air, using the antechamber as a bolthole from the fighting forty kilometers away. The familiar surroundings and the mass of living rock from which the chamber was carved made it an easy resort for relative youths, when hostile fire ripped toward them in the press of battle.

The vaulted chamber was alive with warriors' cries, fear or triumph or simply relief, as they returned to catch their breath and load their weapons before popping back to attack from a new position. One adolescent cackled in splendid glee though his left arm was in tatters from a close-range gunshot: in his right hand the youth carried both an Oltenian shotgun and the mustached head of the human who had owned it before him. The ripe sweat of the warriors mingled with propellant residues from projectile weapons and the dry, arch-of-the-mouth taste of iridium from powerguns which still glowed with the heat of rapid fire.

Sopasian, Ferad's junior by a day and his rival for a long lifetime, sat eighteen meters away, across the width of the chamber. Each of the two theme elders planned in his way to change the face of the three-year war with the humans. Sopasian's face was as taut with strain as that of any post-adolescent preparing for the solo hunt which would make him a warrior.

Sopasian always tried too hard, thought Ferad as he eyed the other theme elder; but that was what worked, had always worked, for Sopasian. In his right hand was not a gun bought from a human trader or looted from an adversary but rather a traditional weapon: a hand-forged dagger, hafted with bone in the days when Molt warriors fought one another and their planet was their own. While Ferad stroked his gunbarrel to permit him to slide it more easily through the interstices of intervening matter, Sopasian's left hand fiercely gripped a disk of synthetic sapphire.

The two elders had discussed their plans with the cautious precision of mutually acknowledged experts who disliked one another. Aloud, Ferad had questioned the premise of Sopasian's plan. Consciously but unsaid, he doubted his rival or *anyone* could execute a plan calling for so perfect a leap to a tiny object in motion.

Still deeper in his heart, Ferad knew that he was rotten with envy at the very possibility that the other theme elder would succeed in a teleportation that difficult. Well, to be old and wise was not to be a saint; and a success by Sopasian would certainly make it easier for Ferad to gain his ends with the humans.

The humans, unfortunately, were only half the problem—and the result Sopasian contemplated would make his fellow Molts even more intransigent. Concern for the repercussions of his plan and the shouts of young warriors like those who had made the war inevitable merged with the background as Ferad's mind tried to grip the electrical ambience of his world. The antechamber itself was a hollow of energy—the crystalline structure of the surrounding rocks, constantly deforming as part of the dynamic stasis in which every planetary crust was held, generated an aura of piezoelectrical energy of high amplitude.

Ferad used the shell of living rock as an anchor as his consciousness slipped out in an expanding circle, searching to a distance his fellows—even Sopasian—found inconceivable. For the younger warriors, such a solid base was almost a necessity unless their goal was very well-known to them and equally rich in energy flux. As they aged, male Molts not only gained conscious experience in teleportation but became better attuned to their planet on a biological level, permitting jumps of increasing distance and delicacy.

In circumstances such as these, the result was that Molts became increasingly effective warriors in direct proportion to their growing distaste for the glory which had animated them in their hot-blooded youth. By the time they had reached Ferad's age . . .

The last object of which Ferad was aware within the antechamber was an internally scored five-centimeter disk, the condensing unit for a sophisticated instrument display. The disk came from a disabled combat car, one of those used by the mercenaries whom the human colonists had hired to support them in their war with the Molts.

Sopasian held the crystal in his left hand as his mind searched for a particular duplicate of it: the location-plotter in the vehicle used by Colonel Alois Hammer himself.

"Largo, vector three-thirty!" called Lieutenant Enzo Hawker as Profile Bourne, his sergeant-driver, disrupted the air-condensed hologram display momentarily by firing his powergun through the middle of it.

A bush with leaves like clawing fingers sprawled over a slab of rock a few meters from the Slammers' jeep. Stems which bolts from the submachine gun touched popped loudly, and the Molt warrior just condensing into local existence gave a strangled cry as he collapsed over his own human-manufactured powergun.

"Via!" the little sergeant shouted as he backed the air-cushion jeep left-handed. "Somebody get this rock over here. Blood and martyrs, that's right on top of us!"

An infantryman still aboard his grounded skimmer caught the shimmer of a Molt teleporting in along the vector for which Hawker had warned. He fired, a trifle too early to hit the attacker whose imminent appearance had ionized a pocket of air which the detection apparatus on the jeep had located. The cyan bolt blew a basin the size of a dinnerplate into the rock face on which the Molt was homing. Then the ten-kilo shaped charge which Oltenian engineers had previously placed shattered the rock and the autochthon warrior himself into a sphere of flying gravel and less recognizable constituents.

Ducking against the shower of light stones, a pair of Oltenians gripping another shaped charge and the bracket that would hold it two meters off the ground scuttled toward the slab on which Bourne's victim quivered in death. A trooper on the right flank of the company, controlled by the other detection jeep, missed something wildly and sent a bolt overhead with a *hiss-thump!* which made even veteran Slammers cringe. The two locals flattened themselves, but they got to their feet again and continued even though one of the pair was visibly weeping. They had balls, not like most of the poofs.

Not like the battalion supposedly advancing to support this thrust by a company of Hammer's infantry reinforced by a platoon of Oltenian combat engineers.

"Spike to Red One," said Hawker's commo helmet—and Bourne's, because the tall, heavy-set lieutenant had deliberately split the feed to his driver through the intercom circuits. Profile was the team's legs; and here on Oltenia especially, Hawker did not want to have to repeat an order to bug out. "Fox Victor—" the Oltenian battalion "—is hung up. Artillery broke up an outcrop, but seems like the Molts are homing on the boulders even. There's some heavy help coming, but it'll be a while. Think you might be able to do some good?"

"Bloody buggerin' *poofs*," Sergeant Bourne muttered as he bent in anticipation of the charge blasting the nearby slab, while the pipper on the map display glowed on a broad gully a kilometer away as "Spike"—the company commander, Henderson—pinpointed the problem.

The pair of detection jeeps were attached to the infantry for this operation, but Hawker's chain of command was directly to Central—Hammer's headquarters—and the idea wasn't one that Henderson was likely to phrase as an order even to someone unquestionably under his control. The Slammers had been on Oltenia for only a few days before the practice of trusting their safety to local support had proven to be the next thing to suicide.

But the present fact was that the company was safe enough only for the moment, with the larger crystalline rocks within their perimeter broken up. The autochthons could—given time to approach the position instead of teleporting directly from some distant location—home on very small crystals indeed. Unless somebody shook loose Fox Victor, the troopers in this lead element were well and truly screwed.

Hawker rubbed his face with his big left hand, squeezing away the prickling caused by Bourne's nearby shots and the nervous quiver inevitable because of what he knew he had to say. "All right," he muttered, "all right, we'll be the fire brigade on this one too."

A hillock six hundred meters distant shattered into shellbursts turbid with dirt and bits of tree. Waves quivered across the ground beneath the jeep for a moment before the blast reached the crew through the air. Bourne cursed again though the artillery was friendly, the guns trying to forestall Molt snipers by pulverizing a site to which they could easily teleport. The attempt was a reminder that no amount of shelling could interdict all outcrops within the line-of-sight range of a powergun.

"Want an escort, Red One?" asked the company commander, flattened somewhere beside his own jeep while his driver's gun wavered across each nearby spray of vegetation, waiting for the warning that it was about to hold a Molt warrior.

"Profile?" asked Lieutenant Hawker, shouting over the fan whine rather than using the intercom.

"What a bloody copping *mess*," grunted the sergeant as his left hand spun the tiller and the fans spun the jeep beneath them. "Hang on," he added, late but needlessly: Hawker knew to brace himself before he said anything that was going to spark his driver into action. "No, we don't want to bloody babysit pongoes!" and the jeep swung from its axial turn into acceleration as smooth as the brightness curve of rheostat-governed lights.

"Cover your own ass, Spike," Hawker reported as the jeep sailed past a trio of grounded infantrymen facing out from a common center like the spokes of a wheel. "We'll do better alone."

The trouble with being a good all-rounder was that you were used when people with narrower capacities got to hunker down and pray. The other detection team, Red Two, consisted of a driver possibly as good as Bourne and a warrant officer who could handle the detection gear at least as well as Hawker. But while no one in the Slammers was an innocent about guns, neither of the Red Two team was the man you really wanted at your side in a firefight. They would do fine, handling detection chores for the entire company during this lull while the autochthons regrouped and licked their wounds.

Red One, on the other hand, was headed for the stalled support force, unaccompanied by skimmer-mounted infantry who would complicate the mad dash Profile intended to make.

Shells passed so high overhead that they left vapor trails and their attenuated howl was lost in the sizzle of brush slapping the jeep's plenum chamber.

"Gimme the push for Fox Victor," Hawker demanded of Central, as his right hand gripped his submachine gun and his eyes scanned the route by which Bourne took them to where the supports were bottlenecked.

The Slammers lieutenant was watching for Molts who, already in position, would not give warning through the display of his detection gear. But if one of those bright-uniformed, totally-incompetent Oltenian general officers suddenly appeared in his gunsights . . .

Enzo Hawker might just decide a burst wouldn't be wasted.

The gorgeous clothing of the officers attending the Widows of the War Ball in the Tribunal Palace differed in cut from the gowns of the ladies, but not in quality or brilliance. General Alexander Radescu, whose sardonic whim had caused him to limit his outfit to that prescribed for dress uniforms in the *Handbook for Officers in the Service of the Oltenian State*, knew that he looked ascetic in comparison to almost anyone else in the Grand Ballroom—his aide, Major Nikki Tzigara, included.

"Well, the lily has a certain dignity that a bed of tulips can't equal, don't you think?" murmured the thirty-two-year-old general as his oval fingernails traced a pattern of lines down the pearly fabric of his opposite sleeve.

Nikki, who had added yellow cuffs and collar to emphasize the scarlet bodice of his uniform jacket, grinned at the reference which he alone was meant to hear in the bustle of the gala. From beyond Tzigara, however, where he lounged against one of the pair of huge urns polished from blue john—columnar fluorspar—by Molt craftsmen in the dim past, Major Joachim Steuben asked, "And what does that leave me, General? The dirt in the bottom of the pot?"

Colonel Hammer's chief of base operations in the Oltenian capital flicked a hand as delicately manicured as Radescu's own across his own khaki uniform. Though all the materials were of the highest quality, Steuben's ensemble had a restrained elegance—save for the gaudily floral inlays of the pistol, which was apparently as much a part of the Slammers dress uniform as the gold-brimmed cap was for an Oltenian general officer. In fact, Major Steuben looked very good indeed in his tailored khaki, rather like a leaf-bladed dagger in an intarsia sheath. Though flawlessly personable, Steuben had an aura which Radescu himself found at best disconcerting: Radescu's mind kept focusing on the fact that there was a skull beneath that tanned, smiling face.

But Joachim Steuben got along well in dealing with his Oltenian counterparts here in Belvedere. The first officer whom Hammer had given the task of liaison and organizing his line of supply from the starport had loudly referred to the local forces as poofs. That was understandable, Radescu knew; but very impolitic.

Nikki, who either did not see or was not put off by the core of Joachim which Radescu glimpsed, was saying, "Oh, Major Steuben, *you* dirt?" when the string orchestra swung into a gavotte and covered the remainder of the pair's smalltalk.

Every man Radescu could see in the room was wearing a uniform of some kind. The regulars, like Nikki Tzigara, modified the stock design for greater color; but the real palm went to the "generals" and "marshals" of militia units which mustered only on paper. These were the aristocratic owners of mines, factories, and the great ranches which were the third leg of human success on Oltenia. They wore not only the finest imported natural and synthetic fabrics, but furs, plumes, and—in one case of strikingly poor taste, Radescu thought—a shoulder cape flayed from the scaly hide of an adolescent Molt. Officers of all sorts spun and postured with their jeweled ladies, the whole seeming to the young general the workings of an ill-made machine rather than a fund-raiser for the shockingly large number of relicts created in three years of war.

Radescu lifted his cap and combed his fingers through the pale, blond hair which was plastered now to his scalp by perspiration. The second blue john vase felt cool to his back, but the memories it aroused increased his depression. The only large-scale celebrations of which the autochthons, the Molts, had not been a part were those during the present war. While not everyone—yet—shared the general's opinion that the war was an unmitigated disaster, the failure of this gathering to include representatives of the fourteen Molt themes made it less colorful in a way that no amount of feathers and cloth-of-gold could repair.

A gust of air, cool at any time and now balm in the steaming swamps, played across the back of Radescu's neck and the exposed skin of his wrists. He turned to see a scarlet Honor Guard disappearing from view as he closed a door into the interior of the Tribunal Palace. The man who had just entered the ballroom was the Chief Tribune and effective ruler of Oltenia, Grigor Antonescu.

"Well met, my boy," said the Chief Tribune as he saw General Radescu almost in front of him. There was nothing in the tone to suggest that Antonescu felt well about anything, nor was that simply a result of his traditional reserve. Radescu knew the Chief Tribune well enough to realize that something was very badly wrong, and that beneath the wall of stony facial control there was a mind roiling with anger.

"Good evening, Uncle Grigor," Radescu said, bowing with more formality than he would normally have shown his mother's brother, deferring to the older man's concealed agitation."I don't get as much chance to see you as I'd like, with your present duties."

There were factory owners on the dance floor who could have bought Alexander Radescu's considerable holdings twice over, but there was no one with a closer path to real power if he chose to travel it.

"You have good sense, Alexi," Antonescu said with an undertone of bitterness that only an ear as experienced as Radescu's own would have heard.

The Chief Tribune wore his formal robes of office, spotlessly white and of a severity unequaled by even the functional uniform of Joachim Steuben . . . who seemed to have disappeared. Another man in Grigor Antonescu's position might have designed new regalia more in line with present tastes or at least relieved the white vestments' severity with jewels and metals and brightly patterned fabrics rather the way Nikki had with his uniform (and where *was* Nikki?).Chief Tribune Antonescu knew, however, that through the starkness of a pure neutral color he would draw eyes like an ax blade in a field of poppies.

"It's time," Antonescu continued, with a glance toward the door and away again, "that I talk to *someone* who has good sense."

On the dance floor, couples were parading through the steps of a sprightly *contre-danse*—country dance—to the bowing of the string orchestra. The figures moving in attempted synchrony reminded Alexander Radescu now of a breeze through an arboretum rather than of a machine. "Shall we . . . ?" the general suggested mildly with a short, full-hand gesture toward the door through which his uncle had so recently appeared.

The man-high urns formed an effective alcove around the door, while the music and the bustle of dancing provided a sponge of sound to absorb conversations at any distance from the speakers. Chief Tribune Antonescu gave another quick look around him and said, gesturing his nephew closer, "No, I suppose I need to show myself at these events to avoid being called an unapproachable dictator." He gave Radescu a smile as crisp as the glitter of shears cutting sheet metal: both men knew that the adjective and the noun alike were more true than not.

"Besides," Antonescu added with a rare grimace, "if we go back inside we're likely to meet my esteemed colleagues—" Tribunes Wraslov and Deliu "—and having just spent an hour with their inanity, I don't care to repeat the dose for some while."

"There's trouble, then?" the young general asked, too softly in all likelihood to be heard even though he was stepping shoulder to shoulder as the older man had directed.

There was really no need for the question anyway, since Antonescu was already explaining, "The great offensive that Marshal Erzul promised has stalled. Again, of course."

A resplendent colonel walked past, a young aide on his arm. They both noticed the Chief Tribune and his nephew and looked away at once with the terrified intensity of men who feared they would be called to book. Radescu waited until the pair had drifted on, then said, "It was only to get under way this morning. Initial problems don't necessarily mean—"

"Stalled. Failed. Collapsed totally," Antonescu said in his smooth, cool voice, smiling at his nephew as though they were discussing the gay rout on the dance floor. "According to Erzul, the only units which haven't fallen back to their starting line decimated are those with which he's lost contact entirely."

"Via, he *can't* lose contact!" Radescu snapped as his mind retrieved the Operation Order he had committed to memory. His post, Military Advisor to the Tribunes, was meant to be a sinecure. That General Radescu had used his access to really study the way the

Oltenian State fought the autochthons was a measure of the man, rather than of his duties. "Every *man* in the forward elements has a personal radio to prevent just that!"

"Every man alive, yes," his uncle said. "That was the conclusion I drew, too."

"And—" Radescu began, then paused as he stepped out from the alcove to make sure that he did not mistake the absence of Major Steuben before he completed his sentence with, "and Hammer's Slammers, were they unable to make headway also? Because if they were . . ." He did not go on by saying, ". . . then the war is patently unwinnable, no matter what level of effort we're willing to invest." Uncle Grigor did not need a relative half his age to state the obvious to him.

Antonescu gave a minute nod of approval for the way his nephew had this time checked their surroundings before speaking. "Yes, that's the question that seems most frustrating," he replied as the *contre-danse* spun to a halt and the complex patterns dissolved.

"Erzul—he was on the screen in person—says the mercenaries failed to advance, but he says it in a fashion that convinces me he's lying. I presume that there has been another failure to follow up thrusts by Hammer's units."

The Chief Tribune barked out a laugh as humorless as the stuttering of an automatic weapon. "If Erzul were a better commander, he wouldn't *need* to be a good liar," he said.

The younger man looked at the pair of urns. At night functions they were sometimes illuminated by spotlights beamed down on their interiors, so that the violet tinge came through the huge, indigo grains and the white calcite matrix glowed with power enchained. Tonight the stone was unlighted, and only reflections from the smooth surfaces belied its appearance of opacity.

"The trouble is," Radescu said, letting his thoughts blend into the words his lips were speaking, "that Erzul and the rest keep thinking of the Molts as humans who can teleport and therefore can never be caught. That means every battle is on the Molts' terms. But they *don't* think the way we do, the way humans do, as a society. They're too individual."

The blue john urns were slightly asymmetric, proving that they had been polished into shape purely by hand instead of being lathe-turned as any human craftsman would have done. That in itself was an amazing comment on workmanship, given that the material had such pronounced lines of cleavage and was so prone to splinter under stress. Even the resin with which the urns were impregnated was an addition by the settlers to whom the gift was made, preserving for generations the micron-smooth polish which a Molt had achieved with no tool but the palms of his hands over a decade.

But there was more. Though the urns were asymmetric, they were precise mirror images of one another.

"If we don't understand the way the Molts relate to each other and to the structure of their planet," said Alexander Radescu with a gesture that followed the curve of the right-hand urn without quite touching the delicate surface, "then we don't get anywhere with the war.

"And until then, there's no chance to convince the Molts to make peace."

The ambience over which Ferad's mind coursed was as real and as mercurial as the wave-strewn surface of a sea. He knew that at any given time there were hundreds, perhaps thousands, of his fellows hurling themselves from point to point in transfers which seemed instantaneous only from the outside. There was no sign of others in this universe of stresses and energy, a universe which was that of the Molts uniquely.

That was the key to the character of male Molts, Ferad had realized over the more than a century that he observed his race and the human settlers. Molt females cooperated among themselves in nurturing the young and in agriculture—they had even expanded that cooperation to include animal husbandry, since the human settlement. The prepubescent males cooperated also, playing together even when the games involved teleportation for the kilometer or so of which they and the females were capable.

But with the hormonal changes of puberty, a male's world

became a boundless, vacant expanse that was probably a psychological construct rather than a "real" place—but which was no less real for all that.

In order to transport himself to a point in the material landscape, a Molt had to identify his destination in the dreamworld of energy patterns and crystal junctions that depended both on the size of the object being used as a beacon and on its distance from the point of departure. Most of all, however, finding a location depended on the experience of the Molt who picked his way across the interface of mind and piezoelectrical flux.

That focus on self deeply affected the ability of males to consider anything but individual performance. Hunters, especially the young who were at pains to prove their prowess, would raid the herds of human ranchers without consideration of the effect that had on settler-autochthon relations. And, even to the voice of Ferad's dispassionate experience, it was clear that there would be human herds and human cities covering the planet like studded leather upholstery if matters continued as they began three centuries before.

But while the war might be a necessary catalyst for change, no society built on continued warfare would be beneficial to Man or Molt.

The greater questions of civilization which had been filling Ferad's time in the material world were secondary now in this fluid moment. Crystals which he knew—which he had seen or walked across or handled—were solid foci within the drift. They shrank as the theme elder's mind circled outward, but they did not quickly lose definition for him as they would have done decades or a century earlier.

The psychic mass of the powergun Ferad held created a drag, but his efforts to bring the weapon into tune with his body by stroking the metal now worked to his benefit. He handled the gun in teleporting more easily than he did its physical weight in the material world. His race had not needed the bulk and power of human hunters because their pursuit was not through muscular effort and they struck their quarry unaware, not aroused and violent. Besides that, Ferad was very old, and gravity's tug on the iridium barrel was almost greater than his shrunken arms could resist.

He would hold the weapon up for long enough. Of that he was sure.

Ferad's goal was of unique difficulty, not only because of the distance over which he was teleporting but also due to the nature of the objects on which he was homing. He had never seen, much less touched them; but an ancestor of his had spent years polishing the great urns from solid blocks of blue john. That racial memory was a part of Ferad, poised in momentary limbo between the central cave system of his theme and the Tribunal Palace in Belvedere.

A part of him like the powergun in his hands.

"Shot," called the battery controller through the commo helmets, giving Hawker and Bourne the warning they would have had a few seconds earlier had the rush of their passage not shut off outside sounds as slight as the first pop of the firecracker round. The initial explosion was only large enough to split the twenty-centimeter shell casing short of the impact point and strew its cargo of five hundred bomblets like a charge of high-explosive buckshot.

"Via!" swore the sergeant angrily, because they were in a swale as open as a whore's cunt and the hologram display which he could see from the corner of his eye was giving a warning of its own. The yellow figures which changed only to reflect the position of the moving jeep were now replaced by a nervous flickering from that yellow to the violet which was its optical reciprocal, giving Lieutenant Hawker the location at which a Molt warrior was about to appear in the near vicinity. It was a lousy time to have to duck from a firecracker round.

But Via, they'd known the timing had to be close to clear the ridge before the jeep took its position to *keep* the bottleneck open. Bourne knew that to kill forward motion by lifting the bow would make the slowing jeep a taller target for snipers, while making an axial 180° turn against the vehicle's forward motion might affect the precision with which the Loot called a bearing on the teleporting autochthon. The driver's left hand released the tiller and threw the lever tilting the fan nacelles to exhaust at full forward angle.

His right hand, its palm covered with a fluorescent tattoo which literally snaked all the way up his arm, remained where it had been throughout the run: on the grip of his submachine gun.

"Splash," said the battery controller five seconds after the warning, and the jeep's inertia coasted it to a halt in the waving, head-high grain. A white glow played across the top of the next rise, mowing undergrowth and stripping bark and foliage from the larger trees. The electrical crackle of the bomblets going off started a second later, accompanied by the murderous hum of an object flung by the explosions, a stone or piece of casing which had not disintegrated the way it should have—deadly in either case, even at three hundred meters, had it not missed Bourne's helmet by a hand's breadth.

"Loot!" the driver called desperately. The burring fragment could be ignored as so many dangers survived had been ignored before. But the Molt warrior who by now was in full control of his body and whatever weapon he held, somewhere beyond the waving curtain of grain . . . "Which *way*, Loot, which way!"

"Hold it," said Lieutenant Hawker, an order and not an answer as he jumped to his full meter-ninety height on the seat of the jeep with his gun pointing over the driver's head. There was a feral hiss as Hawker's weapon spewed plastic casings from the ejection port and cyan fire from the muzzle. Profile Bourne's cheeks prickled, and a line of vegetation withered as the burst angled into the grain.

There was a scream from downrange. The sergeant slammed his throttle and the nacelle angle into maximum drive even as his teammate dropped back into a sitting position, the muzzle of his powergun sizzling as it cooled from white to lambent gray. The scream had been high-pitched and double, so that the driver did not need to hear Hawker say, "*Cop!* It was a female and a kid, but I thought she had a bloody satchel charge!"

It wasn't the sort of problem that bothered Bourne a whole lot, but he didn't like to see the Loot so distressed.

The reason Fox Victor was having problems—beyond the fact that they were poofs who couldn't be trusted in a rainstorm, much less a firefight—was obvious on this, the reverse slope of the gully which formed the actual choke-point for the support column. Low retaining walls curved back into the sloping hillside like arms outstretched by the arched opening in their center: the entrance to what the Oltenians called a Molt nursery cave.

In fact, the underground constructs of which this was a small example were almost never true caves but rather tunnels carved into igneous and metamorphic rocks of dense crystalline structure. The sedimentary rocks which could be cut or leached away into caves by groundwater were of no use as beacons for teleporting autochthons—and thus of no use in training young Molts to use their unique abilities.

By being surrounded from earliest infancy with living rock whose crystals were in a constant state of piezoelectrical flux, Molts—male and female alike—began to teleport for short distances before they could crawl. As they grew older, prepubescents played in the near vicinity of their nurseries and gained a familiarity with the structure of those rocks which was deeper than anything else they would meet in life.

And when called to do so by military need, Molt warriors could home on even the smallest portions of the particular locality in which they had been raised. Shelling that broke up the gross structure of a slab did not affect the ability of warriors to concentrate, though the damage would ordinarily have at least delayed younger Molts trying to locate it for teleportation. The result, at least for poofs without the instruments to detect warriors before the shooting started, would be disastrous.

Now, while the pair of Slammers were flat out with nothing but a 15° slope to retard the jeep, the possibility of a Molt teleporting to point-blank range beside them was the least of Profile Bourne's worries. The bolt that snapped into the hillside thirty meters away, fluffing and dimming shell-set grass fires in its momentary passage, was a more real danger. The microfragments from the firecracker round had cleared the crest and face of the ridge, but a Molt somewhere out there, far from the immediate battle scene, continued to snipe at the jeep undeterred. The autochthons were not, in the main, good marksmen, and the vehicle's speed made it a chance target anyway to a gunman a kilometer distant.

But the chance that let the bolt blow a divot from the soil and splinters from the rock close beneath might easily have turned the jeep into a sizzling corona as electrical storage cells shorted through driver and passenger. It was nothing to feel complacent about, and there was no way to respond while the jeep was at speed.

If only they were about to join one of the Slammers' tank companies instead of a poof battalion! Snipers would learn that they, like dogs, got one bite—and that a second attempt meant the ground around them glowed and bubbled with the energy released by a tank's main gun or a long burst from a tribarrel.

That didn't, of course, always mean that the first bite had not drawn blood. . . .

A less skilled driver would have let his jeep lift bow-high at the crest where the ridge rolled down its other slope. Bourne angled his fan nacelles left, throwing the vehicle into a sideslip which cut upward velocity without stalling the jeep as a target silhouetted in two directions. The grass and low brush of the crest were scarred by the bomblets, and a lump half-hidden by the rock which had sheltered it might have been a warrior caught by the shrapnel.

While Bourne concentrated on his own job, Lieutenant Hawker had been on the horn with the poof battalion commander, their Central-relayed conversation audible to the driver but of no particular interest. All Sergeant Bourne cared was that the Oltenian troops not add their fire to that of the Molts already sniping at the jeep. Men so jumpy from being ripped without recourse might well fire at any target they could hit, even when the intellectual levels of their brains knew that it was the wrong target.

"Profile, a hundred and fifty!" the lieutenant ordered. His left arm reached out through the flashing hologram display in the air before him, converting its digital information into a vector for his driver's gun.

The sergeant grounded the jeep in a stony pocket far enough below the crest to be clear of the Molt marksman who had fired as they climbed the back slope. Molts could teleport in within touching distance, but this time that was the plan; and the rocks jumbled by a heavy shell provided some cover from distant snipers.

Bourne did not fire. He knew exactly where the Molt was going to appear, but spraying the area a hundred and fifty meters down the wash would have been suicidal.

Like most of Hammer's troopers, Sergeant Bourne had seen the wreckage Molt warriors made of Oltenian assaults. He hadn't really appreciated the ease with which disaster happened until he saw what now took place in the swale.

The water cut depression in a fold between crystalline ridges was now studded with rubble cracked from both faces by armor-piercing shells and the blazing remains of half a dozen Oltenian vehicles. The human bodies blended into the landscape better than did equipment marked out by pillars of smoke and sometimes a lapping overlay of kerosene flames, though the corpse halfway out of the driver's hatch of an armored car was obvious with his lifted arms and upturned face—brittle as a charcoal statue.

The single firecracker round had been intended only to clear the Molts briefly from the area. A poof armored car and armored personnel carrier were trying to make a dash across the gully during the lull, however, instead of waiting for the Slammers to get into position as Hawker had directed. Some might have said that showed exemplary courage, but Profile Bourne couldn't care less about fools who died well—which was all this crew was managing.

The automatic weapon in the car's turret traversed the slope toward which the vehicle advanced, making a great deal of dust and racket without affecting in the least the warrior who must have teleported directly between the car and the personnel carrier. Bourne didn't fire at the Molt, knowing that the armored vehicles shielded their attacker and that the poofs across the swale would respond to the submachine gun's "attack" on their fellows, no matter *how* good their fire discipline might be.

"Via! Three more, Profile," Lieutenant Hawker said, his pointing arm shifting 15° to the right as the swale rang with the sound of a magnetic limpet mine gripping the steel side of the vehicle against which it had been slapped.

Rock broken by heavy shells, brush smoldering where the bursting charges of the antipersonnel bomblets had ignited it. No target yet, but Profile loosed a three-round burst to splash the boulders twenty meters from the oncoming APC and warn the poofs.

The armored car dissolved in a sheet of flame so intense that the shock wave a fraction of a second later seemed a separate event. A trio of Molts froze out of the air where Hawker had pointed and Bourne's own shots had left glazed scars on the stone a moment before.

He had a target now and he fired over open sights, two rounds into the back of the first warrior and three at the second, who leaped up into the last bolt when molten stone sprayed from the boulder sheltering him. A storm of fire from at least twenty Oltenian guns broke wildly on the general area. The Loot was shouting, "*Close Profile!*" his big arm pointing behind the jeep, but nothing this side of Hell was going to keep Bourne from his third kill—the Molt crouched behind his steaming powergun, firing into the APC as fast as his finger could pull the trigger.

Only when that Molt crumpled did the sergeant spin to shoot over the racked electronics modules replacing the jeep's back seat. Bourne lifted the heat-shivering muzzle of his gun even as his finger took up slack in the trigger. If he had fired as he intended into the center of mass of the warrior coalescing a meter away, the satchel charge the Molt was clutching to his chest would have gone off and vaporized the jeep. Instead, the distorted face of the autochthon dissolved in a burst so needlessly long that even Profile knew that he had panicked.

"Seventy-five," the Loot was saying, and Bourne rotated toward the new target while the decapitated remains of his previous victim toppled backward. In the swale below, the APC crackled with what sounded like gunfire but was actually the explosion of ammunition within its burning interior. Seventy-five meters, a rough figure but there was a tangled clump of ground cover at about that distance in the direction the Loot was pointing, a flat-topped block jutting like a loggia garden into the gully. Bourne squeezed off what was intended to be a two-round burst alerting the poofs deployed on the further side.

There was a single cyan flicker from the submachine gun—he'd

David Drake

emptied the magazine on the previous Molt, leaving only one lonely disk in the loading pan.

Cursing because the warrior homing on the block was going to get a shot in for sure and the Loot was already pointing at another vector, the sergeant swapped magazines.

His eyes were open and searching the terrain for the new target, two hundred meters to the front and closer to the Oltenian battalion than to the jeep. The right handgrip enclosed the magazine well, and a veteran like Bourne had no need to look down for hand to find hand in an operation as familiar as reloading.

He had no need to worry about the warrior his shot had marked, as it turned out.

The standard poof shoulder weapon, a stubby shotgun, did not, with its normal load of fléchettes, have the range of the target. The outside surface of the gun tube could be used as the launching post for ring-airfoil grenades, however, like the one that hurled a pair of Molts in opposite directions from its yellow flash in the center of the target. Turret guns from armored vehicles were raking the blasted area as well, even hitting the corpses as they tumbled.

Could be some a' the poofs had sand in their craws after all.

A powergun too distant to be a target for Bourne under these circumstances was emptied in the direction of the jeep as fast as some warrior could pull the trigger. The bolts weren't really close— some of them were high enough for their saturated blue-green color to be lost in the sunlight. The trio that spattered rock eighty meters from the jeep—forty meters, twenty—were not less terrifying, however, for the fact that the next three missed by more than the sergeant could track.

Bourne's burst toward the Loot's latest warning was careless if not exactly frightened. He couldn't see anything and it was less of a threat than the snipers now ranging on them anyway . . . and then, when the Molt leaped into his vision while poof guns chopped furiously, the sergeant realized that the warrior was hiding from *him*, from the jeep, and fatally ignoring the Oltenians.

"Fox Victor," Lieutenant Hawker ordered, "roll 'em," and the bolt that shattered a boulder into fist-sized chunks ringing on the jeep came from the angle opposite the previous sniper.

"Loot, it's—" the driver said, reaching for the throttle left-handed. A hilltop barely visible puffed white, shells answering a satellite report of sniping, but that alone wouldn't be enough to save their ass. The trucks and armored vehicles of the poof battalion were rumbling from cover; a couple autochthons fired at them, missing badly. Via! If they could miss the broad, flat sides of an APC, how did they get so bloody close to the sheltered jeep?

"Right," said Hawker as he glanced at his display, still and yellow as it vainly awaited more teleporting autochthons, "let's ro—" and the last word was swept away by his driver's fierce acceleration out of the pocket of stone which had become an aiming point for the enemy far off.

The Loot was on Central's push, now, calling for panzers and a salvo of artillery, while Bourne jinked back up and away and the air winked with ill-aimed sniper fire. The bastards didn't need to be good, just lucky, and the bolt that fried sod a millisecond before the jeep's skirts whisked across it was almost lucky enough. Central was answering calmly, dryly—*their* butts weren't on the line!—but that wasn't something the sergeant had time for anyway. They'd done their job, done it bleedin' *perfectly*, and now it looked like they'd be lucky to get out with a whole skin.

Well, that was what happened when you tried to support the poofs.

As the jeep topped the ridge a second time but in the opposite direction, a bolt snapped past it from the far side of the grain field and coincidentally a truck blew up in the swale behind. The detection team could not prevent the support battalion from taking casualties when it traversed open ground. What the Loot's warnings—and Profile's own submachine gun, its barrel reeking with sublimed iridium and the finish it burned from the breastplate to which the elastic sling held it—*had* accomplished was to eliminate the warriors who knew the terrain so well that they could place themselves within millimeters of an opponent in the gully. There were surely other Molts with a nursery association with this area, but the autochthons—thank the Lord!—didn't have the organization to make a massed response to a sudden threat.

They didn't need to, of course, since a handful of warriors could stall a poof battalion, and weeks of long-range sniping eroded the Slammers' strength to no human purpose.

The shock wave from a six-tube salvo skewed the jeep even though the shells impacted on the far side of the ridge and none closer than a half kilometer to the course down which Bourne was speeding to escape. The Loot was having the Slammers' hogs blast clear the flanks of the Oltenian battalion, crumbling rocks that would otherwise stand as beacons for Molts bouncing closer to shoot down the axis of the swale. The poofs should've done that themselves, but their artillery control wasn't up to civilized standards, and their gun crews minced around in a funk fearing a Molt with a satchel charge would teleport aboard an ammo transporter. Which had happened often enough to give anybody the willies, come to think.

The warrior who had snapped shots at them earlier now had at least a pair of supporters—one of whom was too bloody good. Bourne spun and braked his vehicle, fearing the brief pause during which their original downhill velocity was precisely balanced by thrust in the new direction. Lord help 'em if the Loot's request for heavy armor didn't come through the way the artillery support had done.

Though Colonel Hammer didn't leave his people hanging if there was any way around it.

The dark arch of the nursery tunnel into which Bourne headed the jeep was a perfect aiming point—hitting the center of a large target is easier than nailing a small one. The sergeant expected the entrance to be crisscrossed by the dazzling scatter of bolts squeezed off with all the care of which Molt marksmen were capable. He figured he had no hope save the autochthons' bad aim or bad timing. That there were no shots at all was as pleasant a surprise as he'd had since the night a whore tried to kill him with what turned out to be an empty gun. . . .

The tunnel was three meters wide and of simple design, an angled gallery rather than a labyrinth of interconnected chambers.

The same purpose was achieved either way: the encouragement of the very young to teleport to points separated from them by solid barriers.

The same stone angles were just what the doctor ordered to block sniper fire—and as for anybody teleporting directly into the cave, they were cold meat as soon as the Loot's equipment picked them up.

"Safe!" the driver cried happily as he yanked the tiller left at the first 60° break, an edge of polished black granite that had not been dulled by rubbing shoulders as it would have been in a structure occupied by humans.

The warrior just around that corner pointed his Oltenian shotgun squarely at Profile's face.

Molt cave systems were not unlighted—the autochthons actually saw less well in dim conditions than humans did. The roof of this particular tunnel was painted with a strip of—imported—permanent fluorescent, powered by the same piezoelectrical forces which made the rock a beacon for teleporters. It gave off only a pale glow, however, inadequate for irises contracted by the sun outside, so it was in the jeep's front floods that the Molt's eyes gaped. His shadow against the gleaming stone was half again his real height, and the muzzle of the gun seemed broad as the tunnel.

Bourne fluffed his front fans to full screaming lift with his right hand.

He could have shot, have killed the warrior. Man and Molt were equally surprised, and Profile Bourne's reflexes were a safe bet against just about anybody's in those situations.

And then the charge of fléchettes, triggered by the warrior's dying convulsion, would have shredded both men from the waist upward.

Lieutenant Hawker shouted as he fired through the hologram display which had failed to warn him. The Molt was already within the tunnel before the jeep entered, so there were no indicia of teleportation for the apparatus to detect.They should have thought of that, but the lightning-swift danger of the snipers outside had made the cave mouth a vision of safety like none since Mother's bosom.

That was the sort of instinctive error that got your ass killed, thought Hawker as his energy bolts scarred long ovals across the ceiling's fluorescence, ricocheting further down the tunnel in diminishing deadliness, and the Molt's shotgun blasted deafeningly into the uplifted skirt and plenum chamber of the jeep.

The screech of the jeep striking and skidding along the tunnel wall at a 45° angle was actively painful to Profile Bourne. You didn't get to be as good a driver as he was without empathy for your vehicle, and the shriek of metal crumpling was to the sergeant comparable to skidding along a hard surface himself. But he'd done that too, thrown himself down on gravel when shots slammed overhead. You do what you gotta do; and anyway, the Molt's body when the jeep hit it provided a pretty fair lubricant.

Their forward velocity had been scrubbed off by the contact rather than killed by the vectored fans in normal fashion. Bourne chopped the throttle so that the braking thrust would not slam them back against the far wall. The jeep slumped down onto its skirts again, its back end ringing on the stone a moment before the whole vehicle came to rest.

The sergeant knew that he ought to be watching the next angle in case another warrior, prepared by the racketing death of the first, came around it shooting. Instead he closed his eyes for a moment and squeezed his hands together hard enough to make the thin flesh start up around the print of each fingertip. Lord, he'd almost pissed himself!

When he opened his eyes, he saw the tiny, glittering dimple in the steel flooring just between his boots. It was a fléchette from the shotgun charge which had come within a millimeter of doing the warrior's business—or half of it—despite the fact that the roof of the plenum chamber was in the way.

Lord and martyrs!

"Lord and martyrs," muttered Lieutenant Hawker as he stepped out of the vehicle, and curst if he didn't seem as shook as the driver felt. "Don't worry, got it on aural," he added with a nod toward the hologram display and a left-handed tap on the earpiece of his commo helmet. The data relayed through the headset was less instantly assimilable than what his eyes could intake through the holograms—but there were only two directions from which an attack could come in the tunnel.

Anyhow, Profile figured that he needed to walk out the wobbles he could feel in his legs. Maybe the Loot was the same.

Before the sergeant left the jeep, he switched off the headlights which would otherwise be only a targeting aid to whatever Molts were around. The rock quivered when he stepped onto it, an explosion somewhere, and he cursed or prayed—who knew?—at the thought that another salvo of penetrators on the back slope of the ridge might bring the bloody ceiling down and accomplish what the autochthons had failed to do. What the hell, nobody'd ever told him he'd die in bed.

Bourne skidded at his first step. He glanced down, thinking that the stone beneath his boots must have a glass-smooth polish. It wasn't that—and the Molt with the shotgun deserved worse, it'd been too cursed quick for him.

The two Slammers used handsignals at the next angle, five meters further down the tunnel. They could as easily have subvocalized the plan on the intercom, but Profile's quick tap on his own breastplate and the Loot's grimace of acceptance was all that it took anyway.

Bourne put a single shot against the facing wall, the bolt crackling like shattered brick as it bounced from the stone. A fraction of a second later, the sergeant himself went in low.

The shot might have drawn a reflexive return from anyone poised to meet them around the angle—but there was no one, no adult at least: they were in the nursery itself, a circular room no wider than the tunnel from which it was offset to the left, just around the second angle. There were eighteen reed and moss crèches like the pips on an instrument dial, and about half of them still squirmed with infant Molts.

"S'all right, Loot!" Bourne shouted as he rolled into a sitting position; and for all the encouragement of his words, his ankles were crossed in a firm shooter's rest beneath him. "S'all clear, just the babes."

The flash of the shot was still a retinal memory to Bourne as he glanced around the chamber, blinking as if to wash the spreading orange blot from the black surface of his eyeballs. The scars of the ricochet were marked by powdered stone at a constant chest height along the circular wall. No significant amount of energy would have sprayed the infants, but they were mewing fearfully anyway.

The Loot came in behind the muzzle of his gun—you didn't leave decisions of safety to somebody else, even Sergeant Bourne, not in a place like this.

The Molt in the crèche closest to Bourne teleported neatly into his lap, scaring the sergeant into a shout and a leap upward that ended with the infant clamped hard against him and the muzzle of Lieutenant Hawker's submachine gun pointed dead on. The little Molt squealed even more loudly.

"Let's get the cop outa here before the locals put a flame gun down the tunnel and investigate later," Hawker said as he ported his weapon again, making no apology for aiming it toward a teleporting autochthon, even one in Bourne's lap. "Doesn't seem those Molts'll snipe at us here, what with the little ones in the line of fire."

"Right," said his driver, kneeling to put the infant back in its— his? her?—crèche. There were air shafts cut from the chamber's ceiling to the surface twenty or thirty meters above. Through them now sank, competing with the powergun's ozone prickliness, not only the ash and blast residues of the shelling but the stomach-turning sweetness of diesel fumes. The vehicles of Fox Victor had gained the ridge and should by now be advancing down the reverse slope, covered by shellfire against likely sniper positions.

"No, here," said Lieutenant Hawker, reaching out with a left hand that seemed large enough to encircle the infant Molt which he took from Bourne. "You need to drive. We'll clear these out and then get a squad a' engineers to blow the place before it causes more trouble."

Little bastards looked less human than the adults, Bourne thought as he strode quickly back to the jeep, calm again with the tension of battle released by two sudden shocks within the tunnel. You could only be so scared, and then it all had to let go—or you cracked, and Profile Bourne didn't crack. The limbs of the young Molt were very small, more like those of a newt or lizard than of a human baby. Even as adults, the autochthons were shorter and more lightly built than most humans, but after a few years of age there was no difference in proportions.

"I suppose it's because the ones that crawl least do the other— teleport—better," said the Loot as he swung his big frame into the seat behind the displays, still holding the infant Molt. Via, maybe he *could* read his driver's mind; they'd worked through some curst tight places in the past few years. But it was a natural thing to wonder about if you saw the little ones up close like this, and the Loot was smart, he figured out that sort of thing.

Right now, the only thing Bourne really wanted to figure out was how to find a quiet spot where nobody would try to blow him away for a while. He'd given enough gray hairs to this buggering planet and its buggered poof army already!

There was a centimeter's clearance front and rear to turn the jeep in the tunnel's width, but the sergeant did not even consider backing after he tested his eyeball guesstimate with a brief tap on the throttle as he twisted the tiller to bring the vehicle just short of alignment. Sure that it was going to make it, he goosed the fans again and brought the detection vehicle quickly around, converting spin into forward motion as the bow swung toward the first angle and the entrance. If it could be done with a ground effect vehicle, Profile would do it without thinking. Thinking wasn't his strong suit anyway.

The mercenaries' commo helmets brightened with message traffic as the jeep slid back down the initial leg of the gallery. Even a satellite relay squarely overhead didn't permit radio communication when one of the parties was deep beneath a slab of rock. Ground conduction signals were a way around that, but a bloody poor one when all your troops were mounted on air-cushion vehicles.

Might be nice to have a portable tunnel to crawl into, now and again. When some poof circus needed to have its butt saved again, for instance.

The tunnel mouth gave them a wedge of vision onto the far slope, expanding as the jeep slid smoothly toward the opening where the driver grounded it. Sparkling chains of fire laced the air above the valley, bubbling and dancing at a dozen points from which snipers might have fired earlier.

"'Bout bloody time!" the driver chortled, though support from the Slammers' big blowers had come amazingly quickly, given the care with which the expensive vehicles had to travel on this hostile terrain. "About *bloody* time!"

The tribarreled powerguns raking Molt hiding places with counterfire cycled so quickly that, like droplets of water in a fountain, the individual cyan flashes seemed to hang in the air instead of snapping light-quick across the valley. Afterimages strobed within Bourne's dark-adapted eyes: on a sunny day, the bursts of two-centimeter fire imposed their own definition of brightness. Snipers were still safe if they fired and fled instantly; but if a warrior paused to take a breath or better aim, heat sensors would lock on the glowing barrel of his powergun and crisscrossing automatic fire would glaze the landscape with his remains.

The support was combat cars, not the panzers—the tanks—that Bourne had been hoping for. This'd do, but it'd be nice to see a whole bloody hillside go up in a blue flash!

Lieutenant Hawker, holding the Molt, stepped from the jeep and the tunnel mouth, his gunhand raised as if he were hailing a cab in a liberty port. It wasn't the safest thing in the world, on this world, to do, what with autochthons still firing at the oncoming poof battalion and those locals themselves dangerously trigger-happy. Still, the Molts had proven unwilling to shoot toward their infants, and the poofs were more likely to pitch a bunker-buster into the tunnel mouth than they were to shoot at a Slammer in battledress, three times the size of any Molt who ever lived. Shrugging, Bourne butted the jeep a couple meters further forward to take a look himself.

The leading elements of Fox Victor had reformed on the ridge crest and were advancing raggedly abreast in a mounted assault line. There were thirty or so vehicles in the first wave, armored cars and APCs with a leavening of all-terrain trucks taking the place of armored vehicles destroyed earlier in the operation.

The nearest vehicle was one of the light trucks, this one

equipped with a pintle-mounted machine gun instead of carrying a squad of engineers with blasting charges the way the mercenaries had hoped. The Loot signalled it over peremptorily while his tongue searched the controller of his commo helmet for the setting that would give him Fox Victor's intervehicle push—Hawker's previous radio contact had been with the battalion commander, pointless right now.

The truck, still fifty meters upslope, wavered in its course and did not immediately slow; its driver and vehicle commander, as well as the rest of the six Oltenians aboard, obviously had doubts about the idea of halting on open ground pocked with glassy evidence of Molt gunfire. They *did*, however, turn squarely toward the entrance of the nursery tunnel while the independent axles permitted the four wheels to bobble in nervous disorder over the irregularities of the terrain.

Most important, nobody took a shot at the two Slammers. Profile's tattooed gunhand had swung his own weapon minutely to track the Oltenians; now he relaxed it somewhat. Allies, sure, but curse it, they only had to *look* like they were planning to fire and they were *gone.* . . .

The truck braked to a halt beside the notch in the slope which formed the tunnel entrance. Everybody aboard but the gunner leaped out with the spraddle-legged nervousness of dogs sniffing a stranger's territory. Dust, thrown up by treads that were woven in one piece with the wheel sidewalls from ferrochrome monocrystal, continued to drift downhill at a decreasing velocity.

"Who'n blazes're you!" demanded the close-coupled Oltenian captain who presumably commanded more than the crew of this one truck. Additional vehicles were rolling over the ridge, some of them heavy trucks; and, though the artillery was still crunching away at distant locations, fire from the combat cars in crest positions had slackened for lack of targets.

"We're the fairy godmothers who cleared the back slope for you," said Lieutenant Hawker, pumping his submachine gun toward, and by implication over, the ridge. "Now, I want you guys to go in there and bring out the rest of these, the babies."

He joggled the Molt infant that his left hand held to his breastplate; the little creature made a sound that seemed more like a purr than a complaint. "We get them out—there's maybe a dozen of 'em—and we can pack the tunnel with enough explosives to lift the top off the whole bloody ridge. Let's see 'em use it to snipe from then!"

"You're crazy," said one of the poofs in a tone of genuine disbelief.

"We aren't doing any such thing," agreed his captain. "Just shove the explosives in on top—there'll be plenty room still."

"They're *babies*," Lieutenant Hawker said with the kind of edge that made Bourne smile, not a nice smile, as he checked the damage to the jeep's front skirt. "I didn't risk *my* hide to get a lot of lip from you boys when I saved your bacon. Now, hop!"

Lord knew what the chain of command was in a ratfuck like this situation, but it was a fair bet that the Loot couldn't by protocol give direct orders to a higher-ranking local. Hawker didn't wear rank tabs, nobody did when the Slammers were in a war zone; and no poof with a lick of sense was going to argue with somebody the size and demeanor of the mercenary officer. The captain's short-barreled shotgun twitched on his shoulder where he leaned it, finger within the trigger guard; but it was to the locals around him that he muttered, "Come on, then," as he strode within the lighted tunnel.

The skirt wasn't damaged badly enough to need replacement, but Profile hoped he'd have a chance soon to hose it down. The slime which guttered with Molt scales was already beginning to stink.

The Loot talked to Central, business that Bourne's mind tuned out as effectively as a switch on his helmet could've done. It was relaxing, standing in the sunlight and about as safe as you could be on this bloody planet: there were still the sounds of combat far away, but the jeep was now lost in the welter of other military vehicles, a needle among needles. The Molts were reeling, anyway, and the few hundred casualties this operation had cost them must be a very high proportion of the fighting strength of the theme involved.

Lieutenant Hawker was absently stroking the back of the infant with the muzzle of his submachine gun. In the minutes since the gun was last fired, the iridium had cooled to the point that the little Molt found its warmth pleasurable—or at least it seemed to: its eyes were closed, its breathing placid.

Echoes merged the shots in the tunnel into a single hungry roar.

"Loot, the—" the sergeant began as he knelt beside the skirt, the jeep between him and the gunfire, his own weapon pointed back down the tunnel. He meant a teleporting warrior, of course, but the detector holograms had been within the driver's field of vision and they were calm with no yellow-violet flicker of warning.

Besides, the squad of Oltenians was coming back down the gallery talking excitedly, two of them supporting a third who hopped on one leg and gripped the calf of the other with both hands. But that was only a ricochet; you couldn't blaze away in a confined space and not expect to eat some of your own metal.

Bourne stood up and let his sling clutch the submachine gun back against his breastplate now that he knew there was no problem after all. Wisps of smoke eddied from the barrels of the shotguns, residues of flash suppressant from the propellant charges. The air in the nursery chamber must be hazy with it. . . .

"What in the name of the *Lord* have you done?" Lieutenant Hawker asked the captain in a tone that made Profile Bourne realize that the trouble wasn't over yet after all.

"It's not your planet, renter," the captain said. His face was spattered with what Bourne decided was not his own blood. "You don't capture Molts, you kill 'em. Every cursed chance you get."

"C'mon, somebody get me a medic," the wounded man whined. "This hurts like the very blazes!" The fabric of his trousers was darkening around his squeezing hands, but the damage didn't seem to Bourne anything to lose sleep over.

"I told you . . ." the Loot said in a breathless voice, as though he had been punched hard in the pit of the stomach. The big mercenary was holding himself very straight, the infant against his breastplate in the crook of one arm, towering over the captain and the rest of the poofs, but he had the look of a man being impaled.

A four-vehicle platoon of the combat cars which had been

firing in support now kicked themselves sedately from the ridgeline and proceeded down the slope. Dust bloomed neatly around the margin of the plenum chamber of each, trailing and spreading behind the big, dazzle-painted iridium forms. A powergun bolt hissed so high overhead that it could scarcely be said to be aimed at the cars. Over a dozen tribarrels replied in gorgeous fountains of light that merged kilometers away like strands being spun into a single thread.

"When you've had as many of your buddies zapped as we have," said a poof complacently to the Slammer who had earned his commission on Emporion when he, as ranking sergeant, had consolidated his company's position on the landing zone, "then you'll understand."

"Blood and martyrs, Loot!" said Profile Bourne as he squinted upslope. "That's Alpha Company—it's the White Mice and Colonel Hammer!"

"The only good Molt," said the captain, raising overhead the shotgun he held at the balance and eyeing the infant in Lieutenant Hawker's arms as if it were the nail he was about to hammer, "is a dead—"

And the Loot shot him through the bridge of the nose. Bloody hell, thought Bourne as he sprayed first a poof whose gun was half-pointed, then the one who leaped toward the truck and the weapon mounted there. Had he reloaded after popping the round into the nursery chamber? Bourne's first target was falling forward, tangled with the man the Loot had killed, and the second bounced from the side of the truck, the back of his uniform ablaze and all his muscles gone flaccid in midleap. A bolt that had gotten away from Bourne punched a divot of rock from the polished wall of the tunnel.

"Profile, that's *enough!*" the Loot screamed, but of course it wasn't.

The Oltenian with a bit of his own or a comrade's shot-charge in his calf was trying to unsling his shotgun. Everything in the sergeant's mind was as clear and perfect as gears meshing. The emotion that he felt, electric glee at the unity of the world centered on his gun fight, had no more effect on his functioning than would his fury if the submachine gun jammed. In that case, he would finish the job with the glowing iridium barrel as he had done twice in the past. . . .

The submachine gun functioned flawlessly. Bourne aimed low so that stray shots would clear the Loot, lunging to try to stop his subordinate; and as the trio of poofs doubled up, the second burst hacked into their spines.

This close, a firefight ended when nobody on one side or the other could pull a trigger anymore. The Loot knew that.

Combat cars whining like a pair of restive banshees slid to a dynamic halt to either side of the tunnel archway. The central tribarrel, directly behind the driver's hatch, and one wing gun of each bore on the detection team from close enough to piss if the wind were right. Despite the slope, the cars were not grounded; their drivers held them amazingly steady on thrust alone, their skirts hovering only millimeters above the rocky soil. The offside gunner from either car jumped out and walked around his vehicle with pistol drawn.

Lieutenant Hawker turned very slowly, raising his gunhand into the air. The infant Molt clutched in the crook of the other arm began to greet angrily, disturbed perhaps by the screams and the smell of men's bodies convulsing without conscious control.

A dead man's hand was thrashing at Profile's boot. He stepped back, noticing that the hair on the back of his left hand, clutching the foregrip of his weapon, had crinkled from the heat of the barrel.

"I want you both to unsnap the shoulder loop of your slings," said a voice, clear in Bourne's ears because it came through his commo helmet and not over the rush of the big fans supporting tonnes of combat car so close by.

There was no threat in the words, no emotion in the voice. The quartet of tribarrels was threat enough, and as for emotion—killing wasn't a matter of emotion for men like Profile Bourne and the troopers of Headquarters Company—the White Mice.

Lieutenant Hawker took a long look over his shoulder, past his sergeant and on to the Oltenian vehicles already disappearing over the far ridge—their path to Captain Henderson's infantry cleared by the risks the detection team had taken.

"Aye, aye, Colonel Hammer," Hawker said to the wing gunner in the right-hand car, and he unsnapped his sling.

The hologram display began to flash between yellow and violet, warning that a Molt was about to appear.

"Nikki, I've been looking for you the past half hour," said General Radescu no louder than needful to be heard over the minuet that the orchestra had just struck up. His young aide nonetheless jumped as if goosed with a hot poker, bumping the urn that he had been peering around when Radescu came up behind him. "Alexi, I—" Major Nikki Tzigara said, his face flushed a darker red than the scarlet of his jacket bodice. There were white highlights on Nikki's cheekbones and browridge, and the boy's collar looked too tight. "Well it's a . . ." He gestured toward the whirling tapestry of the dance. "I thought I ought to circulate, you know, since you were so busy with your uncle and important people."

The general blinked, taken aback by the unprovoked sharpness of his aide's tone. Nikki was counterattacking when there'd been no attack, Radescu had only said . . . "Ah, yes, there's no doubt something over a hundred people here I really ought to talk to for one reason or another," he said, filing Tzigara's tone in memory but ignoring it in his response because he hadn't the faintest notion of its cause. Nikki really ought to wear full makeup the way Radescu himself had done ever since he understood the effectiveness of Uncle Grigor's poker face. Antonescu might not have become Chief Tribune, despite all his gifts, had he not learned to rule his expression. Heavy makeup was the edge which concealed the tiny hints from blood and muscle that only the most accomplished politician could wholly control.

And Man, as Aristotle had said, was the political animal.

"Rather like being on the edge of a rhododendron thicket," Radescu continued, looking away from his aide to give Nikki room to compose himself, for pity's sake. Uncle Grigor had worked his way a few meters along the margin of the circular hall so that he was almost hidden by a trio of slender women whose beehive coiffures made them of a height with the tall Chief Tribune. "Very colorful, of course, but one can't see very much through it, can one?

"Which reminds me," he added, rising onto the toes of his gilded boots despite the indignity of it—and finding that he could see no farther across the ballroom anyway, "do you know where the mercenary adjutant is, Major Steuben?"

"Why would I know that? He could be anywhere!"

Makeup wouldn't keep Nikki's voice from being shrill as a powersaw when the boy got excited, Alexander Radescu thought; and thought other things, about the way Nikki's medals were now disarranged, rowels and wreathes and dangling chains caught and skewed among themselves. The back of Radescu's neck was prickling, and the hairs along his arms. He *hoped* it wasn't hormonal, hoped that he had better control of his emotions than that. But dear Lord! He didn't care about Nikki's sexual orientation, but *surely* he had better sense than to get involved with a killer like Steuben . . . didn't he?

Ignoring the whispers in his mind, Radescu eyed the gorgeous show on the ballroom floor and said, "This is *why* the war's being fought, you know, Nikki? The—all the men having to wear uniforms, all the women having to be *seen* with men in uniforms." Except for Uncle Grigor, who distanced himself and his fellow Tribunes from the war by starkly traditional robes. Everyone else—of the aristocracy—gained from the war the chance to cavort in splendid uniforms, while Grigor Antonescu settled for real control of the Oltenian State. . . .

"They don't fight the war—*we* don't fight the war, even the ones of us with regular commissions," Radescu continued, turning to face Nikki again and beginning to straighten the boy's medals, a task that kept his eyes from Tzigara's face. "But it couldn't be fought without our support."

The whole surface of his skin was feeling cold as if the nerves themselves had been chilled, though sweat from the hot, swirling atmosphere still tingled at his joints and the small of his back. The two blue john urns stood tall and aloof just as they had done for centuries, but between them—

"I think maybe the Molts would have something to say about ending the war," said Nikki Tzigara. "I mean, you have your *opinions*, Alexi, but we can't make peace—"

"*Nikki!*" Radescu shouted, for suddenly there was an ancient Molt warrior directly behind the young aide. The Molts hide was the color of an algae-covered stone, soaked for decades in peat water, and his right brow horn was twisted in a way unique in the general's experience. The powergun he held was a full-sized weapon, too heavy for the Molt's stringy muscles to butt it against his shoulder the way one of the Slammers would have done.

The warrior had no need for technique at this range, of course.

Nikki had begun to turn, his mouth still open and saying "—the Molts don't—" when the warrior fired.

The first of his twenty-round magazine.

The human nearest to Ferad flew apart in an explosive cavitation effect, two-thirds of the mass of his thorax having been converted to super-hot steam by the bolt it absorbed from the powergun almost in contact with it. The remainder of the corpse was flung backward by the ball of vaporized matter which coated everything within a five-meter radius, Ferad and the urns included. The flailing yellow sleeves were still attached to the rest of the body, but the scarlet bodice which they had complemented was scooped away to the iridescent white of the membrane covering the inner surface of the victim's spine and ribs.

The taller human in pearl and gold who had been standing behind the first had locked eyes with Ferad. He was an easy target, fallen in a tangle of dancers and only partially covered by the corpse of the companion which had knocked him down . . . but the theme elder's finger paused and twitched only after the muzzle had swung to cover a paunchy man in green and brown and the silvery cape of an immature Molt. Ferad did not need to be fussy about his targets and could not afford the time it would take to pick and choose anyway; but in the case of the human screaming something on the floor, he chose *not* to kill. Perhaps it was the eyes, or something behind them.

The thickly packed humans were trying to surge away from the gun like the waves of compression and rarefaction in a gas. Only those closest to Ferad knew what was happening—the bolts of energy hammered the air and struck with the sound of bombs underwater, but the sounds were not sharp enough to identify them to untrained ears in the noisy ballroom.

The orchestra on the far side of the hall continued to play some incomprehensible human melody, its members aware of the disturbance but stolidly unwilling to emphasize it by falling silent. Ferad shot into fleeing backs trapped by the press.

Sopasian had suggested a bomb in his calm voice that hid a cancer of emotions beneath—envy and scorn, but mostly envy. It was a reasonable suggestion, since a bomb would have killed more than the powergun could in targets as soft and frequent as these. The surface-absorbed, two-centimeter bolts had no penetration, though the amount of energy they released could separate limbs from bodies—and the medals on the first victim's chest were still raining down all across the hall.

But Sopasian missed the point of this attack. They couldn't kill *all* the humans, not even if every Molt on the planet had Ferad's skill or Sopasian's. What Ferad brought to the gala was a personal death, not a sudden blast followed by dust and the screams of the injured. This attack went on and on in the safest place in the world, the victims would have said a moment before.

Cyan light spurted from a gunbarrel so hot that the scales on Ferad's left arm were lifting to trap a blanket of insulating air. The polished wood and stones inlaid into the groined ceiling reflected the shots as they echoed with the screams.

Ferad's peripheral vision was better than that of a human, an adaptation crucial to a Molt teleporting into the confusion of a battle or hunt who had to receive a great deal of data about his immediate surroundings in the first instant. The flash of white drew Ferad to the left, the powergun's barrel shimmering its own arc through the air before him.

None of them were armed. The ballroom was like a nursery tunnel, females and infants and all of them helpless as the veriest newborn—but it had to be done.

One of the Tribunes stood in glistening white, facing Ferad though the three shrieking females in between were scrabbling away. The theme elder fired, clearing a path for his next bolt by taking a female at the point where her bare skin met the ruffles at the base of her spine. Her corpse scissored backward, its upper portion scarcely connected to the splaying legs, and the other two females— now in gowns only half pastel—were thrust from either side to close the gap.

The trio had been caught not by the general confusion but by the grip of the Tribune's arms, protective coloration and, in the event, a shield.

Ferad, wishing for the first time in decades that he had the muscles of a young adult, squeezed off another bolt that parted the white-gowned male from his females, only one of them screaming now and the gown covered with the residues from the flash-heated steam. Had Ferad been younger, he could have leaped on the Tribune, thrusting the heavy powergun against his target and finishing in an instant the business it had taken two shots to prepare. But a young, athletic warrior could never have gotten here, and the Tribune was now sprawled on the floor, his back against the wainscoting and only his palms and spread fingers between his face and the white iridium disk of the powergun muzzle.

The Molt's gun did not fire. Ferad had already spent the last round in his magazine.

The theme leader dropped his useless weapon on the floor, where wood and wax crackled away from the barrel. The hours he had spent in locating the urns here in Belvedere, in gripping them with his mind, were gone from memory. The antechamber of the tunnel system which had been the center of his existence for a hundred and forty years was a dazzling beacon though a thousand kilometers separated it from the theme elder.

For the instant only.

The ballroom and the carnage, almost as dreadful to Ferad as to the humans surviving, trembled for a moment, superimposed on the stone and lamps and shouting warriors of the nursery cave.

Two humans made a final impression on him: the male knocked

down by the first bolt, now trying to rise; and another in the khaki of the mercenaries, so much more dangerous than the forces of the settlers themselves. This mercenary must have wedged his way through a counter-current of bodies in screaming panic. His hand was raised, a pistol in it, and there was a blue-green flash from the muzzle that Ferad did not quite see.

In his millisecond of limbo, the theme elder wondered what success his rival, Sopasian, was having.

"There's a Molt—" said Lieutenant Hawker as the tone in his left earpiece gave him a distance and vector, *bloody* close, but the target designation was figured from the jeep and not where he himself stood a couple paces away.

The trooper sent to collect Hawker's gun snatched the weapon away, nervous to be reaching into the crossed cones of fire of the tribarrels to either flank. "*Drop* it, he said, cophead!" the headquarters trooper snarled, just as somebody shouted to Hammer from the other combat car, "Sir, we've got'n incoming!"

For operations against the Molts, all the Slammers' line armor— the tanks and combat cars—had been fitted with ionization detectors similar to those on the team's jeep. For reasons of space and the need for training to operate more sophisticated gear, however, the detectors which equipped the big blowers were relatively rudimentary. The troops of A Company, Hammer's personal guard, were picked as much for technical skills as they were for ruthlessness and lethality—qualities which were not in short supply in the line companies either. The man calling, "Thirty-five left, eight meters— Colonel, he's coming right beside your car!" was getting more precision from his hardware than Hawker would have thought possible.

The big lieutenant stepped over the body of the Oltenian officer, setting the limbs a-twitch again when the sole of his boot brushed a thigh. The trooper with Hawker's gun holstered his own pistol so that he could level the automatic weapon as he turned toward Hammer and the combat car.

"Loot!" called Profile Bourne, familiar enough with Hawker to know that the lieutenant's disquiet was not simply because a warrior was about to attack. The White Mice could handle *that*, the Lord knew, they weren't poofs who needed a picture to figure which end to piss with.

The trooper who had advanced to take Bourne's gun as his companion did Hawker's was now poised between the sergeant and Hammer, impaled on the horns of a dilemma.

Bourne held his weapon muzzle-high, the barrel vertical and threatening to no one who had not seen how quickly he moved. The left hand, however, was thrust out like a traffic warden's—a barrier in defiance of the pistol which the man from A Company still pointed.

The fellow in the combat car had the vector right and the distance, but there was *something* wrong with what he'd said.

Hawker dropped into his seat in the jeep and laid the infant Molt beside him as Hammer's own combat car slid a few meters upslope, swinging so that the two manned guns still covered the expected target without threatening the dismounted troops besides. The flashing holograms of Hawker's display shifted simultaneously with a subtlety that no tone signal could have conveyed.

"Drop it or you're *dead*, trooper!" the man in front of Profile shouted, but even as he spoke, his pistol and his eyes were shifting to the danger behind him, the tribarrels that might be aligned with his spine.

"Colonel, it's right under you!" shouted the man on the combat car's detector.

Hammer's great car spurted sideways like fluff blown from a seed pod and the digits on Hawker's display shifted as quickly.

"Colonel!" the lieutenant bellowed, trying to make himself heard over the fans of the big blowers roaring in the machine equivalent of muscles bunched for flight. His unit link was to Henderson's infantry company, and tonguing Central wouldn't have given him the direct line to Hammer that he needed now.

"It's *in* your car!" Hawker shouted as he leaped out of the jeep, snatching for the submachine gun that had been taken from him.

The Molt was so old that wrinkles showed like dark striping

on his face as the warrior appeared in the fighting compartment between Hammer and the other gunner, both of them craning their necks to scan the rocky ground beside the car. If their body hairs felt the sudden shift in electrostatic balance as the autochthon appeared behind them, that warning was buried in the subconscious of veterans faced with a known threat.

"Contact!" the A Company detection specialist shouted into the instruments on which his attention was focused, and his companion at the wing tribarrel triggered a shot into the empty soil by reflex. The Molt warrior's wiry arms held, raised, a blade of glittering blue steel; the junction between Hammer's helmet and body armor was bared as the colonel stretched to find a target before him.

Hawker caught his gun, but the trooper holding it wouldn't have been in the White Mice if he were soft. He held the weapon with one hand and rabbit-punched the lieutenant with the other, an instinctive, pointless act since Hawker was wearing body armor; but the trooper *held* the gun as the Molt's sword swung downward, unseen by anyone but Hawker—

—and Sergeant Bourne. The Molt sword blade was a sandwich of malleable iron welded to either side of a core of high carbon steel, quick-quenched to a rich blue after forging. That razor-sharp steel and the black iron which gave the blade resilience glowed momentarily cyan in reflecting the bolt flicking past them, brighter for that instant than the sun.

Hammer flattened behind the iridium bulkhead, his commo helmet howling with static induced by the bolt which had bubbled the plastic surface.

The trooper who should have disarmed Profile Bourne was one of those whose eyes were drawn by the bolt to the warrior in the combat car. The autochthon's sword sparked on the lip of the fighting compartment and bounced out. The Molt himself twisted. His face had two eyesockets but only one eye, and the wrinkles were bulged from his features when his head absorbed the energy of the single shot.

The driver of Hammer's car had no view of the scene behind him. He drew a pistol and presented it awkwardly through his hatch, trying to aim at Bourne while still holding the car steady with one hand.

"No!" cried the trooper who had tried to disarm Bourne, windmilling his arms as he made sure he was between the sergeant and the guns threatening him.

Lieutenant Hawker and the trooper with whom he struggled now separated cautiously, Hawker releasing the submachine gun and the man from A Company licking the scraped knuckles of his left hand. There was a pop in the lieutenant's helmet, static from a message he did not himself receive, and the sound level dropped abruptly as both combat cars grounded and cut their fans.

The Molt's sword had stuck point first in the soil. It rang there, a nervous keening that complemented the cries of the infant Molt, dumped without ceremony on the driver's seat when Hawker had gotten into the jeep. The big lieutenant walked back toward his vehicle and lifted the Molt with both hands to hide the fact that they were both trembling.

Colonel Alois Hammer reappeared, standing up with deliberation rather than caution. He held something in his left hand which he looked at, then flipped like a coin to fall spinning onto the ground near the sword. It was the sapphire condensing plate from a combat car's navigation display, a thick fifty-millimeter disk whose internal cross-hatching made it a spot of fluid brilliance in the sunlight.

"He was holding that," said the colonel, pointing to the disk with the pistol in his right hand. He fired, igniting grass and fusing a patch of soil without quite hitting his target. "I didn't know they could do that," and the condensing plate shattered like a bomb, the scored lines providing a myriad fracture sites.

Hammer fired twice more into the mass of glittering particles that carpeted the ground.

"Now, kid, it could be a lot worse," muttered Enzo Hawker as he patted the shivering infant's back and wondered if that were true for the little Molt, for any of them. The sounds of distant battle were like hogs rooting among the mast, shellfire and diesels and the mighty soughing of the Slammers' ground-effect vehicles.

"Hey!" called Sergeant Bourne, holding his weapon vertical

again and aloft at the length of its sling. "Still want *this*, Colonel?" His voice was high and hectoring, a reaction to having made a shot that he would never have dared attempt had he paused to think about what he was doing. A millimeter, two millimeters to the right, and the bolt would have expended itself on Hammer's face an instant before the sword finished the business.

"Disarm the man," Hammer ordered in a voice as far away as the breeze moving wispy clouds in the high stratosphere.

"Sure, all right," said Profile, and perhaps only Hawker realized that the brittle edge in his voice was terror and not a threat. The sergeant's left hand fumbled with the sling catch while his right hand held clear the submachine gun, though its barrel was by now cool enough to touch.

"Only one thing—" the enlisted man added.

"Profile, don't—" said Hawker, aware that three tribarrels were again aimed at his partner's chest.

"Only you better keep the Loot on his console," Bourne completed as he flung his weapon to the ground. "Until you hunt up somebody else who knows how to use the bloody gear, at least."

Three pistol bolts struck within a palm's scope, the first shattering the urn of blue john. The other two sparkled among the shivered fragments, reducing some of the fluorspar to its ionized constituents. Other chips now ranged in color from gray to brilliant amethyst, depending on how close they had been to the momentary heat. Larger chunks, the upper third of the urn, cascaded over the gun the Molt had dropped and, dropping it, disappeared.

Ozone and nascent fluorine battled for ascendancy between themselves, but neither could prevail over the stench of death.

Someone had kicked Alexander Radescu in the temple as he flopped backward to the floor. His memory of the past thirty seconds was a kaleidoscope rather than a connected series, but he was not sure that the blow had anything to do with his disorganization. The gun muzzle flickering like a strobe light while the white glow of the iridium remained as a steady portent of further death . . .

Radescu's right hand lay across his gilded cap, so he could don it again without looking down. He stumbled on his first step toward Chief Tribune Antonescu, but he knew what was binding his right foot and knew also that he dared not actually view it.

Lifting his foot very carefully to clear what was no longer Nikki or anything human, the young general murmured, "I'm going to be fine if I don't think about it. I just don't want to think about it, that's all." His tone would have been suitable had he been refusing a glass of sherry or commenting on the hang of a uniform. He couldn't keep from remembering and imagining concrete realities, of course, but by acting very carefully he could keep them from being realities of *his* experience.

The screams had not stopped when the Molt warrior disappeared. Most of the crowd still did not know what had happened. Would the *Lord* that Alexander Radescu were as ignorant!

"I was afraid you'd been shot, my boy," said Grigor Antonescu, politic even at such a juncture, "by that—" he nodded toward the spilled crystals of bluejohn, cubic and octahedral, and the gun they lay across like a stone counterpane "—or the other."

Staring over his shoulder, Radescu saw Major Steuben picking his way toward them with a set expression and quick glances all around him, ready now for any target which presented itself. Hammer's bodyguard had been marginally too late for revenge, and not even *his* reflexes would have been quick enough to save Nikki. None of the rest mattered to Radescu, not the dead or the maimed, those catatonic with fear or the ones still screaming their throats raw.

But that was over, and the past could not be allowed to impede what the future required.

"This can't go on, Uncle Grigor," Radescu said with a twist of his neck, a dismissing gesture.

The Chief Tribune, whose face and robes were now as much red as white, said, "Security, you mean, Alexi? Yes, we should have had real guards, shouldn't we? Perhaps Hammer's men. . . ."

In his uncle's reasonable voice, Radescu heard himself—a mind that should have been in shock, but which had a core too tough to permit that in a crisis.

Members of the Honor Guard were running about, brilliant in their scarlet uniforms and almost as useless in a firefight as the unarmed militia "officers" attending the ball. They were waving chrome and rhodium-plated pistols as they spilled in through the doors at which they'd been posted to bar the uninvited. If they weren't lucky, there'd be more shots, more casualties. . . .

"Not security, not here at least," said General Radescu, gesturing curtly at one of the Honor Guards gagging at a tangle of bodies. "It's the war itself that has to be changed."

"We can't do that," Antonescu replied bitterly, "without changing the army."

"Changing its command, Uncle Grigor," said Alexander Radescu as his mind shuddered between Nikki's flailing body and the gunbarrel of the aged Molt. "Yes, that's exactly what we have to do first."

The young general flicked at spots on his jacket front, but he stopped when he saw they were smearing further across the pearl fabric.

"I need two gunmen who won't argue about orders," said Radescu to Colonel Hammer, standing where a granite pillar had been blasted to glittering gravel to prevent Molt warriors from materializing on top of them. The Oltenian general spoke loudly to be heard over the pervasive intake rush of the four command vehicles maneuvering themselves back to back to form the Field Operations Center. The verdigrised black head and cape of an ancient Molt were mounted on a stake welded to the bow of one of the cars.

The aide standing with Hammer smiled, but the mercenary colonel himself looked at Radescu with an expression soured both by the overall situation and specifically by the appearance of Alexander Radescu: young, dressed in a uniform whose gold and pearl fabrics were showing signs of blowing grit only minutes after the general disembarked from his aircraft—and full facial makeup, including lip tint and a butterfly-shaped beauty patch on his right cheekbone.

"There's a whole Oltenian army out there," said Hammer bitterly, waving in the direction of the local forces setting up in the near distance. "Maybe you can find two who know which end of a gun the bang comes out of. Maybe you can even find a couple willing to get off their butts and *move*. Curst if I've been able to find 'em, though."

Radescu had worn his reviewing uniform for its effect on the Oltenian command staff, but it was having the opposite result on the mercenaries. "The Tribunes are aware of that," he said with no outward sign of his anger at this stocky, worn, *deadly* man. Grime and battledress did not lower Hammer in the Oltenian's opinion, but the mercenary's deliberate sneering *coarseness* marked him as incurably common. "That's why they've sent me to the field: to take over and get the army moving again. My uncle—" he added, by no means inconsequently "—is Chief Tribune."

The Oltenian general reached into a breast pocket for his identification—a message tube which would project a hologram of Chief Tribune Antonescu with his arm around his nephew, announcing the appointment "to all members of the armed forces of Oltenia and allied troops." Hammer's aide forestalled him, however, by saying, "This is General Radescu, sir."

"Sure, I haven't forgotten," Colonel Hammer remarked with an even deeper scowl, "but he's not what *I* had in mind when I heard they were going to send somebody out to take charge."

He looked from his aide to Radescu and continued, "Oh, don't look so surprised, General. That's part of what you hired us for, wasn't it? Better communications and detection gear than you could supply on-planet?"

Radescu's tongue touched his vermilion lips and he said, "Yes, of course, Colonel," though it was not "of course" and he was quite certain that Chief Tribune Antonescu would have been even more shocked at the way these outsiders had penetrated the inner councils of the State. Radescu had flown to the front without even an aide to accompany him because of the complete secrecy needed for the success of his mission. Though what the mercenaries knew of his plan was not important . . . so long as they had not communicated what they knew to the Oltenian planetary forces.

Which brought the young general back to the real point at issue. "This time the help I need involves another part of the reason we hired you, though."

"General," said Hammer coldly, "I've lost equipment and I've lost men because local forces didn't support my troops when they advanced. We're going to carry out basic contract commitments from here on . . . but I don't do any favors for Oltenian tarts. No, I don't have two men to spare."

"There's Hawker and Bourne," said the aide unexpectedly. He gave Radescu a sardonic smile as he continued. "Might be a way out of more problems than one."

A trio of Slammers were striding toward their leader from the assembled Operations Center, two men and a woman, who looked too frail for her body armor and the equipment strapped over it. Hammer ignored them for the moment and said to his aide, "Look, Pritchard, we can't afford to lose our bond over something like this."

"Look, I have full—" Radescu interjected.

"We're turning them over to the local authority for processing," said Pritchard, as little impressed with the general in gold and pearl as his colonel was. "Via, Colonel, you don't want to call out a firing party for our own men, not for something like that."

Hammer nodded to the three officers who had halted a respectful two paces from him; then, to Radescu, he said as grimly as before, "General, I'm turning over to you Lieutenant Hawker and Sergeant-Commander Bourne, who have been sentenced to death for the murder of six members of the allied local forces. Whatever action you take regarding them will be regarded as appropriate."

He turned his head from Radescu to the waiting trio. "Captain?" he said on a note of query.

"Hammer to Radescu," the woman said with a nod. "It's being transmitted to the Bonding Authority representative."

"All right, General Radescu," Hammer continued, "you'll find the men in the adjutant's charge, Car four-five-niner. I wish you well of them. They were good men before they got involved with what passes for an army here on Oltenia."

Hammer and his aide both faced toward the trio of other mercenaries as if Radescu had already left them.

"But—" the Oltenian general asked, as unprepared for this development as for the scorn with which the offer was made. "*Why* did they, did they commit these murders?"

Hammer was deep in conversation with one of the other officers, but Pritchard glanced back over his shoulder at Radescu and said, "Why don't you ask *them*, General?" He smiled again without warmth as he turned his head and his attention again.

General Alexander Radescu pursed his lips, but he sucked back the comment he had started to make and quenched even the anger that had spawned it. He had made a request, and it had been granted. He was in no position to object that certain conventions had been ignored by the mercenaries.

"Thank you for your cooperation, Colonel," he said to the commo helmets bent away from him above backs clamshelled in porcelain armor. The woman, the communications officer, cocked an eye at the general only briefly. "I assure you that from here on you will have no call to complain about the cooperation the Oltenian forces offer you."

He strode away briskly, looking for a vehicle with skirt number 459. The set of his jaw was reflected alternately in the gilded toe-caps of his shoes.

"One moment, sir," said a graying man who might have been the adjutant—none of the Slammers seemed to wear rank insignia in the field, and officers wore the same uniforms as enlisted men.

Another of the mercenaries had, without being asked, walked to a room-sized goods container and rapped on the bars closing the front of it. "Profile!" he called. "Lieutenant Hawker! He's here to pick you guys up."

"We were informed, of course, sir," said the probable adjutant who looked the Oltenian up and down with an inward smile that was obvious despite its lack of physical manifestations. "Did you get lost in the encampment?"

"Something like that," said Radescu bitterly. "Perhaps you could find a vehicle to carry me and, and my new aides, to, ah, my headquarters?"

"We'll see about that, of course, sir," said the graying man, and the smile did tug a corner of his mouth.

The Slammers had sprayed the area of their intended base camp with herbicide. Whatever they used collapsed the cell walls of all indigenous vegetation almost completely so that in the lower, wetter areas, the sludge of dissolved plant residue was as much as knee deep. That didn't seem to bother the mercenaries, all of whom rode if they had more than twenty meters to traverse—but it had created a pattern of swamps for Radescu which he finally crossed despite its effect on his uniform. He would look a *buffoon* when he called the command staff together!

Then he relaxed. He dared not hold the meeting without two gunmen behind him, and if the mercenaries' public scorn was the price of those gunmen—so be it. Alexander Radescu had thought a long time before he requested this duty from his uncle. He was not going to second-guess himself now.

"Got your gear over here, Profile," said the mercenary who had opened the crude cell and stepped inside the similar—unbarred—unit beside it. He came out again, carrying a heavy suit of body armor on either arm.

The men who had just been freed took their equipment, eyeing Radescu. The young general stared back at them, expecting the sneering dismissal he had received from other mercenaries. What he got instead was an appraisal that went beneath the muck and his uniform, went deeper into Alexander Radescu than an outsider had ever gone before.

It was insufferable presumption on the part of these hirelings.

Lieutenant Hawker was a large, soft-looking man. There were no sharp angles to his face or frame, and his torso would have been egg-shaped in garments which fit closer than the floppy Slammers battledress. He swung the porcelain clamshell armor around himself unaided, however, an action that demonstrated exceptional strength and timing.

His eyes were blue, and the look in them made Radescu wonder how many of the six Oltenians Hawker had killed himself.

Profile, presumably Sergeant Bourne, was no taller than Colonel Hammer and was built along the lines of Radescu's own whippy thinness rather than being stocky like the mercenary commander. His bold smile displayed his upper incisors with the bluish tinge characteristic of tooth buds grown *in vitro*.

There was a scar on the sergeant's head above his right temple, a bald patch of keloid that he had tried to train his remaining hair to cover, and a streak of fluorescent orange wrapping his bare right forearm. Radescu thought the last was a third scar until he saw that it terminated in a dragon's head laid into the skin of Bourne's palm, a hideous and hideously obtrusive decoration . . . and a sign of scarring as well, though not in the physical sense.

Bourne locked shut his body armor and said, "Well, this is the lot of it, Major?" to the graying adjutant.

That mercenary officer grimaced, but said, "Give them their guns, Luckens."

The Slammer who had brought the armor had already ducked back from the storage container with a submachine gun in either hand and ammunition satchels in the crooks of both elbows, grinning almost as broadly as Sergeant Bourne.

The lieutenant who had just been freed had no expression at all on his face as he started to load his own weapon. His left hand slid a fresh magazine into the handgrip of his powergun, a tube containing not only the disks which would liberate bolts of energy but the liquid nitrogen which worked the action and cooled the chamber between shots. As his hands moved, Hawker's eyes watched the Oltenian general.

"I'll need to brief you men in private," Radescu said, managing to override the unexpected catch in his throat. "I'm General Radescu, and the two of you are assigned at my discretion." How private the briefing could be when Hammer listened to discussions in the Tribunal Palace was an open question . . . but again, it didn't matter what the *mercenary* command knew.

"Major Stanzas," said Hawker to the adjutant, only now rotating his face from the Oltenian, "do you see any problem with me borrowing back my jeep for the, ah, duration of the assignment?"

"General," said the adjutant, thumbing a switch in the oral notepad he pointed toward Radescu, "do you accept on behalf of your government the loan of a jeep with detection gear in it?" That gave Hammer somebody to bill if something went wrong . . . and they must already have a record of the level to which the Tribunes had authorized Radescu's authorization.

"Yes, yes, of course," the general snapped, noticing that Bourne had anticipated the question and answer by striding toward a saucer-shaped air-cushion vehicle. It had been designed to hold four people, but this one had seats for only two because the back was filled with electronics modules.

"You may not be real comfortable riding on the hardware that way," Hawker said, "but it beats having a Molt pop out of the air behind you." He turned his head slowly, taking in the arc of non-descript landscape he could not have seen through the barred front of his cell. "Not," he added, "that we'll see action around here."

Radescu gave the big mercenary a brief, tight smile. "You don't think so, Lieutenant? I wouldn't have come to Colonel Hammer for someone to drive me and—" he appraised Hawker in a different fashion, then made a moue which flapped the wings of his beauty patch before he concluded "—bring me tea at night."

Hawker spat on the ground. He would probably have dropped the conversation even without Sergeant Bourne spinning the jeep to an abrupt halt between the two officers and calling cheerfully, "Hop in, everybody." His submachine gun was now carried across his chest on an inertia-locked sling which gave him access to the weapon the instant he took his right hand from the tiller by which he now guided the jeep.

The general settled himself, finding that the modules had been arranged as the back and sides of a rough armchair, with room enough for his hips in the upper cavity. The handles for carrying the modules made excellent grips for Radescu; but there was no cushion, only slick, hard composite, and he hoped Bourne would not play the sort of game with the outsider which he in fact expected.

"Get us a short distance beyond this position and stop," the Oltenian said, bracing himself for an ejection-seat start. He thought of ordering Hawker to trade places with him, but he was sure such a demand would also turn into an embarrassment for him. "I'll brief you there."

Instead of a jackrabbit start, the mercenary sergeant powered up the jeep in an acceleration curve so smooth that only the airstream was a problem to Radescu on his perch. The Oltenian snatched off his glistening, metalized cap and held it against his lap as he leaned forward into the wind.

Bourne was driving fast, but with an economy of movement on the tiller and such skill that the attitude of the jeep did not change even when it shot up the sloping inner face of the berm around the firebase and sailed above the steep outer contour in momentary free flight. He wasn't trying to dump Radescu off the back: Bourne took too much pride in his skill to drive badly as a joke.

"Colonel won't like the way you're speeding in his firebase," Lieutenant Hawker said mildly to the sergeant.

"What's he going to do?" Bourne demanded. "Sentence me to death?" But he slacked off the trigger throttle built into the grip of the tiller.

Between the encampments, Oltenian and mercenary, was a wooded ridge high enough to block shots fired from either position toward targets in the no man's land between. Radescu had understood the forces were integrated, but obviously the situation in the field had changed in a fashion which had not yet been reported to the Tribunes in Belvedere. Bourne threaded his way into a copse of broad-leafed trees on the ridge while Radescu held his seat firmly, aware that even at their present reduced speed he would be shot over the front of the vehicle if the driver clipped one of the boles around which he maneuvered so blithely.

It was without incident, however, that Bourne set the jeep down out of direct sight of either encampment. He turned and looked up at Radescu with a sardonic grin; and Hawker, still-faced, looked as well.

Radescu laughed harshly. "I was wondering," he said to the

surprised expressions of the mercenaries, "whether I'm speaking to you from the height of a throne—or of a cross." He swung himself to the ground, a trifle awkwardly because the padding in his uniform trousers to exaggerate his buttocks had not been sufficient to prevent the hard ride from cutting blood circulation to his legs.

"That's fitting, in a way," the Oltenian said to the Slammers watching as his hands massaged his thighs, a thumb and forefinger still gripping the gilded brim of his hat, "because the Tribunes have granted me power of life and death over all members of the armed forces of the State—but they haven't taught me how to bring the dead to life."

Without speaking, Lieutenant Hawker slipped from his own seat and stood with one heel back against the ground-effect mantle of the jeep. Bourne shifted only very slightly so that he faced Radescu directly; the head of the dragon on his palm rested on the grip of his submachine gun.

"I have been given *full* authority to take command and get the offensive against the Molts on track again," Radescu continued, "and I have the responsibility as well as authority to deal with the situation. But the present command staff is going to resent me, gentlemen, and I do not believe I can expect to do my job unless I go into my initial meeting with you present."

"You think," said Hawker as something small and nervous shrilled down at the men from a treetop, "that the present officers will arrest you if we aren't there to protect you."

"There's two of us, General," added Profile Bourne, whose index finger traced the trigger guard of his weapon, "and there's three divisions over there." He thumbed toward the encampment. "We can't handle that, friend. No matter how much we might like to."

"The army command, and the commander and chief of staff of each division will be present," said General Radescu, stretching his arms out behind his back because when the muscles were under tension they could not tremble visibly. "And they won't do anything overt, no, it's not what they'll say—"

The young Oltenian straightened abruptly, glaring at the

Slammers. "But I don't care what they say, gentlemen, I didn't come here to preside over an army sinking into a morass of lethargy and failure. I will remove any officer who seems likely to give only lip service to my commands.

"And—" he paused, for effect but also because the next words proved unexpectedly hard to get out his throat "—and if I give the signal, gentlemen, I expect you to kill everyone else in the room without question or hesitation. I will give the signal—" he twirled the band of his hat on his index finger "—by dropping my hat."

Glittering like a fairy crown in a shaft of sunlight, Radescu's hat spun to the forest floor. The only sound in the copse for the next ten seconds was the shrieking of the animal in the foliage above them.

"Via," said Sergeant Bourne, in a voice too soft for its precise emotional loading to be certain.

"Sir," said Lieutenant Hawker, shifting his weight from the jeep so that both feet rested firmly on the ground, "does Colonel Hammer know what you intend? For us?"

Radescu nodded crisply, feeling much lighter now that he had stated what he had not, as it turned out, clearly articulated even in his own mind. He felt as though he were listening to the conversation from a vantage point outside his own body. "I have told no one of my specific plans," his mouth said, "not even Chief Tribune Antonescu, my uncle. But I believe Colonel Hammer did—would not be surprised by anything that happened. The point that caused him to grant my request was your, your special status, gentlemen."

"Via," Sergeant Bourne repeated.

Hawker walked over to the gilded cap and picked it up with his left hand, the hand which did not hold a submachine gun.

"Here, sir," he said as he handed the hat back to General Radescu. "You may be needing it soon."

"Hoo, *Lordy!*" said Sergeant Bourne to the captain who nervously ushered them in to the staff room to wait. "Where's the girls, goodson?" He pinched the Oltenian's cheek, greatly to the man's embarrassment. "Not that you're not cute yourself, dearie."

"This the way you—gentlemen—normally operate in the field?"

Hawker asked as his palm caressed the smooth surface of a nymph in a wall fountain.

"Well, the water's recycled, of course," Radescu said in mild surprise as he considered the matter for the first time.

He looked around the big room, the tapestries—reproductions, of course—and ornately carven furniture, the statues in the wall niches set off by foliage and rivulets. The Slammers lieutenant looked as incongruous here, wearing his scarred armor and unadorned weapon, as a bear would in a cathedral: but it was Hawker, not the fittings, which struck Radescu as out of place. "This does no harm, Lieutenant, beyond adding a little to our transport requirements. A modicum of comfort during staff meetings doesn't prevent officers from performing in a responsible and, and, courageous manner in action."

He was wondering whether there would be enough time to requisition an orderly to clean the muck from his boots. On balance, that was probably a bad idea since the pearl trousers were irredeemably ruined. Better to leave the ensemble as it was for the moment rather than to increase its absurdity. . . .

"Just how do you expect to get bloody Oltenian officers to act courageously, General-sir?" Bourne asked in a tone much more soberly questioning than the sarcasm of the words suggested. The three men were alone in the room, now that the poof captain had banged the door nervously behind him, and Bourne watched Radescu over the decorated palm of his right hand.

"I'm going to lead from the front, Sergeant Bourne," the young general said quietly, noticing that the expression on the mercenary's face was very similar to that on the dead Molt staked to the bow of Hammer's command vehicle.

Radescu had seen no trophies of that sort in their drive through the State encampment. That could be a matter of taste—but equally it might mean that Oltenian forces had failed to kill any of the aliens.

Of the autochthons. Oltenia was, after all, the Molts' world alone until the human settlement three centuries before.

"I . . ." said Radescu, choosing to speak aloud on a subject different from that on which his mind would whisper to him if his mouth remained silent. "Ah. . . . Tell me, if you will, how the charges came to be leveled against you, the two of you."

"Why we blew away those heroes of the Oltenian State, Lieutenant," restated Bourne with a bitter smile.

The big Slammers lieutenant sat down on the coping of the fountain. The seat of his trousers must have been in the water, but he did not appear to notice. "Sure, General," he said in the accentless Oltenia-Rumanian which all the Slammers had been sleep-taught when their colonel took the present contract. "I'll tell you about what happened."

Hawker closed his eyes and rubbed his brow with the knuckles of his right hand. In a heart-stopping flash, Radescu realized that the mercenary was removing his fingers from the grip of his weapon before he called up memories of the past.

"We cleared a bottleneck for a battalion of locals," Hawker said.

"Your boys, General," Sergeant Bourne interjected.

"Killed a few ourselves, pointed some others out with gunfire," the lieutenant continued. "No point in knowing where a Molt's going to appear a minute ahead of time if it took us ten to relay the data. These're a pretty good short-range data link." He patted the gray plastic receiver of his submachine gun.

"You were able to have that much effect yourselves?" Radescu said, seating himself at the head of the long conference table. The richly grained wood hid the ruin of his boots and uniform; though when the time came, he really ought to rise to greet the officers he had summoned. "To clear a corridor, I mean?"

"Got our bag limit that day," said Bourne, wiping his lips with the dragon on his palm. "By the *Lord* we did."

"We took the Molts by surprise," Hawker explained. "There really aren't that many of them, the warriors, and we cleared out the ones who knew the territory before they figured things out."

Hawker's right thumb stripped something from a belt dispenser to give his hands something to play with as he talked. The gesture relaxed Radescu somewhat until he realized that the mercenary was now juggling an eyeball-sized minigrenade.

"We ducked into a nursery tunnel then, to get clear of the

snipers," Hawker said. "Figured that warriors could come at us there, but before we were in danger Profile'd hand 'em one to keep."

"Where the chicken got the ax," said Bourne, running an index finger—his left—across his throat. Radescu thought the gesture was figurative. Then he noticed the knife blade, the length of the finger along which it lay and so sharp that light rippled on its edges as it did on the water dancing down the nymph's stone arms.

Bourne smiled and flicked his left hand close to some of the decorative foliage in the nearest wall niche. A leaf gave a startled quiver; half of it fluttered to the floor, severed cleanly. Satisfied, Bourne stropped both sides of the blade against his thigh to clean any trace of sap from the weapon.

"Thing about the Molts," he went on, leaning closer to Radescu, "is that how far they can pop through the air depends on how old they are." It was the sort of lecture the sergeant would have given a man fresh to the field . . . as Radescu was, but he and his ancestors in unbroken line had been living with the Molts for three hundred years. The Oltenian general listened with an air of careful interest, however; the disquisition indicated a level of positive feeling toward him on the mercenary's part; and for more reasons than his plan for the meeting, Radescu wanted Bourne to like him.

"The old males," the sergeant said, "there's no telling how far they can hop if there's a big enough piece of hard rock for 'em to get a *grip* of, like. With their minds, you know? But the females—not bad looking some of 'em either, in the right light—"

"Profile . . . ?"

"Yes sir." Bourne's right hand nodded a gobbling gesture in front of his mouth as if the dragon's head were swallowing the words he had just spoken. "But the females can hop only maybe ten kays and it takes 'em longer to psych into doing it, even the old ones. And the little babies, they can't jump the length of my prick when they're newborn. So the adults keep 'em in holes in the rock so their minds can get the feel of the rock, like; touch the electrical charge when the rock shifts. And there they were when we got in, maybe a dozen a' the babes."

"And that was about when it dropped in the pot, I s' pose,

General," said Hawker as he stood up deliberately and faced the wall so that he would not have to look at the cosmetic-covered Oltenian face as he finished the story. "A, a local officer . . . I told him to get the little ones out of the tunnel; figured they'd be put in a holding tank somewhere. And he killed them."

Hawker's back muscles strained against his clamshell armor, hunching it. "There was one more I was holding, a little Molt I'd brought out myself."

He turned again, proceeding through stress to catharsis. "I blew that poof to Hell, General Radescu, before he could kill that baby too."

Alexander Radescu had seen the Slammers' powerguns demonstrated. The snap of their blue-green energy was too sudden to be fully appreciated by the senses, though the retinas danced for almost a minute thereafter with afterimages of the discharge's red-orange complement. A shot would be dazzling in a cavern of dark rock lighted by Molt torches and the lamps of the vehicles driven headlong within. The blood and stench of the sudden corpse, that, too, Radescu could visualize—had to be able to visualize or he would not stay functionally sane if this meeting this morning proceeded as he feared it might, planned that it might. . . .

"And you, Bourne," Radescu said, "you were condemned simply for being present?" It was more or less what he had expected, though he had presumed that the sergeant was the principal in the event and Lieutenant Hawker was guilty of no more than failure to control his murderous subordinate. It was the sort of clean sweep Chief Tribune Antonescu would have made. . . .

"Oh, one a' the poofs threw down on the Loot," Bourne said. He was smiling because he had returned to an awareness of the fact that he was alive: when Radescu had first seen the sergeant, Bourne was dead in his own mind; waiting as much for burial as the shot in the back of his neck that would immediately precede interment. "I took him out and, Via, figured better safe'n sorry."

He looked at the mercenary officer, and the set of his jaw was as fierce for the moment as any expression he had thrown Radescu. "I still think so, Loot. There a couple of times, I figured I'd been crazy to hand this over and let them put us in that box." His index finger tapped the submachine gun's receiver, then slipped within the trigger guard as if of its own volition. "And you know, we aren't out of it yet, are we?"

Bourne shifted his torso to confront Hawker, and the muzzle of the slung weapon pointed as well.

"Anybody ever swear you'd get out of the Slammers alive, Sergeant?" Lieutenant Hawker asked in a voice as slick and cold as the iridium barrel of the gun thrusting toward him.

Radescu tensed, but there was no apparent fear in Hawker's grim visage—and no more of challenge, either, than that of a man facing a storm cloud in the knowledge that the rain will come if it will.

"Ah, Via, Loot," Bourne said, the sling slapping the submachine gun back against his chest when he let it go, "I didn't want ta grease the colonel, cop. After all, he gave this poor boy a job didn't he?"

Hawker laughed, and Bourne laughed; and the door beside the sergeant opened as the first of the command staff entered the meeting room, already three minutes after the deadline in Radescu's summons.

The Oltenian general looked from the newcomer to the wall clock and back to the newcomer, Iorga, the Second Division commander. When Radescu himself smiled, Sergeant Bourne was uneasily reminded of a ferret he had once kept as a pet—and Hawker caught a glimpse, too, beneath the beauty patch and lip tint, of a mind as ruthless as the blade of a scythe.

It took the command staff thirty-six minutes to assemble in the large trailer in the center of the Oltenian encampment, though none of the officers were more than a kilometer away at the summons and Radescu had clearly stated that anyone who did not arrive in fifteen minutes put his command in jeopardy for that fact alone. It was not, he thought, that they did not believe the threat: it was simply that the men involved would be *unable* to act that promptly even if it were their lives that depended on it.

Which indeed was the case.

The quarters of the Army Commander, Marshal Erzul, adjoined the conference trailer; but it was to no one's surprise that Erzul arrived last of the officers summoned . . . and it did not surprise Alexander Radescu that the marshal attempted to enter surrounded by his personal aides. The milling, disconsolate troop of underlings outside the doorway of the conference room was warning enough that Radescu hewed precisely to the language of the summons; but Erzul's action was not motivated by ignorance.

Radescu had motioned the six earlier arrivals to chairs while he himself sat on a corner of the conference table and chatted with them—recruiting figures, the season's colors in the capital, the gala for the Widows of the War at which a Molt had appeared with a powergun, firing indiscriminately. "There were two stone urns, no more than that, and the Molt focused on them across over a thousand kays—" he was saying, when the door opened and the divisional officers leaped to their feet to salute Marshal Erzul.

Radescu cocked his head toward the marshal and his entourage, then turned away. He did not rise for Erzul who was not, despite his rank, Radescu's superior officer, and he twisted the gold-brimmed cap furiously in his hands. Around and back, like the glittering spirals of a fly jumped by a spider, both of them together buzzing on the end of the spider's anchor line; around and back.

The young general took a deep breath. By looking at the two officers closest to where he sat at the head of the table, he was able to avoid seeing either of the Slammers poised along the wall where they seemed muddy shadows against the opulence and glitter of the room's furnishings and other occupants. He could not avoid his own imagination, however, and the doubt as to whether there would be any safe place in the room when the guns began to spray. He closed his eyes momentarily, not a blink but part of the momentary tensioning of all his muscles . . . but he *had* to learn whose orders they would take, these men around him.

"Generals Oprescu and Iorga," Radescu said loudly, fixing the commanders of the First and Second Divisions with eyes as pure as the blue enamel on his shoulder boards, "will you kindly put out of the conference room all those who seem to have entered with the marshal? All save General Forsch, that is, since the Tribunes have ordered him to attend as well."

There was a frozen pause. Iorga looked at Oprescu, Oprescu at his manicure as a flush mounted from his throat to the cheeks which he had not had time to prepare with a proper base of white gel.

Erzul was a stocky, jowly bulldog to Radescu's cat. As his aides twitched and twittered, the marshal himself crashed a step forward. "This is *my* command," he thundered to the back of Radescu's head, his eyes drawn unwillingly to the flickering highlights of the cap in the general's hands, "and *I* decide where my aides will be!"

"The summons that brought you here, Marshal," Radescu announced in a voice which became increasingly thin in his own ears, though no one else in the room seemed to hear the difference, "informed you that the Tribunes had placed me in charge of all personnel of the First Army, yourself included."

"The Tribunes," sneered Erzul as everyone else in the room stayed frozen and Sergeant Bourne's eyes focused on something a thousand leagues away. "Your *uncle*."

"Yes," said the young general as he rose to his muddy feet, fanning himself gently with the cap in his hand, "my uncle."

General Iorga made a little gesture with the backs of his hands and fingers as if he were a house servant trying to frighten a wasp out of the room with a napkin. "Go on," he said to the captain closest to him in a voice with a tinge of hysteria and desperation. "Go *on* then, you shouldn't *be* here!"

All of the divisional officers, not just the pair to whom Radescu had directed his order, sprang forward as if to physically thrust their juniors out of the conference room. General Forsch, Erzul's lanky, nervous chief of staff, slid behind the marshal as if for concealment and in fear that the sudden onslaught would force him out the door with subordinate aides.

Neither of the mercenaries changed the expression—lack of expression—on his face. Lieutenant Hawker stretched his left arm to the side and began flexing the fingers of that hand like a man trying to work out a muscle cramp.

"Marshal Erzul," said Radescu as he suppressed a hysterical urge to pat the blood-suffused cheek of the former army commander, "your resignation on grounds of health is regretfully accepted. Your services to the State will be noted in my report to Chief Tribune Antonescu." He paused. "To my uncle."

Radescu expected the older man to hit him, but instead Erzul's anger collapsed, leaving behind an expression that justified the accusation of ill-health. The marshal's flush drained away abruptly so that only the grimy sallowness of pigment remained to color his skin. "I—" he said. "General, don't—"

General Iorga stepped between the two officers, the former army commander and the man who had replaced him. "Go on!" he cried to the marshal. Iorga's hands fluttered on the catches of his holster.

In a final burst of frustration, Marshal Erzul snatched off his cap, formal with ropes of gold and silver, and hurled it blindly across the room. It thudded into the wall near Hawker, who neither smiled nor moved as the hat spun end over end to the floor. Erzul turned and charged the door like a soccer player driving for the goal regardless of who might be in his way.

In this case, Erzul's own chief of staff was the only man who could not step clear in time. General Forsch grunted as his superior elbowed him in the pit of the stomach and then thrust past him through the outside door.

Under other circumstances, Forsch might have followed. Now, however, he watched the marshal's back and the door banging hard against its jamb—the automatic opening and closing mechanisms had been disconnected to permit aides to perform those functions in due deference to their superiors. The divisional officers were scurrying for their places around the table, and Radescu was finally preparing to discuss the main order of business—the war with the Molts.

"It's easy to bully old men who've spent their lives in the service of Man and the Tribunate, isn't it, Master Radescu?" said Forsch in a voice as clear and cutting as a well-played violin. "Do you think the Molts will be so obliging to your whim?"

Radescu slid into the chair at the head of the table, looking back over his shoulder at Forsch. The chief of staff stood with his chin thrust out and slightly lifted, rather as though he were baring his long, angular throat to a slaughterer's knife. Radescu had not realized the man even *had* a personality of his own: everything Antonescu's nephew had been told suggested that Forsch was no more than Erzul's shadow—a gaunt, panicky avatar of the marshal.

"No, General," said Radescu in a voice that did not tremble the way his hands would have done save for the polished tabletop against which he pressed them. "I don't think the Molts are going to be obliging at all. Why don't you sit down and we'll discuss the problem like loyal officers of Oltenia?"

He tapped with the brim of his cap on the chair to his immediate right. Forsch held himself rigid for a moment, his body still awaiting death or humiliation while his brain with difficulty processed the information freeing him from that expected end. Moving like a marionette with a string or two broken, the chief of staff—now Radescu's chief of staff, much to the surprise of both men—seated himself as directed.

"Hawker," said General Radescu as if the mercenary were his batman, "take this until we're ready to leave. I won't need it inside here."

Lieutenant Hawker stepped obsequiously from his place at the wall and took the gilded cap Radescu held out without looking away from his fellow Oltenian generals. The Slammer even bowed as he backed away again . . . but when he reached the fountain in its niche, he flipped the cap deliberately from his hand. The Oltenians, focused on one another, did not or did not seem to notice.

Profile Bourne relaxed and began rubbing his right arm with his left forefinger, tracing the length of the glowing orange dragon. Not that it would have mattered, but Radescu's cap was not on the floor.

It lay atop the hat which Erzul had thrown in anger.

"This war can only be a war of attrition," said pudgy General Oprescu with a care that came naturally to a man who needed to avoid dislocating his makeup. Radescu, watching the divisional commander, understood very well how the preternatural calm of the other man's face could cloak thoughts as violent as any which had danced through Marshal Erzul's features moments before. Radescu's face had been that calm, and he was willing to go to lengths beyond anything the marshal had suspected. Perhaps Oprescu also had a core of rigid capability within . . . but it was very well-hidden if that were the case.

"We can only hurt the Molts when they attack *us*," Oprescu continued as he examined his manicure. "Naturally, they inflict more damage on such occasions than we do . . . but likewise, their population base is much lower than ours."

"I believe the estimate," said the pale-eyed General Vuco, who had been a reasonably effective intelligence officer before promotion to Second Division chief of staff, "is seventy-three to one. That is, we can ultimately wipe the Molts from the face of Oltenia so long as we suffer no more than seventy-three casualties for each of the scaly-headed demons that we bag."

"The *problem* is," Oprescu went on, "that the seventy-three casualties aren't limited to the bunion-heads in the lower ranks, not when a Molt can pop out of the air in the middle of an officers' barracks that chances to be too close to a lump of granite."

Radescu's heart stopped for an instant and his eyes, unbidden, flicked sideways to Sergeant Bourne. The mercenary noncom grinned back at him, as relaxed as the trigger spring of his submachine gun. It struck the young Oltenian that there was a flaw in his plan of engaging gunmen to do what he could not have accomplished with guns alone: you have control over a gun as you do not over a man . . . not over men like those, the soft-featured lieutenant who was willing to kill for a matter of principle, and the scarred sergeant who needed far less reason than that. In Radescu's mind echoed the sergeant's gibe in the jeep: "What's he going to do? Sentence me to death?"

But Bourne smiled now and the moment passed with General Forsch saying, as he gripped his biceps with bony fingers, "Of course the Molts have a—feeling for the casualty ratio, too; and while they're not as formally—organized as we—" he blinked around the conference table, finally fixing Radescu with a look like that of a small animal caught at night in the headlights. "Ahem. Not as structured as we are. Nonetheless, when they feel that the fighting is to their disadvantage, they stop fighting—save for random attacks far behind the 'lines,' attacks in which they almost never suffer losses."

"Then," said Alexander Radescu, wishing that his voice were deep and powerful—though surely it could not be as tinny as it sounded in his own hypercritical ears—" we have to shift our strategy. Instead of advancing slowly—" "ponderously" was the word his mind suppressed a moment before his tongue spoke it; the lavish interior of the conference room had taken on a somewhat different aspect for Radescu since the mercenary lieutenant sneered at it "—into areas which the Molts infest, we shall make quick thrusts to capture the areas which make them vulnerable: the nursery caves."

"We *cannot* advance quickly," said General Vuco, who was more able than the others to treat Radescu as a young interloper rather than as the man with demonstrated control over the career of everyone else in the room, "so long as everyone in the assault must expect attack from behind at every instant. To—" he made a gesture with his left hand as if flinging chaff to the wind "—charge forward regardless, well, that was attempted in the early days of the conflict. Panache did not protect the units involved from total destruction, from massacre.

"Of course," Vuco added, directing his eyes toward a corner of the ceiling, "I'm perfectly willing to die for the State, even by what amounts to an order of suicide."

He dropped his gaze, intending to focus on the play of water in the alcove across the table from him. Instead, the Oltenian's eyes met those of Lieutenant Hawker. Vuco snapped upright, out of his pose of bored indolence. His mouth opened to speak, but no words came out.

"The mercenaries we hire, Hammer's troops," said Radescu, suppressing an urge to nod toward Hawker in appreciation, "manage well enough—or did," he added, glaring at his elders and new subordinates, "until our failure to support them led to what I and the Tribunate agreed were needless and excessive casualties, casualties not covered by the normal war risks of their hiring contract."

Now for the first time, most of the senior officers looked up as though Hawker and Bourne were specimens on display. Vuco instead rubbed his eyes fiercely as if he were trying to wipe an image from their surface. Hawker accepted the attention stolidly, but the sergeant reacted with an insouciance Radescu decided was typical, making a surprisingly graceful genuflection—a form of courtesy unfamiliar on Oltenia and shockingly inappropriate from a man as ruggedly lethal as Profile Bourne.

"All very well," said General Forsch in the direction of the Slammers but answering Radescu's implied question, "if we had the detection capability that the mercenaries do. *They* have time, a minute or more, to prepare for an attack, even when they're moving."

Radescu's eyes traversed the arc of the divisional officers and General Forsch. His mind was too busy with his present words and the action which would develop from those words in the immediate future, however, for him really to be seeing the men around him. "Nonetheless," he heard his voice say, "General Forsch will determine a target suitable for sudden assault by Oltenian forces."

It was the intention he had formed before he accepted his uncle's charge, an intention vocalized here in the conference room for the first time.

"Troops for the exercise will come from Second Division. Generals Iorga, Vuco, your staff will coordinate with mine to determine the precise number and composition of the units to be involved in the exercise."

Radescu blinked. It was almost as if he had just opened his eyes because the staring officers sprang suddenly back into his awareness. "Are there any questions, gentlemen?"

General Forsch leaned forward, almost close enough for his long neck to snake out to Radescu's hand like a weasel snapping. "Youth will be served, I suppose," he said. "But, my leader, you have no idea of what it is like to battle the Molts on their own ground."

"I will before long, though," said Alexander Radescu as he rose in dismissal. "I'll be accompanying the force in person."

The sound of his subordinates sucking in breath in surprise was lost in the roar of blood through the young general's ears.

★ ★ ★ ★

The most brilliant strategy, the most courageous intent, come alike to naught if the troops are marshalled at one point and their transport at another. The command group had scuttled out of the conference room with orders to plan an assault which none of them believed could be carried through successfully.

Radescu waited until he heard the door bang shut behind the last of his generals, Forsch; then, elbows on the table, he cradled his chin in his palms while his fingers covered his eyes. He did not like failure and, as he came nearer to the problem, he did not see any other likely result to his attempts.

It occurred to the young general that his subconscious might have planned the whole operation as a means of achieving not victory but solely an honorable excuse for him not to explain defeat to his uncle. The chances were very slim indeed that Alexander Radescu would survive a total disaster.

His pants legs were not only filthy, they stank. How his generals must be laughing at him!

"Sir . . . ?" intruded a voice whose owner he had forgotten.

"Ah, Lieutenant Hawker," said the Oltenian general, his personality donning its public mien as he looked up at the big mercenary. "Forgive me for not dismissing you sooner. I'll contact your colonel with thanks and—"

"General," Sergeant Bourne interrupted as he strode to the nearest chair and reversed it so that its back was toward the conference table, "those birds're right so far: if you just bull straight in like you're talking, your ass is grass and the Molts'll well and truly mow it. You need support—and that's what you hired us Slammers for, isn't it?"

Bourne sat down, the weight of his gear suddenly evident from the crash it made when it bumped the chair. The sergeant's legs splayed to either side of the seat back which rose like an outer, ornately carven breastplate in front of his porcelain armor. The mercenary's method of seating himself was not an affectation, Radescu realized: the man's belt gear and the bulges of electronics built into the shoulders of his backplate would prevent him from sitting in a chair in the normal fashion.

"I thank you for your concern, Sergeant," Radescu said—had he ever before known the name of an enlisted man? He really couldn't be sure. "Colonel Hammer is no longer willing to divide his own forces and trust the Oltenian army to carry out its own portion of the operation. When I have proved my troops are capable of— active endeavor—on their own, then I believe we can come to an accommodation, he and I."

"For now," Radescu added brusquely as he rose, "I have business that does not concern mercenaries. If you'll be so good—"

"Sir, the colonel *has* offered you troops," said Lieutenant Hawker as loudly as necessary to silence Radescu's voice without shrillness. "Us. All Profile means is you ought to use us, the best curst detection team in the Slammers. And he's right—you *ought* to use us, instead of throwing yourself away."

Radescu sat down again, heavily. The Slammers lieutenant was so much larger than the general that only by tricking his mind could Radescu keep from being cowed physically. "He didn't send you to me for that," he said, "for detection. You—you know that."

Bourne snorted and said, "Bloody *cop* we do."

At his side, with a hand now on the noncom's shoulder, Hawker replied, "The colonel doesn't talk to me, sir. But if you think he doesn't keep up with what's happening with the people who hired him, hired *us*, there you're curst well wrong. Don't ever figure a man like Colonel Hammer isn't one step ahead of you—though he may not be ready to commit openly."

"Not," Bourne completed grimly, "when he's ready to call in the Bonding Authority and void the contract for employer's non-performance."

"My Lord," said Radescu. He looked at the pair of mercenaries without the personal emotion—hope or fear or even disgust—he had always felt before. The implications of what Hawker had just said stripped all emotional loadings from the general's immediate surroundings. Hawker and Bourne could have been a pair of trees, gnarled and gray-barked; hard-used and very, very hard themselves. . . .

"My Lord," the Oltenian repeated, the words scarcely moving

his lips. Then his gaze sharpened and he demanded, "You mean it was, was a game? You wouldn't have . . . ?"

"Try me, General," said Profile Bourne. He did not look at Radescu but at his open palm; and the dragon there bore an expression similar to that of the mercenary.

"It's not a game, killing people," said the lieutenant. "We got into the box where you found us by doing just what we told you we did. And believe me, sir, nobody ever complained about the support Profile and me gave when it came down to cases." The fingers of his right hand smoothed the receiver of the submachinegun where the greenish wear on the plastic showed the owner's touch was familiar.

"It's just I guess we can figure one thing out, now," the sergeant remarked, looking up with the loose, friendly look of a man lifting himself out of a bath in drugs. "We'd heard our sentence four days ago, not that there was a whole lotta doubt. I mean, we'd done it. The colonel watched us."

He gave Radescu the grin of a little boy caught in a peccadillo, sure of a spanking but winkingly hopeful that it might still be avoided. "We don't stand much on ceremony in the Slammers," Bourne went on. "For sure not on something like a shot in the neck. So the Loot'n me couldn't figure what the colonel was waiting for."

"I guess," the sergeant concluded with a very different sort of smile again, "he was waiting for you."

Hawker pulled a chair well away from the table, lifting it off the floor so that it did not scrape. The mercenary handled the chair so lightly that Radescu could scarcely believe that it was made of the same dense, heavily carven wood as the one in which the Oltenian sat.

"You see, sir," the lieutenant said as he lowered himself carefully onto the seat, hunching forward a little to be able to do so, "we can't cover more than a platoon, the two of us—but a platoon's enough, for what you need."

"Any more'n that, they get screwed up," added Bourne. "Even if *we* get the range and bearing right, they don't. Just gives the Molts more targets to shoot at. That's not what we're here for."

"What *are* you here for?" Radescu asked, reaching out to touch Bourne's right palm to the other's great surprise. The skin was dry and calloused, not at all unlike the scaly head of a reptile. "What your colonel may want, I can see. But the danger to you personally—it isn't as though you'd be protected by, by your own, the tanks and the organization that strikes down Molts when they appear."

He withdrew his hand, looking at both the Slammers and marvelling at how stolid they appeared. Surely their like could have no emotion? "I'm an Oltenian," Radescu continued. "This is my planet, my State. Even so, everybody in the room just now—" his fingers waggled toward the door through which his fellow generals had exited "—thinks I'm mad to put myself in such danger. You two aren't lumps like our own peasants. You made it clear that I couldn't even *order* you without your willingness to obey. Would Hammer punish you if you returned to him without having volunteered to accompany me?"

"Guess we're clear on that one, wouldn't you say, Loot?" remarked Sergeant Bourne as he glanced at Hawker. Though the noncom was physically even smaller than Radescu, he did not sink into the ambience of the big lieutenant the way the Oltenian felt he did himself. Profile Bourne was a knife, double-edged and wickedly sharp; size had nothing to do with the aura he projected.

For the first time, Radescu considered the faces of his divisional officers as they watched him in the light of the emotions he tried to hide when he looked at the pair of mercenaries. It could be that the Oltenians saw in him a core of something which he knew in his heart of hearts was not really there.

Hawker's body armor shrugged massively. "Look, sir," he said without fully meeting the Oltenian's eyes, "if we liked to lose, then we wouldn't be in the Slammers. I don't apologize for anything that happened before—" now he did focus his gaze, glacial in a bovine face, on Radescu "—but it wasn't what we were hired to do. Help win a war against the Molts."

Bourne tilted forward to grasp Radescu's hand briefly before the sergeant levered himself back to his feet. "And you know, General," the mercenary said as he rose, "until I met you, I didn't think the poofs had a prayer a' doin' that."

The encampment should in theory have been safe enough, with no chunk of crystalline rock weighing more than a kilogram located within a meter of the ground surface. Nobody really believed that a three-divisional area had been swept so perfectly, however, especially without the help which Hammer had refused to give this time.

The center of the encampment, the combined Army and the Second Division Headquarters, had been set up in a marsh and was probably quite secure. The nervousness of the troops mustered both for the operation and for immediate security was due less to intellectual fear of the Molts than to the formless concern which any activity raised in troops used to being sniped at from point-blank ambush with no time to respond.

Alexander Radescu felt sticky and uncomfortable in his new battledress, though its fabric and cut should have been less stiff than the formal uniforms he ordinarily wore. He could not bring himself to don body armor, knowing that it would cramp and distract him through the next hours when his best hope of survival lay in keeping flexible and totally alert.

Hawker and Bourne wore their own back-and-breast armor, heavier but far more resistant than the Oltenian version which Radescu had refused. They were used to the constriction, after all, and would probably have been more subconsciously hindered by its absence than by the weight.

Radescu would have been even more comfortable without the automatic shotgun he now cradled, a short-barreled weapon which sprayed tiny razor-edged airfoils that spread into a three-meter circle ten meters from the muzzle. The gun was perfectly effective within the ranges at which Molt warriors were likely to appear; but it was the general's dislike of *personal* involvement in something as ignoble as killing, rather than his doubts about how accurately he could shoot, which put him off the weapon.

Still, he had to carry the shotgun for protective coloration. The mercenaries' jeep would stand out from the Oltenian units anyway, and the sole unarmed member of a combat patrol would be an even more certain choice for a Molt with the leisure to pick his target.

"Cop!" snarled Lieutenant Hawker from the side-seat of the jeep as he surveyed the numbers his apparatus projected glowing into the air before him. The mercenary's commo helmet was linked to epaulette speakers issued to the entire Oltenian contingent for this operation. Radescu heard the words both on his own borrowed helmet and, marginally later, directly from the lieutenant's mouth. "Discard Beacon Eighty-seven. Team Seven, that's three duds so far outa this lot, and you've had *all* of 'em. Are you sure you know how to switch the bloody things on?"

"The numbers of the beacons being tested appear—on your screen, then?" General Radescu asked the mercenary sergeant beside him, wiggling his fingers toward the floating yellow numbers. Obviously, there was no screen; but he was uncertain how to describe in any other way what he saw.

"Naw, that's the playback from Central," replied Profile Bourne. He nodded his head toward the distant ridge beyond which sheltered Colonel Hammer and his armored regiment. "Doesn't matter if *we* pick up the signal or not, but How Batt'ry can't bust up rocks for us if they don't get the beacon."

"Yes, well . . ." said General Radescu as he looked at the men and equipment around him. The Oltenian contingent was forty men mounted on ten light trucks—each with a load of explosives and radio beacons, plus a pintle-mounted automatic weapon which, at the flip of a switch, fired either solid shot for long-range targets or beehives of airfoil fléchettes like the hand weapons.

The trucks were somewhat larger than the Slammers' jeep on which Radescu himself would be mounted. More significantly, the Oltenian vehicles rode on wheels spun from spring-wire rather than on air cushions. Ground effect vehicles of sufficient ruggedness and payload for scouting through brush required drive-systems of a better power-to-weight ratio than Oltenia could supply. The mercenaries' jeeps and one-man skimmers had the benefit of cryogenic accumulators, recharged at need—every hundred kilometers or so—from the fusion powerplants of the heavier combat cars and tanks.

The jeep which Sergeant Bourne drove and the energy weapon slung against his chest were thus both of a higher technology level than their Oltenian equivalents—but in neither case was the difference significant to the present mission. The range and quickness of the electronics which detected Molts before they appeared physically, and the needle-threading accuracy which terminal guidance gave the Slammers' rocket howitzers, were absolute necessities if the present operation were to succeed, however; and Colonel Hammer was supplying both.

Despite his public dismissal of Radescu, Hammer was giving him and the State of Oltenia one chance to seize back the initiative in this *accursed* war with the planet's dominant autochthons.

"We're ready, sir," said Lieutenant Hawker with his helmet mike shut off to make the report more personal than a radio message to the general two meters away. "The hardware is."

Radescu nodded. Bourne had already slipped onto his seat on the left side of the jeep. Radescu had eaten a light, perfectly bland, meal of protein supplement an hour earlier. The food now lay like an anvil in his belly while his digestive system writhed in an attempt to crush it.

"Captain Elejash," the young general said, his signal broadcast to every member of the assault party, "are your men ready?" He lifted himself carefully onto his electronic throne on the back of the jeep, pleased to note that the motion decreased his nausea instead of causing him to vomit in the sight of several thousand putative subordinates.

"Yes sir," replied the commander of the Oltenian platoon, a rancher before the war as were most of his men. They were a hard-bitten crew, many of them as old as the general himself, and very different in appearance from the pasty-faced young factory workers who made up the ordinary rank and file of the army. Forsch and Iorga had gone at least that far toward making the operation a success.

"General Radescu, the support battalion is ready," said an unbidden voice over the wailing background which Radescu had learned to associate with recompressed ultra-low frequency transmissions from Army HQ.

Alexander Radescu looked imperiously around him at the faces and heavy equipment and distant, wooded hills, all of which blurred in his fear-frozen mind to gray shadows.

"All right," he said in his cool, aristocratic voice. "Then let's go."

And before the last word had reached the general's throat mike, Profile Bourne was easing the jeep forward at a rapidly accelerating pace.

How smoothly it rides, thought General Radescu as the ground effect jeep sailed up a hillside pocked by the burrows of small grazing animals, and Lieutenant Hawker opened fire from the front seat with shocking unexpectedness.

The ionization detectors had given no warning because the Molt was already sited, a picket waiting near the Oltenian base on a likely course of advance. Hawker's face shield was locked in place, and through its electronic additions to the normal sensory spectrum—passive infrared or motion enhancement—the mercenary had spotted his target as it rose to attack.

Cyan flashes squirted from Hawker's gun at a cyclic rate so high that their afterimage combined to form a solid orange bar on Radescu's dazzled retinas. The vehicles were in line abreast at ten-meter intervals with the Slammers' jeep in the center. A multistemmed bush to the jeep's right front hissed and shrivelled as it drank the energy bolts; then it and recognizable portions of an adolescent Molt were blasted apart by a violent secondary explosion. The autochthon had carried either a satchel charge or an unusually powerful shoulder-launched missile. The red flash of its detonation, though harmless to the assault platoon, caused the driver of the nearest truck to stall his engine. He knew that if Hawker had been seconds slower, the blast would have enveloped the Oltenian vehicle.

"Eight red thirty degrees," said Hawker as unemotionally as though his gun's barrel was not pinging and discoloring the finish of the forward transom on which he rested it to cool. Numbers and symbols, not the ones the mercenary was relaying to the assault force, hung as images of yellow and violet in the air before him. "Four yellow zero degrees."

Most of the pintle-mounted weapons snarled bursts toward the range and bearing each gunner had computed from the Slammer's rough direction. First Hawker gave the number of the truck he chose as a base for that deflection; then red, orange, or yellow for fifty, seventy-five, or hundred meter arcs around that truck; and finally the bearing itself. Molts beyond a hundred meters were rarely dangerous to a moving target, even with the most modern weapons. When possible, the mercenary would point out such warriors with a burst from his own gun or even call in artillery; but there was no need to complicate a system of directions which had to work fast if it were to work at all.

"Cease fire," Hawker ordered as the jeep slid through a line of palmate leaves springing from the hillcrest and Radescu covered his face with one hand. "*Cease* fire, Six, they were going away!"

More pickets, Radescu thought as the echoes of gunfire died away and the line of vehicles rocked down the next slope without immediate incident. The blips of plasma which the mercenaries' detection equipment had caught this time were those resulting from Molts disappearing, not coalescing to attack. The pickets would be returning to their council, their headquarters, with warning of the direction and nature of the attack.

There was the sharp crash of an explosion nearby. The crew of Truck Six had tossed a charge overboard, onto a patch of crystalline rock which their own sensors had identified. Dirt showered the jeep and Radescu, while dual blasts sounded from opposite ends of the patrol line, deadened somewhat by distance. The shaped-charge packets were weighted to land cavity-down—most of the time. Even so, they did not have enough standoff for the pencil of super-heated gas to reach maximum velocity and effectiveness before it struck the rock it was to shatter.

The bombs which the patrol set off could not break up even surface outcrops so effectively that no Molt could home on them. However, the charges did, with luck, lessen and change the piezo-electrical signature by relieving stresses on the crystalline structure. The oldest, most experienced, Molts could still pick their way to the location, sorting through the sea of currents and electrical charges for bits of previous reality which their brains could process like those of paleontologists creating a species from bone fragments.

Even these older warriors were slowed and limited as to the range from which they could project themselves to such damaged homing points, however. Younger Molts, equally deadly with their guns and buzzbombs, were effectively debarred from popping into ambush directly behind the advancing patrol.

Powerguns—and the Molts carried them, though Oltenian regulars did not—had an effective antipersonnel range, even in atmosphere, of line of sight. There was no practical way to prevent Molt snipers from firing into distant human arrays, then skipping back to safety. No way at all, except by killing every male Molt on Oltenia.

Or by ending the war, which everyone high in the government thought was also impossible. Everyone but Alexander Radescu.

"Six red one-eighty!" shouted Lieutenant Hawker, emotionless no longer as his instruments warned him of the Molt blurring out of the air through which Truck Six had just driven. The attacker was in Hawker's own blind spot, even if he had dared take his eyes from the readouts now that the attack had come in earnest. "Ten yellow ninety!"

The jeep dropped a hand's breadth on irregular ground as the general twisted to look over his shoulder. The sinking feeling in his guts was more pronounced than the actual drop when he realized that all the pintle-mounted guns in the patrol had been swung forward at the first contact. The guns on even-numbered trucks were to have covered the rear at all times, but nervousness and enthusiasm had combined to give the autochthons a perfect opening. Now gunners were tugging at the grips of their long-barreled weapons, more handicapped by cramped footing than by the guns' inertia.

Black smoke from the shaped charge dissipated above the scar in the sod and flattened grass. Squarely in the center of the blast circle—so much for the effectiveness of the charges—a shadow thickened to solid form.

The Molt's gray scales had a blue tinge and what Radescu would have called a metallic luster had not the iridium barrel of the creature's powergun showed what luster truly was. The general did not even realize he had fired until the butt of the shotgun slammed him in the ribs: he had loose-gripped the unfamiliar weapon, and its heavy recoil punished the error brutally.

Radescu's shot twinkled like a soap bubble as the cloud of airfoils caught the sunlight twenty meters above their target. The Molt's figure was perfectly clear for a moment as it hulked behind the reflection of its gun; then the autochthon began to shrink and dissolve in a manner that made Radescu think it had teleported itself to another location before firing.

No.

There was a scarlet cloud in the air beyond the Molt as the trucks and jeep bounded away, blood and flesh and chips of yellow bone. An Oltenian soldier with a weapon like Radescu's and a skill the general had never been expected to learn had fired three times. The autochthon crumpled before the machine guns could even be rotated back in its direction.

Half a dozen shaped charges went off almost simultaneously, and there was heavy firing from the right. A powergun bolt sizzled across the ragged line of vehicles, an event so sudden that Radescu, as he turned back, could not be certain from which end it had been fired. Hawker was calling out vectors in the tight, high voice of a sportscaster. The young general hoped his fellows could understand the mercenary's directions; he was baffled by the unfamiliar data himself.

Sergeant Bourne banked the jeep around a copse of trees in a turn so sharp that the left side of the skirt dragged, spilling air in its brief hesitation. "Five red zero!" Hawker was calling, and the blur that focused down into a Molt was directly in front of the Slammers' vehicle. Bourne spun the tiller with his left hand and crossed his chest with his right, firing a burst of cyan bolts which the vehicles own motion slewed across the creature's torso. The Molt fell onto its missile launcher, dead before its psychic jump was complete enough for the creature to be aware of its new surroundings.

Radescu's gun tracked the Molt as the jeep skidded past. He did not fire—it was obviously dead—but his bruised side throbbed as if the butt were pounding him again.

There was a whistle from the sky behind, bird cries which expanded into a roar so overpowering that earth fountained in apparent silence behind nearby trucks as they dropped shaped charges at the same time. The sound was so intense that Radescu felt it as a pressure on the back of his neck, then on his forehead and eyeballs. He wanted very badly to jump to the ground and cower there: the universe was so large and hostile. . . .

Instead, the young general gripped the handle of one of the modules which formed his seat and stood up as straight as he could without losing his hold. He was bent like someone trying to ride a bucking animal but the defiance was real.

A craggy, wooded hilltop three hundred meters ahead of the vehicles dimpled, dirt and fragments of foliage lifting into the air. There were no explosions audible. Radescu, slammed back into his seat when the jeep rose to meet him, thought the shell blasts were lost in the waterfall rush from overhead. That blanket of sound cut off with the suddenness of a thrown switch, its echoes a whisper to ears stunned by the roar itself.

Only then did the sextet of shells explode, their blasts muffled by the depth to which they had penetrated the rocky core of the hill. The slope bulged, then collapsed like cake dough falling. Larger trees sagged sideways, their roots crushed when the substrate was pulverized beneath them. No stones or fragments of shell casing were spewed out by the deep explosions, but a pall of dust rose to hide the immediate landscape—including a pair of Molts, killed by concussion just as they started to aim at the oncoming vehicles.

"Via!" swore Alexander Radescu. He had arranged the fire order himself two days earlier, six penetrator shells to land on a major intrusion of volcanic rock identified by satellite on the patrol's path. The plan had worked perfectly in demolishing what would otherwise have been a bastion for the autochthons.

But it had frightened him into a broil of fury and terror, because he had no personal experience with the tools he was using. Planning the fire order had been much like a game of chess played on holographic maps in the rich comfort of Army HQ. It had never occurred to Radescu that a salvo of twenty-centimeter shells would be louder than thunder as they ripped overhead, or that the ground would ripple at the hammer blows of impact even before the bursting charges went off.

Commanding soldiers is not the same as leading them.

"General, we—" Sergeant Bourne started to say, turning in his seat though it was through Radescu's commo helmet that the words came.

"Teams One through Five, break left," the general said, overriding his driver's voice by keying his own throat mike. "Six through Ten—and Command—" the last an afterthought "—break right, avoid the shelled area."

There was confusion in the patrol line as trucks turned and braked for the unanticipated obstacle—which Radescu knew he should have anticipated. The churned soil and toppled vegetation would have bogged the trucks inextricably; and, while the terrain itself might have been passable for the air-cushion jeep, the dust shrouding it would have concealed fallen trunks and boulders lifted from the shuddering earth.

Bourne's head turned again as he cramped the tiller. His face shield had become an opaque mirror, reflecting Radescu in convex perfection. The Oltenian had forgotten that the Slammers' array of night vision devices included personal sonar which would, when necessary, map a lightless area with the fidelity of eyesight—though without, of course, color vision. The sergeant had been perfectly willing to drive into the spreading cloud, despite the fact that it would have blinded the hologram display of Hawker's detectors. That wasn't the sort of problem Profile Bourne was paid to worry about.

"We're blowing Truck Two in place," said a voice which Radescu recognized with difficulty as that of Captain Elejash. Almost at once, there was a very loud explosion from the left side of the line.

Looking over his shoulder, Radescu could see a black column of smoke extending jaggedly skyward from a point hidden by the undergrowth and the curve of the land. The jeep slowed because the trucks which had been to its right and now led it turned more awkwardly than the ground effect vehicle, slowing and rocking on the uneven ground. The smell of their diesel exhaust mingled with the dry, cutting odor of the dust shaken from the hillside.

Hawker was silent, though the yellow digits hanging in the air before him proved that his instruments were still working. They simply had no Molts to detect.

"Truck Two overturned," resumed Elejash breathlessly. "We've split up the crew and are proceeding."

After blowing up the disabled vehicle, thought Radescu approvingly, to prevent the Molts from turning the gun and particularly the explosives against their makers. The trucks had better cross-country performance than he had feared—wet weather might have been a different story—but it was inevitable that at least one of the heavily laden vehicles would come to grief. Truck Two had been lost without enemy action. Its driver had simply tried to change direction at what was already the highest practical speed on broken ground.

"Sir," said Sergeant Bourne, keying his helmet mike with his tongue-tip as he goosed the throttle to leap a shallow ravine that the Oltenian vehicles had to wallow through, "how'd you convince 'em to pick up the truck's crew?"

It was the first time Bourne had called him "sir" rather than the ironic "general."

"I said I'd shoot—order shot—anyone who abandoned his comrades," Radescu replied grimly, "and I hoped nobody thought I was joking."

He paused. "Speed is—important," he continued after a moment spent scanning the tree-studded horizon. The separated halves of the patrol line were in sight of one another again, cutting toward the center. Boulders shaken by shellfire from the reverse slope of the hill still quivered at the end of trails that wormed through the vegetation. They would need follow-up salvoes, but for the moment the Molts seemed unable to use their opportunities. . . . "But we have a war to win, not just a mission to accomplish. And I won't win it with an army of men who know they'll be abandoned any time there's trouble."

Numbers on Hawker's hologram display flashed back and forth from yellow to the violet that was its complement, warning at last of a resumption of Molt attacks. The mercenary lieutenant said, "Purple One," on a command channel which Radescu heard in his left ear and the other Oltenians did not hear at all.

"What?" he demanded, thinking Hawker must have made a mistake that would give a clear shot to the teleporting autochthon.

"Mark," said Hawker, in response to an answer even the general had not heard.

Bourne, fishtailing to avoid Truck Five—itself pressed by Truck Four, the vehicles had lost their spacing as they reformed in line abreast—said, "They're landing way behind us, sir. Loot's just called artillery on 'em while they're still confused." Then he added, "We told you this was the way. Not a bloody battalion, not a division—one platoon and catch 'em with their pants down."

They were in a belt of broad-leafed vegetation, soft-trunked trees sprouted in the rich, well-watered soil of a valley floor. There was relatively little undergrowth because the foliage ten meters overhead met in a nearly solid mat. The other vehicles of the patrol were grunting impressions, patterns occasionally glimpsed through random gaps in the trees. Amazingly, Truck Two appeared to have been the only vehicle lost in the operation thus far, though the flurry of intense fighting had almost certainly caused human casualties.

But teleporting Molts were vulnerable before they were dangerous, and Radescu had been impressed by the way bursts of airfoils had swept patches of ground bare. He had felt like a step-child, leading men armed with indigenous weapons against an enemy with powerguns bought from traders whose view of the universe was structured by profit, not fantasies of human destiny. Though the energy weapons had advantages in range and effectiveness against vehicles—plus the fact that the lightly built autochthons could not easily have absorbed the heavy recoil of Oltenian weapons—none of those factors handicapped the members of the patrol in their present job.

As trees snapped by and Bourne lifted the jeep a centimeter to keep his speed down but still have maximum maneuvering thrust available, the right earpiece of Radescu's helmet said in a machine voice, "Centralto Party. Halt your forces." They were that close, then, thought the Oltenian general. Without bothering to acknowledge— the satellite net that was Hammer's basic commo system on Oltenia would pick up the relayed order—Radescu said, "All units halt at once. All units halt." If he had tried to key the command channel alone to acknowledge, he might have had trouble with the unfamiliar mercenary helmet. Better to save time and do what was necessary instead of slavishly trying to obey the forms. If only he could get his officers to realize that simple truth. . . .

Sergeant Bourne had the principle of lower-rank initiative well in mind. Without waiting for the general to relay the order from Central, Bourne angled his fans forward and lifted the bow of the jeep to increase its air resistance. The tail skirt dragged through the loam but only slightly, not enough to whip the vehicle to a bone-jarring halt the way a less expert driver might have done in his haste.

Hawker's display was alive with flashes of yellow and violet, but he still did not call vectors to the Oltenian troops. A branch high above the jeep parted with an electric crackle as a bolt from a powergun spent itself in converting pulpy wood into steam and charred fragments.

The leaf canopy had become more ragged as the ground started to rise, so that Radescu could now see the escarpment of the ridge whose further face held their goal. The tilted strata before them were marked with bare patches from which the thin soil had slumped with its vegetation, though the trucks could—General Forsch had assured his commander—negotiate a route to the crest.

If it were undefended.

The world-shaking vibration of shells overhead was Radescu's attempt to meet his chief of staff's proviso.

Somebody should have ordered the members of the patrol to get down, but there was no opportunity now given the all-pervasive racket that would have overwhelmed even the bone-conduction speakers set into the Slammers' mastoids. The *hiss-thump* of powerguns as overeager Molts fired without proper targets also was lost, but the rare flicker of bolts in the foliage was lightning to the sky's own thunder. The thick soil of the valley floor was a warranty that no warrior was going to appear at arm's length of the deafened, cowering patrol, and the Molts' disinclination to cover significant distances on foot made it unlikely that any of them would race into the forest to get at the humans they knew were lurking there.

The initial shellbursts were lost in the rush of later salvoes. The first fire order had been intended to destroy a beacon on which the Molts would otherwise have focused. The present shellfire was turning the escarpment ahead into a killing ground.

Profile Bourne tapped the general's knee for attention, then gestured with the open, savage cup of his tattooed right hand toward the images which now hung over the jeep's bow. The modules projected a three-dimensional monochrome of the escarpment, including the heavy forest at its foot and the more scattered vegetation of the gentle reverse slope.

The Oltenian wondered fleetingly where the imaging sensor could be: all of the patrol's vehicles hid behind the barrier of trees, which concealed the escarpment as surely as it did the trucks. The angle was too flat for satellite coverage, and aircraft reconnaissance was a waste of hardware—with the crews if the aircraft were manned—in a military landscape dominated by light-swift powerguns. Perhaps it was a computer model using current satellite photography enhanced from a data base—of Hammer's, since the State of Oltenia had nothing of its own comparable.

The image of the rock face shattered. Instead of crumbling into a slide of gravel and boulders the way the hillock had done earlier when struck by penetrators, the escarpment held its new, fluid form as does a constantly replenished waterfall.

The rain feeding this spray was of bomblets from the firecracker rounds being hurled by all eighteen tubes of the Slammers' artillery. It was a prodigiously expensive undertaking—mechanized warfare is far more sparing of men than of material—but it was the blow from which Radescu prayed the Molts in this region would be unable to recover.

Each shell split in the air into hundreds of bomblets which in turn burst on the next thing they touched—rock, leaf, or the face of a Molt sighting down the barrel of his powergun. The sea of miniature blasts created a mist of glass-fiber shrapnel devouring life in all its forms above the microscopic—but without significantly changing the piezoelectrical constant of the rock on which the autochthons homed.

Hawker's detectors continued to flash notice of further Molts springing into the cauldron from which none of them would return to warn the warriors who followed them to doom.

Lieutenant Hawker was as still as the jeep, though that trembled with the shells pawned vibration of the earth on which it now rested. Sergeant Bourne watched not the image of the fire-rippled escarpment but the detector display. His grin was alive with understanding, and he tapped together the scarred knuckles of his hands. Every violet numeral was a Molt about to die.

Short bursts were an inevitable hazard, impinging on Radescu's senses not by their sounds—even the wash of the main bombardment was lost in the ballistic roar of the shells themselves—but by the fact that shafts of sunlight began to illuminate the forest floor. Stray bomblets stripped away the foliage they touched, but the low-mass shrapnel was not dangerous more than a meter or two from the center of each blast.

The Oltenian was nonetheless startled to see that the backs of his hands glittered in the sudden sunlight with glass fibers scarcely thicker than the hairs from among which they sprang. He had been too lost in the image of shellfire devouring the Molts to notice that it had put its mark on him as well.

The ionization detectors had been quiescent for almost a minute when the face of the escarpment slumped, no longer awash with firecracker rounds. Through the pulsing silence as the shellfire ceased came the rumble of collapsing rock—the final salvo had been of penetrator shells, now that the Molts had either recognized the killing ground for what it was or had run out of victims to send into the useless slaughter.

Like a bright light, the thunder of shellfire left its own

afterimage on the senses of the men who had been subjected to it. Radescu's voice was a shadow of itself in his own ears with all its high frequencies stripped away as he said, "Platoon, forward. Each crew find its own path to the crest and await further orders."

Lord who aids the needy! thought the general as the jeep rocked onto its air cushion again. He was alive, and he had apparently won this first round of his campaign to end the war.

The second round: the command group of the Army had been his opponent in the first, and he had won that too. Both victories due to the pair of mercenaries before him; and to the harsh, unexpectedly complex, colonel who commanded them.

With no need to match his speed to that of the trucks, Bourne sent his jeep through the remaining half-kilometer of forest with a verve that frightened Radescu—who had thought the initial salvo of shells passing overhead had drained him of any such emotion for months.

A few trees had grown all the way up to the original face of harder rock, but for the most part hard-stemmed scrub with less need for water and nutrient had replaced the more substantial vegetation near the escarpment. Everything, including the thin soil, had been swept away by the salvoes of antipersonnel bomblets. The paths down which tons of rock shattered by the penetrators slid were scarcely distinguishable from the stretches to either side which were untouched by the heavy shells.

The surface of an airless planetoid could not have been more barren; and there, at least, Radescu's nostrils would not have wrinkled at the smell of death.

Bourne took his right hand off his gun butt long enough to pull rearward a dashboard lever while his left squeezed the hand throttle on the tiller wide open. The lever must have affected the angle of the fans within the plenum chamber, because the vehicle began to slide straight up the slope, stern lifted almost to a level with the bow like that of a funicular car.

The original angle of the escarpment had been in the neighborhood of one to one. The salvo of penetrators had shaken portions of the overhang down into a ramp at the foot of the slope, easing the

ascent at the same time it changed the electrical signature. The
sergeant's bow-on assault was still a surprise, to the Oltenian and to
the Slammers' lieutenant, judging from Hawker's quick glance
toward his fellow. The rear fans, those directly beneath Radescu
and the electronics modules, spun with the angry sound of bullets
ricocheting as they drove the vehicle upward.

Both mercenaries had locked their face shields down, less for
visibility than for protection against pebbles still skipping from the
hill's crumbled facade. Dust and grit, though blanketed somewhat
by the overburden of topsoil from the further slope, boiled in the
vortices beneath the skirt of the jeep.

The trucks of the patrol's Oltenian element crawled rather than
loped in their ascent, but they were managing adequately. Their tires
were spun from a single-crystal alloy of iron and chrome, and they
gripped projections almost as well as the fingers of a human climber.
Such monocrystal filaments were, with beef, the main export props
of the economy of human Oltenia.

The Molts provided traders with the lustrous, jewel-scaled pelts
of indigenous herbivores and with opportunities to mine pockets of
high-purity ores. The senses which permitted the autochthons to
teleport were far more sensitive and exact than were the best
mechanical geo surveying devices in the human universe. Even so,
Molt trade off-planet was only a tiny fraction of that of members of
the Oltenian state.

The needs of the autochthons were very simple, however. As
the jeep topped the rise, bounced fully a meter in the air by its
momentum, a bolt from a powergun burst the trunk of one of the
nearby trees mutilated in the hammering by firecracker rounds.

Bourne swore savagely in a language Radescu did not know,
then cried, "Loot?" as he whipped the jeep in a double-S that brought
it to a halt, partly behind another of the stripped boles which were
the closest approach to cover on the blasted landscape.

"Take him," said the lieutenant as he rolled out of his seat
before the jeep had fully grounded. As an afterthought, while he
cleared his own weapon in the vehicle's shelter, he added, "Via,
General, get *down!*"

The shot had come from across a valley three kilometers wide and as sere as the forest behind the patrol was lush. When slabs of granite tilted to form shallow wrinkles, layers of porous aquifer had been dammed and rerouted with startling effects for the vegetation on opposites ides of the impermeable divide. This valley had nothing like the dense canopy which had sheltered the vehicles while they waited for the firecracker rounds to do their work. Direct rainfall, the sole source of water for the vegetation here, had paradoxically stripped away much of the soil which might otherwise have been available because there was no barrier of foliage and strong root systems to break the rush of periodic torrents.

The native grass which fattened terran beefalo as efficiently as imported fodder provided a straggly, russet background to the occasional spike-leafed tree. Hiding places in the knobs and notches of the valley's further slope offered interlocking fields of fire across the entire area, and frequent outcrops among the grass below warned that Molts had free access to the valley floor as well.

The present shot had come from the far escarpment, however: it chopped shorter the trunk it hit at a flat angle. As he tumbled off his seat, obedient to the mercenary lieutenant, Radescu took with him a memory of the terrain three thousand meters away—an undifferentiated blur of gray and pale ochre—a background which could conceal a thousand gunmen as easily as one.

"We can't possibly find him!" the Oltenian whispered to Hawker as Sergeant Bourne scanned for potential targets with only his eyes and weapon above the jeep's front skirt. "We'll have to wait for the artillery to get him."

The shelling had resumed, but it was of a different scale and tenor. Black splotches like oil-soaked cotton bloomed around momentary red cores as Oltenian artillery pummeled the far side of the valley. Hammer's three fully automated batteries of rocket howitzers were not involved in this bombardment. Their accuracy was needless—even indigenous artillery couldn't miss by three kilometers. The greater effectiveness of the mercenaries' shells would not change the fact that no practicable volume of fire could really affect the vast area involved. The shellbursts, though violent, left no significant mark once the puff of combustion products dispersed in the light breeze.

The State could not *afford* to use Hammer's hogs needlessly: the shells were imported over long Transit distances. Quite apart from their high cost in money terms,the length of time for replenishment might be disastrous in an emergency if stocks on Oltenia had been needlessly squandered.

Even as he spoke, General Radescu realized the absurdity of waiting for the shells speckling an area of twenty square kilometers to silence a single marksman. He grimaced, wishing he wore the makeup which would ordinarily have covered his flush of embarrassment.

"We got pretty good at countersniper work here on Oltenia," the lieutenant said mildly. The shellfire was not passing directly overhead, and in any case the trajectories were much higher than when the patrol cowered just short of the impact area of the heavy salvoes. "If this one just tries once more, Profile'll spot the heat signature and nail 'im." Hawker scowled. "Wish those bloody poofs'd get up here before the bastard decides to blow our detection gear all to hell. That first shot was too *cursed* close."

Alexander Radescu got to his feet, feeling like a puppet-master guiding the cunningly structured marionette of his body. He walked away from the jeep and the slender tree trunk which was probably as much an aiming point as protection for the crucial electronics. He stumbled because his eyes were dilated with fear and everything seemed to have merged into a blur of glaucous yellow.

"Sir!" someone cried. Then, in his head phones, *"Sir! Get back here!"*

Poofs could only draw fire, could they? Well, perhaps not even that. Radescu's ribcage hurt where the gun had kicked him the only time he fired a shot. As he lifted the weapon again, his vision steadied to throw boulders and hummocks across the valley into a clear relief that Radescu thought was impossible for unaided vision at that distance. His muscles were still shuddering with adrenaline, though, and the shotgun's muzzle wobbled in an arc between bare sky and the valley floor.

That didn't matter. The short-range projectiles could not reach the far slope, much less hit a specific target there. Radescu squeezed off and the recoil rotated his torso twenty degrees. A bitch of a weapon, but it hadn't really *hurt* this time because he had nestled the stock into him properly before he fired. The Molts were not marksmen either; there was no real danger in what he was doing, no *reason* for fear, only physiological responses to instinct—

The muzzle blast of his second shot surprised him; his trigger finger was operating without conscious control. Earth, ten meters downslope, gouted and glazed in the cyan flash of the sniper's return bolt. As grit flung by the release of energy flicked across Radescu's cheeks and forehead, another powergun bolt splashed a pit in the soil so close to Radescu's boots that the leather of them turned white and crinkled.

The crackling snarl of the bolt reaching for his life almost deafened the Oltenian to the snap of Bourne's submachine gun returning fire with a single round. Radescu was still braced against a finishing shot from the heavy powergun across the valley so that he did not move even as the sergeant scrambled back into the jeep and shouted, "Come *on,* let's get this mother down a *hole!*"

The jeep shuddered off its skirts again before even Lieutenant Hawker managed to jump aboard. Radescu, awakening to find himself an unexpected ten meters away, ran back to the vehicle.

"D'ye get him?" Hawker was asking, neither Slammer using the radio. There were things Central didn't have to know.

"Did I shoot at him?" the sergeant boasted, pausing a moment for Radescu to clamber onto his seat again. "Cop, yeah, Loot—he's got a third hole in line with his eyeballs." As the jeep boosted downslope, gravity adding to the thrust of the fans, Bourne added, "Spoiled the bloody trophy, didn't I?"

Radescu knew that even a light bolt could be lethal at line of sight, and he accepted that magnification through the helmet faceplate could have brought the warrior's image within the appearance of arm's length. Nonetheless, a micron's unsteadiness at the gun muzzle and the bolt would miss a man-sized target three kays away. The general could not believe that anyone, no matter how expert, could rightfully be as sure of his accuracy as the Slammers' gunman was.

But there were no further shots from across the valley as the jeep slid over earth harrowed by the barrage of firecracker rounds and tucked itself into the mouth of the nursery tunnel which was the patrol's objective.

The multiple channels of the commo helmets were filled with message traffic, none of it intended for Radescu. If he had been familiar with the Slammers' code names, he could have followed the progress of the support operation—an armored battalion reinforced by a company of combat engineers—which should have gotten under way as soon as the patrol first made contact with the enemy. For now, it was enough to know that Hammer would give direct warning if anything went badly wrong: not because Radescu commanded the indigenous forces, but because he accompanied Hawker and Bourne, two of Hammer's own.

"Duck," said the helmet with unexpected clarity, Bourne on the intercom, and the general obeyed just as the vehicle switched direction and the arms of the tunnel entrance embraced them.

Though the nursery tunnels were carved through living rock— many of them with hand tools by Molts millennia in the past—the entrances were always onto gentle slopes so that no precocious infant projected himself over a sharp drop. That meant the approach was normally through soil, stabilized traditionally by arches of small ashlars, or (since humans landed) concrete or glazed earth portals.

Here the tunnel was stone-arched and, though the external portion of the structure had been sandblasted by the firecracker rounds, blocks only a meter within the opening bore the patina of great age. Radescu expected the jeep's headlights to flood the tunnel, supplementing the illumination which seeped in past them. Instead Profile Bourne halted and flipped a toggle on the dashboard.

There was a *thud!* within the plenum chamber, and opaque white smoke began to boil out around the skirts. It had the heavy odor of night-blooming flowers, cloying but not choking to the men who had to breathe it. Driven by the fans, the smoke was rapidly filling the tunnel in both directions by the time it rose so high that Radescu, his head raised to the arched roof, was himself engulfed by it.

The last thing he saw were the flashing holograms of Hawker's display, warning of Molt activity in the near distance. Before or behind them in the tunnel in this case, because the rock shielded evidence of ionization in any other direction.

Something touched the side of Radescu's helmet. He barely suppressed a scream before his faceplate slid down like a knife carving a swath of visibility through the palpable darkness. He could see again, though his surroundings were all in shades of saffron and the depth of rounded objects was somewhat more vague than normally was the case. Lieutenant Hawker was lowering the hand with which he had just manipulated the controls of the Oltenian's helmet for him.

"Molts can't see in the smoke," Hawker said. "Want to come with me—" the muzzle of his gun gestured down the tunnel "—or stay here with the sarge?"

"I ought—" Radescu began, intending to say "to join my men." But the Oltenian portion of the patrol under Captain Elejash had its orders—set up on the crest, await support, and let the vehicles draw fire if the Molts were foolish enough to provide data for the Slammers' gunnery computers. Each location from which a satellite registered a bolt being fired went into the data base as a point to be hit not now—the snipers would have teleported away—but at a future date when a Molt prepared to fire from the same known position. In fact, the casualties during the patrol's assault seemed to have left the surviving Molts terrified of shellfire, even the desultory bombardment by Oltenian guns. "Yes, I'm with you," the general added instead.

The nursery tunnel would normally have been wide enough to pass the jeep much deeper within it, but the shock of the penetrators detonating had spalled slabs of rock from the walls, nearly choking the tunnel a few meters ahead.

"Dunno if it's safe," the mercenary said, feeling a facet of the new surface between his left finger and thumb.

"It's bedrock," Radescu responded nonchalantly. He had a fear of heights but no touch of claustrophobia. "It may be blocked, but nothing further should fall."

Hawker shrugged and resumed his careful advance.

The tunnel was marked by several sharp changes of direction in its first twenty meters, natural since its whole purpose was to train immature Molts to sense and teleport to locations to which they had no physical access. There were glowstrips and some light trickling through the airshafts in the tunnel roof, but the angled walls prevented the infants from seeing any distance down the gallery.

Radescu's gun wavered between being pointed straight ahead in the instinctive fear that a Molt warrior would bolt around a corner at him, and being slanted up at 45° in the intellectual awareness that to do otherwise needlessly endangered Lieutenant Hawker, a step ahead and only partially to the side. Noticing that, the Oltenian pushed past the Slammer so as not to have that particular problem on his mind.

When Radescu brushed closer to the wall, he noticed that its surface seemed to brighten. That was the only evidence that he was "seeing" by means of high-frequency sound, projected stereo-scopically from either side of the commo helmet and, after it was reflected back, converted to visible light within microns-thick layers of the face shield.

It was the apparent normalcy of his vision that made so amazing the blindness of the pair of Molts which Radescu encountered in the large chamber around the fourth sharp angle. One of them was crawling toward him on hands and knees, while the other waddled in a half crouch with his arms spread as though playing blindman's bluff.

The shotgun rose—Radescu had instincts that amazed him in their *vulgarity*—but the general instead of firing cried, "Wait! Both of you! I want to talk about peace!"

The crawling Molt leaped upright, an arm going back to the hilt of a slung weapon, while the other adult caught up an infant. Both adults were very aged males, wizened though the yellowish tinge which was an artifact of the helmet's mechanism disconcerted eyes expecting the greenish-black scales of great age. The one who was crouching had a brow horn twisted like that of the old warrior in Belvedere. . . .

Hawker was a presence to his left but the Oltenian general concentrated wholly on the chamber before him, sweat springing out on his neck and on the underside of his jaw. There were not merely two Molts in the chamber but over a score, the rest infants in their neat beds of woven grass scattered across the floor of the room—where the adults, their lamps useless, could find them now only by touch.

"Keir, *stop!*" shouted the Molt who had not reached for a weapon. He was speaking in Rumanian, the only language common among the varied autochthonal themes as well as between Molts and humans. In this case, however, the Molts almost certainly spoke the same dialect, so the choice of language was almost certainly a plea for further forbearance on the part of the guns which, though unseen, must be there. "If they shoot, the young—"

The other Molt lunged forward—but toward a sidewall, not toward the humans. He held a stabbing spear, a traditional weapon with two blades joined by a short wooden handgrip in the center. One blade slashed upward in a wicked disemboweling stroke that rang on the stone like a sack of coins falling.

"We won't hurt your infants—" Radescu said as the spearcarrier rotated toward the sound with his weapon raised. Hawker fired and the Molt sagged in on himself, spitted on a trio of amber tracks: smoke concealed the normal cyan flash of the powergun, but shock-waves from the superheated air made their own mark on the brush of high-frequency sound.

The adult with the twisted horn disappeared, holding the infant he had snatched up as Radescu first spoke.

Alexander Radescu tried to lean his gun against the wall. It fell to the floor instead, but he ignored it to step to the nearest of the infant Molts. The little creature was surprisingly dense: it seemed to weigh a good five kilos in Radescu's arms, twisting against the fabric of his jacket to find a nipple. Its scales were warm and flexible; only against pressure end-on did they have edges which Radescu could feel.

"We'll carry them outside," said the Oltenian. "I'll carry them ... We'll keep them in—" his face broke into a broad smile, hidden behind his face shield "—in the conference room; maybe they'll like the fountains."

"Hostages?" asked Hawker evenly, as faceless as the general, turning in a slow sweep of the chamber to ensure that no further Molts appeared to resume the rescue mission.

The infant Radescu held began to mew. He wondered how many of the females and prepubescent males had been fleeing from the ridge in short hops when the bomblets swept down across them. "No, Lieutenant," Radescu said, noting the ripples of saffron gauze in his vision, heat waves drifting from the iridium barrel of Hawker's powergun. "As proof of my good faith. I've proved other things today."

He strode back toward the exit from the tunnel, realizing that his burden would prevent any hostile action by the Molts.

"Now I'll prove that," he added, as much to himself as to the mercenary keeping watch behind him in the lightless chamber.

The image of Grigor Antonescu in the tank of the commo set was more faithful than face-to-face reality would have been. The colors of the Chief Tribune's skin and the muted pattern of his formal robes glowed with the purity of transmitted light instead of being overlaid by the white glaze of surface reflection as they would have been had General Radescu spoken to him across the desk in his office.

"Good evening, Uncle," Radescu said. "I appreciate your— discussing matters with me in this way." Relays clicked elsewhere in the command car, startling him because he had been told he would be alone in the vehicle. Not that Hammer would not be scowling over every word, every nuance. . . .

"I'm not sure," replied the Tribune carefully, "that facilities supplied by the mercenaries are a suitable avenue for a conversation about State policy, however."

His hand reached forward and appeared to touch the inner surface of the tank in which Radescu viewed him. In fact, the older man's fingers must have been running across the outside of the similar unit in which he viewed his nephew's image. "Impressive, though. I'll admit that," he added.

The Tribune had the slim good looks common to men on his side of Radescu's family. He no longer affected the full makeup his nephew used regularly, because decades of imperious calm had given him an expression almost as artful. The general aped that stillness as he went on. "The key to our present small success has been the mercenaries; similarly, they are the key to the great success I propose for the near future."

"Wiping out an entire theme?" asked Antonescu over fingers tented so that the tips formed a V-notch like the rear sight of a gun.

"Peace with all the themes, Uncle," Radescu said, and no amount of concentration could keep a cheek muscle from twitching and making the wings of his butterfly beauty patch flutter. "An end to this war, a return to peaceful relations with the Molts—which off-planet traders have easily retained. There's no need for men and Molts to fight like this. Oltenia has three centuries of experience to prove there's no need."

Cooling fans began to whirr in a ceiling duct. Something similar must have happened near the console which Antonescu had been loaned by Hammer's supply contingent in Belvedere, because the Chief Tribune looked up in momentary startlement—the first emotion he had shown during the call. "There are those, Alexi," he said to the tank again, "who argue that with both populations expanding, there is no longer enough room on Oltenia for both races. The toll on human farm stock is too high, now that most Molts live to warrior age—thanks to improvements in health care misguidedly offered the autochthons by humans in the past."

"Molt attacks on livestock during puberty rites are inevitable," Radescu agreed, "as more land is devoted to ranching and the number of indigenous game animals is reduced." He felt genuinely calm, the way he had when he committed himself in the conference room with Marshal Erzul. There was only one route to real success, so he need have no regrets at what he was doing. "We can't stop

the attacks. So we'll formalize them, treat them as a levy shared by
the State and by the Molts collectively."

"They don't have the organization to accomplish that,"
Antonescu said with a contemptuous snap of his fingers. "Even if
you think our citizens would stand for the cost themselves."

"What are the costs of having powerguns emptied into crowded
ballrooms?" the younger man shot back with the passionless
precision of a circuit breaker tripping. "What is the cost of this
army—in *money* terms, never mind casualties?"

Antonescu shrugged. Surely he could not really be that calm . . .
He said, "Some things are easier in war, my boy. Emotions can be
directed more easily, centralized decision making doesn't arouse
the—negative comment that it might under other circumstances."

"The Molts," said the young general in conscious return to an
earlier subject, "have been forced by the war to organize in much the
same way that we have rallied behind the Tribunate."

By an effort of will, he held his uncle's eyes as he spoke the
words he had rehearsed a dozen times to a mirror. "There could be
no long-term—no middle-term—solution to Molt-human relations
without that, I agree. But with firm control by the leaders of both
races over the actions of their more extreme members, there *can* be
peace—and a chance on this planet to accomplish things which
aren't within the capacity of *any* solely human settlement, even
Earth herself."

The Chief Tribune smiled in the warm, genuinely affectionate
manner which had made him the only relative—parents included—
for whom Alexander Radescu had cared in early childhood. Radescu
relived a dual memory, himself in a crib looking at his Uncle
Grigor—and the infant Molt squirming against him for sustenance
and affection.

Antonescu said, "Your enthusiasm, my boy, was certainly one
of the reasons we gave the army into your charge when traditional
solutions had failed. And of course—" the smile lapsed into something with a harder edge, but only for a moment "—because you're
my favorite nephew, yes.

"But primarily," the Chief Tribune continued, "because you are a very intelligent youngman, Alexi, and you have a record of doing what you say you'll do . . . which will bring you far, one day, yes."

He leaned forward, just as he had in Radescu's infancy, his long jaw and flat features a stone caricature of a human face. "But how can you offer to end a war that the Molts began—however fortunate their act may have been for some human ends?"

"I'm going to kick them," the general said with a cool smile of his own, "until they ask *me* for terms. And the terms I'll offer them will be fair to both races." He blinked, shocked to realize that he had been speaking as if Chief Tribune Antonescu were one of the coterie of officers he had brought to heel in the conference room. "With your permission, of course, sir. And that of your colleagues."

Antonescu laughed and stood up. Radescu was surprised to see that the Chief Tribune remained focused in the center of the tank as he walked around the chair in which he had been sitting. "Enthusiasm, Alexi, yes, we expect that," he said. "Well, you do your part and leave the remainder to us. You've done very well so far.

"But I think you realize," the older man went on with his hands clasped on the back of a chair of off-planet pattern, "that I've stretched very far already to give you this opportunity." Antonescu's voice was calm, but his face held just a hint of human concern which shrank his nephew's soul down to infancy again. "If matters don't—succeed, according to your plans and the needs of the State, then there won't be further options for you. Not even for you, Alexi."

"I understand, Uncle," said Alexander Radescu, who understood very well what failure at this level would require him, as an Oltenian aristocrat, to do in expiation. "I have no use for failures either."

As he reached for the power switch at the base of the vision tank, he wondered who besides Hammer would be listening in on the discussion—and what *they* thought of his chances of success.

The bolt was a flicker in the air, scarcely visible until it struck an Oltenian armored car. The steel plating burned with a clang and a white fireball a moment before a fuel tank ruptured to add the sluggish red flames of kerosene to the spectacle. The vehicle had been hull down and invisible from the ridge toward which the next assault would be directed; but the shot had been fired from the rear, perhaps kilometers distant.

Three men in Oltenian fatigues jumped from the body of the vehicle while a fourth soldier screamed curses in a variety of languages and squirmed from the driver's hatch, cramped by the Slammer body armor which he wore. The turrets on several of the neighboring armored cars began to crank around hastily, though the sniper was probably beyond range of the machine guns even with solid shot. There was no chance of hitting the Molt by randomly spraying the landscape anyway; Radescu's tongue poised to pass an angry order down when some subordinate forestalled him and the turrets reversed again.

"Nothing to be done about that," Radescu said to the pair of men closest to him. He nodded in the direction of a few of the hundred or so armored vehicles he could see from where he stood. Had he wished for it, satellite coverage through the hologram projector in the combat car would have shown him thousands more. "With a target the size of this one, the odd sniper's going to hit something even if he's beyond range of any possible counterfire."

A second bolt slashed along the side of an armored personnel carrier a hundred meters from the first victim. There was no secondary explosion this time—in fact, because of the angle at which it struck, the powergun might not have penetrated the vehicle's fighting compartment. Its infantrymen boiled out anyway, many of them leaving behind the weapons they had already stuck through gunports in the APC's sides. Bright sunlight glanced incongruously from their bulky infrared goggles, passive night vision equipment which was the closest thing in the Oltenian arsenal to the wide assortment of active and passive devices built into the Slammers' helmets.

Thank the Lord for small favors: in the years before squabbling broke out in open war between men and Molts, the autochthons had an unrestricted choice of imports through off-planet traders. They had bought huge stocks of powerguns and explosives, weapons which made an individual warrior the bane of hundreds of his sluggish human opponents. Since theirs would be the decision of when and where to engage, however, they had seen no need of equipment like the mercenaries' helmets—equipment which expanded the conditions under which one could fight.

"Don't bet your ass there's no chance a' counterfire," growled Profile Bourne; and as he was speaking, the main gun of one of Hammer's tanks blasted back in the direction from which the sniper's bolts had come.

The flash and the *thump!* of air closing back along the trail blasted through it by a twenty-centimeter powergun startled more Oltenians than had the sniper fire itself.

General Forsch had started to walk toward Radescu from one of the command trailers with a message he did not care to entrust either to radio or to the lips of a subordinate. When the tank fired, the gangling chief of staff threw himself flat onto ground which the barrage of two days previous had combed into dust as fine as baby powder. Forsch looked up with the anger of a torture victim at his young commander.

Radescu, seeing the yellow-gray blotches on the uniform which had been spotless until that moment, hurried over to Forsch and offered a hand to help him rise. Radescu had deliberately donned the same stained battledress he had worn during the previous assault, but he could empathize nonetheless with how his subordinate was feeling.

"The meteorologists say there should be a period of still air," the chief of staff muttered, snatching his hand back from Radescu's offer of help when he saw how dirty his palms were.

"Our personnel say that it may last for only a few minutes," Forsch continued, dusting his hands together with intense chopping motions on which he focused his eyes. "The—*technician* from the mercenaries—" he glanced up at Hawker and Bourne, following Radescu to either side "—says go with it." His face twisted. "Just 'go with it.'"

The sky was the flawless ultramarine of summer twilight. "Thank you, General Forsch," Radescu said as he looked upward, his back to the lowering sun. Profile had been right: whether or not the tank blast had killed the sniper, its suddenness had at least driven the Molt away from the narrow circuit of rocks through which he had intended to teleport and confuse counterfire. A single twenty-centimeter bolt could shatter a boulder the size of a house, and the consequent rain of molten glass and rock fragments would panic anyone within a hundred meters of the impact area.

Radescu tongued the helmet's control wand up and to the left, the priority channel that would carry his next words to every man in the attacking force and log him into the fire control systems of the Oltenian and mercenary gun batteries. "Execute Phase One," he said, three words which subsumed hundreds of computer hours and even lengthier, though less efficient, calculations by battery commanders, supply officers, and scores of additional human specialties.

True darkness would have been a nice bonus, but the hour or so around twilight was the only real likelihood of still air—and that was more important than the cloak Nature herself would draw over activities.

"All right," Alexander Radescu said, seeing General Forsch but remembering his uncle. The trailers of the Oltenian operations center straggled behind Forsch because of the slope. A trio of Slammers' combat cars with detectors like those of the jeep guarded the trailers against Molt infiltrators. Hull down on the ridge line, the seventeen tanks of Hammer's H Company waited to support the assault with direct fire. A company of combat cars, vulnerable (as the tanks were not) to bolts from the autochthons' shoulder weapons, would move up as soon as the attack was joined.

Apart from the combat car in which the commander himself would ride, every vehicle in the actual assault would be Oltenian; but all the drivers were Hammer's men.

Forsch saluted, turned, and walked back toward the trailers with his spine as stiff as a ramrod. There was an angry crackle nearby as a three-barreled powergun on one of the combat cars ripped a bubble of ionization before it could become a functioning Molt. There were more shots audible and those only a fraction of the encounters which distance muffled, Radescu knew. A satchel charge detonated—with luck when a bolt struck it, otherwise when a Molt hurled it into a vehicle of humans whose luck had run out.

The autochthons were stepping up their harassing attacks, though their main effort was almost certainly reserved for the moment that humans crowded into the killing ground of the open, rock-floored valley. Bolts fired from positions kilometers to either side would enfilade the attacking vehicles, while satchel charges and buzzbombs launched point-blank ripped even Hammer's panzers. Human counterfire itself would be devastating to the vehicles as confusion and proximity caused members of the assault force to blast one another in an attempt to hit the fleeing Molts.

It might still happen that way.

"Might best be mounting up," said Lieutenant Hawker,whose level of concern was shown only by the pressure-mottled knuckles of the hand which gripped his submachine gun. Bourne was snapping his head around like a dog trying to catch flies. He knew the link from the combat car to the lieutenant's helmet would beep a warning if a Molt were teleporting to a point nearby, but he was too keyed up to accept the stress of inaction. "Three minutes isn't very long."

"Long enough to get your clock cleaned," the sergeant rejoined as he turned gratefully to the heavy vehicle he would drive in this assault.

The first shells were already screaming down on the barren valley and the slope across it. The salvo was time-on-target: calculated so that ideally every shell would burst simultaneously, despite being fired from different ranges and at varying velocities. It was a technique generally used to increase the shock effect of the opening salvo of a bombardment. This time its purpose was to give the Molts as little warning as possible between their realization of Radescu's plan and its accomplishment. The young general sprinted for the combat car, remembering that its electronics would give him a view from one of the tanks already overlooking the valley.

Colonel Hammer and his headquarters vehicles were twenty kilometers to the rear, part of the security detachment guarding the three batteries of rocket howitzers. The mercenary units had been severely depleted by providing drivers for so many Oltenian vehicles, and a single Molt with a powergun could wreak untold havoc among the belts of live ammunition being fed to the hogs.

There was in any case no short-term reason that high officers should risk themselves in what would be an enlisted man's fight. Radescu had positioned his own headquarters in a place of danger so that his generals could rightfully claim a part in the victory he prayed he would accomplish. He was joining the assault himself because he believed, as he had said to Hawker and Bourne when he met them, in the value of leading from the front.

And also because he *was* Alexander Radescu.

There were footpegs set into the flank of the combat car, but Hawker used only the midmost one as a brace from which to vault into the open fighting compartment. The big mercenary then reached down, grasped Radescu by the wrist rather than by the hand he had thought he was offering, and snatched him aboard as well. Hawker's athleticism, even hampered by the weight and restriction of his body armor, was phenomenal.

The detection gear which had been transferred to the combat car for this operation took up the space in which the forward of the three gunners would normally have stood. The pintle-mounted tribarrels were still in place, but they would not be used during the assault. The Slammers' submachine guns and the shotgun which the general again carried would suffice for close-in defense without endangering other vehicles.

The thick iridium sides of the mercenary vehicle made it usable in the expected environment, which would have swept the jeep and any men aboard it to instant destruction. Radescu touched his helmet as he settled himself in the corner of the fighting compartment opposite Hawker: firing from the combat car meant raising one's head above the sidewalls.

The big vehicle quivered as Bourne, hidden forward in the driver's compartment, fed more power to the idling fans. Hawker brought up an image of the valley over the crest, his hands brushing touch plates on the package of additional instruments even before Radescu requested it. Very possibly the lieutenant acted on his own hook, uninterested in Radescu's wishes pro or con. . . .

The hologram was of necessity monochrome, in this case a deep red-orange which fit well enough with what Radescu remembered of the contours of rock covered by sere grass. The shellbursts hanging and spreading over the terrain were the same sullen, fiery color as the ground, however, and that was disconcerting. It made Radescu's chest tighten as he imagined plunging into a furnace to be consumed in his entirety.

The tanks began to shoot across the valley with a less startling effect than the single countersniper blast. These bolts were directed away from the assault force, and they added only marginally to the ambient sound. The bombardment did not seem too loud to Radescu after the baptism he had received from shells plunging down point-blank the previous day. The sky's constant thrum was fed by nearly a thousand gun tubes, some of them even heavier— though slower firing—than the Slammers' howitzers, and the effect was all-pervasive even though it had not called itself to the general's attention.

Dazzling reflections from the 200mm bolts played across even the interior of the combat car, washing Hawker's grim smile with the blue-green cast of death. The bolts did not show up directly on the display, but air heated by their passage roiled the upper reaches of the smoke into horizontal vortices. Across the valley the shots hammered computer-memorized positions from which Molts had sniped in the past. Rock sprayed high in the release of enormous crystalline stresses, and bubbles of heated air expanded the covering of smoke into twisted images larger than the tanks which had caused them.

"Base to Command," said the helmet in the voice of General Forsch, overlaid by a fifty-cycle hum which resulted from its transmission through the mercenaries' commo system. There were spits of static as well, every time a tank main gun released its packet of energy across the spectrum. "Phase One coverage has reached planned levels."

"Terminate Phase One," said Radescu. Across from him, Lieutenant Hawker patted a switch and the image of the valley collapsed. He did not touch other controls, so presumably the detection apparatus had been live all the time. The smile he flashed at Radescu when he saw the general's eyes on him was brief and preoccupied, but genuine enough.

"Phase One terminated," Forsch crackled back almost at once.

There was no effect directly obvious to the assault force, but that was to be expected: the flight time of shells from some of the guns contributing to the barrage was upwards of thirty seconds. "Prepare to execute Phase Two," said Radescu on the command channel as clearly as the hormones jumping in his bloodstream would permit. Everything around him was a fragment of a montage, each existing on a timeline separate from the rest.

"Give 'em ten seconds more," Profile broke in on the intercom. "Some bastard always takes one last pull on the firing lanyard to keep from having to unload the chamber."

"Execute Phase Two," ordered Radescu, his tongue continuing its set course as surely as an avalanche staggers downhill, the driver's words no more than a wisp of snow fencing overwhelmed in the rush of fixed intent.

Whatever Bourne may have thought about the order, he executed it with a precision smoother than any machine. The combat car surged forward, lagging momentarily behind the Oltenian APCs to either flank because the traction of their tires gave them greater initial acceleration than could the air cushion. Seconds later, when the whole line crested the ridge, the Slammers vehicle had pulled ahead by the half length that Bourne thought was safest.

In the stillness that replaced the howl of shells, small arms sizzled audibly among the grumble of diesels as soldiers responded to teleporting Molts—or to their own nervousness. A full charge of shot clanged into the combat car's port side, although Hawker's instruments showed that the gunman in the personnel carrier could not have had a real target.

Radescu raised himself to look over the bulkhead, though the sensible part of his mind realized that the added risk was considerable and unnecessary. To function in a world gone mad, a man goes mad himself: to be ruled by a sensible appreciation of danger in a situation where danger was both enormous and unavoidable would drive the victim into cowering funk—counter survival in a combat zone where his own action might be required to save him. Bracing himself against the receiver of the tribarrel locked in place beside him, Alexander Radescu caught a brief glimpse of the results of his plan—before he plunged into them.

The sweep of the broad valley the assault must cross boiled with the contents of the thousands of smoke shells poured over it by the massed batteries. The brilliant white of rounds from Hammer's guns lay flatter and could be seen still spreading, absorbing and underlying the gray-blue chemical haze gushing from Oltenian shells. The coverage was not—could not be—complete, even within the two-kilometer front of the attack. Nonetheless, its cumulative effect robbed snipers of their targets at any distance from the vehicles.

Molts teleporting to positions readied to meet the attack found that even on the flanking slopes where the warriors were not blanketed by smoke, their gunsights showed featureless shades of gray instead of Oltenian vehicles. The wisest immediately flickered back to cover on the reverse slope. Younger, less perceptive autochthons began firing into the haze—an exercise as vain as hunting birds while blindfolded.

A pillar of crimson flame stabbed upward through the smoke as the result of one such wild shot; but Hammer's tanks and the combat cars joining them on the ridge combed out the frustrated Molts like burrs from a dog's hide. Had the snipers picked a target, fired once, and shifted position as planned, they would have been almost invulnerable to counter measure. Warriors who angrily tried to empty their guns into an amorphous blur lasted five shots or fewer before a tank gun or a burst of automatic fire turned them into a surge of organic gases in the midst of a fireball of liquid rock.

All colors narrowed to shades of yellow as the combat car drove into the thickening smoke and Radescu switched on the sonic vision apparatus of his borrowed helmet. What had been an opaque fog opened into a 60° wedge of the landscape, reaching back twenty or thirty meters. It would not have done for top speed running, but the visibility was more than adequate for an assault line rolling across open terrain at forty kph.

A tree stump, ragged and waist high, coalesced from the fog as the helmet's ultrasonic generators neared it. Bourne edged left to avoid it, the combat car swaying like a leaf in the breeze, while the

Slammer driving the Oltenian vehicle to the right swerved more awkwardly in the other direction.

Alexander Radescu had been loaned a helmet from mercenary stores, but there was no question of equipping enough local troops to drive all the vehicles in the assault. The alternative had been to scatter a large proportion of the Slammers among packets of Oltenian regulars. That Hammer had found the alternative acceptable was praise for Radescu which the Oltenian had only hoped to receive.

A Molt with a buzzbomb on his shoulder, ready to launch, appeared beside the tree stump.

The smoke did nothing to prevent warriors from teleporting into the valley to attack. The autochthons had expected a barrage of high explosives and armor-piercing rounds, which would have had some effect but only a limited one. This valley was the center of a theme's territory; in a jump of a kilometer or two over ground so familiar, a young adult could position himself on a chunk of granite no larger than his head.

What the smoke shells did do was to prevent the autochthons from seeing anything after they projected themselves into the fog. Radescu cried out, raising his shotgun. The Molt was turned half away from them, hunching forward, hearing the diesel engine of the nearest APC but unable to see even that.

The combat car's acceleration and slight change of attitude threw the Oltenian general back against the hard angles of the gun mount beside him. Bourne had brought up power and changed fan aspect in a pair of perfectly matched curves which showed just how relatively abruptly an air-cushion vehicle could accelerate on a downslope, when gravity was on its side and the rolling friction of wheels slowed the conventional vehicles to either flank.

The Molt must have heard the rush of air at the last, because he whirled like a dancer toward the combat car with a look of utter horror as the bow slope rushed down on him. Radescu fired past the car's forward tribarrel, his shot missing high and to the left, as the autochthon loosed his shoulder-launched missile at the vehicle.

The buzzbomb struck the combat car beside the driver's hatch and sprang skyward, its rocket motor a hot spot in the smoke to infrared goggles and a ghostly pattern of vortices in the Slammers' ultrasound. The combat car, which weighed thirty-two tonnes, quivered only minutely as it spread the Molt between the ground and the steel skirt of the plenum chamber.

There was a violent outbreak of firing from the vehicles just behind the combat car. Passive infrared was useless for a driver because terrain obstacles did not radiate enough heat to bring them out against the ambient background. For soldiers whose only duty was to cut down Molts before the warriors could find targets of their own in the smoke, passive infrared was perfect.

The gunners in the armored car turrets and the infantrymen huddled behind vision blocks in the sides of their armored personnel carriers could see nothing—until Molt warriors teleported into the valley.

The autochthons' body temperature made them stand out like flares blazing in a sea of neutral gray. The automatic fire of the turret guns was not very accurate; but the ranges were short, the shot-cones deadly, and there were over fifteen thousand twitching trigger fingers packed into a constricted area. Warriors shimmered out of the smoke, hesitated in their unexpected blindness, and were swept away in bloody tatters by the rattling crossfire. Charges of miniature airfoils sang from one vehicle to another, scarring the light armor and chipping away paint like a desultory sandblasting. The projectiles could not seriously harm the vehicles, however, and the armor was sufficient to preserve the crews and infantry complements as well.

The Molt that Profile had just driven over was a wide blotch to the goggles of the Oltenians in the flanking APCs. Their guns stormed from either side, stirring the slick warmth and ricocheting from the rocky ground.

Lieutenant Hawker touched Radescu with his left hand, the one which did not hold the submachine gun. The combat car yawed as Profile braked it from the murderous rush he had just achieved, but the veteran lieutenant held steady without need to cling to a support as the Oltenian did.

"Arming distance," Hawker said over the intercom now that he had Radescu's attention. "The buzzbomb didn't go off because it was fired too close in. It's a safety so you don't blow yourself up, that's all. Profile wasn't taking any risks."

"Yee-*ha!*" shouted the driver, clearly audible over the windrush.

Alexander Radescu was later surprised at how little he remembered of the assault—and that in flashes as brief and abrupt as the powergun bolt that lanced past him from behind, close enough to heat the left earpiece of his commo helmet before it sprayed dirt from the ground rising in front of the combat car. Bypassed sniper or mercenary gunner forgetting his orders not to fire into the smoke? No way to tell and no matter: all fire is hostile fire when it snaps by your head.

The slope that was their objective on the other side of the valley had been shrouded as thickly as the rest of the ground which the assault needed to cross. The hogs had kicked in final salvoes of firecracker rounds to catch Molts who thought the fog protected them. That explosive whisking, added to the greater time that the curtain had been in place, meant that the smoke had begun to part and thin here where the ground rose.

A crag, faceted like the bow of a great sea vessel, appeared so abruptly in Radescu's vision that the Oltenian instinctively flipped up his face shield. The wedge of granite had a definite purple cast noticeable through the smoke of sun-infused white and gray streaming slowly down into the valley basin, heavier than the air it displaced.

It had been inevitable that the assault lines would straggle. Perhaps it was inevitable also that Profile Bourne would use his experience with his vehicle and its better power-to-weight ratio to race to the objective alone—despite clear orders, from Hawker as well as Radescu, to keep it reined in. There was no other vehicle close to them as the sergeant climbed to the left of the slab with his fans howling out maximum thrust and the ionization detector began flashing its violet and yellow warning, visible as the rock was through a thin neutral mask.

Alexander Radescu looked up and to the right, guided by instinct in the direction that the electronic tocsin was causing

Hawker to turn with his submachine gun. The air solidified into a Molt with scales of as rich a color as the rock he stood on—spitting distance from the car laboring uphill, an easy cast for a satchel charge or a burst of fire into the open-topped compartment.

The Molt did not carry a weapon, and his right horn was twisted.

"No!" Radescu shouted, forgetting his intercom link as he lunged across the fighting compartment to grasp his companion's gun. His fingers locked at the juncture of the barrel and receiver, cold iridium and plastic which insulated too well to have any temperature apart from that which the general's hand gave the outer layer of molecules. "Not this one!"

"Steady," said Enzo Hawker, bracing the Oltenian with the free hand which could have plucked the man away, just as Radescu's slight body would have been no sufficient hindrance had the gunner wished to carry through and fire at the Molt. "Watch your side of the car."

The broad ravine into which Bourne plunged them was a water cut ramp to the crest. It held smoke dense enough to be instantly blinding. The autochthon had already disappeared, teleporting away with a smile which was probably an accident of physiognomy.

"I'm sorry, I—" Radescu said as he straightened, remembering this time to use his intercom. Hawker was as solid as the iridium bulkheads themselves, while the general's own mind leaped with fear and embarrassment and a sense of victory which intellectually he knew he had not yet won. "Shouldn't have touched you, Lieutenant, I was—" He raised his eyes to meet the other man's and saw nothing, even a hand's length apart, because the mercenary's face shield was a perfect mirror from the outside. "I didn't think."

"Just steady," Hawker said quietly. "You've been thinking fine."

Shells were hitting the ground, a considerable distance away but heavily enough that pebbles slid in miniature avalanches as the ravine walls quivered. As soon as the vehicles rolled into the valley, the artillery had shifted its points of aim to rocky areas within a few kilometers of the target of the assault.

These would be staging points for the Molt refugees, the females and the prepubescent males driven from what should have been the inviolable core of the theme holdings. They could stay ahead of human pursuit and would in a matter of a few hops scatter beyond the area which shells could saturate. But since the starting point was known, there was a finite number of initial landing areas available to the Molt noncombatant. Those were the targets for as many fragmentation and high-explosive rounds as the army could pump out.

Alexander Radescu had his own reasons, eminently logical ones, to want peace. He had to give the autochthons a reason whose logic the most high-spirited, glory-longing warrior would accept as overwhelming.

Dead comrades would not achieve that alone: a warrior *could* not accept the chance of dying as a sufficient reason to modify his actions, any more than could a mercenary soldier like Hawker, like Bourne in the forward hatch. Maimed females and children howling as they tried to stuff intestines back into their body cavities were necessary, as surely as the Molt in the ballroom of the Tribunal Palace in Belvedere had been, stooping behind the weight of his powergun—every shot turning a gay costume into burning, bloody rags.

"It's not worth it," the young general said, sickened by the coolness with which he had deliberated slaughter.

Only when Hawker said, "Hey?" did the Oltenian realize he had spoken not only aloud but loudly. He shrugged to the mercenary and their vehicle, sideslipping down the reverse slope, would have put an end to the conversation even had Radescu wished to continue it.

The smoke blanket here was tattered into no more than a memory of what the assault force had first driven into, though it—like a sheet of glass viewed endwise—was still opaque to a sniper trying to draw a bead any distance through it. There was a body sprawled forty meters from the combat car, an adult male killed by one of the shrapnel rounds which interspersed the smoke shells covering the ridge.

"Red two-ninety!" cried Lieutenant Hawker, "*Radescu!* Red two-seventy!" and the general whirled to fire over the bulkhead at the Molt appearing almost beside the combat car, too close for Hawker himself to shoot.

The muzzle blast of the shotgun was a surprise, but this time the properly shouldered stock thrust and did not slam the young general. Neither did the charge hit the autochthon, a male with a powergun, though a bush a meter from him was stripped in a sharp-edged scallop.

The Molt threw his arms up and ran as the car sailed past him. Radescu fired again, missing even worse because he had not figured the vehicle's speed into his attempt to lead the runner; and as the Slammer lieutenant aimed over the back deck, the autochthon dissolved away in a further teleport. Only then did Radescu realize that the Molt had not only been too frightened to shoot, he had dropped his powergun as he fled.

The cave entrance for which Bourne steered was much larger than the one they had captured on the other side of the ridge—larger, in fact, than anything of the sort which Radescu had previously seen. The size was accentuated by the hasty attempts the Molts had made to build a physical barrier across the huge, pillared archway. There was a layer of stones ranging from head-sized down to pebbles in the entrance, the foundation course of a crude wall. Around the stones were more bodies, half a dozen of them—probably adult males, but too close to the epicenter of the firecracker round that burst overhead for the bomblets to have left enough of the corpses for certain identification.

A puff of breeze opened a rent in the smoke through which the evening sky streamed like a comet's violet hair.

"Hang on," said the sergeant on the intercom. He had driven past the archway and now, as he spoke, spun the combat car on its axis to approach from the downhill side.

Radescu, clinging to the gun mount awkwardly because of the personal weapon in his hand, cried, "There's a barrier there, Sergeant—rocks!"

"Hang the cop on!" Bourne replied gleefully, and the combat car, brought to the end of the tether of its downhill inertia, accelerated toward the entrance at a rate that sailed it over the pitiable stones through which a less ebullient driver would have plowed.

There was light in the cavernous chamber beyond, a portable area lamp of Oltenian manufacture, held up at arm's length by a Molt with a twisted horn.

As cool as he had been when he prepared to execute his own command group within minutes of meeting them, General Radescu said, "Neither of you shoot," on the intercom. Then, tonguing the command channel though he was not sure of signal propagation from in side the crystal line rock, he added, "Command to all units. Phase Two is complete. Terminate all offensive activity, shoot only in self-defense."

Bourne had not expected to halt immediately within the entrance, nor had the general specifically ordered him to do so. The sergeant would not have been condemned for murder, however, if he had felt the need to wait for orders before he took action he considered sensible. Now he used the steel skirts of the plenum chamber as physical brakes against the floor of polished rock, screeching and sparking in an orange-white storm instead of depending on the thrust of the fans to halt the heavy vehicle. The dazzling afterimages of saturated blue seemed for a moment brighter than the lamp which the autochthon had continued to hold steady while the car slewed around him in a semicircle.

When the skirts rested solidly on the pavement, Radescu realized that the ground itself was not firm. Earth shocks from the distant impact zones made dust motes dance around the globe of light, and the bulkhead quivered as Radescu dismounted.

Lag time, General Radescu hoped as he stepped toward the wizened Molt, shells fired before his order to desist. Behind him, the combat car pinged and sizzled as metal found a new stasis. There was also the clicking sound of Lieutenant Hawker releasing the transport lock of a tribarrel, freeing the weapon for immediate use.

"I hope you're here to talk of peace," said the Oltenian, reaching out to take the lamp which seemed too heavy for the frail autochthon.

"No," said Ferad who relinquished the lamp willingly, though he would have held it as long as need required—the way he had supported the powergun until he had emptied the magazine. "I am here this time to *make* peace."

The placid landscape had a slightly gritty texture, but Alexander Radescu was not sure whether that was a real residue from the smoke shells or if it was just another result of his own tiredness.

Losing would have taken just as much effort as the triumph he had in fact achieved.

Lieutenant Hawker murmured a reply to his commo helmet, then leaned toward Radescu and whispered, "Seven minutes."

The Oltenian general nodded, then turned to Forsch and the divisional generals assembled behind him, each with a small contingent of troops in dress uniforms. "The Tribunes are expected to arrive in seven minutes," Radescu called, loudly enough for even the enlisted men to hear him.

Radescu had gone to some lengths to give this event the look of a review, not an occupation. Weapons had been inspected for external gloss. Dress uniforms—blue with orange piping for the other ranks, scarlet for officers through field grade, and pearl with gold for the generals—would not remind the watching autochthons of the smoke-shrouded, shot-rippling assault by which the Oltenian Army had entered a theme stronghold.

The Molts would not forget, the survivors watching from distant hills with the representatives of the other themes. There was no need to rub their broad noses in it, that was all.

"General Radescu," said a voice. "Sir?"

Radescu turned, surprised but so much a man living on his nerves that no event seemed significantly more probable than did any other. "Yes?" he said. "General Forsch?"

Profile Bourne watched the chief of staff with the expression of disdain and despair which had summed up his attitude toward all the local forces—until the Oltenian line had made the assault beside him. Even those men were poofs again when they donned their carnival uniforms.

The sergeant's hands were linked on his breastplate, but that put them adequately near to his slung submachine gun. The reason the two Slammers had given for continuing to guard Radescu was a valid one: a single disaffected Molt could destroy all chances of peace by publicly assassinating Alexander Radescu. The general had not been impelled to ask whether or not that was the real reason.

Forsch was nervous, looking back at the divisional generals two paces behind him for support. Iorga nodded to him with tight-lipped enthusiasm.

"Sir," the lanky chief of staff continued, though he seemed to be examining his expression in the mirrors of Radescu's gilded boots, "I—we want to say that . . ."

The hills whispered with the rush of an oncoming aircraft. That, and perhaps the sculptured placidity of Radescu's face, brought Forsch back to full functioning. "You may have sensed," he said, meeting his commander's eyes, "a certain hostility when you announced your appointment to us."

"I surprised you, of course," Radescu murmured to make Forsch easier about whatever he intended to say. The great cargo plane commandeered to bring the Tribunes to sign the accords was visible a kilometer away, its wing rotors already beginning to tilt into hovermode fortheset-down. "All of you performed to the highest expectations of the State."

"Yes," the chief of staff said, less agreement than an acceptance of the gesture which Radescu had made. "Well. In any case, sir— and I speak for all of us—" more nods from the officers behind him "—we were wrong. You *were* the man to lead us. And we'll follow you, the whole army will follow you, wherever you choose to lead us if the peace talks break down."

Lord and his martyrs, thought Alexander Radescu, surveying the faces of men up to twice his age, they really would. They would follow him because he had gotten something done, even though some of the generals must have realized by now that he'd have shot them out of hand if they stood in the way of his intent. Lord and martyrs!

"I—" Radescu began; then he reached out and took Forsch's

right hand in his and laid the other on the tall officer's shoulder. "General—men—the peace talks won't fail." It was hard to view the quick negotiations between Ferad and himself as anything so formal that they could have been "broken off," but it was the same implicit dependence on bureaucratic niceties which had turned the war into a morass on the human side. "But I appreciate your words as, as much as I appreciated the skill and courage, the *great* courage, the whole army displayed in making this moment possible."

The Molts' problem had been the reverse of the self-inflicted wound from which the Oltenian Army had bled. The autochthons were too independent ever to deal the crushing blows that their ability to concentrate suddenly would have permitted them. Each side slashed at one another but struggled with itself, too ineffective either to win or to cease. And the same solution would extricate both from the bloody swamp: leaders who could see a way clear and who were willing to drive all before them.

"She's coming in," said Profile Bourne, not himself part of the formalities but willing to remind those who were of their duties. General Forsch wrung his superior's hand and slipped back to his place a pace to the rear, while the aircraft settled with a whining roar that echoed between the hills.

Debris and bodies had been cleared from the broad archway, and for the occasion the flagstone pavement had even been polished by a crew which ordinarily cared for the living quarters of general officers. Radescu had toyed only briefly with the thought of resodding the shell scars and wheel tracks. The valley's rocky barrenness was the reason it had become a Molt center, and nothing the human attack had done changed its appearance significantly. It was perhaps well to remind the Tribunate that this was not merely a human event, that the autochthons watching from vantage points kilometers distant were a part of it and of the system the treaty would put into effect for the remainder of the planet's history.

The aircraft's turbines thrummed in a rapidly descending rhythm when the oleo struts flexed and rose again as the wheels accepted the load. Dust billowed from among the russet grassblades, bringing General Radescu a flashback of a hillside descending in a welter of Molt bodies as the penetrators lifted it from within. He had been so frightened during that bombardment. . . .

The rear hatchway of the big cargo plane was levering itself down into an exit ramp. "Attention!" Radescu called, hearing his order repeated down the brief ranks as he himself braced. Most of the army was encamped five kilometers away in a location through which the troops had staged to the final assault. There they nervously awaited the outcome of this ceremony, reassured more by the sections of Hammer's men with detection gear scattered among them than they were by Radescu's promises as he rode off.

He'd done that much, at least, built trust between the indigenous and mercenary portions of his army on the way to doing the same between the intelligent species which shared the planet. It occurred to Alexander Radescu as he watched a pair of light trucks drive down the ramp, the first one draped with bunting for the ceremony, that wars could not be won: they could only be ended without having been lost. The skirmishes his troops had won were important for the way they conduced to the ends of peace.

The chairs draped in cloth-of-gold made an imposing-enough background for the Tribunes, but no one seemed to have calculated what uneven ground and the truck's high center of gravity would do to men attempting to sit on such chairs formally. Radescu suppressed a smile, remembering the way he had jounced on the back of the jeep.

That experience and others of recent days did not prevent him from being able to don a dress uniform and the makeup which had always been part of the persona he showed the world; but a week of blood and terror had won him certain pieces of self-knowledge which were, in their way, as important to him as anything he had accomplished in a military sense.

The driver of the lead truck tried to make a sweeping turn in order to bring the rear of his vehicle level with the red carpet which had been cut in sections from the flooring of the living trailers of high officers. An overly abrupt steering correction brought an audible curse from one of the men in the back of the vehicle, men who looked amazingly frail to Alexander Radescu after a week of troops in battledress.

Hawker and Bourne had kept a settled silence thus far during the makeshift procession until the six guards in scarlet—none of them were below the rank of major—jumped from the second truck to help the Tribunes down the steps welded to the back of the first. At the Honor Guard's appearance, Enzo Hawker snorted audibly and Radescu felt an impulse to echo the Slammer's disdain.

And yet those men were very similar to Radescu himself in background; not quite so well connected, but officers of the Tribunal Honor Guard for the same reason that Alexander Radescu was a general. That he was a man who could lead an army while they, with their rhodium-plated pistols, could not have guarded a school crossing, was an individual matter.

Grigor Antonescu, First among Equals, wore a pure white robe of office, while the collars of his two companions were black. Radescu saluted.

Instead of returning the formality the Chief Tribune took his nephew's hand in his own and raised it high in a gesture of triumph and acclamation. "Well done, my boy," the older man said loudly. "*Well* done."

More surprised by his uncle's open praise than he was by the brief scowls with which the other members of the Tribunate, Wraslov and Deliu, responded to it, the young general said, "Ah, Excellency, we all had confidence in the abilities of our men." Nodding to the side, toward the still-faced Bourne, he added in afterthought, "And in our allies, of course, in Colonel Hammer."

The presence of the troops braced to attention behind him vibrated in Radescu's mind like a taut bowstring. "Excellencies," he said, guiding down his uncle's hand and releasing it, "the actual meeting will be within the, the cavern, actually a tunnel complex as extensive as any Molt artifact on the planet, as it chances. The antechamber seemed a particularly suitable location for the signing since it—reminds the representatives of other themes that our troops are here without Molt sufferance."

Chief Tribune Antonescu patted at the front of his robe, frowning minutely when he realized that the marks he left in the fine dust were more disfiguring than the smooth layer which the ride from the plane had deposited over him. "The Molts are inside then, already?" he asked in a voice which, like his static face, gave away nothing save the fact that something was hidden.

"No, Excellency," said Radescu, finding that his slight, ingenuous smile had become a mask which he knew he must maintain, "they're—in sight, I suppose, the representatives."

He gestured with his spread fingers toward a few of the crags where, if he had squinted, he might have been able to see male autochthons waiting as the Oltenian Army waited in camp. "The young and females whom we captured are still at the lower levels within, under parole so to speak, those who might be able to teleport away now that we've stopped shelling."

For a moment, the general lost control of the smile he had been keeping neutral, and the Tribunes were shocked by the face of a man who recalled tumbled bodies and who now grinned that he might not weep. "But the theme elders who'll be signing—they'll arrive in the chamber when we set off a smoke grenade to summon them." The grin flashed back like a spring-knife. "Red smoke, not gray."

The pair of mercenaries, near enough to overhear, smiled as well but the reference escaped the newcomers who had not been part of the assault.

"Then let's go within," said Antonescu, "and we *won't* have the Molts present until you and I—until we all—" taking his nephew's hand again, the Chief Tribune began to walk along the carefully laid carpet "—have had a chance to discuss this among ourselves."

Radescu raised an eyebrow as he stepped into line beside his uncle, but the facial gesture was a restrained one, even slighter than necessary to avoid cracking his makeup. Antonescu, a master both of restraint and interpretation of minute signals, said, "Only for a moment, Alexi."

"I was afraid for a moment," the general said in a carefully modulated voice as he walked along, "a symptom of my youthful arrogance, I'm afraid—" echoing in nervousness his uncle's words and his own "—that you didn't realize that the agreement stands or falls as a piece—that it can't be modified."

He thought as he spoke that he was being overly blunt with the man who was both his protector and a necessary part of final success, but Tribune Antonescu only replied, "Yes, we were in no doubt of that, my boy. Not from the first."

The six Honor Guards fell in behind the Tribunes in what Radescu found himself thinking of as courtly, not military, precision. The two mercenaries drifted along to either side of the procession. The general risked a glance around to see that while Hawker walked to the left and eyed the head of the valley with its smatterings of autochthons, many of them picked out by iridium highlights, Profile Bourne glowered at the gaily caparisoned troops on review to the right.

Radescu had heard the Slammers discussing whether or not they should wear dress uniforms of their own. He agreed with their final assessment: tailored khakis would only accentuate the scarred functionality of the helmets and body armor they would wear regardless.

"The whole army," Radescu said, hoping to direct his uncle's attention to the troops who had sweated as hard for this display as they had in preparation for the assault, "performed in a way to honor the State."

Surely, as the plane circled to land, the Tribunes had seen the burned-out vehicles littering the course of the assault—particularly near the crest of this ridge, up whose gentle reverse slope the entourage now walked. Radescu's plan had made the attack possible and a success: nothing could have made it easy. The general's eyes prickled with emotion as he thought of these men and their comrades plunging into darkness to meet their terrifyingly agile opponents.

"As written," muttered the Tribune, Deliu, who walked behind Radescu, "this treaty permits the Molts to import anything they want without State control—specifically including weapons. Hard to imagine anyone but the most arrant traitor suggesting that the Molts should be allowed powerguns after the way they used one in Belvedere last month."

"Not the place for that, Mikhail," Antonescu said over his shoulder, the very flatness of his remark more damning than an undertone of anger.

Radescu did not miss a step as he paced along in front of men picked not for their smartness on review but because of the way each had distinguished himself in the assault which made this ceremony possible. His mind, however, clicked into another mode at the paired statements which were neither a question nor an answer—yet were both.

Aloud, drowning the other voices in his mind, the general said, "Quite apart from the question of whether Ferad would have agreed to it, Excellency, the prohibition would have been useless—and the past few days have made me extremely intolerant of pointless behavior."

"I didn't care to discuss such matters here where the Molts may be listening through directional microphones," said Antonescu in a louder voice as he passed Captain Elejash and the platoon which had made the preliminary assault.

"Since I've told the leader of the Molts precisely what I'm going to tell you," Alexander Radescu continued with a cool hauteur which he was too fiercely angry to disguise, "you need not be concerned on that score. Oltenia has no effective means of preventing off-planet merchants from dealing directly with the Molts—even now, in the middle of open warfare. Since they, the theme elders as surely as the young bucks, couldn't feel secure in peace without the sort of equipment renewed fighting would require, then I saw no reason to make them even *more* insecure by pretending to embargo it."

Now at midday the threshold of the autochthons' cave complex was bathed in light, but that only emphasized the wall of darkness just within. The high-vaulted antechamber was ancient enough to be set with sconces for rushlights, though the battery-powered floods now secured in them to wash the ceiling were of an efficiency equal to anything on the planet. There was no need to match the brilliance outdoors, however, so it was only as their eyes adapted that the men took in the rich, vaguely purple ambience which white light stroked from polished granite.

The table in the center of the room was of thin, stamped metal which the cloth drapery did little to disguise. Ferad had offered a lustrous pelt of an autochthonal herbivore, but on reflection it had seemed to both that the feathery scales would prove an impossible surface on which to sign the treaty.

"We couldn't be more pleased with the way you broke the Molts in so short a time, my boy," said Grigor Antonescuas the rock enclosed the party. There were three semicircular doorways spaced about the inner face of the antechamber, barricaded now—not in a misguided attempt to keep the Molts hostage further within the cave system, but simply to prevent Oltenian soldiers from wandering into places where they might cause problems. "But there are some matters of judgment in which you are, in all deference to your abilities, too young to make the decisions."

He spoke, thought Alexander Radescu, as if the sharp exchange in the sunlight had not occurred. Deliu's interference was not to be allowed to affect the calm tenor of the tutorial the Chief Tribune had prepared to give his nephew.

Avoiding the real meat of the opening statement, Radescu replied, "I won a couple skirmishes against an unprepared enemy, Uncle. Scarcely a matter of breaking the Molts, or even the one theme primarily involved."

"There were sizable contingents from all across Oltenia," put in the eldest of the Tribunes, Constantin Wraslov, who even in Radescu's earliest recollection had looked too skeletal to be long for the world. His tone lacked the deliberate venom of Deliu's, but it had the querulousness common to even the most neutral of Wraslov's pronouncements. "We've seen the report on the examination of the corpses after the battle."

Radescu looked at the Tribune, surprised at the dispassion with which his mind pictured the old man as one of the victims being examined by the Intelligence Section: the body pulped by a sheet of rock giving way on top of it . . . flayed by microshrapnel from a dozen nearby bomblets . . . halved by a point-blank, chest-high burst from an armored car's gun. . . ."Yes," the general said with the dynamic calm of a fine blade flexing under the pressure of a thrust, "all the themes had representatives here. That made it possible for Ferad to inflate what was really a minor occurrence into enough of an event to panic the other themes into making peace. Ferad himself knows better—as, of course, do I."

"The infants are their weak point," said Tribune Deliu, adding with a grudging approval, "and you fingered that well enough, boy, I grant you." There was no affection in the look he gave Radescu, however; and when the gilt brim of the general's hat threw a band of light across Deliu's eyes, the Tribune's glare could have been that of a furious boar.

"Yes, you've shown us how to exterminate the autochthons," Wraslov agreed gleefully, rubbing his hands and looking around the big chamber with the enthusiasm of an archeologist who had just penetrated a tomb. "Before, we tried to clear areas so that they couldn't attack us, you know, because it seemed they could always escape."

From where he stood, Radescu could not see the aged Tribune's face. The Honor Guard had aligned itself as a short chord across the portion of the curving wall toward which Wraslov was turned. The worried looks that flashed across the bland expressions of the six red-clad officers were a suggestion of what those men thought they saw in the Tribune's eyes.

"Excellencies, we *can't* . . ." Radescu began, breaking off when he realized that he didn't know where to take the words from there. His body felt so dissociated from his mind that his knees started to tremble and he was not sure that he could continue to stand up.

He was not alone in feeling the tension in the chamber. Chief Tribune Antonescu, for all his outward calm, had an inner heat which might have been no more than a well-bred distaste for the scene which he saw developing.

In fact, the only men in the antechamber who did seem relaxed were the two Slammers, and theirs was the calm of soldiers carrying out a familiar task. Hawker and Bourne had their backs to the stone to one side of the entranceway, too close together for a Molt to attempt to teleport between them but still giving their gunhands adequate clearance. They scanned the room, their face shields transparent but already locked in place in case the lights went out and vision aids were required.

Hawker's hands were still. Profile Bourne rubbed the grip of his submachine gun, not with his fingers but with the palm of his right hand. The orange dragon caressed the plastic in a fashion that gave Radescu a thrill of erotic horror before he snatched his eyes away.

His uncle had not pressed when a sense of the futility of words had choked the young general's first attempt at argument. Antonescu still waited with a placid exterior and a core of disdain for the emotional diatribe which he expected to hear. Wraslov was lost in his contemplation of corpses, past and future; but Tribune Deliu was watching the general with a grin of pleasant anticipation.

He would not, thought Alexander Radescu, embarrass Uncle Grigor and give that stupid *animal* Deliu a moment of triumph. For some reason, that seemed more important than the fact that the plan he'd expected to weld together the races of Oltenia had just disintegrated like a sand castle in the surf. Perhaps it was because he had control over himself; and now, as he tumbled from his pinnacle of arrogant certainty, he realized that he had no control over anything else after all.

"The arguments against exterminating the Molts," Radescu said in the tone of cool disinterest with which he would have enumerated to a friend the failings of an ex-lover, "the negative arguments that is—" He paused and raised an eyebrow in question. "Since I presume the positive argument of Oltenia leading the galaxy through its combination of human and autochthonal talents has already been discounted? Yes?"

"We don't *need* to hear your arguments," rasped Deliu, "since we've already decided on the basis of common sense."

"Thought is a beneficial process for human beings, Excellence," said Radescu in a voice as clear and hard as diamond windchimes. "You should try it yourself on occasion."

One of the Honor Guards ten meters across the chamber gasped, but Chief Tribune Antonescu waved the underling to panicked silence without even bothering to look at the man. "Deliu," said the Chief Tribune, "I promised my nephew a discussion, and that he shall have. His merits to the State alone have earned him that."

Antonescu's careful terminology and the edge in his voice were extraordinarily blunt reminders of the difference in the current government between Tribunes and the Chief Tribune. He nodded toward the general. "Alexi," he prompted.

Which left the real situation exactly where Radescu had feared it was, the dream of Man/Molt partnership dissolved in a welter of blood, but there is a pleasure to small triumphs in the midst of disaster. Was this happening to Ferad among *his* fellows as well . . .

Aloud, Radescu continued, "If we could destroy every nursery chamber, and if every infant Molt were within such a chamber, neither of which statements is true—" he did not bother to emphasize his disclaimer, knowing that rhetorical tricks would lessen at least in his own mind the icy purity of what he was saying "—then it would still be two, more realistically, three decades, before the operation would by itself deplete the ranks of effective Molt warriors. Prepubescents, even adolescents with a range of a few kays per hop, have been met on the battlefield only in cases like this one where we have gone to *them*."

"Yes, yes," said Tribune Wraslov, turning to nod at Radescu. The young general felt as if he stood at the shimmering interface between reality and expectation. On the side that was reality, the skeletal tribune agreed with what Radescu had said and gave his thin equivalent of a smile. But surely his assumption that Wraslov was being sarcastic must be correct? It was obvious that everything Radescu had said was a bitter attack on what the Tribunate seemed to have decided.

"And what conclusions do you draw from your analysis, Alexi?" asked Grigor Antonescu, very much the pleased uncle . . . though he beamed, like a moon, coolly.

"That at best, Uncle, we're talking about another generation of war," Radescu replied, walking toward the chintz-covered table because his legs worked normally again and he needed the opportunity to try them out. The whole conversation had the feel of something he might have overheard twenty years before—two aristocrats talking about a planned marriage of peripheral interest to both their households. It *couldn't* be a discussion which would determine the future of Oltenia for the foreseeable future!

And he, Alexander Radescu, wasn't really taking part in it. He could not have shut down his emotions so thoroughly and be proceeding dispassionately in his mind to end game, not if it were Alexi and Uncle Grigor talking here in a Molt cavern. . . .

"Another generation of ballrooms filled with bodies," Radescu continued as his index finger traced the chintz into hills and valleys like those outside, baptized already in blood.

"We've destroyed those urns, of course," snapped Tribune Deliu to the general's back.

"Buildings collapsing because the foundations were on bedrock and a Molt flitted in to set a bomb there," Radescu said calmly to the table. "There've been a few of those already and there'll be more."

His copy of the treaty document, hand-lettered on parchment, crinkled in his breast pocket when he straightened. Ferad would bring the other copy himself, on archival-quality paper imported from Earth—and how long would the Molt leader wait for the red smoke before he realized that there would be no peace after all, not in his lifetime or the lifetime of anyone now on the planet . . .

"Yes, but we'll be killing many of them, very many," said Tribune Wraslov, whose eyes had a glazed appearance that removed him as far from the present as Radescu felt he himself had been removed. The two of them were only reflections, their lips moving without stirring anything around them. Only Chief Tribune Antonescu was real. . . .

"A generation of men walking the streets of Belvedere, of every city and village on Oltenia," the general continued because he could not stop without having made every possible effort to prevent what would otherwise occur, "who have been trained to shoot infants—"

"Shoot Molts," Deliu interrupted.

"Shoot *infants* as harmless and helpless as anything human they're going to find when they go home on leave," Radescu said, feeling his voice tremble as his control began to break. Something terrible would happen if he ever lost control. "*That's* what we'll have if the war goes on!"

"We will have a Tribunate with complete control of the State," said Chief Tribune Antonescu in a voice that penetrated the ears of every listener like a sword blade being slammed home in its sheath. "That's what we'll continue to have for so long as the war goes on."

The six men of the Honor Guard were tense ciphers at the curving wall, nervously watching State policy being made in a scene like an argument over cards. But men were men when personal emotions ran high, thought Alexander Radescu, and nothing could have been more personal than what he had just been told.

How naive of him to assume that Uncle Grigor would divorce personal benefit from matters of State. A political appointee like General Radescu should have known better.

The Chief Tribune walked over to his nephew and put a hand on his shoulder. He no longer towered over little Alexi; they were eye to eye with any difference in height to the younger man. . . . "Do you understand what I'm telling you, my boy?" he asked with the real warmth which almost none of his closest associates had heard in Antonescu's voice. "Surely you understand?"

"I understand that it's wrong," said the general. Loudly, almost shouting as he pulled away from the Chief Tribune, he added, "I understand that it's *evil*, Uncle Grigor!"

"Then understand *this*," roared Antonescu, who had not raised his voice when informed of his son's suicide thirty years before. "You have the authority we choose to give you. To carry out decisions of the Tribunate—and no more!"

"Yes, yes," murmured Wraslov, and Deliu blinked avid, swine-bright eyes beside him.

"You will summon the Molt leader, as planned," the Chief Tribune said in frigid certainty. "We will stand to the side, so that the Molts can be killed as they appear. These mercenaries are capable of that, I presume?"

"Oh yes," General Radescu said with a nonchalance born of a question with an easy answer in the midst of so much that had no answer at all that he cared to accept. It was only after he spoke that he even bothered to look at Bourne and Hawker, gray figures who could so easily be dismissed as age-tattered statues . . . until the sergeant gave Radescu a wink almost veiled beneath the highlights on his face shield.

"I think we'd best leave it to the professionals, then," the Chief Tribune said, dismissing with a nod the motions the hands of the Honor Guard were making toward their gleaming, black-finished pistol holsters.

"Yes, of course," the general agreed, as his mind superimposed every image of Ferad that it held in memory—and one image more, the wizened Molt staggering backward with his chest shot away and the treaty ablaze in his hand.

Antonescu was walking toward the great archway with his nephew, though of course he could not leave the antechamber without warning the Molts of what was prepared. The other Tribunes were drifting for safety toward the young officers of the Honor Guard, out of the line of fire through autochthons appearing beside the flimsy table. "The trouble with you, my boy," said the Chief Tribune, laying his hand again on his nephew's shoulder, "is that you're very clever, but you're young—and you don't understand the use of power."

"Sir?" said General Forsch, waiting just outside in the sunshine. Beside him was Captain Elejash, looking uncomfortable in his scarlet uniform and holding the smoke grenade in big, capable hands.

Radescu shook his head sharply, then turned to look at his uncle and the plea in the older man's eyes that his protégé accept reality without an unpleasant scene.

"Don't I understand power, Uncle Grigor?" the general said, raising his right hand to his brow. "Well, perhaps you're right." The only thing his eyes could see as he looked back into the antechamber was the gape of the dragon that Bourne's palm stroked across the grip of his weapon.

Alexander Radescu tossed his cap toward the table in a scintillating arc.

The Honor Guard was crumpling before the cyan flashes which killed them were more than a stroboscopic effect to the men in the chamber. One Guard managed to open his holster flap, but his chest was lit by smoky flames which seemed to spring from the scarlet dye rather than the black craters the powergun had punched in the uniform.

Radescu could forget that afterward, could forget the way Deliu's bladder and bowels stained his white robes as the bolts hit him and the look of ecstasy on Wraslov's face as his eyeballs reflected the blue-green glare from the muzzle of Hawker's submachine gun.

What he would never forget, however, was the wetness on his face, his fingertips coming down from his cheek red with the splattered blood of his Uncle Grigor.

When the weapons detector chimed, the man behind the console shouted, "The little one's holding!" and three shotguns pointed instinctively at Hawker and Bourne in the anteroom of the Chief Executive's residence.

"Hey, it's Profile," said one of the quartet of guards, lifting the muzzle of his weapon in embarrassment. Down the hall, the bell responder in the guard commander's office shut off when that worthy bolted toward the anteroom.

"What's this cop?" Bourne snapped in outrage, not so angry, however, as to take a blustering step toward the leveled shotguns. "We off loaded our bloody hardware 'fore we came over!"

"Don't care if he's the Lord himself come to take me to heaven," rejoined a guard with his gun still centered. He was dressed in issue battledress, but the yellow bandana worn as a head covering and the paired pistols in cross-draw holsters gave him a piratical air. "If he's packin' he stays where he is."

"Excuse me, Sergeant Bourne," said the guard at the detector console as the guard commander—Elejash, now Colonel Elejash—burst into the anteroom with yet another shotgun, "but if you'd check your left forearm, the underside . . . ?"

"That's all right, Culcer," said Elejash, lifting his own weapon and stepping across the line of fire from his men to their targets. "You did right, but we're to admit this pair as is."

"Via," said Profile Bourne, blushing for the first time in his partner's memory.

He twitched his left hand, and the spring clip on his wrist flipped the knife into his waiting grip. "Lord and martyrs, man, you're right," the sergeant said to the shimmering blade in a voice of wonder. "I forgot it."

Enzo Hawker laughed, both in amusement and from a need to release the rigid lock into which he had set his muscles at the unexpected challenge. The Oltenian guards, all of them men he and Bourne had helped train, joined with various levels of heartiness.

"That's all right, Sergeant," Elejash said as Bourne strode over to the console and offered his knife pommel-first to the guard seated there.

"Like hell it is," Bourne muttered, laying the little weapon on the console when the guard refused to take it. "I couldn't even bitch if they'd blown me away, could I?"

Elejash looked at Hawker and the big mercenary, shrugging, said, "Well, we weren't expecting any special treatment, but I think I'd have been disappointed in you fellows if you'd shot us now, yeah."

"Briefly disappointed," said the guard at the console.

"Well," muttered Profile Bourne, starting to regain his composure—mistakes about weapons weren't the sort of thing the sergeant accepted in anyone, least of all himself, "it wouldn't be the first time I'd missed Embarkation Muster—but usually I was drunk'r in jail."

"You can go on in," said the guard commander. "The Chief Executive told me to expect you."

"Or both," Bourne added to the nearer pair of guards. All the Oltenians wore personal touches on their uniforms, and the fatigues of the man at the console were patterned with a loose gray mesh in which he could have passed at a distance for a Molt warrior.

"Hey, how in blazes did he know that?" Bourne asked Colonel Elejash. "We didn't—you know, want to intrude when things were still settling out. This was pretty much spur a' the moment, with us gonna lift ship in a couple hours."

The guard commander shrugged, a gesture similar enough to

that of the mercenary lieutenant earlier to be an unconscious copy. Others of the Slammers had helped to train the new Executive Guard, but Hawker and Bourne had had a particular impact because of their earlier association. "Why don't you ask him?" the Oltenian said, making a gesture that began as a wave toward the inner door and ended by opening it.

"The Slammers are here, sir," Elejash called through the doorway.

"Two of us, anyhow," said Bourne as he squared his shoulders and, swaggering to cover his nervousness—it wasn't the sort of thing he was used to, but the Loot was right to say they *had* to do it—he led the way into the circular Reception Chamber.

Across from the door, against the wall behind the desk and Chief Executive Radescu rising from his seat, was an urn of large blue and indigo crystals in a white matrix.

"Enzo, Profile," Radescu said, holding out his hands to either man. He was wearing trousers and a loose tunic, both of civilian cut and only in their color—pearl gray, with gold piping on the pants legs—suggestive of anything else. "I'd—well, I didn't want to order you in here, but I was really hoping to see you again before lift-off."

"Well, you were busy," the lieutenant said uncomfortably as he shook the hand offered him, "and we, we had training duties ourselves." Funny; they'd *made* him what he was, but Radescu was fully a planetary ruler now in Hawker's mind . . . while he and Profile were better'n fair soldiers in the best outfit in the galaxy.

"What do you think of them?" Radescu asked brightly, drawing the mercenaries to the trio of chairs beside his desk—prepared for them, apparently, for the Oltenian leader seated himself in the middle one and guided the others to either side. "What do you think of them, then? The new Guards?"

"They'll do," said Profile Bourne, wriggling his back against a chair he found uncomfortable because it was more deeply upholstered than he was used to.

"We told a couple of them," Hawker amplified, "that the Slammers were always hiring if they felt like getting off-planet."

"Via, though, they still don't *look* like soldiers," the sergeant said, miming with his left hand the bandana of the guard with the evident willingness to have blown him away.

"Conversely," said Alexander Radescu, "you know that there's a job here for you if you decide to stay. I'll clear it with Colonel Ham—"

"Sure, Profile," interrupted the big lieutenant, "and when's the last time you wore a fatigue shirt with a right sleeve on it? *Talk* to me about issue uniforms!"

Sometimes the best way to give a negative answer to a question, an offer, was to talk about something else instead. Well, Radescu thought, he could appreciate the courtesy, though he would much have preferred the other response.

To the Slammers, the Chief Executive said, "There's been a tradition here on Oltenia that officers could modify their outfits according to personal taste—when they weren't on field service, that is. I decided that the same standards should apply to the Exec—to my personal guard. A—" he spread and closed his fingers as his mind sorted words and found some that were close enough "—mark of the honor in which I hold them."

He laughed aloud, knowing as he heard the sound that there was very little humor in it. "After all," he said, "they keep me alive."

Sergeant Bourne had been eyeing the room, spacious and looking the more so for its almost complete lack of furnishings: the trio of chairs which seemed out of place; the large desk with an integral seat; and the blue john urn toward which Profile now nodded and asked, "That there what I think it is?"

"Yes, the surviving one of the pair," agreed the Chief Executive, following the sergeant's eyes. Neither mercenary had ever been in this building when it was the Tribunal Palace, but that story would have gotten around. "I'd been told it was destroyed also, but it appears that my uncle had instead removed it to storage in a warehouse. It permits Ferad to visit me at need." He smiled. "Or at whim. We've gotten to be friends, in a way, in the month since the shooting stopped."

Radescu got up and stepped toward the circular wall, his arm describing a 90° arc of the plain surface. "That's going to be covered with a twenty-centimeter sheet of black granite," the leader—the dictator—of Oltenia said. "It's been quarried by machinery, but the polish is being put to it by Molts—by hand. From every theme, and all of them who want to help. Ferad tells me that mothers are bringing infants as small—"

He coughed, clearing away the constriction of memory from his throat "—as small as the one I took out of the nursery chamber myself. They're putting the little ones' hands on the stone and sliding them along it, so that in the future, they'll be able to find this room as they can anything on the planet."

Sergeant Bourne guffawed, but anything he might have intended to say was swallowed when Radescu continued bitterly, "That means, I suppose, that my human enemies will find a way to hire a Molt warrior to assassinate me. No doubt my spirit will lie more easily for having helped achieve that degree of cooperation between the two intelligent races on the planet."

"Problems, General?" Bourne asked, levering himself out of the chair with an expression which did not seem so much changed from what he had worn a moment before but rather was a refinement of it. As when a fresh casting is struck to remove the sand clinging to its surface, thus the lines of the sergeant's face sprang into full relief when the thought of action rang in the little man's mind.

"I meant it about the job," replied the young Oltenian evenly, meeting the mercenary's eyes.

"We've been moving around a lot," said Hawker, with the same calm and the same underlying determination as had been in Radescu's voice when he repeated the offer. "Being with the Regiment, it more or less keeps an edge on without it getting—you know, outa control."

Profile Bourne looked quizzically at his lieutenant, not at all unwilling himself, at this point, to have heard more about what Radescu wanted—and needed. Hawker, knowing that and determined to forestall the discussion, went on, "If we left Hammer and tried to settle down here, either we'd dump it all, all we'd been—doing, you know, you aren't talking about a couple detection specialists now, are you?"

He took a deep breath, raising his hand to hold the floor for the moment he had to pause before continuing, "We'd lose it, or we'd—" his eyes flicked toward Sergeant Bourne in a gesture so minute that Radescu could not be certain that it had been intentional "—go the other way, turn into something you couldn't have around anyplace you'd—be wearing civilian clothes, put it that way."

Alexander Radescu nodded brusquely and turned again to face the wall that would be replaced by a surface of polished granite. He did not speak.

To his back, Lieutenant Hawker said in a tone that reminded Bourne of the way the Loot had stroked the little Molt, "You're having trouble with the Chief Tribune's relatives, then? Sort of thought you might. . . ."

"Them?" said Alexander Radescu with sardonic brightness as he turned again to the Slammers. "Oh, no, not at all. For one thing, they're my relatives, too, you know. They think they're sitting well—which they are, since they're the only pool of people I can trust, besides the army. And anyway, nobody on either side of the family was close enough to Uncle Grigor to think of, of avenging him.

"Nobody but me."

Radescu began to pace, his left hand swinging to touch the wall at intervals as he circled it. Bourne rotated to watch him, but Lieutenant Hawker remained seated, his eyes apparently on the backs of his hands. "Things are settling in quite well, people forgetting the war—and the Molts putting it behind them as well, from what Ferad says and the other reports, the *lack* of incidents."

"There's been shooting," Sergeant Bourne interjected.

He talked to Oltenians, now, to members of the Guard and to the soldiers *they* talked to. It gave him more awareness of the planet on which he served than he could ever before remember having. Planets, to one of Hammer's Slammers, were generally a circumscribed round of fellows, "recreation establishments," and gun fight pictures. For the past month, Profile Bourne had found fellows among the local forces.

"There's always *been* incidents," Radescu snapped. His cheeks were puffier than they had been in the field, thought Lieutenant Hawker as he glanced sidelong. . . . "There's going to be shootings in mining camp bars and ranch dormitories as long as there's men, much less men and Molts. But it's no worse than, oh, ten years ago— I can get the exact figures. Having the Slammers around for an additional month to settle what *anybody* started, that was useful; but basically, three years of war haven't undone three centuries of peace, or as close to peace as Nature seems ready to allow anyone."

"Well," said Bourne, still standing, figuring that they'd done what, Via, courtesy demanded in making the call. He didn't look real great, the general didn't, but at least he wasn't a tarted-up clown the way he had been that first day, through the bars of the holding cell. . . . "Glad things are workin' out, and you know that if you need the Slammers again—"

"It's the Tzigara family," said Radescu, speaking through the sergeant's leave-taking as if oblivious to it. "Isn't that amusing?"

Lieutenant Hawker met the Chief Executive's painted smile with calm eyes and no expression of his own, waiting to hear what would be dragged out by the fact that when he and Bourne upped ship there would be no one for Radescu to speak to. That was what they had come for, though Profile didn't know it. That, and the one thing Hawker needed to say to pay their debt to the man who, after all, had saved their lives. . . .

"You never met Nikki, did you?" Radescu continued in a bantering tone. "He was my aide, k-killed at the, in the ballroom . . . that night."

He cleared his throat, forced unwillingly to pause, but neither of the Slammers showed any sign of wanting to break in on the monologue. "He had a cousin, and I don't think I even knew that, in the, you know, in the Honor Guard. And it couldn't have made any difference, I don't mean *that*, but the family blames me now for both deaths."

"He was one a' the ones we blew away in the cave, you mean?" the sergeant asked, not particularly concerned but hoping that if the question were clarified he would be able to understand what in blazes the general was driving at.

"You did what I ordered you to do, what *had* to be done!" Alexander Radescu replied in a tone more fitting for condemnation than approval. But it was the world which he wanted to condemn, not the pair of mercenaries . . . and not even himself, though that was increasingly easy to do, when he lay awake at three in the morning. "There's been one attempt to kill me already, poison, and I've had word of others planned. . . ."

Radescu tented his fingers in front of him and seemed to carry out a brief series of isometrics, pressing the hands together and letting them spring back. "Sometimes I think that I won't be safe so long as there's a single one of the Tzigaras alive," he said. Then, with his eyes still determinedly focused on his fingertips, he added, "I'd be—very pleased if you gentlemen changed your minds, you know."

Lieutenant Hawker rose from the chair without using his arms to lift him, despite the depth and give of the upholstery. The lack of body armor made him feel lighter; and, though most of his waking hours were spent as he was now, without the heavy porcelain clamshell latched to him, being around Radescu made the Slammers lieutenant feel that he *ought* to be in armor. Habituated response, he supposed.

"I think we'd best be getting back to the Regiment, sir," said Enzo Hawker, stretching out his hand to shake Radescu's.

"Of course," agreed the Chief Executive, clasping the mercenary's firmly. "Colonel Hammer performed to the perfect satisfaction of his contract. What you two did was more."

"Don't worry 'bout missing us, general," said Profile as he took the hand offered him in turn. "You got boys out there—" he nodded to the anteroom "—can handle anything we would."

He laughed, pleasantly in intention, though the harshness of the sound made Radescu think of the fluorescent dragon on the palm wringing his. "Dudn't take a world a' smarts, dudn't even take a lotta training. Just to be willing, that's all." He laughed again and stepped toward the door.

Hawker touched the sergeant on the shoulder, halting and turning him. "Sir," the big lieutenant said as his subordinate watched and waited with a frown of confusion, "you're where you are now because you were willing to do what had to be done. Everybody else wanted an easy way out. Wanted to kill Molts instead of ending a war."

"Where I am now," Alexander Radescu repeated, quirking his lips into a smile of sorts.

"If you didn't have the balls to handle a tough job," said Hawker sharply, "you'd have seen the last of me 'n the sarge a long while back, mister."

Hawker and Radescu locked eyes while Bourne looked from one man to the other, puzzled but not worried; there was nothing here to worry about.

"I appreciate the vote of confidence," said the Oltenian as he broke into a grin and reached out to shake the lieutenant's hand again.

"Oh, there's one thing more," Hawker added in a gentle voice as he willingly accepted the handclasp. "Profile, I'll bet the Chief Executive thinks we were firing long bursts there when we cleared the cave."

"What?" said Radescu in amazement, pausing with the mercenary's hand still in his.

"Oh, Via, no," Profile Bourne blurted, *his* surprise directed at the suggestion rather than the fact that the Loot had voiced it. "Blood 'n martyrs, General, single shots only. Lord, the polish that stone had, the ricochets'd fry us all like pork rinds if we'd just tried to hose things down." He stared at Radescu in the hopeful horror of a specialist who prays that he's been able to prevent a friend from doing something lethally dangerous through ignorance.

"That's right sir," said Enzo Hawker as he met the Chief Executive's wondering eyes. "You have to know exactly what you're doing before you decide to use guns."

Radescu nodded very slowly as the two guns for hire walked out of his office.

M2A4, HATCH OPEN, HULL DOWN

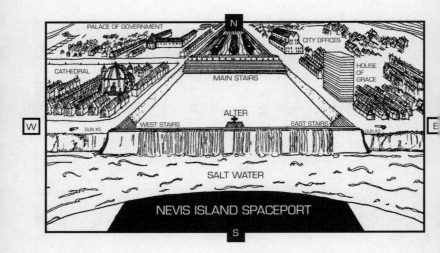

COUNTING THE COST

To Sergeant Ronnie Hembree
Who did good work.

CHAPTER ONE

They'd told Tyl Koopman that Bamberg City's starport was on an island across the channel from the city proper, so he hadn't expected much of a skyline when the freighter's hatches opened. Neither had he expected a curtain of steam boiling up so furiously that the sun was only a bright patch in mid-sky. Tyl stepped back with a yelp. The crewman at the controls of the giant cargo doors laughed and said, "Well, you were in such a *hurry*, soldier."

The Slammers issue-pack Tyl carried was all the luggage he'd brought from six months' furlough on Miesel. Strapped to the bottom of the pack was a case of homemade jalapeño jelly that his aunt was sure—correctly—was better than any he could get elsewhere in the galaxy.

But altogether, the weight of Tyl's gear was much less than he was used to carrying in weapons, rations, and armor when he led a company of Alois Hammer's infantry. He turned easily and looked at the crewman with mild sadness—the visage of a dog that's been unexpectedly kicked . . . and maybe just enough else beneath the sadness to be disquieting.

The crewman looked down at his controls, then again to the

151

mercenary waiting to disembark. The squealing stopped when the triple hatches locked open. "Ah," called the crewman, "it'll clear up in a minute er two. It's always like this on Bamberg the first couple ships down after a high tide. The port floods, y'see, and it always looks like half the bloody ocean's waiting in the hollows t' burn off."

The steam—the hot mist; it'd never been dangerous, Tyl realized now—was thinning quickly. From the hatchway he could see the concrete pad and, in the near distance, the bulk of the freighter that must have landed just before theirs. The flecks beyond the concrete were the inevitable froth speckling moving water, the channel or the ocean itself—and the water looked cursed close to somebody who'd just spent six months on a place as dry as Miesel.

"Where do they put the warehouses?" Tyl asked. "Don't they flood?"

"Every three months or so they would," the crewman agreed. "That's why they're on the mainland, in Bamberg City, where there's ten meters of cliff and seawall t' keep 'em dry. But out here's flat, and I guess they figured they'd sooner the landing point be on the island in case somebody, you know, landed a mite hard."

The crewman grinned tightly. Tyl grinned back. They were both professionals in fields that involved risks. People who couldn't joke about the risks of the jobs they'd chosen tended to find other lines of work in a hurry.

The ones who survived.

"Well, I guess it's clear," Tyl said with enough question in his tone to expect a warning if he were wrong. "There'll be ground transport coming?"

"Yeah, hovercraft from Bamberg real soon," the crewman agreed. "But look, there's a shelter on the other side a' that bucket there. You might want to get over to it right quick. There's some others in orbit after us, and it can be pretty interesting t' be out on the field when it's this wet and there's more ships landing."

Tyl nodded to the man and strode down the ramp that had been the lower third of the hatch door. He was nervous, but it'd all be fine soon. He'd be back with his unit and not alone, the way he'd been on the ship—

And for the whole six months he'd spent with his family and a planet full of civilians who understood his words but not his language.

The mainland shore, a kilometer across Nevis Channel, was a corniche. The harsh cliffs were notched by the mouth of the wide river which was responsible for Bamberg City's location and the fact it was the only real city on the planet. Tyl hadn't gotten the normal briefing because the regiment shifted employers while he was on furlough, but the civilian sources available on Miesel when he got his movement orders were about all he needed anyway.

Captain Tyl Koopman wasn't coming to the planet Bamberia; he was returning to Hammer's Slammers. After five years in the regiment and six months back with his family, he had to agree with the veterans who'd warned him before he went on furlough that he wasn't going home.

He had left home, because the Slammers were the only home he'd got.

The shelter was a low archway, translucent green from the outside and so unobtrusive that Tyl might have overlooked it if there had been any other structure on the island. He circled to one end, apprehensive of the rumbling he heard in the sky—and more than a little nervous about the pair of star freighters already grounded in the port.

The ships were quiescent. They steamed and gave off pings of differential cooling, but for the next few days they weren't going to move any more than would buildings of the same size. Nevertheless, learned reflex told Tyl that big metal objects were tanks . . . and no infantryman lived very long around tanks without developing a healthy respect for them.

The door opened automatically as Tyl reached for it, wondering where the latch was. Dim shadows swirled inside the shelter, behind a second panel that rotated aside only when the outside door had closed again.

There were a dozen figures spaced within a shelter that had room for hundreds. All those waiting were human; all were male; and all but one were in civilian garb.

Tyl walked toward the man in uniform—almost toward him, while almost meeting the other man's eyes so that he could stop and find a clear spot at the long window if the fellow glared or turned his head as the Slammers officer approached.

No problem, though. The fellow's quirking grin suggested that he was as glad of the company as Tyl was.

It was real easy to embarrass yourself when you didn't know the rules—and when nobody wore the rank tabs that helped you figure out what those rules might be.

From within the shelter, the windows had an extreme clarity that proved they were nothing as simple as glass or thermoplastic. The shelter was unfurnished, without even benches, but its construction proved that Bamberia was a wealthy, high-technology world.

There was a chance for real profit on this one. Colonel Hammer must have been delighted.

"Hammer's Regiment?" the waiting soldier asked, spreading his grin into a look of welcome.

"Captain Tyl Koopman," Tyl agreed, shaking the other man's hand. "I'd just gotten E Company when I went on furlough. But I don't know what may've happened since, you know, since we've shifted contracts."

He'd just blurted the thing that'd been bothering him ever since Command Central had sent the new location for him to report off furlough. He'd sweated blood to get that company command— sweated blood and spilled it . . . and the revised transit orders made him fear that he'd have to earn it all over again because he'd been gone on furlough when the colonel needed somebody in the slot.

Tyl hadn't bothered to discuss it with the folks who'd been his friends and relatives when he was a civilian; they already looked at him funny from the time one of them asked about the scrimshaw he'd given her and he was drunk enough to tell the real story of the house-to-house on Cachalot. But this guy would understand, even though Tyl didn't know him and didn't even recognize the uniform.

"Charles Desoix," the man said, "United Defense Batteries." He flicked a collar tab with his finger. "Lieutenant and XO of Battery D, if you don't care what you say. It amounts to gopher, mainly. I just broke our Number Five gun out of Customs on Merrinet."

"Right, air defense," Tyl said with the enthusiasm of being able to place the man in a structured universe. "Calliopes?"

"Yeah," agreed Desoix with another broad grin, "and the inspectors seemed to think somebody in the crew had stuffed all eight barrels with drugs they were going to sell at our transfer stop on Merrinet. Might just've been right, too—but we needed the gun here more than they needed the evidence."

The ship that had been a rumble in the sky when Tyl ducked into the shelter was now within ten meters of the pad. The shelter's windows did an amazing job of damping vibration, but the concrete itself resonated like a drum to the freighter's engine note. The two soldiers fell silent. Tyl shifted his pack and studied Desoix.

The UDB uniform was black with silver piping that muted to non-reflective gray in service conditions. It was a little fancier than the Slammers' khaki—but Desoix's unit wasn't parade-ground pansies.

The Slammers provided their own defense against hostile artillery. Most outfits didn't have the luxury that Fire Central and the vehicle-mounted powerguns gave Hammer. Specialists like United Defense Batteries provided multi-barreled weapons— calliopes—to sweep the sky clear over defended positions and to accompany attacking columns which would otherwise be wrecked by shellfire.

It wasn't a job Tyl Koopman could imagine himself being comfortable doing; but Via! he didn't see himself leading a tank company either. A one-man skimmer and a 2cm powergun were about all the hardware Tyl wanted to handle. Anything bigger cost him too much thought that would have been better spent on the human portion of his command.

"Your first time here?" Desoix asked diffidently. The third freighter was down. Though steam hissed away from the vessel with a high-pitched roar, it was possible to talk again.

Tyl nodded. Either the tide was falling rapidly or the first two ships had pretty well dried the pad for later comers. The billows of white mist were sparse enough that he could still see the city across the channel: or at any rate, he could see a twenty-story tower of metal highlights and transparent walls on one side of the river, and a domed structure across from it that gleamed gold—except for the ornate cross on the pinnacle whose core was living ruby.

"Not a bad place," Desoix said judiciously. He looked a few years older than the Slammers officer, but perhaps it was just that, looks, dark hair and thin features contrasting with Tyl's broad pale face and hair so blond that you could hardly see it when it was cropped as short as it was now.

"The city, I mean," Desoix said, modifying his earlier comment. "The sticks over on Continent Two where it looks like the fighting's going to be, well—they're the sticks."

He met Tyl's eyes. "I won't apologize for getting a quiet billet this time 'round."

"No need to," Tyl said . . . and they were both lying, because nobody who knows the difference brags to a combat soldier about a cushy assignment; and no combat soldier but wishes, somewhere in his heart of hearts, that he'd gotten the absolutely necessary assignment of protecting the capital while somebody else led troops into sniper-filled woodlands and endured the fluorescent drumbeat of hostile artillery.

But Via! *Somebody* had to do the job.

Both of them.

"Hey, maybe the next time," Tyl said with a false smile and a playful tap on the shoulder of the man who wasn't a stranger anymore.

Several boats—hovercraft too small to haul more than a dozen men and their luggage—were putting out from Bamberg City, spraying their way toward the island with an enthusiasm that suggested they were racing.

Tyl's view of them was unexpectedly cut off when a huge surface-effect freighter slid in front of the shelter and settled. The freighter looked like a normal subsonic aircraft, but its airfoils were canted to double their lift by skimming over water or smooth ground. The bird couldn't really fly, but it could carry a thousand tonnes of cargo at 200 kph—a useful trade-off between true ships and true aircraft.

"Traders from Two," Desoix explained as men began scuttling from the freighter before its hydraulic outriggers had time to lock it firmly onto the pad. "They circle at a safe distance from the island while the starships are landing. Then, if they're lucky, they beat the Bamberg factors to the pad with the first shot at a deal."

He shrugged. "And if their luck's *really* out, there's another starship on its way in about the time they tie up. Doesn't take much of a shock wave to make things real interesting aboard one of those."

Tyl squinted at the men scuttling from the surface-effect vehicle. Several of those waiting in the shelter were joining them, babbling and waving documents. "Say, those guys're—"

"Yeah, rag-heads," Desoix agreed. "I mean, I'm sure they're in church every day, kissing crosses and all the proper things, but . . . yeah, they're looking at some problems if President Delcorio gets his crusade going."

"Well, that's what we're here for," Tyl said, looking around horizons that were hemmed by starships to the back and side and the surface-effect vehicle before him.

"Now," he added, controlling his grimace, "how do we get to the mainland if we're not cargo?"

"Ah, but we are," Desoix noted as he raised the briefcase that seemed to be all the luggage he carried. "Just not very valuable cargo, my friend. But I think it's about time to—"

As he started toward the door, one of the hovercars they'd watched put out from the city drove through the mingled cluster of men from the starships and the surface freighter. Water from the channel surrounded the car in a fine mist that cleared its path better than the threat of its rubber skirts. While the driver in his open cab exchanged curses with men from the surface freighter, the rear of his vehicle opened to disgorge half a dozen civilians in bright garments.

"Our transportation," Desoix said, nodding to the hovercar as he headed out of the shelter. "Now that it's dropped off the Bamberg factors to fight for their piece of the market. Everybody's got tobacco, and everybody wants a share of what may be the last cargoes onto the planet for a while."

"Before the shooting starts," Tyl amplified as he strode along with the UDB officer. They hadn't sent a briefing cube to Miesel for him . . . but it didn't take that or a genius to figure out what was going to happen shortly after a world started hiring mercenary regiments.

"That's the betting," Desoix agreed. He opened the back of the car with his universal credit key, a computer chip encased in noble metal and banded to his wrist.

"Oh," said Tyl, staring at the keyed door.

"Yeah, everything's up to date here in Bamberg," said the other officer, stepping out of the doorway and waving Tyl through. "Hey!" he called to the driver. "My friend here's on me!"

"I can—" Tyl said.

"—delay us another ten minutes," Desoix broke in, "trying to charge this one to the Hammer account or pass the driver scrip from Lord knows where."

He keyed the door a second time and swung into the car, both men moving with the trained grace of soldiers who knew how to get on and off air-cushion vehicles smoothly—because getting hung up was a good way to catch a round.

"Goes to the UDB account anyway," Desoix added. "Via, maybe we'll need a favor from you one of these days."

"I'm just not set up for this place, coming off furlough," Tyl explained. "It's not like, you know, Colonel Hammer isn't on top of things."

The driver fluffed his fans and the car began to cruise in cautious arcs around the starships, looking for other passengers. All the men they saw were busy with merchants or with the vessels themselves, preparing the rails and gantries that would load the vacuum-sealed one-tonne bales of Bamberg tobacco when the factors had struck their deals.

No one looked at the car with more than idle interest. The driver spun his vehicle back into the channel with a lurch and building acceleration.

CHAPTER TWO

"One thing," Desoix said, looking out the window even though the initial spray cloaked the view. "Money's no problem here. Any banking booth can access Hammer's account and probably your account back home if it's got a respondent on one of the big worlds. Perfectly up to date. But, ah, don't talk to anybody here about religion, all right?"

He met Tyl's calm eyes. "No matter how well you know them, you don't know them that well. Here. And don't go out except wearing your uniform. They don't bother soldiers, especially mercs; but somebody might make a mistake if you were in civilian clothes."

Their vehicle was headed for the notch in the sea cliffs. It was a river mouth as Tyl had assumed from the spaceport, but human engineering had overwhelmed everything natural about the site. The river was covered and framed into a triangular plaza by concrete seawalls as high as those reinforcing the corniche.

Salt water from the tide-choked sea even now gleamed on the plaza, just as it was streaming from the spaceport. Figures—women as well as men, Tyl thought, though it was hard to be sure between the spray and the loose costumes they wore—were pouring into the plaza as fast as the water had left it.

For the most part the walls were sheer and ten meters high, but there were broad stairs at each apex of the plaza—two along the seaside east and west and a third, defended by massive flood works, that must have been built over the channel of the river itself.

"What's the problem?" Tyl asked calmly. From what he'd read, the battle lines on Bamberia were pretty clearly drawn. The planetary government was centered on Continent One—wealthy and very centralized, because the Pink River drained most of the arable land on the continent. All the uniquely flavorful Bamberg tobacco could be barged at minimal cost to Bamberg City and loaded in bulk onto starships.

There hadn't been much official interest in Continent Two for over a century after the main settlement. There was good land on Two, but it was patchy and not nearly as easy to develop profitably as One proved.

That didn't deter other groups who saw a chance that looked good by their standards. Small starships touched down in little market centers. Everything was on a lesser scale: prices, quantities, and profit margins. . . .

But in time, the estimated total grew large enough for the central government to get interested. Official trading ports were set up on the coast of Two. Local tobacco was to be sent from them to Bamberg City, to be assessed and transshipped.

Some was; but the interloping traders continued to land in the back country, and central government officials gnashed their teeth over tax revenues that were all the larger for being illusory.

It didn't help that One had been settled by Catholic Fundamentalists from Germany and Latin America, and that the squatters on Two were almost entirely Levantine Muslims.

The traders didn't care. They had done their business in holographic entertainment centers and solar-powered freezers, but there was just as much profit in powerguns and grenades.

As for mercenaries like Alois Hammer—and Tyl Koopman . . . They couldn't be said not to care; because if there wasn't trouble, they didn't have work.

Not that Tyl figured there was much risk of galactic peace being declared.

Desoix laughed without even attempting to make the sound humorous. "Well," he said, "do you know when Easter is?"

"Huh?" said Tyl. "My family wasn't, you know, real religious . . . and anyway, do you mean on Earth or here or where?"

"That's the question, isn't it?" Desoix answered, glancing around the empty cabin just to be *sure* there couldn't be a local listening to him.

"Some folks here," he continued, "figure Easter according to Earth-standard days. You can tell them because they've always got something red in their clothing, a cap or a ribbon around their sleeve if nothing else. And the folks that say, 'We're on Bamberia so

God meant us to use Bamberg days to figure his calendar . . . well, they wear black."

"And the people who wear cloaks, black or red," Desoix concluded. "Make sure they know you're a soldier. Because they'd just as soon knock your head in as that of any policeman or citizen—but they won't, because they know that killing soldiers gets expensive fast."

Tyl shook his head. "I'd say I didn't believe it," he said with the comfortable superiority of somebody commenting on foolishness to which he doesn't subscribe. "But sure, it's no screwier than a lot of places. People don't need a reason to have problems, they make their own."

"And they hire us," agreed Desoix.

"Well, they hire us to give 'em more control over the markets on Two," Tyl said, not quite arguing. "This time around."

Their vehicle was approaching the plaza. It stood two meters above the channel, barely eye-height to the men in the back of the hovercar. A pontoon-mounted landing stage slid with the tides in a vertical slot in the center of the dam blocking the river beneath the plaza; the car slowed as they approached the stage.

"If they dam the river—" Tyl started to say, because he wouldn't have commanded a company of the Slammers had he not assessed the terrain about him as a matter of course.

Before Desoix could answer, slotted spillways opened at either end of the dam and whipped the channel into froth with gouts of fresh water under enough pressure to fling it twenty meters from the concrete. The hovercar, settling as it made its final approach to the stage, bobbed in the ripples; the driver must have been cursing the operator who started to drain the impoundment now instead of a minute later.

"Hydraulics they know about," Desoix commented as their vehicle grounded on the stage with a blip of its fans and the pontoons rocked beneath them. "They can't move the city—it's here because of the river, floods or no. But for twenty kilometers upstream, they've built concrete levees. When the tides peak every three months or so—as they just did—they close the gates here and divert the river around Bamberg City."

He pointed up the coast. "When the tide goes down a little, they vent water through the main channel again until everything's normal. In about two days, they can let barges across to the spaceport."

The hovercar's door opened, filling the back with the roar of the water jetting from a quarter kilometer to either side. "Welcome to Bamberg City," Desoix shouted over the background as he motioned Tyl ahead of him.

The Slammers officer paused outside the vehicle to slip on his pack again.

Steel-mesh stairs extended through the landing stage, up to the plaza—but down into the water as well: they did not move with the stage or the tides, and they were dripping and as slick as wet, polished metal could be.

"No gear?" he asked his companion curiously. Desoix waved his briefcase. "Some, but I'm leaving it to be off loaded with the gun. Remember, I'm travelling with a whole curst calliope."

"Well, you must be glad to have it back," said Tyl as he gripped the slick railing before he attempted the steps.

"Not as glad as my battery commander, Major Borodin," Desoix said with a chuckle. "It was his ass, not mine, if the Merrinet authorities had decided to keep it till it grew whiskers."

"But—" he added over the clang of his boots and Tyl's as they mounted the stairs "—he's not a bad old bird, the major, and he cuts me slack that not every CO might be willing to do."

The stairs ended on a meter-wide walkway that was part of the plaza but separated from it by a low concrete building, five meters on the side parallel to the dam beneath it and narrower in the other dimension. On top, facing inward to the plaza, was an ornate, larger than life crucifix.

Tyl hesitated, uncertain as to which way to walk around the building. He'd expected somebody from his unit to be waiting here on the mainland if not at the spaceport itself. He was feeling alone again. The raucous babble of locals setting up sales kiosks on the plaza increased his sense of isolation.

"Either way," Desoix said, putting a hand on the other man's shoulder—in comradeship as well as direction. "This is just the mechanical room for the locks except—"

Desoix leaned over so that his lips were almost touching Tyl's ear and said, "Except that it's the altar of Christ the Redeemer, if you ask anybody here. I *really* put my foot in it when I tried to get permission to site one of my guns on it. Would've been a perfect place to cover the sea approaches, but it seems that they'd rather die here than have their cross moved.

"Of course," the UDB officer added, a professional who didn't want another professional to think that he'd done a bad job of placing his guns, "I found an all-right spot on a demolition site just east of here."

Desoix nodded toward the thronged steps at the eastern end of the plaza. "Not quite the arc of fire, but nothing we can't cover from the other guns. Especially now we've got Number Five back."

In the time it had taken the hovercar to navigate from the space-port to the mainland, a city of small shops had sprung up in the plaza. Tyl couldn't imagine the development could be orderly—but it was, at least to the extent that a field of clover has order, because the individual plants respond to general stimuli that force them into patterns.

There were city police present, obvious from their peaked caps, green uniforms, and needle stunners worn on white cross-belts . . . but they were not organizing the ranks of kiosks. Men and women in capes were doing that; and after a glance at their faces, Tyl didn't need Desoix to tell him how tough they thought they were.

They just might be right, too; but things have a way of getting a lot worse than anybody expected, and it was then that you got a good look at what you and the rest of your crew were really made of.

Traffic in the plaza was entirely pedestrian. Vehicles were blocked from attempting the staircases at either seafront corner by massive steel bollards, and the stairs at the remaining apex were closed by what seemed to be lockworks as massive as those venting the river beneath the plaza. They'd *have* to be, Tyl realized, because there needed to be some way of releasing water from the top of its levee-channeled course in event of an emergency.

But that wasn't a problem for Captain Tyl Koopman just now. What *he* needed was somebody wearing the uniform of Hammer's Slammers, and he sure as blazes didn't see such in all this throng.

"Ah," he said, "Lieutenant . . . do you—"

The transceiver implanted in his mastoid bone beeped, and an unfamiliar voice began to answer Tyl's question before he had fully formed it.

"Transit Base to Captain Tyl Koopman," said the implant, scratchy with static and the frustration of the man at the other end of the radio link. "Captain Koopman, are you reading me? Over."

Tyl felt a rush of relief as he willed his left little finger to crook. The finger didn't move, but the redirected nerve impulse triggered the transmitter half of his implant. "Koopman to Transit," he said harshly. "Where in *blazes* are you, anyway? Over."

"Sir," said the voice, "this is Sergeant Major Scratchard, and you don't need to hear that I'm sorry about the cock-up. There's an unscheduled procession, and I can't get into the main stairs until it's over. If you'll tell me where you are, I swear I'll get t' you as soon as the little boys put away their crosses and let the men get back to work."

"I'm—" Tyl began. Desoix was turned half aside to indicate that he knew of the conversation going on and knew it wasn't any of his business. That gave the Slammers officer the mental base he needed for a reasoned decision rather than nervously agreeing to wait in place.

"All, sir," Scratchard continued; he'd paused but not broken the transmission. "There's a load of stuff for you here from Central. The colonel wants you to read the draft over when you report to Two. And, ah, the President, ah, Delcorio,wants to see you ASAP because you're the ranking officer now. Over."

"The main stairs," Tyl said, aloud rather than sub-vocalizing the way he had done thus far through the implant. Desoix could hear him. To underscore that he *wanted* the UDB officer to listen, Tyl pointed toward the empty stairs at the third apex. "That's at the end farthest from the sea, then?"

Desoix nodded. Scratchard's voice said, "Ah, yessir," through the static.

"Fine, I'll meet you there when you can get through," Tyl said flatly. "I'm in uniform and I have one pack is all. Koopman out."

He smiled to Desoix. "It'll give me a chance to look around," he explained. Now that his unit had contacted him he felt confident—whole, for the first time in . . . Via, in six months, just about.

Desoix smiled back. "Well, you shouldn't have any real problems here," he said. "But—" his head tilted, just noticeably, in the direction of three red-cloaked toughs "—don't forget what I told you. Myself, I'm going to check Number Three gun so long as I'm down on the corniche anyway. See you around, soldier."

"See you around," Tyl agreed confidently. He grinned at his surroundings with a tourist's vague interest. Captain Tyl Koopman was home again, or he would be in a few minutes.

CHAPTER THREE

Charles Desoix thought about the House of Grace as he mounted the eastern stairs from the plaza. The huge hospital building, Bishop Trimer's latest but not necessarily last attempt to impose his presence on Bamberg City, was about all a man could see as he left the plaza in this direction. For that matter, the twenty glittering stories of the House of Grace were the only portions of the city visible from the floor of the plaza, over the seawalls.

It was like looking at a block of blue ice; and it was the only thing about being stationed in Bamberg City that Desoix could really have done without. But the Bishop certainly wasn't enough of a problem that Desoix intended to transfer to one of the batteries out in the boonies on Two, rumbling through valleys you could be *sure* the rag-heads had mined and staked for snipers.

Thousands of people, shoppers as well as shopkeepers, were still pouring into the plaza; Desoix was almost alone in wanting to go in the opposite direction. He wasn't in a big hurry, so he kept his temper in check. An unscheduled inspection of Gun Three was a good excuse for the battery XO to be there, not just sneaking around. . . .

He had some business back at the Palace of Government, too; but he wasn't so horny from the trip to Merrinet that he was willing to make that his first priority. Quite.

Three prostitutes, each of them carried by a pair of servants to save their sandals and gossamer tights, were on their way to cribs in the plaza below. Desoix made way with a courteous bow; but uniform or not, he was going to make way. The phalanx of red-cloaked guards surrounding the girls would have made sure of that.

One of the girls smiled at Desoix as she rocked past. He smiled back at her, thinking of Anne McGill . . . but Blood and *Martyrs*! he could last another half hour. He'd get his job done first.

There was an unusual amount of congestion here, but that was because the main stairs were blocked. Another procession, no doubt; Bishop Trimer playing his games while President Delcorio and his wife tried to distract the populace with a crusade on Two.

As for the populace, its members knocked in each other's heads depending on what each was wearing that day.

Just normal politics, was all. Normal for places that hired the United Defense Batteries and other mercenary regiments, at any rate.

At dawn, the shadow of the House of Grace lay across the cathedral on the other side of the plaza, so that the gilded dome no longer gleamed. Desoix wrinkled his nose and thought about dust-choked roads on Two with a sniper every hundred meters of the wooded ridges overlooking them.

To blazes with all of them.

There was even more of a crush at the head of the stairs. Vehicles slid up to the bollards to drop their cargo and passengers—and then found themselves blocked by later-comers, furious at being stopped a distance from where they wanted to be. A squad of city police made desultory efforts to clear the jam, but they leaped aside faster than the bystanders did when the real fighting started.

Two drivers, one with a load of produce and the other carrying hand bags,were snarling. Three black-cloaked toughs jumped the driver with the red headband, knocked him down, and linked arms in a circle about the victim so that they could all three put the boot in.

At least a dozen thugs in red coalesced from nowhere around the fight. It grew like a crystal in a supersaturated solution of hate.

The police had their stunners out and were radioing for help, but they kept their distance. The toughs wore body armor beneath their cloaks, and Desoix heard the slam of at least one slug-throwing pistol from the ruck.

He willed his body to stay upright and to stride with swift dignity between vehicles and out of the potential line of fire. It would have griped his soul to run from this scum; but more important, anyone who ducked and scurried was a worthy victim, while a recognized mercenary was safe except by accident.

Anyway, that was what Desoix told himself.

But by the Lord! it felt good to get out of the shouted violence and see Gun Three, its six-man crew alert and watching the trouble at the stair head with their personal weapons ready.

The calliope's eight stubby barrels were mounted on the back of a large air-cushion truck. Instead of rotating through a single loading station as did the 2cm tribarrels on the Slammers' combat cars, each of the calliope's tubes was a separate gun. The array gimballed together to fire on individual targets which the defenders couldn't afford to miss.

Any aircraft, missile, or artillery shell that came over the sector of the horizon which Gun Three scanned—when the weapon was live—would be met by a pulse of high-intensity 3cm bolts from the calliope's eight barrels. Nothing light enough to fly through the air could survive that raking.

A skillful enemy could saturate the gun's defensive screen by launching simultaneous attacks from several directions, but even then the interlocking fire of a full, properly sited six-calliope battery should be able to hold out and keep the target it defended safe.

Of course, proper siting was an ideal rather than a reality, since every irregularity of terrain—or a building like the House of Grace— kept guns from supporting one another as they could do on a perfectly flat surface. Bamberg City wasn't likely to be surrounded by hostile artillery batteries, though, and Charles Desoix was proud of the single-layer coverage he had arranged for the whole populated area.

He did hope his gunners had sense enough not to talk about saturating coverage when they were around civilians. Especially civilians who looked like they'd been born to squatter families on Two.

"Good to see you back, sir," said Blaney, the sergeant in command of Gun Three on this watch.

He was a plump man and soft looking, but he'd reacted well in an emergency on Hager's World, taking manual control of his calliope and using it in direct fire on a party of sappers that had made it through the perimeter Federal forces were trying to hold.

"Say," asked a blond private Desoix couldn't call by name until his eye caught stenciling on the fellow's helmet: Karsov. "Is there any chance we're going to move, sir? Farther away from all this? It gets worse every day."

"What's . . ." Desoix began with a frown, but he turned to view the riot again before he finished the question—and then he didn't have to finish it.

The riot that Desoix had put out of his mind by steely control had expanded like mold on bread while he walked the three hundred meters to the shelter of his gun and its crew. There must have been nearly a thousand people involved—many of them lay-folk with the misfortune of being caught in the middle, but at least half were the cloaked shock troops of the two Easter factions.

Knives and metal bars flashed in the air. A shotgun thumped five times rapidly into a chorus of screams.

"Via," Desoix muttered.

A firebomb went off, spraying white trails of burning magnesium through the curtain of petroleum flames. Police aircars were hovering above the crowd on the thrust of their ducted fans while uniformed men hosed the brawlers indiscriminately with their needle stunners.

"This is what we're defending?" Blaney asked with heavy irony.

Desoix squatted, motioning the gun crew down with him. No

point in having a stray round hit somebody. The men were wearing their body armor, but Desoix himself wasn't. He didn't need it on shipboard or during negotiations on Merrinet, and it hadn't struck him how badly the situation in Bamberg City could deteriorate in the two weeks he was gone.

"Well,"he said, more or less in answer. "They're the people paying us until we hear different. Internal politics, that's not our business. And anyhow, it looks like the police have it pretty well under control."

"For now," muttered Karsov.

The fighting had melted away, as much in reaction to the firebomb as to the efforts of the civil authorities. Thugs were carrying away injured members of their own parties. The police tossed the disabled battlers whom they picked up into aircars, with angry callousness.

"It'd be kinda nice, sir," said Blaney, turning his eyes toward the House of Grace towering above them, "if we could maybe set up on top of there. Get a nice view all around, you know, good for defense; and, ah, we wouldn't need worry about getting hit with the odd brick or the like if the trouble comes this way next time."

The chorus of assent from the whole crew indicated that they'd been discussing the point at length among themselves.

Desoix smiled. He couldn't blame the men, but wishing something strongly didn't make it a practical solution.

"Look," he said, letting his eyes climb the sculptured flank of the hospital building as he spoke. The narrower sides of the House of Grace, the north and south faces, were of carven stone rather than chrome and transparent panels.

The south face, toward Gun Three and the seafront, was decorated with the miracles of Christ: the sick rising from their beds; the lame tossing away their crutches; loaves and fishes multiplying miraculously to feed the throng stretching back in low relief.

On the opposite side were works of human mercy: the poor being fed and lodged in church kitchens; orphans being raised to adulthood; medical personnel with crosses on their uniforms healing the sick as surely as Christ did on the south face.

But over the works of human mercy, the ascetic visage of Bishop Trimer presided in a coruscance of sun-rays like that which haloed Christ on the opposite face. A determined man, Bishop Trimer. And very sure of himself.

"Look," Desoix repeated as he reined in his wandering mind. "In the first place, it's a bad location because the gun can only depress three degrees and that'd leave us open to missiles skimming the surface."

Karsov opened his mouth as if to argue, but a snarled order from Sergeant Blaney shut him up. Lieutenant Desoix was easy-going under normal circumstances; but he was an officer and the Battery XO . . . and he was also hard as nails when he chose to be, as Blaney knew by longer experience than the private had.

"But more important . . ." Desoix went on with a nod of approval to Blaney. "Never site a gun in a spot where you can't drive away if things really get bad. Do you expect to ride down in the elevators if a mob decides what they really ought to do tomorrow is burn the hospital?"

"Well, they wouldn't . . ." Karsov began.

He looked at the wreckage and smoke near the plaza stairs and thought the better of saying what a mob would or wouldn't do.

"Were you on Shinano, Sergeant?" Desoix asked Blaney.

"Yes sir," the noncom said. "But I wasn't in the city during the riots, if that's what you mean."

"I was a gun captain then," Desoix said with a smile and a biting voice, because it was always nice to remember the ones you survived. "The Battery Commander—this was Gilt, and they sacked him for it—sited us on top of the Admin Building. Ten stories in a central park.

"So we had a *really* good view of the mob, because parts of it were coming down all five radial streets with torches. And they'd blown up the transformer station providing power to the whole center of town."

He coughed and rubbed his face. "There were aircars flying every which way, carrying businessmen who knew they weren't going to get out at ground level . . . but we didn't have a car, and we couldn't even get the blazes off the roof. It didn't have a staircase, just the elevator—and that quit when the power went off."

Blaney was nodding with grim agreement; so were two of the other veterans in the gun crew.

"How—how'd you get out, sir?" Karsov asked in a suitably chastened tone.

Desoix grinned again. It wasn't a pleasant expression. "Called to one of those businessmen on a loud-hailer," he said. "Asked him to come pick us up. When he saw where we had the calliope pointed, he decided that was a good idea."

The slim officer paused and looked up at the House of Grace again. "Getting lucky once doesn't mean I'm going to put any of my men in that particular bucket again, though," he said. "Down here—" he smiled brightly, but there was more than pure humor in this expression, too "—at the worst, you've got the gun to keep anybody at a distance."

"Think it's going to be that bad, sir?" one of the crewmen asked.

Desoix shrugged. "I need to report to the Palace," he said. "I guess it's clear enough to do that now."

As he turned to walk away from the gun position, he heard Sergeant Blaney saying, "Not for us and the other mercs, maybe. But yeah, it's going to get that bad here. You wait and see."

CHAPTER FOUR

Tyl Koopman strolled through a series of short aisles into which the plaza was marked by freshly erected kiosks. In most cases the shop proprietors were still setting out their goods, but they were willing to call Tyl over to look at their merchandise. He smiled and walked on—the smile becoming fixed in short order.

He'd learned Spanish when the Slammers were stationed on Cartagena three years before, so he could have followed the local language without difficulty. It was interesting that most of the shop-keepers recognized Tyl's uniform and spoke to him in Dutch, fluent at least for a few words of enticement.

It was interesting also that many of those keeping shops in the plaza were of Levantine extraction, like the merchants who had disembarked from the surface-effect freighter. They were noticeable not only for their darker complexions but also because their booths and clothing were so bedecked with crosses that sometimes the color of the underlying fabric was doubtful.

Not, as Lieutenant Desoix had suggested, that their desperate attempts to belong to the majority would matter a hoot in Hell when the Crusade really got moving. Tyl wasn't a cynic. Like most line mercenaries, he wasn't enough of an intellectual to have abstract positions about men and politics.

But he had a good mind and plenty of data about the way things went when politicians hired men to kill for them.

The section Tyl was walking through was given over to tobacco and smoking products—shops for visitors rather than staples for the domestic market which seemed to fill most of the plaza.

Tobacco from Bamberia had a smooth melding of flavors that remained after the raw leaf was processed into the cold inhalers in which most of the galaxy used imported tobacco. Those who couldn't afford imports smoked what they grew in local plots on a thousand worlds . . . but those who could afford the best and wanted the creosote removed before they put the remainder of the taste into their bodies, bought from Bamberia.

Most of the processing was done off-planet, frequently on the user world where additional flavorings were added to the inhalers to meet local tastes. There were a few inhaler factories on the outskirts of Bamberg City, almost the only manufacturing in a metropolis whose wealth was based on transport and government. Their creations were displayed on the tables in the plaza, brightly colored plastic tubes whose shapes counterfeited everything from cigarillos to cigars big enough to pass for riot batons.

But the local populace tended to follow traditional methods of using the herb that made them rich. Products for the local market posed here as exotica for the tourists and spacers who wanted something to show the folks back home where they'd been.

Tourists and spacers and mercenaries. The number of kiosks

serving outsiders must have increased radically since President Delcorio started hiring mercenaries for his Crusade.

Tyl passed by displays of smoking tobacco and hand-rolled cigars—some of the boxes worth a week's pay to him, even now that he had his captaincy. There were cigar cutters and pipe cleaners, cigarette holders and pipes carved from microporous meerschaum mined on the coasts of Two.

Almost all the decoration was religious: crosses, crucifixes, and other symbols of luxuriant Christianity. That theme was almost as noticeable to Tyl as the fact that almost everyone in the plaza—and every kiosk—was decorated with either black or red, and never both.

Each staggering aisle was of uniform background. To underscore the situation, cloaked toughs faced off at every angle where the two colors met, glowering threats that did not quite—while Tyl saw them—come to open violence.

Great place to live, Bamberg City. Tyl was glad of his khaki uniform. He wondered how often the silver and black of the United Defense Batteries was mistaken for black by somebody with a red cloak and a brick in his hand.

Grimacing to himself, the Slammers officer strode more swiftly toward his goal, the empty stairs at the north end of the plaza. The scene around him was colorful, all right, and this was probably one of the few chances he'd have to see it.

You served on a lot of worlds in a mercenary regiment, but what you mostly *saw* there were other soldiers and the wrack of war . . . which was universal, a smoky gray ambiance that you scanned and maybe shot at before you moved on.

Even so, Tyl didn't want to spend any longer than he had to in this plaza. He could feel the edge of conflict which overlay it like the cloaks that covered the weapons and armor of the omnipresent bullies, waiting for an opportunity to strike out. He'd seen plenty of fighting during his years with the Slammers, but he didn't want it hovering around him when he was supposed to be in a peaceful rear area.

The stairs were slimy with water pooling in low spots, but Nevis Island and its spaceport shielded the plaza from most of the seaweed and marine life that the high tides would otherwise have washed up.

Tyl picked his way carefully, since he seemed to be the first person to climb them since the tide dropped.

A procession, Scratchard had said, blocking normal traffic. Maybe that would be a little easier to take than the human bomb waiting to go off below in the plaza.

At the top of the stairs were ten pairs of steel-and-concrete doors. Each side-hung panel was five meters across and at least three meters high. The doors—lock-gates—were fully open now. They rotated out toward the plaza on trunnions in slotted rails set into the concrete. As Tyl neared them on his lonely climb, he heard the sound of chanted music echoing from beyond the doors.

Tyl had expected to see gaily bedecked vehicles when he reached the top of the stairs and could look into the covered mall beyond. Instead there were people on foot, and most of *them* were standing rather than marching from left to right.

The mall was at least a hundred meters wide; its pavement was marked to pass heavy ground traffic from one side of the river to the other. At the moment, a sparse line of priests in full regalia was walking slowly down the center of the expanse, interspersed with lay-folk wearing robes of ceremonially drab coarseness.

Some carried objects on display. Ornate crucifixes were the most common, but there were banners and a reliquary borne by four women which, if *pure* gold, must have cost as much as a starship.

Every few paces, the marchers paused and chanted something in Latin. When they began to move again, a refrain boomed back from the line of solid-looking men in white robes on either side of the procession route. The guards—they could be nothing else— wore gold crosses on the left shoulders of their garments, but they also bore meter-long staffs.

There was no need for the procession to be blocking the whole width of the mall; but when Tyl stepped through the door, the nearest men in white gave him a look that made it real clear what would happen to anybody who tried to carry out secular business in an area the Church had marked for its own.

Tyl stopped. He stood in a formal posture instead of lounging against a column while he waited. No point in offending the fellows who watched him with hard eyes even when they bellowed verses in a language he knew only well enough to recognize.

No wonder Scratchard hadn't been able to make it to the plaza as he'd intended. The other two staircases were open and in use, but the procession route certainly extended some distance to either side of the river; and Scratchard, with business of his own to take care of, would have waited till the last minute before setting out to collect an officer returning from furlough.

No problem. But it calmed Tyl to remember that there *were* other Slammers nearby, in event of a real emergency.

The gorgeous reliquary was the end of the procession proper. When that reached the heavy doors at the west end of the mall, a barked order passed down the lines of guards, repeated by every tenth man.

The men in white turned and began to double-time in the direction the procession was headed, closing up as they moved. They carried their staffs vertically before them, and their voices boomed a chant beginning, *"Fortis iuventus, virtus audax bellica . . ."* as they strode away.

They marched in better order than any mercenary unit Tyl could remember having seen—not that close-order drill was what folks hired the Slammers for.

And there were a lot of them, for the double lines continued to shift past and contract for several minutes, more and more quick-stepping staff-wielders appearing from farther back along the procession route to the east. They must have timed their withdrawal so that the whole route would be cleared the instant the procession reached its destination, presumably the cathedral.

At least *something* in this place was organized. It just didn't appear to be what called itself the government.

CHAPTER FIVE

Tyl didn't follow the procession when the route cleared, nor did he try to raise Sergeant Major Scratchard on his implant again.

He'd told Scratchard where he'd be; and if the noncom couldn't find him, then that was important information for Captain Tyl Koopman to know.

There was a surge of civilians—into the mall and through it down the stairs to the plaza—as soon as the procession was clear. Normal folk, so far as Tyl could tell from the loose-fitting fashions current here. Most of them wore a red ribbon or a black one, but there was no contingent of cloaked thugs.

Which meant that the bullies, the enforcers, had gotten word that the main stairs would be blocked when the tide cleared the plaza—although Scratchard and apparently a lot of civilians had been caught unaware. That could mean a lot of things: none of them particularly good, and none of them, thank the Lord, the business of Tyl Koopman or Hammer's Slammers.

He caught sight of a uniform of the right color. Sergeant Major Scratchard muscled his way through the crowd, his rank in his eyes and his grizzled hair. His khaki coveralls were neat and clean, but there were shiny patches over the shoulders where body armor had rubbed the big man's uniform against his collarbone.

Tyl hadn't recognized the name, but sight of the man rang a bell in his mind. He swung away from the pillar and, gripping the hand the noncom extended to him, said, "Sergeant Major Scratchard? Would that be Ripper Jack?"

Scratchard's professional smile broadened into something as real and firm as his handshake. "Cap'n Koopman, then? Yeah, when I was younger, sir . . . Maybe when I was younger."

He shifted his right leg and the hand holding Tyl's, just enough to point without apprising the civilians around of the gesture.

Scratchard wore a knife along his right calf. Most of the sheathed blade was hidden within his boot but the hand-filling grip was strapped to mid-calf. "Pistols jam on you, happen," the big man half bragged, half explained. "This'n never did."

His face hardened. "Though they got me pretty much retired to Admin now with my bum knees."

"Didn't look that quiet a billet just now," Tyl said, pitching his voice lower than the civilians, scurrying on their own errands, could have overheard. "Down in the plaza just now, the enforcers in cloaks . . . And I was talking to a UDB lieutenant landed the same time I did."

"Yeah, you could maybe figure that," Scratchard said in a voice too quietly controlled to be really neutral. "Open your leg pocket, sir, and stand real close."

Tyl, his face still, ran a finger across the seal of the bellows pocket on the right leg of his coveralls . He and the noncom pressed against one of the door pillars, their backs momentarily to the crowd moving past them. He felt the weight of what Scratchard had slipped into his pocket.

Tyl didn't need to finger the object to know that he'd been given a service pistol, a 1cm powergun. In the right hands, it could do as much damage as a shotgun loaded with buck.

Tyl's were the right hands. He wouldn't have been in the Slammers if they weren't. But the implications. . . .

"We're issuing sidearms in Bamberg City, then?" he asked without any emotional loading.

Scratchard, an enlisted man reporting to an officer, said stiffly, "Sir, while I was in charge of the Transit Detachment, I gave orders that none of the troopers on port leave were to leave barracks in groups of less than three. And no, sidearms aren't officially approved. But I won't have men under my charge disarmed when I sure as blazes wouldn't be disarmed myself. You can change the procedures if you like."

"Yes, Sergeant Major, I can," Tyl said with just enough iron to emphasize that he was well aware of their respective ranks. "And if I see any reason to do so, I will."

He smiled, returning the conversation to the footing where he wanted to keep it. "For now, let's get me to the barracks and see just what it is the colonel has on line."

Pray to the Lord that there'd be orders to take over E Company again.

Scratchard hesitated, looking first toward the east, then the western lock doors. "Ah, sir," he said. "We're billeted in the City Offices—" he pointed toward the eastern end of the mall, the side toward the huge House of Grace. "Central's cut orders for you to carry the Transit Detachment over to Two for further assignment . . . but you know, nothing that can't wait another couple days. We've still got half a dozen other troopers due back from furlough."

"All right," Tyl said, to show that he wasn't going to insist on making a decision before he'd heard Scratchard's appraisal of the situation. "What else?"

"Well, sir," said the noncom. "President Delcorio really wants to see the ranking Slammers officer in the city. Didn't call the message over, his nephew brought it this morning. I told him you were in orbit, due down as soon as the port cleared—'cause *I'm* bloody not the guy to handle that sort of thing. I checked with Central, see if they'd courier somebody over from Two, but they didn't want. . . ."

Tyl understood why Colonel Hammer would have turned down Scratchard's request. It was obvious what President Delcorio wanted to discuss . . . and it wasn't something that Hammer wanted to make a matter of official regimental policy by sending over a staff officer.

The Slammers hadn't been hired to keep public order in Bamberg City, and Colonel Hammer wanted all the time he could get before he had to officially make a decision that might involve the Bonding Authority either way.

"Central said you should handle it for now,"Scratchard concluded. "And I sure think *somebody* ought to report to the President ASAP."

"Via," muttered Tyl Koopman.

Well, he couldn't say that he hadn't been given a responsible job when he returned from furlough.

He shrugged his shoulders, settling the pack more comfortably. "Right," he said. "Let's do it then, Sergeant Major."

"Palace of Government," Scratchard said in evident relief, pointing west in the direction the procession had been headed. He stepped off with a stiff-legged stride that reminded Tyl that the noncom had complained about his knees.

The crowd had thinned enough that the Slammers officer could trust other pedestrians to avoid him even if he glanced away from his direction of movement. "You go by Jack when you're with friends?" he asked,looking at the bigger man.

"Yes sir, I do," Scratchard replied.

He grinned, and though the expression wasn't quite natural, the noncom was working on it.

Mercenary units were always outnumbered by the indigenous populations that hired them—or they were hired to put down. Mercenaries depended on better equipment, better training—and on each other, because everything else in the world could be right and you were still dead if the man who should have covered your back let you down.

Tyl and Scratchard both wanted—needed—there to be a good relationship between them. It didn't look like they'd be together long . . . but life itself was temporary, and that wasn't a reason not to make things work as well as they could while it lasted.

"This way," said Scratchard as the two soldiers emerged from the mall crossing the river. "Give you a bit of a view, and we don't fight with trucks."

There was a ramp from the mall down to interlocking vehicular streets—one of them paralleling the river, the plaza, and then sweeping west along the corniche. The other was a parklike boulevard which tied into the first after separating the gold-domed cathedral from a large, three-story building whose wings enclosed a central courtyard open in the direction of the river.

"That's the . . . ?" Tyl said, trying to remember the name.

"Palace of Government, yeah," Scratchard replied easily. He was taking them along the pedestrian walk atop the levee.

Glancing over the railing to his right, Tyl was shocked to see the water was within two meters of the top of the levee. He could climb directly aboard the scores of barges moored there, silently awaiting for the locks to open. All he'd have to do was swing his legs over the guard rail.

"Via!" he said, looking from the river to the street and the buildings beyond it. "What happens if it comes up another couple meters? All that down there floods, right?"

"They've got flood shutters on all the lower floors," Scratchard explained/agreed. "They say it happened seventy-odd years ago when everything came together—tides and a storm that backed up the outlet channels up-coast. But they know what they're doing, their engineers."

He paused, then added in a tone of disgust, "Their politicians, now . . . But I don't suppose they know their asses from a hole in the ground, any of 'em anywhere."

He didn't expect an argument from an officer of Hammer's Slammers; and Tyl Koopman wasn't about to give him one.

Bamberg City was clean, prosperous. The odor of toasted tobacco leaf permeated it, despite the fact that the ranks of hogsheads on the waiting barges were all vacuum-sealed; but that was a sweet smell very different from the reeks that were the normal concomitant of bulk agriculture.

Nothing wrong here but the human beings.

A flagpole stood in the courtyard of the Palace of Government. Its twelve-man honor guard wore uniforms of the same blue and gold as the fabric of the drooping banner.

In front of the cathedral were more than a thousand of the men in cross-marked white robes. They were still chanting and blocking vehicles, though the gaps in the ranks of staff-armed choristers permitted pedestrians to enter the cathedral building. The dome towered above this side of the river, though it in turn was dwarfed by the House of Grace opposite.

There was a pedestrian bridge from the embankment to the courtyard of the Palace of Government, crossing the vehicular road. As they joined the traffic on it, heavy because of the way vehicles were being backed up by the tail end of the procession, Tyl asked, "Who wears white here? The ones who hold Easter on Christmas?"

"Umm," said the sergeant major. The noncom's tone reminded Tyl of the pistol that weighted his pocket—and the reason it was there.

In a barely audible voice, Scratchard went on, "Those are orderlies from the House of Grace. They, ah, usually turn out for major religious events."

Neither of the mercenaries spoke again until they had reached the nearly empty courtyard of the government building. Then, while the honor guard was still out of earshot, Tyl said, "Jack, they don't look to me like they empty bedpans."

"Them?" responded the big sergeant major. "They do whatever Bishop Trimer tells them to do, sir."

He glanced over his shoulder in the direction of the massed orderlies. His eyes held only flat appraisal, as if he were estimating range and the length of the burst he was about to fire.

"Anything at all," he concluded.

Tyl Koopman didn't pursue the matter as he and Scratchard—the latter limping noticeably—walked across the courtyard toward the entrance of the Palace of Government.

He could feel the eyes of the honor guard following them with contempt. It didn't bother him much, anymore.

Five years in the Slammers had taught him that parade-ground soldiers always felt that way about killers in uniform.

CHAPTER SIX

The flood shutters of the Palace of Government were closed, and Charles Desoix wasn't naive enough to think that the thick steel plates had been set against the chance of a storm surge. Bamberg City had really come apart in the two weeks he was gone.

Or just maybe it was starting to come together, but President John Delcorio wasn't going to be part of the new order.

Desoix threw a sharp salute to the head of the honor guard. The Bamberg officer returned it while the men of his section presented arms.

Striding with his shoulders back, Desoix proceeded toward the front entrance—the only opening on the first two stories of the palace that wasn't shuttered.

As Desoix looked at it, the saluting was protective coloration. It was purely common sense to want the respect of the people around you . . . and when you've wangled billets for yourself and your men in the comfort of the Palace of Government, that meant getting along with the Executive Guard.

By thumbing an epaulet loop, Desoix brightened the gray-spattered markings of his uniform to metallic silver—and it was easy to learn to salute, as easy as learning to hold the sight picture that would send a bolt of cyan death downrange at a trigger's squeeze. There was no point in not making it easy on yourself.

He thought of making a suggestion to the Slammers officer who'd just arrived, but . . . Tyl Koopman seemed a good sort and as able as one of Colonel Hammer's company commanders could be expected to be.

But Koopman also seemed the sort of man who might be happier with his troops in the police barracks beneath the City Offices than he would be in the ambiance of the Palace.

The captain in command of the guards at the entrance was named Sanchez; he roomed next door to Desoix in the officers' quarters in the West Wing. Instead of saluting again, Desoix took the man's hand and said, "Well, Rene, I'm glad to be back on a civilized planet again . . . but what on *earth* has been going on in the city since I left?"

The Guard captain made a sour face and looked around at the sergeant and ten men of his section. Everyone in the Executive Guard was at least sponsored by one of the top families on the planet. Not a few of them were members of those families, asserting a tradition of service without the potential rigors of being stationed on Two if the Crusade got under way.

"Well, you know the people," Sanchez said, a gentleman speaking among gentlemen. "The recent taxes haven't been popular, since there are rumors that they have more to do with Lady Eunice's wardrobe than with propagation of Christ's message. Nothing that we need worry about."

Desoix raised an eyebrow. The Executive Guard carried assault rifles whose gilding made them as ornamental as the gold brocade on the men's azure uniforms . . . but there were magazines in the rifles today. That was as unusual as the flood shutters being in place.

"Ah, you can't really stay neutral if things get . . . out of hand, can you?" the UDB officer asked. He didn't like to suggest that he and Sanchez were on different standards; but that was better than using "we" when the word might seem to commit the United Defense Batteries.

The guardsman's face chilled. "We'll follow orders, of course," he said. "But it isn't the business of the army to get involved in the squabbles of the mob: or to attempt to change the will of the people."

"Exactly," said Desoix, nodding enthusiastic agreement. *"Exactly."*

He was still nodding as he strode into the entrance rotunda. He hoped he'd covered his slip with Sanchez well enough.

But he certainly *had* learned where the army—or at least the Executive Guard stood on the subject of the riots in the streets.

There was a small, separately guarded elevator off the rotunda which opened directly onto the Consistory Room on the third floor. Desoix hesitated. The pager inset into his left cuff had lighted red with Major Borodin's anxiety, and Desoix knew what his commander wanted without admitting his presence by answering.

It would be a *very* good idea to take the elevator. Borodin was awkward in the company of President Delcorio and his noble advisors; the major, the battery, and the situation would all benefit from the presence of Lieutenant Charles Desoix.

But Desoix had some personal priorities as well, and. . . .

There was traffic up and down the central staircase—servants and minor functionaries, but not as many of them as usual. They had an air of nervousness rather than their normal haughty superiority.

When the door of the small meeting room near the elevator moved, Desoix saw Anne McGill through the opening.

Desoix strode toward her, smiling outwardly and more relieved than he could admit within. He wasn't the type who could ever admit being afraid that a woman wouldn't want to see him again—or that he cared enough about her that it would matter.

The panel, dark wood placed between heavy engaged columns of pink and gray marble, closed again when he moved toward it.

She'd kept it ajar, watching for his arrival, and had flashed a sight of herself to signal Desoix closer.

But Lady Anne McGill, companion and confidante of the President's wife, had no wish to advertise her presence here in the rotunda.

Desoix tapped on the door. He heard the lock click before the panel opened, hiding Anne behind it from anyone outside. Maybe her ambivalence was part of the attraction, he thought as he stepped into a conference room. There was a small, massively built table, chairs for six, and space for that many more people to stand if they knew one another well.

All the room held at the moment was the odor of heavy tobaccos, so omnipresent on Bamberia that Desoix noticed it only because he'd been off-planet for two weeks . . . and Anne McGill in layers of silk chiffon which covered her like mist, hiding everything while everything remained suggested.

Desoix put his arms around her.

"Charles, it's very dangerous," she said, turning so that his lips met her cheek.

He nuzzled her ear and, when she caught his right hand, he reached for her breast with his left.

"Ah . . ." he said as a different level of risk occurred to him. "Your husband's still stationed on Two, isn't he?"

"Of course," Anne muttered scornfully.

She was no longer fighting off his hands, but she was relaxing only slightly and that at a subconscious level. "You don't think Bertrand would be *here* when things are like this, do you? There's a Consistory Meeting every morning now, but things are getting worse. *Anyone* can see that. Eunice says that they're all cowards, all the men, even her husband."

She let her lips meet his. Her body gave a shudder and she gripped Desoix to her as fiercely as her tension a moment before had attempted to repel him. "You should be upstairs now," she whispered as she turned her head again. "They need you and your major, he's very upset."

"My call unit would have told me that if I'd asked it," the UDB officer said as he shifted the grip of his hands. Anne was a big woman, large boned and with a tendency toward fat that she repressed fiercely with exercise and various diets. She wore nothing beneath the bottom layer of chiffon except the smooth skin which Desoix caressed. His hand ran up her thigh to squeeze the fat of her buttock against the firm muscle beneath.

"Then don't be long . . ." Anne whispered as she reached for the fly of his trousers.

Desoix didn't know quite what she meant by that.

But he knew that it didn't matter as he backed his mistress against the table, lifting the chiffon dress to spill over the wood where there would be no risk of staining the fabric.

CHAPTER SEVEN

"Captain Tyl Koopman, representing Hammer's Regiment," boomed the greeter, holding the door of the Consistory Room ajar—and blocking Tyl away from it with her body, though without appearing to do so.

"Enter," said someone laconically from within. The greeter swept the panel open with a flourish, bowing to Tyl.

Machines could have done all the same things, Tyl thought with amusement; but they wouldn't have been able to do them with such pomp. Even so, the greeter, a plump woman in an orange and silver gown, was only a hint of the peacock-bright gathering within the Consistory Room.

There were twenty or thirty people, mostly men, within the domed room above the rotunda. Natural lighting through the circumference of arched windows made the Slammers officer blink. It differed in quality (if not necessarily intensity) from the glow-strips in the corridors through which he had been guided to reach the room.

The only men whose garments did not glitter with metallic threads were those whose clothing glowed with internal lambency from powerpacks woven into the seams. President John Delcorio, in black velvet over which a sheen trembled from silver to ultraviolet, was the most striking of the lot.

"Good to see you at last, Captain," Delcorio boomed as if in assurance that Tyl would recognize him—as he did from the holograms set in niches in the hallways of the Palace of Government. "Maybe your veterans can put some backbone into our own forces, don't you think? So that we can all get down to the real business of cleansing Two for Christ."

He glowered at a middle-aged man whose uniform was probably that of a serving officer, because its dark green was so much less brilliant than what anyone else in the room seemed to be wearing.

John Delcorio was shorter than Tyl had assumed, but he had the chest and physical presence of a big man indeed. His hair, moustache, and short beard were black with gray speckles that were probably works of art: the President was only thirty-two standard years old. He had parlayed his position as Head of Security into the presidency when the previous incumbent, his uncle, died three years before.

Delcorio's eyes sparkled, and the flush on his cheeks was as much ruddy good health as a vestige of his present anger. Tyl could understand how a man with eyes that sharp could cut his way to leadership of a wealthy planet.

But he could also see how such a man's pushing would bring others to push back, push hard. . . .

Maybe too hard.

"Sir," Tyl replied, wondering what you were *supposed* to call the President of Bamberia when you met him. "I haven't been fully briefed yet on the situation. But Hammer's Slammers carry out their contracts."

He hoped that was neutral enough; and he hoped to the *Lord* that Delcorio would let him drop into the background now.

"Yes, well," said Delcorio. The quick spin of his hand was more or less the dismissal Tyl had hoped for. "Introduce Major Koopman to the others, Thomas. Have something to drink—" There was a well-stocked sideboard beneath one of the windows, and most of those present had glasses in their hands. "We're waiting for Bishop Trimer, you see."

"How *long* are you going to wait before you send for him, John?" asked the woman in the red dress that shimmered like a gasoline flame. She wasn't any taller than the President; but like him, she flashed with authority as eye-catching as her clothes. "You *are* the President, you know."

It struck Tyl that Delcorio and this woman who could only be his wife wore the colors of the Easter factions he had seen at daggers-drawn in the plaza. That made as little sense as anything else in Bamberg City.

"Major, then, is it?" murmured a slender fellow at Tyl's elbow, younger than the mercenary had been when he joined the Slammers. "I'm Thom Chastain, don't you see, and this is my brother Richie. What would you like to drink?"

"Ah, I'm really just a captain," Tyl said, wondering whether Delcorio had misheard, was being flattering—or was incensed that Hammer had sent only a company commander in response to a summons from his employer. "Ah, I don't think. . . ."

"Eunice," the President was saying in a voice like a slap, "this is *scarcely* the time to precipitate disaster by insulting the man who can stabilize the situation."

"The *army* can stabilize—" the woman snapped.

"It isn't the business of the army—" boomed the soldier in green.

The volume of his interruption shocked him as well as the others in the wrangle. All three paused. When the discussion resumed, it was held in voices low enough to be ignored if not unheard.

"Queen Eunice," said Thom Chastain, shaking his head. There was a mixture of affection and amusement in his voice, but Tyl had been in enough tight places to recognize the flash of fear in the young man's eyes. "She's really a terror, isn't she?"

"Ah," Tyl said while his mind searched for a topic that had nothing to do with Colonel Hammer's employers. "You gentlemen are in the army also, I gather?"

There were couches around most of the walls. Near one end was a marble conference table that matched the inlaid panels between the single-sheet vitril windows. Nobody was sitting down, and the groups of two or three talking always seemed to be glancing over their collective shoulders toward the door, waiting for the missing man.

"Oh, well, these," said the other Chastain brother, Richie—surely a twin. He flicked the collar of his blue and gold uniform, speaking with the diffidence Tyl had felt at being addressed as "Major."

"We're honorary colonels in the Guards, you know," said Thom. "But it's because of our grandfather. We're not very inter. . . ."

"Well, Grandfather Chastain was, you know," said Richie, taking up where his brother's voice trailed off. "He was president some years ago. Esteban Delcorio succeeded him, but Thom and I are something like colonels for life—"

"—and so we wear—"

They concluded, both together, "But we aren't soldiers the way you are, Major."

"Or Marshal Dowell, either," Thom Chastain added later, nodding to the man in green who had broken away from the Delcorios—leaving them to hiss at one another. "Now, what would you like to drink?"

Just about anything, thought Tyl. So long as it had enough kick to knock him on his ass . . . which, in a situation like this, would get him sacked if the colonel didn't decide he should instead be shot out of hand. Why in *blazes* hadn't somebody from the staff been couriered over on an "errand" that left him available to talk informally with the civil authorities?

"Nothing for me, thank you," Tyl said aloud. "Or, ah, water?"

Marshal Dowell had fallen in with a tall man whose clothes were civilian in cut, though they carried even more metallic brocade than trimmed the military uniforms. The temporary grouping broke apart abruptly when Dowell turned away and the tall man shouted at his back, "No, I *don't* think that's a practical solution, Marshal! Abdicating your responsibilities makes it impossible for me to carry out mine."

"Berne is the City Prefect," Thom whispered into Tyl's ear. The Chastain brothers were personable kids—but "kid" was certainly the word for them. They *seemed* even younger than their probable age—which was old enough to ride point in an assault force, in Tyl's terms of reference.

From the other side, Richie was saying, "There's been a lot of trouble in the streets recently, you know. Berne keeps saying that he doesn't have enough police to take care of it."

"It is *not* in the interests of God or the State," responded Marshal Dowell, his voice shrill and his face as red as a flag, "that we give up the Crusade on Two because of some rabble that the police would deal with if they were used with decision!"

Tyl saw a man in uniform staring morosely out over the city. The uniform was familiar; desire tricked the Slammers officer into thinking that he recognized the man as well.

"'Scuse me," he muttered to the Chastains and strode across the circular room. "Ah, Lieutenant Desoix?"

Tyl's swift motion drew all eyes in the room to him—so he felt/knew that everyone recognized his embarrassment when the figure in silhouette at the window turned: a man in his mid-forties, jowls sagging, paunch sagging . . . Twenty years older than Charles Desoix and twenty kilos softer.

"Charles?" the older man barked as his eyes quested the room for the subject of Tyl's call.

"Where have you—"

Then he realized, from the way the Slammers officer's face went from enthusiastic to stricken, what had happened. He smiled, an expression that reminded Tyl of snow slumping away from a rocky hillside in the spring, and said, "You'd be Hammer's man? I'm Borodin, got the battery of the UDB here that keeps them all—" he nodded toward nothing in particular, pursing his lips to make the gesture encompass everyone in the room "—safe in their bed."

The scowl with which Major Borodin followed the statement made a number of the richly dressed Bamberg officials turn their interest to other parts of the room.

Tyl was too concerned with controlling his own face to worry about the reason for Borodin's anger—which was explained when the UDB officer continued, "I gather we're looking for the same man. And I must say, if *you* could get down from orbit in time to be here, I don't understand what Charles' problem can be."

"He—" said Tyl. Then he smiled brightly and replaced his intended statement with, "I'm sure Lieutenant Desoix will be here as soon as possible. It's very—difficult out there, getting around, it seems to me."

"Tell me about it, boy," Borodin grunted as he turned again to the window, not so much rude as abstracted.

They were looking out over the third-story porch which faced the front of the Palace of Government. In the courtyard below were the foreshortened honor guard and the flag, still drooping and unrecognizable. The river beyond was visible only by inference. Its water, choked between the massive levees, was covered with barges ten and twelve abreast, waiting to be passed through beneath the plaza.

On the other side of the river—

"That's the City Offices, then?" Tyl asked.

Where he and the men under his temporary charge were billeted. And where now police vehicles swarmed, disgorging patrolmen and comatose prisoners in amazing numbers.

"Claims to be," Borodin grunted. "Don't see much sign that anything's being run from there, do you?"

He glanced around. He was aware enough of his surroundings to make sure that nobody but the other mercenary officer would overhear the next comment. "Or from here, you could bloody well say."

The door opened. The scattered crowd in the Consistory Room turned toward the sound with the sudden unanimity of a school of fish changing front.

"Father Laughlin, representing the Church," called the greeter in a clear voice that left its message unmistakable.

The President's face settled as if he had just watched one wing of the building crumble away. Eunice Delcorio swore like a transportation sergeant.

"Wait out here, boys," said a huge man—soft-looking but not far short of two meters in height—in white priestly vestments. "You won't be needed."

He was speaking, Tyl saw through the open door, to a quartet of "hospital orderlies." They looked even more like shock troops than they had in the street, though these weren't carrying their staffs.

Eunice Delcorio swore again. The skin over her broad cheekbones had gone sallow with rage.

Father Laughlin appeared to be at ease and in perfect control of himself, but Tyl noticed that the priest ducked instinctively when he entered the room—though he would have had to be a full meter taller to bump his head on any of the lintels in the Palace of Government.

"Where's Trimer?" Delcorio demanded in a voice that climbed a note despite an evident attempt to control it.

"Bishop Trimer, you—" Laughlin began smoothly.

"Where's Trimer?"

"Holding a Service of Prayer for Harmony in the cathedral," the priest said, no longer trying to hide the ragged edges of emotion behind an unctuous wall.

"He was told to be here!" said Berne, the City Prefect, breaking into the conversation because he was too overwhelmed by his own concerns to leave the matter to the President. He stepped toward the priest, his green jacket fluttering—a rangy mongrel snarling at a fat mastiff, which will certainly make a meal of it should the mastiff deign to try.

"Bishop Trimer appreciated the President's invitation," Laughlin said, turning and nodding courteously toward Delcorio. "He sent me in response to it. He was gracious enough to tell me that he had full confidence in my ability to report your concerns to him. But his first duty is to the Church—and to all members of his flock, rather than to the secular authorities who have their own duties."

The Chastain brothers were typical of those in the Consistory Room, men of good family gathered around the President not so much for their technical abilities but because they controlled large blocks of wealth and personnel on their estates. They watched from the edges of the room with the fascination of spectators at a bloody accident, saying nothing and looking away whenever the eyes of one of the principals glanced across them.

"All right," said Eunice Delcorio to her husband. Her eyes were as calm as the crust on a pool of lava. "Now you've got to recall troops. Tell him."

She pointed toward Marshal Dowell, scorning to look at the military commander directly.

"Your will, madam—" Dowell began with evident dislike.

"My *will* is that you station two regiments in the city at once, Marshal Dowell," Eunice Delcorio said with a voice that crackled like liquid oxygen flowing through a field of glass needles. "Or that you wait in the cells across the river until some successor of my husband chooses to release you."

"With your leave, sir," Dowell huffed in the direction of the President.

The Marshal was angry now, and it wasn't the earlier flashing of someone playing dangerous political games with his peers. He was lapsing into the normal frustration of a professional faced with laymen who didn't understand why he couldn't do something they thought was reasonable.

"Madam," Dowell continued with a bow to Eunice Delcorio, "your will impresses me, but it doesn't magically make transport for three thousand men and their equipment available on Two. It doesn't provide rations and accommodations for them here. And if executed with no more consideration than I've been able to give it in this room, away from my staff, it will almost certainly precipitate the very disasters that concern you."

"You—" Dowell went on.

"You—" Eunice Delcorio snapped.

"You—" the City Prefect shouted.

"You—" Father Laughlin interrupted weightily.

"You will all be silent!" said John Delcorio, and though the President did not appear to raise his voice to an exceptional level, none of the angry people squabbling in front of him continued to speak.

The two mercenary officers exchanged glances. It had occurred to both of them that any situation was salvageable if the man in charge retained the poise that President Delcorio was showing now.

"Gentlemen, Eunice," Delcorio said, articulating the thought the mercenaries had formed. "We are the *government*, not a mob of street brawlers. So long as we conduct ourselves calmly but firmly, this minor storm will be weathered and we will return to ordinary business."

He nodded to the priest. "And to the business of God, to the Crusade on Two. Father Laughlin, I trust that Bishop Trimer will take *all* necessary precautions to prevent his name from being used by those who wish to stir up trouble?"

Delcorio's voice was calm, but nobody in the room doubted how intense the reaction might be if the priest did not respond properly.

"Of course, President Delcorio," Laughlin said, bowing low.

There was a slight motion on the western edge of the room as a door opened to pass a big woman floating in a gown of white chiffon. She wasn't announced by a greeter, and she made very little stir at this juncture in the proceedings as she slipped through the room to stand near Eunice Delcorio.

"Lord Berne," Delcorio continued to his tall prefect, "I expect your police to take prompt, firm action wherever trouble erupts." His eyes were piercing.

"Yes sir," Berne said, his willing enthusiasm pinned by his master's fierce gaze. Alone of the civilians in the room, he owed everything he had to his position in the government. The richness of his garments showed just how much he had acquired in that time.

"I've already done that," he explained. "I've canceled leaves and my men have orders that all brawling is to be met with overwhelming force and the prisoners jailed. I've suspended normal release procedures for the duration of the emergency also."

Berne hesitated as the implications of what he had just announced struck him anew. "Ah, in accordance with your previous directions, sir. And your assurance that additional support would be available from the army as required."

Nobody spoke. The President nodded as he turned slowly to his military commander and said, "Marshal, I expect you to prepare for the transfer of two regular regiments back to the vicinity of the capital."

Dowell did not protest, but his lips pursed.

"*Prepare*, Marshal," Delcorio repeated harshly. "Or do you intend to inform me that you're no longer fit to perform your duties?"

"Sir," Dowell said. "As you order, of course."

"And you will further coordinate with the City Prefect so that the Executive Guard is ready to support the police if and when I order it?"

Not a command but a question, and a fierce promise of what would happen if the wrong answer were given.

"Yes sir," Marshal Dowell repeated. "As you order." Berne was nodding and rubbing his hands together as if trying to return life to them after a severe chill.

"Then, gentlemen . . ." Delcorio said, with warmth and a smile as engaging as his visage moments before had threatened. "I believe we can dismiss this gathering. Father Laughlin, convey my regrets to the Bishop that he couldn't be present, but that I trust implicitly his judgment as to how best to return civil life to its normal calm."

The priest bowed again and turned toward the door. He was not the same man in demeanor as the one who had entered the meeting, emphasizing his importance by blatantly displaying his bodyguards.

"Praise the Lord," Tyl muttered, more to himself than to Major Borodin. "I've been a lotta places I liked better 'n this one—and some of them, people were shooting at me."

Nodding to take his leave of the UDB officer, Tyl started for the door that was already being opened from the outside.

"Lieutenant Desoix of United Defense Batteries," the greeter announced.

"You there," Eunice Delcorio called in a throaty contralto—much less shrill than her previous words had led Tyl to imagine her ordinary voice would be. "Captain Koopman. Wait a moment."

Father Laughlin was already out of the room. Borodin was bearing down on his subordinate with obvious wrath that Desoix prepared to meet with a wry smile.

Everybody else looked at Tyl Koopman.

She'd gotten his name and rank right, he thought as his skin flashed hot and his mind stumbled over itself wondering what to say, what she wanted, and why in *blazes* Colonel Hammer had put him in this bucket. He was a *line* officer and this was a job for the bloody staff.

"Yes, ma'am," he said aloud, turning toward his questioner. His eyes weren't focusing right because of the unfamiliar strain, so he was seeing the President's wife as a fiery blur beneath an imperious expression.

"How many men are there under your command, Captain?" Eunice continued. There was no hostility in her voice, only appraisal. It was the situation that was freezing Tyl's heart having to answer questions on this level, rather than the way in which the questions were being asked.

"Ma'am, ah?" he said. What had Scratchard told him as they walked along the levee? "Ma'am, there's about a hundred men here. That's twenty or so in the base establishment, and the rest the transit unit that, you know, I'll be taking to Two in a few days."

"No," the woman said, coolly but in a voice that didn't even consider the possibility of opposition. "We certainly aren't sending any troops away, now."

"Yes, that's right," Delcorio agreed.

A tic brushed the left side of the President's face. The calm with which he had concluded the meeting was based on everything going precisely as he had choreographed it in his mind. Eunice was adding something to the equation, and even something as minor as that was dangerous to his state of mind if he hadn't foreseen it.

"Ah . . ." said Tyl. "I'll need to check with Cen—"

"Well, *do* it, then!" Delcorio blazed. "Do I need to be bothered with details that a *corporal* ought to be able to deal with?"

"Yes *sir!*" said the Slammers officer.

He threw the President a salute because it felt right.

And because that was a good opening to spinning on his heel and striding rapidly toward the door, on his way *out* of this room.

CHAPTER EIGHT

Headquarters and billets for the enlisted men of Battery D were in a basement room of the Palace of Government, converted to the purpose from a disused workers' cafeteria. Desoix sighed to see it again, knowing that here his superior would let out the anger he had bottled up while the two of them stalked through hallways roamed by folk from outside the unit.

Control, the artificial intelligence/communications center, sat beside a wall that had been pierced for conduits to antennas on the roof. It was about a cubic meter of electronics packed into thirty-two resin-black modules, some of them redundant.

Control directed the battery in combat because no human reactions were fast enough to deal with hypersonic missiles—though the calliopes, pulsing with light-swift violence, could rip even those from the sky if their tubes were slewed in the right direction.

The disused fixtures were piled at one end of the room. Control's waste heat made the room a little warmer, a little drier; but the place still reminded Desoix of basements in too many bombed-out cities.

Major Borodin pulled shut the flap of the curtain which separated his office from the bunks on which the off-duty shift was relaxing or trying to sleep. In theory, the curtain's microprocessors formed adaptive ripples in the fabric and canceled sounds. In practice—

Well, it didn't work that badly. And if you're running an eighty-man unit in what now had to be considered combat conditions, you'd better figure your troops were going to learn what was going on no matter how you tried to conceal it.

"You should have called in at once!"the battery commander said, half furious, half disappointed, like a parent whose daughter has come home three hours later than expected.

"I needed you at that meeting," he added, the anger replaced by desperate memory. "I . . . you know, Charles, I never know what to say to them up there. We're supposed to be defending the air space here, not mixed up in riots."

"I got a good look at that this morning, Sergei," Desoix said quietly. He seated himself carefully on the collapsible desk and, by his example, urged Borodin into the only chair in the curtained-off corner. "I think we need to reposition Gun Three. It's too close to where—things are going on. Some of our people are going to get hurt."

Borodin shook his craggy head abruptly. "We can't do that," he said. "Coverage."

"Now that Five's back on-planet—" Desoix began.

"You were with that woman, weren't you?" Borodin said, anger hardening his face as if it were concrete setting. "That's really why you didn't come to me when I needed you. I *saw* her slip in just before you did."

Yes, Daddy, Desoix thought. But Borodin was a good man to work for—good enough to humor.

"Sergei," he said calmly, "now that we've got a full battery again, I can readjust coverage areas. We can handle the seafront from the suburbs east and west, I'm pretty—"

"Charles, you're going to get into really terrible trouble," Borodin continued, his voice now sepulchral. "Get us all into trouble."

He looked up at his subordinate and added, "Now, I was younger too, I understand . . . But believe me, boy, there's plenty of it going around on a businesslike basis. And that's a *curst* sight safer."

Desoix found himself getting angry—and that made him even angrier, at himself, because it meant that Anne mattered to him.

Who you screwed wasn't nearly as dangerous as caring about her.

"Look," he said, hiding the edge in his voice but unable to eliminate the tremble. "I just shook a calliope loose on Merrinet, and it cost the unit less than three grand plus my transportation. I *solve* pro—"

"You paid a fine?"

"Via, no! I didn't pay a fine," Desoix snapped.

Shifting into a frustrated and disappointed tone of his own—a good tactic in this conversation, but exactly the way Desoix was really feeling at the moment also—he continued, "Look, Sergei, I bribed the Customs inspectors to switch manifests. The gun was still being held in the transit warehouse, there wasn't a police locker big enough for a calliope crated for shipment. If I'd pleaded it through the courts, the gun would be on Merrinet when we were old and gray. I—"

He paused, struck by a sudden rush of empathy for the older man.

Borodin was a fine combat officer and smart enough to find someone like Charles Desoix to handle the subtleties of administration that the major himself could never manage. But though he functioned ably as battery commander, he was as lost in the job's intricacies as a man in a snowstorm. Having an executive officer to guide him made things safe—until they weren't safe, and he wouldn't know about the precipice until he plunged over it.

Desoix was just as lost in the way he felt about Lady Anne McGill; and, unlike Borodin, he didn't even have a guide.

He gripped Borodin's hand. "Sergei," he said, "I won't ask you to trust me. But I'll ask you to trust me not to do anything that'll hurt the battery. All right?"

Their eyes met. Borodin's face worked in a moue that was as close to assent as he was constitutionally able to give to the proposition.

"Then let's get back to business," Charles Desoix said with a bright smile. "We need to get a crew to Gun Five for setup, and then we'll have to juggle duty rosters for permanent manning—unless we can get Operations to send us half a dozen men from Two to bring us closer to strength."

Borodin was nodding happily as his subordinate outlined ordinary problems with ordinary solutions.

Desoix just wished that he could submerge his own concerns about what he was doing.

CHAPTER NINE

"Locked on," said the mechanical voice of Command Central in Tyl's ears. "Hold f—"

There was a wash of static as the adaptive optics of the satellite failed to respond quickly enough to a disturbance in the upper atmosphere.

"—or soft input," continued the voice from Colonel Hammer's headquarters, the words delayed in orbit while the antenna corrected itself.

The air on top of the City Office building was still stirred by the fans of aircars moving to and from the parking area behind. Their numbers had dropped off sharply since the last remnants of the riot were dispersed. In the twilight, it was easier to smell the saltiness from the nearby sea—or else the breezes three stories up carried scents trapped in the alleys lower down.

The bright static across Tyl's screen coalesced into a face, recognizable as a woman wearing a commo helmet like Tyl's own. Noise popped in his earphones for almost a second while her lips moved on the screen—the transmissions were at slightly different frequencies. Then her voice said, "Captain Koopman, how secure are these communications on your end?"

"Ma'am?" Tyl said, too recently back from furlough not to treat the communicator as a woman instead of an enlisted man. "I'm using a portable laser from the top of the police station. It's—I think it's pretty safe, but if the signal's a problem, I can use—"

"Hold one, Captain," the communicator said with a grin of sorts. Her visage blanked momentarily in static again.

A forest of antennas shared the roof of the building with the Slammers officer: local, regional, and satellite communications gear. Instead of borrowing a console within to call Central, Tyl squatted on gritty concrete.

His ten-kilo unit included a small screen, a twenty centimeter rectenna that did its best to align itself with Hammer's satellites above, and a laser transmitting unit which probably sent Central as fuzzy a signal as Tyl's equipment managed to receive.

But you can't borrow commo without expecting the folks who loaned it to be listening in; and if Tyl did have to stay in Bamberg City with the transit detachment, he didn't want the locals to know that he'd been begging Central to withdraw him.

The screen darkened into a man's face. "Captain Koopman?" said the voice in his helmet. "I appreciate your sense of timing. I'm glad to have an experienced officer overseeing the situation there at the moment."

"Sir!" Tyl said, throwing a salute that was probably out of the restricted field of the pickup lens.

"Give me your appraisal of the situation, Captain," said the voice of Colonel Alois Hammer. His flat-surface image wobbled according to the vagaries of the upper atmosphere.

"At the moment . . ." Tyl said. He looked away from the screen in an unconscious gesture to gain some time for his thoughts.

The House of Grace towered above him. At the top of the high wall was the visage of Bishop Trimer enthroned. The prelate's eyes were as hard as the stone in which they were carved.

"At the moment, sir, it's quiet," Tyl said to the screen. "The police cracked down hard, arrested about fifty people. Since then—"

"Leaders?" interrupted the helmet in its crackling reproduction of the colonel's voice. Hammer's eyes were like light-struck diamonds, never dull—never quite the same.

"Brawlers, street toughs," Tyl said contemptuously. "A lot of 'em, is all. But it's been quiet, and . . ."

He paused because he wasn't sure how far he ought to stick his neck out with no data, not really—but his commanding officer waited expectantly on the other end of the satellite link.

"Sir," Tyl said, determined to do the job he'd been set, even though this stuff scared him in a different way from a firefight. There he *knew* what he was supposed to do. "Sir, I haven't been here long enough to know what's normal, but the way it feels out there now . . ."

He looked past the corner of the hospital building and down

into the plaza. Many of the booths were still set up and a few were lighted—but not nearly enough to account for the numbers of people gathering there in the twilight. It was like watching gas pool in low spots, mixing and waiting for the spark that would explode it.

"The only places I been that felt like this city does now are night positions just before somebody hits us."

"Rate the players, Captain," said Hammer's voice as his face on the screen flickered and dimmed with the lights of an aircar whining past, closer to the roof than it should have been for safety.

The vehicle was headed toward the plaza. Its red and white emergency flashers were on, but the car's idling pace suggested that they were only a warning.

As if *he* knew anything about this sort of thing, Tyl thought bitterly. But the colonel was right, he could give the same sort of assessment that any mercenary officer learned to do of the local troops he was assigned to support. It didn't really matter that these weren't wearing uniforms.

Some of them weren't wearing uniforms.

"Delcorio's hard but he's brittle," Tyl said aloud. "He'd do all right with enough staff to take the big shocks, but what he's got . . ."

He paused, collecting his thoughts further. Hammer did not interrupt, but the fluctuation of his image on the little screen reminded Tyl that time was passing.

"All right," the Slammers captain continued. "The police, they seem to be holding up pretty well. Berne, the City Prefect, don't have any friends and I don't guess much support. On that end, it's gone about as far as it can and keep the lid on."

Hammer was nodding, but Tyl ignored that too. He had his data marshalled, now, and he needed to spit things out while they were clear to him. "The army, Dowell at least, he's afraid to move and he's not afraid not to move. He won't push anything himself, but Delcorio won't get much help from there.

"And the rest of 'em, the staffs—" Tyl couldn't think of the word the group had been called here "—they're nothing, old men and young kids, nobody that matters . . . ah, except the wife, you know, sir? Ah, Lady Eunice. Only she wants to push harder than

I think they can push here with what they got and what they got against 'em."

"The mob?" prompted the colonel. Static added a hiss to words without sibilants.

Tyl looked toward the plaza. The sky was still blue over the western horizon, behind the cathedral's dome and the Palace of Government. The sunken triangle of the plaza was as dark as a volcano's maw, lighted only by the sparks of lanterns and apparently open flames.

"Naw, not the mobs," Tyl said, letting his helmet direct his voice while his eyes gathered data instead of blinking toward his superior. "Them, they'd handle each other if it wasn't any more. But—"

He looked up. The sunset slid at an angle across the side of the House of Grace. The eyes of Bishop Trimer's carven face were as red as blood.

"Sir," Tyl blurted, "it's the Church behind it, the Bishop, and he's going to walk off with the whole thing soon unless Delcorio's luckier 'n anybody's got a right to expect. I think—"

No, say it right.

"Sir," he said, "I recommend that all regimental forces be withdrawn from Bamberg City at once, to avoid us being caught up in internal fighting. There are surface-effect freighters at the port right now. With your authorization, I'll charter one immediately and have the unit out of here in three hours."

Two hours, unless he misjudged the willingness and efficiency of the sergeant major; but he'd promise what he was sure of and surprise people later by bettering the offer if he could.

Hammer's lips moved. Tyl thought that the words were delayed by turbulence, but the colonel was only weighing what he was about to say before he put it into audible syllables. After a moment, the voice and fuzzy screen said in unison, "Captain, I'm going to tell you what my problem is."

Tyl's lungs filled again. He'd been holding his breath unknowingly, terrified that his colonel was about to strip him of his rank for saying too much, saying the wrong thing. Anything else, that was all right. . . .

Even command problems that weren't any business of a captain in the line.

"Our contract," Hammer said carefully, "is with the government of Bamberia, not precisely with President Delcorio."

The image of the screen glared as if reading on Tyl's face the interjection his subordinate would never have spoken aloud. "The difference is the sort that only matters in formal proceedings—like a forfeiture hearing before the Bonding Authority, determining whether or not the Regiment has upheld its end of the contract."

"Yes *sir*!" Tyl said.

Hammer's face lost its hard lines. For a moment, Tyl thought that the hint of grayness was more than merely an artifact of the degraded signal.

"There's a complication," the colonel said with a precision that erased all emotional content from the statement. "Bishop Trimer has been in contact with the Eagle wing Division regarding taking over conduct of the Crusade in event of a change of government."

He shrugged. "My sources," he added needlessly. "It's a small community, in a way."

Then, with renewed force and no hint of the fatigue of moments before, Hammer went on, "In event of Trimer taking over, as you accurately estimated was his intention, we're out of work. That's not the end of the world, and I *certainly* don't want any of my men sacrificed pointlessly—"

"No *sir*," Tyl barked in response to the fierceness in his commander's face.

"—but I need to know whether a functional company like yours might be able to give Delcorio the edge he needs."

Hammer's voice asked, but his eyes demanded. "Stiffen Dowell's spine, give Trimer enough of a wild card to keep him from making his move before the Crusade gets under way and whoever's in charge won't be able to replace units that're already engaged."

And do it, Tyl realized, without a major troop movement that could be called a contract violation by Colonel Hammer, acting against the interests of a faction of his employers.

It might make a junior captain—acting on his own initiative—guilty of mutiny, of course.

"Sir," Tyl said crisply, vibrant to know that he had orders now that he could understand and execute. "We'll do the job if it can be done. Ripper Jack's a good man, cursed good. I don't know the others yet, most of 'em, but it's three-quarters veterans back from furlough and only a few newbie recruits coming in."

"Understand me, Captain," Hammer said—again fiercely. "I *don't* want you to become engaged in fighting unless it's necessary for your own safety. There aren't enough of you to make any difference if the lid really comes off, and I *won't* throw away good men just to save a contract. But if your being in the capital keeps President Delcorio in power for another two weeks . . . ?"

"Yes *sir*!" Tyl repeated brightly, marvelling that his commander seemed relieved at his reaction. Via, he was an officer of Hammer's Slammers, wasn't he? Of *course* he'd be willing to carry out orders that were perfectly clear—or as clear as combat orders ever could be.

Keep the men in battledress and real visible; hint to Dowell that there was a company of panzers waiting just over the horizon to land and *really* kick butt as soon as he said the word. Make waves at the staff meetings. They couldn't bother him now with their manners and fancy clothes.

The colonel had told Tyl Koopman what to do, and a few rich fops weren't going to affect the way he did it.

"Then carry on, Captain," Hammer said with a punctuation of static in the middle of the words that did not disguise the pleasure in his voice. "There's a lot—"

The sky was a lighter gray than the ground or the sea, but the sun had fully set. The cyan flash of a powergun lanced the darkness like a scream in silence.

"Hold!" Tyl shouted to his superior, rising from his crouch to get a better view past the microwave dish beside him.

A volley of bolts spat from at least half a dozen locations in the plaza. The orbiting police aircar staggered and lifted away. Its plastic hull had been hit. The driver's desperate attempt to increase speed fanned the flames to sluggish life; a trail of smoke marked the vehicle's path.

A huge roar came from the crowd in the plaza. Led by a line of torches and light wands, it crawled like a living thing up both the central and eastern stairs.

They weren't headed for the Palace of Government across the river. They were coming here.

Tyl flipped his helmet's manual switch to the company frequency. "Sar'ent Major," he snapped, "all men in combat gear and ready t' move *soonest*! Three days rations and all the ammo we can carry."

He switched back to the satellite push and began folding the screen—not essential to the transmission while the face of Colonel Alois Hammer still glowed on it with tigerish intensity.

"Sir," Tyl said without any emotion to waste on the way he was closing his report, "I'll tell you more when I know more."

Then he collapsed the transceiver antenna. Hammer didn't have anything as important to say as the mob did.

CHAPTER TEN

The mob was pulsing toward the City Offices like the two heads of a flood surge. Powergun bolts spiked out of the mass, some aimed at policemen but many were fired at random.

That was the natural reaction of people with the opportunity to destroy something—an ability which carries its own imperatives. Tyl wasn't too worried about that, not if he had his men armed and equipped before they and the mob collided.

But when he clumped down the stairs from the trap door in the roof, he threw a glance over his shoulder. The north doors of the House of Grace had opened, disgorging men who marched in ground-shaking unison as they sang a Latin hymn.

That was real bad for President Delcorio, for Colonel Hammer's chances of retaining his contract—

And possibly real bad for Tyl Koopman and the troops in his charge.

The transit detachment was billeted on the second floor, in what was normally the turn-out room. Temporary bunks, three-high, meant the troops on the top layer couldn't sit up without bumping the ceiling. What floor space the bunks didn't fill was covered by the foot-lockers holding the troops' personal gear.

Now most of the lockers had been flung open and stood in the disarray left by soldiers trying to grab one last valuable—a watch; a holoprojector; a letter. They knew they might never see their gear again.

For that matter, they knew that the gear was about as likely to survive the night as they themselves were—but you had to act as if you were going to make it.

Sergeant Major Scratchard stumped among the few troopers still in the bunk room, slapping them with a hand that rang on their ceramic helmets. "Move!" he bellowed with each blow. "It's yer *butts*!"

If the soldier still hesitated with a fitting or to grab for one more bit of paraphernalia, Scratchard gripped his shoulder and spun him toward the door. As Tyl stuck his head into the room, a female soldier with a picture of her father crashed off the jamb beside him, cursing in a voice that was a weapon itself.

"All clear, sir," Scratchard said as the last pair of troopers scampered for the door ahead of him, geese waddling ahead of a keeper with a ready switch. "Kekkonan's running the arms locker, he's a good man."

Tyl used the pause to fold the dish antenna of his laser communicator. The sergeant major glanced at him. He said in a voice as firm and dismissing as the one he'd been using on his subordinates, "Dump that now. We don't have time fer it."

"I'll gather 'em up outside," Tyl said. "You send 'em down to me, Jack."

He clipped the communicator to his equipment belt. Alone of the detachment, he didn't have body armor. Couldn't worry about that now.

The arms locker, converted from an interrogation room, was next door to the bunk room. The hall was crowded with troopers waiting to be issued weapons and those pushing past, down the stairs with armloads of lethal hardware that they would organize in the street where there was more space.

Tyl joined the queue thumping its way downstairs. As he did so, he glanced over his shoulder and called, "We'll *have* time, Sar'ent Major. And by the Lord! We'll have a secure link to Central when we do."

CHAPTER ELEVEN

For a moment, the exterior of the City Offices was lighted by wall sconces as usual. A second or two after Tyl stepped from the door into the bulk of his troops, crouching as they awaited orders, the sconces, the interior lights, and all the streetlights visible on the east side of the river switched off.

There was an explosion louder than the occasional popping of slug throwers in the distance. A transformer installation had been blown up or shorted into self-destruction.

That made the flames, already painting the low clouds pink, more visible.

A recruit turned on his hand light. The veteran beside him snarled, "Fuckhead! Use infrared on your helmet shield!"

The trooper on the recruit's other side—more direct—slapped the light away and crushed it beneath her boot.

"Sergeants to me," Tyl ordered on the unit push. He flashed momentarily the miniature lightwand that he carried clipped to a breast pocket—for reading and for situations like this, when his troops needed to know where he was.

Even at the risk of drawing fire when he showed them.

He hadn't called for noncoms, because the men here were mostly veterans with a minimum of the five-years service that qualified them for furlough. Seven sergeants crawled forward, about what Tyl had expected and enough for his purposes.

"Twelve-man squads," he ordered, using his commo helmet instead of speaking directly to the cluster of sergeants. That way all his troops would know what was happening.

As much as Tyl did himself, at any rate.

"Gather 'em fast, no screwing around. We're going to move as soon as everybody's clear." He looked at the sergeants, their face shields down, just as his was—a collection of emotionless balls, and all of them probably as worried as he was: worried about what they knew was coming, and more nervous yet about all the things that might happen in darkness, when nobody at all knew which end was up.

"And no shooting, troopers. Unless we got to."

If they had to shoot their way out, they were well and truly screwed. Just as Colonel Hammer had said—there weren't enough of them to matter a fart in a whirlwind if it came down to that.

A pair of emergency vehicles—fire trucks swaying with the weight of the water on board them—roared south along the river toward the City Offices. A huge block of masonry hurtled from the roof of an apartment building just up the street. Tyl saw its arc silhouetted against the pink sky for a moment.

The stone hit the street with a crash and half-bounced, and half-rolled, into the path of the lead truck. The fire vehicle slewed to the side, but its wheels weren't adequate to stabilize the kiloliters of water in its ready-use tank. The truck went over and skidded, rotating on its side in sparks and the scream of tortured metal— even before its consort rammed it from behind.

Someone began to fire a slug thrower from the roof. The trucks were not burning yet, but a stray breeze brought the raw, familiar odor of petroleum fuel to the hunching Slammers.

There wasn't anything in Hell worse than street fighting in somebody else's city—

And Tyl, like most of the veterans with him, had done it often enough to be sure of that.

A clot of soldiers stumbled out the doorway. Scratchard was the last, unrecognizable for a moment because of the huge load of equipment he carried.

Looked as if he'd staggered out with everything the rest of the company had left in the arms locker, Tyl thought. A veteran like Jack Scratchard should've known to—

Reinforced windows blew out of the second floor with a cyan flash, a bang, and a deep orange *whoom!* that was simultaneously a sound and a vision. The sergeant major hadn't tried to empty the arms locker after all.

"Put this on, sir," Scratchard muttered to the captain as the fire trucks up the street ignited in the spray of burning fragments hurled from the demolition of the Slammers' excess stores. The actinics of the powergun ammunition detonating in its storage containers made exposed skin prickle, but the exploding gasoline pushed at the crouching men with a warm, stinking hand.

Roof floodlights, driven by the emergency generator in the basement, flared momentarily around the City Offices. Shadows pooled beneath the waiting troops. They cursed and ducked lower— or twisted to aim at the lights revealing them.

Volleys of shots from the mob shattered the lenses before any of the Slammers made up their minds to shoot. The twin pincers, from the plaza and from the House of Grace, were already beginning to envelope the office building.

The route north and away was awash in blazing fuel. The police aircar that roared off that way, whipping the flames with its vectored thrust, pitched bow-up and stalled as an automatic weapon raked it from the same roof as the falling masonry had come.

Scratchard had brought a suit of clamshell body armor for Tyl to wear—and a submachine-gun to carry along with a bandolier holding five hundred rounds of ammo in loaded magazines.

"We're crossing the river," Tyl said in a voice that barely danced on the spikes of his present consciousness. "By squad."

He hadn't gotten around to numbering the squads. There was a clacking sound as the sergeant major latched Tyl's armor for him.

Tyl pointed at one of the sergeants—he didn't know *any* bloody names!—with his lightwand. "You first. And you. Next—"

In the pause, uncertain in the backlit darkness where the other noncoms were, Scratchard broke in on the command frequency saying, "Haskins, third. Hu, Pescaro, Bogue, and Hagemann. Move, you dickheads!"

Off the radio, his head close to Tyl's as the captain clipped his sling reflexively to the epaulet tab of his armor and shrugged the heavy bandolier over the opposite shoulder, the sergeant major added, "You lead 'em, sir—I'll hustle their butts from here."

Even as Tyl opened his mouth to frame a reply, Scratchard barked at one of the men who'd appeared just ahead of him, "Kekkonan—you give 'im a hand with names if he needs it, right?"

Sergeant Kekkonan, short and built like one of the tanks he'd commanded, clapped Tyl on the shoulder hard enough that it was just as well the captain had already started in the direction of the thrust—toward the river and the squad running toward the levee wall as swiftly as their load of weapons and munitions permitted.

A column of men came around the northern corner of the building. Their white tunics rippled orange in the glare of the burning vehicles. The leaders carried staffs as they had when they guarded the procession route, but in the next rank back winked the iridium barrels of powerguns and the antennas of sophisticated communications gear.

They were no more than three steps from the nearest of the nervous Slammers. When the leading orderlies shouted and threw themselves out of the way, there were almost as many guns pointed at the troops as pointed by them.

"*Hold!*" Tyl Koopman ordered through his commo helmet as his skin chilled and his face went stiff. Almost they'd made it, but now—

He was running toward the mob of orderlies—Via! *They* weren't a mob!—with his hands raised, palms forward.

"This isn't our fight!" he cried, hoping he was close enough to the orderlies to be understood by them as well as by the troops on his unit push. "Squads, keep moving—over the levee!"

The column of orderlies had stopped and flattened like the troops they were facing, but there were three men erect at the new head of the line. One carried a shoulder-pack radio; one a bull-horn; and the man in the middle was a priest with a crucifix large enough to be the standard that the whole column followed.

Tyl looked at the priest, wondering if he could grab the butt of his slung weapon fast enough to take some of them with him if the words the priest murmured to the man with the bull-horn brought a blast of shots from the guns aimed at the Slammers captain.

The burning trucks roared. Sealed parts ruptured with plosive sounds and an occasional sharp crack.

"Go on, get out of here," the bull-horn snarled, its crude amplification making the words even harsher than they were when they came from the orderly's throat.

Tyl spun and brandished his lightwand. "Third Squad," he ordered. "Move!"

A dozen of his troopers picked themselves up from the ground and shambled across the street behind him—toward the guns leveled on the mob from the levee's top. The first two squads were deployed there with the advantages of height and a modicum of cover if any of the locals needed a lesson about what it meant to take on Hammer's Slammers.

Tyl's timing hadn't been quite as bad as he'd thought. Hard to tell just what might have happened if the column from the House of Grace had arrived before Tyl's company had a base of fire across the street.

Two more squads were moving together. The leaders of the mob's other arm, bawling their way up the river road, had already reached the south corner of the City Offices. The cries of *"Freedom, Freedom!"* were suddenly punctuated with screams as a dozen or so of the leaders collapsed under a burst of electrostatic needles fired by one of the policemen inside.

Tyl heard the shots that answered the stunner, slug throwers as well as powerguns, but the real measure of the response was the barely audible clink of bottles shattering.

Then the gasoline bombs ignited and silhouetted the building from the south.

Tyl stood on the pedestrian way atop the levee, wondering when somebody would get around to taking a shot at him just because he *was* standing.

"Three and four," he ordered as the heavily laden troops scrambled up the steps to join him. "Across the river, climb over the barges. Kekkonan, you lead 'em, set up a perimeter on the other side.

"And *wait!*" he added, though Kekkonan didn't look like the sort you had to tell that to.

The rest of the company was moving in a steady stream, lighted between the two fires of the trucks and the south front of the building they had abandoned.

"Take 'em across, take 'em across!" Tyl shouted as the Slammers plodded past. The noncoms would take the words as an order, and the rest of the troops would get the idea.

The first two squads squirmed as they waited, their guns now aimed toward both pincers of the mob. Fifty meters of the west frontage of the City Offices were clear of the rioters who would otherwise have lapped around it. It wasn't a formal standoff; just the tense waiting of male dogs growling as they sidled toward each other, not quite certain what the next seconds would bring.

The last man was Sergeant Major Scratchard, falling a further step behind his troops with every step he took.

"We're releasing the prisoners!" boomed the array of loud-speakers on the building roof. Simultaneous words from a dozen locations echoed themselves by the amount of time that sound from the mechanical diaphragms lagged behind the electronic pulses feeding them.

"Second Squad, withdraw," Tyl ordered. He felt as if his load of gear had halved in weight when the eyes of the rioters, orange flecks lighted by the fires of their violence, turned away from him and his men to stare at the City Offices.

Tyl jumped back down the steps and put his left arm—the submachine-gun was under his right armpit—around the sergeant major's chest. Scratchard weighed over a hundred kilos, only a little of it in the gut that had expanded with his desk job. Tyl's blood jumped with so much adrenalin that he noticed only Scratchard's inertia—not his weight.

"Lemme go!" Scratchard rasped in a voice tight with the ache in his knees.

"Shut the hell up!" Tyl snarled back. The laser communicator was crushed between them, biting both men's thighs. If he'd had a hand free, he'd have thrown the cursed thing against the concrete levee.

The mob's chanted "Freedom!" gave way suddenly to a long bellow, loud and growing like a peal of thunder. Tyl's back was to the City Offices, and the rolling triumph had started on the far side anyway, where the jail entrance opened onto the parking area. He knew what was happening, though.

And he knew, even before the shouts turned to "*Kill* them! *Kill* them!" that this mob wasn't going to be satisfied with freeing their fellows.

Likely the police trapped inside the building had known that too; but they didn't have any better choices either.

"You, give us a hand!" Tyl ordered as he and Scratchard stumbled toward the railing across the walkway. He pointed to the nearest trooper with the gun that filled his right hand. She jumped to her feet and took the sergeant major's other arm while Tyl boomed over the radio, "First Squad, withdraw. Kekkonan, make sure you've got us covered."

The river here was half a kilometer wide between the levees, but with night sights and powerguns, trained men could sweep the far walkway clear if some of the rioters decided it'd be safe to pursue.

The river had fallen more than a meter since Tyl viewed it six hours before. The barges still floated a safe jump beneath the inner walkway of the levee—but not safe for Jack Scratchard with a load of gear.

"Gimme my arms free," the sergeant major ordered.

Tyl nodded and stepped away with the trooper on the other side. Scratchard gripped the railing with both hands and swung himself over. He crouched on the narrow lip, choosing his support, and lowered himself onto the hogsheads with which the barge was loaded. The troopers waiting to help the senior noncom had the sense to get out of the way.

"I'm fine now," Scratchard grunted. "Let's move!"

The barges were moored close, but there was enough necessary slack in the lines that some of them were over a meter apart while their rubber bumpers squealed against those of the vessel on the opposite flank. Tyl hadn't thought the problem through, but Kekkonan or one of the other sergeants had stationed pairs of troopers at every significant gap. They were ready to guide and help lift later-comers over the danger.

"Thank the Lord," Tyl muttered as four strong arms boosted him from the first barge to the next in line. He wasn't sure whether he meant for the help or for the realization that the men he commanded were as good as anybody could pray.

CHAPTER TWELVE

Charles Desoix wore a commo helmet to keep in touch with his unit, but he was looking out over Bamberg City with a handheld image intensifier instead of using the integral optics of the helmet's face shield. The separate unit gave him better illumination, crisper details. He held the imager steady by resting his elbows on the rail of the porch outside the Consistory Room, overlooking the courtyard and beyond—

The railing jiggled as someone else leaned against it, bouncing Desoix's forty-magnification image of a window in the City Office building off his screen.

"*Lord* cur—" Desoix snarled as he spun. He wasn't the sort to slap the clumsy popinjay whom he assumed had disturbed him, but he was willing to give the contrary impression at the moment.

Anne McGill was at the rail beside him.

"They told me—" Desoix blurted.

"Yes, but I couldn't—" Anne said, both of them trying to cover the angry outburst that would disappear from reality if they pretended it hadn't occurred.

She'd closed the clear doors behind her, but Desoix could see into the Consistory Room. Enough light fell onto the porch to illuminate them for anyone looking in their direction.

He put his arms around Anne anyway, being careful not to gouge her back with a corner of the imaging unit. She didn't protest as he thought she might—but she gasped in surprise as her breasts flattened against her lover.

"Ah," Desoix said. "Yeah, I thought I'd wear my armor while I was out . . . Ah, maybe we ought to go inside."

"No," Anne said, squeezing him tighter. "Just hold me."

Desoix stroked her back with his free hand while the breeze brought screams and the smell of smoke from across the river.

His helmet hissed with the sound of a Situation Report. He'd programmed Control to call for a sitrep every fifteen minutes during the night. That was the only way you could be sure an outlying unit hadn't been wiped out before they could sound an alarm. . . .

That wasn't a way Charles Desoix liked to think. "Just a second, love," he muttered, blanking his mind of what the woman with her arms around him had started to say.

"Two to Control, all clear," a human voice said. "Over."

Gun Two was north of the city on a bluff overlooking the river. It had a magnificent field of fire—and there was very little development in the vicinity, which made it fairly safe in the present circumstances.

"Control to Three," said the emotionless artificial intelligence in the Palace basement. "Report, over."

The hollow sound of gasoline bombs igniting, deadened by the pillow of intervening air, accompanied the gush of fresh orange flames from across the river. One side of the City Offices was covered with crawling fire.

"Three t' Control," came the voice of Sergeant Blaney.

There was a whining noise behind the words, barely audible through the commo link. It nagged at Desoix's consciousness, but he couldn't quite remember. . . .

"It's all right here," the human voice continued, "but there's a lot of traffic in and out of the plaza. There's fires north of us, and there's shots all round."

The sergeant paused. He wasn't speaking to Control but rather in the hope that Borodin or Desoix were listening even without an alert—and that they'd do something about the situation.

"Nothing aimed at us, s' far as we can tell," Blaney concluded. "Over."

The mechanical whining had stopped some seconds before.

Men, lighted by petroleum flares in both directions, were headed from the City Offices to the adjacent levee. Desoix couldn't make out who they were without the imaging unit, but he had a pretty good idea.

His left hand massaged Anne McGill's shoulders, to calm her and calm himself as well. He reached for his helmet's commo key with his right hand, careful not to clash the two pieces of sophisticated hardware together, and said, "Blue to Three. Give me an azimuth on your gun, Blaney. Over."

Major Borodin was Red. With luck, he wasn't monitoring the channel just now.

Blaney hesitated, but he knew the XO could get the data from Control as easily—and that if Desoix asked, he already knew the answer even though Gun Three was far out of direct sight of the Palace of Government. "Sir," he said at last. "It's two-five-zero degrees. Over."

Normal rest position for Gun Three was 165° pointing out over Nevis Channel in the direction from which hostile ship-launched missiles were most likely to come. The crew had just re-aimed their weapon to cover the east stairs of the plaza. That was what *they* obviously thought was the most serious threat of their own well-being.

"Blue to Three," said Charles Desoix. "Out."

He wasn't down there with them, and he wasn't about to overrule their assessment of the situation from up here.

"Eunice is so angry," Anne McGill murmured. Communicating with the man beside her was as important to her state of mind as the strength of his arm around her shoulders. "I'm afraid, mostly—" and the simplicity of the statement belied its truth "—and so's John, I think, though it's hard to tell with him. But Eunice would like to hang them all, starting with the Bishop."

"Not going to be easy to do," Desoix said calmly while he adjusted the imager one-handed and prayed that it wouldn't show what he thought he saw in the shuddering flames.

It did. Men and women in police uniforms were being thrown

from the roof of the office building. They didn't fall far: just a meter or two, before they were halted jerking by the ropes around their necks.

Within the Consistory Room, voices burbled. Light brightened momentarily as someone turned up a wall sconce. It dimmed again as abruptly when common sense overcame a desire for gleaming surroundings.

The clear panels surrounding the circular room were shatter-proof vitril. They were supposed to stop bricks or a slug from any weapon a man could fire from his shoulder, and the layer of gold foil within the thermoplastic might even deflect a powergun bolt.

But only a fool would insist on testing them while he was on the other side of the panel. That kind of test was a likely result of making the Consistory Room a beacon on a night like this.

Anne straightened slightly when she heard the sounds in the room behind them, but she didn't move away as Desoix had expected her to do. "There!" she said in a sharp whisper, pointing down toward the river. "They're moving . . . They—are they coming for us?"

Desoix used both hands to steady the imager, though he kept the magnification down to ten power. The fuel fires provided quite a lot of light, and the low clouds scattered it broadly for the intensification circuits.

"Those are Hammer's men," the UDB officer said as the scene glowed saffron in the imager's field of view.

The troopers crossing the river on the barges moored there were foreshortened by the angle and flattened into two dimensions by the imaging circuitry, but there were a lot of them. Enough to be the whole unit, the Lord willing—and better the Slammers have the problems than United Defense Batteries.

Desoix's helmet said in Control's calm voice, "Captain Koopman of Hammer's Regiment has been calling the officer of the day on the general frequency. The OOD has not replied. Now Captain Koopman is calling you. Do you wish—"

"Patch him through," Desoix ordered. Anne's startled expression reminded him that she would think he was speaking to her, but there wasn't time to clear that up now.

"—warn the guards not to shoot at us?" came the voice of the Slammers captain he'd met just that morning. "I can't raise the bastards and I *don't* want any trouble."

"Desoix to Slammers, over?" the UDB officer said.

"Roger Desoix, over," Koopman responded instantly. The relief in the infantry captain's voice was as obvious as the threat in the previous phrase: if anybody started shooting at him and his men, he was planning to finish the job and worry later about the results.

"Tyl, I'm headed down to the front entrance right now," Desoix said. "It's quiet on this side, so don't let some recruit get nervous at the wrong time."

He'd lowered the imager and was stroking Anne's back fiercely with his free hand, feeling the soft cloth bunch and ripple over skin still softer. Her arm was around his hips, beneath the rim of his armor, caressing him as well. Hard to believe this was the woman who'd always refused to lie down on a bed with him, because if her hairdo was mussed, people might guess what she'd been doing.

Desoix turned and kissed her, vaguely amazed that the tension of the moment increased his sexual arousal instead of dampening it.

"Love," he said, and *meant* "love," for the first time in a life during which he'd used the word to a hundred woman on a score of planets. "I'm going downstairs for a moment. I'll be back soon, but wait inside."

Even as he kissed her warm lips again, he was moving toward the door and carrying the woman with him by the force of his arm as well as by his personality.

Desoix felt a moment's concern as he strode for the elevator across the circular room that he'd left his mistress to be spiked by the wondering eyes of the dozen or more men who stood in nervous clumps amidst the furniture. Anne was going to have to handle that herself, because he couldn't take her with him into what he was maybe getting into.

And if he didn't go, well—he didn't need what he'd heard in Tyl Koopman's voice to know how a company of Hammer's Slammers was going to respond if a bunch of parade-ground soldiers tried to bar their escape from a dangerous situation.

CHAPTER THIRTEEN

The way some of the Executive Guard in the rotunda were waving their weapons around would have bothered Desoix less if he'd believed the men involved had ever fired their guns deliberately. A couple of them might honestly not know the difference between the trigger and the safety catch, making the polished-marble room as dangerous as a foxhole at the sharp end of the front.

If Koopman's unit blew off the flood shutters and tossed in grenades, the rotunda was going to be as dangerous as an abattoir.

Captain Rene Sanchez must have been off-duty by now, but there were more guards in the rotunda than the usual detachment and he was among them.

"Rene," Desoix called cheerfully as he stepped off the elevator, noticing that the Bamberg officer had unlatched the flap covering his pistol. "I've come to give you a hand. We're getting some reinforcements, Hammer's men. They're on the way now."

Sanchez turned with a wild expression. "Nobody comes in or out," he said in a voice whose high pitch increased the effect of his eyes being focused somewhere close to infinity. The Guardsman was either drugged to a razor's edge, or his nerves unaided had honed him to the same dangerous state.

"We're going to take care of this, Rene," Desoix said, putting a friendly hand on Sanchez's shoulder.

The local man was quivering and it wasn't just fear. Sanchez was ready to go, go off in *any* direction. He was in prime shape to lead a night assault with knives and grenades—and he was just about as lethal as a live grenade, too.

You could never tell about the ones who'd never in their lives done anything real. They could react any way at all when the universe forced itself to their attention. About all a professional like Charles Desoix knew to expect was that he wouldn't like the result, whatever it turned out to be.

The Guard Commandant, Colonel Drescher, was present.

Arm in arm with Sanchez, the UDB officer walked toward him. Desoix had nodded to Drescher in the past, but they had never spoken.

"Colonel," he said, using Rene Sanchez and a brisk manner as his entree. "We've got some reinforcements coming in a few moments. I'm here to escort them in."

"Charles, I got a squad in the courtyard now," said Desoix's helmet. "Let's get a door open, all right? Over."

He didn't respond to Koopman's call, because the Guards colonel was saying, "You? UDB? I'm sorry, mister mercenary, the marshal has given orders that the shutters not be opened."

"I just came from Marshal Dowell in the Consistory Room," Desoix said, letting his voice rise as only control had kept it from doing earlier. The best way to play this was to pretend to be on the edge of blind panic. That wasn't so great a pretense as he would have wished.

"He *ordered* me down here to inform you," Desoix continued. He thought he'd glimpsed Dowell upstairs. Certainly that was possible, at any rate. "By the Lord! man. Do you realize what the marshal will do if you endanger him by keeping out his reinforcements? He'll have you—well, it's obvious."

The Guards colonel blinked. "Jorge Dowell doesn't give *me* orders!" he snapped, family pride overwhelming whatever trace of military obedience was in Drescher's makeup.

The Executive Guard was enough a law unto itself that Desoix had been sure that Drescher's references to army orders was misdirection—though Dowell might well have given such orders if anybody had bothered to ask him.

But because they hadn't . . . Desoix's present bluff wasn't beyond the realm of Dowell's possible response either.

"Still," Colonel Drescher continued. "Since you're here, we'll make an exception for courtesy's sake."

The waxen calm of his expression lapsed into gray fear for a moment. "But be quick, Lieutenant, or I swear I'll shut you out with them and the animals across the river."

Soldiers who'd been listening to the exchange touched the

undogging mechanism without orders, but they paused and drew back instead of engaging the gears to slide the shutters away.

"Well get on with it!" cried another voice.

One of the guards pressed the switch before Desoix's hand reached it; the UDB officer glanced at the speaker instead.

There were four men together. They were wearing civilian clothes now in place of the ornate uniforms they'd worn in the Consistory Room this morning and in days past. The considerable entourage behind them stretched beyond the rotunda: servants, very few of them real bodyguards—but most of the males were now armed with rifles and pistols which looked as though they came from government stores.

"Charles, how we holding?" came Tyl Koopman's voice through the commo helmet. "Over."

The words lacked the overtone of threat that had been in his earlier query. The Slammers could see or at least hear that a door was opening.

"Blue to Slammers," Desoix responded. He could feel a smile starting to twitch the corners of his mouth. "Just a second. There's some restructuring going on in here and we're, ah, making room for you in the guest quarters. Let these folks pass."

Desoix made sure that he was with the quartet of wealthy landholders as they forced their way through the door ahead of their servants.

"No, no," one of the men was saying to another. "My townhouse will have to take care of itself. I'm off to my estates to rally support for the President. I'll inform John of what I'm doing just as soon as I get there, but of course I couldn't waste time now with goodbyes."

Desoix thought for a moment that Captain Sanchez would step outside with him because that was the direction in which the Guards officer had last been pointed. Sanchez was lost in the turmoil, though, and Desoix stood alone beside the door as minor rats streamed out past him, following the lead of the noble rats they served.

Fires glowed against the cloud cover from at least a dozen directions in the city, not just the vicinity of the City Offices directly across the river. The smell of burning was more noticeable here than it had been on the porch six meters high.

Desoix looked up. The porch was a narrow roof above him. He couldn't tell from this angle whether Anne McGill had stayed inside as he'd ordered, or if she were out in the night again watching for him, watching for hope.

"You, sir," a soldier said with enough emphasis to make the question a demand. "You our UDB liaison?"

"Roger," Desoix said. "I'm—"

But the close-coupled soldier in Slammers battledress was already relaying the information on his unit frequency.

There were several dozen of Hammer's men in the courtyard already. More were arriving with every passing moment. He didn't see Captain Koopman or the sergeant major he'd met once or twice before Tyl had arrived to take command.

The troopers jogged across the open street, hunched over. When they reached the courtyard they slowed. The veterans swept the Palace's empty, shuttered walls with their eyes, waiting for the motion that would unmask gunports and turn the paved area into a killing ground unless they shot first.

The new recruits only stared, more confused than frightened but certainly frightened enough.

"They know something we don't?" asked the Slammers noncom with KEKKONAN stenciled on his helmet. He nodded in the direction of the servants, the last of whom were clearing the doorway.

"They know they're scared," Desoix said.

Kekkonan laughed. "That just shows they're breathin'," he said.

He grunted something into his commo helmet—waved left-handed to Desoix because his right hand was on the grip of his slung submachine-gun—and trotted into the rotunda with his troopers filing along after him.

The UDB officer had intended to lead the Slammers inside to avoid problems with the Bamberg guards. He hadn't moved quickly enough, but that wasn't likely to matter. Nobody with good sense was going to get in the way of *those* jacked-up killers.

Ornamental lighting still brightened the exterior of the Palace, though the steel-shuttered facade looked out of place in a glittering myriad of tiny spotlights. It illuminated well the stooped forms in khaki and gray ceramic armor as they arrived, jogging because their loads were too heavy for them to run faster.

There were six in the last group, four troopers carrying a fifth while Captain Tyl Koopman trotted along behind with a double load of guns and bandoliers.

Casualty, Desoix thought, but Sergeant Major Scratchard was cursing too fluently for anyone to think his wound was serious.

"Listen, you idiots," Scratchard said in a voice of sudden calm as the UDB officer ran up to help. "If you don't let me down now we're under the lights, I got no authority from here on out. Your choice, Cap'n."

"Right, we'll all walk from here," said Koopman easily. He handed one of the guns he carried to Scratchard while looking at Desoix. "Lieutenant," he added, "I'm about as glad to see you as I remember being."

Desoix looked over the other officer's shoulder toward the fires and shouts across the river. For a moment he thought it was his imagination that the sounds were coming closer.

Light flickering through the panels of the mall disabused him of his hopes. A torch-lit column was marching over the river. What the rioters had done to the City Offices suggested that they weren't headed for the cathedral now to pray for peace.

"Let's get inside," said Charles Desoix. "When this is all over, then you can thank me."

He didn't need to state the proviso: *assuming either of us is still alive.*

CHAPTER FOURTEEN

Tyl hadn't ridden in the little elevator off the back of the rotunda before. He and the UDB officer just about filled it, and neither of them was a big man.

Of course, in his armor and equipment Tyl wasn't the slim figure he would have cut in coveralls alone.

"Don't like to leave the guys before we know just what's happening here," he said aloud, though he was speaking as much to his own conscience as to the UDB officer beside him.

Tyl would have hated to be bolted behind steel shutters below, where the sergeant major was arranging temporary billets for the troops. The windowed Consistory Room was the next best thing to being outside—

And headed *away* from this Lord-stricken place!

"Up here is where we learn what's happening,"Desoix said reasonably, nodding toward the elevator's ceiling. "Or at least as much as anyone in the government knows," he added with a frown which echoed the doubt in his words.

The car stopped with only a faint burring from its magnetic drivers. The doors opened with less sound even than that. Tyl strode into the Consistory Room.

He was Colonel Hammer's representative and the ranking Slammer on this continent. So long as he remembered that, nobody else was likely to forget.

There were fewer people in the big room than there had been in the morning, but their degree of agitation made the numbers seem greater. Marshal Dowell was present with a pair of aides, but those three and the pair of mercenaries were the only men in uniform.

The Chastain brothers smiled with frozen enthusiasm when Tyl nodded to them. They wore dark suits of conservative cut—and of natural off-planet fabrics that gave them roughly the value of an aircar. Everyone else in the room was avoiding the Chastains. Backs turned whenever one of the twins attempted to make eye contact.

Berne, the City Prefect, didn't have even a twin for company. He huddled in the middle of the room like a clothes pole draped with the green velour of his state robe.

"Where are—" Tyl began, but he'd already lost his companion. Lieutenant Desoix was walking briskly toward the large-framed woman who seemed to be an aide to the President's wife. Neither the President nor Eunice Delcorio were here at—

Servants opened the door adjacent to the elevator. John Delcorio entered a step ahead of his wife, but only because of the narrowness of the portal. Eunice was again in a flame-red dress. This one was demure in the front but cut with no back at all and a skirt that stretched to allow her legs to scissor back and forth as she moved.

Tyl hadn't found a sexual arrangement satisfactory to him on the freighter that brought him to Bamberia, and there'd been no time to take care of personal business since he touched down. He felt a rush of lust. It was a little disconcerting under the circumstances—

But on the other hand, it was nice to be reminded that there was more to life than the sorts of things that'd been going on in the past few hours.

"You there!" President Delcorio said unexpectedly. He glared at Tyl, his black eyes glowing like coal in a coking furnace. "Do you have to wear *that*?"

Tyl glanced down at where Delcorio pointed with two stubby, sturdy fingers together.

"This?" said the Slammers officer. His submachine-gun hung from his right shoulder in a patrol sling that held it muzzle forward and grip down at his waist. He could seize it by reflex and spray whatever was in front of him without having to aim or think.

"Yessir," he explained. He spoke without concern, because it didn't occur to him that anyone might think he was offering insolence instead of information. "Example for the troops, you know. I told 'em nobody moved without a gun and bandolier— sleeping, eating, whatever."

Tyl blinked and looked back at the President. "Besides," he added. "I might *need it*, the way things are."

Delcorio flushed. Tyl realized that he and the President were on intersecting planes. Though the two of them existed in the same universe, almost none of their frames of reference were identical.

That was too bad. But it wasn't a reason for Tyl Koopman to change; not now, when it was pretty curst obvious that the instincts he'd developed in Hammer's Slammers were the ones most applicable here.

Eunice Delcorio laughed, a clear, clean sound that cut like a knife. "At least there's somebody who understands the situation," she said, echoing Tyl's thought and earning the Slammers officer another furious glance by her husband.

"I think we can all agree that the situation won't be improved by silly panic," Delcorio said mildly as his eyes swept the room. "Dowell, what do you have to report?"

There had been movement all around the room with the arrival of the Delcorios but it was mostly limited to heads turning. Major Borodin, who'd been present after all—standing so quietly by a wall that Tyl's quick survey had missed him—was marching determinedly toward his executive officer. Desoix himself was alone. His lady friend had left him at once to join her mistress, the President's wife.

But at the moment, everyone's attention was on Marshal Dowell, because that was where the President was looking.

"Yes, well," the army chief said. "I've given orders that a brigade be returned from Two as quickly as possible. You must realize that it's necessary for the troops to land as a unit so that their effect won't be dissipated."

"What about *now*?" cried the City Prefect. He stepped forward in an access of grief and rage, fluttering his gorgeous robes like a peacock preparing to fly. "You said you'd support my police, but your precious soldiers did *nothing* when those scum attacked the City Offices!"

One of Dowell's aides was speaking rapidly into a communicator with a shield that made the discussion inaudible to the rest of the gathering. The marshal glanced at him, then said, "We're still not sure what the situation over there is, and at any rate—"

"They took the place," Tyl said bluntly.

In the Slammers you didn't stand on ceremony when your superiors had bad data or none at all in matters that could mean the life of a lot of people. "Freed their friends, set fire to the building— hung at least some of the folks they caught. Via, you can see it from here, from the window."

He gestured with an elbow, because to point with his full arm would have moved his hand further from the grip of his weapon than instinct wanted to keep it at present.

Perhaps because everyone followed the gesture toward the panels overlooking the courtyard, the chanted . . . *freedom* . . . echoing from that direction became suddenly audible in the Consistory Room.

Across the room, the concealed elevator suctioned and snapped heads around. The officer Desoix had nodded to downstairs, the CO of the Executive Guard, stepped out with a mixture of arrogance and fear. He moved like a rabbit loaded with amphetamines. "Gentlemen?" he called in a clear voice. "Rioters are in the courtyard with guns and torches!"

Tyl was waiting for a recommendation—*Do I have your permission to open fire?* was how a Slammers officer would have proceeded—but this fellow had nothing in mind save the theatrical announcement.

What Tyl didn't expect—nobody expected—was for Eunice Delcorio to sweep like a torch flame to the door and step out onto the porch.

The blast of noise when the clear doors opened was a shocking reminder of how well they blocked sound. There was an animal undertone, but the organized chant of *"Freedom!"* boomed over and through the snarl until the mob recognized the black-haired, glass-smooth woman facing them from the high porch.

Tyl moved fast. He was at Eunice's side before the shouts of surprise had given way to the hush of a thousand people drawing breath simultaneously. He thought there might be shots. At the first bang or spurt of light he was going to hurl Eunice back into the Consistory Room, trusting his luck and his clamshell armor.

Not because she was a woman; but because if the President's wife got blown away, there was as little chance of compromise as there seemed to be of winning until the brigade from Two arrived.

And maybe a little because she was a woman. "What will you have, citizens?" Eunice called. The porch was designed for speeches. Even without amplification, the modeling walls threw her powerful contralto out over the crowd. "Will you abandon God's Crusade for a whim?"

The uplifted faces were a blur to Tyl in the scatter of light sources that the mob carried. The crosses embroidered in white cloth on the left shoulders of their garments were clear enough to be recognized, though, and that was true whether the base color was red or black. There was motion behind him, but Tyl had eyes only for the mob.

Weapons glinted there. He couldn't tell if any of them were being aimed. The night-vision sensors in his face shield would have helped; but if he locked the shield down he'd be a mirror-faced threat to the crowd, and that might be all it took to draw the first shots. . . .

Desoix'd stepped onto the porch. He stood on the other side of Eunice Delcorio, and he was cursing with the fluency of a mercenary who's sleep-learned a lot of languages over the years.

The other woman was on the porch too. From the way the UDB officer was acting, she'd preceded rather than followed him.

The crowd's silence had dissolved in a dozen varied answers to Eunice's question, all underlain by blurred attempts to continue the chant of "Freedom!"

Something popped from the center of the mob. Tyl's left arm reached across Eunice's waist and was a heartbeat short of hurling the woman back through the doors no matter who stood behind her. A white flare burst fifty meters above the courtyard, harmless and high enough that it could be seen by even the tail of the mob stretching across the river.

The mob quieted after an anticipatory growl that shook the panels of the doors.

There was a motion at the flagstaff, near where the flare had been launched. Before Tyl could be sure what was happening, a handheld floodlight glared over the porch from the same location.

He stepped in front of the President's wife, bumping her out of the way with his hip, while his left hand locked the face shield down against the blinding radiance. The muzzle of his submachine-gun quested like an adder's tongue while his finger took up slack on the trigger.

"Wait!" boomed a voice from the mob in amplified startlement. The floodlight dimmed from a threat to comfortable illumination.

"I'll take over now, Eunice," said John Delcorio as his firm hand touched Tyl's upper arm, just beneath the shoulder flare of the clamshell armor.

The Slammers officer stepped aside, knowing it was out of his hands for better or for worse, now.

President Delcorio's voice thundered to the crowd from roof speakers, "My people, why do you come here to disturb God's purpose?"

Through his shield's optics, Tyl could see that there were half a dozen priests in dark vestments grouped beside the flagpole. They had a guard of orderlies from the House of Grace, but both the man with the light and the one raising a bull-horn had been ordained. Tyl thought, though the distance made uncertain, that the priest half-hidden behind the pole was Father Laughlin.

None of the priests carried weapons. All the twenty or so orderlies of their bodyguard held guns.

"We want the murderer Berne!" called the bull-horn. The words were indistinct from the out-of-synchronous echoes which they waked from the Palace walls. "Berne sells justice and sells lives!"

"Berne!" shouted the mob, and their echoes thundered BERNE berne berne.

As the echoes died away, Tyl heard Desoix saying in a voice much louder than he intended, "Anne, for the *Lord's* sake! Get back inside!"

"Will you go back to your homes in peace if I replace the City Prefect?" Delcorio said, pitching his words to make his offered capitulation sound like a demand. His features were regally arrogant as Tyl watched him sidelong behind the mirror of his face shield.

The priest with the bull-horn leaned sideways to confer with the bigger man behind the flagpole, certainly Father Laughlin. While the mob waited for their leaders' response, the President used the pause to add, "One man's venality can't be permitted to jeopardize God's work!"

"Give us Berne!" demanded the courtyard.

"I'll replace—" Delcorio attempted.

GIVE give give roared the mob. GIVE give give. . . .

Eunice leaned over to say something to her husband. He held up a hand to silence the crowd. The savage voices boomed louder, a thousand of them in the courtyard and myriads more filling the streets beyond.

A woman waved a doll in green robes above her head. She held it tethered by its neck.

Delcorio and his wife stepped back into the Consistory Room. Their hands were clasped so that it was impossible to tell who was leading the other. The President reached to slide the door shut for silence, but Lieutenant Desoix was close behind with an arm locked around the other woman's waist. His shoulder blocked Delcorio's intent.

Tyl Koopman wasn't going to be the only target on the balcony while the mob waited for a response it might not care for. He kept his featureless face to the front—with the gun muzzle beneath it for emphasis—as he retreated after the rest.

CHAPTER FIFTEEN

"Firing me won't—" Berne began even before Tyl slid the door shut on the thunder of the mob.

"I'm not sure we can defend—" Marshal Dowell was saying with a frown and enough emphasis that he managed to be heard.

"Be silent!" Eunice Delcorio ordered in a glass-sharp voice.

The wall thundered with the low notes of the shouting in the courtyard.

Everyone in the Consistory Room had gathered in a semicircle. They were facing the porch and those who had been standing on it.

There were only a dozen or so of Delcorio's advisors present. Twice that number had awaited when Tyl followed Eunice out to confront the mob, but they were gone now.

Gone from the room, gone from the Palace if they could arrange it—and assuredly gone from the list of President Delcorio's supporters.

That bothered Tyl less than the look of those who remained.

They glared at the City Prefect with the expression of gorgeously attired fish viewing an injured one of their number . . . an equal moments before, a certain victim now. The eyes of Dowell's aides were hungry as they slid over Berne.

Eunice Delcorio's voice had carved a moment of silence from the atmosphere of the Consistory Room. The colonel of the Executive Guard filled the pause with, "It's quite *im*possible to defend the Palace from numbers like that. We can't even think of—"

"Yeah, we could hold it," Tyl broke in.

He'd forgotten his face shield was locked down until he saw everyone start away from him as if he were something slime-covered that had just crawled through a window. With the shield in place, the loudspeaker built into his helmet cut in automatically so they *weren't* going to ignore him if he raised his voice.

He didn't want to be ignored, but he flipped up the shield to be less threatening now that he had the group's attention.

"You've got what, two companies?" he went on, waving his left index finger toward the glittering colonel. All right, they weren't the Slammers; but they had assault rifles and they weren't exactly facing combat infantry either.

"We've got a hundred men," he said. "*Curst* good ones, and the troops the UDB's got here in the Palace know how to handle—"

Tyl had nodded in the direction of Lieutenant Desoix, but it was Borodin, the battery commander, who interrupted, "I have no men in the Palace."

"Huh?" said the Slammers officer.

"What?" Desoix said. "We have the off-duty c—"

"I'm worried about relieving the crews with the, ah—" Borodin began.

He looked over at the President. The mercenary commander couldn't whisper the explanation, not now. "The conditions in the streets are such that I wasn't sure we'd be able to relieve the gun crews normally, so I ordered the reserve crews to billet at the guns so that we could be sure that there'd be a full watch alert if the enemy tries to take advantage of . . . events."

"*Events!*" snarled John Delcorio.

The door behind him rattled sharply when a missile struck it. The vitril held as it was supposed to do.

"John, they aren't after *me*," Berne cried with more than personal concern in his voice. He was right, after all, everybody else here must know that, since it was so obvious to Tyl Koopman in his first day on-planet. "You mustn't—"

"If you hadn't failed, none of this would be happening," Eunice said, her scorn honed by years of personal hatred that found its outlet now in the midst of general catastrophe.

She turned to her husband, the ends of her black hair emphasizing the motion. "Why are you delaying? They want this criminal, and that will give us the time we need to deal with the filth properly with the additional troops."

Vividness made Eunice Delcorio a beautiful woman, but the way her lips rolled over the word "properly" sent a chill down the spine of everyone who watched her.

Berne made a break for the door to the hall.

Tyl's mind had been planning the defense of the Palace of Government. Squads of the local troops in each wing to fire as soon as rioters pried or blasted off a flood shutter to gain entrance. Platoons of mercenaries poised to react as fire brigades, responding to each assault with enough violence to smother it in the bodies of those who'd made the attempt. Grenadiers on the roof; they'd very quickly clear the immediate area of the Palace of everything except bodies and the moaning wounded.

Easy enough, but they were answers to questions that nobody was asking anymore. Besides, they could only hold the place for a few days against tens of thousands of besiegers—only long enough for the brigade to arrive from Two, if it came.

And Tyl was a lot less confident of that point than the President's wife seemed to be.

A middle-aged civilian tripped the City Prefect. One of Dowell's aides leaped on Berne and wrestled him to the polished floor as he tried to rise, while the other aide shouted into his communicator for support without bothering to lock his privacy screen in place.

Tyl looked away in disgust. He caught Lieutenant Desoix's eye. The UDB officer wore a bland expression.

But he wasn't watching the scuffle and the weeping prefect either.

"All right," said the President, bobbing his head in decision. "I'll tell them."

He took one stride, reached for the sliding door, and paused. "You," he said to Tyl. "Come with me."

Tyl nodded without expression. Another stone or possibly a light bullet whacked against the vitril. He set his face shield and stepped onto the porch ahead of the Regiment's employer.

He didn't feel much just now, though he wanted to take a piss real bad. Even so, he figured he'd be more comfortable facing the mob than he was over what had just happened in the Consistory Room.

The crowd roared. Behind his shield, Tyl grinned—if that was the right word for the way instinct drew up the corners of his mouth to bare his teeth. There was motion among the upturned faces gleaming like the sputum the sea leaves when it draws back from the strand.

Something pinged on the railing. Tyl's gun quivered, pointed—

"Wait!" thundered the bull-horn.

"My people!" boomed the President's voice from the roofline. He rested his palms wide apart on the railing.

He'd followed after all, a step behind the Slammers officer just in case a sniper was waiting for the first motion. Delcorio wasn't a brave man, not as a professional soldier came to appraise courage, but his spirit had a tumbling intensity that made him capable of almost anything.

At a given moment.

The mob was making a great deal of disconnected noise. Delcorio trusted his amplified voice to carry him through as he continued, "I have dismissed the miscreant Berne as you demanded. I will turn him over to the custody of the Church for safekeeping until the entire State can determine the punishment for his many crimes."

"Give us Berne!" snarled the bull-horn with echoing violence. It spoke in the voice of a priest but not a Christian; and the mob that took up the chant was not even human.

Delcorio turned and tried to shout something into the building with his unaided voice. Tyl couldn't hear him.

The President raised a hand for silence from the crowd. The chant continued unabated, but Delcorio and the Slammers officer were able to back inside without a rain of missiles to mark their retreat.

There was a squad of the Executive Guard in the Consistory Room. Four of the ten men were gripping the City Prefect. Several had dropped their rifles in the scuffle and no one had thought to pick the weapons up again.

Delcorio made a dismissing gesture. "Send him out to them," he said. "I've done all I can. Quickly, so I don't have to go out there—"

His face turned in the direction of his thoughts, toward the porch and the mob beneath. The flush faded and he began to shiver uncontrollably. Reaction and memory had caught up with the President.

There were only four civilian advisors in the room besides Berne. Five. A man whose suit was russet or gold, depending on the direction of the light, had been caught just short of getting into the elevator by Delcorio's return.

The Guards colonel was shaking his head. "No, no," he said. "That won't do. If we open a shutter, they'll be in and, well, the way the fools are worked up, who knows what might happen?"

"But—" the President said, his jaw dropping. He'd aged a decade since he stepped off the porch. Hormonal courage abandoned him to reaction and remembrance. "But I *must*. But I promised them, Drescher, and if I don't—"

His voice would probably have broken off there anyway, but a bellow from the courtyard in thunderous synchrony smothered all sound within for a moment.

"Pick him up, then," said Eunice Delcorio in a voice as clear as a sapphire laser. "You four—pick him up and follow. We'll give them their scrap of bone."

She strode toward the door, the motion of her legs a devouring flame across the intarsia.

Berne screamed as the soldiers lifted him. Because he was screaming, no one heard Tyl Koopman say in a choked voice, "Lady, you *can't*—"

But of course they could. And Tyl had done the same or worse, checking out suspicious movements with gunfire, knowing full well that nine chances in ten, the victims were going to be civilians trying to get back home half an hour after curfew. . . .

He'd never have spent one of his own men this way; and he'd never serve under an officer who did.

Colonel Drescher threw open the door himself, though he stood back from the opening with a care that was more than getting out of the way of the President's wife.

Tyl stepped out beside her, because he'd made it his job . . . or Hammer had made it his job . . . and who in blazes cared, he was there and the animal snarl of the mob brought answering rage to the Slammer's mind and washed some of the sour taste from his mouth.

The Guardsmen in azure uniforms and Berne in green made a contrast as brilliant as a parrot's plumage as they manhandled the prefect to the railing under the glare of lights. Floods were trained from at least three locations in the courtyard now, turned high; but that was all right, they needed to watch this, sure they did.

Eunice cried something inaudible but imperious. She gestured out over the railing. The soldiers looked at one another.

Berne was screaming wordlessly. His eyes were closed, but tears poured from beneath the lids. He had fouled himself in his panic. The smell added the only element necessary to make the porch a microcosm of Hell.

Eunice gestured again. The Guards threw their prisoner toward the courtyard.

Berne grabbed the railing with both hands as he went over. His legs flailed without the organization needed to boost him back onto the porch, but his hands clung like claws of east bronze.

Eunice gave a furious order that was no more than a grimace and a quick motion of her lips. Two of the soldiers tried gingerly to push Berne away. The prefect twisted his head and bit the hands of one. His eyes were open now and as mad as those of a backward psychotic. Bottles and stones began to fly from the crowd, clashing on the rail and floor of the porch.

The Guardsmen drew back into a huddle in the doorway. The man who still carried his rifle raised it one-handed to shield his face.

A bottle shattered on Tyl's breastplate. He didn't hear the shot that was fired a moment later, but the howl of a light slug ricocheting from the wall cut through even the roar of the crowd.

"Get inside!" Tyl's speakers bellowed to Eunice Delcorio as he stepped sideways to the railing where Berne thrashed. Tyl hammered the man's knuckles with the butt of his submachine-gun. One stroke, two—bone cracked—

Three and the prefect's screaming changed note. His broken left hand slipped and his right hand opened. Berne's throat made a sound like a siren as he fell ten meters to the mob waiting to receive him.

Tyl turned. If the Guardsmen had still been blocking the doorway, he might have shot them . . . but they'd fled inside and Eunice Delcorio was sweeping after them. Her head was regally high, and she was ignoring the streak of blood over one cheekbone where a stone had cut her.

Tyl turned for a last look into the courtyard. The rioters were passing Berne hand to hand, over their heads, like a bit of green algae seen sliding through the gut of a paramecium. There was greater motion also; the mob was shifting back—only a compression in the crowd at the moment, but soon to turn into real movement that would clear the courtyard.

They were leaving, now that they had their bone.

As the City Prefect was passed along, those nearest were ripping bits away. For the moment, the bits were mostly clothing.

Tyl stepped into the Consistory Room and slammed the door behind him hard enough to shatter a panel that hadn't been armored. He left his face-shield down, because if none of them could see his expression, he could pretend that he wasn't really here.

"Lieutenant Desoix," said Major Borodin. He wasn't speaking loudly, but no one else in the room was speaking at all. "Gun Three needs to be withdrawn. Will you handle that at once."

The battery commander's face looked like a mirror of what Tyl thought was on his own features.

"Nobody's withdrawing," said President Delcorio. He had his color back, and he stroked his hands together briskly as if to warm them. His eyes shifted like a sparkling fire and lighted on the Guards colonel. The hands stopped.

"Colonel Drescher," Delcorio said crisply. "I want your men on combat footing at once. Don't you have some other sort of uniforms? Like those."

One spade-broad hand gestured toward Tyl in khaki and armor. "Something suitable. This isn't a *parade*. We're at war. War."

"Well, I—" Drescher began. Everyone in the room was in a state of shock, hammered by events into a state that made them ready to be pressed in any direction by a strong personality.

For a moment, until the next stimulus came along.

"Well, get on with it!" the President snapped. While the squad of gay uniforms was just shifting toward the hall door, Delcorio's attention had already flashed across the other faces in the Consistory Room.

And found very few.

"Where's—" Delcorio began. "Where's—" His voice rose, driven by an emotion that was either fury or panic—and perhaps had not yet decided which it would be.

"Sir," said one of the Chastains, stepping forward to take the President by the hand. "Thom and I will—"

"*You!*" Delcorio screamed. "What are you doing here?"

"Sir," said Thom Chastain with the same hopeful puppy expression as his brother. "We know you'll weather this—"

"You're spying, aren't you?" Delcorio cried, slapping at the offered hands as if they were beasts about to bite him. "Get out, don't you think I know it!"

"Sir—" said the two together in blank amazement.

The President's nephew Pedro stepped between the Chastains and Delcorio. "Go on!" he snarled, looking like a bulldog barking at a pair of gangling storks. "We don't need you here. Get *out*!"

"But—" Richie Chastain attempted helplessly. Pedro, as broadly built as his uncle, shoved the other men toward the door.

They fled in a swirl of robes and words whimpered to one another or to fate.

"You there," the President continued briskly. "Dowell. You'll have the additional troops in place by noon tomorrow. Do you understand? I don't care if they have to loot shops for their meals, they'll be here."

Delcorio spoke with an alert dynamism. It was hard to imagine that the same man had been on the edge of violent madness a moment before, and in a funk brief minutes still earlier.

Dowell saluted with a puzzled expression. He mumbled something to his aides. The three of them marched out the hall door without looking backward.

If they caught the President's eye again, he might hold them.

"And *you*, Major Borodin, you aren't going to strip our city of its protection against the Christ-deniers," Delcorio said as he focused back on the battery commander.

The President should have forgotten the business of moving the gun—so much had gone on in the moments since. He hadn't forgotten, though. There *was* a mind inside that skull, not just a furnace of emotions.

If John Delcorio were as stupid as he was erratic, Tyl might have been able to figure out what in the Lord's name he ought best to be doing.

"*Do* you understand?" Delcorio insisted, pointing at the battery commander with two blunt fingers in a gesture as threatening as anything short of a gun muzzle could be.

"Yes sir," replied Major Borodin, his voice as stiff as the brace in which he held his body. "But I must tell you that I'm obeying under protest, and when I contact my superiors—"

"You needn't tell me anything, mercenary," the President interrupted without even anger to leaven the contempt in his words. "You need only do your job and collect your pay—which I assure you, your superiors show no hesitation in doing either."

"John," said Eunice Delcorio with a shrug that dismissed everything that was going on around her at the moment. "I'm going to call my brother again. They said they couldn't raise him when I tried earlier."

"Yes, I'll talk to him myself," the President agreed, falling in step beside the short woman as he headed toward the door to their private apartments. "He'd have nothing but a ten-hectare share-crop if it weren't for me. If he thinks he can duck his responsibilities now. . . ."

"Anne," Desoix said in a low voice as Eunice's aide hesitated. She looked from her mistress to the UDB officer—and stayed.

Pedro Delcorio raised an eyebrow, then nodded to the others as he followed his uncle out of the Consistory Room. There were only four of them left: the three mercenaries and Desoix's lady friend.

The four of them, and the smell of fear.

CHAPTER SIXTEEN

"Let's get out of here," Koopman said.

Charles Desoix's heart leaped in agreement—then bobbed back to normalcy when he realized that the Slammers officer meant only to get out of the Consistory Room, onto the porch where the air held fewer memories of the immediate past.

Sure, Koopman was the stolid sort who probably didn't realize how badly things were going . . . and Charles Desoix wasn't going to support a mutiny, wasn't going to desert his employers because of trouble that hadn't—if you wanted to be objective about it—directly threatened the United Defense Batteries at all.

It was hard to be objective when you were surrounded by a mob of perhaps fifty thousand people, screaming for blood and quite literally tearing a man to pieces.

They were welcome to Berne—he was just as crooked as the bull-horn had claimed. But. . . .

"What did you say, Charles?" Anne asked—which meant that Desoix had been speaking things that he shouldn't even have been thinking.

He hugged her reflexively. She jumped, also by reflex because she didn't try to draw further away when she thought about the situation. Major Borodin didn't appear to notice her to care.

The courtyard was deserted, but the mob had left behind an amazing quantity of litter—bottles, boxes, and indefinable scraps; even a cloak, scarlet and apparently whole in the light of the wall sconces. It was as if Desoix were watching a beach just after the tide had ebbed.

Across the river, fires burned from at least a score of locations. Voices echoed, harsh as the occasional grunt of shots.

Like the tide, the mob would return.

"We've got to get out of here," Desoix mused aloud.

"She'll leave," Anne said with as much prayer in her voice as certainty. "If she stays, they'll do terrible things to . . . She *knows* that, she won't let it happen."

"Colonel wants me to hold if there's any chance to keep Delcorio in power," Koopman said to the night. There was a snicker of sound as he raised his face shield, but he did not look at his companions as he spoke. "What's your bet on that, Charles?"

"Something between zip and zero," Desoix said. He was careful not to let his eyes fall on Anne or the major when he spoke; but it was no time to tell polite lies.

"'Bout what I figured too," the Slammers officer said mildly. He was leaning on his forearms while his fingers played with a dimple in the rail. After a moment, Desoix realized that the dimple had been hammered there by a bullet.

"I don't see any way we can abandon our positions in defiance of a direct order," Major Borodin said.

The battery commander set his fingers in his thinning hair and squeezed firmly, as though that would change the blank rotation of his thoughts. He took his hands away and added hurriedly to the Slammers officer, "Of course, that has nothing to do with you, Captain. My problem is that I have to defend the city, so I'm in default of the contract if I move my guns. Well, Gun Three. But that's the only one that seems to be in danger."

"Charles, you'll protect her if we leave, won't you?" asked Anne in sudden fierceness. She pulled on Desoix's shoulder until he turned to face her worries directly. "You won't let them have her to, to escape yourself, will you?"

He cupped her chin with his left hand. "Anne," he said. "If Eunice and the President just say the word, we'll have them safely out of here within the hour. Won't we, Tyl?" he added as he turned to the Slammers officer.

"Colonel says, maybe just a week or two," Koopman said unexpectedly. When his index finger burnished the bullet scar, the muzzle of his own slung weapon chinked lightly against the rail. "Suppose Delcorio could hold out a week?"

"Suppose we could hold out five minutes if they come back hard?" Desoix snapped, furious at the infantryman's response when finally it looked as if there were a chance to clear out properly. There wasn't any doubt that Eunice Delcorio could bend her husband to her own will. She was inflexible, with none of John Delcorio's flights and falterings.

If Anne worked on her mistress, it could all turn out reasonably. Exile for Delcorio on his huge private estates; safety for Anne McGill, whose mistress wasn't the only one with whom the mob would take its pleasure.

And release for the mercenaries who were at the moment trapped in this place by ridiculous orders.

"Yeah," said Koopman with a heavy sigh. He turned at last to face his companions. "Well, I'm not going to get any of my boys wasted for nothing at all. We aren't paid to be heroes. Guess I'll go down and tell Jack to pack up to move at daylight."

The Slammers officer quirked a grin to Desoix and nodded to Anne and the major as he stepped toward the door.

"Tyl, wait . . ." Desoix said as a word rang echoes. "Can you . . . Major, how many men do you have downstairs still?"

Borodin shrugged out of the brown study into which he had fallen as he watched the fires burning around him. "Men?" he repeated. "Senter and Lachere is all. We're still short—"

"Tyl, can you, ah—" Desoix went on. He paused, because he didn't want to use the wrong word, since what he was about to ask was no part of the Slammers' business.

"I need to get down to the warehouses on the corniche," Desoix said, rephrasing the question to make the request personal rather than military. "All I've got here are the battery clerks and they're not, ah, trained for this. Could you detail a few men, five or six, to go along with me in case there was a problem?"

"Lieutenant," Borodin said gruffly. "What do—"

"Sir," Desoix explained as the plan drew itself in glowing lines in his mind, the alternative sites and intersecting fields of fire. "When we get Gun Five set up, we can move Three a kilometer east on the corniche and still be in compliance. Five on the outskirts of town near Pestini's Chapel, Three on Guizer Head—and we've got everything Delcorio can demand under the contract."

"Without stationing any of our men down. . . ." Borodin said as the light dawned. He might have intended to point toward the plaza, but as his gaze turned out over the city, his voice trailed off instead. Both UDB officers stared at Tyl Koopman.

Koopman shrugged. "I'll go talk to the guys," he said.

And they had to be satisfied with that, because he said nothing more as he walked back into the building.

CHAPTER SEVENTEEN

Tyl's functional company had taken over the end of a second-floor hallway abandoned by the entourage of six noble guests of the President. The hundred troopers had a great deal more room than there'd been in the City Office billet—or any normal billet.

And, though they'd lost their personal gear when the office building burned, the nobles' hasty departure meant that the soldiers could console themselves for the objects they'd lost across the river. Jewelry and rich fabrics peeked out the edges of khaki uniforms as Tyl strode past the corridor guard and into the billeting area.

Too bad about Aunt Sandra's jelly, though. He could turn over a lot of rich folks' closets and not find anything to replace that.

Troopers with makeshift bedrolls in the hallway were jumping to attention because somebody else had. The heads that popped from doorways were emptying the adjoining guest suites as effectively as if Tyl had shouted, "Fall in!"

Which was about the last thing he wanted.

"Settle down," he said with an angry wave of his arm, as if to brush away the commotion. They were all tight. The troops didn't know much, and that made them rightly nervous.

Tyl Koopman knew a good deal more, and what he'd seen from the porch wasn't the sort of knowledge to make anybody feel better about the situation.

"Captain?" said Jack Scratchard as he muscled his way into the hall.

Tyl motioned the sergeant major over. He keyed his commo helmet with the other hand and said loudly—most of the men didn't have their helmets on, and only the senior noncoms were fitted with implants—"At present, I'm expecting us to get the rest of the night's sleep here, but maybe not be around much after dawn. When I know more, you'll hear."

Scratchard joined him. The two men stepped out of the company area for the privacy they couldn't find within it. Tyl paused and called over his shoulder, "Use a little common sense in what you try to pack, all right?"

He glared at a corporal with at least a dozen vibrantly colored dresses in her arms.

The remaining six suites off the hallway were as empty as those Scratchard had appropriated. He must have decided to keep the troops bunched up a little under the present circumstances, and Tyl wasn't about to argue with him.

The doors of all the suites had been forced. As they stepped into the nearest to talk, Tyl noticed that the richly appointed room had been turned over with great care, although none of his soldiers were at present inside continuing their looting.

Loot and mud were the two constants of line service. If you couldn't get used to either one, you'd better find a rear-echelon slot somewhere.

"Talk to the Old Man?" Scratchard muttered when he was sure they were alone in the tumbled wreckage.

Tyl shrugged. "Not yet," he said. "Sent an all clear through open channels, is all. It's mostly where we left it earlier, and I don't want Central—" he wasn't comfortable saying "Hammer" or even "the Old Man" "—thinking they got to wet-nurse me."

He paused, and only then got to the real business. "Desoix—the UDB Number Two," he said. "He wants a few guys to cover his back while he gets a calliope outa storage down to the seafront. Got everybody but a couple clerks out with the other tubes."

The sergeant major knuckled his scalp, the ridge where his helmet rode. "What's that do for us, the other calliope?" he asked.

"Bloody zip," Tyl answered with a shrug. He was in charge, but this was the sort of thing that the sergeant major had to be brought into.

Besides, nothing he'd heard about Ripper Jack Scratchard suggested that there'd be an argument on how to proceed.

"What it does," Tyl amplified, "is let them withdraw the gun they got down by the plaza. Desoix doesn't like having a crew down there, the way things're going."

Scratchard frowned. "Why can't he—" he began.

"Don't ask," Tyl said with a grimace.

The question made him think of things he'd rather forget. He thumbed in what might have been the direction of the Consistory Room and said, "It got real strange up there. Real strange."

He shook his head to rid it of the memories and added, "You know, he's the one I finally raised to get us into here before it really dropped in the pot. None of the locals were going to do squat for us."

"Doing favors is a good way t' get your ass blown away," Scratchard replied, sourly but without real emphasis. "But sure, I'll look up five guys that'd like t' see the outside again."

He grinned around the clothing strewn about them from forced clothes presses. "Don't guess it'll be too hard to look like civilians, neither."

"Ah," said Tyl. He was facing a blank wall. "Thought I might go along, lead 'em, you know."

"Like hell," said the sergeant major with a grin that seemed to double the width of his grizzled face. "I might, except for my knees. You're going to stay bloody here, in charge like you're supposed t' be."

His lips pursed. "Kekkonan'll take 'em. He won't buy into anything he can't buy out of."

Tyl clapped the noncom on the shoulder. "Round 'em up," he said as he stepped into the hall. "I'll tell Desoix. This is the sort of thing that should've been done, you know, last week."

As he walked down the hall, the Slammers officer keyed his helmet to learn where Desoix was at the moment. Putting this sort of information on open channels didn't seem like a great idea, unless you had a lot more confidence in the Bamberg army than Tyl Koopman did.

Asking for volunteers in a business like this was a waste of time. They were veteran troops, these; men and women who would parrot "never volunteer" the way they'd been told by a thousand generations of previous veterans . . . but who knew in their hearts that it was boredom that killed.

You couldn't live in barracks, looking at the same faces every waking minute, without wanting to empty a gun into one of them just to make a change.

So the first five soldiers Scratchard asked would belt on their battle gear with enthusiasm, bitching all the time about "When's it somebody else's turn to take the tough one?" They didn't want to die, but they didn't think they would . . . and just maybe they would have gone anyway, whatever they thought the risk was, because it was too easy to imagine the ways a fort like the Palace of Government could become a killing bottle.

They were Hammer's Slammers. They'd done that to plenty others over the years.

Tyl didn't have any concern that he'd be able to hand Desoix his bodyguards, primed and ready for whatever the fire-shot night offered.

And he knew that he'd give three grades in rank to be able to go along with them himself.

CHAPTER EIGHTEEN

The porch off the Consistory Room didn't have a view of anything Tyl wanted to see—the littered courtyard and, across the river, the shell of the City Offices whose windows were still outlined by the sullen glow in its interior. The porch was as close as he could come to being outside, though, and that was sufficient recommendation at the moment.

The top of the House of Grace was barely visible above the south wing of the Palace. The ghost of firelight from the office building painted the eyes and halo of the sculptured Bishop Trimer also.

Tyl didn't want company, so when the door slid open behind him, he turned his whole body. That way his slung submachine-gun pointed, an "accident" that he knew would frighten away anyone except his own troopers—whom he could order to leave him alone.

Lieutenant Desoix's woman stopped with a little gasp in her throat, but she didn't back away.

"Via!" Tyl said in embarrassment, lifting the gun muzzle high and cursing himself in his head for the dumb idea. One of those dandies, he'd figured, or a smirking servant . . . except that the President's well-dressed advisors seemed to have pretty well disappeared, and the flunkies also.

Servants were getting thin on the ground, too.

"If you'd like to be alone . . . ?" the woman said, either polite or real perceptive.

"Naw, you're fine," Tyl said, feeling clumsy and a lot the same way as he had a few months ago. Then he'd been to visit a girl he might have married if he hadn't gone off for a soldier the way he had. "You're, ah—Lady Eunice's friend, aren't you?"

"That too," said the woman drily. She took the place Tyl offered at the railing and added, "My name's Anne McGill. And I believe you're Captain Koopman?"

"Tyl," the soldier said. "Rank's not form—" He gestured. "Out here."

She didn't look as big as she had inside. Maybe because he had his armor on now that he was standing close to her.

Maybe because he'd recently watched five big men put looted cloaks on over their guns and armor to go off with Lieutenant Desoix.

"Have you known Charles long?" she asked, calling Tyl back from a stray thought that had the woman wriggling out of her dark blue dress and offering herself to him.

He shook his head abruptly to clear the thought. Not his type, and he *sure* wasn't hers.

"No," he said, forgetting that she thought he'd answered with the shake of his head. "I just got in today, you see. I don't recall we ever served with the UDB before. Anyhow, mostly you don't see much of anybody's people but your own guys."

It wasn't even so much that he was horny. Screwing was just something he could really lose himself in.

Killing was that way too.

"It's dangerous out there, isn't it?" she said. She wasn't looking at the city because her face was lifted too high. From the way her capable hands washed one another, she might well have been praying.

"Out there?" Tyl repeated bitterly. "Via, it's dangerous *here*, and we can't do anything but bloody twiddle our thumbs."

Anne winced, as much at the violence as the words themselves.

Instantly contrite, Tyl said, "But you know, if things stay cool a little longer—no spark, you know, setting things off . . . It may all work out."

He was repeating what Colonel Hammer had told him a few minutes before, through the laser communicator now slung at his belt again. To focus on the satellite from here, he'd had to aim just over the top of the House of Grace. . . .

"When the soldiers from Two come, there'll be a spark, won't there?" she asked. She was looking at Tyl now, though he didn't expect she could see any more of his face in the darkness than he could of her. Firelight winked on her necklace of translucent beads.

The scent she wore brought another momentary rush of lust.

"Maybe not," he said, comfortable talking to somebody who might possibly believe the story he could never credit in discussions with himself. "Nobody really wants that kind a' trouble."

Not the army, that was for sure. *They* weren't going to push things.

"Delcorio makes a few concessions—he already gave 'em Berne, after all. The troops march around with their bayonets all polished to look pretty. And then everybody kisses and makes up."

So that Tyl Koopman could get back to the business of a war whose terms he understood.

"I hope . . ." Anne was murmuring.

She might not have finished the phrase even if they hadn't been interrupted by the door sliding open behind them.

Tyl didn't recognize Eunice Delcorio at first. She was wearing a dress of mottled gray tones and he'd only seen her in scarlet in the past. With the fabric's luminors powered up, the garment would have shone with a more-than-metallic luster; but now it had neither shape nor color, and Eunice's voice guttered like that of a brittle ghost as she said, "Well, my dear, I wouldn't have interrupted you if I'd known you were entertaining a gentleman."

"Ma'am," Tyl said, bracing to attention. Eunice sounded playful, but so was a cat with a field mouse—and he didn't *know* what she could do to him if she wanted, it wasn't in the normal chain of command. . . .

"Captain Koopman and I were discussing the situation, Eunice," Anne said evenly. If she were embarrassed, she hid the fact; and there was no trace of fear in her voice. "You could have called me."

Eunice toyed with the hundred millimeter wand that could either page or track a paired unit. "I thought I'd find you instead, my dear," she said.

The President's wife wasn't angry, but there was fierce emotion beneath the surface sparkle. The wand slipped from her fingers to the floor.

Tyl knelt swiftly—you don't bend when you're wearing a ceramic back-and breast—and rose as quickly with the wand offered in his left hand.

Eunice batted the little device out into the courtyard. It was some seconds before it hit the stones below.

"I told the captain," Anne said evenly, "that I was concerned about your safety in view of the trouble that's occurring here in the city."

"Well, that should be over very shortly, shouldn't it?" Eunice said. Nothing in her voice hinted at the way her body had momentarily lost control. "Marshal Dowell has gone to Two himself to expedite movement of the troops."

The technical phrase came from her full lips with a glitter that made it part of a social event. Which, in a manner of speaking, it was.

"Blood and Martyrs," Tyl said. He wasn't sure whether or not he'd spoken the curse aloud, and at this point he didn't much care.

He straightened. "Ma'am," he said, nodding stiffly to the President's wife. "Ah, ma'am," with a briefer nod to Anne.

He strode back into the building without waiting for formal leave. Over his shoulder, he called, "I need to go check on the dispositions of my troops."

Especially the troops out there with Desoix, in a city that the local army had just abandoned to the rebels.

CHAPTER NINETEEN

There were at least a dozen voices in the street outside, bellowing the bloodiest hymn Charles Desoix had ever heard. They were moving on, strolling if not marching, but the five Slammers kept their guns trained on the door in case somebody tried to join them inside the warehouse.

What bothered Desoix particularly was the clear soprano voice singing the descant, "Sew their manhood to our flags. . . ."

"All right," he said, returning his attention to the business of reconnecting the fusion powerplant which had been shut down for shipping. "Switch on."

Nothing happened.

Desoix, half inside the gun carriage's rear access port, straightened to find out what was happening. Lachere, the clerk he'd brought along because he needed another pair of hands, leaned hopefully from the open driver's compartment forward. "It's on, sir," he said.

"Main *and* Start-up are on?" Desoix demanded. And either because they hadn't been or because a contact had been a little sticky, he heard the purr of the fusion bottle beginning to bring up its internal temperature and pressure.

Success. In less than an hour—

"The representative of Hammer's Regiment has an urgent message," said Control's emotionless voice. "Shall I patch him through?"

"Affirmative," Desoix said, blanking his mind so that it wouldn't flash him a montage of disaster as it always did when things were tight and the unexpected occurred.

Wouldn't show him Anne McGill in the arms of a dozen rioters, not dead yet and not to die for a long time. . . .

"We got a problem," Koopman said, as if his flat voice and the fact of his call hadn't already proved that. "Dowell just did a bunk to Two. I don't see the situation holding twenty-four hours. Over."

Maybe not twenty-four minutes.

"Is the Executive Guard . . ." Desoix began. While he paused to choose his phrasing, Koopman interrupted with, "They're still here, but they're all in their quarters with the corridor blocked. I figure they're taking a vote. It's that sorta outfit. And I don't figure the vote's going any way I'd want it to. Over."

"All right," Desoix said, glancing toward the pressure gauge that he couldn't read in this light anyway. "All right, we'll have the gun drivable in thirty, that's three-oh, minutes. We'll—"

"Negative. Negative."

"Listen," the UDB officer said with his tone sharpening. "We're this far and we're not—"

Kekkonan, the sergeant in charge of the detachment of Slammers, tapped Desoix's elbow for attention and shook his head. "He said negative," Kekkonan said. "Sir."

The sergeant was getting the full conversation through his mastoid implant. Desoix didn't have to experiment to know it would be as much use to argue with a block of mahogany as with the dark, flat face of the noncom.

"Go ahead, Tyl," Desoix said with an inward sigh. "Over."

"You're not going to drive a calliope through the streets tonight, Charles," Koopman said. "Come dawn, maybe you can withdraw the one you got down there, maybe you just spike it and pull your guys out. This is save-what-you-got time, friend. And *my* boys aren't going to be part a' some fool stunt that sparks the whole thing off."

Kekkonan nodded. Not that he had to.

"Roger, we're on the way," Desoix said. He didn't have much emotion left to give the words, because his thoughts were tied up elsewhere.

Via, she was *married*. It was her bloody husband's business to take care of her, wasn't it?

CHAPTER TWENTY

"Go," said Desoix without emphasis.

Kekkonan and another of the Slammers flared from the door in opposite directions. Their cloaks—civilian and of neutral colors, green and gray—fluffed widely over their elbows, hiding the submachine-guns in their hands.

"Clear," muttered Kekkonan. Desoix stepped out in the middle of the small unit. He felt as much a burden to his guards as the extra magazines that draped them beneath the loose garments.

It remained to be seen if either he or the ammunition would be of any service as they marched back to the Palace.

"Don't remember *that*," Lachere said, looking to the west.

"Keep moving," Kekkonan grunted. There was enough tension in his voice to add a threat of violence to the order.

One of the warehouses farther down the corniche—half a kilometer—had been set on fire. The flames reflected pink from the clouds and as a bloody froth from sea foam in the direction of Nevis Island. The boulevard was clogged by rioters watching the fire and jeering as they flung bodies into it.

Desoix remembered the descant, but he clasped Lachere's arm and said, "We weren't headed in that direction anyway, were we?"

"Too bloody right," murmured one of the Slammers, the shudder in his tone showing that he didn't feel any better about this than the UDB men did.

"Sergeant," Desoix said, edging close to Kekkonan and wishing that the two of them shared a command channel. "I think the faster we get off the seafront, the better we'll be."

He nodded toward the space between the warehouse they'd left and the next building—not so much an alley as a hedge against surveyors' errors.

"Great killing ground," Kekkonan snorted.

Flares rose from the plaza and burst in metallic showers above the city. Shots followed, tracers and the cyan flicker of powergun bolts aimed at the drifting sparks. There was more shooting, some of it from building roofs. Rounds curved in flat arcs back into the streets and houses.

A panel in the clear reflection of the House of Grace shattered into a rectangular scar.

"Right you are," said Kekkonan as he stepped into the narrow passage.

They had to move in single file. Desoix saw to it that he was the second man in the squad. Nobody objected.

He'd expected Tyl to give him infantrymen. Instead, all five of these troopers came from vehicle crews, tanks and combat cars. The weapon of choice under this night's conditions was a submachine-gun, not the heavier, 2cm semiautomatic shoulder weapon of Hammer's infantry. Koopman or his burly sergeant major had been thinking when they picked this team.

Desoix's submachine-gun wasn't for show either. Providing air defense for frontline units meant you were right in the middle of it when things went wrong . . . and they'd twice gone wrong very badly to a battery Charles Desoix crewed or captained.

Though it shouldn't come to that. The seven of them were just another group in a night through which armed bands stalked in a truce that would continue so long as there was an adequacy of weaker prey.

The warehouses fronted the bay and the spaceport across the channel, but their loading docks were in the rear. Across the mean street were tenements. When Desoix's unit shrugged its way out of the cramped passage, they found every one of the windows facing them lighted to display a cross as large as the sashes would allow.

"Partytime," one of the troopers muttered. Some of the residents were watching the events from windows or rooftops, but most of them were down in the street in amorphous clots like those of white cells surrounding bacteria. There were shouts, both shrill and guttural, but Desoix couldn't distinguish any of the words.

Not that he had any trouble understanding what was going on without hearing the words. There were screams coming from the center of one of the groups . . . or perhaps Desoix's mind created the sound it knew would be there if the victim still had the strength to make it.

A dozen or so people were on the loading dock to the unit's right, drinking and either having sex or making as good an attempt at it as their drinking permitted. Somebody threw a bottle that smashed close enough to Kekkonan that the sergeant's cloak flapped as he turned; but there didn't appear to have been real malice involved. Perhaps not even notice.

Party time.

"All right," Kekkonan said just loudly enough for the soldiers with him to hear. "There's an alley across the way, a little to the left. Stay loose, don't run . . . and *don't* bunch up, just in case. Go."

Except for Lachere, they were all veterans; but they were human as well. They didn't run, but they moved much faster than the careless saunter everybody knew was really the safest pace.

And they stayed close, close enough that one burst could have gotten them all.

Nothing happened except that a score of voices followed them with varied suggestions, and a woman naked to the waist stumbled into Charles Desoix even though he tried his best to dodge her.

She was so drunk that she didn't notice the contact, much less that she'd managed to grab the muzzle of his submachine-gun for an instant before she caromed away.

The alley stank of all the garbage the rains hadn't washed away; somebody, dead drunk or dead, was sprawled just within the mouth of it.

Desoix had never been as eager to enter a bedroom as he was that alley.

"Ah, sir," one of the Slammers whispered as the foetor and its sense of protection enclosed them. "Those people, they was rag-heads?"

The victims, he meant; and he was asking Desoix because Desoix was an officer who might know about things like that.

The Lord knew he did.

"Maybe," Desoix said.

They had enough room here to walk two abreast, though the lightless footing was doubtful and caused men to bump. "Landlords—building superintendents. The guy you owe money to, the guy who screwed your daughter and then married the trollop down the hall."

"But . . . ?" another soldier said.

"Any body you're quick enough to point a dozen of your neighbors at," Desoix explained forcefully. "Before he points them at you. Party time."

The alley was the same throughout its length, but its other end opened onto more expensive facades and, across the broad street, patches of green surrounding the domed mass of the cathedral.

Traffic up the steps to the cathedral's arched south entrance was heavy and raucous. The street was choked by ground vehicles. Some of them trying to move but even these blocked by the many which had been parked in the travel lanes.

"Hey there!"shouted the bearded leader of the group striding from the doorway just to the left of the alley. He wore two pistols in belt holsters; the cross on the shoulder of his red cape was perfunctory. "Where're *you* going?"

"Back!" said Kekkonan over his shoulder, twisting to face the sudden threat.

Even before the one syllable order was spoken, the torchlight and echoing voices up the alley behind them warned the unit that they couldn't retreat the way they had come without shooting their way through.

Which would leave them in a street with five hundred or a thousand aroused residents who had pretty well used up their local entertainment.

"Hey!" repeated the leader. The gang that had exited the building behind him were a dozen more of the same, differing only in sex, armament, and whether or not they carried open bottles.

Most of them did.

They'd seen Kekkonan's body armor—and maybe his gun— when he turned toward them.

"Hey," Desoix said cheerfully as he stepped in front of the sergeant. "You know us. We're soldiers."

He'd been stationed in Bamberg City long enough that his Spanish had some of the local inflections that weren't on the sleep-learning cube. He wouldn't pass for a local, but neither did his voice put him instantly in the foreign—victim—category to these thugs.

"From the Palace?" asked the leader. His hand was still on a pistol, but his face had relaxed because Desoix was relaxed.

Desoix wasn't sure his legs were going to hold him up.

He'd been this frightened before, but that was when he was under fire and didn't have anything to do except crouch low and swear he'd resign and go home if only the Lord let him live this once.

"Sure," he said aloud, marvelling at how well his voice worked. "Say, chickie— got anything there for a thirsty man?"

"Up your ass with it!" a red-caped female shrieked in amazement.

All the men in the group bellowed laughter.

One of them offered Desoix a flask of excellent wine, an off-planet vintage as good as anything served in the Palace.

"You're comin' to the cathedral, then?" the leader said as Desoix drank, tasting the liquid but feeling nothing. "Well, come on, then. The meeting's started by now or I'll be buggered."

"Not by me, Easton!" one of his henchmen chortled.

"Come on, boys," Desoix called, waving his unit out of the alley before there was a collision with the mob following. "We're already late for the meeting!"

Thank the Lord, the troopers all had the discipline or common sense to obey without question. Hemmed by the gang they'd joined perforce, surrounded by hundreds of other citizens wearing crosses over a variety of clothing, Desoix's unit tramped meekly up the steps of the cathedral.

Just before they entered the building, Desoix took the risk of muttering into his epaulet mike, "Tyl, we're making a necessary detour, but we're still coming back. If the Lord is with us, we're still coming back."

CHAPTER TWENTY-ONE

The nave was already full. Voices echoing in debate showed that the gang leader had been correct about the meeting having started. Hospital orderlies with staves guarded the entrance—keeping order rather than positioned to stop an attack.

Bishop Trimer and those working with him knew there would be no attack—until they gave the order.

Easton blustered, but there was no bluffing the white-robed men blocking the doorway. One of the orderlies spoke into a radio with a belt-pack power source, while the man next to him keyed a handheld computer. A hologram of the bearded thug bloomed atop the computer in green light.

"Right, Easton," the guard captain said. "Left stairs to the north gallery. You and your folks make any trouble, we'll deal with it. Throw anything into the nave and you'll all decorate lamp posts. Understood?"

"Hey, I'm important!" the gang boss insisted. "I speak for the whole Seventeenth Ward, and I belong down with the bosses on the floor!"

"Right now, you belong on the Red side of the gallery," said the orderly. "Or out on your butts. Take your pick."

"You'll regret this!" Easton cried as he shuffled toward the indicated staircase. "I got friends! I'll make it hot fer you!"

"Who're you?" the guard captain asked Charles Desoix. His face was as grizzled as that of the Slammers sergeant major; his eyes were as flat as death.

If Desoix hadn't seen the platoon of orderlies with assault rifles rouse from the antechamber when the gang boss threatened, he would have been tempted to turn back down the steps instead of answering. He couldn't pick his choice of realities, though.

"We're soldiers," he said, leaving the details fuzzy as he had before. "Ah—this isn't official, we aren't, you see. We just thought we'd, ah . . . be ready ourselves to do our part. . . ."

He hoped that meant something positive to the guard captain, without sounding so positive that they'd wind up in the middle of real trouble.

The fellow with the radio was speaking into it as his eyes locked with Desoix's.

The UDB officer smiled brightly. The guard captain was talking to another of his men while both of them also looked at Desoix.

"All right," the captain said abruptly. "There's plenty of room in the south gallery. We're glad to have more converts to the ranks of active righteousness."

"We shoulda bugged out," muttered one of the troopers as they mounted the helical stairs behind Desoix.

"Keep your trap shut and do what the el-tee says," Sergeant Kekkonan snarled back.

For good or ill, Charles Desoix was in command now.

Given the sophistication of the commo unit the orderly at the door held, Desoix didn't dare try to report anything useful to those awaiting him back in the Palace. He hoped Anne would have had sense enough to flee the city before he got back to the Palace.

Almost as much as another part of him prayed that she would

be waiting when he returned; because he was very badly going to need the relaxation she brought him.

CHAPTER TWENTY-TWO

In daytime the dome would have floated on sunlight streaming through the forty arched windows on which it was supported. The hidden floods directed from light troughs to reflect from the inner surface were harsh and metallic by contrast, even though the metal was gold.

Desoix and his unit muscled their way to the railing of colored marble overlooking the nave. It might have been smarter to hang back against the gallery windows, but they were big men and aggressive enough to have found a career in institutionalized murder.

They were standing close to the east end and the hemicycle containing the altar, where the major figures in the present drama now faced the crowd of their supporters and underlings.

Between the two groups was a line of orderlies kneeling shoulder to shoulder. Even by leaning over the rail, Desoix could not see the faces of those on the altar dais.

But there were surprises in the crowd.

"That's Cerulio," Desoix said, nudging Kekkonan to look at a sumptuously dressed man in the front rank. His wife was with him, and the four men in blue around them were surely liveried servants. "He was in the Palace an hour ago. Said he was going to check his townhouse, but that he'd be back before morning."

"Don't know him," grunted Kekkonan. "But that one, three places over—" he didn't point, which reminded Desoix that pointing called attention to both ends of the out stretched arm "—he's in the adjutant general's staff, a colonel I'm pretty sure. Saw him when we were trying to requisition bunks."

Desoix felt a chill all the way up his spine. Though it didn't change anything beyond what they had already determined this night.

The man speaking wore white and a mitre, so that even from above there could be no mistaking Bishop Trimer.

"—wither away," his voice was saying. "Only in the last resort would God have us loose the righteous indignation that this so-called president has aroused in our hearts, in the heart of every Christian on Bamberia."

One shot, thought Charles Desoix.

He couldn't see Trimer's face, but there was a line of bare neck visible between mitre and chasuble. No armor there, no way to staunch the blood when a cyan bolt blasts a crater the size of a clenched fist.

And no way for the small group of soldiers to avoid being pulled into similarly fist-sized gobbets when the mob took its revenge in the aftermath. "Not our fight," Desoix muttered to himself.

He didn't have to explain that to any of his companions. He was pretty sure that Sergeant Kekkonan would kill him in an eye-blink if he thought the UDB officer was about to sacrifice them all.

"We will wait a day, in God's name," the Bishop said. He was standing with his arms outstretched.

Trimer had a good voice and what was probably a commanding manner to those who didn't see him from above—like Charles Desoix and God, assuming God was more than a step in Bishop Trimer's pursuit of temporal power. He could almost have filled the huge church with his unaided voice, and the strain of listening would have quieted the crowd that was restive with excitement and drink.

As it was, Trimer's words were relayed through hundreds of speakers hidden in the pendentives and among the acanthus leaves of the column capitals. Multiple sources echoed and fought one another, creating a busyness that encouraged whispering and argument among the audience.

Desoix had been part of enough interunit staff meetings to both recognize and explain the strain that was building in the Bishop's voice. Trimer was used to being in charge; and here, in his own cathedral, circumstances had conspired to rob him of the absolute control he normally exercised.

The man seated to Trimer's right got up. Like the Bishop, he was recognizable by his clothing—a red cape and a red beret in which a bird plume of some sort bobbed when he moved his head.

The Bishop turned. The gallery opposite Desoix exploded with cheers and catcalls. Red-garbed spectators in the nave below were jumping, making their capes balloon like bubbles boiling through a thick red sauce, despite the efforts of the hospital orderlies keeping the two factions separate.

All the men on the dais were standing with their hands raised. The noise lessened, then paused in a great hiss that the pillared aisles drank.

"Ten minutes each, we agreed," one of the faction leaders said to the Bishop in a voice amplified across the whole cathedral.

"Speak, then!" said the Bishop in a voice that was short of being a snarl by as little as the commotion below had avoided being a full-fledged riot.

Trimer and most of the others on the dais seated themselves again, leaving the man in red to stand alone. There was more cheering and, ominously, boos and threats from Desoix's side of the hall. Around the soldiers, orderlies fought a score of violent struggles with thugs in black.

The man in red raised his hands again and boomed, "Everybody siddown, curse it! We're *friends* here, friends—"

When the sound level dropped minusculy, he added, "Rich friends we're gonna be, every one of us!"

The cheers were general and loud enough to make the light troughs wobble.

"Now all you know there's no bigger supporter of the Bishop than I am," the gang boss continued in a voice whose nasality was smoothed by the multiple echoes. "But there's something else you all know, too. I'm not the man to back off when I got the hammer on some bastid neither."

He wasn't a stupid man. He forestalled the cheers—and the threats from the opposing side of the great room—that would have followed the statement by waving his arms again for silence even as he spoke.

"Now the way I sees it," he went on. "The way *anybody* sees it—is we got the hammer on Delcorio. So right now's the time we break 'is bloody neck for 'im. Not next week or next bloody year when somebody's cut another deal with 'im and he's got the streets full a' bloody soldiers!"

In the tumult of agreement, Desoix saw a woman wearing black cross-belts fight her way to the front of the spectators' section and wave a note over the heads of the line of orderlies.

The black-caped gang boss looked a question to the commo-helmeted aide with him on the dais. The aide shrugged in equal doubt, then obeyed the nodded order to reach across the orderlies and take the note from the woman's hand.

"Now the Bishop says," continued the man in red, "Give him a little time, he'll waste right away and nobody gets hurt. And that's fine, sure . . . but maybe it's time a few a' them snooty bastids *does* get hurt, right?"

The shouts of "yes" and "kill" were punctuated with other sounds as bestial as the cries of panthers hunting. It was noticeable that the front rank of spectators, the men and women with estates and townhouses, either sat silent or looked about nervously as they tried to feign enthusiasm.

While the red leader waited with his head thrown back and arms akimbo, the rival gang boss read the note he had been passed. He reached toward Bishop Trimer with it and, when another priest tried to take the document from his hand, swatted the man away. Trimer leaned over to read the note.

"Now I say," the man in red resumed in a lull, "allright, we give Delcorio time. We give the bastid as much time as it takes fer us to march over to the Palace and pull it down—"

The black-caped gang boss got up, drawing the Bishop's gaze to follow the note being thrust at the leader of the other street gang.

The timbre of the shouting changed as the spectators assessed what was happening in their own terms—and prepared for the immediate battle those terms might entail.

"The rightful President of Bamberia is Thomas Chastain," cried the black-caped leader as the cathedral hushed and his rival squinted at the note in the red light.

The man in red looked up but did not interrupt as the other leader thundered in a deep bass, "He was robbed of his heritage by the Delcorios and held under their guards in the Palace—but now he's escaped! Thom Chastain's at his house right now, waiting for us to come and restore him to his position!"

Everyone on the dais was standing. Some of the leaders, Church and gangs and surely the business community as well, tried to speak to one another over the tumult. Unless they could read lips, that was a useless exercise.

Desoix was sure of that. He'd been caught in an artillery barrage, and the decibel level of the bursting shells had been no greater than that of the voices reverberating now in the cathedral.

Bishop Trimer touched the gang bosses. They conferred with looks, then stepped back to give the Bishop the floor again. Though they did not sit down, they motioned their subordinates into chairs on the dais. After a minute or two, the room had quieted enough for Trimer to speak.

"My people," he began with his arms outstretched in benediction. "You have spoken, and the Lord God has made his will known to us. We will gather at dawn here—"

The gang bosses had been whispering to one another. The man in black tugged the Bishop's arm firmly enough to bring a burly priest—Father Laughlin?—from his seat. Before he could intervene, the red-garbed leader spoke to Trimer with forceful gestures of his hand.

The Bishop nodded. Desoix couldn't see his face, but he could imagine the look of bland agreement wiped thinly over fury at being interrupted and dictated to by thugs.

"My people," he continued with unctuous warmth, "we will meet at dawn in the plaza, where all the city can see me anoint our rightful president in the name of God who rules us. Then we will carry President Chastain with us to the Palace to claim his seat—and God will strengthen our arms to smite anyone so steeped in sin that they would deny his will. At dawn!"

The cheering went on and on. Even in the gallery, where the floor and the pillars of colored marble provided a screen from the worst of the noise, it was some minutes before Kekkonan could shout into Desoix's ear, "What's that mean for us, sir?"

"It means," the UDB officer shouted back, "that we've got a couple hours to load what we can and get the hell out of Bamberg City."

He paused a moment, then added, "It means we've had a good deal more luck the past half hour than we had any right to expect."

CHAPTER TWENTY-THREE

"We got 'em in sight," said Scratchard's voice through Tyl's commo helmet. The sergeant major was on the roof with the ten best marksmen in the unit. "Everybody together, no signs they're being followed."

Tyl started to acknowledge, but before he could Scratchard concluded, "Plenty units out tonight besides them, but nobody seems too interested in them nor us. Over."

"Out," Tyl said, letting his voice stand for his identification.

He locked eyes with the sullen Guards officer across the doorway from him, Captain Sanchez, and said, "Open it up, sir. I got a team coming in."

There were two dozen soldiers in the rotunda: the ordinary complement of Executive Guard and the squad Tyl had brought with him when Desoix blipped that they were clear again and heading in.

Earlier that night, the UDB officer had talked Tyl and his men through the doors that might have been barred to them. Tyl wasn't at all sure his diplomacy was good enough for him to return the favor diplomatically.

But he didn't doubt the locals would accept any suggestion he chose to make with a squad of Slammers at his back.

Sanchez didn't respond, but the man at the shutter controls punched the right buttons instantly. Warm air, laced with smoke more pungent than that of the omnipresent cigars, puffed into the circular hall.

Tyl stepped into the night.

The height and width of the House of Grace was marked by a cross of bluish light, a polarized surface discharge from the vitril glazing. It was impressive despite being marred by several shattered panels.

And it was the only light in the city beyond hand carried lanterns and the sickly pink-orange-red of spreading fires. Streetlights that hadn't been cut when transformers shorted were tempting targets for gunmen.

So were lighted windows, now that the meeting in the cathedral had broken up and the gangs were out in force again.

Tyl clicked his face shield down in the lighted courtyard and watched the seven soldiers jogging toward him with the greenish tinge of enhanced ambient light.

"All present 'n accounted for, sir," muttered Kekkonan when he reached Tyl, reporting because he was the senior Slammer in the unit.

"Sergeant major's got a squad on the roof," Tyl explained. "Make sure your own gear's ready to move, then relieve Jack. All right?"

"Yes *sir*," said Kekkonan and ducked off after his men. The emotion in his agreement was the only hint the noncom gave of just how tight things had been an hour before.

"Lachere, make sure Control's core pack's ready to jerk out," Desoix said. "We've got one jeep, so don't expect to leave with more than you can carry walking."

The clerk's boots skidded on the rotunda's stone flooring as he scampered to obey.

Desoix put his arm around Tyl's shoulders as they followed their subordinates through armored doors which the guard immediately began to close behind them. Tyl was glad of the contact. He felt like a rat in a maze in this warren of corridors and blocked exits.

"I appreciate your help," Desoix said. "It might have worked. And without those very good people you lent me, it would—"

He paused. "It wouldn't have been survivable. And I'd have

probably made the attempt anyway, because I didn't understand what it was like out there until we started back."

"I guess . . ." Tyl said. "I guess we better report to, to the President before we go. Unless he was tapping the push. I guess we owe him that, for the contract."

They stepped together into the small elevator. It was no longer separately guarded. The Executive Guardsmen watched them without expression.

A few of the Slammers stationed in the rotunda threw ironic salutes. They were in a brighter mood than they'd been a few minutes before. They knew from their fellows who'd just come in that the whole unit would be bugging out shortly.

"You're short of transport too?" Tyl asked, trying to keep the concern out of his voice as he watched Desoix sidelong.

"I can give my seat to your sergeant major, if that's what you mean," Desoix replied. "I've hiked before. But yes, this was the base unit they robbed to outfit all the batteries on Two that had to be mobile."

That was exactly what Tyl had meant.

The elevator stopped. In the moment before the door opened, Desoix added, "There's vehicles parked in the garage under the Palace here. If we're providing protection, there shouldn't be a problem arranging rides."

If it's safe to call attention to yourself with a vehicle, Tyl thought, remembering the fire trucks. Luxury cars with the presidential seal would be even better targets.

Tyl expected Anne McGill to be at the open door connecting the Consistory Room with the presidential suite, where she could be in sight of her mistress and still able to hear the elevator arrive. She was closer than that, arm's length of the elevator—and so was Eunice Delcorio.

The President was across the room, in silhouette against the faint glow which was all that remained of the City Offices toward which he was staring. His nephew stood beside him, but there was no one else—not even a servant—in the darkened room.

"Charles?" Anne said. Her big body trembled like a spring, but she did not reach to clasp her lover now, in front of Eunice.

Tyl let Desoix handle the next part. They hadn't discussed it, but the UDB officer knew more about things like this . . . politics and the emotions that accompany politics.

Desoix stepped forward and bowed to Eunice Delcorio, expertly sweeping back the civilian cape he still wore over his gun and armor. "Madam," he said. "Sir—" John Delcorio had turned to watch them,though he remained where he was. "I very much regret that it's time for you to withdraw from the city."

The President slammed the bottom of his fist against the marble pillar beside him. Anne was nodding hopeful agreement; her mistress was still, though not calm.

"There's still time to get out," Desoix continued. Tyl marvelled at Desoix's control. *He* wanted to get out, wanted it so badly that he had to consciously restrain himself from jumping into the elevator and ordering the unit to form on him in the courtyard.

"But *barely* enough time. The—they are going to anoint Thom Chastain President at dawn in the plaza, and then they'll come here. Even if they haven't gotten heavy weapons from one of the military arsenals, there's no possible way that the Palace can be defended."

"I knew the swine were betraying me,"Delcorio shouted. "I should never have let them live, never!"

"We can cover the way out if you move fast enough," Tyl said aloud. "Ten minutes, maybe."

What he'd seen in the Consistory Room and heard from Desoix's terse report on the way back to the Palace convinced him that Delcorio, not Thom Chastain, was responsible for the present situation. But *why* didn't matter anymore.

"All right," the President said calmly. "I've already packed the seal and robes of state. I had to do it myself because they'd all run, even Heinrich. . . ."

"No," said Eunice Delcorio. *"No!"*

"Eunice," begged Anne McGill.

"Ma'am," said Tyl Koopman desperately. "There's no way."

He was unwilling to see people throw themselves away. You

learn that when you fight for hire. There's always another contract, if you're around to take it up. . . .

"I've been mistress of this city, of this planet," the President's wife said in a voice that hummed like a cable being tightened. "If they think to change that, well, they can burn me in the Palace first."

She turned to stare, either at her husband or at the smoldering night beyond him. "It'll be a fitting monument, I think," she said.

"And I'll set the fires *myself*—" whirling, her eyes lashed both the mercenary officers "—if no one's man enough to help me defend it."

Anne McGill fell to her knees, praying or crying.

"Madam," said Major Borodin, entering from the hall unannounced because there was no greeter in the building to announce him.

The battery commander looked neither nervous nor frustrated. There was an aura of vague distaste about him, the way his sort of officer always looked when required to speak to a group of people.

This was a set speech, not a contribution to the discussion.

"I urge you," Borodin went on, reeling the words off a sheaf of mental notes, "to use common sense in making personal decisions. So far as public decisions go, I must inform you that I am withdrawing my battery from the area affected by the present unrest, under orders of my commander—and with the concurrence of our legal staff."

"I said—" John Delcorio began, ready to blaze up harmlessly at having his nose rubbed in a reality of which he was already aware.

"No, of *course* we can defeat them!" said Eunice, pirouetting to Borodin's side with a girlish sprightliness that surprised everyone else in the room as much as it did the major.

"No, no," the President's wife continued brightly, one hand on Borodin's elbow while the other hand gestured to her audience. "It's really quite possible, don't you see? There's many of them and only a few of us—but if they're in the plaza, well, we just hold the entrances."

She stroked Borodin's arm and waved, palm up, to Tyl and Desoix. Her smile seemed to double the width of her face. "You brave lads can do that, can't you? Just the three stairs, and you'll have the Executive Guard to help you. The Bishop won't make any trouble about coming to the Palace alone to discuss matters if the choice is. . . ."

Eunice paused delicately. This wasn't the woman who moments before had been ready—*had* been ready—to burn herself alive with the Palace. "And this way, all the trouble ends and no one more gets hurt, all the rioting and troubles. . . ."

"No," said Major Borodin. His eyes were bulging and he didn't appear to be seeing any of his present surroundings. His mental notes had been hopelessly disarrayed by this—

"Yes, yes, of *course!*" President Delcorio said, rubbing his hands together in anticipation. "We'll see how much Trimer blusters when he's asked to come and there's a *gun* at his head to see that he does!"

Tyl had pointed enough guns to know that they weren't the kind of magic wand Delcorio seemed to be expecting. He looked at Desoix, certain of agreement and hopeful that the UDB officer would be able to express the plan's absurdity in a more tactful fashion than Tyl could.

Desoix had lifted Anne McGill to her feet. His hand was on the woman's waist, but she wasn't paying any conscious attention to him. Instead, her eyes were on Eunice Delcorio.

"No," muttered Borodin. "No, no! We've got to withdraw at once."

Maybe it was the rote dismissal by the battery commander that made Tyl really start thinking, Colonel Hammer wanted Delcorio kept in power for another week—and no deal Trimer cut with the present government was likely to last *longer* than that, but a week . . . ?

Two hundred men and a pair of calliopes—blazes, maybe it *would* work!

"Of course," Tyl said aloud, "Marshal Dowell's on the other side, sure as can be, so the Guard downstairs . . . ?"

"Dowell isn't the Executive Guard," said the President dismissively. "He's nothing but a jumped-up shopkeeper. I was a fool to think he'd be loyal because he owed everything to me."

Like City Prefect Berne, Tyl thought. He kept his mouth shut.

"But the Guard, they're the best people in the State," Delcorio continued with enthusiasm. "They won't give in to trash and gutter sweepings now that we've found a way to deal with them."

"Lieutenant," said the battery commander, "I'll oversee the loading. Give the withdrawal orders as soon as you've determined the safest routes."

He pivoted on his left heel, rotating his elbow from Eunice's seductive touch. He stamped out of the room.

"Yes sir," Desoix said crisply, but he made no immediate motion to follow his superior.

"Well," said Tyl, feeling the relief that returned with resignation—it'd been a crazy notion, but just for a minute he'd thought . . . "Well, I better tell—"

"Wait!" Anne McGill said. She stepped toward her mistress, but she was no longer ignoring Charles Desoix. Halfway between the two she spun toward her lover and set a jewel-ringed hand at the scooped collar of the dress she wore beneath her cloak. She pulled fiercely.

The hem of lustrous synthetic held. White and red creases sprang out where the straps crossed her shoulders.

"Anne?" the President's wife called from behind her companion.

Anne wailed, "Mary, Queen of Heaven!" and tugged again, pulling the left strap down to her elbow instead of trying again to tear the fabric. Her breast, firm but far too heavy not to sag, flopped over the bodice which had restrained it.

"Is this what you want to give to them?" she cried. Her eyes were blind, even before she shut them in a vain attempt to hold back the tears. "Give the, the *mob*? I won't go! I won't leave Eunice even if you *are* all cowards?"

"Anne," Desoix pleaded. "President Delcorio—the front row in the cathedral *was* the best people in the State. Some of them were here with you this morning. Colonel Drescher isn't going to—"

"How do you know until you ask him?" Eunice demanded in a voice like a rapier. Her arm was around Anne McGill now, drawing the dark cloak over the naked breast. Tyl couldn't say whether the gesture was motherly or simply proprietary.

This hasn't got anything t' do with . . . his surface mind started to tell him; but deeper down, he knew it did. Like as not it always did, one way or another; who was screwing who and how everybody felt about it.

"All right!" Desoix shouted. "We'll go ask him!"

"I'll go myself," said President Delcorio, sucking in his belly and adding a centimeter to his height by straightening up.

"That's not safe, Uncle John," said Pedro Delcorio unexpectedly. "I'll go with the men."

"Well . . ." Tyl said as the President's nephew gestured him toward the elevator. Desoix, his face set in furious determination, was already inside.

It was going to be cramped with three of them. "Via, why not?" Tyl said. It was easier to go along than to refuse to, right now. Nothing would come of it. He'd seen too many parade-ground units to expect this one to find guts all of a sudden.

But if just maybe it did work . . .Via, nobody liked to run with their tail between their legs, did they?

CHAPTER TWENTY-FOUR

Koopman's idiotic grin was just one more irritation to Charles Desoix as the elevator dropped.

"Bit of a chance you're taking, isn't it?" the Slammers officer asked. "Going against your major's orders and all?"

Desoix felt himself become calm and was glad of it. None of this made any sense. If Tyl decided to laugh—well, that was a saner response than Desoix's own.

"Only if something comes of it," he said,wishing that he didn't sound so tired. Wrung out.

He *was* wrung out. "And if I'm alive afterward, of course."

Pedro's eyes were darting between the mercenaries. His bulky body—soft but not flabby—would have given him presence under some circumstances. In these tight quarters he was overwhelmed by the men in armor—and by the way they considered the future in the light of similar pasts.

The car settled so gently that only the door opening announced the rotunda. Desoix swung out to the left side, noticing that identical reflex had moved Koopman to the right—as if they were about to clear a defended position.

Half a dozen powerguns were leveled at the opening door, though the Slammers here on guard jerked their muzzles away when they saw who had arrived.

The rotunda was empty except for Hammer's men.

"Where's the guards?" Koopman demanded in amazement.

One of his men shrugged. "A few minutes back, they all moved out."

He pointed down the corridor that led toward the Guard billets. "I called the sar'ent major, but he said hold what we got, he and the rest a' the company'd be with us any time now."

"Let's go, then!" said Pedro Delcorio, trotting in the direction of the gesture.

Desoix followed, because that was what he'd set out to do. He hunched himself to settle his armor again. When he felt cold, as now, he seemed to shrink within the ceramic shell.

"Carry on," Koopman said to his guard squad. As the Slammers officer strode along behind the other two men, Desoix heard him speaking into his commo helmet in a low voice.

The barracks of the Executive Guard occupied the back corridor of the Palace's south wing. It had its own double gate of scissor-hinged brass bars over a panel of imported hardwood, both portions polished daily by servants.

The bars were open, the panel—steel-cored, Desoix now noticed—ajar. Captain Sanchez and the squad he'd commanded in the rotunda stood in the opening, arguing with other Guardsmen in the corridor beyond. When they heard the sound of boots approaching, they whirled. Several of them aimed their rifles.

Charles Desoix froze, raising his hands and moving them out from his sides. He had been close to death a number of times already this night.

But never closer than now.

"What do you men think you're doing?" Pedro demanded in a voice tremulous with rage. "Don't you recognize me? I'm—"

"*No!*" Sanchez snapped to the man at his side. The leveled assault rifle wavered but did not fire—as both Desoix and the Guards captain had expected.

"Wha . . . ?" Delcorio said in bewilderment.

"Rene, it's me," Desoix called in an easy voice. He sidled a step so that Sanchez could see him clearly past the President's nephew. Walking *forward* was possible suicide. "Charles, you know? We came to discuss the present situation with Colonel Drescher."

The words rolled off Desoix's tongue, amazing him with their blandness and fluency. Whatever else that scene upstairs with Anne had done, it had burned the capacity to be shocked out of him for a time.

Drescher stepped forward when his name was spoken. He had been the other half of the argument in the gateway. The lower ranking Guardsmen grounded their weapons as if embarrassed to be touching real hardware in the presence of their commander.

"Master Desoix," said Drescher, "we're very busy just now. I have nothing to discuss with you or any of John Delcorio's by-blows."

"*What?*" Pedro Delcorio shouted, able this time to get the full syllable out in his rage.

Koopman put a hand, his left hand, on the young civilian's shoulder and shifted him back a step without being too obvious about the force required.

Desoix walked forward, turning his spread arms into gestures as he said, "Sir, it's become possible to quell the rioting without further bloodshed or the need for additional troops. We'd like to discuss the matter with you for a moment."

As if Drescher's deliberate ignorance of his military rank didn't bother him, Desoix added with an ingratiating smile, "It will make you the hero of the day, sir. Of the century."

"And who's that?" Drescher said, waving his swagger stick in the direction of the Slammers officer. "Your trained dog, Desoix?"

Recent events had shocked the Guard Commandant into denial so deep that he was being more insulting than usual to prove that civilization and the rule of law still maintained in his presence. Charles Desoix knew that, but Tyl Koopman with a submachine-gun under his arm—

"No sir," said the Slammers officer. "I'm Captain Koopman of Hammer's Regiment. My unit's part of the defense team."

"Sir," Desoix said in the pause that followed Koopman's response and sudden awareness of what the mercenary's response *could* have been. "The mob will have gathered in the plaza by dawn. By sealing the three exits, we can bring their, ah, leaders, to a reasonable accommodation with the government."

"The government of the State," said Drescher icily, cutting through Desoix's planned next phrase, "is what God and the people choose it to be. The Executive Guard would not presume to interfere with that choice."

"Colonel," Desoix said. He could feel his eyes widening, but he didn't see the Guardsmen in front of him. In his mind, a dozen men were raping Anne McGill while shrill-voiced women urged them on. "If they attack the Palace, there'll be a bloodbath."

"Then it's necessary to evacuate the Palace, isn't it?" Drescher replied. "Now, if you *gentle*—"

"Don't you boys take oaths?" Koopman asked curiously. There wasn't any apparent emotion in his tone. "Don't they matter to you?"

Colonel Drescher went white. "You foreign mercenaries have a vision of Bamberg politics," he said, "that a native can only describe as bizarre." His voice sounded as though he would have been screaming if his lungs held enough air. "Now get *away* from here!"

Charles Desoix bowed low. "Gentlemen," he murmured to his companions as he turned. "We have no further business here."

They didn't look behind them as they marched to where the corridor jogged and the wall gave them cover against a burst of shots into their backs. Pedro Delcorio was shaking.

So was Koopman, but it showed itself as a lilt in his voice as he said, "Well, they're frightened. Can't blame 'em, can we, Charles? And they'd not have been much use, just stand there and nobody who'd seen 'em in their prettiness was going to be much scared, eh?"

Adrenalin was babbling through the lips of the Slammers officer.

His right hand was working in front of him where the Guardsmen couldn't see it, clenching and unclenching, because if it didn't move, it was going to find its home on the grip of his submachine-gun. . . .

Anne was waiting around the comer. She looked at the faces of the three men and closed her eyes.

"Anne, we can't—" Desoix began. He was sure there had to be something he could say that would keep her from the suicide she'd threatened, at the hands of the mob or more abruptly here with a rope or the gun he knew she kept in her bedroom.

"Sure we can," said Tyl Koopman. His voice had no emotion, and his eyes had an eerie, thousand-meter stare.

"You've got a calliope aimed at both side stairs, sure, they won't buck that, one burst and that's over. And me and the boys, sure, we'll take the main stairs, those lock gates, they're like vaults, *no* problem."

"Then it's all right?" Anne said in amazement. Her beautiful face was lighting as if she were watching a theophany. "You can still save us, Charles?"

She touched her fingertips to his chest, assuring herself of her lover's continuing humanity.

"I—" said Charles Desoix. He looked at the Slammers officer, then back into the eyes of Anne McGill.

They'd have to do something about Major Borodin—literally put the old man under restraint. Maybe Delcorio still had a few servants around who could handle that.

"I—" Desoix repeated.

Then he squared his shoulders and said, "Certainly, darling, Tyl and I can handle it without the help of *those* fools."

It amazed the UDB officer to realize how easily he had decided to ruin his life. The saving grace was the fact that there wouldn't be many hours of life remaining to him after this decision.

CHAPTER TWENTY-FIVE

Tyl watched the antenna of his laser communicator quest on the porch outside the Consistory Room, making a keening sound as it searched for its satellite. The link was still thirty seconds short of completion when his commo helmet said, "Four-six to Six, over."

Tyl jumped, ringing the muzzle of his submachine-gun against the rail as he spun.

"Go ahead, Four-six," he said to Sergeant Major Scratchard when he realized that the call was on the unit push, not the laser link he'd been setting up. He was a hair late in his response, but nobody else knew the unexpected call had scared him like that.

"Sir," said Scratchard, "the Palace troops, they're all marching out one a' the side doors right now. Over."

Good riddance, Tyl thought. "Let 'em go, Jack," he said. "Six out."

"Six?"

"Go ahead, Four-six."

"Sir, should we secure the doors after them? Over."

"Negative, Four-six," Tyl snapped. "Ignore this bloody building and carry out your orders! Six out."

It hadn't been that silly a question. Jack was nervous because he didn't know much, because Tyl hadn't told him very much. The noncom was trying to cross all possible tees because he couldn't guess which ones would turn out to be of critical importance.

Neither could his captain. Which was the real reason Tyl had jumped down the sergeant major's throat.

A dim red light pulsed on the antenna's tracking head, indicating that the unit had locked on. Tyl switched modes on his helmet, grimaced, and said, "Koopman to Central, over."

Seconds of flickering static, aural and visual, took his mind off the cross dominating the skyline toward which the laser pointed. It was only an hour before dawn. The streets were alive with bands of men and women, ant-small at this distance and moving like foraging ants toward the plaza.

"Hold one," said the helmet. The screen surged into momentary crystal sharpness. Colonel Hammer glared from it.

He looked very tired. All but his eyes.

"Go ahead, Captain," Hammer said, and the static fuzzing his voice blurred his image a moment later as well, as though a bead curtain had been drawn between Tyl and his commander.

Tyl found that a lot more comfortable. Funny the things you worry about instead of the really worrisome things. . . .

"Sir," he said, knowing that his voice sounded dull—it had to, he couldn't let emotion get out during this report because he hadn't any idea of what emotion he'd find himself displaying. "I've alerted my men for an operation at dawn to bottle up the rioters and demand the surrender of their leaders. We'll be operating in concert with elements of the UDB."

There was no need to say "over," since the speakers could see one another—albeit with a lag of a few seconds. Tyl keyed the thumb-sized unit on his sending head, a module loaded with the street plan, routes, and makeup of the units taking part in the operation. The pre-load burped out like an angry katydid.

Hammer's eyes, never at rest, paused briefly on a point to the left of the pickup feeding Tyl's screen. A separate holotank was displaying the schematic, while Tyl's face continued to fill the main unit.

Hammer's face wore no expression as it clicked to meet Tyl's eyes again. "What are the numbers on the other side?" he asked emotionlessly.

"Sir, upwards of twenty kay. Maybe fifty, the plaza'd hold that much and more."

Tyl paused. "Sir," he added, "we can't fight 'em, we know that. But maybe we can face them down, the leaders."

People were moving in the courtyard beneath him, four cloaked figures sopping out of the Palace on their missions. Desoix and his two clerks to the warehouse and the calliope they'd set up only hours before. And. . . .

"How are you timing your assault?" the colonel asked calmly. "If the ringleaders aren't present, you've gained nothing. And if you wait too long . . . ?"

"Sir, one of the women from the Palace," Tyl explained. "She's, ah, getting in position right now in the south gallery of the cathedral. There's a view to the altar on the seafront, that's where the big ones'll be. She'll cue us when she spots the ones we need."

He thought he was done speaking, but his tongue went on

unexpectedly, "Sir, we thought of using a man, but a woman going to pray now—it's not going to upset anything. She'll be all right."

The colonel frowned as if trying to understand why a line captain was apologizing for using a female lookout. It didn't make a lot of sense to Tyl either, after he heard his own words—but he'd been away for a long time.

And anyway, the only similarity between Anne McGill and the dozen females in Tyl's present command was that their plumbing was the same.

"What happens if they don't back down?" Hammer said in a voice like a whetstone, apparently smooth but certain to wear away whatever it rubs against, given time and will.

"We bug out," Tyl answered frankly. "The mall at the main stairs, that's where we'll be, it's got gates like bank vaults on all four sides. Things don't work out, Trimer ducks instead of putting his hands up and his buddies start shooting—well, we slam the plaza side doors and we're gone."

"And your supports?" Hammer asked. His mouth wavered in what might have been either static or an incipient grin.

"Desoix's men, they're mounted," Tyl said. It was an open question whether or not you could really load a double crew on a calliope and drive away with it, but that was one for the UDB to answer. "Worst case, there's going to be too much confusion for organized pursuit. Unless . . ."

"Unless the streets are already blocked behind you," said Colonel Hammer,who must have begun speaking before Tyl's voice trailed off on the same awareness. "Unless there's a large enough group of rioters between your unit and safety to hold you for their fifty thousand friends to arrive."

"Yes sir," said Tyl.

He swallowed. "Sir," he said, "I can't promise it'll work. If it does, it'll give you the time you wanted for things to hot up over there. But I can't promise."

"Son," said Colonel Hammer. He was grinning like a skull. "When you start making promises on chances like this, I'll remove you from command so fast your ears'll ring."

His face straightened into neutral lines again. "For the record," Hammer said, "you're operating without orders. Not in violation of orders, just on your own initiative."

"Yes *sir*," Tyl said.

Hammer hadn't paused for agreement. He was saying, "I expect you to withdraw as soon as you determine that there is no longer a realistic chance of success. Nobody's being paid to be heroes, and—"

He leaned closer to the pickup. His face was grim and his eyes glared like gun muzzles. "Captain, if *you* throw my men away because you want to be a hero, I'll shoot you with my own hand. If you survive."

"Yes *sir*," Tyl said through a swallow. This time his commander had waited for an acknowledgment.

Hammer softened. "Then good luck to you, son," he said. "Oh—and son?"

"Yes sir?"

The colonel grinned with the same death's-head humor as before. "Bishop Trimer decided Hammer's Slammers weren't worth their price," Hammer said. "It wouldn't bother me if by the end of today, His Eminence had decided he was wrong on that."

Hammer touched a hidden switch and static flooded the screen.

"Four-six to Six," came Scratchard's voice, delayed until the laser link was broken. "We're ready, sir. Over."

"Four-six," Tyl said as he shrugged his armor loose over his sweating torso. "I'm on my way."

He left the laser communicator set up where it was. He'd need it again after the operation was over.

In the event that he survived.

CHAPTER TWENTY-SIX

"—gathered together at the dawn of a new age for our nation, our planet, and our God," said the voice.

Bishop Trimer's words had a touch of excitement remaining to them, despite being attenuated through multiple steps before they got to Tyl's helmet. Anne McGill aimed a directional microphone from the cathedral to the seafront altar, below her and over a kilometer away.

Trimer's speech was patched through the commo gear hidden between the woman's breasts, then shuttled by the UDB artificial intelligence over the inter-unit frequency to Tyl Koopman.

"We could shoot the bastard easy as listen to him," Scratchard said as he held out a shoulder weapon to his captain.

Only the two of them among the ninety-eight troopers in the rotunda had helmets that would receive the transmission. The other Slammers watched in silence as varied as their individual personalities: frightened; feral; cautious; and not a few with anticipation that drew back their lips in memory of past events. . . .

"Might break the back of the rebellion," Tyl said.

He had to will his eyes to focus on Scratchard's face, on anything as near as the walls of the big room. "Sure as blood that lot—" he touched his helmet over the tiny speaker "—they'd burn the city down to bricks 'n bare concrete. Might as well nuke 'em as that."

His voice didn't sound, even to him, as if he much cared. He wasn't sure he did care. He wasn't really involved with things that could be or might be . . . or even were.

"With dawn comes the light," the Bishop was saying. "With this dawn, the Lord brings us also the new light of freedom in the person of the man he has commanded me to anoint President of Bamberia."

"Jack, I don't need that," Tyl said peevishly. Sight of the 2cm weapon being pushed toward him had brought him back to reality; irritation had succeeded where abstracts like survival and success could not. "I got a gun, remember?"

He slapped the receiver of the submachine-gun under his arm, then noticed that the whole company was carrying double as well as being festooned with bandoliers and strings of grenades.

"UDB's weapons stores were here in the Palace," the sergeant major explained patiently. "Their el-tee, he told us go ahead. Sir, we don't got far to go. And I swear, they all jam."

Scratchard grinned sadly. He lifted his right boot to display the hilt of his fighting knife, though with his hands full he couldn't touch it for emphasis. "Even these, the blade can break. When you really don't want t' see that."

"Sorry," said Tyl, glad beyond words to be back in the present with sweaty palms and an itch between his shoulder blades that he couldn't have scratched even if it weren't covered by his clamshell armor.

"Blazes," he added as he checked the load—full magazine, chamber empty. "Here's my treatment a' choice anyhow. I'll take punch over pecka-pecka-pecka any day."

He looked up and glared around the circle of his troops as if seeing them for the first time. Pretty nearly he was. Good men, good soldiers; and just the team to pull the plug on Trimer and the bully boys who thought they owned the streets when the Slammers were in town.

"Thomas Chastain has mounted the dais," said Anne McGill. She sounded calm, but the distance in her voice was more than an electronic artifact. "Both Chastain brothers. The faction heads are present, and so are several churchmen, standing beneath the crucifix."

Tyl keyed the command channel while ducking through the bandolier of 2cm magazines the sergeant major held for him.

"Orange to Blue Six," he said, using the code he and the UDB officer had set up in a few seconds when they realized that they'd need it. "Report."

"Blue Six ready," said Desoix's voice.

"Orange to Blue Three. Report."

"Blue Three ready," said a voice Tyl didn't recognize, the non-com in charge of the Gun Three near the east entrance to the plaza.

"Orange Six to Blue," Tyl said. "We're moving into position . . . now."

He cut down with his right index finger. Before the gesture ended, Sergeant Kekkonan was leading the first squad into the incipient dawn over Bamberg City.

CHAPTER TWENTY-SEVEN

"I figured they'd a' burned it down, the way they was going last night," said Lachere, blinking around the warehouse from the driver's seat.

"Tonight," he said, correcting himself in mild wonder.

"Senter, what's the street look like?" Desoix asked from the gun saddle. Beneath him the calliope quivered like a sleeping hound, its being at placid idle—but ready to rend and bellow the instant it was aroused.

Desoix couldn't blame his subordinate for thinking more than a few hours had passed since they first entered this warehouse. It seemed like a lifetime—

And that wasn't a thought Lieutenant Charles Desoix wanted to pursue, even in the privacy of his own mind.

"I don't see anybody out, sir," the other clerk called from the half-open pedestrian door. "Maybe lookin' out a window, I can't tell. But none a' the big mobs like when we got here."

Reentering the warehouse without being caught up—or cut down—by the bands of bravos heading toward the plaza had been the trickiest part of the operation so far. Stealth was the only option open to Desoix and his two companions. Even if Koopman had been willing—been able, it didn't matter—to spare a squad in support, a firefight would still mean sure disaster for the plan as well as for the unit.

"All right, Senter," Desoix said. "Open the main doors and climb aboard."

Lachere was bringing the fans up to driving velocity without orders. He wasn't a great driver, but he'd handled air-cushion vehicles before and could maneuver the calliope well enough for present needs.

The suction roar boomed in the cavernous room while Senter struggled with the unfamiliar door mechanism. The warehouse staff—manager, loaders, and guards—had disappeared at the first sign of trouble, leaving nothing behind but crated goods and the heavy effluvium of tobacco to be stirred into a frenzy by the calliope's drive fans.

The door rumbled upward; Senter scampered toward the gun vehicle. Desoix smiled. He'd been ready to clear their way with his eight 3cm guns if necessary.

He had ordered Control to lock the general frequency out of his headset. Captain Koopman was in charge of this operation, so Desoix didn't have to listen to the running commentary about what the mob in the plaza was doing.

If he listened on that frequency, he would hear Anne; and he would have to remember where she was and how certainly she would die if he failed.

"Ready, sir?" Lachere demanded, shouting as though his voice weren't being transmitted over the intercom channel.

Desoix raised a hand in bar. "Blue Six to all Blue and Orange units," he said. "We're moving into position—now."

He chopped his hand.

Lachere accelerated them into the street with a clear view of the plaza's south stair head, two blocks away.

Metal shrieked as Lachere sideswiped the door jamb, but none of the calliope's scratch crew noticed the sound.

CHAPTER TWENTY-EIGHT

"I'm with you!" said Pedro Delcorio, gripping Tyl's shoulder from behind. He was almost with the angels, because Tyl spun and punched the young noble in the belly with the weapon he'd just charged, his finger taking up slack.

"Careful, sonny," the Slammers officer said as intellect twitched away the gun that reflex had pointed.

Tyl felt light, as though his body were suspended on wires that someone else was holding. His skin was covered with a sheen of sweat that had nothing to do with the night's mild breezes.

Pedro wore a uniform—a service uniform, probably; though the clinking, glittering medals on both sides of the chest indicated that the kid still had something to learn about combat conditions. He also wore a determined expression and a pistol in a polished holster.

"You're doing this for my family," Pedro said. "One of us should be with you."

"That why we're doing it?" Tyl asked, marvelling at the lilt in his own voice. Tyl wasn't sure the kid knew how close he'd come to dying a moment before. "Well, it'll do unless a better reason comes along. Stick close, boy, and leave that—" he nodded toward the gun "—in its holster."

He had a squad on the levee and a squad deployed to cover the boulevard and medians separating the Palace from the cathedral. The rest of the Slammers were moving at a nervous shuffle down the river drive bunched more than he liked, than anybody'd like, but they were going to need all the firepower available to clear the mall in a hurry. Those hydraulic gates were the key to the operation: the key to bare safety, much less success.

No one seemed to be out, but Tyl could hear occasional shouts in the distance as well as the antiphonal roars from the plaza— though the latter were directed upward,into the sulphurous dawn, by the flood walls. Litter of all sorts splotched the pavement, waste and shattered valuables as well as a few bodies.

One of the crumpled bodies jumped up ahead of them. The drunk tottered backward when his foot slipped on the bottle which had put him there in the first place.

Tyl's point man fired a ten-shot burst—far too long—at the drunk. The bolts splashed all around the target, cyan flashes and the white blaze of lime burned out of the concrete. None of the rounds hit the intended victim.

A sergeant jumped to the shooter's side and slapped him hard on the helmet. "Cop-head!" he snarled. "Cop-head! Get your ass behind me. And if you shoot again without orders, you better have the muzzle in your mouth!"

The drunk scrambled in the general direction of the cathedral, stumbling and rolling on the ground to rise and stumble again. The air bit with the odors of ozone and quicklime.

The company shuffled onward with a squad leader in front.

"Blue Six to all Blue and Orange units," said Tyl's commo helmet. Desoix sounded tight, a message played ten percent faster than it'd been recorded. "We're moving into position—now."

The point man paused at the base of the ramp to the mall and the plaza's main stairs.

"Check your loads, boys," said Sergeant Major Scratchard over the unit push.

Jack was back with the three squads of the second wave, but Tyl didn't expect him to stay there long when the shooting started.

"Sir," reported the point sergeant, using the command channel, "the gates are shut on this side."

"Orange Six to all Blue and Orange," Tyl ordered as he ran the ten meters to where the noncom paused. "Don't bloody move. We got a problem."

The gates separating the mall from the west river drive were as massive and invulnerable as those facing the plaza itself.

They were closed, just as the point man had said.

Tyl ran up the ramp, his bandoliers clashing against one another. The slung submachine-gun gouged his hip beneath the flare of his armor. The gates were solid, solid enough to shrug away tidal surges with more power than a battery of artillery.

There was no way one company without demolition charges or heavy weapons was going to force its way through.

The small vitril windows in the gate panels were too scarred and dirty to show more than hinted movement, but there was a speaker plate in one of the pillars. Nothing ventured. . . .

Tyl keyed the speaker and said, "Open these gates at once, in the name of Bishop Trimer!"

The crowd in the plaza cheered deafeningly, shaking the earth like a distant bomb blast.

Shadows, colors, shifted within the closed mall. The plate replied in the voice of Colonel Drescher, "Go away, little lapdog. The Executive Guard is neutral, as I told you. And this is where we choose to exercise our neutrality."

The crowd thundered, working itself into bloodthirsty enthusiasm.

Tyl turned his back on the reinforced concrete and touched his commo helmet. His troops were crouching, watching him. Those who wore their shields down had saffron bubbles for faces, painted by the glow which preceded the sun.

"Orange to Blue Six," Tyl said. "We're screwed. The Guards're holding the mall and they got it shut up. We can't get in, and if we tried we'd bring the whole bunch down on us. Save what you can, buddy. Over."

He'd forgotten that Anne McGill had access to the circuit. Before Desoix could speak, her voice rang like shards of crystal through Tyl's helmet, saying, "The river level has dropped. You can go under the plaza on a barge and come up beneath the altar."

The cross on the cathedral dome was beginning to blaze with sunlight. McGill's angle was on the seafront. She couldn't see any of the troops, Tyl's or the pair of calliopes, and she wouldn't have understood a *bloody* thing if she had been able to watch them. Bloody woman, bloody planet. . . .

Bloody fool, Captain Tyl Koopman, to be standing here. Nobody he saw was moving except Scratchard, clumping up the ramp to his captain's side. If Ripper Jack were bothered by his knees or the doubled load of weaponry, there was no sign of it on his expectant face.

"Tyl, she's right," Desoix was saying. "Most of the louvers are still closed, so there's no risk of drifting out to sea, but the maintenance catwalks lead straight up to the control house. The altar."

"Roger on the river level," the sergeant major muttered with his lips alone. He must've spoken to the noncom on the levee, using one of the support frequencies so as not to tie up the command push.

Tyl looked up at the sky, bright and clear after a night that was neither.

"Tyl, we'll give the support we can," Desoix said. Both officers knew exactly what the change of plan would mean. They weren't going to be able to *talk* to the mob when they came up into the plaza. Desoix was apparently willing to go along with the change.

Wonder what the colonel would say?

Colonel Hammer wasn't here. Tyl Koopman was, and he was ready to go along with it too. More fool him.

"Orange Six to all Orange personnel," he said on the unit push. "We're going to board the nearest barge and cut it loose so we drift to the dam at the other end of the plaza. . . ."

CHAPTER TWENTY-NINE

Some of the men were still scrambling aboard the barge, the second of the ten in line rather than the nearest, because it seemed less likely to scrape the whole distance along the concrete channel. Tyl didn't hear the order Jack Scratchard muttered into his commo helmet, but troopers standing by three of the four cables opened fire simultaneously.

Arm-thick ropes of woven steel parted in individual flashes. The barge sagged outward, its stern thumping the fenders of the vessel to port. Only the starboard bow line beside Tyl and the sergeant major held their barge against the current sucking them seaward.

The vertical lights on the walls, faintly green, merged as the channel drew outward toward the river's broad mouth and the dam closing it. They reflected from the water surface, now five meters beneath the concrete roof though it was still wet enough to scatter the light back again in turn.

"Hold one, Jack," Tyl said as he remembered there was another thing he needed to do before they slipped beneath the plaza. He keyed his helmet on the general interunit frequency and said, "Orange Six to all Orange personnel. I am ordering you to carry out an attack on the Bamberg citizens assembled in the plaza. Anyone who refuses to obey my order will be shot."

"Via!" cried one of the nearer soldiers. "I'm not afraid to go, sir!"

"Shut up, you fool!" snarled Ripper Jack. "Don't you understand? He's just covered your ass for afterward!"

Tyl grinned bleakly at the sergeant major. Everybody seemed to have boarded the vessel, clinging to one another and balancing on the curves of hogsheads.

"Cut 'er loose," he said quietly.

Scratchard's powergun blasted the remaining cable with a blue-green glare and a gout of white sparks whose trails lingered in the air as the barge lurched forward.

Their stern brushed along the portside barge until they drifted fully clear. The grind of metal against the polymer fenders was unpleasant. Friction spun them slowly counterclockwise until they swung free.

They continued to rotate for the full distance beneath the widening channel. One trooper vomited over his neighbor's back-plate, though that was more likely nerves than the gentle, gently frustrating motion.

Light coming through the louvered flood gates was already brighter than the greenish artificial sources on either wall. It was still diffuse sky-glow rather than the glare of direct sun, but the timing was going to be very close.

The barge grounded broadside with a crash that knocked down anybody who was standing. Perhaps because of their rotation, they'd remained pretty well centered in the channel. Individually and without waiting for orders, the troopers nearest the catwalk jumped to it and began to lower a floating stage like the one on the dam's exterior.

"They must've heard something," Tyl grumbled. The variety of metallic sounds the barge made echoed like a boiler works among the planes of water and concrete. But as soon as the barge had slipped its lines, Tyl had been unable to hear even a whisper of what he knew was a sky-shattering clamor from the crowded plaza. Probably those above were equally insulated.

And anyway, it didn't matter now. Tyl pressed forward to the pontoon-mounted stage and the stairs of steel grating leading up to the open hatch of the control room. Tyl's rank took him through his jostling men, but it was all he could do not to use his elbows and gun butt to force his way faster.

He had to remember that he was commanding a unit, not throwing his life away for no reason he could explain even to himself. He had to act as if there were military purpose to what he was about to do.

Only two men could stand abreast on the punched-steel stair treads, and that by pressing hard against the rails. The control room was almost as tight, space for ten men being filled by a dozen. Tyl squeezed his way in, pausing in the hatchway. When he turned to address his troops, he found the sergeant major just behind him.

It would have been nice to organize this better; but it would have been nicer yet for somebody else to be doing it. Or no one at all.

"Stop bloody pushing!" Tyl snapped on the unit frequency. Inside the control room, his signal would have been drunk by the meter-thick floor of the plaza. No wonder sound didn't get through.

Motion stopped, except for the gentle resilience of the barge's fenders against the closed floodgates.

"There's one door out into the plaza," Tyl said simply. "We'll deploy through it, spread out as much as possible. If it doesn't work out, try to withdraw toward the east or west stairs, maybe the calliopes can give us some cover. Do your jobs, boys, and we'll come through this all right."

Scratchard laid a hand on the captain's elbow, then keyed his own helmet and said, "Listen up. This is nothin' you don't know. There's a lot of people up there."

He pumped the muzzle of his submachine-gun toward the ceiling. "So long as there's one of 'em standing, none of us 're safe. Got that?"

Heads nodded, hands stroked the iridium barrels of powerguns. Some of the recruits exchanged glances.

"Then let's go," the sergeant major said simply. He hefted himself toward the hatchway.

Tyl blocked him. "I want you below, Jack," he said. "Last man out."

Scratchard grinned and shook his head. "I briefed Kekkonan for that," he said.

Tyl hesitated.

Scratchard's face sobered. "Cap'n," he said. "This don't take good knees. What it takes, I got."

"All right, let's go," said Tyl very softly. "But I'm the first through the door."

He pushed his way to the door out onto the plaza, hearing the sergeant major wheezing a step behind.

CHAPTER THIRTY

Anne McGill couldn't see the sun, but the edges of the House of Grace gleamed as they bent light from the orb already over the horizon to the northeast.

The crucifix on the seafront altar was golden and dazzling. The sun had not yet reached it, but Bishop Trimer was too good a showman not to allow for that: the gilt symbol was equipped with a surface-discharge system like that which made expensive clothing shimmer. What was good enough for the Consistory Room was good enough for God—as he was represented here in Bamberg City.

"Anne, what's happening in the plaza?" said the tiny phone in her left ear. "Do you see any sign of the, of Koopman? Over."

She was kneeling as if in an attitude of prayer, though she faced the half-open window. There were scores of others in the cathedral this morning, but no one would disturb another penitent. Like her, they were wrapped in their cloaks and their prayers.

And perhaps all of their prayers were as complex and uncertain as those of Anne McGill, lookout for a pair of mercenary companies and mistress of a man whom she had prevented from retreating with her to a place of safety.

"Oh Charles," she whispered. "Oh Charles." Then she touched the control of her throat mike and said in a firm voice, "Chastain is kneeling before Bishop Trimer in front of the crucifix. He's putting a—I don't know, maybe the seal of office around his neck but I thought that was still in the Palace. . . ."

The finger-long directional microphone was clipped to the window transom which held it steady and unobtrusive. UDB stores included optical equipment as powerful and sophisticated as the audio pickup; but in use, an electronic telescope looked like exactly what it was—military hardware, and a dead giveaway of the person using it.

She had only her naked eyes. Though she squinted she couldn't be sure—

"The Slammers, curse it!" her lover's voice snapped in her ear. Charles' tongue suppressed the further words, "you idiot," but they were there in his tone. "Is there any sign of them?"

"No, no," she cried desperately. She'd forgotten to turn on her microphone. "Charles, no," she said with her thumb pressing the switch as if to crush it. "Chastain is rising and the crowds—"

Anne didn't see the door beneath the altar open the first time. There was only a flicker of movement in her peripheral vision, ajar and then closed.

Her subconscious was still trying to identify it when a dozen flashes lighted the front of the crowd facing the altar.

For another moment, she thought those were part of the celebration, but people were sprawling away from the flashes. A second later, the popping sound of the grenades going off reached her vantage point.

Men were spilling out of the altar building. The bolts from their weapons hurt Anne's eyes, even shielded by distance and full dawn.

"Charles!" she cried, careless now of who might hear her in the gallery. "It's started! They're—"

The air near the seafront echoed with a crashing hiss like that of a dragon striking. Anne McGill had never heard anything like it before. She didn't know that it was a calliope firing—but she knew that it meant death.

Buildings hid her view of the impact zone at the west stair head of the plaza, but some of the debris flung a hundred meters in the air could still be identified as parts of human bodies.

CHAPTER THIRTY-ONE

When the grenades burst, Scratchard jerked the metal door open again—a millisecond before a slow fuse detonated the last of their greeting cards. A scrap of glass-fiber shrapnel drew a line across the back of Tyl's left thumb.

He didn't notice it. He was already shooting from the hip at the first person he saw as he swung through the doorway, a baton-waving orderly whose face was almost as white as his robe except where blood spattered both of them.

Tyl's target was a meter and a half away from his gun muzzle. He missed. The red cape and shoulder of a woman beside the orderly exploded in a cyan flash.

The orderly swung his baton in desperation, but he was already dead. Jack Scratchard put a burst into his face before pointing his submachine-gun at the group on the altar above and behind them. Trimer flattened, carrying Thom Chastain with him, but blue-green fire flicked the chests of both gang bosses.

Tyl hadn't appreciated the noise. It beat on him, a pressure squeezing him into his armor and engulfing the usual *thump!* of his bolts heating the air like miniature lightning. He butted his weapon firmly against his shoulder and fired three times to clear the area to his right.

The targets fell. Their eyes were still startled and blinking, though the 2cm bolts had scooped their chests into fire and a sludge of gore.

Tyl strode onward, making room for the troopers behind him as he'd planned, as he'd ordered in some distant other universe.

An army officer leaped from the altar with a pistol in his hand, either seeking shelter in the crowd or fleeing Scratchard's quick gun in blind panic. The Bamberg soldier doubled up as fate carried him past Tyl's muzzle and reflex squeezed the powergun's trigger.

Short range but a nice crossing shot. Tyl was fine and the noise, the shouting, was better protection than his helmet and clamshell. But there were too many of the bastards, a mass like the sea itself, and Tyl was all alone in a tide that would wash over him and his men no matter what they—

One calliope, then the other, opened fire. Not even crowd noise and the adrenalin coursing through his blood could keep the Slammers officer from noticing that.

He stepped forward, his right shoulder against the altar building to keep him from slipping. Each shot was aimed, and none of them missed.

In a manner of speaking, Tyl Koopman's face wore a smile.

CHAPTER THIRTY-TWO

The bollards at the stair head were hidden by the units on guard, thugs wearing the colors of both factions and a detachment of hospital orderlies.

There were at least fifty heavily armed men and women in plain sight of Desoix's calliope—and it was only a matter of moments before one of them would turn from the ceremony and look up the street.

There weren't many options available then.

"Is there any sign of them?" Desoix shouted to—at his mistress as she nattered on about what Trimer was using as he swore in his stooge as President.

Lachere was twisted around in the driver's saddle, peering back at his lieutenant and chewing the end of a cold cigar, a habit he'd picked up in the months they'd been stationed here. He didn't look worried, but Senter had enough fear in his expression for both clerks as he stared at Desoix's profile from his station at the loading console.

"Charles!" cried the voice he had let through to him again for necessity. "It's—"

Desoix had already heard the muffled exclamation points of the grenades.

"Blue Six to Blue Three," he said, manually cutting a way to the unit frequency. "Open fire."

As his mouth voiced the final flat syllable, his right foot rocked forward on the firing pedal. Traversing left to right, Desoix swept the stair head clear of all obstructions with the eight ravening barrels of his calliope.

The big weapon was intended for computer-directed air defense. Under manual control, its sights were only a little more sophisticated than those of shoulder-fired powerguns: a hologrammatic sight picture with a bead in the center to mark the point of impact.

Nothing more was required.

Several of the guards turned when the grenades went off, instinctively looking for escape and instead seeing behind them the calliope's lowered muzzles. One of the orderlies got off a burst with his submachine-gun.

The bullets missed by a hundred meters in the two blocks they were meant to travel. Concrete, steel, and flesh—most particularly flesh—vaporized as the calliope chewed across the stair head in a three-second burst.

Desoix switched to intercom with the hand he didn't need for the moment on the elevation control and said, "Lachere, advance toward the stair head at a—"

Faces appeared around the seawall just north of where the bollards had been before the gun burned them away. The high-intensity 3cm ammunition had shattered concrete at the start of the burst before Desoix traversed away. His right hand rolled forward on the twist-grip, reversing the direction in which the barrel array rotated on its gimbals.

More of the wall disintegrated in cyan light and the white glare of lime burned free of the concrete by enormously concentrated energy. Most of the rioters had time to duck back behind the wall before the second burst raked it.

The wall didn't save them. Multiple impacts tore it apart and then flash-heated the water in their own bodies into steam explosions.

Beneath Desoix, the skirts of the calliope's plenum chamber dragged the pavement. Air had enough mass to recoil when it was heated to a plasma and expelled from the eight tubes as the gun fired. Lachere drove forward, correcting inexpertly against the calliope's pitch and yaw.

Gunfire was a blue-green shield against the roar from the plaza, but in the moments between bursts the mob's voice asserted itself over the numbness of ringing breech blocks and slamming air. The stair head was now within a hundred meters as the gun drove onward. There was a haze over the target area—steam and dust, burnt lime and burning bodies.

Desoix's face shield protected him from the sun-hot flash of his guns. Events, thundering forward as implacably as an avalanche, shielded him from awareness that would have been as devastating to him as being blinded.

With no target but the roiling haze, Desoix triggered another burst when they were ten meters from the stair head. Fragments blown clear by the impacts proved that there had been people sheltering beneath eye level but accessible to the upper pair of gun tubes.

"Sir?" a voice demanded, Lachere slowing and ready to ground the vehicle before they lurched over the scars where the bollards had been and their bow tilted down the steps.

"Go!" Desoix shouted, knowing that the plenum chamber would spill its air in the angle of the stair treads and that their unaided fans would never be able to lift the calliope away once they had committed.

Koopman and his company of Slammers weren't going anywhere either, unless they all succeeded in the most certain and irrevocable way possible.

The stench of ozone and ruin boiled out from beneath the drive fans an instant before the calliope rocked forward. Gravity aided its motion for an instant before the friction of steel against stone grounded the skirts. The plaza was a sea of faces with a roar like the surf.

Bullets rang off the hull and splashed the glowing iridium of one port-side barrel. The doors of the mall at the head of the main stairs were open toward the plaza. Men there were firing assault rifles at the calliope. Some of them were either good or very lucky.

Desoix rotated his gun carriage.

"Sir!" Senter cried with his helmet against the lieutenants. "Those aren't the mob! They're the Guard!"

"Feed your guns, soldier!" said Charles Desoix. The open flood gates filled his sight hologram.

He rocked the firing pedal down and began to traverse his target in a blaze of light.

CHAPTER THIRTY-THREE

Tyl's index finger tightened. The gunstock pummeled his shoulder. The center of his face shield went momentarily black as it mirrored away the flash that would otherwise have blinded him.

A finger of plastic flipped up into his sight picture, indicating that he'd just fired the last charge in his weapon. He reached for another magazine.

A hospital orderly stopped trying to claw through the mass of other panicked humans and turned to face Tyl. He was less than ten meters away and held a pistol.

Tyl raised the tube of 2cm ammunition to the loading gate in the forestock and burned the nail and third knuckle of all the fingers on his left hand. He'd already put several magazines through the powergun, so its barrel was white hot.

He dropped the magazine. The orderly shot him in the center of the chest.

There was no sound anymore in the plaza. Tyl could see everything down to the last hair on the moustache of the orderly collapsing around a bolt from somebody else's powergun. His armor spread the bullet's impact, but it felt as if they'd driven a tank over his chest. Maybe if he didn't move. . . .

The calliope which was canted down the west staircase opened fire again.

Only three of the eight barrels were live at the moment. Individual bolts made a thump as ionized air ripped from the barrel; they crossed the plaza a few meters over Tyl's head as a microsecond *hiss!* and a flash of light so saturated that it seemed palpable.

Everything the bolts hit was disintegrated with a crash sharper than a bomb going off, solids converted to gas and plasma as suddenly as the light-swift bursts of energy had snapped through the air. The plaza's concrete flooring gouted in explosions of dazzling white—

But the crowd was packed too thickly for that to happen often. The calliope's angle allowed its crew to rake the mob from above.

Each 3cm bolt hit like the hoof of a horse galloping over soft ground, hurling spray and bits of the footing in every direction before lifting to hammer the surface again.

Bodies crumpled in windrows. Screaming rioters climbed the fallen on their way toward the main stairs, already packed with their fellows. The guns continued to fire.

"If I can hear, I can move," Tyl said, mouthing the words because that *was* his first movement since the bullet hit him.

He knelt to pick up the magazine he had dropped. The pain that flooded him, hot needles being jabbed into his whole chest, made him drop the empty gun instead.

He couldn't breathe. He didn't fall down because his muscles were locked in a web of flesh surrounding a center of pulsing red agony.

The spasm passed.

Tyl's troopers were spread in a ragged semicircle, centering on the building from which they'd deployed. He was near the east stairs; the treads were covered with bodies.

Rebels had been shot in the back as they tried to run from the soldiers and the blue-green scintillance of hand weapons. If they reached the top of the stairs, Gun Three on the seafront hurled them back as a puree and a scattering of fragments.

The west stairs were relatively empty, because the mob had time to clear it in the face of the calliope staggering toward them. They died on the plaza floor, because they'd run toward the debouching infantry; but the steps gleamed white in the sunlight and provided a pure contrast to the bodies and garments crumpled everywhere else in muddy profusion.

Tyl left the 2cm weapon where he'd dropped it; he raised his submachine-gun. It felt light by contrast with the thick iridium barrel of the shoulder weapon, but he still had trouble aiming.

It was hot, and Tyl was as thirsty as he ever remembered being. Ozone had lifted all the mucus away from the membranes of his nose and throat. The mordant gas was concentrated by shooting in the enclosed wedge of the plaza. The skin of Tyl's face and hands prickled as if sunburned.

He aimed at a face and missed high, the barrel wobbling, sending the round into the back of somebody a hundred meters away on the main stairs.

He lowered the muzzle and fired again, fired again, fired again.

Single shots, aimed at anyone who looked toward him instead of trying to get away. Second choice for targets were the white robes of orderlies, most of whom had been armed—though few enough had the discipline to stand in chaos against the mercenaries' armor and overwhelming firepower.

Third choice was whoever filled the sight picture next. None of the mercenaries were safe so long as one of the others was standing.

The calliope opened up again. Desoix had unjammed and reloaded six of the barrels. A thick line staggered through the mob like the track of a tornado across a corn field.

Tyl fired; fired again; fired again. . . .

CHAPTER THIRTY-FOUR

It was very quiet.

Desoix watched the men from Gun Three's doubled crew as they picked their way across the plaza at his orders. Sergeant Blaney was leading the quartet himself. They were carrying their submachine-guns ready and moving with a gingerly awkwardness, trying to avoid stepping in the carnage.

Nobody could get down the east stairs without smearing his boots to the ankles with blood.

"They could hurry up with the water," Lachere muttered.

"They didn't see it happen," Desoix said. He lay across the firing console, his chin on his hands and his elbows on the control grips he no longer needed to twist.

He closed his eyes for a moment instead of rubbing them.

Desoix's hands and face, like those of his men, were black with iridium burned from the calliope's bores by the continuous firing. The vapor had condensed in the air and settled as dust over everything within ten meters of the muzzles. Rubbing his eyes before he washed would drive the finely divided metal under the lids, into the orbits.

Desoix kept reminding himself that it would matter to him someday, when he wasn't so tired.

"They just shot when somebody ran up the stairs and gave them a target," he continued in the croak that was all the voice remaining to him until Blaney arrived with the water. "It wasn't like—"

He wanted to raise his arm to indicate the plaza's carpet of the dead, but waggling an index finger was as much as he had need or energy to accomplish. "It wasn't what we had, all targets, and it. . . ."

Desoix tried to remember how he would have felt if he had come upon this scene an hour earlier. He couldn't, so he let his voice trail off.

A lot of them must have gotten out when somebody opened the gates at either end of the mall. Desoix had tried to avoid raking the mall and the main stairs. The mercenaries had to end the insurrection and clear the plaza for their own safety, but the civilians swept out by fear were as harmless as their fellows who filled the sight picture as the calliope coughed and traversed.

There'd been just the one long burst which cleared the mall of riflemen.

Cleared it of life.

"Here you go, sir," said Blaney, skipping up the last few steps with a four-liter canteen and hopping onto the deck of the calliope.

"Took yer bloody time," Lachere repeated as he snatched the canteen another of the newcomers offered him. He began slurping the water down so greedily that he choked and sprayed a mouthful out his nostrils.

Senter was drinking also. He hunched down behind the breeches of the guns he had been feeding, so that he could not see any of what surrounded the calliope. Even so, the clerk's eyelids were pressed tightly together except for brief flashes that showed his dilated pupils.

"Ah, where's Major Borodin, sir?" Blaney asked.

Desoix closed his eyes again, luxuriating in the feel of warm water swirling in his mouth.

Gun Three had full supplies for its double crew before the shooting started. Desoix hadn't thought to load himself and his two clerks with water before they set out.

He hadn't been planning; just reacting, stimulus by stimulus, to a situation over which he had abdicated conscious control.

"The major's back at the Palace," Desoix said. "President Delcorio told me he wanted a trustworthy officer with him, so I commanded the field operations myself."

He didn't care about himself anymore. He stuck to the story he had arranged with Delcorio because it was as easy to tell as the truth . . . and because Desoix still felt a rush of loyalty to his battery commander.

They'd succeeded, and Major Borodin could have his portion of the triumph if he wanted it.

Charles Desoix wished it had been him, not Borodin, who had spent the last two hours locked in a storeroom in the Palace. But his memory would not permit him to think that, even as a fantasy.

"Blaney," he said aloud. "I'm putting you in command of this gun until we get straightened around. I'm going down to check with Captain Koopman." He nodded toward the cluster of gray and khaki soldiers sprawled near the altar.

"Ah, sir?" Blaney said in a nervous tone. Desoix paused after swinging his leg over the gunner's saddle. He shrugged, as much response as he felt like making at the moment.

"Sir, we started taking sniper fire, had two guys hurt," Blaney went on. "We—I laid the gun on the hospital, put a burst into it to, you know, get their attention. Ah, the sniping stopped."

"Via, you really did, didn't you?" said the officer, amazed that he hadn't noticed the damage before.

Gun Three had a flat angle on the south face of the glittering building. Almost a third of the vitril panels on that side were gone in a raking slash from the ground floor to the twentieth. The bolts wouldn't have penetrated the hospital, though the Lord knew what bits of the shattered windows had done when they flew around inside.

Charles Desoix began to laugh. He choked and had to grip the calliope's chassis in order to keep from falling over. He hadn't been sure that he would ever laugh again.

"Sergeant," he said, shutting his eyes because Blaney's stricken face would set him off again if he watched it. "You're afraid you're in trouble because of *that*?"

He risked a look at Blaney. The sergeant was nodding blankly.

Desoix gripped his subordinate's hand. "Don't worry," he said. "Don't. I'll just tell them to put it on my account."

He took the canteen with him as he walked down the stairs toward Tyl Koopman. Halfway down, he stumbled when he slipped on a dismembered leg.

That set him laughing again.

CHAPTER THIRTY-FIVE

"Got twelve could use help," said the sergeant major as Tyl shuddered under the jets of topical anesthetic he was spraying onto his own chest.

Scratchard frowned and added, "Maybe you too, hey?"

"Via, I'm fine," Tyl said, trying to smooth the grimace that wanted to twist his face awry. "No dead?"

He looked around sharply and immediately wished he hadn't tried to move quite that fast.

Tyl's ceramic breastplate had stopped the bullet and spread its impact across the whole inner surface of the armor. That was survivable; but now, with the armor and his tunic stripped off, Tyl's chest was a symphony of bruising. His ribs and the seams of his tunic pockets were emphasized in purple, and the flesh between those highlights was a dull yellow-gray of its own.

Scratchard shrugged. "Krasinski took one in the face," he said. "Had 'er shield down too, but when your number's up. . . ."

Tyl sprayed anesthetic. The curse that ripped out of his mouth could have been directed at the way the mist settled across him and made the bruised flesh pucker as it chilled.

"Timmons stood on a grenade," Scratchard continued, squatting beside his captain. "Prob'ly his own. Told 'em not to screw with grenades after we committed, but they never listen, not when it gets . . .”

Scratchard's fingers were working with the gun he now carried, a slug-firing machine pistol. The magazine lay on the ground beside him. The trigger group came out, then the barrel tilted from the receiver at the touch of the sergeant major's experienced fingers.

Jack wasn't watching his hands. His eyes were open and empty, focused on the main stairs because there were no fallen troopers there. They'd been his men too.

"One a' the recruits," Scratchard continued quietly, "he didn't want to go up the ladder."

Tyl looked at the noncom.

Scratchard shrugged again. "Kekkonan shot him. Wasn't a lotta time to discuss things."

"Kekkonan due another stripe?" Tyl asked.

"After this?" Scratchard replied, his voice bright with unexpected emotion. "We're *all* due bloody something, sir!"

His face blanked. His fingers began to reassemble the gun he'd picked up when he'd fired all the ammunition for both the power-guns he carried.

Tyl looked at their prisoners, the half-dozen men who'd survived when Jack sprayed the group on the altar. Now they clustered near the low building, under the guns of a pair of troopers who'd been told to guard them.

The soldiers were too tired to pay much attention. The prisoners were too frightened to need guarding at all.

Thom Chastain still wore a gold-trimmed scarlet robe. A soldier had ripped away the chain and pendant Tyl remembered vaguely from earlier in the morning. Thom smiled like a porcelain doll, a hideous contrast with the tears which continued to shiver down his cheeks.

The tears were particularly noticeable because one of the gang bosses beside Thom on the altar had been shot in the neck. He'd been very active in his dying, painting everyone nearby with streaks of bright, oxygen-rich blood. The boy's tears washed tracks in the blood.

Bishop Trimer and three lesser priests stood a meter from the Chastains—and as far apart as turned backs and icy expressions could make them.

Father Laughlin was trying to hunch himself down to the height of other men. His white robes dragged the ground when he forgot to draw them up with his hands; their hem was bloody.

The prisoners weren't willing to sit down the way the Slammers did. But *nobody* was used to a scene like this.

"I never saw so many bodies," said Charles Desoix.

"Yeah, me too," Tyl agreed.

He hadn't seen the UDB officer walk up beside him. His eyes itched. He supposed there was something wrong with his peripheral vision from the ozone or the actinics—despite his face shield.

"Water?" Desoix offered.

"Thanks," Tyl said, accepting the offer though water still sloshed in the canteen on his own belt. He drank and paused, then sipped again.

Where the calliope had raked the mob, corpses lay in rows like flotsam thrown onto the strand by a storm. Otherwise, the half of the plaza nearer the seafront was strewn rather than carpeted with bodies. You could walk that far and, if you were careful, step only on concrete.

Bloody concrete.

Where the plaza narrowed toward the main stairs, there was no longer room even for the corpses. They were piled one upon another . . . five in a stack . . . a ramp ten meters deep, rising at the same angle as the stairs and composed of human flesh compressed by the weight of more humans—each trying to escape by clambering over his fellows, each dying in turn as the guns continued to fire.

The stench of scattered viscera was a sour miasma as the sun began to warm the plaza.

"How many, d'ye guess?" Tyl asked as he handed back the canteen.

He was sure his voice was normal, but he felt his body begin to shiver uncontrollably. It was the drugs, it *had* to be the anesthetic.

"Twenty thousand, thirty thousand," Desoix said. He cleared

his throat, but his voice broke anyway as he tried to say, "They did, they . . ."

Desoix bent his head. When he lifted it again, he said in a voice as clear as the glitter of tears in his eyes, "I think as many were crushed trying to get away as we killed ourselves. But we killed enough."

Something moved at the head of the main stairs. Tyl aimed the submachine-gun he'd picked up when he stood. Pain filled his torso like the fracture lines in breaking glass, but he didn't shudder anymore. The sight picture was razor sharp.

An aircar with the gold and crystal markings of the Palace slid through the mall and cruised down the main stairs. The vehicle was being driven low and slow, just above the surface, because surprising the troops here meant sudden death.

Even laymen could see that.

Tyl lowered his weapon, wondering what would have happened if he'd taken up the last trigger pressure and spilled John and Eunice Delcorio onto the bodies of so many of their opponents.

The car's driver and the man beside him were palace servants, both in their sixties. They looked out of place, even without the pistols in issue holsters belted over their blue livery.

Major Borodin and Colonel Drescher rode in the middle pair of seats, ahead of the presidential couple.

The battery commander was the first to get out when the car grounded beside the mercenary officers. The electronic piping of Borodin's uniform glittered brighter than sunlight on the metal around him. He blinked at his surroundings, at the prisoners. Then he nodded to Desoix and said, "Lieutenant, you've, ah—carried out your orders in a satisfactory fashion."

Desoix saluted. "Thank you, sir," he said in a voice as dead as the stench of thirty thousand bodies.

Colonel Drescher followed Borodin, moving like a marionette with a broken wire. The flap of his holster was closed, but there was no gun inside. One of the Guard commander's polished boots was missing. He held the sole of the bare foot slightly above the concrete, where it would have been if he were fully dressed.

President Delcorio stepped from the vehicle and handed out his

wife as if they were at a public function. Both of them were wearing
cloth of gold, dazzling even though the cat's fans had flung up bits
of the carnage as it carried them through the plaza.

"Gentlemen," Delcorio said, nodding to Tyl and Desoix. His
throat hadn't been wracked by the residues of battle, so his voice
sounded subtly wrong in its smooth normalcy.

Pedro Delcorio was walking to join his uncle from the control
room beneath the altar. He carried a pistol in his right hand. The
bore of the powergun was bright and not scarred by use.

The President and his wife approached the prisoners. Major
Borodin fluffed the thighs of his uniform; Drescher stood on one
foot, his eyes looking out over the channel.

President Delcorio stared at the Bishop. The other priests
hunched away, as if Delcorio's gaze were wind-blown sleet.

Trimer faced him squarely. The Bishop was a short man and
slightly built even in the bulk of his episcopal garments, but he was
very much alive. Looking at him, Tyl remembered the faint glow
that firelight had washed across the eyes of Trimer's face carven on
the House of Grace.

"Bishop," said John Delcorio. "I'm so glad my men were able
to rescue you from this—" his foot delicately gestured toward the
nearest body, a woman undressed by the grenade blast that killed
her "—rabble."

Father Laughlin straightened so abruptly that he almost fell
when he kicked the pile of communications and data transfer equipment which his two fellows had piled on the ground. No one had
bothered to strip the priests of their hardware, but they had done so
themselves as quickly as they were able.

Perhaps the priests felt they could distance themselves from
what had gone before . . . or what they expected to come later.

"Pres . . ." said Bishop Trimer cautiously. His voice was oil
smooth—until it cracked. "President?"

"Yes, very glad," Delcorio continued. "I think it must be that the
Christ-denying elements were behind the riot. I'm sure they took
you prisoner when they heard you had offered all the assets of the
Church to support our crusade."

Laughlin threw his hands to his face, covering his mouth and a look of horror.

"Yes, all Church personalty," said Trimer. "Except what is needed for the immediate sustenance of the Lord's servants."

"All assets, real and personal, is what I'd heard," said the President. His voice was flat. The index finger of his right hand was rising as, if to make a gesture, a cutting motion.

"Yes, personal property and all the estates of the Church outside of Bamberg City itself," said Bishop Trimer. He thrust out his chin, looking even more like the bas relief on the shot-scarred hospital.

Delcorio paused, then nodded. "Yes," he said. "That's what I understood. We'll go back to—"

Eunice Delcorio looked at Tyl. "You," she said in a clear voice, ignoring her husband and seemingly ignoring the fact that he had spoken. "Shoot these two."

She pointed toward the Chastains.

Tyl raised his submachine-gun's muzzle skyward and stepped toward the President's wife.

"Sir!" shouted Ripper Jack Scratchard, close enough that his big hand gripped Tyl's shoulder. "Don't!"

Tyl pulled free. He took Eunice's right hand in his left and pressed her palm against the grip of the submachine-gun. He forced her fingers closed. "Here," he said. "You do it."

He hadn't thought he was shouting, but he must have been from the way all of them stared at him, their faces growing pale.

He spun Eunice around to face the ramp of bodies. She was a solid woman and tried to resist, but that was nothing to him now. "It's easy," he said. "See how bloody easy it is?

Do you see?"

A shot cracked. He *had* been shouting. The muzzle blast didn't seem loud at all.

Tyl turned. Scratchard fired his captured weapon again. Richie Chastain screamed and stumbled across his twin; Thom was already down with a hole behind his right ear and a line of blood from the corner of his mouth.

Scratchard fired twice more as the boy thrashed on his belly. The second bullet punched through the chest cavity and ricocheted from the ground with a hum of fury.

Tyl threw his gun down. He turned and tried to walk away, but he couldn't see anything. He would have fallen except that Scratchard took one of his arms and Desoix the other, holding him and standing between him and the Delcorios.

"Bishop Trimer," he heard the President saying. "Will you adjourn with us, please, to the Palace." There was no question in the tone. "We have some details to work out, and I think we'll be more comfortable there, though my servant situation is a—"

Tyl turned.

"Wait," he said. Everyone was watching him. There was a red blotch on the back of Eunice's hand where he'd held her, but he was as controlled as the tide, now. "I want doctors for my men."

He lifted his hand toward the House of Grace, glorying in the pain of moving. "You got a whole hospital, there. I want doctors, *now*, and I want every one of my boys treated like he was Christ himself. Understood?"

"Of course, of course," said Father Laughlin in the voice Tyl remembered from the Consistory Meeting.

The big priest turned to the man who had been wearing the commo set and snarled, "Well, get *on* it, Ryan. You heard the man!"

Ryan knelt and began speaking into the handset, glancing sometimes up at the hospital's shattered facade and sometimes back at the Slammers captain. The only color on the priest's face was a splotch of someone else's blood.

Trimer walked to the aircar, arm in arm with President Delcorio.

Borodin and Drescher had already boarded. Neither of them would let their eyes focus on anything around them. When Pedro Delcorio squeezed in between them, the two officers made room without comment.

Father Laughlin would have followed the Bishop, but Eunice Delcorio glanced at his heavy form and gestured dismissingly. Laughlin watched the car lift into a hover; then, sinking his head low, he strode in the direction of the east stairs.

Tyl Koopman stood between his sergeant major and the UDB lieutenant. He was beginning to shiver again.

"What's it mean, d'ye suppose?" he whispered in the direction of the main stairs.

"Mean?" said Charles Desoix dispassionately. "It means that John Delcorio is President—President in more than name—for the first time. It means that he really has the resources to prosecute his Crusade, the war on Two, to a successful conclusion. I doubt that would have been possible without the financial support of the Church."

"But who *cares*!" Tyl shouted. "D'ye mean we've got jobs for the next two years? Who bloody cares? Somebody'd 've hired us, you know that!"

"It means," said Jack Scratchard, "that we're alive and they're dead. That's all it means, sir."

"It's *got* to mean more than that," Tyl whispered.

But as he looked at the heaps and rows of bodies, tens of thousands of dead human beings stiffening in the sun, he couldn't put any real belief into the words.

CHAPTER THIRTY-SIX

The Slammers were gone.

Ambulances had carried their wounded off, each with a guard of other troopers ready to add a few more bodies to the day's bag if any of Trimer's men seemed less than perfectly dedicated to healing the wounded. Desoix thought he'd heard the sergeant major say something about bivouacking in the House of Grace, but he hadn't been paying much attention.

There was nothing here for him. He ought to leave himself.

Desoix turned. Anne McGill was walking toward him. She had thrown off the cloak that covered her in the cathedral and was wearing only a dress of white chiffon like the one in which she had greeted him the day before.

Her face was set. She was moving very slowly, because she

would not look down and her feet kept brushing the things that she refused to see.

Desoix began to tremble. He had unlatched his body armor, but he still had it on. The halves rattled against one another as he watched the woman approach.

There was nothing there. There couldn't be anything left there now.

It didn't matter. That was only one of many things which had died this morning. No doubt he'd feel it was an unimportant one in later years.

Anne put her arms around him, crushing her cheek against his though he was black with iridium dust and dried blood. "I'm so sorry," she whispered. "Charles, I—we . . . Charles, I love you."

As if love could matter now.

Desoix put his arms around her, squeezing gently so that the edges of his armor would not bite into her soft flesh.

Love mattered, even now.

AFTERWORD TO COUNTING THE COST:

HOW THEY GOT THAT WAY

I gained my first real insight into tanks when I was about eight years old and the local newspaper ran a picture of one, an M41 Walker Bulldog, on the front page.

The M41 isn't especially big. It's longer than the Studebaker my family had at the time but still a couple feet shorter than the 1960 Plymouth we owned later. At nine feet high and eleven feet wide, the tank was impressive but not really out of automotive scale.

What was striking about it was the way it had flattened a parked car when the tank's driver goofed during a Christmas Parade in Chicago. That picture proved to me that the power and lethality of a tank are out of all proportion to the size of the package.

I learned a lot more about tanks in 1970 when I was assigned to the 11th Armored Cavalry Regiment in Viet Nam.

Normally, interrogators like me were in slots at brigade level or higher. The Eleventh Cav was unusual in that each of its three squadrons in the field had a Battalion Intelligence Collection Center—pronounced like the pen—of four to six men. After a week or two at the rear-echelon headquarters of my unit, I requested assignment to a BICC. A few weeks later, I joined Second Squadron in Cambodia.

Our BICC had a variety of personal and official gear—the tent was our largest item—which fitted into a trailer about the size of a middling-big U-Haul-It. We didn't have a *vehicle* of our own. When the squadron moved (as it generally did every week or two), the trailer was towed by one of the Headquarters Troop tracks; and we, the personnel, were split up as crew among the fighting vehicles.

The tanks were M48s, already obsolescent because the 90mm main gun couldn't be trusted to penetrate the armor of new Soviet tanks. That wasn't a problem for us, since most of the opposition wore black pajamas and sandals cut from tire treads.

M48s have a normal complement of four men, but that was exceptionally high in the field. In one case, I rode as loader on a tank which would have been down to two men—driver and commander— without me. The Eleventh Cav was at almost double its official (Table of Organization) strength, but the excess personnel didn't trickle far enough from headquarters to reach the folks who were expected to do the actual fighting.

While I was there, a squadron in the field operated as four linked entities. Squadron headquarters (including the BICC) was a firebase, so called because the encampment included a battery of self-propelled 155mm howitzers—six guns if none were deadlined.

Besides How Battery, the firebase included Headquarters Troop with half a dozen Armored Cavalry Assault Vehicles—ACAVs. These were simply M113 armored personnel carriers modified at the factory into combat vehicles. Each had a little steel cupola around a fifty caliber machine-gun and a pintle-mounted M60 machine-gun (7.62mm) on either flank.

There were also a great number of other vehicles at the firebase: armored personnel carriers modified into trucks, high-sided command vehicles, and mobile flamethrowers (Zippos); maintenance vehicles with cranes to lift out and replace engines in the field; and a platoon of combat engineers with a modified M48 tank as well as the bulldozers that turned up an earthen berm around the whole site.

Apart from these headquarters units, the squadron was made up of a company of (nominally) seventeen M48 tanks; and three line troops with twelve ACAVs and six Sheridans apiece. The Sheridan is a deathtrap with a steel turret, an aluminum hull, and a 152mm cannon whose ammunition generally caught fire if the vehicle hit a forty-pound mine.

Either a line troop or the tank company laagered at the firebase at night for security. The other three formed separate night defensive positions within fire support range of How Battery.

I talked with a lot of people in the field, and I got a good firsthand look at the way an armored regiment conducts combat operations.

When I got back to the World, I resumed my hobby of writing fantasies. I'd sold three stories to August Derleth in the past; now I sold him a fourth, set in the late Roman Empire. Mr. Derleth paid for that story the day before he died.

With him gone, there was no market for what I was writing: short stories in the heroic fantasy subgenre. I kept writing them anyway, becoming more and more frustrated that they didn't sell. (I wasn't real tightly wrapped back then. It was a while before I realized just how screwy I was.)

Fortunately, writer friends in Chapel Hill, Manly Wade Wellman and Karl Edward Wagner, suggested that I use Viet Nam as a setting. I tried it with immediate success, selling a horror fantasy to *F&SF* and a science fiction story to *Analog*.

I still had a professional problem. There were very few stories that someone with my limited skills could tell which were SF or fantasy, and which directly involved the Eleventh Cav. I decided to get around the issue by telling a story that was SF because the characters used ray guns instead of M16s . . . but was otherwise true, the way it had been described to me by the men who'd been there.

The story was "The Butcher's Bill," and for it I created a mercenary armored regiment called Hammer's Slammers.

The hardware was easy. I'd spent enough time around combat vehicles to have a notion of their strengths and weaknesses. Hammer's vehicles were designed around the M48s and ACAVs I'd ridden, with some of the most glaring faults eliminated.

All the vehicles in the field with the Eleventh Cav were track laying; that is, they had caterpillar treads instead of wheels. This was necessary because we never encamped on surfaced roads. Part of any move, even for headquarters units, was across stretches of jungle cleared minutes before by bulldozers fitted with Rome Plow blades.

The interior of a firebase was also bulldozed clear. Rain turned the bare soil either gooey or the consistency of wet soap. In both cases, it was impassable for wheeled vehicles. Our daily supplies came in by helicopter.

Tracks were absolutely necessary; and they were an absolute curse for the crewmen who had to maintain them.

Jungle soils dry to a coarse, gritty stone that abrades the tracks as they churn it up. When tracks wear, they loosen the way a bicycle chain does. To steer a tracked vehicle, you brake one tread while the other continues to turn. If the tracks are severely worn, you're certain to throw one.

If they're not worn, you may throw one anyway.

Replacing a track in the field means the crew has to break the loop; drive off it with the road wheels and the good track while another vehicle stretches the broken track; reverse onto the straightened track, hand feeding the free end up over the drive sprocket and along the return rollers; and then mate the ends into a loop again.

You may very well throw the same track ten minutes later.

Because of that problem (and suspension problems. Want to guess how long torsion bars last on a fifty-ton tank bouncing over rough terrain?) I decided my supertanks had to be air-cushion vehicles. That would be practical only if fuel supplies weren't a problem, so that the fans could be powerful enough to keep the huge mass stable even though it didn't touch the ground.

I'm a writer, not an engineer. I didn't have any difficulty in giving my tanks and combat cars (ACAVs with energy weapons) the fusion powerplants without which they'd be useless.

Armament required the same sort of decision. Energy weapons have major advantages over projectile weapons; but although tanks may some day mount effective lasers, I don't think an infantryman will ever be able to carry one. I therefore postulated guns that fired bolts of plasma liberated—somehow—from individual cartridges.

That took care of the hardware. The organization was basically that of the Eleventh Cav, with a few changes for the hell of it.

The unit itself was *not* based on any US unit with which I'm familiar. Its model was the French Foreign Legion; more precisely, the French Foreign Legion serving in Viet Nam just after World War Two—when most of its personnel were veterans of the SS who'd fled from Germany ahead of the Allied War Crimes Commission.

The incident around which I plotted "The Butcher's Bill" was the capture of Snuol the day before I arrived in Cambodia. That was the only significant fighting during the invasion of Cambodia, just as Snuol was the only significant town our forces reached.

G, one of the line troops, entered Snuol first. There was a real street, lined with stucco-faced shops instead of the grass huts on posts in the farming hamlets of the region. The C-100 AntiAircraft Company, a Viet Cong unit, was defending the town with a quartet of fifty-one caliber machine-guns.

A fifty-one cal could put its rounds through an ACAV the long way, and the aluminum hull of a Sheridan wasn't much more protection. Before G Troop could get out, the concealed guns had destroyed one of either type of vehicle.

The squadron commander responded by sending in H Company, his tanks.

The eleven M48s rolled down the street in line ahead. The first tank slanted its main gun to the right side of the street, the second to the left, and so on. Each tank fired a round of canister or shrapnel into every structure that slid past the muzzle of its 90mm gun.

On the other side of Snuol, they formed up to go back again. There wasn't any need to do that.

The VC had opened fire at first. The crews of the M48s didn't know that, because the noise inside was so loud that the clang of two-ounce bullets hitting the armor was inaudible. Some of the slugs flattened and were there on the fenders to be picked up afterward. The surviving VC fled, leaving their guns behind.

There was a little looting—a bottle of whiskey, a sack of ladies' slippers, a step through Honda (which was flown back to Quan Loi in a squadron helicopter). But for all practical purposes, Snuol ceased to have human significance the moment H Company blasted its way down the street.

The civilian population? It had fled before the shooting started. Not that it would have made any difference to the operation.

So I wrote a story about what wars cost and how decisions get made in the field—despite policy considerations back in air-conditioned offices. It was the best story I'd written so far, and the first time I'd tackled issues of real importance.

Only problem was, "The Butcher's Bill" didn't sell.

Mostly it just got rejection slips, but one very competent editor said that Joe Haldeman and Jerry Pournelle were writing as much of that sort of story as his magazine needed. (Looking back, I find it interesting that in 1973 magazine terms, the stories in *The Forever War*, *The Mercenary*, and *Hammer's Slammers* were indistinguishable.)

One editor felt that "The Butcher's Bill" demanded too much background, both SF and military, for the entry-level anthology he was planning. That was a good criticism, to which I responded by writing "Under the Hammer."

"Under the Hammer" had a new recruit as its viewpoint character, a kid who was terrified that he was going to make an ignorant mistake and get himself killed. (I didn't have to go far to find a model for the character. Remember that I hadn't had advanced combat training before I became an ad hoc tank crewman.) Because the recruit knew so little, other characters could explain details to him and to the reader.

I made the kid a recruit to Hammer's Slammers, because I already had that background clear in my mind. I hadn't intended to write a series, it just happened that way.

"Under the Hammer" didn't sell either.

I went about a year and a half with no sales. This was depressing, and I was as prone as the next guy to whine, "My stuff's better 'n some of the crap they publish."

In hindsight, I've decided that when an author doesn't sell, it's because:

1) he's doing something wrong; or

2) he's doing something different, and he isn't good enough to get away with being different.

In my case, there was some of both. The two Hammer stories were different—and clumsy; I was new to the job. Most of the other fiction I wrote during that period just wasn't very good.

But the situation was very frustrating.

The dam broke when Gordy Dickson took "The Butcher's Bill" for an anthology he was editing. It wasn't a lot of money, but I earned my living as an attorney. This was a sale, and it had been a long time coming.

Almost immediately thereafter, the editor at *Galaxy* (who'd rejected the Hammer stories) was replaced by his assistant, a guy named Jim Baen. Jim took the pair and asked for more.

I wrote three more stories in the series before Jim left to become SF editor of Ace Books. One of the three was the only piece I've written about Colonel Hammer himself instead of Hammer's Slammers. It was to an editorial suggestion: tell how it all started. Jim took that one, and though he rejected the other two, they sold elsewhere. The dam really had broken.

I moved away from Hammer and into other things, including a fantasy novel. Then Jim, now at Ace, asked for a collection of the 35,000 words already written plus enough new material in the series to fill out a book. Earlier I'd had an idea that seemed too complex to be done at a length a magazine would buy from me. I did it— "Hangman"—for the collection and added a little end-cap for the volume also—"Standing Down."

To stand between the stories, I wrote essays explaining the background of the series, social and economic as well as the hardware. In some cases I had to work out the background for the first time. I hadn't started with the intention of writing a series.

Hammer's Slammers came out in 1979. That was the end of the series, so far as I was concerned. But as the years passed, I did a novelette. Then the setting turned out to be perfect for my effort at using the plot of the *Odyssey* as an SF novel *(Cross the Stars)*. I did a short novel, *At Any Price,* that was published with the earlier novelette and a story I did for the volume. . . .

And I'm going to do more stories besides this one in the series, because Hammer's Slammers have become a vehicle for a message that I think needs to be more widely known. Veterans who've written or talked to me already understand, but a lot of other people don't.

When you send a man out with a gun, you create a policymaker. When his ass is on the line, he will do whatever he needs to do. And if the implications of that bother you, the time to do something about it is before you decide to send him out.

Dave Drake

Chapel Hill, N.C.

M2A4F HERMAN'S WHORE

ROLLING HOT

CHAPTER ONE

The camera light threw the shadow of the Slammers officer harshly across the berm which the sun had colored bronze a few moments ago as it set. Her hair was black and cut as short as that of a man.

"For instance, Captain Ranson," Dick Suilin said, "here at Camp Progress there are three thousand national troops and less than a hundred of your mercenaries, but—"

shoop

Ranson's eyes widened, glinting like pale gray marble. Fritzi Dole kept the camera focused tightly on her face. He'd gotten an instinct for a nervous subject in the three years he'd recorded Suilin's probing interviews.

"—the cost to our government—"

shoop-shoop

"—is greater for your handful of—"

"Incoming!" screamed Captain June Ranson as she dived for the dirt. It wasn't supposed to be happening here—

But for the first instant, you *never* really believed it could be happening, not even in the sectors where it happened every bleeding night. And when things were bad enough for one side or the other to hire Hammer's Slammers you could be pretty sure that there were no safe sectors.

319

Camp Progress was on the ass end of Prosperity's inhabited continent—three hundred kilometers north of the coast and the provincial capital, Kohang, but still a thousand kays south of where the real fighting went on in the areas bordering the World Government enclaves. Sure, there'd been reports that the Conservatives were nosing around the neighborhood, but nothing the Yokel troops themselves couldn't handle if they got their thumbs out.

For a change.

Camp Progress was a Yokel—was a National Army—training and administrative center, while for the Slammers it served as a maintenance and replacement facility. In addition to those formal uses, the southern sector gave Hammer a place to post troops who were showing signs of having been at the sharp end a little too long.

People like Junebug Ranson, for instance, who'd frozen with her eyes wide open during a firefight that netted thirty-five Consies killed-in-action.

So Captain Ranson had been temporarily transferred to command the Slammers' guard detachment at Camp Progress, a "company" of six combat cars. There'd been seventeen cars in her line company when it was up to strength; but she couldn't remember a standard day in a war zone that they *had* been up to strength. . . .

And anyway, Ranson knew as well as anybody else that she needed a rest before she got some of her people killed.

shoop

But she wasn't going to rest here.

The bell was ringing in the Slammers' Tactical Operations Center, a command car in for maintenance. The vehicle's fans had all been pulled, leaving the remainder as immobile as a 30-tonne iridium boulder; but it still had working electronics.

The Yokel garrison had a klaxon which they sounded during practice alerts. It was silent *now* despite the fact that camp security was supposedly a local responsibility.

Slammers were flattening or sprinting for their vehicles, depending on their personal assessment of the situation. The local reporter gaped at Ranson while his cameraman spun to find out what was going on. The camera light sliced a brilliant swath through the nighted camp.

Ranson's left cheek scraped the gritty soil as she called, "All Red Team personnel, man your blowers and engage targets beyond the berm. Blue Team—" the logistics and maintenance people "—prepare for attack from within the camp."

She wasn't wearing her commo helmet—that was in her combat car—but commands from her mastoid implant would be rebroadcast over her command channel by the base unit in the TOC. With her free hand, the hand that wasn't holding the submachine-gun she always carried, even here, Ranson grabbed the nearer of the two newsmen by the ankle and jerked him flat.

The Yokel's squawk of protest was smothered by the blast of the first mortar shell hitting the ground.

"I said *hold* it!" bellowed Warrant Leader Ortnahme, his anger multiplied by echoes within the tank's plenum chamber. "Now slide the bloody nacelle all across the bloody baseplate!"

"Yes sir," said Tech 2 Simkins. "Yes, Mr. Ortnahme!"

Simkins gripped his lower lip between his prominent front teeth and pushed.

The flange on the fan nacelle slid a little farther from the bolt holes in the mounting baseplate. "Ah . . . Mr. Ortnahme?"

It was hot and dry. The breeze curling through the access port and the fan intakes did nothing but drift grit into the eyes of the two men lying on their backs in the plenum chamber. It had been a hard day.

It wasn't getting any easier as it drew to a close.

The lightwand on the ground beneath the baseplate illuminated everything in the scarred, rusty steel cavern—including the flange, until Simkins tried to position the nacelle and his arms shadowed the holes. The young technician looked scared to death. The good Lord knew he had reason to be, because if Simkins screwed up one more time, Ortnahme was going to reverse his multitool and use the welder end of it to—

Ortnahme sighed and let his body relax. He set down the

multitool, which held a bolt ready to drive, and picked up the drift punch to realign the cursed holes.

Henk Ortnahme was tired and sweaty, besides being a lot older and fatter than he liked to remember . . . but he was also the Slammers' maintenance chief at Camp Progress, which meant it was his business to get the job done instead of throwing tantrums.

"No problem, Simkins," he said mildly. "But let's get it right this time, huh? So that we can knock off."

The tank, *Herman's Whore*, had been squarely over the blast of a hundred-kilogram mine. The explosion lifted the tank's 170-tonne mass, stunning both crewmen and damaging the blades of five of the six fans working at the time.

By themselves, bent blades were a field repair job—but because the crew'd been knocked silly, nobody shut down the system before the fans skewed the shafts . . . which froze the bearings . . . which cooked the drive motors in showers of sparks that must've been real bloody impressive.

Not only did the entire fan nacelles have to be replaced now—a rear-echelon job by anybody's standards—but three of the cursed things had managed to weld their upper brackets to the hull, so the brackets had to be replaced also.

It was late. Ortnahme'd kept his assistant at it for fourteen hours, so he couldn't rightly blame Simkins for being punchy . . . and the warrant leader knew his own skills and judgment weren't maybe all they bloody oughta be, just at the moment. They should've quit an hour before; but when this last nacelle was set, they were done with the cursed job.

"I got it, kid," he said calmly.

Simkins hesitated, then released the nacelle and watched nervously as his superior balanced the weight on his left palm. The upper bracket was bolted solidly, but there was enough play in the suspension to do real harm if the old bastard dropped—

A bell rang outside in the company area—rang and kept on ringing. Simkins straightened in terrified surmise and banged his head on the tank's belly armor. He stared at Ortnahme through tear-blinded eyes.

The warrant leader didn't move at all for a moment. Then his left biceps, covered with grit sticking to the sweat, bunched. The nacelle slid a centimeter and the drift punch shot through the realigned holes.

"Kid," Ortnahme said in a voice made tight by the tension of holding the fan nacelle, "I want you to get into the driver's seat and light her up, but don't—"

White light like the flash of a fuse blowing flickered through the intakes. The *blam!* of the mortar shell detonating was almost lost in the echoing clang of shrapnel against the skirts of the tank. Two more rounds went off almost simultaneously, but neither was quite as close.

Ortnahme swallowed. "But don't spin the fans till I tell you, right? I'll finish up with this myself."

"S—" Simkins began. Ortnahme had let the drift punch slide down and was groping for the multitool again. His arm muscles, rigid under their covering of fat, held the unit in place.

Simkins set the multitool in his superior's palm, bolt dispenser forward, and scuttled for the open access plate. "Yes sir," he called back over his shoulder.

The multitool whirred, spinning the bolt home without a shade of difficulty.

Simkins' boots banged on the skirts as the technician thrust through the access port in the steel wall. It was a tight enough fit even for a young kid like him, and as for Ortnahme—Ortnahme had half considered cutting a double-sized opening and welding the cover back in place when he was done with this cursed job.

Just as well he hadn't done that. With a hole that big venting the plenum chamber, the tank woulda been anchored until it was fixed.

Tribarrels fired, the thump of expanding air preceded minutely by the hiss of the energy discharge that heated a track to the target. Another salvo of mortar shells landed, and an earth shock warned of something more substantial hitting in the near distance.

Not a time to be standing around outside, welding a patch on a tank's skirts.

With the first bolt in place, the second was a snap. Or maybe

Herman's Whore had just decided to quit fighting him now that the shooting had started. The bitch was Slammers equipment, after all.

The tank shuddered. It was just Simkins hitting the main switch, firing up the containment/compression lasers in the fusion bottle that powered the vehicle, but for a moment Ortnahme thought the fan he held was live.

And about to slice the top half of his body into pastrami as it jiggled around in its mounting.

Shrapnel glanced from the thick iridium of the hull. It made a sharp sound that didn't echo the way pieces did when they rang on the cavernous steel plenum chamber. Ortnahme found the last hole with the nose of a bolt and triggered the multitool. The fastener spun and stopped—too soon. Not home, not aligned.

Another earth shock, much closer than the first. *Herman's Whore* shuddered again, and the bolt whirred the last centimeter to seat itself properly.

Warrant Leader Henk Ortnahme, wheezing with more than exertion, squirmed on his belly toward the access port. He ignored the way the soil scraped his chest raw.

He started to lift himself through the access port—carefully: the mine had stripped half the bolts holding down the cover plate, so there was sharp metal as well as a bloody tight fit.

Tribarrels ripped outward, across the berm. To the south flares and tracers— mostly aimed high, way too high—from the Yokel lines brightened the sky.

Ortnahme was halfway through the access port when, despite the crash and roar of gunfire, he heard the whisper of more incoming mortar shells.

The 20cm main gun of another tank fired, blotting every other sight and sound from the night with its thunderous cyan flash.

When Ranson hit the deck, Dick Suilin's first reaction was that the woman officer was having convulsions. He turned to call for help, blinking because Fritzi's light had flared across him as the cameraman spun to record a new subject: half-clad soldiers sprinting or sprawling all across the detachment area. Somebody was ringing a raucous bell that—

Ranson, flat on the ground, grabbed Suilin's right ankle and jerked forward.

"Hey!" the reporter shouted, trying to pull away.

Standing straight, the woman didn't even come up to his collarbone, but she had a grip like a wire snare. Suilin overbalanced, flailing his arms until his butt hit the coarse soil and slammed all the air out of his lungs.

There was a white flash, a bang, and—about an inch above Suilin's head—something that sounded like a bandsaw hitting a pineknot. Fritzi grunted and flung his camera in the opposite direction. Its floodlights went out.

"Fritzi, what are you—" Suilin shouted, stopping when his words were punctuated by two more blasts.

They were being *shelled* for God's sake! Not two hours' ride from Kohang!

The Slammers captain had disappeared somewhere, but when Suilin started to get up to run for cover, Fritzi Dole fell across him and knocked him flat again.

Suilin started to curse, but before he got the first word out a nearby combat car lighted the darkness with a stream of bolts from a tribarrel.

The chunk of shrapnel which grated past Suilin a moment before had chopped off the back of his cameraman's skull. Fritzi's blood and brains splashed Suilin's chest.

Dick Suilin had seen death before; he'd covered his share of road accidents and nursing home fires as a junior reporter. Even so, he'd been on the political beat for years now. *This* was a political story; the waste of money on foreign mercenaries when the same sums spent on the National Army would give ten times the result.

And anyway, covering the result of a tavern brawl wasn't the same as feeling Fritzi's warm remains leak over the neat uniform in which Suilin had outfitted himself for this assignment.

He tried to push the body away from him, but it was heavy

and as flexible as warm bread dough. He thought he heard the cameraman mumbling, but he didn't want to think that anyone so horribly wounded wouldn't have died instantly. Half of Fritzi's brains were gone, but he moaned as the reporter thrust him aside in a fit of revulsion.

Suilin rolled so that his back was toward the body.

The ground which he'd chosen for his interview was bare of cover, but a tank was parked against the berm twenty meters from him. He poised to scuttle toward the almost astronomical solidity of the vehicle and cower under the tarpaulin strung like a lean-to from its flank.

Before the reporter's legs obeyed his brain's decision, a man in the Slammers' dull khaki ran past. The mercenary was doubled over by the weight of equipment in his arms and fear of shrapnel.

He was the only figure visible in what had been a languorously busy encampment. Suilin ran after him, toward the combat car almost as close as the tank, though to the opposite side.

The reporter needed companionship now more than he needed the greater bulk of steel and iridium close to his yielding flesh.

The combat car's driver spun its fans to life. Dust lifted, scattering the light of the tribarrel firing from the vehicle.

Three more mortar shells struck. Through the corner of his eye, Suilin saw the tarp plastered against the side of the tank.

The cloth was shredded by the blast that had flung it there.

"Hey, snake," said DJ Bell, smiling like he always had, though he'd been dead three months. "How they hangin'?"

Sergeant Birdie Sparrow moaned softly in his sleep. "Go away,DJ," his dreamself murmured. "I don't need this."

"Via, Birdie," said the dead trooper. "You need all the friends you can get. We—"

The short, smiling man started to change, the way he did in this dream.

"—all do."

Birdie didn't sleep well in the daytime, but with a tarp shading him, it was okay, even with the heat.

He couldn't sleep at all after dark, not since DJ bought it but kept coming back to see him.

DJ Bell was a little guy with freckles and red hair. He kept his helmet visor at ninety degrees as an eyeshade when he rode with his head and shoulders out of the commander's hatch of his tank, but his nose was usually peeling with sunburn anyways.

He'd had a bit of an attitude, DJ did; little-guy stuff. Wanted to prove he was as tough as anybody alive, which he was; and that he could drink anybody under the table—which he couldn't, he just didn't have the body weight, but he kept trying.

That stuff only mattered during stand-downs, and not even then once you got to know DJ. Birdie'd known DJ for five years. Been his friend, trusted him so completely that he never had to think about it when things dropped in the pot. DJ'd covered Birdie's ass a hundred times. They were the kind of friends you only had when you were at the sharp end, when your life was on the line every minute, every day.

It'd been a routine sweep, G Company's combat cars had pushed down a ridge-line while the tanks of M Company's 3d Platoon held a blocking position to see what the cars flushed. One tank was deadlined with problems in its main-gun loading mechanism, and Lieutenant Hemmings had come down with the rolling crud, so Birdie Sparrow was in charge of the platoon's three remaining tanks.

Being short a tank didn't matter; G Company blew a couple of deserted bunkers, but they couldn't find any sign of Consies fresher than a month old. The combat cars laagered for the night on the ridge, while the tanks headed back for Firebase Red.

They were in line abreast. Birdie'd placed his own *Deathdealer* on the right flank, while DJ's *Widowmaker* howled along forty meters away in the center of the short line. They were riding over fields that'd been abandoned years before when the National Government cleared the area of civilians in an admission that they could no longer defend it from Conservative guerrillas slipping across the enclave borders.

All three tank commanders were head-and-shoulders out of their cupolas, enjoying the late afternoon sun. DJ turned and waved at Birdie, calling something that wasn't meant to be heard over the sound of the fans.

The motion sensor pinged a warning in Birdie's helmet, but it was too late by then.

Later—there was plenty of time later to figure out what had happened—they decided that the standoff mine had been set almost three years before. It'd been intended to hit the lightly armored vehicles the Yokels had been using in the region back then, so its high-sensitivity fuse detonated the charge 200 meters from the oncoming tanks.

Birdie's tanks didn't have—*none* of the Hammer's tanks had— its detection apparatus set to sweep that far ahead, because at that range the mine's self-forging projectile couldn't penetrate the armor even of a combat car. What the motion sensor had caught was the warhead shifting slightly to center on its target.

The mine was at the apex of an almost perfect isosceles triangle, with the two tanks forming the other corners. It rotated toward *Widowmaker* instead of *Deathdealer*.

Both tank commanders' minds were reacting to the dirty, yellow-white blast they saw in the corner of their eyes, but there hadn't been time for muscles to shift enough to wipe away DJ's grin when the projectile clanged against *Widowmaker*'s sloping turret and glanced upward. It was a bolt of almost-molten copper, forged from a plate into a spearpoint by the explosive that drove it toward its target.

DJ wore ceramic body armor. It shattered as the projectile coursed through the trooper's chest and head.

As Birdie Sparrow hosed the countryside with both his tribarrel and main gun, trying to blast an enemy who'd been gone for years, all he could think was, *Thank the Lord it was him and not me.*

"Look, y' know it's gonna happen, Birdie," said DJ's ghost earnestly. "It don't mean nothin'."

His voice was normal, but his chest was a gaping cavity and his face had started to splash—the way Birdie'd seen it happen three months before; only slowly, very slowly.

DJ had a metal filling in one of his molars. It glittered as it spun out through his cheek.

"DJ, you gotta stop doin' this," Birdie whimpered. His body was shivering and he wanted to wake up.

"Yeah, well, you better get movin', snake," DJ said with a shrug of his shoulders almost separated from what was left of his chest. The figure was fading from Birdie's consciousness. "It's starting again, y' know."

shoop

Birdie was out of his shelter and climbing the recessed steps to *Deathdealer*'s turret before he knew for sure he was awake. He was wearing his boots—he hadn't taken them off for more than a few minutes at a time in three months—and his trousers.

Most troopers kept their body armor near their bunks. Birdie didn't bother with that stuff anymore.

Despite the ringing alarm bell, there were people still standing around in the middle of the company area; but that was their problem, not Birdie Sparrow's.

He was diving feet-first through the hatch when the first mortar shell went off, hurling a figure away from its blast.

The body looked like DJ Bell waving goodbye.

When the third mortar shell went off, June Ranson rolled into a crouch and sprinted toward her combat car. The Consies used 100mm automatic mortars that fired from a three-round clip. It was a bloody good weapon—a lot like the mortars in Hammer's infantry platoons, and much more effective than the locally made tube the National Army used.

The automatic mortar fired three shots fast, but the weight of a fresh clip stretched the gap between rounds three and four out longer than it would have been from a manually loaded weapon.

Of course, if the Consies had a *pair* of mortars targeted on Ranson's detachment area, she was right outa luck.

Guns were firing throughout the encampment now, and the Yokels had finally switched on their warning klaxon. A machine-gun sent a stream of bright-orange Consie tracers snapping through the air several meters above Ranson's head. One tracer hit a pebble in the earthen berm and ricocheted upward at a crazy angle.

A strip charge wheezed in the night, a nasty, intermittent sound like a cat throwing up. A drive rocket was uncoiling the charge through the wire and minefields on which the Yokels depended for protection.

The charge went off, hammering the ground and blasting a corridor through the defenses. It ignited the western sky with a momentary red flash like the sunset's afterthought.

Ranson caught the rear handhold of her combat car, *Warmonger*—Tootsie One-three—and swung herself into the fighting compartment. The fans were live, and both wing guns were firing.

Beside the vehicle were the scattered beginnings of an evening meal: a catalytic cooker, open ration packets, and three bottles of local beer spilled to stain the dust. *Warmonger*'s crew had been together for better than two years. They did everything as a team, so Ranson could be nearly certain her command vehicle would be up to speed in an emergency.

She was odd man out: apart from necessary business, the crewmen hadn't addressed a dozen words to her in the month and a half since she took over the detachment.

Ranson didn't much care. She'd seen too many people die herself to want to get to know any others closely.

Hot plastic empties ejecting from Stolley's left wing gun spattered over her. One of the half-molten disks clung to the hair on the back of her wrist for long enough to burn.

Ranson grabbed her helmet, slapped the visor down over her face, and thumbed it from optical to thermal so that she could see details again. That dickheaded Yokel reporter had picked a great time to blind her with his camera light. . . .

A mortar shell burst; then everything paused at the overwhelming crash of a tank's main gun. At least one of the panzers sent to Camp Progress for maintenance was up and running.

Figures, fuzzy and a bilious yellow-green, leaped from concealment less than a hundred meters from the berm. Two of them intersected the vivid thermal track of Stolley's tribarrel. The third flopped down and disappeared as suddenly as he'd risen.

A cubical multi-function display, only thirty centimeters on a side and still an awkward addition to the clutter filling the blower's fighting compartment, was mounted on the front bulkhead next to Ranson's tribarrel. She switched it on and picked up her back-and-breast armor.

"Janacek!" She ordered her right gunner over the pulsing thump-*hiss* of the tribarrels to either side of her. "Help me on!"

The stocky, spike-haired crewman turned from the spade grips of his gun and took the weight of Ranson's ceramic armor. She shrugged into the clamshell and latched it down her right side.

All six blowers in the guard detachment were beads of light in the multi-function display. Their fusion bottles were pressurized, though that didn't mean they had full crews.

"Now your own!" she said, handing the compartment's other suit to Janacek.

"Screw it!" the gunner snarled as he turned to his tribarrel.

"*Now*, trooper!" Ranson shouted in his ear.

Janacek swore and took the armor.

Two bullets clanged against the underside of the splinter shield, a steel plate a meter above the coaming of the fighting compartment. One of the Consie rounds howled off across the encampment while the other disintegrated in red sparks that prickled all three of the Slammers.

Stolley triggered a long burst, then a single round. "*My* trick, sucker!" he shouted.

The air was queasy with the bolts' ionized tracks and the sullen, petrochemical stink of the empty cases.

The blowers of the guard detachment were spaced more or less evenly around the 500-meter arc of the Slammers' area, because they were the only vehicles Ranson could depend on being combat ready. Two tanks were in Camp Progress for maintenance, and a third one—brand new—had been delivered here for shake-down before being sent on to a line company.

All three of the panzers *might* be able to provide at least fire support. If they could, it'd make a lot of difference.

Maybe the difference between life and death.

Ranson poked the control to give her all units with live fusion powerplants in a half-kilometer area. She prayed she'd see three more lights in her display—

Somebody who at least *said* he was Colonel Banyussuf, the camp commander, was bleating for help on the general channel. "*. . . are overrunning headquarters! They're downstairs now!*"

Likely enough, from the crossfire inside the berm at the other end of the camp. And Banyussuf's own bloody problem until Ranson had her lot sorted out.

There were ten blips: she'd forgotten the self-propelled howitzer in because of a traversing problem. Somebody'd brought it up, too.

Ranson switched on her own tribarrel. A blurred figure rose from where the two Consies Stolley'd killed were cooling in her visor's image. She ripped the new target with a stream of bolts that flung his arm and head in the air as his torso crumpled to the ground.

They were Hammer's Slammers. They'd been brought to Prosperity to kick ass, and that's just what they were going to do.

CHAPTER TWO

Hans Wager, his unlatched clamshell flapping against his torso, lifted himself onto the back deck of his tank and reached for the turret handhold.

He hated mortars, but the shriek of incoming didn't scare him as much as it should've. He was too worried about the bleeding cursed, *huge* whale of a tank he was suddenly in charge of in a firefight.

And Wager was pissed: at Personnel for transferring him from combat cars to tanks when they promoted him to sergeant; at himself, for accepting the promotion if the transfer came with it; and at his driver, a stupid newbie named Holman who'd only driven trucks during her previous six months in the regiment.

The tank was brand new. It didn't have a name. Wager'd been

warned not to bother naming the vehicle, because as soon as they got the tank to D Company it'd be turned over to a senior crew while he and Holman were given some piece of knackered junk.

Wager grabbed the hatch—just in time, because the tank bucked as that dickhead Holman lifted her on her fans instead of just building pressure in the plenum chamber. "Set—" Wager shouted. The lower edge of his body armor caught on the hatch coaming and jolted the rest of the order out as a wheeze.

Curse this bloody machine that didn't have any bloody *room* for all its size!

The berm around the Yokel portion of Camp Progress was four meters high—good protection against incoming, but you couldn't shoot over it. They'd put up guard towers every hundred meters inside the berm to cover their barbed wire and minefields.

As Wager slid at last into his turret, he saw the nearest tower disintegrate in an orange flash that silhouetted the bodies of at least three Yokel soldiers.

Holman had switched on the turret displays as soon as she boarded the tank, so Wager had access to all the data he could possibly want. Panoramic views in the optical, enhanced optical, passive thermal, active infrared, laser, millimetric radar, or sonic spectra. Magnified views in all the above spectra.

Three separate holographic screens, two of which could be split or quadded. Patching circuits that would display similar data fed from any other Slammer vehicle within about ten kays.

Full readouts through any of the displays on the status of the tank's ammunition, its fans, its powerplant, and all aspects of its circuitry.

Hans Wager didn't understand *any* of that cop. He'd only been assigned to this mother for eighteen hours.

His commohelmet pinged. "This is Tootsie Six," said the crisp voice of Captain Ranson from the guard detachment. "Report status. Over."

Ranson didn't have a call sign for Wager's tank, so she was highlighting his blip on her multi-function display before sending.

Wager didn't have a call sign either.

"Roger, Tootsie Six," he said. "Charlie Three-zero—" the C Company combat car he'd crewed for the past year as driver and wing gunner "—up and running. Over."

Holman'd got her altitude more or less under control, but the tank now hunched and sidled like a dog unused to a leash. Maybe Wager ought to trade places with Holman. He figured from his combat car experience that he could *drive* this beast, so at least one of the seats'd be filled by somebody who knew his job.

Wager reached for the seat lever and raised himself out of the cold electronic belly of the turret. He might not have learned to be a tank commander yet, but . . .

The night was bright and welcoming. Muzzle flashes erupted from the slim trees fringing the stream 400 meters to Wager's front. Short bursts without tracers. He set his visor for persistent display—prob'ly a way to do that with the main screens, too, but who the cop cared?—to hold the aiming point in his vision while he aligned the sights of the cupola tribarrel with them.

The first flash of another burst merged with the crackling impact of Wager's powergun. There wasn't a second shot from *that* Consie.

Wager walked his fire down the course of the stream, shattering slender tree trunks and igniting what had been lush grass an instant before the ravening cyan bolts released their energy. The tank still wasn't steady, but Wager'd shot on the move before. He knew *his* job.

A missile exploded, fuel and warhead together, gouging a chunk out of the creekbank where the tribarrel had found it before its crew could align it to fire.

Hans Wager's job was to kill people.

The helmeted Slammers trooper—with twenty kilos of body armor plus a laden equipment belt gripped in his left arm—caught the handle near the top of the car's shield, put his right foot in the step cut into the flare of the plenum chamber skirt, and swung himself into the vehicle.

Suilin's skin was still prickling from the hideous, sky-devouring flash/*crash!* that had stunned him a moment before. He'd thought a bomb had gone off, but it was a tank shooting because it happened again. He'd pissed his pants, and that bothered him more than the way Fritzi was splashed across the front of his uniform.

Suilin grabbed the handle the way the soldier had. The metal's buzzing vibration startled him; but it was the fans, of course, not a short circuit to electrocute him. He put his foot on the step and jumped as he'd seen the soldier do. He *had* to get over the side of the armor which would protect him once he was there.

His chest banged the hard iridium, knocking the breath out of him. His left hand scrabbled for purchase, but he didn't have enough strength to—

The trooper Suilin had followed to the combat car leaned over and grabbed the reporter's shoulder. He jerked Suilin aboard with an ease that proved it was as much a knack as pure strength—

But the fellow *was* strong, and Dick Suilin was out of shape for this work. He didn't belong here, and now he was going to die in this fire-struck night. . . .

"Take the left gun!" shouted the trooper as he slapped the armor closed over his chest. He lowered his helmet visor and added in a muffled voice, "I got the right!"

A trio of sharp, white blasts raked the National Army area. Something over flew the camp from south to north with an accelerating roar that dwarfed even the blasts of the tank gun. It was visible only as the dull glow of a heated surface.

Suilin picked himself up from the ice chest and stacked boxes which halved the space available within the fighting compartment. One man was already bent over the bow gun, ripping the night in short bursts. Suilin's guide seized the grips of the right-hand weapon and doubled the car's weight of fire.

Two of the guard towers were burning. Exploding flares and ammunition sent sparkles of color through the smoky orange flames. The fighting platforms were armored, but the towers were constructed of wood. Suilin had known that—but he hadn't considered until now what the construction technique would mean in a battle.

There wasn't supposed to *be* a battle, here in the south.

Suilin bent close to the third tribarrel, hoping he could make some sense of it. He'd had militia training like every other male in the country over the age of sixteen, but Prosperity's National Army wasn't equipped with powerguns.

He took the double grips in his hands, that much was obvious. The weapon rotated easily, though the surprising mass of the barrels gave Suilin's tentative swings more inertia than he'd intended.

When his thumbs pressed the trigger button between the grips, nothing happened. The tribarrel had a switch or safety somewhere, and in the dark Suilin wasn't going to be able to overcome his ignorance.

The gun in a tank's cupola snapped a stream of cyan fire south at a flat angle. There was a huge flash and a separate flaring red streak in the sky above the National Army positions. Two other missiles detonated on the ground as three of the earlier salvo had done.

The mercenaries claimed they could shoot shells and missiles out of the air. Suilin hadn't believed that was more than advertising puffery, but he'd just seen it happen. The Slammers' vehicles couldn't protect the National Army positions, but missiles aimed high enough to threaten the mercenaries' own end of Camp Progress were being gutted by computer-aimed powerguns.

The back of Suilin's mind shivered to realize that just now he really didn't care what happened to his fellow citizens, so long as those Consie missiles couldn't land on *him*.

The tribarrel was useless—the reporter knew he was useless with it—but a short-barreled grenade launcher and bandolier lay across the ice chest beside him. He snatched it up and found the simple mechanical safety with his left thumb.

Suilin had never been any good with a rifle, but his shotgun had brought down its share of birds at the estates of family friends. In militia training he'd taken to grenade launchers like a child to milk.

A bullet passed close enough to crack in Suilin's left ear. He didn't have any idea where the round came from, but both the other men in the fighting compartment swung their tribarrels and began hosing a swale only a hundred meters from the berm. So . . .

Suilin lifted his grenade launcher and fired. He didn't bother with the sights, just judged the angle of the barrel. The *chook!* of the shot was a little sharper than he'd expected; the Slammers used lighter projectiles with a higher velocity than the weapons he'd trained on.

They used a more potent bursting charge, too. The grenade's yellow flash, fifty meters beyond Suilin's point of aim, looked like an artillery piece firing.

He lowered the muzzle slightly and squeezed off. This time the projectile burst just where he wanted it, in the swale whose lips were lighted by the tribarrel's crackling bolts.

Suilin didn't see the figure leap from concealment until the powerguns clawed the Consie dazzlingly apart.

"That's right!" his guide screamed from the right-hand gun. "Flush the bastards for us!"

The grenade launcher's recoil woke a familiar warmth from the reporter's shoulder. He swung his weapon slightly and walked three shots down the hidden length of the swale. The last was away before the first was cratering the darkened turf.

An empty clip ejected from the weapon after the fifth round. Both tribarrels fired. There was a disemboweled scream as Dick Suilin reached for the bandolier, groping for more ammunition. . . .

The turret hatch clanged above Birdie Sparrow; he wasn't shivering any more. Albers, his driver, hadn't boarded yet, so Birdie brought *Deathdealer* up himself by touching the main switch. The displays lighted softly on auxiliary power while the fusion bottle built pressure.

Deathdealer's hull deadened most sounds, but mortar fragments rang on her skirts like sleet on a window. "Booster, Screen Three," Birdie said, ordering the tank's artificial intelligence to bring up Screen Three, which he habitually used for non-optical sensor inputs.

The tracks of mortar shells were glowing holographic arcs, red for the first salvo and orange for the second. Birdie computed a vector and overlaid it on his main screen at the same time he fed the data to fire control. The turret began to rotate on its frictionless magnetic bearings; the breech of the main gun raised a few centimeters as the muzzle dipped onto its aiming point.

Deathdealer grunted as her fans took a first bite of air. Albers had boarded, so they were fully combat ready.

Light enhancement on the main screen showed the shell tracks arcing from a copse 1800 meters from the berm at a deflection of 43° east of true north. The orange pipper on Screen Two, the gunnery display, was centered on that point.

The Consies might be in a gully hidden by the trees, and there was a limit to the amount of dirt and rock even a 20cm powergun could excavate, but—

Birdie rocked his foot switch, sending two rounds from his main gun crashing downrange.

Deathdealer shook. The amount of copper plasma being expelled was only a few grams, but when even that slight mass was accelerated to light speed, its recoil force shifted the tank's 170 tonnes. Spent casings ejected onto the turret floor, overwhelming the air conditioning with the stench of hot matrix.

The copse exploded in a ball of fire and live steam. A tree leaped thirty meters skyward, driven by the gout of energy that had shattered the bole at root level.

Birdie chuckled and coughed in the atmosphere of reeking plastic. The mortar crew might not've bought it this time, but they bloody sure weren't going to call attention to themselves for a while. DJ'd have appreciated that.

The main screen highlighted movement in blue: two figures hunched with the weight of the burden they carried between them toward the berm.

Birdie's left thumb rocked the gun control from main to coax while his right hand expertly teased the joystick to bring the pipper onto his targets. They went to ground just as his foot was tensing on the gunswitch, disappearing into a minute dip that meant the difference between life and death.

Birdie started to switch back to the main gun and do the job by brute force, but—

Y' know it's gonna happen, DJ had said in his dream. Birdie waited, ten seconds, twenty. . . .

The Consies popped up from cover, their figures slightly blurred by phosphor delays in the enhanced hologram. Birdie's foot pressed down the rest of the way. A drive motor whirred as the cupola tribarrel thumped out its five-round burst. Cyan impacts flung the targets to left and right as parts of their bodies vaporized explosively.

Death had waited; thirty seconds for that pair, years for other men. But Death didn't forget.

Birdie was safe. He was inside the heaviest piece of land-based armor in the human universe.

Three artillery rockets hit in the near distance. A fourth rumbled overhead, shaking *Deathdealer* and Birdie's vision of safety. Those were definitely big enough to hurt anything in their impact zone.

Even a tank.

The reflexes of five years' combat, including a year as platoon sergeant, took over. Birdie kept one eye on the panoramic main screen while his hands punched data out of his third display.

The other tanks in the encampment were powered up. The tribarrel couldn't override it without codes he didn't have. The third tank, an H Company repair job named *Herman's Whore*, didn't respond when he pinged it, and a remote hookup indicated nobody was in the turret.

From his own command console, Birdie rotated the *Whore*'s tribarrel to the south and slaved it to air defense. Until somebody overrode his command, the gun would engage any airborne targets her sensors offered her.

That left Birdie to get back to immediate business. An alarm pinged to warn him that a laser rangefinder painted *Deathdealer*'s armor. The gunnery computer was already rotating the turret, while a pulsing red highlight arrowed the source: an anti-tank missile launcher 1200 meters away, protected only by night and distance.

Which meant unprotected.

Deathdealer's close-in defense system would detonate the missile at a distance with a sleet of barrel-shaped steel pellets, but the

Consies needed to learn that you didn't target Colonel Hammer's tanks.

Birdie Sparrow thumbed the gunswitch, preparing to teach the Consies a main-gun lesson.

Henk Ortnahme, panting as he mounted the turret of *Herman's Whore*, didn't notice the cupola tribarrel was slewed until the bloody thing ripped out a bloody burst that almost blew his bloody head off.

The plasma discharge prickled his scalp and made the narrow fringe that was all the hair he had stand out like a ruff.

Ortnahme ducked blindly, banging his chin on the turret. He couldn't see a bloody thing except winking afterimages of the bolts, and he was too stunned to be angry.

The southern sky flashed and bled as one warhead detonated vainly and another missile's fuel painted the night instead of driving its payload down into the Slammers' positions. Sure, somebody'd slaved the cupola gun to air defense, and that was fine with Ortnahme.

Seeing as he'd managed to survive learning about it.

He mounted the cupola quickly and lowered himself into the turret, hoping the cursed gun wouldn't cut loose again just now. The hatch was a tight fit, but it didn't have sharp edges like the access port.

The port had torn Ortnahme's coveralls so he looked like he'd been wrestling a tiger. Then the bloody coverplate—warped by the mine that deadlined the tank to begin with—hadn't wanted to bolt back in place.

But Ortnahme was in the turret now, and *Herman's Whore* was ready to slide.

The radio was squawking on the command channel. Ortnahme'd left the hatch open, and between the racket of gunfire and incoming—most of *that* well to the south by now—the warrant leader couldn't hear what was being said. If he'd known he was in for a deal like this, he'd've brought the commo helmet stashed in his quarters against the chance that someday he'd get back out in the field. . . .

For now he rolled the volume control up to full and blasted himself with, "—DO YOU HAVE A CREW? O—"

Ortnahme dumped some of the volume.

"—ver."

"Roger, Tootsie Six," the warrant leader reported. "*Herman's Whore* is combat ready. Over."

He sat down, the first chance he'd had to do that since sunup, and leaped to his feet again as the multitool he'd stowed in his cargo pocket clanged against the frame of the seat. Blood and martyrs!

Ortnahme was itching for a chance to shoot something, but he'd spent too long with the fan and the coverplate. There weren't any targets left on *his* displays, and he suspected that most of the bolts still hissing across the berm were fired by kids who didn't have the sense God gave a goose.

The Consies had hit in a rush, figuring to sweep over the encampment by sheer speed and numbers. You couldn't *do* that against the firepower the Slammers put out.

The rest of Camp Progress, though . . .

"Tootsie Six to all Red and Blue personnel," Junebug Ranson continued. "The Yokels report that bandits have penetrated their positions. Red units will form line abreast and sweep south through the encampments. Mobile Blue units—"

The three tanks. Ortnahme's tank, by the Lord's blood!

"—will cross the berm, form on the TOC, and sweep counter-clockwise from that point to interdict bandit reinforcements. *Deathdealer* has command."

Sergeant Sparrow. Tall, dark, and as jumpy as a pithed frog. Usually Ortnahme got crewmen to help him when he pulled major maintenance on their vehicles, but he'd given Sparrow a wide berth. *That* boy was four-plus crazy.

"Remaining Blue elements," Ranson concluded, "hold what you got, boys. We got to take care of this now, but we'll be back. Tootsie Six over."

Remaining Blue elements. The maintenance and logistics people, the medic and the light-duty personnel. The people who were crouched now in bunkers with their sidearms and their prayers, hoping that when the armored vehicles shifted front, the Consies wouldn't be able to mount another attack on the Slammer positions.

"*Deathdealer*, roger."

"Charlie Three-zero, roger."

"*Herman's Whore*, roger," Ortnahme reported. He didn't much like being under the command of Birdie Sparrow, a flake who was technically his junior; but Sparrow was a flake because of years of line service, and it wasn't a point that the warrant leader would even think of mentioning after it all settled down again.

Assuming.

He switched to intercom. "You heard the lady, Simkins," he said. "Lift us over the bloody berm!"

And as the fan note built from idle into a full-throated roar, Ortnahme went back to looking for targets.

The combat car drove a plume of dust from the berm as it started to back and swing. The man who'd been firing the forward tribarrel turned so that Dick Suilin could see the crucifix gilded onto the plastron of his body armor. He flipped up his visor and said, "Who the cop 're you?"

"I'm, ah—" the reporter said.

His ears rang. Afterimages like magnified algae rods filled his eyes as his retinas tried to redress the chemical imbalances burned into them by the glaring powerguns.

He waggled the smoking muzzle of the grenade launcher.

That must have been the right response. The man with the crucifix looked at the trooper who'd guided Suilin to the vehicle and said, "Where the cop's Speed, Otski?"

The wing gunner grimaced and said, "Well, Cooter, ah—his buddy in Logistics got in, you know, this morning."

"Bloody buggered *fool!*" Cooter shouted. He'd looked a big man even when he hunched over his tribarrel; straightening in rage made him a giant. "*Tonight* he's stoned?"

"Cut him some slack, Cooter," Otski said, looking aside rather than meeting the bigger soldier's eyes. "This ain't the Strip, you know."

Suilin rubbed his forehead. The Strip. The no-man's-land surrounding the Terran Government enclaves in the north.

"Tonight it's the bleeding Strip!" Cooter snapped.

Cooter's helmet spoke something that was only a tinny rattle to Suilin. "Tootsie Three, roger," the big man said. Otski nodded.

A multiple explosion hammered the center of the camp. Munitions hurled themselves in sparkling tracks from a bubble of orange flame.

"Blood 'n martyrs," Cooter muttered as angry light bathed his weary face.

He lifted a suit of hard armor from the floor of the fighting compartment. "Here," he said to Suilin, "put this on. Wish I could give you a helmet, but that dickhead Speed's got it with him."

Their combat car was sidling across the packed earth, keeping its bow southward—toward the flames and the continued shooting. The car passed close to where Fritzi Dole lay. The photographer's clothing swelled in the draft blasting from beneath the plenum chamber.

Dust whipped and eddied. The other combat cars were maneuvering also, forming a line. Here at the narrow end of the encampment, the separations between vehicles were only about ten meters apiece.

"The gun work?" Cooter demanded, patting the breech of the tribarrel as Suilin put on the unfamiliar armor. The clamshell seemed to weigh more than its actual twenty kilos; it was chafing over his left collarbone even before he got it latched.

"Huh?" the reporter grunted. "I think—I mean, I don't—"

Making a bad guess *now* meant someone might die rather than just a libel suit.

Meant Dick Suilin might die.

"Oh, right," Cooter said easily. He poked with a big finger at where the gun's receiver was gimballed onto its pedestal. A green light glowed just above the trigger button. "No sweat, turtle. I'll just slave it to mine. You just keep bombin' 'em like you been doing."

The helmet buzzed again. "Tootsie Three, roger," Cooter

repeated. He tapped the side of his helmet and ordered, "Move out, Shorty, but keep it to a walk, right?"

Cooter and Otski bent over their weapons. When the big trooper waggled his handgrips, the left tribarrel rocked in parallel with his own.

"What are we doing?" Suilin asked, swaying as the combat car moved forward. The big vehicle had the smooth, unpleasant motion of butter melting as a grill heats.

The reporter pulled another loaded clip from the bandolier to have it ready. He squinted toward the barracks ahead of them, silhouetted in orange light.

"Huh?" said Cooter. His face was a blank behind his lowered visor as he looked over his shoulder in surprise.

"We're gonna clear your Consie buddies outa Camp Progress," Otski said with a feral grin in his voice.

"Yeah, right, you don't have a commo," Cooter said/apologized. "Look, anybody you see in a black uniform, zap him. Anybody shoots at us, *zap* him. Fast."

"Anything bleedin' moves," said Otski, "you zap it. Any mistake you gotta make, make it in favor of *our* ass, right?"

Suilin nodded tightly. There was a howl and *whump!* behind them. For a moment he thought the noise was a shell, but it was only one of the huge tanks lifting its mass over the berm.

A combat car on the right flank fired down one of the neat boulevards which served the National Army's portion of the camp.

"Hey, turtle?" the right wing gunner said. "You got a name?"

"Dick," Suilin said. He'd lifted the grenade launcher to his shoulder twice already, then lowered it because he felt like a fool to be aiming at no target. The noise around him was hideous.

"Don't worry, Dick," Otski said. "We'll tell yer girl you was brave."

He chuckled, then lighted the wide street ahead of them with a burst from his tribarrel.

"You must send the 4th Armored Brigade to relieve us!" Colonel Banyussuf was ordering his superiors in Kohang. Since June

Ranson's radio was picking up the call down in the short-range two-meter push, there was about zip possibility that anybody 300 kilometers away could hear the Yokel commander's panicked voice.

Two men in full uniform poked their rifles gingerly southward, around the corner of a barracks. Light reflected from their polished leather and brightly-nickeled Military Police gorgets. The MPs stared in open-mouthed amazement as the combat car slid past them.

"About zip" was still a better chance than that District Command in Kohang would do anything about Banyussuf's problems.

Trouble here meant there was *big* trouble everywhere on Prosperity. District Command wasn't going to send the armored brigade based on the coast near Kohang haring off into the sticks to relieve Banyussuf.

"Watch it," Willens, their driver, warned.

Warmonger slid into an intersection. A crowd of thirty or so women and children screamed and ran a step or two away from them, then screamed again and flattened as another car crossed at the next intersection east. Dependents of senior noncoms, looking for a place to hide. . . .

Ranson wouldn't have minded having a Yokel armored brigade for support, but it'd take too long to reach here. Her team could do the job by themselves.

"Two o'clock!" she warned. Movement on the second floor of a barracks, across the wide boulevard that acted as a parade square every morning for the Yokels.

The left corner of her visor flashed the tiny red numeral 2. Her helmet's microprocessor had gathered all its sensor inputs and determined that the target was of Threat Level 2.

Cold meat under most circumstances, but in Camp Progress there were thousands of National Army personnel who looked the same as the Consies to scanners. With her visor on thermal, Ranson couldn't tell whether the figure wore black or a green-on-green mottled Yokel uni—

The figure raised its gun. 2 blinked to 1 in Ranson's visor, then vanished—

Because a dead man doesn't have any threat level at all. Ranson's burst converged with Janacek's; the upper front of the barracks flew apart as the powerguns ignited it.

Willens slewed the car left. Somebody leaned out of a window of the same barracks and fired—missed even the combat car except for one bullet ricocheting from the dirt street to whang on the skirts.

Ranson killed the shooter, letting *Warmonger*'s forward motion walk the flashing cyan cores of her burst down the line of barracks windows. Janacek was raking the lower story, and as they came abreast of the building, the One-five blower to *Warmonger*'s right laid on a crossfire from two of its tribarrels.

A single bolt from the other car sizzled through gaps already blown in the structure and hit the barracks on the other side of the street. The cyan track missed Ranson by little enough that the earphones in her helmet screamed piercingly with harmonics from the energy release.

She noticed it the way she'd notice a reflection in a shop window. Everything around her seemed to be reflected or hidden behind sheets of thick glass. Nothing touched her. Her skin felt warm, the way it did when she was on the verge of going to sleep.

A tank's main gun flashed beyond the berm. Ranson would've liked the weight of the panzers with her to push the Consies out, but their 20cm cannon were too destructive to use within a position crammed with friendly troops and their dependents. If things got hot enough that the combat cars needed a bail-out—

She'd give the orders she had to give and worry about the consequences later. But for now . . .

A group of armed men ran from a cross street into the next intersection. Some of them were still looking back over their shoulders when *Warmonger*'s three tribarrels lashed them with converging streams of fire.

Figures whirled and disintegrated individually for a moment before a bloom of white light—a satchel charge, a buzzbomb's warhead; perhaps just a bandolier strung with grenades—enveloped the group. The shockwave slammed bodies and body fragments in every direction.

Ranson was sure they'd been wearing black uniforms. Pretty sure.

"—*must help me!*" whimpered the radio. "*They have captured the lower floor of my headquarters!*"

She hand-keyed the microphone and said, "Progress Command, this is Slammers Command. Help's on the way, but be bloody sure your own people don't shoot at *us*. Out."

Or *else*, her mind added, but she didn't want that threat on record. Anyway, even the Yokels were smart enough to know what happened when somebody shot at the Slammers. . . .

"Tootsie Six to Red elements," Ranson heard herself ordering. "Keep moving even if you're taking fire. Don't let 'em get their balance or they'll chop us."

Her voice was echoing to her down corridors of glass.

CHAPTER THREE

Callsign Charlie Three-zero hit halfway up the berm's two-meter height. Holman had the beast still accelerating at the point of impact.

Even though Wager'd seen it coming and had tried to brace himself, the collision hurled his chest against the hatch coaming. His clamshell armor saved his ribs, but the shock drove all the breath from his body.

Air spilled from the tilted plenum chamber. The tank sagged backward like a horse spitted on a wall of pikes.

Hans Wager hoped that the smash hadn't knocked his driver's teeth out. He wanted to do that himself, as soon as things got quiet again.

"Holman," he wheezed as he keyed his intercom circuit. He'd never wanted to command a tank. . . . "Use lift, not your bloody speed. You can't—"

Dust exploded around Charlie Three-zero as if a bomb had gone off. Holman kept the blades' angle of attack flat to build up fan speed before trying to raise the vehicle again. She wasn't unskilled, exactly; she just wasn't used to moving something with this much inertia.

"—just ram through the bloody berm!" Wager concluded; but as they backed, he got a good look at the chunk they'd gouged from the protective dirt wall and had to wonder. They bloody near *had* plowed their way through, at no cost worse than bending the front skirts.

Rugged mother, this tank was. Might be something to be said for panzers after all, once you got to know 'em.

And got a bleedin' driver who knew 'em.

Something in the middle of the Yokel positions went off with walloping violence. Other people's problems weren't real high on Hans Wager's list right now, though.

The acting platoon leader, Sergeant Sparrow, had assigned Wager to the outside arc of the sweep and taken the berm side himself. Wager didn't like Sparrow worth spit. When Wager arrived at Camp Progress, he'd tried to get some pointers from the experienced tank sergeant, but Sparrow was an uncommunicative man whose eyes focused well beyond the horizon.

The dispositions made sense, though. The action was likely to be hottest right outside the camp. Sparrow's reflexes made him the best choice to handle it. Wager wasn't familiar with his new hardware, but he was a combat trooper who could be trusted to keep their exposed flank clear.

The middle slot of the sweep was a tank cobbled into action by the maintenance detachment. The lord *only* knew what they'd be good for.

The Red team's six combat cars had formed across the detachment area and were starting toward the bubbling inferno of the Yokel positions. As they did so, Sparrow's *Deathdealer* eeled over the berm with only two puffs where the skirts dug in and kicked dirt high enough for it to go through the fan intakes.

Even the blower from maintenance had made the jump without a serious problem. While Wager and his *truck*driver—

Holman had the fans howling on full power. A lurching *clack* vibrated through Charlie Three-zero's fabric as the driver rammed all eight pitch controls to maximum lift.

"Via!" Wager screamed over the intercom. "Give her a *little* for—"

Their hundred and seventy tonnes rose—bouncing on thrust instead of using the cushion effect of air under pressure in the plenum chamber. The tank teetered like a plate spinning on a broomhandle.

"—ward!"

The stern curtsied as Holman finally tilted two of her fan nacelles to direct their thrust to the rear. Charlie Three-zero slid forward, then hopped up as the skirts gouged the top of the berm like a cookie cutter in soft dough.

The tank sailed off the front of the berm and dropped like the iridium anvil she was as soon as her skirts lost their temporary ground effect. They hit squarely, ramming the steel skirts ten centimeters into the ground and racking Wager front and back against the coaming.

Somehow Holman managed to keep a semblance of control. The tank's bow slewed right—and Charlie Three-zero roared off counterclockwise, in pursuit of the other two members of their platoon.

They continued to bounce every ten meters or so. Their skirts grounded, rose till there was more than a hand's breadth clearance beneath the skirts—and spilled pressure in another hop.

But they were back in the war.

The reason Warrant Leader Ortnahme fired into the rockpile 300 meters to their front was that the overgrown mound—a dump for plowed-up stones before the government took over the area from Camp Progress—was a likely hiding place for Consie troops.

The reason Ortnahme fired the main gun instead of the tribarrel was that he'd never had an excuse to do *that* before in his twenty-three years as a soldier.

His screens damped automatically to keep from being overloaded, but the blue flash was reflected onto Ortnahme through the open hatch as *Herman's Whore* bucked with the recoil.

The rockpile blew apart in gobbets of molten quartz and blazing vegetation. There was no sign of Consies.

Via! but it felt good!

Simkins was keeping them a hundred meters outside Sparrow's *Deathdealer*, the way the acting platoon leader had ordered. Simkins had moved his share of tanks in the course of maintenance work, but before now, he'd never had to drive one as fast as twenty kph. He was doing a good job, but—

"Simkins!" he ordered. "*Don't* jink around them bloody bushes like they was the landscaping at headquarters. Just drive over 'em!"

But the kid was doing fine. The Lord *only* knew where the third tank with its newbie crew had gotten to.

The air above the Yokels' high berm crackled with hints of cyan, the way invisible lightning backlighted clouds during a summer storm. The Red team was finding somebody to mix with.

The tanks might as well be practicing night driving techniques. The Consies that'd hit this end of the encampment must all be dead or runnin' as fast as they could to save their miserable—

WHANG!

Herman's Whore slewed to the right and grounded, then began staggering crabwise with the left side of her skirts scraping. They'd been hit, *hard*, but there wasn't any trace of the shot in the screens whose sensors should've reported the event even if they hadn't warned of it.

"Sir, I've lost plenum chamber pressure," Simkins said, a triumph of the obvious that even a bloody civilian with a bloody *rutabaga* for a brain wouldn't've bothered to—

"Did the access door blow open again?" Simkins continued.

Blood and Martyrs. Of course.

"Lord, kid, I'm sorry," the warrant leader blurted, apologizing for what he hadn't said—and for the fact he hadn't been thinking. "Put 'er down and I'll take care of it."

The tank settled. Ortnahme raised his seat to the top of its run, then prepared to step out through the hatch. Down in the hull, the sensor console pinged a warning.

Ortnahme couldn't see the screens from this angle, and he didn't have a commo helmet to relay the data to him in the cupola.

He didn't need the electronic sensors. His eyes and the sky-glow from the ongoing destruction of Camp Progress showed him a Consie running toward *Herman's Whore* with an armload of something that wasn't roses.

"Simkins!" the warrant leader screamed, hoping his voice would carry either to the driver or the intercom pickup in the hull. "Go! Go! Go!"

The muscles beneath Ortnahme's fat bunched as he swung the tribarrel. The gun tracked as smoothly as wet ice, but it was glacially slow as well.

Ortnahme's thumbs clamped on the trigger, lashing out a stream of bolts. The Consie flopped down. None of the bolts had cracked through the air closer than a meter above his head. The bastard was too close for the cupola gun to hit him.

Which the Consie figured out just as quick as Ortnahme did. The guerrilla picked himself up and shambled toward the tank again, holding out what was certainly a magnetic mine. It would detonate a few seconds after he clamped it onto the *Whore*'s steel skirts.

Ortnahme fired again. His bolts lit the camouflaged lid of the hole in which the Consie had hidden—twenty meters from where the target was now.

There was a simple answer to this sort of problem: the close-in defense system built into each of Hammer's combat vehicles, ready to blast steel shot into oncoming missiles or men who'd gotten too close to be handled by the tribarrel.

Trouble was, Ortnahme was a very competent and experienced mechanic. He'd dismantled the defense system before he started the rebuild. If he hadn't, he'd've risked killing himself and fifty other people if his pliers slipped and sent a current surge down the wrong circuit. He'd been going to reconnect the system in the morning, when the work was done. . . .

The intake roar of the fans resumed three Consie steps before the tank began moving, but finally *Herman's Whore* staggered forward again. They were a great pair for a race—the tank crippled, and the man bent over by the weight of the mine he carried. A novelty act for clowns. . . .

Down in the hull the commo was babbling something—orders, warnings; Simkins wondering what the *cop* his superior thought he was up to. Ortnahme didn't dare leave the cupola to answer—or call for help. As soon as they drew enough ahead of the Consie, he'd blast the bastard and then fix the access plate so they could move properly again.

The trouble with *that* plan was that *Herman's Whore* had started circling. The tank moved about as fast as the man on foot, but the Consie was cutting the chord of the arc and in a few seconds—

The warrant leader lifted himself from the hatch and let himself slide down the smooth curve of the turret. He fumbled in his cargo pocket. Going in this direction, his age and fat didn't matter. . . .

The Consie staggered forward, bent over his charge, in a triumph of will over exhaustion. He must have been blowing like a whale, but the sound wasn't audible over the suction of the tank's eight fans.

Ortnahme launched himself from the tank and crushed the guerrilla to the ground. Bones snapped, caught between the warrant leader's mass and the mine casing.

Ortnahme didn't take any chances. He hammered until the grip of the multitool thumped slimy dirt instead of the Consie's head.

Herman's Whore was circling back. Ortnahme tried to stand, then sat heavily. He waved his left arm.

By the time Simkins pulled up beside him, the warrant leader would be ready to get up and *weld* that cursed access cover in place.

Until then, he'd figured he'd just sit and catch his breath.

Terrain is one thing on a contour map, where a dip of three meters in a hundred is dead flat, and another thing on the ground, where it's enough difference to hide an object the size of a tank.

Which is just what it seemed to have done to call sign Tootsie Four, the maintenance section's vehicle, so far as Hans Wager could tell from his own cupola.

It wasn't Holman's fault.

What with the late start, they'd had to drive like a bat outa Hell to get into position. It would've taken the Lord and all his martyrs to save 'em if they'd stumbled into the Consies while Wager was barely able to hang on, much less shoot.

But since they caught up, she'd been keeping Charlie Three-zero about 300 meters outboard of Sparrow's blower, just like orders. Only thing was, there was supposed to be another tank between them.

Sparrow was covering a double arc, with his tribarrel swung left and his main gun offset to the right. It was the main gun that fired, kicking a scoop load of fused earth skyward in fiery sparkles.

Wager didn't see what the platoon leader'd shot at, but three figures jumped to their feet near the point of impact. Wager tumbled them to the ground again as blazing corpses with a burst from his tribarrel.

They were doing okay. Wager was doing okay. His facial muscles were locked in a tight rictus, and he took his fingers momentarily from the tribarrel's grips to massage the numbness out of them.

His driver was doing all right too, now that it was just a matter of moving ahead at moderate speed. *Deathdealer* was travelling at about twenty kph, and Holman had been holding Charlie Three-zero to the same speed since they caught up with the rest of the platoon.

Because Sparrow's tank was on the inside of the pivot, it was slowly drawing ahead of them. Wager felt the hull vibration change as Holman fiddled with her power and tilt controls, but the tank's inertia took much longer to adjust.

The fan note built into a shriek.

Wager scanned the night, wishing he had the eyes of two wing gunners to help the way he would on a combat car. Having the main gun was all well and good, but he figured the firepower of another pair of tribarrels—

Via! What did Holman think they were doing? Running a race?

—would more than make up for a twenty centimeter punch in *this* kind of war.

"Holman!" he snarled into his intercom. "Slow us bloody—"

Charlie Three-zero's mass had absorbed all the power inputs and was now rocketing through the night at twice her previous speed. *Way* too fast in the dark for anything but paved roads. Rocks clanged on the skirts as the tank crested a knoll—

And plunged down the other side, almost as steep as the berm they'd crashed off minutes before.

"—*down!*"

The ravine was full of Consies, jumping aside or flattening as Charlie Three-zero hurtled toward them under no more control than a 170-tonne roundshot.

Wager's bruised body knew *exactly* how the impact would feel, but reflex kept that from affecting anything he did. Charlie Three-zero hit, bounced. Wager's left hand flipped the protective cage away from the control on the tribarrel's mount—the same place it was on a combat car. He rammed the miniature joystick straight in, firing the entire close-in defense system in a single white flash from the top of the skirts.

Guerrillas flew apart in shreds.

The door of a bunker gaped open in the opposite side of the gully. Holman had been trying to raise Charlie Three-zero's bow to slow their forward motion. As the tank hopped forward, the bow *did* lift enough for the skirts to scrape the rise instead of slamming into it the way they had when trying to get out of Camp Progress.

"Bring us—" Wager ordered as he rotated his tribarrel to bear on the Consies behind them, some squirming in their death throes but others rising again to point weapons.

—*around*, he meant to say, but Holman reversed her fans and sucked the tank squarely down where she'd just hit. The unexpected impact rammed Wager's spine against his seat. His tribarrel was aimed upward.

"You dickheaded fool!" he screamed over the intercom as he lowered his weapon and the tank started to lift in place.

A Consie threw a grenade. It bounced off the hull and exploded in the air. Wager felt the hot *flick* of shrapnel beneath the cheekpiece of his helmet, but the grenadier himself flopped backward with most of his chest gone.

The tribarrel splattered the air, then walked its long burst across several of the guerrillas still moving.

Holman slammed the tank down again. They hit with a crunch, followed by a second shudder as the ground collapsed over the Consie bunker.

Holman rocked her fans. Dust and quartz pebbles flew back, covering the corpses in the gully like dirt spurned by a cat over its dung.

"Sergeant?" called the voice in Wager's intercom. "Sergeant? Want to make another pass?"

Wager was trying to catch his breath. "Negative, Holman," he managed to say. "Just bring us level with *Deathdealer* again.

"Holman," he added a moment later. "You did just fine."

Their position in line was second from the left, but Dick Suilin glimpsed the remaining combat car on his side only at intersections—and that rarely.

Its powerguns lit the parallel street in a constant reminder of its lethal presence. A burst quivering like a single blue flash showed Suilin a hump on what should have been the straight slope of a barracks roofline across the next intersection.

The reporter fired; the empty clip ejected with the *choonk* of his weapon.

Before Suilin's grenade had completed its low-velocity arc toward its target, the figure fired back with a stream of tracers that looked the size of bright orange baseballs. They sailed lazily out of the flickering muzzle flashes, then snapped past the reporter with dazzling speed.

The splinter shield above Suilin rang, and impacts sparkled on the iridium side armor. *How could the Consie have missed*—the reporter thought.

A tremendous blow knocked him backward.

His grenade detonated on the end wall of the building, a meter below the machine-gunner. Cooter, screaming curses or orders to their driver, squeezed his trigger button. Cyan fire ripped from both the weapon he gripped and the left wing gun, slaved to follow the point gun's controls.

Suilin didn't hurt, but he couldn't feel anything between his neck and his waistband. He tried to say, "I'm all right,"to reassure himself, but he found there was no air in his lungs and he couldn't breathe. There were glowing dimples in the splinter shield where the machine-gun had hammered it.

I'm dead, he thought. It should have bothered him more than it did.

His grenade had missed the Consie. Tracers sprayed harmlessly skyward as the fellow jumped back while keeping a death grip on his trigger.

Cooter's powerguns lit and shattered roof tiles as they sawed toward, then through, their target. The machine-gun's ammunition drum blew up with a yellow flash.

Suilin's hands hurt like *hell*. "Via!" he screamed. A flash of flaming agony wrapped his chest and released it as suddenly, leaving behind an ache many times worse than what he remembered from the time he broke his arm.

Both the mercenaries, faceless in their visored helmets, were bending over him. "Where you hit?" Cooter demanded as Otski lifted the reporter's right forearm and said, "Via! But it's just fragments, it's okay."

Cooter's big index finger prodded Suilin in the chest. "Yeah," he said. "No penetration." He tugged at something.

Suilin felt a cold, prickling sensation over his left nipple. "What're you—" he said, but the Slammers had turned back to their guns.

The car must have paused while they checked him. Now it surged forward faster than before.

They swept by the barracks. Cooter's long double burst had turned it into a torch.

Suilin lay on his back. He looked down at himself. There was a charred circle as big as a soup dish in the fabric cover of his clamshell. In the center of *that* was a thumb-sized crater in the armor itself.

The pockmark in the ceramic plate had a metallic sheen, and there were highlights of glittering metal in the blood covering the backs of both Suilin's hands. When the bullet hit the clamshell armor and broke up, fragments splashed forward and clawed the reporter's bare hands.

He rose, pushing himself up with his arms. For a moment, his hands burned and there were ice picks in his neck and lower back.

Coolness spreading outward from his chest washed over the pain. There were colored tabs on the breast of the armor. Suilin had thought they were decorations, but the one Cooter had pulled was obviously releasing medication into Suilin's system.

Thank the Lord for that.

He picked up the grenade launcher and reloaded it. Shock, drugs, and the tiny bits of metal that winked when he moved his fingers made him clumsy, but he did it.

Like working against a deadline. Your editor didn't care why you *hadn't* filed on time; so you worked when you were hung over, when you had flu. . . .

When your father died before you had had time to clear things up with him. When your wife left you because you didn't care about *her*, only your cursed *stories*.

Dick Suilin raised his eyes and his ready weapon just as both the combat car and the immediate universe opened up with a breathtaking inferno of fire.

They'd reached the Headquarters of Camp Progress.

It was a three-story building at the southern end of the encampment. Nothing separated the pagoda-roofed structure from the berm except the camp's peripheral road. The berm here, like the hundred-meter square in front of the building, had been sodded and was manicured daily.

There were bodies sprawled on the grass. Suilin didn't have time to look at them, because lights flared in several ground-floor windows as Consies launched buzzbombs and ducked back.

The grenade launcher's dull report was lost in the blurred crackling of the three tribarrels, but the reporter knew he'd gotten his round away as fast as the veterans had theirs.

Unlike the rest of Camp Progress, the Headquarters building was a masonry structure. At least a dozen powerguns were raking the two lower floors. Though the stones spattered out pebbles and molten glass at every impact, the walls themselves held and continued to protect the Consies within them.

The grenade was a black dot against the window lighted by bolts from the powerguns. It sailed through the opening, detonated with a dirty flash, and flung a guerrilla's corpse momentarily into view.

The oncoming buzzbomb filled Suilin's forward vision. He saw it with impossible clarity, its bulbous head swelling on a thread of smoke that trailed back to the grenade-smashed room.

The close-in defense system went off, spewing miniature steel barrels into the path of the free-flight missile. They slashed through the warhead, destroying its integrity. When the buzz bomb hit the side of the combatcar between the left and center gun positions, the fuse fired but the damaged booster charge did not.

The buzzbomb bounced from the armor with a bell sound, then skittered in tight circles around the grass until its rocket motor burned out.

Cooter's driver eased the vehicle forward, onto the lawn, at barely walking speed. The square was normally lighted after sunset, but all the poles had been shot away.

Dick Suilin had spent three days at or close to the Headquarters building while he gathered the bulk of his story. Clean-cut, *professional* members of the National Army, doing their jobs with quiet dedication—to contrast with ragged, brutal-looking mercenaries (many of whom were female!), who absorbed such a disproportionate share of the defense budget.

"Hey turtle!" Otski called. "Watch that—"

To either side of the grassed area were pairs of trailers, living quarters for Colonel Banyussuf and his favored staff. The one on the left end was assigned to Sergeant Major Lee, the senior noncom at Camp Progress. Suilin was billeted with him. The door was swinging in the light breeze, and a dozen or so bulletholes dimpled the side-wall at waist height, but Suilin could at least hope he'd be able to recover his gear unharmed when this was over.

The car to their left fired a short burst at the trailer. The bolts blew the end apart, shattering the plywood panels and igniting the light metal sheathing. The reporter swore at the unnecessary destruction.

The air crisscrossed with machine-gun bullets and the smoke trails of at least a dozen buzzbombs. All four of the silent trailers were nests of Consie gunners.

Suilin ducked below the car's armored side.

Bullets hit the iridium and rang louder than things that small could sound. The defense system, a different portion of the continuous strip, went off. The light reflected from the underside of the splinter shield was white and orange and cyan, and there was no room in the universe for more noise.

The reporter managed to raise himself, behind the muzzle of his grenade launcher, just in time to see Sergeant Major Lee's trailer erupt in a violent explosion that showered the square with shrapnel and blew the trailer behind it off its slab foundation.

There was a glowing white spot on the armor of the combat car to Suilin's left. As he watched, the driver's hatch popped open and a man scrambled out. Another crewman rolled over the opposite side-wall of the fighting compartment.

The car blew up.

Because the first instants were silent, it seemed a drawn-out affair, though the process couldn't have taken more than seconds from beginning to end. A streak of blue-green light shot upward, splashed *on* the splinter shield and *through* the steel covering almost instantaneously.

The whole fighting compartment became a fireball that bulged the side armor and lifted the remnants of the shield like a bat-wing.

A doughnut of incandescent gas hung for a moment over the wreckage, then imploded and vanished.

Suilin screamed and emptied the clip of his grenade launcher into the other trailer on his side. It was already burning; Cooter didn't bother to fire into its crumpled remains as their car accelerated toward the Headquarters building.

Two flags—one white, the other the red-and-gold of the National Government—fluttered from the top floor of the building on short staffs. No one moved at those windows.

Now the lower floors were silent also. Otski raked the second story while Cooter used the car's slow drift to saw his twin guns across the lowest range of windows. Cooter's rotating iridium barrels were glowing white, but a ten-meter length of the walls collapsed under the point-blank jackhammer of his bolts.

Suilin reloaded mechanically. He didn't have a target. At this short range, his grenades were more likely to injure himself and the rest of the crew than they were to find some unlikely Consie survivor within the Headquarters building.

He caught motion in the corner of his eye as he turned.

The movement came from a barracks they'd passed moments before, on the north side of the square. Tribarrels, Otski's and that of the next combat car in line, had gnawed the frame building thoroughly and set it alight.

A stubby black missile was silhouetted against those flames.

Gear on the floor of the fighting compartment trapped the reporter's feet as he tried to swing his grenade launcher. The close-in defense system slammed just above the skirts. The buzzbomb exploded in a red flash, ten meters away from the combat car.

A jet of near-plasma directed from the shaped-charge warhead skewered the night.

The spurt of light was almost lost to Suilin's retinas, dazzled already by the powerguns, but the blast of heat was a shock as palpable as that of the bullet that had hit him in the chest.

Otski fell down. Something flew past the reporter as he reeled against the armor.

The barrel of the grenade launcher was gone. Just gone, vaporized ten centimeters from the breech. If the jet had struck a finger's breadth to the left, the grenade would have detonated and killed all three of them.

The shockwave had snatched off Otski's helmet. The gunner's left arm was missing from the elbow down. That explained the stench of burned meat.

Suilin vomited onto his legs and feet.

"I'm all right," Otski said. He must have been screaming for Suilin to be able to hear him. "It don't mean nothin'."

A line was charred across the veteran's clamshell armor. A finger's breadth to the left, and . . .

There were two tabs on the front of Otski's back-and-breast armor. Suilin pulled them both.

"Is it bleeding?" Cooter demanded. "Is it bleeding?"

The bone stuck out a centimeter beyond where the charred muscle had shrunk back toward the gunner's shoulder. "He's—" Suilin said. "It's—"

"Right," shouted Cooter. He turned back to his tribarrel.

"I'm all right," said Otski. He tried to push himself erect. His stump clattered on the top of an ammunition box. His face went white and pinched in.

Don't mean nothin', Otski's lips formed. Then his pupils rolled up and he collapsed.

The combat car spun in its own length and circled the blasted Headquarters building. There were figures climbing the berm behind the structure. Cooter fired.

Dick Suilin leaned over Otski and took the grips of his tribarrel. Another car was following them; a third had rounded the building from the other side.

When Suilin pressed the thumb button, droplets of fire as constant as a strobe-lit fountain streamed from his rotating muzzles.

Sod spouted in a line as the reporter walked toward the black-clad figure trying desperately to climb the steep berm ahead of them. At the last moment the guerrilla turned with his hands raised, but Suilin couldn't have lifted his thumbs in time if he'd wanted to.

Ozone and gases from the empty cases smothered the stink of Otski's arm.

For a moment, Consies balanced on top of the berm. A scything cross fire tumbled them as the tanks and combat cars raked their targets from both sides.

When nothing more moved, the vehicles shot at bodies in case some of the guerrillas were shamming. Twice Suilin managed to explode the grenades or ammunition that his targets carried.

Cooter had to pry the reporter's fingers from the tribarrel when Tootsie Six called a ceasefire.

CHAPTER FOUR

"I've got authorization," said Dick Suilin, fumbling in the breast pocket of his fatigues. The "*Extend all courtesies*" card signed by his brother-in-law, Gover nor Samuel Kung, was there, along with his Press ID and his Military Status Papers.

Suilin's military status was Exempt-III. That meant he would see action only in the event of a call-up of all male citizens between the ages of sixteen and sixty.

He was having trouble getting the papers out because his fingers were still numb from the way they'd been squeezing the tribarrel's grips.

For that matter, the National Government might've proclaimed a general call-up overnight—if there *was* still a National Government.

"Buddy," snarled the senior noncomat the door of the communications center, "I can't help you. I don't care if you got authorization from God 'n his saints. I don't care if you *are* God 'n his saints!"

"I'm not that," the reporter said in a soft, raspy voice. Ozone and smoke had flayed his throat. "But I need to get through to Kohang—and it's your ass if I don't."

He flicked at his shirtfront. Some of what was stuck there came off.

Suilin's wrist and the back of his right hand were black where vaporized copper from the buzzbomb had recondensed.All the fine hairs were burned off, but the skin beneath hadn't blistered. His torso was badly bruised where the bullet-struck armor had punched into him.

The butt of the pistol he now carried in his belt prodded the bruise every time he moved.

"Well, I'm not God neither, buddy," the noncom said, his tone frustrated but suddenly less angry.

He waved toward his set-up and the two junior technicians

struggling with earphones and throat mikes. "The land lines're down, the satellites're down, and there's jamming right across all the bands. If you think *you* can get something through, you just go ahead and try. But if you want my ass, you gotta stand in line."

The National side of Camp Progress had three commo centers. The main one was—had been—in the shielded basement of Headquarters. A few Consies were still holed up there after the rest of the fighting had died down. A Slammers' tank had managed to depress its main gun enough to finish the job.

The training detachment had a separate system, geared toward the needs of homesick draftees. It had survived, but Colonel Banyussuf—who'd also survived—had taken over the barracks in which it was housed as his temporary headquarters. Suilin hadn't bothered trying to get through the panicked crowd now surrounding the building.

The commo room of the permanent maintenance section at Camp Progress was installed in a three-meter metal transport container. It was unofficial—the result of scrounging over the years. Suilin hadn't ever tried to use it before; but in the current chaos, it was his only hope.

"What do you mean, the satellites are down?" he demanded.

He was too logy with reaction to be sure that what he'd heard the noncom say was as absurd as he thought it was. The microwave links were out? Not all of them, surely. . . .

"Out," the soldier repeated. "Gone. Blitzed. Out."

"Blood and martyrs," Suilin said.

The Consie guerrillas couldn't have taken down all the comsats. The Terran enclaves had to have become directly involved. That was a stunning escalation of the political situation—

And an escalation which was only conceivable as part of a planned deathblow to the National Government of Prosperity.

"I've *got* to call Kohang," said Dick Suilin, aloud but without reference to the other men nearby. All he could think of was his sister, in the hands of Consies determined to make an example of the governor's wife. "Suzi . . ."

"You can forget bloody Kohang," said one of the techs as he stripped off his headphones. He ran his fingers through his hair. The steel room was hot, despite the cool morning and the air conditioner throbbing on the roof. "It's been bloody overrun."

Suilin gripped the pistol in his belt. "What do you mean?" he snarled as he pushed past the soldier in the doorway.

"They said it was," the technician insisted. He looked as though he intended to get out of his chair, but the reporter was already looming over him.

"*Somebody* said it was," argued the other tech. "Look, we're still getting signals from Kohang, it's just the jamming chews the bugger outa it."

"There's fighting all the hell over the place," said the senior noncom, putting a gently restraining hand on Suilin's shoulder." 'Cept maybe here. Look, buddy, nobody knows what the hell's going on anywhere just now."

"Maybe the mercs still got commo," the first tech said. "Yeah, I bet they do."

"Right," said the reporter. "Good thought."

He walked out of the transport container. He was thinking of what might be happening in Kohang.

He gripped his pistol very hard.

The chip recorder sitting on the cupola played a background of guitar music while a woman wailed in Tagalog, a language which Henk Ortnahme had never bothered to learn. The girls on Esperanza all spoke Spanish. And Dutch. And English. Enough of it.

The girls all spoke money, the same as everywhere in the universe he'd been since.

The warrant leader ran his multitool down the channel of the close-in defense system. The wire brush he'd fitted to the head whined in complaint, but it never quite stalled out.

It never quite got the channel clean, either. Pits in the steel were no particular problem—*Herman's Whore* wasn't being readied for a parade, after all. But crud in the holes for the bolts which both anchored the strips and passed the detonation signals . . . that was something else again.

Something blew up nearby with a hollow sound, like a grenade going off in a trash can. Ortnahme looked around quickly, but there didn't seem to be an immediate problem. Since dawn there'd been occasional shooting from the Yokel end of the camp, but there was no sign of living Consies around here.

Dead ones, sure. A dozen of 'em were lined up outside the TOC, being checked for identification and anything else of intelligence value. When that was done—done in a pretty cursory fashion, the warrant leader expected, since Hammer didn't have a proper intelligence officer here at Camp Progress—the bodies would be hauled beyond the berm, covered with diesel, and barbecued like the bloody pigs they were.

Last night had been a bloody near thing.

Ortnahme wasn't going to send out a tank whose close-in defenses were doubtful. Not after he'd had personal experience of what that meant in action.

He bore down harder. The motor protested; bits of the brush tickled the face shield of his helmet. He'd decided to wear his commo helmet this morning instead of his usual shop visor, because—

Via, why not admit it? Because he'd really wished he'd had the helmet the night before. He couldn't change the past, couldn't have all his gear handy back *then* when he needed it; but he could sure as hell have it on him now for a security blanket.

There was a 1cm pistol in Ortnahme's hip pocket as well. He'd never seen the face of the Consie who'd chased him with the bomb, but today the bastard leered at Ortnahme from every shadow in the camp.

The singer moaned something exceptionally dismal. Ortnahme backed off his multitool, now that he had a sufficient section of channel cleared. He reached for a meter-long strip charge.

Simkins, who should've been buffing the channels while the warrant leader bolted in charges, had disappeared minutes after they'd parked *Herman's Whore* back in her old slot against the berm. The kid'd done a bloody good job during the firefight—but that didn't mean he'd stopped being a bloody maintenance tech. Ortnahme was going to burn him a new asshole as soon as—

"Mr. Ortnahme?" Simkins said. "Look what I got!"

The warrant leader turned, already shouting. "Simkins, where in the name of all that's holy have—"

He paused. "Via, Simkins," he said. "Where did you get that?"

Simkins was carrying a tribarrel, still in its packing crate.

"Tommy Dill at Logistics, sir," the technician answered brightly. "Ah, Mr. Ortnahme? It's off the books, you know. We set a little charge on the warehouse roof, so Tommy can claim a mortar shell combat-lossed the gun."

Just like that was the only question Ortnahme wanted to ask.

Though it was sure-hell *one* of 'em, that was God's truth.

"Kid," the warrant leader said calmly, more or less. "What in the bloody hell do you think you're gonna do with that gun?"

From the way Simkins straightened, "more or less" wasn't as close to "calmly" as Ortnahme had thought.

"Sir!" the technician said. "I'm gonna mount it on the bow. So I got something to shoot, ah . . . you know, the next time."

The kid glanced up at the blaring recorder. He was holding the tribarrel with no sign of how much the thing weighed. He wouldn't have been able to do that before Warrant Leader Ortnahme started running his balls off to teach him his job.

Ortnahme opened his mouth. He didn't know which part of the stupid idea to savage first.

Before he figured out what to say, Simkins volunteered, "Mister Ortnahme? I figured we'd use a section of engineer stake for a mount and weld it to the skirt. Ah, so we don't have to chance a weld on the iridium, you know?"

Like a bloody puppy, standin' there waggling his tail—and *how* in bloody hell had he got Sergeant Dill to agree to take a tribarrel off manifest?

"Kid," he said at last, "put that down and start buffing this channel for me, all right?"

"Yes, Mister Ortnahme."

The klaxon blurted, then cut off.

Ortnahme and every other Slammer in the compound froze. Nothing further happened. The Yokels must've been testing the system now that they'd moved it.

The bloody cursed fools.

"Sir,"the technician said with his face bent over the buzz of his own multi tool. "Can I put on some different music?"

"I like what I got on," Ortnahme grunted, spinning home first one, then the other of the bolts that locked the strip of explosive and steel pellets into its channel.

"Why, sir?" Simkins prodded unexpectedly. "The music, I mean?"

Ortnahme stared at his subordinate. Simkins continued to buff his way forward, as though cleaning the channel were the only thing on his mind.

"Because," Ortnahme said. He grimaced and flipped up the face shield of his helmet. "Because that was the kinda stuff they played in the bars on Esperanza, my first landfall with the Regiment. Because it reminds me of when I was young and stupid, kid. Like you."

He slid another of the strip charges from its insulated packing, then paused. "Look," he said, "this ain't our tank, Simkins."

"It's our tank till they send a crew to pick it up," the technician said over the whine of his brush. "It's our tank tonight, Mister Ortnahme."

The warrant leader sighed and fitted the strip into place. It bound slightly, but that was from the way the skirt had been torqued, not the job Simkins was doing on the channel.

"All right," Ortnahme said, "but we'll mount it solid so you swing the bow to aim it, all right? I don't want you screwing around with the grips when you oughta be holding the controls."

Simkins stopped what he was doing and turned. "*Thank* you, Mister Ortnahme!" he said, as though he'd just been offered the cherry of the most beautiful woman on the bloody planet.

"Yeah, sure," the warrant leader said with his face averted. "Believe me, you're gonna do the work while I sit on my butt 'n watch."

Ortnahme set a bolt,then a second. "Hey kid?" he said. "How the hell did you get Tommy to go along with this cop?"

"I told him it was you blasted the Consie with the satchel charge when Tommy opened his warehouse door."

Ortnahme blinked. "Huh?" he said. "Somebody did that? It sure wasn't me."

"Tommy's got a case of real French brandy for you, sir," the technician said. He turned and grinned. "And the tribarrel. Because I'm your driver, see? And he didn't want our asses swingin' in the breeze again like last night."

"Bloody hell," the warrant leader muttered. He placed another bolt and started to grin himself.

"We won't use engineer stakes," he said. "I know where there's a section of 10cm fuel-truck hose sheathing. We'll cut and bend that. . . ."

"Thank you, Mister Ortnahme."

"And I guess we could put a pin through the pivot," Ortnahme went on. "So you could unlock the curst thing if, you know, we got bogged down again."

"*Thank* you, Mister Ortnahme!"

Cursed little puppy. But a smart one.

Two blocks from the commo room, Dick Suilin passed the body of a man in loose black garments. The face of the corpse was twisted in a look of ugly surprise. An old scar trailed up his cheek and across an eyebrow, but there was no sign of the injury that had killed him here.

The Slammers' TOC was almost two kilometers away. Suilin was already so exhausted that his ears buzzed except when he tried to concentrate on something. He decided to head for the infantry-detachment motor pool and try to promote a ride to the north end of the camp.

It occurred to the reporter that he hadn't seen any vehicles moving in the camp since the combat cars reformed and howled back to their regular berths. As he formed the thought, a light truck drove past and stopped beside the body.

A lieutenant and two soldiers wearing gloves, all of them looking morose, got out. Before they could act, a group of screaming dependents, six women and at least as many children, swept around the end of one of the damage buildings. They pushed the soldiers away, then surrounded the corpse and began kicking it.

Suilin paused to watch. The enlisted men glanced at one another, then toward the lieutenant, who seemed frozen. One of the men said, "Hey, we're s'posed to take—"

A woman turned and spat in the soldier's face.

"*Murdering Consie bastard! Murdering little Consie bastard!*"

Two of the older children were stripping the trousers off the body. A six-year old boy ran up repeatedly, lashed out with his bare foot, and ran back. He never quite made contact with the corpse.

"*Murdering Consie Bastard!*"

The officer drew his pistol and fired in the air. The screaming stopped. One woman flung herself to the ground, covering a child with her body. The group backed away, staring at the man with the gun.

The officer aimed at the guerrilla's body and fired. Dust puffed from the shoulder of the black jacket.

The officer fired twice more, then blasted out the remainder of his ten-round magazine. The hard ground sprayed grit in all directions; one bullet ricocheted and spanged into a doorjamb, missing a child by centimeters at most.

The group of dependents edged away. Bullets had disfigured still further the face of the corpse.

"Well, get on with it!" the lieutenant screamed to his men. His voice sounded tinny from the muzzle blasts of his weapon.

The soldiers grimaced and grasped the body awkwardly in their gloved hands. A glove slipped as they swung the guerrilla onto the tailgate of the truck. The body hung, about to fall back.

The lieutenant grabbed a handful of the Consie's hair and held it until the enlisted men could get better grips and finish their task.

Suilin resumed walking toward the motor pool. He was living in a nightmare, and his ears buzzed like wasps. . . .

"Now, to split the screen," said squat Joe Albers, *Deathdealer*'s driver,"you gotta hold one control and switch the other one whatever way."

Hans Wager set his thumb on the left hold button and clicked the right-hand magnification control of the main screen to *x4*. The turret of the unnamed tank felt crowded with two men in it, although Wager himself was slim and Albers was stocky rather than big.

"Does it matter which control you hold?" asked Holman, peering down through the hatch.

"Naw, whichever you want," Albers said while Wager watched the magical transformations on his screen.

The left half of the main screen maintained its portion of a 360° panorama viewed by the light available in the human visual spectrum. Broad daylight, at the moment. The right portion of the screen had shrunk into a 90° arc whose field of view was only half its original height.

Wager twisted the control dial, rotating the magnified sector slowly around the tank's surroundings. Smoke still smoldered upward from a few places beyond the berm; here and there, sunlight glittered where the soil seared by powerguns had enough silicon to glaze.

The berth on the right side of the tank was empty. The combat car assigned there had bought it in the clearing operation. Buzzbombs. The close-in defense system hadn't worked or hadn't worked well enough, same difference. Albers said a couple of the crew were okay. . . .

Wager's field of view rolled across the Yokel area. The barracks nearest the Slammers were in good shape still; but by focusing down one of the streets and rolling the magnification through *x16* to *x64*, he could see that at least a dozen buildings in a row had burned.

A few bolts from a powergun and those frame structures went up like torches. . . .

The best protection you had in a combat car wasn't armor or even your speed: it was the volume of fire you put on the other bastard and anywhere the other bastard might be hiding.

Tough luck for the Yokels who'd been burned out. Tougher

luck, much tougher, for the Consies who'd tried to engage Hammer's Slammers.

"For the driver," Albers said with a nod up toward Holman's intent face, "it's pretty much the same as a combat car."

"The weight's not the bloody same," Holman said.

"Sure, you gotta watch yer inertia," the veteran driver agreed, "but you do the same things. You get used to it."

He looked back over at Wager. The right half-screen was now projecting a magnified slice of what appeared at one-to-one on the left.

On the opposite side of the encampment, a couple of the permanent maintenance staff worked beside another tank. The junior tech looked on while his boss, a swag-bellied warrant three, settled a length of pipe in the jig of a laser saw.

"Turret side, though," Albers went on, "you gotta be careful. About half what you know from cars, that's the wrong thing in the turret of a panzer."

"I don't like not having two more pair of eyes watchin' my back," Wager muttered as his visuals swam around the circumference of the motionless tank.

"The screens'll watch for you," Albers said gently.

He touched a key without pressing it. "You lock one of 'em onto alert at all times. The AI in here, it's like a thousand helmet systems all at once. It's faster, it catches more, it's better at throwing out the garbage that just looks like it's a bandit."

The hatches of the Tactical Operations Center, a command car without drive fans, were open, but from this angle Wager couldn't see inside. The backs of two Slammers, peering within from the rear ramp, proved there was a full house—a troop meeting going on. What you'd expect after a contact like last night's.

"Not like having tribarrels pointing three ways, though," Holman said. Dead right, even though she'd never crewed a combat vehicle before.

Albers looked up at her. "If you want," he said, "you can slave either of the guns to the threat monitor. It'll swing 'em as soon as it pops the alert."

Deathdealer, Albers' own tank, was parked next to the TOC. A tarpaulin slanted from the top of the skirts to the ground, sheltering the man beneath. "Via," Wager muttered. "He's racked out now?"

Birdie Sparrow's right hand was visible beneath the edge of the tarp. It was twitching. Albers looked at the magnified screen, then laid his fingers over Eager on the dial and rolled the image away.

"Birdie's all right," the veteran driver said. "He takes a little getting used to, is all. And the past couple months, you know, he's been a little, you know . . . loose."

"That's why they sent you back here with the blower instead of using some newbies for transit?" Holman asked.

Bent over this way, Holman had to keep brushing back the sandy brown curls that fell across her eyes. Her hair was longer than Wager had thought, and the strands appeared remarkably fine.

"Yeah, something like that, I guess," Albers admitted. "Look, Birdie's great when it drops in the pot like last night. Only . . . since his buddy DJ got zapped, he don't sleep good, is all."

"Newbies like us," Wager said bitterly. *Not new to war, not him at least; but new to* this *kind of war.*

"I can see this gear can do everything but tuck me goodnight. But I'm bloody sure that *I* won't remember what to do the first time I need to. And that's liable to be my ass." He glanced upward. "Our ass."

Holman flashed him a tight smile.

"Yeah, well," Albers agreed. "Simulators help, but on-the-job training's the only game there's ever gonna be for some things."

Albers rubbed his scalp, grimacing in no particular direction. "You know," he went on, "you can take care a' most stuff if you know what button to push. But some things, curst if I know where the button is."

It seemed to Hans Wager that Albers' eyes were searching for the spot on the main screen where his tank commander lay shivering beneath a sunlit tarp.

When Dick Suilin was twenty meters from the motor pool, a jeep exploded within the wire-fenced enclosure. The back of the vehicle lurched upward. The contents of its fuel tank sprayed in all directions, then *whoomped* into a fireball that rose on the heat of its own combustion.

No one was in the jeep when it blew up, but soldiers throughout the area scattered, bawling warnings.

A few men simply cowered and screamed. One of them continued screaming minutes after the explosion.

Suilin resumed walking toward the entrance.

The combined motor pool held well over three hundred trucks, from jeeps to articulated flatbeds for hauling heavy equipment. The only gate in and out of Camp Progress was visible a block away. A pair of bunkers, massive structures with three-meter walls of layered sandbags and steel planking, guarded the highway where it passed through the wire, minefields, and berm.

The sliding barrier was still in place across the road. When the Consies came over the berm, they took the bunkers from behind. Satchel charges through the open doors set off the munitions within, and the blasts lifted the roofs.

The bunkers had collapsed. The craters were still smoldering.

One of the long sheds within the motor pool had been hit by an artillery rocket. The blast folded back its metal roof in both directions. Grenades and automatic weapons had raked and ignited some of the trucks parked in neat rows, but there were still many undamaged vehicles.

A three-tonne truck blew up. The driver jumped out of the cab and collapsed. Diesel from the ruptured fuel tank gushed around him in an iridescent pool. Nobody moved to help, though other soldiers stared in dazed expectation.

Two officers were arguing at the entrance while a number of enlisted men looked on. A lieutenant wearing the green collar tabs of Maintenance & Supply said in a voice that wavered between reasonableness and frustration, "But Major Schaydin, it isn't *safe* to take any of the vehicles yet. The Consies have booby—"

"God curse you for a fool!" screamed the major. His summer dress uniform was in striking contrast to the lieutenant's fatigues, but a nearby explosion had ripped away most of the right trouser leg and blackened the rest. "*You* can't deny me! I'm the head of the Intelligence Staff! My orders supersede any you may have received. Any orders at all!"

Schaydin carried a pair of white gloves, thrust jauntily through his left epaulet. His hat hadn't survived the events of the evening.

"Sir,"the lieutenant pleaded,"this isn't orders, it isn't *safe*. The Consies booby-trapped a bunch of the vehicles during the attack, time delays and pressure switches, and they—"

"You bastards!" Schaydin screamed. "D' you want to find yourselves playing pick-up-sticks with your butt cheeks?"

He stalked past the lieutenant, brushing elbows as though he really didn't see the other man.

A sergeant moved as though to block Schaydin. The lieutenant shook his head in angry frustration. He, his men, and Suilin watched the major jump into a jeep, start it, and drive past them in a spray of dust.

"I need a jeep and driver," Suilin said, enunciating carefully. "To carry me to the Slammers' TOC." He deliberately didn't identify himself.

The lieutenant didn't answer. He was staring after Major Schaydin.

Instead of following the road, the intelligence officer pulled hard left and drove toward the berm. The jeep's engine lugged for a moment before its torque converter caught up with the demand. The vehicle began to climb, spurning gravel behind it.

"He'd do better," said the lieutenant, "if he at least tried it at a slant."

"Does he figure just to drive through the minefields?" asked one of the enlisted men.

"The Consies blew paths all the cop through the mines," said a sergeant. "If he's lucky, he'll be okay."

The jeep lurched over the top of the berm to disappear in a rush and a snarl. There was no immediate explosion.

"Takes more 'n luck to get through the Consies themselfs," said the first soldier. "Wherever he thinks he's going. Bloody officers."

"I don't need an argument," said Dick Suilin quietly.

"Then take the bloody jeep!" snapped the lieutenant. He pointed to a row of vehicles. "Them we've checked, more or less, for pressure mines in the suspension housings and limpets on the gas tanks. They must've had half a dozen sappers working the place over while their buddies shot up the HQ."

"No guarantees what went *into* the tanks," offered the sergeant. "Nothin' for that but waiting—and I'd as soon not wait on it. You want to see the mercs so bad, why don't you walk?"

Suilin looked at him. "If it's time," the reporter said, "it's time."

The nearest vehicle was a light truck rather than a jeep. He sat in the driver's seat, feeling the springs sway beneath him. No explosion, no flame. Suilin felt as though he were manipulating a marionette the size and shape of the man he had been.

He pressed the starter tit on the dash panel. A flywheel whirred for a moment before the engine fired normally.

Suilin set the selector to Forward and pressed the throttle. No explosion, no flame.

As he drove out of the motor pool, Suilin heard the sergeant saying, ". . . no insignia and them eyes—he's from an Insertion Patrol Group. Just wish them and the Consies'd fight their war and leave us normal people alone. . . ."

"Here he is, Captain Ranson," said the hologram of the commo tech at Firebase Purple. The image shifted.

Major Danny Pritchard looked exhausted even in hologram, and he was still wearing body armor over his khaki fatigues. He rubbed his eyes. "What do you estimate the strength of the attack on Camp Progress, Junebug?" he asked.

"Maybe a battalion," Ranson replied, wondering if her voice was drifting in and out of timbre the way her vision was. "They hit all sides, but it was mostly on the south end."

"Colonel Banyussuf claims it was a division," Pritchard said with a ghost of a smile. "He claims his men've killed over five thousand Consies already."

An inexperienced observer could have mistaken for transmission noise the ripping sounds that shook the hologram every ten or twenty seconds. Even over a satellite bounce, Ranson recognized the discharge of rocket howitzers.

Hammer's headquarters was getting some action too.

Cooter laughed. "If the Yokels killed anybody, it was when one of 'em fell out a window and landed on 'im. We got maybe three hundred."

"Stepped on?" demanded the image of Hammer's executive officer—and some said, heir.

"Stepped on and gun camera, maybe two hundred," Ranson said. "But there's a lot of stuff won't show up till they start sifting the ashes. Cooter's right, maybe three. It was a line battalion, and it won't be bothering anybody else for a while."

The command car was crowded. Besides Ranson, it held a commo tech named Bestwick at the console, ready if the artificial intelligence monitoring the other bands needed a human decision; Cooter, second in command of the detachment; and Master Sergeant Wylde, who'd been a section leader before, and would be again as soon as his burns healed.

Wylde was lucky to be alive after the first buzzbomb hit his car. He shouldn't have been present now; but he'd insisted, and Ranson didn't have the energy to argue with him. Anyway, between pain and medications, Wylde was too logy to be a problem except for the room his bandaged form took up.

"Hey?" said Cooter. He lifted his commo helmet slightly with one hand so that he could knuckle the line of his sweat-darkened auburn hair. "Major? What the hell's happening, anyway? Is this all over?"

Danny Pritchard smiled a great deal; usually it was a pleasant expression.

Not this smile.

"They hit the three firebases and all but one of the line companies," the major said. "We told everybody hold what they got; and then the hogs—" Pritchard nodded; a howitzer slashed the sky again from beyond the field of view "—scratched everybody's back with fire-cracker rounds. Each unit swept its circuit before the dust settled from the shellbursts."

The smile hardened still further. "Kinda nice of them to concentrate that way for us."

Ranson nodded, visualizing the white flare of precisely directed cluster bomb-lets going off. The interlocking fields of fire from Firebases Red, Blue, and Purple covered the entire Strip. Guerrillas rising in panic, to be hosed down by the tribarrels in the armored vehicles. . . .

"Yeah," said Sergeant Wylde in a husky whisper. The wounded man's face didn't move and his eyes weren't focused on the hologram. "But how about the Yokels? Or is this a private fight fer us 'n the Consies?"

"Right," said Pritchard with something more than agreement in his tone of voice. "Hold one, Junebug."

The sound cut off abruptly as somebody hit the muting switch of the console at HQ. Major Pritchard turned his head. Ranson could see Pritchard's lips moving in profile as he talked to someone out of the projection field. She was in a dream, watching the bust of a man who spoke silently. . . .

What's your present strength in vehicles and trained crews?

Junebug?

Captain Ranson?

Ranson snapped alert. Cooter had put his big arm around her shoulders to give her a shake.

"Right," she said, feeling the red prickly flush cover her, as though she'd just fainted and come around. She couldn't remember where she was, but in her dream somebody had been asking—

"We've got—" Cooter said.

"We're down a blower," Ranson said, facing Pritchard's worried expression calmly. "A combat car."

"Mine," said Wylde to his bandaged hands. Ranson wasn't sure whether or not the sergeant was within the hologram pickup.

"My crews, two dead," Ranson continued. "Three out for seven days or more. Sergeant Wylde, my section leader, he's out."

"Oh-yew-tee," Wylde muttered. "Out."

"Can you pick anybody up from the Blue side?" Pritchard asked.

"There's the three panzers," Ranson said. "Only one's got a trained crew, but they came through like gangbusters last night."

She frowned, trying to concentrate. "Personnel, though . . . Look, you know, we're talking newbies and people who're rear echelon for a reason."

People even farther out of it than Captain June Ranson, who nodded off while debriefing to Central. . . .

"Look, sir," Cooter interjected. "We shot the cop outa the Consies. I don't know about no 'five thousand' dead cop, But if they'd had more available, they'da used it last night. They bloody sure don't have enough left to try anytime soon."

"I believe you, Lieutenant," Pritchard said wearily. "But that's not the only problem." He rubbed the palms of his hands together firmly. "Hold one," he repeated as he got up from the console.

Colonel Alois Hammer sat down in Pritchard's place.

The hologram was as clear as if Hammer were in the TOC with Ranson. The colonel was madder than hell; so mad that his hand kept stabbing upward to brush away the tic at the corner of his left eye.

"Captain . . ." Hammer said. He fumbled with the latches of his clamshell armor to give himself time to form words—or at least to delay the point at which he had to speak them.

He glared at June Ranson. "*We* kicked the Consies up one side and down the other. The National Army had problems."

"That's why they hired us, sir," Ranson said. She was very calm. Thick glass was beginning to form between her and the image of the regimental commander.

"Yeah, that's why they did, all right," Hammer said. He ground at his left eye.

He lowered his hand. "Captain, you saw what happened to the structure of Camp Progress during the attack?"

"What structure?" Cooter muttered bitterly.

Ranson shivered. The glass wall shivered also, falling away as shards of color that coalesced into Hammer's face.

"Sir, the Consies were only a battalion," Ranson said. "They could've done a lot of damage—they did. But it was just a spoiling attack, they couldn't 've captured the base in the strength they were."

"They can capture Kohang, Captain," Hammer said. "And if they capture a district capital, the National Government is gone. The people who pay us."

Ranson blinked, trying to assimilate the information.

It didn't make any sense. The Consies were beat—beaten *good*. Multiply what her teams had done at Camp Progress by the full weight of the Regiment—with artillery and perfect artillery targets for a change—and the Conservative Action Movement on Prosperity didn't have enough living members to bury its dead. . . .

"Nobody was expecting it, Captain Ranson," Hammer said. The whiskers on his chin and jowls were white, though the close-cropped hair on the colonel's head was still a sandy brown. "The National Government wasn't, *we* weren't. It'd been so quiet the past three months that we—"

His eye twitched. "*Via!*" he cursed. "*I* thought, and if anybody'd told me different I'd 've laughed at them. I thought the Consies were about to pack it in. And instead they were getting ready for the biggest attack of the war."

"But Colonel," Cooter said. His voice sounded desperate. "They *lost*. They got their butts kicked."

"Tell that to a bunch of civilians," Hammer said bitterly. "Tell that to your Colonel Banyussuf—the bloody fool!"

Somebody at Central must have spoken to Hammer from out of pickup range, because the colonel half-turned and snarled, "Then *deal* with it! Shoot 'em all in the neck if you want!"

He faced around again. For an instant, Ranson stared into eyes as bleak and merciless as the scarp of a glacier. Then Hammer blinked, and the expression was gone; replaced with one of anger and concern. Human emotions, not forces of nature.

"Captain Ranson," he resumed with a formality that would have been frightening to the junior officer were she not drifting again into glassy isolation. "In a week, it'll all be over for the Consies. They'll have to make their peace on any terms they can get—even if that means surrendering for internment by the National

Government. But if a district capital falls, there won't *be* a National Government in a week. All they see—"

Hammer's left hand reached for his eye and clenched into a fist instead. "All they see," he repeated in a voice that trembled between a whisper and a snarl, "is what's been lost, what's been destroyed, what's been disrupted. You and I—"

His hand brushed out in a slighting gesture. "We've expended some ammo,we've lost some equipment. We've lost some people. Objectives cost. Winning costs."

Sergeant Wylde nodded. Blood was seeping from cracks in the Spray Seal which replaced the skin burned from his left shoulder.

"But the politicians and—and what passes for an army, here, they're in a panic. One more push and they'll fold. The people who pay us will fold."

One more push. . . . Ranson thought/said; she wasn't sure whether the words floated from her tongue or across her mind.

"Captain Ranson," Hammer continued, "I don't like the orders I'm about to give you, but I'm going to give them anyway. Kohang has to be relieved soonest, and you're the only troops in position to do the job."

June Ranson was sealed in crystal, a tiny bead that glittered as it spun aimlessly through the universe. "Sir," said the voice from her mouth, "there's the 4th Armored at Camp Victory. A brigade. There's the Yokel 12th and 23rd Infantry closer than we are."

Her voice was enunciating very clearly. "Sir, I've got eight blowers."

"Elements of the 4th Armored are attempting to enter Kohang from the south," Hammer said. "They're making no progress."

"How hard are they trying?" shouted Cooter. "How hard are they bloody trying?"

"It doesn't matter," Ranson thought/said.

"Lieutenant, that doesn't matter," said Hammer, momentarily the man who'd snarled at an off-screen aide. "They're not doing the job. We're going to. That's what we're paid to do."

"Cooter," said Ranson, "shut up."

She shouldn't say that with other people around. Screw it. She focused on the hologram. "Sir," she said, "what's the enemy strength?"

"We've picked up the call signs of twenty-seven Consie units in and around Kohang, company-size or battalion," Hammer said, in a tone of fractured calm. "The data's been downloaded to you already."

Bestwick glanced up from the console behind the projected image and nodded; Ranson continued to watch her commanding officer.

"Maybe three thousand bandits," Ranson said.

"Maybe twice that," Hammer said, nodding as Ranson was nodding. "Concentrated on the south side and around Camp Victory."

"There's two hundred thousand people in Kohang," Ranson said. "There's three thousand *police* in the city."

"The Governmental Compound is under siege," Hammer said coldly. "Some elements of the security forces appeared to be acting in support of the Consies." He paused and rubbed his eye.

"A battalion of the 4th Armored left Camp Victory without orders yesterday afternoon," he continued. "About an hour before the first rocket attack. Those troops aren't responding to messages from their brigade commander."

"Blood and martyrs," somebody in the TOC said. Maybe they all said it.

"Sir," said Ranson, "we can't, we can't by ourself—"

"Shoot your way into the compound," Hammer said before she could finish. "Reinforce what's there, put some backbone into 'em. They *got* enough bloody troops to do the job themselves, Captain . . . they just don't believe it."

He grimaced. "Even a couple blowers. That'll do the trick until G and H companies arrive. Just a couple blowers."

"Cop," muttered Wylde through his bandages.

"Bloody hell," muttered Cooter with the back of his hand set tightly against his mouth.

"May the Lord have mercy on our souls," said/thought June Ranson.

"Speed's essential," Hammer resumed. "You have authorization to combat-loss vehicles rather than slow down. The victory bonus'll cover the cost of replacement."

"I'll be combat-lossing crews, Colonel," Ranson's voice said. "But they're replaceable too. . . ."

Cooter gasped. Wylde grunted something that might have been either laughter or pain.

Hammer opened his mouth, then closed it with an audible clop. He opened it again and spoke with a lack of emotion as complete as the white, colorless fury of a sun's heart. "You are not to take any unnecessary risks, Captain Ranson. It *is* necessary that you achieve your objective. You will accept such losses as are required to achieve your objective. Is that understood?"

"Yes sir," said Ranson without inflection. "Oh, yes sir."

Hammer turned his head. The viewers at Camp Progress thought their commander was about to call orders or directions to someone on his staff. Instead, nothing happened while the hologram pickups stared at the back of Alois Hammer's head.

"All right," Hammer said at last, beginning to speak before he'd completely faced around again. His eyes were bright, his face hard. "The Consies' night vision equipment isn't as good as ours for the most part, so you're to leave as soon as it's dark. That gives you enough time to prepare and get some rest."

"*Rest*," Wylde murmured.

"The World Gov satellites'll tell the Consies where we are to the millimeter," Ranson said. "We'll have ambush teams crawling over us like flies on a turd, all the way to Kohang."

Or however far.

"Junebug," said Hammer, "I'm not hanging you out to dry. Thirty seconds before you start your move, all the WG satellites are going to go down, recce and commo both. They'll stay down for however long it suits me that they do."

Ranson blinked, "Sir," she said hesitantly, "if you do that . . . I mean, that means—"

"It means that our commo and reconnaissance is probably going to go out shortly thereafter, Captain," Hammer said. "So you'll be on your own. But you don't have to worry about tank killers being vectored into your axis of advance."

"Sir, if you hit their satellites—" Ranson began.

"They'll take it and smile, Captain," Hammer said. "Because if they don't, there won't *be* any Terran World Government enclaves here on Prosperity to worry about. I guarantee it. They may think they can cause me trouble on Earth, but they *know* what I'll do to them here!"

"Yes sir," June Ranson said. "I'll check the status of my assets and plot a route, then get back to you."

"Captain," Hammer said softly, "if I didn't think it could be done, I wouldn't order it. No matter how much it counted. Good luck to you and your team."

The hologram dissolved into a swirl of phosphorescent mites, impingement points of the carrier wave itself after the signal ceased. Bestwick shut down the projector.

"Cooter," Ranson said, "get the guard detachment ready. I'll take care of the tanks myself."

Cooter nodded over his shoulder. The big man was already on the way to his blower. It was going to be tricky, juggling crews and newbies to fill the slots that last night's firefight had opened. . . .

If Hammer took on the World Government, he was going to lose. Not here, but in the main arena of politics and economics on Earth.

That bothered June Ranson a lot.

But not nearly as much as the fact that the orders she'd just received put her neck on the block, sure as Death itself.

CHAPTER FIVE

Speedin' Steve Riddle sat by Platt's cot in the medical tent, listening to machines pump air in and out of his buddy's lungs.

And thinking.

They sat on the lowered tailgate of Platt's truck, staring at the sky and giggling occasionally at the display. At first there'd been only the lesser moon edging one horizon while the other horizon was saffron with the sunset.

Lights, flames . . . ? streaks of tracers that painted letters in the sky for the drug-heightened awareness of the two men. Neither Platt nor Riddle could read the words, but they knew whatever was being spelled was excruciatingly funny . . . ?

"Speed," called Lieutenant Cooter, "get your ass back to the blower and start running the prelim checklist. We're moving out tonight."

"Wha . . . ?" Riddle blurted, jerking his head up like an ostrich surprised at a waterhole. He was rapidly going bald. To make up for it, he'd grown a luxuriant moustache that fluffed when he spoke or exhaled.

"Don't give me any lip, you stupid bastard!" Cooter snapped, though Speed's response had been logy rather than argumentative. "If I didn't need you bad, you'd be findin' your own ticket back to whatever cesspit you call home."

"Hey, El-Tee!" Otski called, sitting up on his cot despite the gentle efforts of Shorty Rogers to keep him flat. "How they hangin', Cooter-baby?"

He waggled his stump.

"Come on, Otski," Rogers said. Shorty was *Flamethrower*'s driver and probably the best medic in the guard detachment as well as being a crewmate of the wounded man. "Just take it easy or I'll have to raise your dosage, and then it won't feel so good. All right?"

The medicomp metered Platt's breathing, in and out.

"Hey, lookit," Otski burbled, fluttering his stump again though he permitted Shorty to lower him back to the cot.

An air injector spat briefly, but the gunner's voice continued for a moment. "Lookit it when I wave, Cooter. I'm gonna get a flag. Whole bunch of flags, stick 'em in there 'n wave 'n wave. . . ."

"Shorty, you're gonna have to get back to the car too," Cooter said. "We'll turn 'em over to the Logistics staff until they can be lifted out to a permanent facility."

"Cop! None a' the Logistics people here'd know—"

Riddle thought:

The parts shed bulged around a puff of orange flame. The shockwave threw Riddle and Platt flat on the sloping tailgate; they struggled to sit up again. It was hilarious.

The Consie sapper rose from his crouch, silhouetted by the flaming shed he'd just bombed. He carried a machine pistol in a harness of looped rope, so that the weapon swung at waist height. His right hand snatched at the grip.

"Lookie, Speed!" Platt cackled. "He's just as bald as you are! Lookie!"

"Lookie!" Riddle called. He threw up his arms and fell backward with the effort.

The machine pistol crackled like the main truss of a house giving way. Its tracers were bright orange, lovely orange, as they drew spirals from the muzzle. One of them ricocheted around the interior of the truck box, dazzling Riddle with its howling beauty. He sat up again.

"Beauty!" *he cried. Platt was thrashing on his back. Air bubbled through the holes in his chest.*

The machine pistol pointed at Riddle. Nothing happened. The sapper cursed and slapped a magazine into the butt-well to replace the one that had ejected automatically when the previous burst emptied it.

The Consie's body flung itself sideways, wrapped in cyan light as a powergun from one of the combat cars raked him. The fresh magazine exploded. A few tracers zipped crazily out of the flashing yellow ball of detonating propellant.

"Beauty," *Steve Riddle repeated as he fell backward.*

Platt's chest wheezed.

"—a medicomp when it bit 'em on the ass!"

Air from the medicomp wheezed in and out of Platt's nostrils.

"Screw you!" called a supply tech with shrapnel wounds in his upper body.

"Then get 'em over to the Yokel side!" Cooter said. "They got facilities. Look, I'm not lookin' for an argument: we're movin' out at sunset, and none of my able-bodied crew are stayin' to bloody screw around here. All right?"

"Yeah, all right. One a' the newbies had some training back

home, he says." Rogers stood up and gave a pat to the sleeping Otski. "Hey, how long we gonna be out?"

"Don't bloody ask," Cooter grunted bitterly. "Denzil, where's your driver?"

The left wing gunner from Sergeant Wylde's blower turned his head—all the motion of which he was capable the way he was wrapped. "Strathclyde?" he said. His voice sounded all right. The medicomp kept his coverings flushed and cool with a bath of nutrient fluid. "Check over to One-one. He's got a buddy there."

"Yeah, well, One-five needs a driver," Cooter explained. "I'm going to put him on it."

Shorty Rogers looked up. "What happened to Darples on One-five?" he asked.

"Head shot. One a' the gunners took over last night, but I figure it makes sense to transfer Strathclyde for a regular thing."

"Cop," muttered Rogers. "I'll miss that snake." Then, "Don't mean nuthin'."

"Riddle!" Cooter snarled. "What the bloody hell are you doing still here? Get your ass moving, or you won't bloody have one!"

Riddle walked out of the medical tent. The direct sunlight made him sneeze, but he didn't really notice it.

Bright orange tracers, spiraling toward his chest.

He reached his combat car, *Deathdealer*. The iridium armor showed fresh scars. There was a burnished half-disk on the starboard wall of the fighting compartment—copper spurted out by a buzzbomb. The jet had cooled from a near-plasma here on the armor. Must've been the round that took out Otski. . . .

Riddle sat on the shaded side of the big vehicle. No one else was around. Cooter and Rogers had their own business. They wouldn't get here for hours.

Otski wouldn't be back at all. Never at all.

Bright orange tracers. . . .

Riddle took a small cone-shaped phial out of his side pocket. It was dull gray and had none of the identifying stripes that marked ordinary stim-cones, the ones that gave you a mild buzz without the aftereffects of alcohol.

He put the flat side of the cone against his neck, feeling for the carotid pulse. When he squeezed the cone, there was a tiny hiss and a skin-surface prickling.

Riddle began to giggle again.

Troops were moving about the Slammers' portion of the encampment in a much swifter and more directed fashion than they had been the afternoon before, when Dick Suilin first visited this northern end of Camp Progress.

The reporter glanced toward the bell—a section of rocket casing—hung on top of the Tactical Operations Center. Perhaps it had rung, unheard by him while he drove past the skeletons of National Army barracks . . . ?

The warning signal merely swayed in the breeze that carried soot and soot smells even here, where few sappers had penetrated.

Suilin had figured the commo gear would be at the TOC, whether Captain Ranson was there or not. In the event, the black-haired female officer sat on the back ramp of the vehicle, facing three male soldiers who squatted before her.

She stood, thumping out her closing orders, as Suilin pulled up; the men rose a moment later. None of the group paid the local reporter any attention.

Suilin didn't recognize the men. One of them was fat, at least fifty standard years old, and wore a grease-stained khaki jumpsuit.

"No problem, Junebug," he called as he turned away from the meeting. "We'll be ready to lift—if we're left alone to *get* ready, all right? Keep the rest a' your people and their maintenance problems off my back—" he was striding off toward a parked tank, shouting his words over his shoulder "—and we'll be at capacity when you need us."

Suilin got out of his truck. *They called their commanding officer Junebug?*

"Yeah, well," said another soldier, about twenty-five and an average sort of man in every way. He lifted his helmet to rub his scalp, then settled the ceramic/plastic pot again. "What do you want for a call sign? Charlie Three-zero all right?"

Ranson shook her head. "Negative. You're Blue Three," she said flatly.

Blue Three rubbed his scalp again. "Right," he said in a cheerless voice. "Only you hear 'Charlie Three-zero,' don't have kittens, okay? I got a lot to learn."

He turned morosely, adding, "And you know, this kinda on-the-job training ain't real survivable."

Suilin stood by, waiting for the third male mercenary to go before he tried to borrow the Slammers' communications system to call Kohang.

Instead of leaving, the soldier turned and looked at the reporter with a disconcertingly slack-jawed, vacant-eyed stare. The green-brown eyes didn't seem to focus at all.

Captain Ranson's eyes followed her subordinate's. She said angrily, "Who the bloody hell are you?"

It wasn't the same face that Suilin had been interviewing the night before.

There were dark circles around Ranson's eyes, and her left cheek was badly scratched. Her face, her hands, and her neck down to the scallop where she'd been wearing armor were dingy with fouling spewed from the breeches of her tribarrel when jets of nitrogen expelled the empty cases.

Ranson had been angry at being forced into an interview. She'd known the power was in the reporter's hands: the power to probe for answers she didn't want to give; the power to twist questions so that they were hooks in the fabric of her self-esteem; the power to make a fool out of her, by the words he tricked her into saying—or the form into which he edited those words before he aired them.

Now . . .

Now Suilin wondered what had happened to Fritzi Dole's body. He was *almost* certain that this small, fierce mercenary wouldn't shoot a reporter out of hand to add to the casualty count, no matter how angry and frustrated she was now. . . .

"I'm, ah," he said, "Dick Suilin. I'm, ah, we met yesterday when the—"

"The reporter," Ranson said. "Right, the bloody fool who didn't know t' hit the dirt for incoming. The interview's off."

She started to turn. "Beat it," she added.

"It's not—" Suilin said. "Captain Ranson, I need to talk to some-body in Kohang, and your commo may be the—"

"Buddy," said Ranson with a venom and disgust that shocked the reporter more than the content of the words did, "you must be out of your mind. Get *out* of here."

The other soldier continued to watch without expression.

"Captain, you don't understand," Suilin called to Ranson's back. "I need to make sure my sister's all right."

The woman bent to reenter the immobile command blower.

"Curse it! She's the wife of the District Governor. *Now* will you—"

Ranson turned. The reporter thought he'd seen her angry before.

"The District Governor," she repeated softly. "The District Bleeding Governor."

She walked toward Suilin. He poised, uncertain as to what the female officer intended.

She tapped him on the chest as she said, "Your brother-in-law doesn't have any balls, buddy." The tip of her index finger was like a mallet.

"Captain—"

"He's got a brigade of armor," Ranson continued, "and maybe ten battalions of infantry and gendarmes, according to the order of battle in my data banks."

She tapped even harder. Suilin backed a step. "But no balls a'tall."

The reporter set his leg to lock him into place. "Captain, you can't—"

Ranson slapped him, forehand and then back across the other cheek. Her fingers were as hard as the popper of a bullwhip. "And he's got an ass, so we're going to get *our* ass shot off to save his!"

She spun on her heel. "Sparrow, get him out of my sight," she called over her shoulder as she entered her TOC.

Suilin viewed the world through a blur of tears. Sparrow put a hand on his shoulder and turned him with a detached gentleness that felt like compassion to the reporter at the moment.

"S'okay, turtle," the mercenary said as he walked Suilin toward the truck he'd borrowed. "We just got orders to relieve the District Governor ourself, and we got bugger-all t' do it with."

"What?" the reporter said. "In Kohang?"

His right cheek burned, and his left felt as if someone had flayed the skin from it. He wondered if Ranson had been wearing a ring. "Who's relieving Kohang?"

Sparrow waved an arm as deliberately as a stump speaker gesturing. "You're lookin'at it, turtle," he said. "Three tanks, five cars . . . and maybe crews for most of 'em."

The veneer of careless apathy dropped away. Sparrow shivered. He was tall and thin with an olive complexion several shades darker than Suilin's own.

"Via," the mercenary muttered. "Via!"

Sparrow turned and walked, then trotted in a loose-limbed way toward the tank across the enclosure from the TOC. He climbed the shallow steps up its skirts and battered hull, then popped into the turret with the haste of a man boarding under fire.

The hatch clanged loudly behind him.

Dick Suilin sat in his truck, blinking to clear his eyes and mind. He started the vehicle and turned it in a tight circle, heading back toward National Army Headquarters.

His own gear had been destroyed in the firefight, but he thought the barracks in which Fritzi Doyle was billeted had survived. The cameraman had worn fatigues. One of his spare sets would fit Suilin well enough.

Fritzi wouldn't mind.

The corpse of a National Army sergeant was sprawled at the doorway of a bombed-out building. He'd thrown on a uniform shirt, but he had no shoes or trousers. His left arm was outstretched while his right was folded under his face as though cushioning it from the ground.

He'd been carrying a grenade launcher and a satchel of reloads for it. They lay beside his body.

Suilin stopped the truck, picked up the weapon and ammunition, and set the gear on the passenger seat. As an afterthought, he tried to lift the dead man. The body was stiff and had already begun to blacken in the bright sun.

Someone whose job it was would deal with the sergeant. Not Dick Suilin.

Suilin's hands felt slimy. He accelerated away, kicking gravel over the corpse in his haste to be shut of it.

"Blue One," said Captain June Ranson, checking the artificial intelligence in her multi-function display. A digit on the holographic map blinked twice in yellow, then twice more in blue light when the transponder in *Deathdealer* answered the call automatically.

"Go ahead, Tootsie Six," said Sergeant Sparrow's voice.

"Linkage check," Ranson said. "Blue Two."

Deathdealer led the line-to-be, quivering on its fans just ahead of Ranson's *Warmonger*.

There wasn't enough room in the Slammers' end of the encampment to form up completely until the blowers started to move south, toward the gate. Sound, re-echoing from the berm and the sloped iridium sides of the vehicles, vibrated the flesh of everyone around.

Exclusion circuits in Ranson's commo helmet notched out as much of the fan's racket as possible, but the sound of multiple drive nacelles being run up to speed created an ambiance beyond the power of electronics to control. Air forced beneath the lips of eight plenum chambers picked up grit which ricocheted into standing waves where the currents from two or three blowers intersected.

Deathdealer's turret was already buttoned up. Nothing wrong with that—it'd be quieter inside, though the fan-driven chaos would penetrate even the massive iridium castings that stopped all but direct point-blank hits by the largest powerguns.

Ranson had never seen Birdie Sparrow man his tank from the open cupola. A tank's electronics were better than human senses, even when those senses were augmented by the AI and sensors in a commo helmet. The screens within a panzer's turret gave not only crisper definition on all the electro-optical bands but also gave multiple simultaneous options.

That information glut was one of the reasons most tank commanders chose to fight their vehicles from the cupola instead of the closed turret whenever possible.

It was difficult to get experienced crewmen to transfer from combat cars to the panzers, even though it usually meant promotion. Most tank commanders were promoted from driver, while the driver slots were filled by newbies with no previous combat experience in the Slammers.

Ranson had checked Birdie Sparrow's personnel file—this afternoon; she'd had no reason to call up the records from Central's database before. . . .

Before Colonel Hammer handed her command of a suicide mission.

Sparrow had five standard years, seven months, service with the Regiment. All but the training in the first three months had been in line companies, so there was no need to wonder how he handled combat: *just fine or he wouldn't 've lasted out his fourth month.* Hammer's Slammers weren't hired by people who needed them to polish their gear in barracks.

A few problems on stand-down; a more serious one with a platoon leader in the field that had cost Sparrow a pay-grade—but it was the lieutenant who'd been transferred back to Central and, after the discreet interval required for discipline, out of the Slammers. Sparrow had an excellent record and must have been in line for his own platoon—

Instead of which, he'd been sent down here to the quiet south for a little time off.

Junebug Ranson had an even better service record than Sparrow did. She knew curst well what *she* was doing down here at Camp Progress.

Task Force Ranson was real lucky to have a company commander as experienced as Junebug Ranson to lead the mission, and a tanker as good as Birdie Sparrow to head up the unit's tank element.

The trouble was, they were both bughouse bleeding crazy, and Ranson knew it.

It was her job to know it, and to compensate the best way she could.

"Roger, Tootsie Six," said her helmet in the voice of Warrant Leader Ortnahme as the digit 2 flickered on the map display.

"Linkage check," responded Captain Ranson. "Blue Three."

Needs must, when the Devil drives.

"Cooter," said Chief Lavel over the commo helmet's Channel 3. It was a lock-out push normally reserved for vehicle intercoms, so that even Tootsie Six couldn't overhear without making a point of it. "I found 'im. The sonuvabitch."

Flamethrower shuddered violently and began to skid as the tank to starboard ran up its fans to full pitch and thrust for a test.

The panzer's driver had his nacelles vertical, so the hundred and seventy tonnes of tank simply rose a hand's breadth off the ground. The air bleeding beneath the skirts was at firehose pressure, though; the smack of it pushed the lighter combat car away until Shorty Rogers grounded *Flamethrower* to oppose the friction of steel on soil to the blast of wind.

Cooter keyed Channel 3 and said, "Can you get him here, Chief? We're gonna get the word any time now."

"Cooter," said his friend, "I think you better take a look at this one yourself."

Chief Lavel had been a gun captain. He knew about time and about movement orders; and he knew what he was saying.

"Cop!" Cooter swore. "He in his doss, then?"

The tank, the nameless one crewed by a couple newbies, settled back onto its skirts. The sergeant in the cupola looked down at Cooter. In formation, they'd be running well ahead of *Flamethrower*'s Tailass Charlie slot.

"Negative," said Chief. "He's in his buddy's bunk—you know, Platt's? In the Logistics doss."

Night fell like an axe at Camp Progress. Except for the red blur on the western horizon, the sun had disappeared completely in the past three minutes.

Cooter switched his visor to enhancement and checked to make sure the nameless tank was between him and Tootsie Six, then cut back to standard optical.

Depth perception was never quite as good on enhanced mode. There were enough lights on in the encampment for Cooter to find his way to the Logistics bunker/barracks.

Cooter tapped the shoulder of Gale, the right wing gunner from Tootsie One-four, transferred to *Flamethrower* now that Otski and the other blower had both become casualties. Speaking on 12, the other lock-out push, to be heard over the fan noise, Cooter said, "Hold the fort, Windy. I'll be back in a couple minutes max."

"We'll be bloody *gone* in a couple minutes, Cooter," Gale replied.

He was an older man, nearly thirty; not a genius, but bright and competent enough that he'd 've had a blower of his own years before had he not adamantly refused the promotion.

"Yeah, well," Cooter said, climbing awkwardly past Speed Riddle's clamshell and helmet stacked in front of the left tribarrel. "We're last in line. Worst case, Shorty'll have to make up a little time."

Worst case, Captain Ranson would notice her second-in-command hadn't pulled out on time and would check *Flamethrower*'s own sensors. If she found Cooter gone from his post now, she'd have him dragged behind a blower all the way back to Camp Progress as soon as the mission was over.

Which was pretty much what Cooter had in mind for Speed Riddle.

He lumbered across the ground, burdened by his armor and half-blinded by dust despite his lowered visor. Cooter was a big man, but no man was significant in an area packed with the huge, slowly maneuvering masses of armored vehicles.

Logistics section—the warehouses, truck park, and bunkered sleeping quarters for the associated personnel—formed the boundary between the Slammers' positions and the remainder of Camp Progress. Sappers who'd gotten through the Yokel defenses had bombed a parts shed and shot up a few trucks, but the Red section's counterattack put paid to the Consies here before they'd really gotten rolling.

The doss—half dug into the berm, half sandbagged—was undamaged except for six plate-sized cups which a tribarrel had blasted from the front wall. There was a gap in the line of glassy impact craters where one round had splashed a Consie sapper instead of hitting the sandbags.

Chief Lavel stood in the doorway. He gestured to Cooter but hunched his way into the doss before the lieutenant arrived.

Chief tried to give himself a little advantage when there was anything tricky to do, like negotiating the double step that put the floor of the doss below ground level for safety. He got around amazingly well for a man missing his left arm and leg, though.

Outside the bunker, armored vehicles filled the evening with hot lubricant and the sharpness of ozone arcing away from dirty relays. The bunker's interior stank of human waste.

"What the . . . ?" Cooter muttered as he followed Chief down the narrow hallway along the front wall of the structure. A glowstrip was tacked to the ceiling; Cooter's helmet scraped it. He swore, ducked, and then straightened to bump again.

Board partitions made from packing cases divided the doss into rooms—decent-sized ones for Lavel and his permanent staff and, at the far end, tiny cubicles to house transients like the drivers making supply runs. The rooms were empty; the personnel were either involved with the departure or watching it.

Except for the last cubicle, where Speed Riddle lay sprawled on a cot with a broad smile. The balding gunner had fouled himself thoroughly enough that waste was dripping from his pants leg onto the floor.

Riddle's fingers held a drug phial. Two more empties lay beside his hand.

Cooter stared at the gunner for several seconds. Then he turned around and strode back down the aisle.

His helmet brushed the glowstrip. He punched upward with his knotted right fist, banging the flat fixture against the ceiling of steel plank and causing grit to drift down through the perforations from the sandbagged top cover.

"Coot!" Lavel called, stumping along behind him. "Hey Coot. Slow down."

"Chief," Cooter said without slowing or turning, "I want that bastard tied up until he can be delivered to Central. With wire. Barbed wire'd be fine. Somethin' happens to me, you take care of the Court Martial, right?"

The end of Lavel's long crutch shot across the doorway, blocking Cooter's exit. "*Wait* a bloody minute!" Chief said.

Lavel was leaning against the right wall. The crutch was strapped to his stump, since he didn't have a left hand with which to grip it. He lowered it, a slim wand of boron monocrystal, when Cooter turned at last to face him.

"Going to use one of the newbies in Riddle's place?" he asked.

Cooter shook his head violently, as much to clear it as for a gesture. "Put the last one I could trust on One-five for a driver," he said. "I'll be better off watching that side myself than trusting some hick who's still got both thumbs up his ass."

"Take me, Cooter," said Chief Lavel.

Cooter looked at his friend with a cold lack of passion. Chief was so tall that he also had to duck to clear the ceiling. His shoulders were massive. Lavel had been thin when he was a whole man, but the inertia of his years of injury gave him a grotesque pot belly.

"Please, Coot," he said. "You won't regret it."

"I need you here, Chief," Cooter said as he turned. "You take care of Riddle, you hear?"

"*Coot?*"

"Gotta go now," Cooter muttered as he took both steps to the exterior with one stretch of his long, powerful legs.

The armored vehicles were snorting, running up the speed of their fans again; and, as Cooter strode toward *Flamethrower,* a tank fired its main gun skyward.

There were too bloody many vehicles in too little space, and the bloody drivers had too much on their minds.

A combat car was drifting toward *Herman's Whore.* The lighter vehicle was already so close that Ortnahme had to crank down his display to read the number stenciled on its skirts. "Tootsie One-two!" he snarled. "You're fouling—"

The tank lurched. For an instant, Ortnahme thought Simkins was trying to back away from the oncoming car. That wouldn't work, because *Herman's Whore* had rotated in place and her skirts were firmly against the berm.

"—us, you dickheaded—"

The man in the fighting compartment of Tootsie One-two turned, his face a ball of blank wonder as he stared at the tank looming above him. He was probably gabbling to his driver over the intercom, but there was no longer time to avoid the collision. The skirts of both vehicles were thick steel, but the combined mass would start seams for sure.

"—fool! Watch your—"

The bow of *Herman's Whore* lifted slightly. Simkins had run up his fans and vectored them forward. The tank couldn't slide backward because of the berm, so its bow skirts blasted a shrieking hurricane of air into the combat car.

Tootsie One-two, *Flamethrower*, pitched as though it had just dropped into a gully. The trooper in the fighting compartment bounced off the coaming before he could brace himself on the grips of two of the tribarrels.

Why in blazes was there only *one* man in the back of *Flamethrower* when the task force was set to move out?

The combat car slid two meters under the thrust of the tank's fans before Shorty Rogers dumped his own ground effect and sparked to a halt on bits of gravel in the soil.

The figure in the fighting compartment stood up again and gave *Herman's Whore* an ironic salute. "Blue Two," said Ortnahme's helmet. "Sorry 'bout that."

"Tootsie One-two," the warrant leader responded. He felt expansive and relieved, now that he was sure they wouldn't be deadlined at the last instant by a stupid mistake. "No harm done. It's prob'ly my bloody fault for not seeing your nacelles were aligned right when we had time to screw with 'em."

Herman's Whore settled, a little abruptly. Their skirts gave the ground a tap that rattled Ortnahme's teeth and probably cut a centimeter-deep oval in the hard soil.

"Simkins—" the warrant leader began, the word tripping the helmet's artificial intelligence to intercom mode.

"Sir, I'm sorry," his driver was already blurting. "I let the sucker—"

"Blood'n martyrs, Simkins," Ortnahme interrupted, "don't worry about that! Where dja learn that little maneuver, anyhow?"

"Huh?" said the helmet. "Sir, it was just, you know, the leverage off the berm . . .?"

He sounded like he thought Ortnahme was gonna chew his head off. Which had happened maybe a little too often in the past . . . but bloody hell, you had t' break 'em in the start. . . .

"Sir?" Simkins added in a little voice.

"Yeah?"

"Sir, I really like tanks. D'ye suppose that—"

"Like bloody hell!" the warrant leader snapped." Look, kid, you're more good to me and Colonel Hammer right where you bloody are!"

"Yes sir."

Which, come t' think about it, was driving a panzer. Well, there'd be time t' worry about that later.

Or there wouldn't.

The turret interior had darkened as the sky did, because the main screen was set on direct optical. Ortnahme frowned, then set the unit for progressive enhancement, projecting images at sixty percent of average daylight ambiance.

The visual display brightened suddenly, though the edges of the snarling armored vehicles lacked a little of the definition they would have had in unaided sunlight. No matter what the sky did—sun, moons, or the Second Coming—the main screen would continue to display at this apparent light level until Ortnahme changed its orders.

Henk Ortnahme *knew* tanks. He knew their systems backward and forward, better than almost any of the panzers' regular crews.

Line troops found a few things that worked for them. Each man used his handful of sensor and gunnery techniques, ignoring the remainder of his vehicle's incredibly versatile menu. You don't fool around when your life depends on doing instinctively something that works *for you*.

The maintenance chief had to be sure that everything worked, every time. He'd spent twenty years of playing with systems that most everybody else forgot. He could run the screens and sensors by reflex and instantly critique the performance of each black box.

What the warrant leader *hadn't* had for those twenty years was combat experience. . . .

"Sir," said the helmet. "Ah, when are we supposed to pull out?"

A bloody stupid question.

Sunset, and Simkins could see as well as Ortnahme that it was sunset plus seven. Captain Ranson had said departure time would be coordinated by Central, so probably the only people who knew why Task Force Ranson was on hold were a thousand kilometers north of—

Screen Two, which in default mode—as now—was bore sighted to the main gun, flashed the orange warning director control. As the letters appeared, the turret of *Herman's Whore* began to rotate without any input from Warrant Leader Ortnahme.

The turret was being run by Fire Central, at Headquarters. Henk Ortnahme had no more to say about the situation than he did regarding any *other* orders emanating directly from Colonel Hammer.

"Sir?" Simkins blurted over the intercom.

"Blue Two—" demanded at least two other vehicles simultaneously, alerted by the squealing turret and rightly concerned about what the hell was going on. Screwing around with a tank's main gun in these close quarters wasn't just a *bad* idea.

"Simkins," Ortnahme said. His fingers stabbed buttons. "It's all right. The computer up in Purple's just took over."

As he spoke, Ortnahme set his gunnery screen to echo on Screen Three of the other tanks and the multi-function displays with which the combat cars made do. That'd answer their question better 'n anything he could say—

And besides, he was busy figuring out what Central thought it was doing with his tank.

The warrant leader couldn't countermand the orders coming from Firebase Purple, but he *could* ask his own artificial intelligence to tell him what firing solution was being fed to it. Screen Three obligingly threw up the figures for azimuth, elevation, and range.

"Blood 'n martyrs," Henk Ortnahme whispered.

Now he knew why the departure of Task Force Ranson had been delayed.

They had to wait for the Terran World Government's recce satellite to come over the horizon—

Herman's Whore fired its main gun; cyan lightning and a thunderclap through the open hatch, a blast of foul gases within the turret.

—so they could shoot it down.

The unexpected bolt didn't blind Cooter because his visor reacted in microseconds to block the intense glare. The shock stunned him for a moment anyway; then the big man began to run through the mass of restive vehicles.

A tank—*Deathdealer*, Blue One—slid forward. When the big blower was clear, entering the Yokel area between the demolished shed and a whole one, Captain Ranson's *Warmonger* fell in behind it. It was as though the echoing blast from *Herman's Whore* had triggered an iridium avalanche.

The third vehicle, another combat car, sidled up to the line of departure. That'd be One-five, its driver a newbie on whom Cooter had decided to take a chance. The fellow was matching his blower's speed to that of the leading vehicles, but he had his bow pointing 30° off the axis of motion.

Some dickhead Yokel had parked a light truck just inside the Slammer's area. One-five's tail skirts managed to tap the little vehicle and send it spinning halfway up the berm, a graphic illustration of the difference between a tonne at rest and thirty tonnes in motion.

Cooter reached his car panting with exertion, anger, and a relieved awareness of how bloody *near* that asshole Riddle had made him cut it. One-one was already pulling into line for the run through Camp Progress, though the second and third combat cars would spread left and right as outriders as soon as they left the gate.

A Yokel wearing fatigues cut for somebody shorter put a hand on Cooter's shoulder as he set his foot on *Flamethrower*'s skirt. The fellow carried a slung grenade launcher, a kitbag, and a satchel of ammunition.

Cooter had never seen him before.

"Who the hell are you?" he snarled over the fans' intake howl. The skirts were quivering with repressed violence, and the nameless Blue Three was already headed into the Yokel compound.

"I'm Dick," the fellow shouted. "From last night. Lieutenant, can you use a grenadier for this run?"

Cooter stared at him a second, five seconds . . . ten. One-six was pulling out. . . .

"You bet your ass I can, turtle," Cooter said. "Welcome aboard!"

CHAPTER SIX

The upper half of June Ranson's visor showed a light-enhanced view of her surroundings. It flicked from side to side as her head bobbed in the nervous-pigeon motions of somebody with more things to worry about than any human being could handle.

Deathdealer led the column. Even from 200 meters ahead, the wake of the tank's vast passage rocked *Warmonger*'s own considerable mass. Willens was driving slightly left of the center of *Deathdealer*'s track, avoiding some of the turbulence and giving himself a better direct view forward. It raised the danger from mines, though; the tank would set off anything before the combat car reached it, if their tracks were identical. . . .

She let it go for now. The roadway between Camp Progress and the civilian settlement over the ridge had been cleared in the fighting the night before.

Stolley had his tribarrel cocked forward, parallel to the car's axis of motion instead of sweeping the quadrant to the left side like he ought to. Stolley figured—and they all figured, Junebug Ranson as sure as her wing gunner—that first crack at any Consies hereabouts would come from the front.

But a ninety percent certainty meant one time in ten you were dead. *Deathdealer* and the bow gunner, June Ranson, could handle the front. Stolley's job—

Ranson put her fingers on the top barrel of Stolley's weapon, well ahead of the mounting post, and pushed.

The wing gunner's hands tightened on the grips for a moment before he relaxed with a curse that he didn't even try to muffle. The gun muzzles swung outward in the direction they ought to be pointed.

Stolley stared at his commanding officer. His face was a reflecting ball behind his lowered visor.

"If you don't like your job," Ranson said, speaking over the wind noise instead of using intercom, "I can arrange for you to drive. Another blower."

Stolley crouched behind his gun, staring into the night.

Ranson nodded in approval of the words she'd been listening to, the words coming from her mouth. Good command technique—under the circumstances, under field conditions where it was more important to be obeyed than to be liked. This crew wasn't going to like its blower captain anyway . . . but they'd obey.

Ranson shook her head violently. She wasn't an observer, watching a holographic record from command school on Friesland. She was . . .

The images on the lower half of her visor wobbled at a rate different from that of the combat car and didn't change when Ranson darted her head to the left or right. She'd slaved its display to that of the sensors on *Deathdealer* in the lead. The tank's intakes sucked the tops of low bushes toward her from the roadside. Then, as *Deathdealer* came alongside, the air leaking beneath her skirts battered them away.

Moments later, *Warmonger* swept by the bushes. The top of Ranson's visor repeated the images of the lower section as if on a five-second delay.

Ranson shook her head again. It didn't help.

By an emergency regulation—which had been in place for fourteen years—there were to be no private structures within two kilometers of a military base. Colonel Banyussuf had enforced that reg pretty stringently. There'd been drink kiosks all along the road to within a hundred meters of the gate, but they were daylight use only.

Since the panzers swept through the night before, nothing remained of the flimsy stands but splinters and ash that swirled to the passage of Task Force Ranson.

Permanent civilian dwellings, more serious entertainment—whores, hard drugs, gambling—as well as the goods and services you'd normally find in a town the size of Camp Progress, were in Happy Days. That settlement was just over the ridge the road climbed as it ran southeast from the camp. Technically, Happy Days was within the two-kilometer interdict; but out of sight, out of mind.

Being over the ridge meant line-of-sight bolts from the Slammers' powerguns wouldn't 've hurt the civilians. The National Army might've dropped some indirect fire on Happy Days during the fighting, but Ranson doubted the Yokels had been that organized.

Janacek had taped a red-patterned bandanna to the lower rear edge of his commo helmet. At rest, it kept sun from the back of his neck, but when the car was moving, it popped and fluttered like a miniature flag.

When Task Force Ranson got beyond the settlement, they could open their formation and race cross-country through the night; but the only practical place to cross the wooded ridge was where the road did.

There were probably Consies hidden among the civilians of Happy Days. One of them might try a shot as the armored vehicles howled past. . . .

The lead tank crested the rise in a cloud of as hand charredwood. There'd been groves of mighty trees to either side of the road. Panels of bright silk strung from trunk to trunk sectioned the copses into open-air brothels in fine weather.

Before. During the previous night, return fire and the backblasts of bombardment rockets had torched the trees into ash and memories. That permitted *Deathdealer*'s driver to swing abruptly to the right, off the roadway and any weapons targeted on it, just before coming into sight of Happy Days.

Debris momentarily blanked the lower half of Ranson's visor. It cleared with a view of the settlement. The ground across the ridge dropped away more steeply than on the side facing Camp Progress, so the nearest of the one-and two-story houses were several hundred meters away where the terrain flattened.

Happy Days was a ghost town.

Deathdealer was proceeding at forty kph, fractionally slower than her speed a few moments before. *Warmonger* started to close the 200-meter separation, but Willens throttled back and swung to the left of the road as the combat car topped the rise. Ranson's left hand switched her visor off remote; her right was firm on the tribarrel's grip.

Happy Days hadn't been damaged in the previous night's fighting. The buildings crowded the stakes marking the twenty-meter right of way, but their walls didn't encroach—another regulation Banyussuf had enforced, with bulldozers when necessary.

Half the width was road surface which had been stabilized with a plasticizer, then pressure-treated. The lead tank slipped down the incline on the right shoulder behind a huge cloud of dust.

Nothing moved in the settlement.

A few of the structures were concrete prefabs, but most were built of laths covered with enameled metal. Uncut sheets already imprinted with the logos of soups or beers gleamed in an array more colorful than that of a race course. Behind the buildings themselves, fabric barriers enclosed yards in which further business could be conducted in the open air.

The lead tank was almost between the rows of buildings. Ranson's visor caught and highlighted movement of the barred window of a popular knocking-shop across the street and near the far end of the strip. She switched her display to thermal.

Stolley swung his tribarrel toward the motion.

"No!" June Ranson shouted.

The wing gunner's short burst snapped through the air like a

single streak of cyan, past *Deathdealer* and into a white coruscance
as the window's iron grillwork burned at the impacts.

A buzzbomb arced from the left and exploded in the middle of
its trajectory as the tank's close-in defense system fired with a
vicious crackling.

At least twenty automatic weapons volleyed orange tracers
from Happy Days. The bullets ricocheted from *Deathdealer* and
clanged like hammer blows on *Warmonger*'s hull and gunshields.

"All Tootsie elements!" Ranson shouted. Willens had chopped
his throttles; *Warmonger*'s skirts tapped the soil. "Bandits! Blue
One—"

But it was too late to order Blue One to lay a mine-clearing
charge down the road. The great tank accelerated toward Happy
Days in a spray of dust and pebbles, tribarrel and main gun blasting
ahead of it.

"Hey, snake?" said DJ Bell from the main screen as bolts from a
powergun cracked past *Deathdealer*. "Watch out for the Pussycat,
okay?"

"Go '*way*, DJ!" Birdie Sparrow shouted. "Albers! Goose it! Fast!
Fast!"

The sound of bullets striking their thick armor was lost in the
roar of the fans whose intakes suddenly tried to gulp more air than
fluid flow would permit. The impacts quivered through Sparrow's
boots on the floorplate like the ticks of a mechanical clock gone
haywire.

Sparrow gripped a gunnery joystick in either hand. Most
tankers used only one control, thumb-switching from main gun to
tribarrel and back at need. He'd taught himself years ago to operate
with both sticks live. You didn't get sniper's precision that way, but—

"Bandits!" cried the captain. "Blue One—"

Whatever she wanted would wait.

—when it was suppressing fire you needed, like now—

Whatever anybody else wanted could wait.

Using the trigger on the right joystick, Sparrow rapped a five-
round burst from the tribarrel across a shop midway down the Strip

on the left side. Sheet metal blew away from the wood beneath it, fluttering across the street as if trying to escape from the sudden blaze behind it.

The main screen was set on a horizontally compressed 360° panorama. Sparrow was used to the distortion. He caught the puff of a buzzbomb launch before his electronics highlighted the threat.

A defensive charge blasted from above *Deathdealer*'s skirts. It made the hull ring as none of the hostile fire had managed.

Sparrow's tribarrel raked shopfronts further down the Strip in a long burst. The bolts flashed at an increasing separation because the tank was accelerating.

Deathdealer's turret rotated counterclockwise, independently of the automatic weapon in the cupola. The left pipper, the point-of-aim indicator for the main gun, slid backward across the facade of one of the settlement's sturdier buildings.

The neon sign was unlighted, but Sparrow knew it well—a cat with a Cheshire grin, gesturing with a forepaw toward her lifted haunches.

That was where the buzzbomb had come from. Three more sparks spat in the darkness—light, lethal missiles, igniting in the whorehouse parlor—just as Sparrow's foot stroked the pedal trip for his 20cm cannon.

Deathdealer's screens blacked out the cyan flash. The displays were live again an instant later when dozens of ready missiles went off in a secondary explosion that blew the Pussycat's walls and roof into concrete confetti.

"Blue Three," the command channel was blatting, "move forward and—"

Albers brought *Deathdealer* into the settlement with gravity aiding his desperately accelerating fans. He was hugging the right side of the Strip, too close for a buzzbomb launched from that direction to harm. Anti-personnel mines banged harmlessly beneath them.

"—lay a clearing charge before anybody else proceeds!"

Across the roadway, shopfronts popped and sizzled under the

fire of Sparrow's tribarrel and the more raking bolts of combat cars pausing just over the ridgeline as Tootsie Six had ordered.

Deathdealer brushed the front of the first shop. The building collapsed like a bomb going off.

The tank accelerated to eighty kph. Albers used his mass and the edge of his skirts like a router blade, ripping down the line of flimsy shops. The fragments scattered in the draft of his fans.

A Consie took two steps from a darkened tavern, knelt, and aimed his buzz-bomb down the throat of the oncoming tank.

Sparrow's foot twitched on the firing pedal. The main gun crashed out a bolt that turned a tailor's shop across the road into a fireball with a plasma core. The blast was twenty meters from the rocketeer, but the Consie flung away his weapon in surprise and tried to run.

A combat car nailed him, half a pace short of the doorway that would have provided concealment if not protection.

Sparrow had begun firing with his tribarrel at a ten o'clock angle. As *Death-dealer* raced toward the far end of the settlement, he panned the weapon counterclockwise and stuttered bursts low into shopfronts. Instants after the tribarrel raked a facade, his main gun converted the entire building into a self-devouring inferno.

Two controls, two pippers sliding across a compressed screen at varying rates. The few bullets that still spattered the hull were lost in the continuous rending impact of Albers' 170-tonne wrecking ball.

Choking gases from the cannon breech, garbled orders and warnings from the radio.

No sweat, none of it. Birdie Sparrow was in control, and they couldn't none of 'em touch him.

Another whorehouse flew apart at the touch of *Deathdealer*'s skirt. A meter by three-meter strip of metal enameled with a hundred and fifty bright Lion Beer logos curled outward and slapped itself over the intake of #1 Starboard fan.

The sudden loss of flow dipped the skirt to the soil and slewed *Deathdealer*'s bow before plenum-chamber pressure could balance the mass it carried. The stern swung outward, into the *clang-clang* impact of bolts from a combat car's tribarrel. Fist-sized chunks vaporized from iridium armor that had ignored Consie bullets.

Sparrow rocked in his turret's stinking haze, clinging grimly to the joysticks and bracing his legs as well. The standard way to clear a blocked duct was to reverse the fan. That'd ground *Deathdealer* for a moment, and with the inertia of their present speed behind *that* touchdown—

Albers may have chopped his #1S throttle but he didn't reverse it—or try to straighten *Deathdealer*'s course out of the hook into which contact had canted it. They hit the next building in line, bow-on at seventy kph—shattering panels of pre-stressed concrete and sweeping the fan duct clear in the avalanche of heavy debris.

Deathdealer bucked and pitched like a bull trying to pin a tiger to the jungle floor. The collision was almost as bad as the one for which Sparrow had prepared himself, but the tank never quite lost forward way. They staggered onward, cascading chunks of wall, curtains, and gambling tables.

The tank's AI threw up a red-lit warning on Screen Three. *Deathdealer*'s ground-penetrating radar showed a thirty-centimeter tunnel drilled beneath the road's hard surface from the building they'd just demolished. The cavity was large enough to contain hundreds of kilos of explosive—

And it almost certainly did.

Without the blocked fan, *Deathdealer* would've been over the mine before the radar warning. Maybe past the mine before the Consie at the detonator could react—that was the advantage of speed and the shattering effect of heavy gunfire, the elements Sparrow'd been counting on to get them through.

And their armor. Even a mine that big. . . .

"All Mike—T-tootsie elements," Sparrow warned. "The road's mined! Mines!"

He'd frozen the gunnery controls as he waited for the collision. Now, while Albers muscled the tank clear of the wreckage and started to build speed again, Sparrow put both pippers on the building across the road from them. He vaporized it with a long burst and three 20cm rounds, just in case the command detonator was there rather than in the shattered gambling den.

It might have a pressure or magnetic detonator. Speed wouldn't 've helped *Deathdealer* then, if luck hadn't slewed them off the road at the right moment.

"Can't touch us!" Birdie Sparrow muttered as he fired back over the tank's left rear skirts. "Can't touch us!"

"Not this time, snake," said DJ Bell as bitter gases writhed through the turret.

If he'd bothered to look behind him, Hans Wager could've seen that the tail end of the column had yet to pass the gates of Camp Progress.

Just over the ridge, all hell was breaking loose.

Wager's instinctive reaction was the same as always when things really dropped in the pot: to hunker down behind his tribarrel and hope there were panzers close enough to lend a hand.

It gave him a queasy feeling to realize that this time, *he* was the tank element and it was for him, Blue Three, that the CO was calling.

"—move forward and lay a clearing charge!"

Something big enough to light the whole sky orange blew up behind the ridge. Pray the Lord it was Consies eating some of their own ordnance rather than a mine going off beneath a blower.

The lead tank and Tootsie Six had both dropped over the ridgeline. One-five any One-one pulled forward. The first car slid to the right in a gush of gray-white ash colored blue by gunfire while the other accelerated directly up the road.

Blue Three shuddered as her driver poured the coal to her. Through inexperience, Holman swung her fan nacelles rearward too swiftly. Their skirts scraped a shower of sparks for several meters along the pavement.

Wager found his seat control, not instinctively but fast enough. He dropped from cupola level while the tank plowed stabilized gravel with a sound like mountains screaming.

Tracers stitched the main screen and across the sky overhead, momentary flickers through the open hatch.

One-five vanished behind the crest. One-one swung to the right and stopped abruptly with a flare of her skirts, still silhouetted on the ridgeline. Blue Three was wallowing toward the same patch of landscape under full power.

Wager shouted a curse, but Holman had their mount under control. The nameless tank pivoted left like a wheeled vehicle whose back end had broken away, avoiding the combat car. They could see now that One-one had pulled up to keep from overrunning Tootsie Six.

Blue Three began to slide at a slight sideways angle down the ridge they'd just topped. The three cars ahead of them were firing wildly into the smoke and flying debris of the settlement.

Sparrow's Blue One had just smashed a building. It pulled clear with the motion of an elephant shrugging during a dust bath.

"All Mike—T-tootsie elements," came a voice that a mask on the main screen would identify (if Wager wondered) as Blue One, used to his old call sign. "Mines! Mines!"

"Blue Three!" snarled Captain Ranson. "Lay the bloody charge! Now!"

If the bitch wanted to trade jobs, she could take this cursed panzer and all its cursed hardware! She could take it and shove it up her ass!

It wasn't that Hans Wager had never used a mine-clearing charge before. On a combat car, though, they were special equipment bolted to the bow skirts and fired manually. All the tanks were fitted with integral units, controlled by the AI. So. . . .

"Booster," Wager ordered crisply. "Clearance charge."

The gun fight pipper on Screen Two dimmed to half its previous orange brilliance. ARMED appeared in the upper left corner of the screen, above RANGE TO TARGET and LENGTH OF FOOTPRINT.

Magenta tracks, narrowed toward the top by foreshortening, overlay the image of the settlement toward which Blue Three was slipping with the slow grace of a beer stein on a polished bar.

Instead of aligning with the pavement, the aiming tracks skewed across the right half of the Strip.

"Holman!" Wager screamed. "Straighten up! Straighten the fuck out! With the road!"

Sparrow's *Deathdealer* had reached the end of the built-up Strip. The turret was rotated back at a 220° angle to the tank's course. Its main gun fired, a blacked-out streak on Blue Three's screens and a dazzle of cyan radiance through her open hatch.

Wager heard the fan note rise as his driver adjusted nacelles #1S and #2S and boosted their speed. The nameless tank seemed to hesitate, but its attitude didn't change.

"Range,"Wager called to his artificial intelligence. They were about a hundred meters from the nearest buildings. Since they were still moving forward maybe he ought to—

Whang!

Wager looked up in amazement. The bullet that had flattened itself against the cupola's open hatch dropped onto his cheek. It was hotter than hell.

"Sonuvabitch!" Wager shouted.

"Blue Two," ordered the radio, "move into position and lay down a clearance charge!"

"Sergeant," begged Holman over the intercom channel, "do you want me to stop us or—"

She'd straightened 'em out all right, for about a millisecond before the counterclockwise rotation began to swing the tank's bow out of alignment again in the opposite direction. The aiming tracks marched across the screen with stately precision.

The volume of fire from the combat cars slackened because Wager's tank blocked their aim. Another bullet rang against the hatch; this one ricocheted glowing into the darkness. Bloody good thing Wager wasn't manning the cupola tribarrel himself just now. . . .

"Fire!" Wager ordered his AI.

He didn't know what the default setting was. He just knew he wasn't going to wait in his slowly revolving tank and get it right some time next week.

Blue Three chugged, a sound much like that of a mortar firing nearby. The charge, a net of explosive filaments deploying behind a sparkling trio of rocket drivers, arched from a bow compartment.

As soon as the unit fired, the computed aiming tracks

transformed themselves into a holographic overlay of the charge being laid—the gossamer threads would otherwise have been invisible.

The net wobbled outward for several seconds, shuddering in the flame-spawned air currents. It settled, covering 500 meters of pavement, the road's left shoulder, and the fronts of most of the buildings on the left side.

Muzzle flashes continued to wink from the stricken ruins of Happy Days.

The charge detonated with a white flash as sudden as that of lightning. Dust and ash spread in a dense pall that was opaque in the thermal spectrum as well as to normal optics.

Hundreds of small mines popped and spattered gravel. The explosive-filled cavity whose image, remoted from *Deathdealer* and frozen for reference on Wager's Screen Three, didn't go off.

Fuckin' A.

Hans Wager shifted Screen Two to millimetric radar and gripped his gunnery control. "Holman, drive on," he ordered, aware as he spoke that Blue Three was already accelerating.

Holman hadn't waited to be told. She knew as sure as Wager did that if the big mine went off, it was better that a tank take the shock than the lesser mass of a combat car.

Better for everybody except maybe the tank's crew.

Wager triggered the main gun and coaxially locked tribarrel simultaneously, throwing echoing swirls onto his display as the dense atmosphere warped even the radar patterns.

"Tootsie Six," he said as he felt the tank beneath him build to a lumbering gallop. "This is Blue Three. We're going through."

Flamethrower cleared the rise. The settlement was a scene from Brueghel's Hell, and Dick Suilin was being plunged into the heart of it.

Cooter looked back over his shoulder at the reporter. His voice in Suilin's earphones said, "Watch the stern, turtle. Don't worry about the bow—we'll go through on Ortnahme's coattails."

Gale, the veteran trooper, had already shifted his position

behind the right wing gun so that he was facing backward at 120° to the combat car's direction of travel. Suilin obediently tried to do the same, but he found that stacked ammo boxes and the large cooler made it difficult for him to stand. By folding one knee on the cooler, he managed to aim at the proper angle, but he wasn't sure he'd be able to hit anything if a target appeared.

Flamethrower was gathering speed. They'd crawled up the slope, matching their speed to that of the tank ahead of them. That vehicle in turn was trying not to overrun the combat cars pausing at the hillcrest.

The first series of the loud shocks occurred before Suilin's car was properly beyond the berm of Camp Progress. After that, the hidden fighting settled down to the vicious sizzle of powerguns. Each bolt sounded like sodium dropping into water in blazing kilogram packets.

When *Flamethrower* topped the ridgeline, offset to the left of the last tank in Task Force Ranson, Suilin saw the remains of Happy Days.

Four days before, he'd thought of the place as just another of the sleazy Strips that served army bases all over Prosperity—all over the human universe. Now it was a roiling pit, as smoky as the crater of a volcano and equally devoid of life.

"Blue Two," said a voice in Suilin's earphones, "this is Tootsie One-two. We're comin' through right up yer ass, so don't change yer mind, all right?"

It was probably Cooter speaking, but the reporter couldn't be sure. The helmets transmitted on one sideband, depriving the voices of normal timbre, and static interrupted the words every time a gun fired.

"Roger that, Tootsie One-two," said a different speaker. "Simkins, you heard the man. Keep yer bloody foot in it, right?"

Suilin's visual universe was a pattern of white blurs against a light blue background. The solidity and intensity of the white depended on the relative temperature of the object viewed.

I put it on thermal for you, Gale had said as he slapped a commo helmet onto the reporter's head with the visor down.

The helmet was loose, slipping forward when Suilin dipped his head and tugging back against its chin strap in the airstream when the combat car accelerated uphill. There was probably an adjustment system, but Suilin didn't know where it was . . . and this wasn't the time to ask.

Their own car, *Flamethrower*, slid over the crest and slowed as a billow of dust and ash expanded from the bow skirts like half a smoke ring. The driver had angled his fans forward; they lifted the bow slightly and kicked light debris in the direction opposite to their thrust against the vehicle's mass.

The tank had offset to the right on the hilltop as *Flamethrower* pulled left. Now it blew forward a similar but much larger half-doughnut. The arc of dust sucked in on itself, then recoiled outward when the cannon fired. The gun's crash was deafening to Suilin, even over the howl of the fans.

There was nothing to see on the flank Suilin was supposed to be guarding except the slight differential rate at which rocks, gravel, and vegetation lost the heat they'd absorbed during daylight. He risked a look over his shoulder, just as the tank fired again and Cooter ripped a burst from his tribarrel down the opposite side of what had been the settlement.

A combat car was making the run through Happy Days. The preceding vehicles of the task force waited in line abreast on the rising ground to the east of the settlement. Their hulls, particularly the skirts and fan intakes, were white; the muzzles of their power-guns were as sharp as floodlights.

The settlement was a pearly ambiance that wrapped and shrouded the car speeding through its heart. A gout of rubble lifted. It had fused to glass under the impact of the tank's 20cm bolt.

Suilin couldn't see any sign of a target—for the big gun or even for Cooter's raking tribarrel. The car racing through the wreckage was firing also, but the vehicles waiting on the far side of the gauntlet were silent, apparently for fear of hitting their fellow.

The road was outlined in flames over which smoke and ash

swept like a dancer's veils. Molten spatters lifted by the tank cannon cooled visibly as they fell. There was no return fire or sign of Consies.

There were no structures left in what had been a community of several thousand.

The tank beside *Flamethrower* shrugged like a dog getting ready for a fight. Dust and ash puffed from beneath it again, this time sternward.

"Hang on, turtle!" a voice crackled in Suilin's ears as *Flamethrower* began to build speed with the deceptive smoothness characteristic of an air-cushion vehicle.

Suilin gripped his tribarrel and tried to see something—*any-thing*—over the ghost-ring sight of the weapon. The normal holographic target display wasn't picked up by his visor's thermal imaging. The air stank of ozone and incomplete combustion.

The car rocked as its skirts clipped high spots and debris flung from the buildings. The draft of *Flamethrower*'s fans and passage shouldered the smoke aside, but there was still nothing to see except hot rubble.

Cooter and Gale fired, their bursts producing sharp static through Suilin's headset. The helmet slipped back and forth on the reporter's forehead.

In desperation, Suilin flipped up his visor. Glowing smoke became black swirls, white flames became sullen orange. The bolts from his companions' weapons flicked the scene with an utter purity of color more suitable for a church than this boiling inferno.

Suilin thumbed his trigger, splashing dirt and a charred timber with cyan radiance. He fired again, raising his sights, and saw a sheet of metal blaze with the light of its own destruction.

They were through the settlement and slowing again. There were armored vehicles on either side of *Flamethrower*. Gale fired a last spiteful burst and put his weapon on safe.

Suilin's hands were shaking. He had to grip the pivot before he could thumb the safety button.

It'd been worse than the previous night. This time he hadn't known what was happening or what he was supposed to do.

"Tootsie Six to all Tootsie elements," said the helmet. "March order, conforming to Blue One. Execute."

The vehicles around them were moving again, though *Flamethrower* held a nervous, greasy balance on its fans. They'd move out last again, just as they had when Task Force Ranson left the encampment.

Minutes ago.

"How you doing, turtle?" Lieutenant Cooter asked. He'd raised his visor also. "See any Consies?"

Suilin shook his head. "I just . . ." he said. "I just shot, in case . . . Because you guys were shooting, you know?"

Cooter nodded as he lifted his helmet to rub his scalp. "Good decision. Never hurts t' keep their heads down. You never can tell. . . ."

He gazed back at the burning waste through which they'd passed.

Suilin swallowed. "What's this 'turtle' business?" he asked.

Gale chuckled through his visor.

Cooter smiled and knuckled his forehead again. "Nothin' personal," the big lieutenant said. "You know, you're fat, you know? After a while you'll be a snake like the rest of us."

He turned.

"Hey," the reporter said in amazement. "I'm not fat! I exercise—"

Gale tapped the armor over Suilin's ribs. "Not fat *there*, turtle," the reflective curve of the veteran's visor said. "Newbie fat, you know? Civilian fat."

The tank they'd followed from Camp Progress began to move. "Watch your arcs, both of you," Cooter muttered over the intercom. "They may have another surprise waiting for us."

Suilin's body swayed as the combat car slipped forward. He still didn't know what the mercenaries meant by the epithet.

And he was wondering what had happened to all the regular inhabitants of Happy Days.

"Go ahead, Tootsie," said the voice of Slammer Six, hard despite all the spreads and attenuations that brought it from Firebase Purple to June Ranson's earphones. "Over."

"Lemme check yer shoulder," said Stolley to Janacek beside her. "C'mon, crack the suit."

"Roger," Ranson said as she checked the positioning of her force in the multifunction display. "We're okay, no casualties, but there was an ambush at the Strip settlement just out the gate."

Blue One was ghosting along 200 meters almost directly ahead of *Warmonger* at sixty kph. That was about the maximum for an off-road night run, even in this fairly open terrain.

One-one and One-five had taken their flanking positions, echeloned slightly back from the lead tank. The remaining four blowers were spaced tank-car, tank-car, behind *Warmonger* like the tail of a broadly diamond-shaped kite.

Just as it ought to be . . . but the ratfuck at Happy Days had cost the task force a good hour.

"We couldn't 've avoided it," Ranson said, "so we shot our way through."

If she'd known, *known*, there was a company of Consies in Happy Days, she'd 've bypassed the place by heading north cross-country and cutting east, then south, near Siu Mah. It'd 've been a hundred kilometers out of their way, but—

"Look, bugger off," said Janacek. "I'm fine. I'll take another pill, right?"

"Any of the bypass routes might 've got you in just as deep," said Colonel Hammer, taking a chance that, because of the time lag, his satellited words were going to step on those of his junior officer. "It's really dropped in the pot, Captain, all the hell over this country. But you don't see any reason that you can't carry out your mission?"

The question was so emotionless that concern stuck out in all directions like barbs from a burr. "Over."

"Quit screw'n around, Checker," Stolley demanded. "You got bits a' jacket metal there. I get 'em out and there's no sweat."

Ranson touched the scale control of her display. The eight discrete dots shrank to a single one, at the top edge of a large-scale moving map that ended at Kohang.

Latches clicked. Janacek had opened his clamshell armor for his buddy's inspection. A bullet had disintegrated on the shield of

Janacek's tri barrel during the run through Happy Days; bits of the projectile had sprayed the wing gunner.

Ranson felt herself slipping into the universe of the map, into a world of electronic simulation and holographic intersections that didn't bleed when they dropped from the display.

That was the way to win battles: move your units around as if they *were* only units, counters on a game board. Do whatever was necessary to check your enemy, to smash him, to achieve your objective.

Commanders who thought about blood, officers who saw with their mind's eye the troops they commanded screaming and crawling through muck with their intestines dangling behind them . . . those officers might be squeamish, they might be hesitant to give the orders needful for victory.

The commander of the guerrillas in this district understood that perfectly. Happy Days was a deathtrap for anybody trying to defend it against the Slammers. There was no line of retreat, and the vehicles' power guns were sure to blast the settlement into ash and vapor, along with every Consie in it.

The company or so of patriots who'd tried to hold Happy Days on behalf of the Conservative Action Movement almost certainly didn't realize that; but the man or woman who gave them their orders from an office somewhere in the Terran Government enclaves on the North Coast did. The ambush had meant an hour's delay for the relief operation, and that was well worth the price—on the North Coast.

Men and munitions were the cost of doing business. You needed both of them to win.

You needed to spit them both in the face of the enemy. They could be replaced after the victory.

Stolley's handheld medikit began to purr as it swallowed bits of metal that it had separated from the gunner's skin and shoulder muscles. Janacek cursed mildly.

Colonel Hammer knew the rules also.

"Slammer Six," June Ranson's voice said, "we're continuing. I don't know of any . . . I mean, we're not worse off than when we received the mission. Not really."

She paused, her mouth miming words while her mind tried to determine what those words should be. Hammer didn't interrupt. "We've got to cross the Padma River. Not a lotta choices about where. And we'll have the Santine after that, that'll be tricky. But we'll know more after the Padma."

Warmonger's fans ruled the night, creating a cocoon of controlled sound in which the electronic dot calling itself Junebug Ranson was safe with all her other dots.

Her chestplate rapped the grips of the tribarrel. She'd started to doze off again.

"Tootsie Six, over!" she said sharply. Her skin tingled, and all her body hairs were standing up straight.

There was a burst of static from her headset, but no response.

"Tootsie Six, over," she repeated.

Nothing but carrier hum.

Ranson craned her neck to look upward, past the splinter shield. There was a bright new star in the eastern sky, but it was fading even as she watched.

For fear of retribution, the World Government had spared the Slammers' recon and comsats when they swept the Yokels' own satellites out of orbit. When Alois Hammer raised the stakes, however, the Terrans stayed in the game.

"Now a little Spray Seal," Stolley muttered, "and we're done. Easier 'n bitchin', ain't it?"

Task Force Ranson was on its own now.

But they'd been on their own from the start. Troops at the sharp end were always on their own.

"Awright, then latch me up, will ya?" Janacek said. Then, "Hey, Stolley. When ya figure we get another chance t' kick butt?"

Warmonger howled through the darkness.

CHAPTER SEVEN

"I think it's a little tight now," Suilin said, trying gingerly to lift the commo helmet away from his compressed temples.

"Right," said Cooter. "Now pull the tab over the left ear. Just a cunt hair."

"Time t' stoke the ole furnaces," said Gale, handing something small to Cooter while the reporter experimented with the fit of his helmet.

When Suilin drew down on the tab as directed, the helmet lining deflated with an immediate release of pressure. It felt good—but he didn't want the cursed thing sliding around on his head, either; so maybe if he pulled the right tab again, just a—

"And one for you, buddy," Gale said, offering Suilin a white-cased stim cone about the size of a thumbnail. "Hey, what's your name?"

"Dick," the reporter said. "Ah—what's this?"

Cooter set the base of his cone against the inner side of his wrist and squeezed to inject himself. "Wide-awakes," he said. "A little something to keep you alert. Not much of a rush, but it beats nodding off about the time it all drops in the pot."

"Like Tootsie Six," Gale said, thumbing forward with a grin.

The front of the column was completely hidden from *Flamethrower*. Task Force Ranson had closed to fifty-meter separations between vehicles as soon as they entered the forest, but even Blue Two, immediately ahead of them, had been only a snorting ambiance for most of the past hour.

"Junebug's problem ain't she's tired," Cooter said with a grimace. "She's . . ." He spun his finger in a brief circle around his right ear. "It happens. She'll be okay."

"But won't this . . . ?" Suilin said, rolling the stim cone between his fingers. "I mean, what are the side effects?"

As a reporter, he'd seen his share and more of burn-outs, through his business and in it.

Cooter shrugged. "After a couple days," the big man said, raising his arm absently to block a branch swishing past his gun-shield, "it don't help anymore. And your ears ring like a sonuvabitch about that long after. Better 'n getting your ass blown away."

"Hey," said Gale cheerfully. "Promise me I'll be *around* in a couple days and I'll drink sewage."

Suilin set the cone and squeezed it. There was a jet of cold against his skin, but he couldn't feel any other immediate result.

Flamethrower broke into open terrain, a notch washed clean when the stream below was in spate. The car slid down the near bank, under control but still fast enough that their stern skirts sparked and rattled against the rocky soil. Water exploded in a fine mist at the bottom as Rogers goosed his fans to lift the car up the far side. They cleared the upper lip neatly, partly because the bank had already been crumbled into a ramp by the passage of earlier vehicles.

Blue Two had been visible for a moment as the tank made its own blasting run up the bank. Now *Flamethrower* was alone again, except for sounds and the slender-boled trees through which the task force pushed its way.

"Lord, why can't this war stop?" Dick Suilin muttered.

"Because," said Cooter, though the reporter's words weren't really meant as a question, "for it to stop, either your folks or the World Government has gotta throw in the towel. Last we heard, that hadn't happened."

"May a' bloody happened by now," Gale grunted, looking sourly at the sky where stars no longer shared their turf with commo and recce satellites. "Boy, wouldn't that beat hell? Us get our asses greased because we didn't know the war was over?"

"It's *not* the *World* Government," the reporter snapped. "It's the Terran Government, and that hasn't been the government on *this* world for the thirty years since we freed ourselves."

Neither of the mercenaries responded. Cooter lowered his head over his multifunction display and fiddled with its dials.

"Look, I'm sorry," Suilin said after a moment. He lifted his helmet and rubbed his eyes. Maybe the Wide-awake was having an effect after all. "Look, it's just that Prosperity could be a garden spot, a paradise, if it weren't for outsiders hired by the Terrans."

"Sorry, troop," said Gale as he leaned past Suilin to open the cooler on the floor of the fighting compartment. "But that's a big negative."

"Ninety percent of the Consies're born on Prosperity," Cooter agreed without looking up. "And I don't mean in the enclaves, neither."

"Ninety-bloody-eight percent of the body count," Gale chuckled. He lifted the cap off a beer by catching it on the edge of his gunshield and thrusting down. "Which figures, don't it?"

He sucked the foam from the neck of the bottle and handed it to Cooter. When he opened and swigged from the second one, Gale murmured, "I'll say this fer you guys. You brew curst good beer."

He gave the bottle to Suilin.

It was a bottle of 33, cold and wonderfully smooth when the reporter overcame his momentary squeamishness at putting his lips on the bottle that the mercenary had licked. Suilin didn't realize how dry his throat was until he began to drink.

"Look," he said, "there's always going to be malcontents. They wouldn't be a threat to stability if they weren't being armed and trained in the enclaves."

"Hey, what do I know about politics?" Gale said. He patted the breech of his tribarrel with his free hand.

A branch slapped Suilin's helmet; he cursed with doubled bitterness. "If Coraccio'd taken the enclaves thirty years ago, there wouldn't be any trouble now."

"Dream on, turtle," Gale said over the mouth of his own beer.

"Coraccio *couldn't* take the WG's actual bases," Cooter remarked, quickly enough to forestall any angry retort. "The security forces couldn't hold much, but they sure-hell weren't givin' up the starports that were their only chance of going home to Earth."

Gale finished his beer, belched, and tossed the bottle high over the side. The moonlit glitter seemed to curve backward as *Flamethrower* ground on, at high speed despite the vegetation.

"You shoulda hired us," he said. "Well, you know—somebody like us. But we'll take yer money now, no sweat."

Suilin sluiced beer around in his mouth before he swallowed it. "Only a fraction of the population supported the Consies," he said. "The Conservative Action Movement's just a Terran front."

"Only a fraction of the people here 're really behind the Nationals, either," Cooter said. He raised his hand, palm toward

Suilin in bar. "All right, sure—a bigger fraction. But what most people want's for the shooting to stop. Trust me, turtle. That's how it *always* is."

"We've got a right to decide the government of our own planet!" the reporter shouted.

"You bet," agreed the big lieutenant. "And that's what you're paying Hammer's Slammers for. So their fraction gets tired of havin' its butt kicked quicker'n your fraction does."

"They're payin' us," said Gale, caressing his tribarrel again, "because there's no damn body in the Yokel army who's got any balls."

Suilin flushed. His hand tightened on his beer bottle.

"All Tootsie elements," said a voice from Suilin's commo helmet. "We're approaching Phase Line Mambo, so look sharp."

The reporter didn't fully understand the words, but he knew by now what it meant when both mercenaries gripped their tribarrels and waggled the muzzles to be sure they turned smoothly on their gimbals.

Dick Suilin dropped the bottle with the remainder of his beer over the side. His hands were clammy on the grips of his weapon.

That was the trouble with his learning to understand things. Now he knew what was coming.

When Henk Ortnahme rocked forward violently, he reacted by bracing his palms against the main screen and opening his mouth to bellow curses at Tech 2 Simkins.

Herman's Whore didn't ground 'er bloody skirts, though, as Simkins powered her out of the unmanned gully between Adako Creek and the Padma River . . . and Warrant Leader Ortnahme wouldn't a' been bouncing around the inside of his tank like a pea in a whistle if he'd had brains enough to strap himself into his bloody seat.

He didn't shout the curses. When he rehearsed them in his mind, they were directed as much at himself as the kid, who was doing pretty good. Night, cross-country, through forested mountains— pretty *bloody* good.

"*All Tootsie elements*," boomed the command channel. "*We're approaching Phase Line Mambo, so look sharp.*"

Phase Line Mambo: Adako Beach, and the only bridge for a hundred kays that'd carry tanks over the Padma River. Consie defenses for sure. Maybe alerted defenses.

Simkins wasn't the only guy in *Herman's Whore* who was getting a crash course tonight in his new duties.

"Company," said somebody on the unit push, musta been Sparrow, because the view remoted onto Ortnahme's Screen Three had the B1 designator in its upper left corner.

The lead tank overlooked the main east-west road through the forest; Sparrow must've eased forward until *Deathdealer* was almost out of the trees. Half a dozen light vehicles were approaching from the east, still a kilometer away. They were moving at about fifty kph—plenty fast enough for anything on wheels that had to negotiate the roads in this part of the continent.

A dull blue line began jumping through the remoted image, three centimeters from the right edge of the screen. Nothing wrong with the equipment: *Death-dealer*'s transmission was just picking up interference from another circuit, the one that aligned the tank's main gun. . . .

"*Don't Shoot!*" June Ranson snarled on the command channel before she bothered with proper communications procedures.

Then, "Tootsie Six to all Tootsie elements. Form on Blue One, east along the roadcut. *Don't* expose yourselves, and don't shoot without *my* orders. These 're probably civilians. We'll wait till they clear the bridge, then we'll blast through ourselves while the guards 're relaxing."

Herman's Whore rocked as Simkins shifted a bit to the left, following the track of the car ahead. They'd intended to enter the roadcut in line ahead, where the slope was gentlest; now they'd have to slide down abreast.

A sputter of static on the commo helmet indicated one of the subordinate leaders, Sparrow or Cooter, was talking to Tootsie Six on a lock-out channel.

Ranson didn't bother to switch off the command push to reply,

"Negative, Blue One. Getting there twenty minutes later doesn't matter. The bridge guards'll 've seen the truck lights too; they'll be trigger-happy until they see there's no threat to them."

No big deal. Line abreast was a little trickier for the drivers, but it was about as fast . . . and it put Task Force Ranson in a perfect ambush position, just in case the trucks weren't civilian after all.

Herman's Whore nosed to the edge of the trees, swung to put her port side to the roadcut, and halted. She quivered in dynamic stasis.

Ortnahme cranked up the magnification on his gunnery screen, feeding enhanced ambient light to his display. He had a better angle on the trucks than Blue One did, and when he focused on the figures filling the canvas-topped bed of the lead vehicle—

Blood 'n martyrs!

"Tootsie Six," hissed the general unit push before Ortnahme could call his warning, "this is One-six. They ain't civilians."

The leading truck had National Army fender stencils and a Yokel crest on the passenger door, but the troops in back wore black uniforms. Ortnahme scanned their faces at a hundred magnifications. Bored, nervous—yeah, you could be both at the same time, he knew that bloody well himself. And very bloody young.

"Roger," said the command channel crisply. "All Tootsie elements, I'm highlighting your primary targets. On command, take 'em out before you worry about anybody else."

That truckload wasn't going to get much older.

Ortnahme's remote screen pinged as the view from *Deathdealer* vanished and was replaced by the corner tag R6, for Red Six, and a simple string of magenta beads, one for each truck. The second bead from the end was brighter and pulsing.

"Blue Two, roger," the warrant leader said, knowing the AI would transmit his words as a green dot on Ranson's display—even if all seven responses came in simultaneously.

"When the shooting starts, team," the command channel continued, "go like hell. Six out."

The first soft-skin had passed beneath *Herman's Whore* and was continuing toward the bridge. The armored vehicles would have burning trucks to contend with in their rush, but Ortnahme realized Ranson couldn't pop the ambush until all six targets were within the killing ground.

The second truck was a civilian unit with a mountain landscape painted on the passenger door and MASALLAH in big metalized letters across the radiator. Other than that, it was the same as the first: a stake-bed with twelve rubber tires and about sixty bloody Consies in back.

MASALLAH. God help us. They'd *need* God's help when the tribarrels started slicing into 'em.

The third truck came abreast with its gearbox moaning. Yokel maintenance was piss-poor, at least from what Ortnahme'd seen of it. Guess it didn't matter, not if they were handing over their hardware to the Consies.

Nobody in the trucks looked up, though they were within fifty meters of Task Force Ranson. Half the distance was vertical . . . which was a problem in itself for Ortnahme, since the guns in the turret and cupola of *Herman's Whore* couldn't depress as low as the pintle-mounted weapons of the combat cars.

"Tootsie, this is Blue One," said the radio. "Vehicles approaching the bridge from the west, too."

"Bloody marvelous," somebody muttered on the general push. It might have been the warrant leader himself.

"Roger, Blue One," replied Ranson coolly. "They're stopping, so it shouldn't affect us. Six out."

The gunnery pipper didn't bear on the trucks when they were directly below *Herman's Whore*. Life being what it bloody was, that's where Ortnahme's target would be when the balloon went up.

"Simkins," the warrant leader said, "when I give the word, get us over the edge. Got that? Not even a bloody eyeblink later."

"Yes sir," agreed the intercom. "Ah, sir . . . ?"

Ortnahme grimaced. The fourth truck was below them. "Go ahead."

"Sir, won't the guards be even more alerted if we start shooting before we cross the bridge? Than if we'd gone sooner, I mean?"

"Yeah," Ortnahme said, stating the bloody obvious, but this

wasn't the time to tear a strip off the kid. "But we don't want a Consie battalion waiting for us on the other side, do we? It's the hand we got, kid, so we play it."

"Yes sir," Simkins agreed. "I just wondered."

From his voice, that's all it was.

Maybe Simkins hadn't figured out that one *real* likely response from an altered guard detachment would be to blow the bloody bridge—maybe with most of Task Force Ranson learning to fly a hundred meters above the Padma River.

The fifth truck, Yokel Army again, grunted and snarled its way onto Screen Two. Ortnahme's pipper quivered across the canvas top, bloody useless unless the Consies all died of fright when the main gun ripped over their heads, but he still had a view of the troops. There was something funny about this lot. They were wearing armbands, and their uniforms—

"*All Tootsie elements—*"

"Simkins, *go!*" the warrant leader shouted.

Herman's Whore lurched sideways and down. Startled faces glanced upward in the magnified display, warned at last but only a microsecond before the command push added, "*Fire!*"

The pure, heart-wrenching blue of powerguns firing saturated the roadcut. Ortnahme's foot took up the slack in the gun pedal as his tank slid—and the orange pipper slid down onto one of the mouths screaming in the back of the fifth truck.

The 20cm bolt merged with a white and orange explosion. The whole truck was a fireball. Heated by the plasma, the steel chassis blazed with even greater venom than the contents of the fuel tanks and the flesh of the soldiers at the point of impact.

Ortnahme switched to his tribarrel as the tank rushed down the slope, its fans driving into a sea of flame.

Not that it mattered, but the troops in the truck he'd just destroyed weren't wearing black uniforms.

Three blazing figures lurched out of the inferno. Ortnahme shot them down, more as an act of mercy than of war.

They were in camouflaged National Army fatigues with black armbands, and they were carrying National Army assault rifles.

Not that it mattered.

"Fire!" June Ranson heard her voice say. Her visor opaqued, shutting out the double microsecond dazzles of *Deathdealer*'s main gun firing almost on top of her, but the momentary blindness didn't matter. The battle was taking place within a holographic screen while Ranson watched it from above.

Her tribarrel scissored bolts across those of Stolley's weapon, turning fist-sized chunks of the leading truck into meter-diameter flashes colored by material that vaporized and burned: rubber/metal/wood across the truck; cloth/flesh/munitions as the muzzles lifted into the bed.

Metals burned with a gorgeous intensity of color, white and red and green.

The target exploded into a lake of fire that screamed. Willens kept *Warmonger* as high on her fans as he could as the combat car entered the roadcut at a barely controlled slide and cranked hard right to follow *Deathdealer* up the bridge approach.

The filters of Ranson's helmet snapped into place as flames *whuffed* out like crinolines encircling the combat car. For a moment, everything was orange and hot; then *Warmonger* was through.

Junebug Ranson was back in the physical world in which her troops were fighting.

The Adako Beach community was a few hovels on this east side of the Padma River. There were twenty or thirty more dwellings, still unpretentious, beyond the gravel strand across the stream. The bridge itself was a solid concrete structure with a sandbagged blockhouse on the far end and a movement-control kiosk in the center of the span.

The blockhouse and kiosk had been added in reaction to the worsening security situation. When *Deathdealer*'s main gun punched the center of the blockhouse twice, the low building blew apart with an enthusiasm which the ammunition going off within did little more than color. Swatches of fiberglass fabric from the sandbags burned red as they drifted in the updraft.

A bus was waiting on the other side to cross the bridge. It lurched off the road and heeled slowly over onto its side, its headlights still burning. The truck behind it didn't move, but both cab doors flew open and figures scuttled out.

A man without pants ran from one of the huts near the bridge approach and began firing an automatic rifle at *Deathdealer*. Sparrow ignored—or was unaware of—the fleabites, but Stolley triggered a burst in the Consie's direction.

The hovel disintegrated into burning debris under the touch of the cyan bolts. The Consie dropped flat and continued firing, sheltered by the rocky irregularity of the ground. Another set of muzzle flashes sparkled yellow from closer to the streambed. A bullet rang on *Warmonger*'s hull.

The long span between the concrete guardrails of the bridge had been narrowed by coils of concertina wire, reducing the traffic flow to a single lane past the central checkpoint. A round, pole-mounted signal board, white toward the east and presumably red on the other face, reached from the kiosk.

An attendant bolted out of the kiosk, waving his empty hands above his head. He was running toward the armored vehicles rather than away, but he didn't have a prayer of reaching safety in either direction.

The flash of *Deathdealer*'s main gun ended the possibility of a threat lurking within the kiosk and crisped the attendant on his third stride.

"All Tootsie!" Ranson shouted. "Watch the left of the near side, there's bandits!"

The gunners on her combat cars were momentarily blind as they bucked out of the fireball to which they had reduced the trucks. That made them a dangerously good target for the riflemen firing from the downslope.

Those Consies were good. Caught completely by surprise, hideously outgunned—and still managing to make real pests of themselves. Hammer could use more recruits of their caliber—

To replace the troops this run was going to use up.

Sparks cascaded in all directions as *Deathdealer* entered the bridge approach and Albers, the only experienced tank driver in the task force, dropped his skirts so low they scraped. The truck-width passage across the bridge was too narrow for the blowers, and there wasn't time for the lengthy spooling and restringing of the barriers that would've been required during a normal down-time move.

June Ranson felt the satisfaction common to any combat soldier when circumstances permit him to use the quick and dirty way to achieve his objective. But that didn't mean there weren't risks. . . .

Deathdealer hit the first frame and smashed it to kindling while loops of wire humped like terrified caterpillars. Strands bunched and sparkled. The tank slid forward at forty kph, grinding the concertina wire between the guardrail and the vehicle's own hundred and seventy tonnes.

The wire couldn't *stop* a tank or even a combat car, but any loop that snaked its way into a fan intake would lock up the nacelle as sure as politicians lie. A bulldozer with treads for traction was the tool of choice for clearing this sort of entanglement; but, guided by a driver as expert as Albers, a tank would do the job just fine.

Warmonger followed *Deathdealer* at a cautious fifty meters, in case a strand of wire came whipping back unexpectedly. Willens drove with his hatch buttoned up above him, while Ranson and her two gunners crouched behind their weapons. The blades of a drive fan weren't the only thing you could strangle with a loop of barbed wire.

Steel rubbed concrete in an aural counterpart of the hell-lit road the task force had left behind them. Sparks ricocheted in wild panic, scorching when they touched. Ranson smelled a lock of her hair that had grown beyond the edge of her helmet.

Deathdealer's tribarrel fired. Ranson didn't bother remoting an image of Sparrow's target, and there was nothing to see from behind the tank's bulk now.

"Six," said her commo helmet, "Blue One. The bus 'n truck 're—"

Deathdealer swung onto the western approach, pushing as well as dragging tangled masses of concertina wire. The tank shook herself like a whore waggling a come-on. A touch of her skirts pulverized half a meter of bridge abutment.

"—civvie, no threat. Over."

As Albers accelerated forward, *Deathdealer*'s stern rebounded from the concrete and slapped the three-axled truck that had been waiting to cross the bridge. The lighter vehicle danced away from the impact with the startled delicacy of a horse shying. Ten meters from the pavement, the crumpled wreckage burst into flame.

"All Tootsie elements," Ranson relayed. "Vehicles at the west approach are no threat, repeat, no threat. Six out."

Warmonger blasted through a cloud of powdered concrete as Willens pulled them clear of the bridge. Blue One fired its tribarrel into the houses to the right. There was no sign of hostile activity or even occupation. A ball of wire still dragged twenty meters behind the tank, raising a pall of dust.

One of the tires of the overturned bus revolved lazily. The vehicle lay on both its doors. Figures were climbing out of the windows. They flattened as *Warmonger* swept by behind the tank.

Stolley's tribarrel snapped over the civilians as he fired across the river, trying to nail the Consie riflemen from this better angle. Rock flashed and gouted, but the muzzle flashes bloomed again.

A trooper screamed on the unit push.

Junebug Ranson's eyes were glazed. Her mouth was open.

Ozone and matrix residues from her tribarrel flayed her throat as she fired into the village, shattering walls and roofslates.

It was very beautiful in the hologram of her mind.

Five-year-old Dickie Suilin screamed, "*Suzi!*" as his older sister squeezed his nostrils shut and clapped her other hand over his mouth. The flames arcing over the skirts of *Flamethrower* roared their laughter.

He could breathe after all. A mask of some sort had extended from the earpieces of the commo helmet as soon as the inferno waved an arm of blazing diesel fuel to greet the combat car plunging toward it. Suilin could breathe, and he could see again when over-load reset his visor from thermal display to optical.

Though there wasn't much to see except flames curling around black steel skeletons, the chassis of trucks whose flammable portions were already part of the red/orange/yellow/white billows.

Even steel burned when Suilin raked it with his tribarrel. Faces bloomed into smears of vapor and calcined bones. . . .

Blue Two grunted head-on down the road, spewing a wake of blazing debris to either side. Cooter's driver followed, holding *Flamethrower* at a 45° degree angle along the edge of the cut.

The slant threw the men in the fighting compartment toward the fire their vehicle was skirting. Gale clung to the starboard coaming. Cooter must have locked his tribarrel in place, because he was frozen like a statue of Effort on its grips.

And Dick Suilin, after a hellish moment of feeling his torso swing out and down toward the bellowing flames, braced his feet against the inner face of the armor and grabbed Cooter by the waist. If the big lieutenant minded, they could discuss it later.

Something as soft-featured and black as a tar statue reached out of the flames and gripped the coaming to either side of Suilin's tribarrel. The only parts of the figure that weren't black were the teeth and the great red cracks writhing in what had been the skin of both arms. The thing fell away without trying to speak.

Only a shadow. Only a sport thrown by the flames.

"Help me, Suzi," the reporter whispered. "Help me, Suzi."

Blue Two sucked fire along with it for an instant as the tank cleared the ambush site. Then the return flow, cool sweet air, pistoned Hell back into its proper region and washed Suilin in its freedom as well.

This car was *Flamethrower*. For the first time, Suilin realized how black was the humor with which the Slammers named their vehicles.

The driver brought them level with a violence that banged the skirts on the roadway. Suilin grunted. He reached for the grips of his tribarrel, obeying an instinct to hang onto something after he lost his excuse to hold Cooter.

Powerguns punctuated the night with flashes so intense they remained for seconds as streaks across the reporter's retinas. His mind tried desperately to process the high-pitched chatter from the commo helmet—a mixture of orders, warnings, and shouted exclamations.

It was all meaningless garbage; and it was all terrifying.

The downslope to the left of the roadway was striped orange by the firelight and leaping with shadows thrown from outcrops anchored too firmly in the fabric of the planet to be uprooted when the Padma River flooded. Muzzle flashes pulsed there, shockingly close.

A bottle-shaped yellow glow swelled and shrank as the gunman triggered his burst. The gun wasn't firing tracers, but the corner of Suilin's eyes caught a flicker as glowing metal snapped from the muzzle.

Specks of light raked the car ahead of Blue Two. Red sparks flashed up the side armor.

On the commo helmet, someone screamed *lord lord lord*.

The tribarrel wouldn't swing fast enough. Dick Suilin was screaming also. He unslung his grenade launcher.

Blue Two's main gun lit the night. Rock and the damp soil beneath it geysered outward from the point of impact, a white track glowing down the slope for twenty meters.

Flamethrower's driver flinched away from the bolt, throwing the thirty-tonne car into a side-step as dainty as that of a nervous virgin.

Blue Two and the combat car both accelerated up the bridge approach. The tank's turret continued to rotate to bear on the cooling splotch which its first bolt had grazed. If it fired from *that* angle, the bolt would pass within ten meters of *Flame*—

The tribarrel in Blue Two's cupola fired instead of the main gun.

Suilin straightened and fired a burst from his own tribarrel in the same general direction. He'd dropped the grenade launcher when he ducked in panic behind the hull armor. He was too rattled now to be embarrassed by his reaction—

And anyway, both the veterans sharing the fighting compartment had ducked also.

You couldn't be sure of not being embarrassed unless you were dead. The past night and day had been a gut-wrenching exposition of just what it meant to be dead. Dick Suilin would do anything at all to avoid *that*.

Traces of barbed wire clung to the cast-in guardrail supports. Large sections of the rail had been shattered by gunfire or smashed at the touch of behemoths like *Flamethrower*. Blue Two swung its turret forward again, releasing a portion of the fear that knotted Suilin's stomach, but only a portion.

Gale fired his tribarrel over *Flamethrower*'s stern. Bolts danced off the left guardrail and streaked through the ambush scene. Their cyan purity glared even in the heart of the kerosene pyre which consumed the trucks and their cargo. The bolts vanished only when they touched something solid.

Flamethrower was the last vehicle in the column. Suilin turned also and hosed the fire-shot darkness, praying that there would be no wobbling muzzle flashes to answer as a Consie rifleman raked *Flamethrower* as he had the car ahead of them.

They slid past the further abutments at fifty kph. There'd been a blockhouse there, but it lay in steaming ruins licked by rare red tongues of flame. A truck burned brightly, well down the steep embankment supporting the approach to the bridge.

On its side, between *Flamethrower* and the truck, lay a tipped-over bus. A Consie gunman silhouetted by the truck, aimed at Suilin from a bus window.

Liquid nitrogen sprayed into the chambers of Suilin's tribarrel as it cycled, kicking out the spent cases and cooling the glowing iridium of the chamber before the next round was loaded. The gas was a hot kiss blowing back across the reporter's hands as he horsed his weapon onto the unexpected threat. The tribarrel was heavy despite being perfectly balanced on its gimbals, and it swung with glacial torpor.

"*Not that—*" screamed Suilin's headset. Two-cm bolts ripped across the undercarriage of the bus, bright flashes that blew fuel lines, air lines, hydraulic lines into blazing tangles and opened holes the size of tureens in the sheet metal.

The line of bolts missed by millimeters the man whose raised hand had been shadowed into a weapon by the flames behind him. The civilian fell back into the interior of the bus.

No-no-no—

Suilin's screams didn't help any more than formal prayers would have done if he'd had leisure to form them.

When it first ignited, the ruptured fuel tank engulfed the rear half of the bus. The flames had sped all the way to the front of the vehicle before any of the flailing figures managed to crawl free.

Somebody patted the reporter's forearms; gently at first, but then with enough force to detach his death grip from the tribarrel.

" S'okay, turtle," a voice said. "All okay. Don't mean nothin'."

Suilin opened his eyes. He'd flipped up his visor, or one of the mercenaries had raised it for him. Cooter was holding his forearms, while Gale watched the reporter with obvious concern. He wasn't sure which of the veterans had been speaking.

The river lay as a black streak behind them as the road climbed. Adako Beach was a score of dull fires, big enough to throw orange highlights on the water but nothing comparable to the holocaust of the truck convoy.

And the similar diesel-fed rage which consumed the bus.

"No sweat," Cooter said gently. "Don't mean nothin'."

"It means something to *them!*" the reporter screamed. He couldn't see for tears, but when he closed his eyes every terrified line of the civilian at the bus window cleared from the surface of his mind. "*To them!*"

"Happens to everybody, turtle," Gale said. "There's always somebody don't get the word. This time it was you."

"It won't matter next century," Cooter said. "Don't sweat what you can't change."

Flamethrower slowed as Blue Two entered the woods ahead. When the trees closed about the combat car, Dick Suilin could no longer see the flames.

Memory of the fire began to dull. Only a minute. Only a few seconds. . . .

"Trust me, turtle," Gale added with a chuckle. "You stick with us and it won't be the last time, neither."

CHAPTER EIGHT

Birdie Sparrow curled and uncurled his hands, working out the stiffness from their grip on the gunnery joysticks.

Gases from the breech of the main gun swirled as if fleeing the efforts of the air-conditioning fans which tried to scavenge them. The twisted vapors picked up the patterns glowing in the holographic screens, mixed and softened the colors, and turned the turret interior into a sea of gentle pastels.

The radio crackled with reports of damage and casualties. That didn't touch Birdie. *Deathdealer*'s finish had been scratched by a bullet or two, and there were some new dents in her skirts; but the Consies hadn't so much as fired a buzzbomb.

Tough about the crew of One-six, but a combat car . . . what'd they expect? That was worse 'n ridin' with your head out the cupola.

DJ Bell pointed from a wisp of mauve vapor toward the yellow warning that had just blinked alive in the corner of Screen Two.

Sparrow hit the square yellow button marked automatic air defense—easy to find now, because it started to glow a millisecond after the *Aircraft Warning* header came up on the gunnery screen. The tribarrel in the cupola whined, rousing to align itself with the putative target.

Piss off, DJ, Sparrow thought/said to the phantom of his friend that grinned until the inevitable change smeared its features.

Aloud, certainly aloud, Sparrow reported, "Tootsie Six, this is Blue One. Aircraft warning. Sonic signature only."

He was reading off the data cascading in jerks down the left edge of his screen like the speeded-up image of a crystal growing. The pipper remained in the center of the holofield, but the background displayed on the screen jumped madly. The tracking system was trying to find gaps that would permit it to shoot through the dense vegetation.

"AAD has a lock but not a window." Sparrow paused then pursed his lips. "Signature is consistent with a friendly recce drone. We expectin' help? Over."

The bone-deep hum of *Deathdealer* grinding her way southward was the only response for several seconds.

"Blue One," Captain Ranson's voice said at last, "it may be friendly—but let your AAD make the choice. I'd rather shoot down a friendly drone with a bad identification transponder than learn the Terrans were giving some smart-help to their Consie buddies. Out."

The pipper jumped and quivered among the tree images, like an attack dog straining on its leash.

"No, sweat, snake," whispered DJ Bell. "It's all copacetic. This time. . . ."

"Blue Two lock," said Ranson's headset as the B2 designator glowed air-defense yellow in her multi-function display.

Warmonger went airborne for an unplanned instant. Willens boosted his fans when he realized the ground had betrayed him, but the car landed again like a gymnast dropping three meters onto a mat.

The three mercenaries in the fighting compartment braced for it, splay-legged and on their toes. Shock gouged the edge of Ranson's breastplate into the top of her thighs.

"Blue Three, ah, locked," said Sergeant Wager, but the designator *didn't* come on, not for a further five seconds.

Wager, the recent transfer from combat cars, was having problems with his hardware. Understandable but a piss-poor time for it. His driver, that was Holman, she wasn't any better. The nameless Blue Three kept losing station, falling behind or speeding up to the point the tank threatened to overrun the car directly ahead of it.

"Janacek!" Ranson snapped. "Don't point your gun! Now! Lower it!"

"Via, Cap'n—" the wing gunner said fiercely. His tribarrel slanted upward at a 30° angle on the rough southwest vector he'd gleaned from seeing *Deathdealer*'s cupola gun rouse.

"*Lower* it, curse you!" Ranson repeated. "And then take your cursed hands away from it. *Now!*"

There was almost nil chance of a hand-aimed tribarrel doing any good if three tank units failed on air-defense mode. There was a bloody good chance that a human thumb would twitch at the wrong time and knock down a friendly drone whose IFF handshake had passed the tank computers, though. . . .

Deathdealer had to be the leading panzer. Blue Three in the rear-guard slot wouldn't tear gaps the way it did in the middle of the line, but Wager's inexperience could be an even worse disaster there if the task force were hit from behind. Maybe if she put *Deathdealer*'s driver in the turret of Blue Three and moved an experienced driver from one of the cars to—

Command exercises. Arrange beads of light in a chosen order, then step back while the grading officer critiques your result.

"*Tight-ass bitch*," the intercom muttered. Hand-keyed, Janacek or Stolley, either one, or even Willens.

Veterans don't like to be called down by their new CO. But veterans screw up too, just like newbies . . . just like COs who drift in and out of an electronic non-world, where the graders snarl but don't shoot.

Ranson thought she heard the aircraft's engine over the howl of *Warmonger*'s fans and the constant slap of branches against their hull. That was impossible.

"Six, it's friendly!" Sparrow called, echoing the relayed information that flashed on the display which in turn cross-checked the opinion of the combat car's own electronics. And they could all be wrong, but—

The aircraft *was* friendly. Its data dump started.

Maps and numerals scrolled across the display, elbowing one another aside as knowledge became chaos by its volume. Ranson was so focused on her attempt to sort the electronic garbage with a combat car's inadequate resources that she didn't notice the drone when it passed overhead a few seconds later.

The Slammers' reconnaissance drones were slow, loping along at less than a thousand kph instead of sailing around the globe at a satellite's ninety-minute rate. On the other hand, no satellite could survive in a situation where the enemy had powerguns and even the very basic fire-direction equipment needed to pick up a solid object against the vacant backdrop of interstellar space.

Stolley whispered inaudibly as the drone flicked past, barely visible against the slats of the trees. The aircraft had a long, narrow-chord wing mounted high so as not to interfere with the sensors in its belly.

The drone's high-bypass turbofan sighed rather than roared,

and the exhaust dumped from its twin outlets was within fifty degrees C of ambient. Except for the panels covering the sensor bays, the plastic of the wings and fuselage absorbed radio—radar—waves, and the material's surface adapted its mottled coloration to whatever the background might be.

Task Force Ranson could still have gulped the drone down with the ease of a frog and a fly. The Consies operating here weren't nearly as sophisticated—

And that was good, because even a cursory glance at the down-loaded data convinced June Ranson that the task force was cold meat if it continued along the course she'd planned originally.

Information wriggled on her multi-function display. Task Force Ranson didn't have a command car, but the electronics suite of one of the panzers would do about as well. . . .

"Blue One," she ordered, "how close is the nearest clearing where we can laager for—half an hour? Six over."

That should be time enough. There were wounded in One-six to deal with besides. Cooter could shift crews while she—

"Six," said Sparrow in his usual expressionless voice, "there's a bald half a kay back the way we came. It'll give us a clear shot over two-seventy, maybe three-hundred degrees. Blue One over."

"Roger, Blue One," Ranson said. Weighing the alternatives, knowing that the grader would demonstrate that any decision she made was the wrong one, because there are no right decisions in war.

Knowing also that there is no decision as bad as no decision at all.

"All Tootsie elements," her voice continued, "halt and prepare to reverse course."

Warmonger bobbed, its fan chuffing as Willens tried to scrub off momentum smoothly while his eyes darted furiously over the display showing his separation from the huge tanks before and behind him.

"Tootsie, One-two, lead on the new course as displayed." Better to have a tank as a lead vehicle, but there wasn't much chance of trouble here in the boonies, and it was only half a kilometer. . . .

Warmonger touched the ground momentarily, then began to rotate on its axis. A twenty-centimeter treebole, thick for this area, this forest, this planet, obstructed the turn. Willens backed them grudgingly to the altered course.

Anyway, she wasn't sure she wanted Blue Two leading. Ortnahme didn't have much field experience either.

"We'll laager on the bald. Break. Blue Three, I'll be borrowing your displays. I want you to take over my position while we're halted. Over."

"Roger, Tootsie Six. Blue Three out."

"All Tootsie elements, execute new course. Tootsie Six out."

She'd get an eighty percent for that. Down on reversing, down on halting, down on not swapping Cooter's combat car for one of the panzers. But she'd be down on those points whichever way she'd chosen. . . .

Ranson rubbed her eyes, vaguely surprised to find that they were open. Her body braced itself reflexively as Willens brought *Warmonger* up to speed.

She'd use Blue Three's displays. And she'd use the tank's commo gear also, because that was going to get tricky.

Of course, it was always tricky to talk with Colonel Hammer.

The bald was a barren, hundred-meter circle punched in the vegetation of a rocky knoll by fire, disease, or the chemistry of the underlying rock strata. *Flamethrower* scudded nervously across the clearing and settled, not to the ground on idle but in a dynamic stasis with its fans spinning at high speed.

Cooter spoke to his multi-function display, then poked a button on the side of it. Suilin's tribarrel shivered.

"Just let it be," the big lieutenant said, nodding toward the weapon. "I put all the guns on air defense." He gripped the rear coaming and swung his leg over the side of the vehicle.

"There's not much chance of 'em helping, using car sensors," he added. "But it's what we got till the panzers arrive."

As Cooter spoke, Blue Two came bellowing out of the trees. The tank's vast size was emphasized by the narrow compass of the bald.

The warrant leader from Maintenance, his bulky form unmistakable, waved from the cupola as his driver pulled to a location 120° around the circle from *Warmonger*. Further vehicles were following closely.

"What's going on?" the reporter asked Gale. "Why are we in the, the clear?"

In only a few hours, Suilin had gotten so used to the forest canopy that he felt naked under the open sky. Both moons were visible, though wisps of haze blotted many of the stars. He didn't suppose the leaves really provided much protection—but, like his childhood bedcovers, they'd served to keep away the boogeymen of his imagination.

The veteran gestured toward the horizon dominated by a long ridge twenty kilometers away. "Air attack," he said. "Or arty. While we're movin' it's okay, but clumpin' all together like this, we could get our clocks cleaned. If we see it comin', we're slick, we shoot it down. But with powerguns, if a leaf gets in the way, the bolt don't touch the incoming shell it's s'posed t' get, does it?"

"The Consies don't have air . . . ?" Suilin began, but he broke the statement off on a rising inflection.

Gale grinned viciously. "Right," he said. "Bet on that and kiss yer ass goodbye."

He glanced at the combat car which had just pulled up beside them and grounded. "Not," he added, "like we're playin' it safe as is."

Cooter clambered aboard the grounded car. Its sides were scratched, like those of all the vehicles, but the words *Daisy Belle* could be read on the upper curve of the armorplate.

A cartoon figure had been drawn beside the name, but it would have been hard to make out even under better lighting. A bullet had struck in the center of the drawing, splashing the paint away without cratering the armor. A second bullet had left a semicircle of lead on the coaming.

There was only one mercenary standing erect in the fighting compartment to greet Cooter.

"Wisht we had a better field that way," Gale mused aloud, nodding toward the crags that lurched up to the immediate north of the bald, cutting off vision in that direction. "Still, with the panzers—" a second tank had joined Blue Two and the third was an audible presence "—it oughta be okay. Whatever hardware does best, them big fuckers does best."

Suilin climbed out of the fighting compartment and jumped to the ground. He staggered when he found himself on footing that didn't vibrate. Despite the weight of his armor, the reporter mounted the rear slope of *Daisy Belle* without difficulty. He'd learned where the steps in the armor were—

And he was no longer entering an alien environment.

Cooter was examining the right forearm of the standing crewman. The trooper's sleeve had been torn away. The bandage across the muscles was brilliantly white in the moonlight except for the dots of blood on opposite sides.

He must have bandaged himself, because the other two crewmen lay on the floor of the fighting compartment—one dead, the other breathing but comatose.

"I'm okay," the wounded man said sullenly.

"Sure you are, Titelbaum," Cooter replied. "Tootsie One-five," he continued, keying his helmet. "This is Tootsie Three. Tommy, send one a'your boys—send Chalkin—to One-six. Over."

"I kin *handle* it!" Titelbaum insisted as the lieutenant listened to the reply.

"One-five," Cooter said in response to a complaint Suilin couldn't hear. "*I'd* like to be in bed with a hooker. Get Chalkin over here, right? I need 'im to take over. Three out."

"I kin—"

"You got one hand," Cooter snapped. "Just shut it off, okay?"

"I'm left—"

"You're a bloody liar." Cooter looked at Suilin, balanced on the edge of the armor, for the first time. "Good. Gimme a hand with McGwire. We'll sling her to the skirts and get a little more space for Chalkin."

Suilin nodded. He didn't trust himself to speak.

"Here, take the top," Cooter said. He reached beneath McGwire's shoulders and lifted the corpse with surprising gentleness.

McGwire had been a small woman with sharp features and a fine shimmer of blonde hair. Her head was bare. A bullet had entered beneath her right mastoid at an upward slant that lifted the commo helmet when it exited with a splash of brains.

McGwire's flesh was still warm. Suilin kept his face rigid as his hands took the weight from Cooter.

"Titelbaum," the lieutenant said, "where's your—oh."

The wounded crewman was already offering a flat dispenser of cargo tape. Cooter thrust it into a pocket and grasped the corpse by the boots.

"Okay, turtle," he said as he raised his leg over the side coaming— careful not to step on the comatose soldier on the floor of the compartment. "Easy now. We'll fasten her to the tarp tie-downs."

Cooter paused for a moment on the edge, using a tribarrel to support his elbow. Then he swung his other leg clear and slid from the bulge of the skirts to the ground without jerking or dropping his burden.

Suilin managed to get down with his end also. It was a difficult job, even though he had proper steps for his feet.

Gear—stakes, wire mesh, bedding, and the Lord knew what all else—was fastened along the sides of all the combat cars. Cooter spun a few centimeters of tape into a loop and reached behind a footlocker to hook the loop to the hull. He took two turns around McGwire's ankles before snugging them tight to the same tie-down.

A trooper carrying a submachine-gun and a bandolier of ammunition jogged up to *Daisy Belle*, glancing around warily at the vehicles which snorted and shifted across the bald. "This One-six?" he demanded. "Oh, hi, Coot."

"Yeah, try 'n keep Titelbaum trackin', will you?" the lieutenant said. "He's takin' it pretty hard, you know?"

"Aw, cop," the newcomer muttered, looking past Suilin. "Nandi bought it? Aw, cop."

"Foran's not in great shape neither, but he'll be okay," Cooter said.

The lieutenant's big, capable fingers wrapped tape quickly around McGwire's shoulders.

The corpse leaked on Suilin's hands and wrist. The reporter's face didn't move except for a slight flaring of his nostrils.

Chalkin climbed into the fighting compartment. The barrel of his submachine-gun rang against the armor. "Dreamer," he said. "None of us'll be okay unless some fairy godmother shows up real quick."

"Okay, let's get back," Cooter said. He touched the reporter's shoulder, turned him. "Dunno how long Junebug's gonna stay here."

He glanced up at the moons. "No longer 'n she has to, I curst well hope."

Suilin found he had a voice. "It gets easier from here?" he asked.

"Naw, but it gets over," the big man said as he waved Suilin ahead of him at the steps of their vehicle.

Suilin paused, looking at the hull beneath the tribarrel he served. He hadn't had a good look at the cartoon painted on the sides of the combat car before. Above *Flamethrower* in crude Gothic letters, a wyvern writhed so that its tail faced forward. Jets of blue fire spouted from both nostrils, and the creature farted a third flame as well.

He wondered whether a bullet would blast away the grinning drawing an instant before another round lifted the top of Dick Suilin's head.

"It gets over," Cooter mused aloud. "One way or the other."

"Sir, are we s'posed to be watchin' this?" Simkins murmured through the intercom link. The map sliding across the main turret screen was reproduced in miniature on one of the driver's displays as well.

"Junebug didn't put a bloody lock on it, did she?" Ortnahme grunted. "Besides, we got all the data the drone dumped ourselves."

But the men on *Herman's Whore* didn't know what the Task Force commander was going to do with the recce data; and therefore, what she was going to do with them.

Warrant Leader Ortnahme was pretty sure Captain Ranson didn't realize *Herman's Whore* was echoing the displays from Blue

Three; but as he'd told Simkins, she hadn't thrown the mechanical toggle that would've prevented them from borrowing the signals.

And hell, it was their asses too!

"Sir," said Simkins, "where 're we?"

"We're off-screen, kid," Ortnahme replied, just as the image rotated eight degrees from Grid North to place as much as possible of the Santine River on the display at one time. The estuary was on the right edge of the screen.

Symbols flashed at a dozen points—bridges, ferries; fords if there'd been any, which there weren't, not this far down the Santine's course.

The image jerked leftward under June Ranson's control in the nameless tank. More symbols, but not so very many more; and none of 'em a bloody bit of good until you'd gone 300 kays in the wrong bloody direction. . . .

"Which way are we going to go, sir?" the technician asked.

The display lurched violently back to the southward. The image jumped as Ranson shrank the map scale, focusing tightly on la Reole. The numeral "I" overlay the main bridge in the center of the town. The symbol was flashing yellow.

"Which bloody way do you think we're gonna go?" Ortnahme snarled. "You think we're pushin' babycarts? There's only one tank-capable bridge left on the Santine till you've gone all the way north t' bloody bumfuck! And *that* bridge's about to fall into the river by itself, it looks!"

"W-warrant Leader Ortnahme? I'm sorry, sir."

Blood 'n martyrs.

It musta been lonely, closed up in the driver's compartment.

The Lord knew it was lonely back here in the turret. Wonder if the background whisper of a voice singing in Tagalog came through the intercom circuit?

"S'okay, kid," Ortnahme muttered. "Look, it's just—ridin' on air don't mean we're light, you see? There's still a hundred seventy tonnes t' support, even if the air cushion spreads it out as good as you can. And there's not a bloody lotta bridges that won't go flat with that much weight on 'em."

Ortnahme stared grimly at the screens. Besides la Reole, there were two "I" designators—bridges of unlimited capacity—across the lower Santine, as well as four Category II bridges that might do in a pinch. Updated information from the drone had colored all six of those symbols red—destroyed.

"'Specially with the Consies blowing every curst thing up these coupla days," he added.

"I see, sir," the technician said with the nervous warmth of a puppy who's been petted after being kicked. "So we're going through la Reole?"

Ortnahme stared glumly at the screen. The bridge designators weren't the only updated symbols the reconnaissance drone had painted on the map from the Slammers' database.

"Well, kid," the warrant leader said, "there's some problems with that, too. . . ."

"Tootsie Six to Slammer Six," June Ranson said, loading the cartridge that would be transmitted to Firebase Purple in a precisely calculated burst. "Absolute priority."

Even if you got your dick half into her, Colonel, you need to hear this now.

"The only tank-crossing point on the lower Santine is la Reole, which is in friendly hands but is encircled by dug-in hostiles. The bridge is damaged besides. The forces at my disposal are not sufficient to overwhelm the opposition, nor is it survivable to penetrate the encirclement and proceed to the bridge with the bulk of the hostile forces still in play behind us."

She paused, though the transmission would compress the hesitation out of existence. "Unless you can give us some support, Colonel, I'm going to have to swing north till the river's fordable. It'll add time." *Three days at least.* "Maybe two days."

A deep breath, drawn against the unfamiliar, screen-lighted closeness of the tank turret. "Tootsie Six, over."

Would the AI automatically precede the transmission with a map reference so that the colonel could respond?

"Slug the transmission with our coordinates and execute," she ordered the unit as she stared bleakly at the holographic map filling her main screen.

Nothing else was working out the way she wanted. Why should the tank's artificial intelligence have the right default?

"Tootsie Three, this is Six," she said aloud. "You got One-six sorted out, Cooter?"

It might be minutes before her own message went out, and the wait for Hammer's response would be at least that long again. The heavens had their own program. . . .

"Tootsie Six, roger," her second-in-command replied, panting slightly. "I gave Chalkin the blower. Mc—"

The transmitting circuit *zeep*ed, pulsing Ranson's message skyward in a tight packet which would bounce from the ionized track that a meteor had just streaked in the upper atmosphere.

Meteorites, invisible to human eyes during daytime, burned across the sky every few seconds. It was just a matter of waiting for the track which would give the signal the narrowest, least interceptive path to the desired recipient. . . .

"—Gwire bought it and Foran's not a lot better, but there's no damage to the car. Over."

"Tootsie Three, how are the mechanicals holding—"

The inward workings of the console beneath Screen Three gave a satisfied chuckle; its amber Stand-by light flashed green.

That quick.

"Cooter," Ranson said, "forget—no—" she threw a toggle "—listen in."

Staring at the screen—though she knew the transmission would be voice only—she said, "Play burst."

Despite the nature of the transmission, the voice was as harshly clear as if the man speaking were stuffed into the turret with his task force commander. For intelligibility, the AI expanded the bytes of transmitted information with sound patterns from its database. If the actual voice wasn't on record, the AI created a synthesis that attempted to match sex, age, and even accent.

In this case, the voice of Colonel Alois Hammer was readily available for comparison with the burst transmission.

"Slammer Six to Tootsie Six," the colonel rasped. "Absolute priority. You must not, I say again, must not, delay. I believe we can provide limited artillery support for you when you break through at la Reole. If that isn't sufficient, I'm ordering you to detach your tank element and proceed with your combat cars by the quickest route feasible to the accomplishment of your mission. I repeat, I order you to carry on with combat cars alone if you can't cross your tanks at la Reole. Over."

Over indeed.

"Send target overlay," June Ranson said aloud. Her index finger traced across the main screen the symbols of Consie positions facing la Reole. "Execute."

Artillery support? Had Hammer sent down a flying column including a hog or two, or was he expecting them to risk their lives—and mission—on Yokel tubes crewed by nervous draftees?

The transmitter squealed again.

She didn't like being inside a tank. The view was potentially better in every respect than what her eyes and helmet visor could provide from *Warmonger*'s deck, but it was all a simulation. . . . "What do you think, Lieutenant Cooter?" Ranson said, as though she were testing him for promotion.

"Junebug," the lieutenant's worried voice replied, "let's run the gauntlet at la Reole, even with the bridge damaged. Trying t' bust what they got at Kohang without the panzers, that'll be our butts sure."

So, Lieutenant . . . You'd commit your forces on a vague suggestion of artillery support—when you know that the enemy is in bunkers, with heavy weapons already targeted on the route your vehicles must take from the point you penetrate the encirclement?

Ranson slapped blindly to awaken herself, wincing with pleasure and a rush of warmth when her fingers rapped something hard. Her skin was flushed.

"Right," she said—aloud, alert. "Let's see what kind of artillery we're talking about."

She looked at the blank relay screen. "Tootsie Six to Hammer Six," *No need for priority now.* "I and my XO judge the Blue Element to be necessary for the successful completion of our mission. Transmit details of proposed artillery support. Over."

Ranson rubbed her eyes. "Execute," she ordered the AI.

"Blue Two to Tootsie Six," her headset said.

She should've involved Ortnahme—and Sparrow, he was Blue Element Leader—in the planning. She had to think like a task force commander, not a grading officer. . . .

"Junebug, if the friendlies can lay some sorta surface covering on the bloody water," the warrant leader was saying, "agricultural film on a wood frame, that'd do, just enough to spread the effect, we can—"

"Negative, Blue Two," Ranson interrupted. "This is a river, not a pond. The current'd disrupt any covering they could cobble together, even if the Consies weren't shelling. I don't want you learning to swim. Over."

"Tootsie Six," grunted Ortnahme: twice her age and in a parallel—though noncommand—pay grade. "That bloody bridge has major structural damage. I don't want to learn to dive bloody tanks from twenty meters in the air, neither. Blue Two out."

If you want it safe, Blue Two, you're in the wrong line of work tonight.

Chuckle; green light. "Play burst."

"Slammer Six to Tootsie Six. There's an operable hog at Camp Progress with nineteen rounds in storage. Using extended-range boosters, it can cover la Reole. One of the transit-company staff is ex-artillery; he's putting together a crew. By the time you need some bunkers hit, the tube'll be ready to do it."

Zip from the console, as the AI replaced the pause which the burst compression had edited out.

"Speed is absolutely essential. If you don't get to Kohang within the next six hours, we may as well all have stayed home. Over."

"Tootsie Six to Slammer Six," Ranson said with textbook precision. She could feel her soul merging with that of the nameless tank, viewing the world through its sensors and considering her data in an electronic balance. "Task Force Ranson will proceed in accordance with the situation as it develops. We will transmit further data if a fire mission is required. Tootsie Six, out. Execute."

She was the officer on-site. She would make the final decision. And if Colonel Hammer didn't like it, what was he going to do? Put her in command of a suicide mission?

"Tootsie Six," said her headset, "this is Blue Two. The hog's operable, all right. The trouble's in the turret-traversing mechanism, and that won't matter for a few rounds to a single point. But I dunno about the bloody crew. Over."

"Six, Three," Cooter's voice responded. "Chief Lavel's solid as they come. He'll handle the fire control, and the rest—that's just lift 'n carry, right? Getting the shells on the conveyor? Nothin' even a newbie with a room-temperature IQ's going t' screw up. Over."

She would make the final decision.

"All Tootsie elements," June Ranson heard her voice ordering calmly. Her touch shrank the map's scale; then her index finger traced the course to la Reole on the screen.

"Transmit," she said. "We will proceed on the marked trace to Phase Line Piper—" fingertip stroking the crest across a shadowy valley from the Consie positions above the beleaguered town on the Santine Estuary "—and punch through enemy lines to the bridge after a short artillery preparation. Prepare to execute in five minutes. Tootsie Six out."

She used the seat as a step instead of raising herself to the hatch with its power lift. Clouds streaked the sky, but the earlier thin overcast was gone.

The Lord have mercy on our souls.

CHAPTER NINE

"Sarge," said Holman on the intercom, "why aren't we just crossing the river instead of fooling with a damaged bridge? When I was in trucks, we'd see the line companies go right around us while we was backed up for a bridge. Down, splash, up the far bank, and gone."

Now that the task force had moved into open country, Holman

was doing a pretty good job of keeping station. You couldn't take somebody straight out of a transport company and expect them to drive blind *and* over broken terrain—with no more than forty hours of air-cushion experience to begin with.

If your life depended on it, though, that was just what you did expect.

"Combat cars have that much lift," Wager explained bitterly. "*These* mothers don't. Via! but I wish I was back in cars."

He was down in the turret, trying to get some sort of empathy with his screens and controls before the next time he needed them. He was okay on mine-clearing, now; he had the right reflexes.

But the next time, Tootsie Six wouldn't be ordering him to lay a mine-clearance charge, it'd be some other cursed thing. It'd be the butt of Hans Wager and the whole cursed task force when he didn't know what the hell to do.

"Look, Holman," he said, because lift was something he *did* understand, lift and tribarrels laying fire on the other mother before he corrected his aim at you. "We're in ground effect. The fans pressurize the air in the plenum chamber underneath. The ground's the bottom of the pressure chamber, right? And that keeps us floating."

"Right, but—"

Holman swore. The column was paralleling the uphill side of a wooded fenceline. She'd attempted to correct their tank's tendency to drift downslope, but the inertia of 170 steel and iridium tonnes had caught up with her again. One quadrant of Wager's main screen exploded in a confetti of splintered trees and fence posts.

"Bleedin' motherin' martyrs!" snarled the intercom as Holman's commo helmet dutifully transmitted to the most-recently accessed recipient.

Friction from the demolished fence and vegetation pulled the tank farther out of its intended line, despite the driver's increasingly violent efforts to swing them away. When the cumulative over-corrections swung the huge pendulum *their* way, the tank lurched upslope and grounded its right skirt with a shock that rattled Wager's head against the breech of the main gun.

Bloody amateur!

Like Hans Wager, tank commander.

Blood and martyrs.

"S'okay, Holman," Wager said aloud, more or less meaning it. "Any one you walk away from."

He'd finally cleared the mines at Happy Days, hadn't he?

"Look, the lift," he went on. "Without something pretty solid underneath, these panzers drop. Sink like stones. But combat cars, the ones you been watchin', they've got enough power for their weight they can use thrust to keep 'em up, not just ground effect."

Wager wriggled the helmet. It'd gotten twisted a little on his brow when he bounced a moment ago. Their tank was now sedately tracking the car ahead, as though the mess behind them had been somebody else's problem.

"Only thing is," Wager continued, "A couple of the cars, they're running shorta fan or two themselves by now. Talkin' to the guys on One-one while we laagered. Stuff that never happens when you're futzing around a firebase, you get twenty kays out on a route march and *blooie.*"

"We're all systems green," Holman said. "Ah, Sarge? I think I'm gettin' the hang of it, you know? But the weight, it still throws me."

"Yeah, well," Wager said, touching the joystick cautiously so as not to startle the other vehicles. The turret mechanism whined restively; Screen Two's swatch of rolling farmland, centered around the orange pipper, shifted slightly across the panorama of the main screen.

"Look, when we get to the crossing point, if we do, get across that cursed bridge *fast*, right?" he added. "It's about ready to fall in the river, see, from shelling? So put'cher foot on the throttle 'n keep it there."

"No, Sarge."

"*Huh?*"

"Sarge, I'm sorry,"Holman said, "but if we do that,we bring it down for sure. And us. Sarge, look, I'm, you know, I'm not great on tanks. But I took a lotta trucks over piddly bridges, right? We'll take it slow and especially no braking or acceleration. That'll work if anything does. I promise. Okay?"

She sounded nervous, telling a veteran he was wrong.

She sounded like she curst well thought she was right, though.

Via, maybe she was. Holman didn't have any line experience . . . but that didn't mean she didn't have *any* experience. They needed everything they could get right now, her and him and everybody else in Task Force Ranson. . . .

"They say she's a real space cadet," Wager said aloud. "Her crew does. Cap'n Ranson, I mean."

"Because she's a woman," Holman said flatly.

"Because she flakes out!" Wager snapped. "Because she goes right off into dreamland in the middle a' talking."

He looked at the disk of sky speeding past his open hatch. It didn't seem perceptibly brighter, but he could no longer make out the stars speckling its sweep.

"At least," said Holman with a touch more emotion than her previous comment, "Captain Ranson isn't so much of a flake that she'd go ahead with the mission without her tanks."

"Yeah," said Sergeant Hans Wager in resignation. "Without us."

Camp Progress stank of death: the effects of fire on scores of materials; rotting garbage that had been ignored among greater needs; and the varied effluvia each type of shell and cartridge left when it went off.

There was also the stench of the wastes which men voided as they died.

It was a familiar combination to Chief Lavel, but some of the newbies in his work crew still looked queasy.

A Consie had died of his wounds beneath the tarp covering the shells off loaded from the self-propelled howitzer. It wasn't until the shells were needed that the body was found. The corpse's skin was as black as the cloth of the uniform which the gas-distended body stretched.

They'd get used to it. They'd better.

Lavel massaged the stump of his right arm with his remaining hand as he watched eight men cautiously lift a 200mm shell, then lower it with a clank onto the gurney. They paused, panting.

"Go on," he said, "One more and you've got the load."

"Via!" said Riddle angrily. There were bright chafe lines on both of the balding man's wrists. "We can rest a bloody—"

"Riddle!" Level snapped. "If you want to be wired up again, just say the word. Any word!"

Two of the work crew started to lower their clamp over the remaining shell in the upper of the two layers. The short, massive round was striped black and mauve.Ridges impressed in the casing showed where it would separate into three parts at a predetermined point in its trajectory.

"Not that one!" Level ordered sharply. "Nor the other with those markings. Just leave them and bring the—bring one of the blue-and-whites."

Firecracker rounds that would rain over four hundred anti-personnel bomblets apiece down on the target area. No good for smashing bunkers, but much of the Consies' hasty siege works around la Reole lacked overhead cover. The Consies'd die in their trenches like mice in a mincer when the firecracker rounds burst overhead. . . .

Level stumped away from the crew, knowing that they could carry on well enough without him. He was more worried about the team bolting boosters onto the shells already loaded onto the hog. A trained crew could handle the job in a minute or less per shell, but the scuts left at Camp Progress when the task force pulled out. . . .

Scuts like Chief Level, a derelict who couldn't even assemble artillery rounds nowadays. A job he could do drunk in the dark a few years ago, back when he'd been a man.

But he had to admit, he felt alive for almost the first time since Gresham's counter-battery salvo got through the net of cyan bolts that should've swept it from the sky. It wasn't any part of Level's fault, but he'd paid the price.

That's how it was in war. You trusted other people and they trusted you . . . so when you screwed up—

—and Chief knew he'd screwed up lots of times in the past, you couldn't live and not transpose a range figure *once*—

—it was some other bastard got it in the neck.

Or the arm and leg. What goes around, comes around.

Lavel began whistling "St.James' Infirmary" between his teeth as he approached the self-propelled howitzer. *His* self-propelled howitzer for the next few hours.

Craige and Komar, transit drivers who hadn't been promoted to line units after a couple years service each, seemed to have finished their task. Six assembled rounds waited on the hog's loading tray.

Between each 200mm shell (color-coded as to type) and its olive-drab base charge was a white-painted booster. The booster contained beryllium-based fuel to give the round range sufficient to hit positions around la Reole.

Lavel checked each fastener while the two drivers waited uneasily. "Allright," he said at last, grudging them credit for the task he could no longer perform. "All right. They should be coming with the next load now."

He climbed the three steps into the gun compartment carefully. The enclosure smelled of oil and propellant residues. It smelled like home.

Lavel powered up, listening critically to the sound of each motor and relay as it came live. The bank of idiot lights above the targeting console had a streak of red and amber with a green expanse: the traversing mechanism failed regularly when the turret was rotated over fifteen degrees to either side.

Thank the Lord for that problem. Without it, the howitzer wouldn't 've been here in Camp Progress when it was needed.

Needed by Task Force Ranson. Needed by Chief Lavel.

He sat in the gun captain's chair, then twisted to look over his shoulder. "Are you clear?" he shouted to his helpers. "Keep clear!"

For choice, Lavel would have stuck his head out the door of the gun compartment to make sure Craige and Komar didn't have their hands on the heavy shells. That would mean picking up his crutch and levering himself from the chair again. . . .

Level touched the execute button to start the loading sequence.

The howitzer had arrived at Camp Progress with most of a basic load of ammunition still stowed in its hull. For serious use, the hog would have been fed from one or more ammunition haulers, connected to the loading ramp by conveyor belts.

No problem. The nineteen rounds available would be enough for *this* job.

Seventeen rounds. Two of the shells couldn't be used for this purpose. But seventeen was plenty.

The howitzer began to swallow its meal of ammunition, clanking and wobbling on its suspension. Warrant Leader Ortnahme had ordered the shells off loaded and stored at a safe distance—from him—as soon as the hog arrived for maintenance. That quantity of high explosive worried most people.

Not Chief Level, who'd worked with it daily—until some other cannon-cocker got his range.

CLUNK. CLUNK. The first six rounds would go into the ready-use drum, from which the gun could cycle them in less than fifteen seconds.

CLUNK. CLUNK. Each round would be launched as an individually targeted fire mission. The hog's computer chose from the ready-use drum the shell that most nearly matched the target parameters.

For bunkers, an armor-piercing shell or delay-fused high explosive if no armor piercing was in the drum. Soon down the line until, if nothing else were available, a paint-filled practice round blasted out of the tube.

CLUNK. The loading system refilled the ready-use drum automatically, until the on-board stowage was exhausted and the outside tray no longer received fresh rounds. Level could hear the second gurney-load squealing closer.

CLUNK.

The drum was loaded—six green lights on the console. He could check the shell-types by asking the system, but there was no need. He'd chosen the first six rounds to match the needs of his initial salvo.

A touch threw the target map up on the screen above the gunnery console. The drone's on-board computer had processed the data before dumping it.

Damage to buildings within la Reole—shell burst patterns as well as holes—provided accurate information as to the type and bearing of the Consie weapons. When that data was superimposed on the raw new siege works, it was easy for an artificial intelligence to determine the location of the enemy's heavy weapons, the guns that were dangerous to an armored task force.

One more thing to check. "TOC," Lavel said to his commo helmet.

No response for ten seconds, thirty . . . The first shell of the new batch clanged down on the loading ramp.

"Tech 2 Helibrun," a harried voice responded at last. "Go ahead, Yellow Six."

Yellow Six. Officer in command of Transit. Lavel's lips curled.

"I'm waiting for the patch to Tootsie Six," he said, more sharply than the delay warranted. "Why haven't I been connected?"

"The bl—" the commo tech began angrily. He continued after a pause to swallow. "Chief, the patch is in place. We don't have contact with the task force yet, is all. From the data we've got from Central, it'll be about an hour before they're on ground high enough that we can reach them from here."

Another pause; instead of an added, *you cursed fool,* simply, "We'll connect you when we do. Over."

Lavel swallowed his own anger. He was getting impatient; which was silly, since he'd waited more than seven years already. . . .

"Roger," he said. "Yellow Six out."

Another shell dropped onto the ramp. There would be plenty of time to load and prepare all seventeen rounds before the start of the fire mission.

Over an hour to kill, and to kill. . . .

The lower half of June Ranson's visor was a fairy procession of lanterns. They hung from tractor-drawn carts and bicycles laden with cargo.

"Action front!" Ranson warned. She was probably the only person in the unit who was trying to follow a remote viewpoint as well as keeping watch on her immediate surroundings.

The reflected cyan crackle from *Deathdealer*'s stabilized tribarrel provided an even more effective warning.

The main road from the southwest into la Reole and its bridge across the Santine Estuary was studded with figures and crude vehicles. Hundreds of civilians, guided—guarded—by a few black-clad guerrillas, were lugging building materials uphill to the Consie siege lines.

The lead tank of Task Force Ranson had just snarled into view of them.

Sparrow's first burst must have come from the bellowing darkness so far as the trio of Consies, springing to their feet from a lantern-lit guardpost, were concerned. The guerrillas spun and died at the roadside while civilians gaped in amazement. Without light-enhanced optics, the tank cresting a plowed knoll 500 meters away was only sound and a flicker of lethal cyan.

Civilians flung down their bicycles and sought cover in the ditches beside the road. Bagged cement; hundred-kilo loads of reinforcing rods; sling-loads of brick—building materials necessary for a work of destruction—lay as ungainly lumps on the pavement.

The loads had been pushed for kilometers under the encouragement of armed Consies. Bicycle wheels spun lazily in the air.

A rifleman stood up on a tractor-drawn cart and fired in the general direction of *Deathdealer*. Sparrow's tribarrel spat bolts at a building on the ridgeline, setting off a fuel pump in a fireball.

Ranson, Janacek, and at least two gunners from car One-five, the left outrider, answered the rifleman simultaneously.

The Consie's head and torso disappeared with a blue stutter. The canned goods which filled the bed of the cart erupted in a cloud of steam. The tractor continued its plodding uphill progress. Its driver had jumped off and was running down the road, screaming and waving his arms in the air.

There were no trucks or buses visible in the convoy. The Consies must have commandeered ordinary transport for more critical purposes, using makeshifts to support the sluggish pace of siegework.

In the near distance to the east of Task Force Ranson, the glare of a powergun waked cyan echoes from high clouds. One of the weapons which the Consies had brought up to bombard la Reole—a pedestal-mounted powergun. The weapon was heavy enough to hole a tank or open a combat car like a can of sardines. . . .

"Booster!" Ranson shouted to her AI. "Fire mission Able. Break. Tootsie Three, call in Fire Mission Able directly—in clear—as soon as you raise Camp Progress. Break. All Tootsie elements, follow the road. They can't 've mined it if they're using it like this. Go! Go! Go!"

Warmonger bucked and scraped the turf before clearing a high spot. Willens had wicked up his throttles. Though he'd lifted the car for as much ground clearance as possible, *Warmonger*'s present speed guaranteed a bumpy ride on anything short of a pool table.

Speed was life now. These terrified civilians and their sleepy guards had nothing to do with the mission of Task Force Ranson, but a single lucky slug could cause an irreplaceable casualty. Colonel Hammer was playing this game with table stakes. . . .

In the roar of wind and gunfire, Ranson hadn't been able to hear the chirp of her AI transmitting.

If it *had* transmitted. If the electronics of a combat car jolting along at speed were good enough to bounce a transmission a thousand kays north from a meteor track. If Fire Central would relay the message to Camp Progress in time. If the hog at Camp Progress . . .

Two men shot at *Warmonger* from the ditch across the road.

Ranson fired back. Bolts ripped from the rotating muzzles of her powergun and vanished from her sight. It wasn't until the lower half of her visor blacked momentarily and the upper half quivered with cyan reflections that she realized that she'd been aiming at the remote image from *Deathdealer*.

Part of June Ranson's mind wondered what her bolts had hit, might have hit. The part in physical control continued to squeeze the butterfly trigger of her powergun and watch the cyan light vanish in the divided darkness of her mind. . . .

★ ★ ★ ★

The night ahead of Dick Suilin was lit spitefully by the fire of the other armored vehicles. He clung to the coaming of *Flamethrower*'s fighting compartment with his left hand; his right rested on the grip of his tribarrel, but his thumb was curled under his fingers as if to prevent it from touching the trigger.

There were no signs of Consies shooting back, but a farm tractor had collapsed into a fuel fire that reminded Suilin of the bus after his bolts raked it.

Oh dear Lord. Oh dear Lord.

Gale was lighting his quarter with short bursts. So far as the reporter could tell, the veteran's bolts were a matter of excitement rather than a response to real targets. Lieutenant Cooter gripped the armor with both hands and shouted so loudly into his helmet microphone that Suilin could hear the sounds though not the words.

Both veterans had a vision of duty.

Dick Suilin had his memories.

When the armored vehicles prickled with cyan bolts, they reentered the reporter's universe. It had been very easy for Suilin to believe that the three of them in the back of *Flamethrower* were the only humans left in the strait bounds of existence. The darkness created that feeling; the darkness and the additional Wide-awake he'd accepted from Gale.

Perhaps what most divorced Suilin from that which had been reality less than two days before was the buzzing roar of the fans. Their vibration seemed to jelly both his mind and his marrow.

Since the driver slid his throttles to the top of their range, *Flamethrower*'s skirt jolted repeatedly against the ground. Suilin found the impacts more bearable than the constant, enervating hum of the car at moderate speed.

Task Force Ranson swung raggedly at an angle to the left. Each armored vehicle followed a separate track, though the general line was on or parallel to the paved highway.

Suilin had ridden the la Reole/Bunduran road a hundred times in the past. It was easy to follow the road's course now with his eyes,

because of the fires lit by powerguns all along its course. The truckers'
cafe and fuel point at the top of the ridge, three kilometers from la
Reole, was a crown of flames.

Flamethrower lurched over a ditch and sparked her skirts on the
gravel shoulder. The driver straightened his big vehicle with port,
then starboard sidethrusts. The motion rocked Suilin brutally but
seemed to be expected by the veterans with him in the fighting compartment.

Gale shot over the stern, and Cooter's weapon coughed bursts
so short it appeared to be clearing its triple throats.

A dozen civilians huddled in the ditch on Suilin's side of the car.
All but one of them were pressed face-down in the soft earth. Their
hands were clasped over the back of their heads as if to force themselves still lower.

The exception lay on her back. A powergun had decapitated her.

Suilin tried to scream, but his throat was too rigid to pass the
sound.

"*Shot!*" crackled his headphones, but there was shooting everywhere. As armored vehicles disappeared over the brow of the ridge,
all their weapons ripped the horizon in volleys. Cooter had explained
that the Consie siegeworks were just across a shallow valley from
where Task Force Ranson would regain the road.

A Consie wearing crossed bandoliers rolled upright in the ditch
fifty meters ahead of *Flamethrower*. He aimed directly at Suilin.

Cooter saw the guerrilla, but the big lieutenant had been raking
the right side of the road while Gale covered the rear. He shouted
something and tried to turn his tribarrel.

Suilin's holographic sights were a perfect image of the Consie,
whose face fixed in a snarl of hate and terror. The guerrilla's cheeks
bunched and made his moustache twitch, as though he were trying
to will his rifle to fire without pulling the trigger.

The muzzle flashes were red as heart's blood.

Flamethrower jolted over debris in the road. A bicycle flew
skyward; the air was sharp with quicklime as bags of cement ruptured.
Three bullets rang on the armor in front of Dick Suilin and
ricocheted away in a blaze of sparks.

As the car settled again, Suilin's tribarrel lashed out: one bolt short, one bolt long . . . and between them, the guerrilla's hair and the tips of his moustache ablaze to frame what had been his face.

Flamethrower was past.

The sky overhead began to scream.

Hans Wager was strapped into his seat. He hated it, but at least the suspended cradle preserved him from the worst of the shocks.

The tank grounded on the near ditch; sparked its skirts across the pavement in red brilliance; and grounded sideways on the ramp of the drainage ditch across the road. Holman hadn't quite changed their direction of travel, though she'd pointed them the right way.

The stern skirts dragged a long gouge up the road as Holman accelerated with the bow high. The main screen showed a dazzling roostertail of sparks behind the nameless tank. Wager didn't care. He had too much on his own plate.

Deathdealer fired its main gun.

That was all right for Birdie Sparrow, an experienced tanker and riding the lead vehicle. Wager'd set the mechanical lock-out on his own 20cm weapon.

He didn't trust the electronic selector when there were this many friendly vehicles around. A bolt from the main gun would make as little of a combat car as it would of a church choir.

Hans Wager was determined that he'd make this *cursed, bloody* tank work for him. Nothing would ever convince him that a tank's sensors were really better than three sets of human eyeballs, sweeping the risks of a battlefield—

But there weren't three sets of eyeballs, just his own, so he *had* to make the hardware work.

The threat sensor flashed a Priority One carat onto the main screen. Wager couldn't tell what the target was in the laterally compressed panorama. The cupola gun, slaved to the threat sensor the way Albers explained it could be, was already rotating left. It swung the magnified gunnery display of Screen Two with it.

Two bodies and one body still living, a Consie huddling beside what had been a pair of civilian females. The guerrilla's rifle was slung across his back, forgotten in his panic. He was too close for the tribarrel to bear.

The tank's skirts swept a bicycle and sling-load of bricks from the road, flinging the debris ahead and aside of its hundred-and-seventy-tonne rush. Chips and brickdust pelted the Consie. He leaped up.

His chest exploded in cyan light and a cloud of steam which somersaulted the corpse a dozen meters from the ditch.

There'd been a major guardpost at the truckstop on the hill, but *Deathdealer* and the crossfire of the two leading combat cars had already ended any threat from that quarter. Fuel roared in an orange jet from the courtyard pump. The roof of the cafe had buried who-ever was still inside when tribarrels cut the walls away.

"*Shot,*" said his commo helmet. The voice of whoever was acting as fire control was warning that friendly artillery would impact in five seconds.

Three bodies sprawled: a step, another step, and a final step, from the front door of the cafe.

Deathdealer dropped over the hill. Its main gun lighted the far valley. The nameless tank topped the ridgeline with a roar. Their speed and Holman's inexperience lofted the vehicle thirty centimeters into the air at the crest.

Hans Wager, bracing himself in his seat, toggled the main gun off safe.

The low ridge a kilometer away paralleled the Santine River and embraced the western half of la Reole. The Consies had used the road to bring up their heavy weapons and building materials for substantial bunkers.

Three shells, dull red with the friction of their passage through air, streaked down onto the enemy concentration. The earth quivered.

The initial results were unremarkable. A knoll shifted, settled; a hundred meters south of that knoll, dust rose in a spout like that of a whale venting its lungs; a further hundred meters south, black smoke puffed—not from the hilltop but well beneath the crest where raw dirt marked the mouth of a recently excavated tunnel.

The knoll erupted, then settled again into a cavity that could have held a tank.

Blue light fused and ignited dust as a store of powergun ammunition devoured itself and the weapon it was meant to feed.

The tunnel belched orange flame; sucked in its breath and blazed forth again. The second time, the edge of the shock wave propelled a human figure.

Three more shells streaked the sky. One of them hit well to the south. The others were aimed at targets across the estuary.

Deathdealer raked the far ridge with both main gun and tribarrel. The combat cars shot up sandbag-covered supply dumps on both sides of the road. Most of the armed Consies would be in bunkers, but any figure seen *now* was fair game for as many guns as could bear on it.

Long before they topped the ridge, Wager had known what his own target would be.

A mortar firing at night illuminates a thirty-meter hemisphere with its skyward flash. There'd been such a flash, needlessly highlighted by the tank's electronics, before the Consies realized they were being taken in the rear.

Wager hated mortars. Their shells angled in too high to be dealt with by the close-in defense system, and a direct hit would probably penetrate the splinter shield of a combat car.

Now a mortar and its crew were in the center of Wager's gunnery screen.

Normally the greatest danger to a mortar was counterfire from another mortar. A shell's slow, arching trajectory was easy for radar to track, and the most rudimentary of ballistic computers could figure a reciprocal. The guerrillas here had been smart: they'd mounted their tube on the back of a cyclo, a three-wheeled mini-truck of the sort the civilians on Prosperity used for everything from taxis to hauling farm produce into town.

At the bottom of the slope, work crews had cleared a path connecting several firing positions. The cyclo had just trundled into a revetment. Shell cartons scattered outside the position 200 meters up the track showed where the crew had fired the previous half-dozen rounds.

The Consie mortarmen were turned to stare with amazement at the commotion behind them. The sparkling impact as Wager's tank landed, half on the pavement and half off, scattered the crew a few paces, but the tanker's shot was in time. . . .

The center of the cyclo vanished: Wager had used his main gun. The 20cm bolt was so intense that the explosion of cases of mortar ammo followed as an anticlimax.

Several of the mortar shells were filled with white phosphorous. None of the crewmen had run far enough to be clear of the smoky tendrils whose hearts would blaze all the way through the victims on which they landed.

The nameless tank swept past flaming heaps of food, bedding, and material. Ammunition burned in harmless corkscrews through the sky and an occasional *ping* on the armor.

More shells from Camp Progress howled overhead and detonated, six of them almost simultaneously this time. A curtain of white fire cloaked the siege lines as hundreds of anti-personnel bomblets combed crevices to lick Consie blood.

The leading vehicles, *Deathdealer* and two combat cars, had slowed deliberately to let the salvo land. Holman matched her tank's attitude to the slope and drew ahead with the inertia she'd built on the downgrade. She spun the nameless tank with unexpected delicacy around the shell crater gaping at the hillcrest.

The artillery had flung dozens of bodies and bodyparts out of eviscerated bunkers. Holman slowed to a crawl so that Wager could pick his targets on the reverse slope.

Men in black uniforms were climbing or crawling from trenches which shells had turned into abattoirs. Wager ignored them. His AI highlighted the firing slits of bunkers which the shells had spared.

Every time his pipper settled, his foot trod out another 20cm bolt.

Jets of plasma from powerguns travelled in a straight line and liberated all their energy on the first solid object they touched. Wager's bolts couldn't penetrate the earth the way armor-piercing projectiles did—but their cyan touch could shake apart hillsides in sprays of volcanic glass.

The interior of a bunker when a megajoule of plasma spurted through the opening was indescribable Hell.

Deathdealer pulled over the crest a hundred meters to the left of Wager's tank. Its main gun spat bolts at the pace of a woodpecker hammering. Sparrow's experience permitted him to fire in a smooth motion, again and again, without any pause greater than that of his turret rotating to bear on the next target.

La Reole sprawled half a kilometer away. The nearest buildings had been shattered by shellfire and the first flush of hand-to-hand fighting before the Consies retreated to lick their wounds and blast the Yokel garrison into submission.

Smoke lifted from a dozen points within the town. A saffron hint of dawn gaped on hundreds of holes in the tile roofs.

An amphibious landing vehicle pulled down from the protection of a courtyard in the town and opened fire with its machine gun. Consies emerging from a shell-ravaged bunker stumbled and fell. Wager remembered the Yokels had a Marine Training Unit here at la Reole. . . .

The tank's turret was thick with fumes. Wager breathed through filters, though he didn't remember them clamping down across his mouth and nose.

He stamped on the firing pedal. The gun wheezed instead of firing: he'd shot off the entire thirty-round basic load, and the tank had to cycle more main gun ammunition from storage deep in the hull.

There weren't any worthwhile targets anyway. Every slit that might have concealed a cannon or powergun was a glowing crater. Streaks of turf smoldered where bolts had ripped them.

Deathdealer was advancing again. The muzzle of its main gun glowed white.

"Sarge, should I . . . ?" Wager's intercom demanded.

"Go, go!" he snapped back. "And Via! be careful with the bridge!"

He hoped the Yokels would have sense enough not to shoot at them. For the moment, that seemed like the worst danger.

Three more shells from Camp Progress screamed overhead.

The howitzer still rocked with the sky-tearing echoes of its twelfth round. Chief Lavel was laughing. Only when he turned and met Craige's horrified eyes did he realize that he wasn't alone in the crew compartment.

Craige massaged her ears with her palms. "Ah," she said. "The guys wanta know, you know . . . are we dismissed now?"

Drives moaned as the gun mechanism filled its ready-use drum with the remaining shells in storage. Lavel put his palm against an armored side-panel to feel every nuance of the movement. It was like being reborn. . . .

"Not yet," he said. "When the last salvo's away, we'll police up the area."

The crew compartment was spacious enough to hold a full eight-man crew under armor when the howitzer was changing position. The 200mm shells and their rocket charges were heavy, and no amount of hardware could obviate the need for humans during some stages of the preparation process.

The actual firing sequence required only one man to pick the targets. The howitzer's AI and electromechanical drives did the rest.

It didn't even require a whole man. A ruin like Chief Lavel was sufficient.

He glanced at the panoramic screen mounted on the slanted armor above the gun mantlet. A light breeze had dissipated much of the smoke from the sustainer charges. They burned out in the first seven seconds after ignition. High in the heavens, streaking south were dense white trails where the ramjet boosters cut in.

The beryllium fuel was energetic—but its residues were intensely hygroscopic and left clouds thick enough to be tracked on radar.

The residues were lethal at extreme dilution as well . . . but the boosters ignited at high altitude, and it wasn't Alois Hammer's planet.

Besides, Via! this was a war, wasn't it? There was always collateral damage in war.

"Ah . . ." said Craige. "Sir? When are you going to shoot off the rest?"

"When I get the bloody update from the task force, aren't I?" Lavel snarled. He patted the console. "It's thirty-three seconds to splash from here. We don't fire the last five rounds till we see what still needs to be hit and where the bloody friendlies are!"

The console in front of Lavel began to click and whine. He had a voice link to the task force, but the electronically sensed information, passed from one AI to another, was faster by an order of magnitude.

It was also less subject to distortion, even when, as now, it had to be transmitted over VHF radio.

Besides, the crews of Task Force Ranson had plenty to occupy them without spotting for the guns.

The new data swept all the previous highlights from the targeting overlay. Green splotches marked changes in relief caused by shellbursts and secondary explosions. Denser pinheads of the same hue showed where bolts from the 20cm powerguns of tanks had glazed the terrain, sealing firing positions whether or not the bunkers themselves were destroyed.

No worthy targets remained on the west side of the Santine.

Lavel's light pen touched a bunker on the near bank of the estuary anyway. It had been built to hold a heavy gun, though the AI was sure nothing was emplaced in it yet. That accomplished, Lavel checked the eastern arc of the siege lines.

The east side was lightly held, because most of the Consie forces across the Santine were concentrated on Kohang. The Marine Unit in la Reole could probably have broken out—but in doing so, they would have had to surrender the town and the crucial crossing point. Somebody—somebody with more brains and courage than any of the Yokels at Camp Progress—had decided to hold instead of running.

Lavel had two high-explosive shells, one target solid, and a firecracker round remaining. He chose three east-side bunkers for the HE and the solid. The solid was intended to test the air-defense system of friendly units, but its hundred and eighty kilos weren't going to do anybody it landed on any good. He set his firecracker round to detonate overhead ten seconds after the others splashed.

The console chittered, then glowed green.

Green for ready. Probably the last time Chief Lavel would ever see that message.

He sighed and slapped execute.

The door to the crew compartment was open. Craige wasn't wearing a commo helmet, but she got her hands to her ears at the *chunk!* of the ignition charge expelling the first round from the tube.

The seven-second ROAR-R-R-R-R-R-R-R-R! of the sustainer motor shook the world.

The remaining four rounds blasted out at one-a-second intervals like beads on a rosary of thunder. Their back blasts shoved the howitzer down on its suspension and raised huge doughnuts of dust from the surrounding soil.

All done. The fire mission, and the last shred of meaning in Chief Lavel's life.

There was still a green light on the ready-use indicator.

"Booster!" Lavel snapped. "Shell status!"

"One practice ready," said the console in a feminine voice. "Zero rounds in storage."

Lavel turned, rising from his seat with a face like a skull. "You!" he said to Craige. "How many rounds did you load this last time?"

"What?" said Craige. "How . . . ? Six, six like you told us. Isn't that—"

"*You stupid bastards!*" Lavel screamed as his hand groped with the patch to Task Force Ranson, changing it from digital to voice. "Those last two shells were anti-tank rounds with seeker heads! You killed 'em all!"

All the displays of *Herman's Whore* pulsed red with an Emergency Authenticator Signal. A voice Ortnahme didn't recognize bellowed, "Task Force! Shoot down the friendly incoming! Tank Killer rounds! Ditch your tanks! Ditch!"

Ortnahme pushed the Air Defense selector. It was already uncaged. He'd been willing to take the chance of bumping it by accident so long as he knew it would be that many seconds quicker to activate when he might need it.

Like now.

"Simkins," he said, surprised at his own calm, "cut your fans and ditch. *Soonest!*"

His calm wasn't so surprising after all. There'd been emergencies before.

There'd been the time a jack began to sink—thin concrete over a bed of rubble had counterfeited a solid base. Thirty tonnes of combat car settling toward a technician. The technician was dead, absolutely, if he did anything except block the low side of the car with the fan nacelle he'd been preparing to fit.

Ortnahme had said, "Kid, slide the fan under the skirt *now!*"— calmly—while he reached under the high side of the car. The technician obeyed as though he'd practiced the movement—

And for the moment that the sturdy nacelle supported the car's weight, Warrant Leader Ortnahme had gripped Tech 2 Simkins by the ankle and jerked him out of the deathtrap.

The kid was all thumbs when it came to powertools, but he took orders for a treat. *Herman's Whore* stuttered for a moment as the inertia of the air in her intake ducts drove the fans. The big blower grounded hard and skidded a twenty-meter trench in the soil as she came to rest.

Ortnahme's seat was raising him, not as fast as a younger, slimmer man could've jumped for the hatch without power assist— but Henk Ortnahme *wasn't* bloody young and slim.

He squeezed his torso out of the cupola hatch. The tribarrel was rotating on its Scarf ring, the muzzles lifting skyward in response to the air-defense program.

Blood and martyrs! It was going to—

The powergun fired. Ortnahme couldn't help but flinch away. Swearing, bracing himself on the coaming, he tried to lever himself out of the hatch as half-melted plastic burned the back of his hands and clung to his shirt sleeves.

He stuck. His pistol holster was caught on the smoke grenades he'd slung from a wire where he could reach them easily when he was riding with the hatch open.

Blood and martyrs.

The northern sky went livid with cyan bolts and the white

winking explosions they woke in the predawn haze. *Herman's Whore* and the other tanks were firing preset three-round bursts—not one burst but dozens, on and on.

The incoming shells had been cargo rounds. They had burst, spilling their sheaves of submunitions.

There were hundreds of blips, saturating the armored vehicles' ability to respond. Given time, the tribarrels could eliminate every target.

There wouldn't be that much time.

Simkins rolled to the ground, pushed clear by the tank's own iridium flank as its skirts plowed the sod. He stared up at the warrant leader in amazement.

Ortnahme sucked in his chest, settled onto the seat cushion to get a centimeter's greater clearance, and rose in a convulsive motion like a whale broaching. His knees rapped the coaming, but he would've chewed his legs bloody off if that was what it took to get away *now*.

Hundreds of targets. A firecracker round, anti-personnel and surely targeted on the opposite side of the river. Harmless except for the way the half-kilo bomblets screened the three much heavier segments of an anti-tank—

Ortnahme bounced from the skirt of *Herman's Whore* and somersaulted to the ground. His body armor kept him from breaking anything when he hit on his back, but his breath wheezed out in an animal gasp.

Two brighter, bigger explosions winked in the detonating mist above him.

The third anti-tank submunition triggered itself. It was an orange flash and a streak of white, molten metal reaching for *Deathdealer* like a mounting pin for a doomed butterfly.

It took Birdie Sparrow just under three seconds to absorb the warning and slap the air defense button. The worst things you hear for heartbeats before you understand, because the mind refuses to understand.

The tribarrel slewed at a rate of 100 degrees per second, so even the near one-eighty it turned to bear on the threat from the sky behind was complete in less than two seconds more.

Four and a half seconds, call it. *Deathdealer* was firing skyward scarcely a half second after small charges burst the cases of both cargo shells and spilled their submunitions in overwhelming profusion.

It wasn't the first time that the distance between life and death had been measured in a fraction of a second.

Albers cut the fans and swung *Deathdealer* sideways on residual energy so that they grounded broadside on, carving the sod like a snowplow and halting them with a haste that lifted the tank's off-side skirts a meter in the air.

Sparrow's seat cradled him in the smoky, stinking turret of his tank. Screen Two showed a cloud of debris that jumped around the pipper like snow in a crystal paperweight.

A redlight winked in a sidebar of the main screen, indicating that *Deathdealer*'s integrity had been breached: the driver's hatch was open. In the panoramic display Albers, horizontally compressed by the hologram, was abandoning the vehicle.

"Better ditch too, Birdie," said the horribly ruined corpse of DJ Bell. "This is when it's happening."

"Booster!" Sparrow screamed to his AI. "Air defense! Sort by size, largest first!"

If it'd been two anti-tank rounds, no sweat. The handful of submunitions in each cargo shell would've been blasted in a few seconds, long before they reached their own lethal range and detonated.

"Hey, there's still time." DJ's face was changing; but this time his features knitted, healed, instead of splashing slowly outward in a mist of blood and bone and brains. "Not a lot, but there's time. You just gotta leave, Birdie."

A pair of firecracker rounds, that was fine too. Their tiny bomblets wouldn't more than etch *Deathdealer*'s dense iridium armor when they went off. Hard lines for the combat cars, but that was somebody else's problem . . . and anyway, none of the bomblets were going to land within a kilometer of the task force.

The heavy anti-tank submunitions weren't aimed at this side of the river either. If the shell had been of ordinary construction, it would've impacted on a bunker somewhere far distant from the friendly tanks.

But the submunitions had seeker heads. As they spun lazily from the casing that bore them to the target area, sophisticated imaging systems fed data to their on-board computers.

A bunker would've done if no target higher in the computers' priorities offered.

A combat car would've done very well.

But if the imaging system located a tank, then it was with electronic glee that the computer deployed vanes to brake and guide the submunition toward that prime target.

Too little time.

Birdie Sparrow slammed the side of his fist into the buckle to disengage himself from the seat restraints. A fireball lighted the gunnery screen as *Deathdealer*'s reprogrammed tribarrel detonated a larger target than the anti-personnel bomblets to which the law of averages had aimed it.

"Birdie, *quick*," DJ pleaded. His face was almost whole again.

Sparrow sank back onto his seat as the screen flared again. "No," he whispered. "No. Not out there."

DJ Bell smiled at his friend and extended a hand. "Welcome home, snake," he said.

There was a white flash.

CHAPTER TEN

"Watch it," warned Cooter, ducking beneath the level of his gunshield. Part of Dick Suilin's mind understood, but he continued to stand upright and stare.

The dawn sky was filthy with rags of black smoke, tiny mothholes streaming back in the wind when bomblets exploded. That was nothing, and the crackle of two tank tribarrels still firing as the remaining anti-personnel cloud impacted on the far ridge was little more.

Deathdealer was devouring itself.

The submunition's location, as well as its attitude and range in respect to *Deathdealer*, were determined by a computer more sophisticated than anything indigenously built on Prosperity. The computer's last act was to trigger the explosion that shattered it in an orange fireball high above the tank.

The blast spewed out a projectile that rode the shockwave, molten with the energy that forged and compressed it. It struck *Deathdealer* at a ninety degree angle where the tank's armor was thinnest, over the rear turtleback covering the powerplant.

Hammer's anti-tank artillery rounds were designed to defeat the armor of the most powerful tanks in the human universe. This one performed exactly as intended, punching its self-forging fragment through the iridium armor and rupturing the integrity of the fusion bottle that powered the huge vehicle's systems.

Plasma vented skyward in a stream as intensely white as the heart of a star. It etched and ate away the edges of the hole without rupturing the unpierced portion of the armor. The internal bulkheads gave way.

Plasma jetted from the driver's hatch an instant before the cupola blew open. Stored ammunition flashed from underdeck compartments. It stained the blaze cyan and vaporized the joint between hull and skirts.

The glowing husk of what had been *Deathdealer* settled to the ground. Where the hull overlay portions of the skirt, the thick steel plates melted from the iridium armor's greater residual heat.

The entire event was over in three seconds. It would be days before the hull had cooled to the temperature of the surrounding air.

The thunderclap, air rushing to fill the partial vacuum of the plasma's track, rocked the thirty-tonne combat cars. Suilin's breastplate rapped the grips of his tribarrel.

Across the river, Consie positions danced in the light of hundreds of bomblets. They looked by contrast as harmless as rain on a field of poppies.

"All units," said Suilin's helmet. "Remount and move on. We've got a job to do. Six out."

Another combat car slid between *Deathdealer* and the figure of the tank's driver. He'd been running away from his doomed vehicle until the initial blast knocked him down. He rose to his feet slowly and climbed aboard the car whose bulk shielded him both from glowing metal and remembrance of what had just happened/almost happened.

Flamethrower rotated on its axis so that all three tribarrels could cover stretches of the bunker line the task force had just penetrated.

"We're the rear guard," Cooter said. "Watch for movement."

The lieutenant triggered a short burst at a figure who stumbled along the ridgeline—certainly harmless since he'd crawled from a shattered bunker; probably unaware even when the two cyan bolts cut him down.

Suilin thought he saw a target. He squinted. It was a tendril of smoke, not a person.

He wasn't sure he would have fired anyway.

Other cars were advancing toward the town, but it took some moments for the crews of the surviving tanks to reboard. One of the tanks jolted forward taking *Deathdealer*'s former place at the head of the column.

The fat maintenance officer who captained *Herman's Whore* was still climbing into the cupola of the other giant vehicle. His belt holster flapped loosely against his thigh.

"Here," said Gale, handing Suilin an open beer.

Cooter was already drinking deeply from a bottle. He fired a short burst with his left hand, snapping whorls in the vapor above the ridge.

The Consie siege lines were gray with blasted earth and the smoke of a thousand fires. There must have been survivors from the artillery and the pounding, bunker-ripping fury of the powerguns, but they were no longer a danger to Task Force Ranson.

Suilin's beer was cold and so welcome to his parched throat that he'd drunk half of it down before he realized that it tasted—

Tasted like transmission fluid. Tasted worse than the plastic residues of the empty cases flung from his tribarrel. He stared at the bottle in amazement.

Flamethrower spun cautiously again and fell in behind *Herman's Whore*. Cooter dropped his bottle over the side of the vehicle. He began talking on the radio, but Suilin's numbed ears heard only the laconic rhythm of the words.

Gale broke a ration bar in half and gave part to the reporter. Suilin bit into it, feeling like a fool with the food in one hand and a horribly spoiled beer in the other. He thought about throwing the bottle away, but he was afraid the veteran would think he was spurning his hospitality.

The ration bar tasted decayed.

Gale, munching stolidly, saw the reporter's eyes widen and said, "Aw, don't worry. It always tastes like that."

He wiped his mouth with the back of his hand, grimy with recondensed vapors given off when his tribarrel fired. "It's the Wide-awakes, you know." He fished more of the cones from the pouch beside the cooler, distributing two of them to Cooter and Suilin.

Suilin dropped the cone into a sidepocket. He forced himself to drink the rest of his beer. It was horrible, as horrible as everything else in this bleeding dawn.

He nodded back toward *Deathdealer*, still as bright as the filament of an incandescent lightbulb. "Is it always like . . . ? Is it always like that?"

"Naw, that time, they got the fusion bottle, y' know?" Gale said, gazing at the hulk with only casual interest.

Internal pressures lifted *Deathdealer's* turret off its ring. It slid a meter down the rear slope before welding itself onto the armor at a skew angle. "S' always differ'nt, I'd say."

"Except for the guys who buy it," Cooter offered, looking backward also. "Maybe it's the same for them."

Suilin bit another piece from the chalk-textured, vile-flavored ration bar.

"I'll let you know," he heard his voice say.

"Blue Two," said Captain June Ranson, watching white light from *Deathdealer* quiver on the inner face of her gunshield, "this is Tootsie Six. You're acting head of Blue Section. Six out."

"Roger, Tootsie."

Sergeant Wager's nameless tank, now the first unit in Task Force Ranson, was picking its way through rubble and shell craters at the entrance to la Reole. It had been a new vehicle at the start of this ratfuck. Now it dragged lengths of barbed wire—and a fencepost—and its skirts were battered worse than those of *Herman's Whore*.

The tank's newbie driver swung wide to pull around a pile of bricks and roof tiles. Too wide. The wall opposite collapsed in a gout of brick dust driven by the tank's fans. Uniformed Yokels, looking very young indeed, scurried out of the ruin, clutching a machine gun and boxes of ammunition.

Warmonger slid into the choking cloud. Filters clapped themselves over Ranson's nose. Janacek swore. Ranson hoped Willens had switched to sonic imaging before the dust blinded him.

Dust enfolded her in a soft blur. Static charges kept her visor clear, but the air a millimeter beyond the plastic was as opaque as the silicon heart of a computer.

Sparrow was dead, vaporized; out of play. But his driver had survived, and she could transfer him to Blue Three. Take over from the inexperienced driver—or perhaps for Sergeant Wager, also inexperienced with panzers but an asset to the understrength crew of One-six.

Mix and match. *What is your decision on this point, Candidate Ranson . . . ?*

Something jogged her arm. She could see again.

The tracked landing vehicle had backed into a cross-street again, making way for the lead tank. The dust was far behind *Warmonger*. The third car in line was stirring it back to life.

A helmeted major in fatigues the color of mustard greens—a Yokel Marine—waved toward them with a swagger stick while he shouted into a hand communicator.

"Booster, match frequencies," Ranson ordered.

She saw through the corners of her eyes that Stolley and Janacek were exchanging glances. How long had her eyes been staring blankly before Stolley's touch brought her back to the physical universe?

". . . onsider yourselves under my command as the ranking National officer in the sector!" the headphones ordered Ranson as her AI found the frequency on which the major was broadcasting. "Halt your vehicles now until I can provide ground guides and reform my defensive perimeter."

"Local officer," Ranson said, trusting her transmitter to overwhelm the handheld unit even if the Yokel was still keying it, "this is Captain Ranson, Hammer's Regiment. That's a negative. We're just passing through."

The Yokel major was out of sight behind *Warmonger*. A ridiculous little man with creased trousers even now, and a coating of dust on his waxed boots and moustache.

A little man who'd held la Reole with a battalion of recruits against an attack much heavier than that which crumpled three thousand Yokels at Camp Progress. Maybe not so ridiculous after all. . . .

"Local officer," Ranson continued, "I think you'll find resistance this side has pretty well collapsed. We'll finish off anything we find across the river. Slammers out."

La Reole had been an attractive community of two-and three-story buildings of stuccoed brick. Lower floors were given over to shops and restaurants for bridge traffic. Shattered glass from display windows now jeweled the pavement, even where shellfire had spared the remainder of the structures.

The highway kinked into a roundabout decorated with a statue, now headless; and kinked again as it proceeded to the bridge approaches. The buildings on either side of the dogleg had been reduced to rubble. The Consie gunners hadn't been able to get a clear shot at the bridge with their direct-fire weapons or to spot the shells their mortars and howitzers lobbed toward the span.

"No! No! No!" shouted the major, his voice buzzy and attenuated by interference from drive fans. "You're needed here! I order you to stop—and anyway, you can't cross the bridge, it's too weak. Do you hear me! Halt!"

Another landing vehicle sheltered in a walled forecourt with its diesel idling. The gunner lifted his helmet to scratch his bald scalp, then saluted Ranson. He was at least twice the age of any of the six kids in the vehicle's open bay, but they were all armed to the teeth and glaring out with wild-eyed fury.

The Consies had attempted a direct assault on la Reole before they moved their heavy weapons into position. That must've gotten interesting.

A few civilians raised their heads above window sills, but they ducked back as soon as any of the mercenaries glanced toward them.

"Local Officer," Ranson said as echoes of drive fans hammered her from the building fronts, "I'm sorry but we've got our orders. You'll have to take care of your remaining problems yourself. Slammers out."

She split her visor to take the remote from the new lead tank. The controls had reverted to direct view when transmission from *Deathdealer* ceased.

The bridge at la Reole was a suspension design with a central tower in midstream and slightly lower towers on either bank to support the cables. Consie gunners had battered the portions of the towers which stuck up above the roof peaks. They had shattered the concrete and parted the cable on the upstream side.

The span sagged between towers, but the lowest point of its double arc was still several meters above the water. The downstream cable continued to hold, although it now stretched over piles of rubble instead of being clamped firmly onto the towers. A guardpost of Marines with rocket launchers, detailed to watch for raft-borne Consies, gaped at the huge tank that approached them.

"Willens," Ranson ordered her driver, "hold up."

The lower half of her visor swayed as the tank moved onto the raised approach.

"All Tootsie units, hold up. One vehicle on the bridge at a time. Take it easy. Six out."

The lead tank was taking it easy. Less than a walking pace, tracking straight although the span slanted down at fifteen degrees to the left side. Flecks of gravel and dust flew off in the fan draft, then drifted toward the sluggish water.

There were cracks in the asphalt surface of the bridge. Sometimes the cracks exposed the girders beneath.

The Yokel major was shouting demands at June Ranson,but she heard nothing. Her eyes watched the bridge span swaying, the images in the top and bottom of her visor moving alternately.

"Just drive *through* it, kid," snarled Warrant Leader Ortnahme as he felt *Herman's Whore* pause. Close to the bridge, la Reole had taken a tremendous pasting from Consie guns. Here, collapsed buildings cascaded bricks and beams from either side of the street.

The tank seemed to gather itself on a quivering column of air. "Like every bloody body else did!" Ortnahme added in a raised voice.

Simkins grabbed handfuls of his throttles instead of edging them forward in the tiny increments with which he normally adjusted the tank's speed and direction. The pause had cost them momentum, but *Herman's Whore* still had plenty of speed and power to batter through the obstacle.

Larger chunks of building material parted to either side of the blunt prow like bayou scum before a barge. Dust billowed out from beneath the skirts in white clouds. It curled back to feed through the fan intakes.

Behind the great tank, wreckage settled again. The pile had spread a little from the sweep of the skirts, but it was built up again by blocks and bits which the thunder of passage shook from damaged buildings.

"Sorry, sir," muttered Simkins over the intercom.

The kid's trouble wasn't that he couldn't drive the bloody tank: it was that he was too bloody careful. Maybe he didn't have the smoothness of, say, Albers from . . .

Via. Maybe not think about that.

Simkins didn't have the smoothness of a veteran driver, but he had plenty of experience shifting tanks and combat cars in and out of maintenance bays where centimeters counted.

Centimeters didn't count in the field. All that counted was

getting from here to there without delay, and doing whatever bloody job required to be done along the way.

Ortnahme sighed. The way he'd reamed the kid any time Simkins brushed a post or halted *in* the berm instead of *at* it, he didn't guess he could complain now if his technician was squeamish about dingin' his skirts.

Simkins eased them to a halt just short of the bridge approach. Cooter's blower was making the run—the walk, rather—and bleedin' Lord 'n martyrs, how the *hell* did they expect that ruin to hold a tank?

The near span rippled to the rhythm of *Flamethrower*'s fans, and the span beyond the crumbling central support towers still danced with the weight of the car that'd crossed minutes before. This was bloody *crazy*!

The Yokels guarding the bridge must've thought so too, from the way they stared in awe at *Herman's Whore*.

Ortnahme, hidden in the tank's belly, glared at their holographic images. They'd leaned their buzzbomb launchers against the sand-bagged walls of their bunker.

Hard to believe that ten-kilo missiles could really damage something with the size and weight of armor of *Herman's Whore*, but Henk Ortnahme believed it. He'd rebuilt his share of tanks after they took buzzbombs the wrong way—and, regretfully, had combat-lossed others when the cost of repair would exceed the cost of buying a new unit in its place.

There were costs for crew training and, less tangibly, for the loss of experience with veteran crewmen; but those problems weren't in Ortnahme's bailiwick.

"Sir?" the intercom asked. "The . . . you know, the guns they been hitting this place with. Wasn't that a, you know, an awful lot?"

"Don't worry about it, kid," the warrant leader said smugly. "Our only problem now's this bloody bridge."

Ortnahme adjusted his main screen so that the panorama's stern view was central rather than being split between the two edges.The shattered bunkers were hidden by the same buildings that'd protected the bridge from Consie gunfire. Smoke, turgid and foul, covered the western horizon.

"Ah, sir?" Simkins said. "What I mean is, you know, we been fighting guerrillas, right? But all this heavy stuff, this was like a war."

A Yokel jeep jolted its way over the rubble pile in the wake of Task Force Ranson. The driver was young and looked desperately earnest. The Marine major who'd gestured in fury as *Herman's Whore* swept into la Reole at the end of the Slammers' column sat/stood beside the driver.

The officer was covering his mouth and nose with a handkerchief in his left hand while his right gripped the windshield brace to keep his ass some distance in the air. The jeep could follow where air cushions had taken the Slammers, but the wheeled vehicle's suspension and seat padding were in no way sufficient to make the trip a comfortable one.

"This war's been goin' on for bloody years, kid," Ortnahme explained.

His thumb rotated the panorama back to its normal orientation. Bad enough watching the bridge sway, without having the screen's image split *Flamethrower* right down the middle that way.

"They got, the Consies, they been hauling stuff outa the Enclaves all that time, sockin' it away. Bit by bit till they needed it for that last big push. All that stuff—" Ortnahme nodded toward the roiling destruction behind them, though of course the technician couldn't see the gesture "—that means the Consies just shot their bolt."

Ortnahme scratched himself beneath the edge of his armor and chuckled. "Course, it don't mean they didn't *hit* when they shot their bloody bolt."

Cooter's blower had just reached the far end of the bridge—safely, Via! but this tank weighed five, six, times as much—when the image on the main screen changed sharply enough to recall the warrant leader from his grim attempt to imagine the next few minutes.

Though *Herman's Whore* pretty well blocked the bridge approach, the driver of the Yokel jeep managed to slide around them with two wheels off on the slope of the embankment. As the jeep gunned its way back onto the concrete, its image filled a broad swath of Ortnahme's screen.

What the bloody *hell?*

The major threw down his makeshift dust filter, rose to his full height, and began to shout and gesture toward the tank. The young Marines at the bunker beside *Herman's Whore* snapped to attention— eyes front, looking neither toward the tank nor their screaming officer.

Ortnahme could've piped the Yokel's words in through a commo circuit, scrubbed of all the ambient noise. Thing was, whatever the fellow was saying, it sure as hell wasn't anything Warrant Leader Henk Ortnahme wanted to hear.

"Simkins!" he said. "Can you get by these meatballs?"

"Ah . . . Without hitting the jeep?"

"Can you get bloody *by*, you dickhead?"

Herman's Whore shifted sideways like a beerstein on a slick, wet bar. The fan note built for a moment; then, using all his maintenance-bay skills, Simkins slid them past the jeep closer than a coat of paint.

The wheeled vehicle shrank back on its suspension as the sidedraft from the plenum chamber buffeted it, but metal didn't touch bloody metal!

That Yokel major was probably still pissed off. When the jeep bobbed in the windthrust, he fell sideways out of his seat. Let him file a bloody complaint with Colonel Hammer—in good time.

The left side of the tank tilted down, but that didn't bother the warrant leader near as much as the motion. It'd been bad watching the bridge sway when another vehicle was on it. The view on Ortnahme's screens hadn't made his stomach turn, though, as the reality bloody well did. Blood and martyrs, they were—

They were opening wide cracks in the asphalt surface as they passed over it. The tank's weight was stretching the underlying girders beyond their design limits.

The cracks spread forward, outrunning *Herman's Whore* in its sluggish progress toward the supporting pier in the center of the estuary.

And that *bloody* fool of a major had climbed back into his jeep. His driver had two wheels and most of the jeep's width on the narrow downstream sidewalk, using the span's tilt to advantage because it prevented the tank's sidedraft from flipping the lighter vehicle right through the damaged guardrail.

Those sum'bitch Yokels were trying to pull around the tank and block it on this shuddering nightmare of a bridge.

"Kid," Ortnahme began, "don't let 'em—"

He didn't have to finish the warning, because Simkins was already pouring the coal to his fans.

The water of the Santine Estuary was sluggish and black with tannin from vegetable matter that fed it on the forested hills of its drainage basin. Glutinous white bubbles streaked the surface, giving the current's direction and velocity. The treetrunks, crates, and other solid debris were more or less hidden by the fluid's dark opacity.

Ortnahme had a very good view of the water because of the way *Herman's Whore* tilted toward it.

They were approaching the central pier now while the span behind them flexed like the E-string of a bass guitar. The jeep, caught in the pulses and without the tank's weight to damp them, bounced all four wheels off the gaping roadway while the two Yokels clung for dear life.

Consie shells and the bolts from their one bunkered powergun had reduced the central towers to half their original height. The Yokels at the guardpost there were already climbing piles of rubble to be clear of the oncoming tank. *Herman's Whore* wasn't rocketing forward, but a tank head-on at twenty kph looks like Juggernaut on a joyride.

Their speed was four times what Ortnahme had planned, given the flimsy structure of the bridge. He just hadn't realized *how* bloody flimsy.

They *had* to go fast!

Ortnahme's helmet crackled with angry demands from the east bank. He switched the sound off at the console.

Tootsie Six could burn him a new one if she wanted, just as soon as *Herman's Whore* reached solid ground again. Until then, he didn't give a hoot in Hell what anybody but his driver had to say.

They reached the central pier in a puff of dust and clanging gravel, debris from the towers. Task Force Ranson's previous vehicles had rammed a track clear, but the kid was moving too fast to be nice about what his skirts scraped.

The Yokel jeep halted on the solid pier. The major shook his fist, but he didn't seem to be ordering his guards to try buzzbombs where verbal orders had failed.

Via, maybe they were going to make it after all. That newbie crew in Blue Three had crossed, hadn't—

A cable parted, whanging loud enough to be clearly audible. A second *whang!*, a third—

The bow of *Herman's Whore* was tilting upward. The intake howl of her fans proved that Simkins had both throttle banks slid wide flat open.

It wasn't going to be enough.

The cables parting were the short loops every meter or so, attaching the main support cable to the bridge span. Each time one broke, the next ahead took the doubled strain of the tank's weight—and broke in turn. The asphalt roadway crumbled instantly, but the unsupported stringers beneath continued to hold for a second or two longer—until they stretched beyond steel's modulus of tension.

Thirty meters behind *Herman's Whore*, the span fell away from the central pier and splashed into the estuary. Froth from its impact drifted sullenly downstream.

The tank was accelerating toward safety at fifty kph and rising, but their bow was pointing up at thirty-five, forty, forty-five—

For an instant, *Herman's Whore* was climbing at an angle of 47° with the east tower within a hundred meters and the round, visored faces of everybody in the task force staring at them in horror. Then the spray of the tank bellying down into the estuary hid everything for the few seconds before her roaring fans stalled out in the thicker medium.

Warrant Leader Ortnahme lifted his foot to the top of his seat and thrust his panting body upward. His eyes had just reached the level of the cupola hatch when water rushing in the opposite direction met him.

Easy, easy. He was fine if he didn't bloody panic. . . . The catches of his body armor, top and bottom; shrugging sideways, feeling them release, feeling the ceramic weight drop away instead of sinking even *his* fat to a grave in the bottom muck.

The water was icy and tasted of salt. Bubbles of air gurgled past Ortnahme as *Herman's Whore* gave its death rattle. Violet sparks flickered in the blackness as millions of dollars worth of superb, state-of-the-art electronics shorted themselves into melted junk.

Ortnahme's skin tingled. His diaphragm contracted, preventing him from taking the breath he intended as a last great gurgling shivered past his body to empty the turret of air. He shoved himself upward to follow the bubble to the surface.

He was halfway through the hatch when his equipment belt hooked on the string of grenades again.

The warrant leader reached down for the belt buckle. The drag of water on his shirt sleeves slowed the movement, but it was all going to be—

The belt had twisted. He couldn't find the buckle though his fingers scrabbled wildly and his legs strained upward in an attempt to break web gear from which Ortnahme's conscious mind knew you could support a bloody *howitzer* in midair.

Air. Blood and martyrs. He tried to scream.

Herman's Whore grounded with a slurping impact that added mud to the taste of salt and blood in Ortnahme's mouth. They couldn't be more than three meters down; but a millimeter was plenty deep enough if it was over your mouth and nose.

Plenty deep enough to drown.

The darkness pressing the warrant leader's eyes began to pulse deep red with his heartbeats, a little fainter each time. He thought he felt something brush his chest, but he couldn't be sure and he didn't think his fingers were moving anymore.

The wire parted. A grip on Ortnahme's belt added its pull to the warrant leader's natural buoyancy.

Sunlight came as a dazzling explosion. Ortnahme bobbed, sneezed in reaction. Water sprayed from his nostrils.

Tech 2 Simkins was dog-paddling with a worried look. He was

trying to retract the cutting blade of his multitool, but his face kept dipping beneath the surface.

One of the combat cars had just waddled down the bank. It was poised to lift across the water as soon as the man in the stern— Cooter, it was, from his size and the crucifix on his breastplate— unlimbered a tow line for the swimmers to grab as the car skittered by.

"Sir," Simkins said. His face was wet from dunking, but Ortnahme would swear there were tears in his eyes as well. "Sir, I'm sorry. I tried to hold it but I—"

He was blubbering, all right, but the black water slapped him again when he forgot to paddle. Sometimes being hog fat and able to float had advantages. . . .

"Sir—" the kid repeated as his streaming visage lifted again.

"Via, kid!" Ortnahme said, almost choking on his swollen tongue. He'd bitten the bloody hell out of it as he struggled. "Will you shut yer bleedin' trap?"

Flamethrower roared as it moved onto the water.

"If I ever have a son," Ortnahme shouted over the fan noise, "I'll name the little bastard Simkins!"

CHAPTER ELEVEN

"I thought," said Dick Suilin, looking down at the silent trench line as *Flamethrower* accelerated past, "that we'd have to fight our way out of la Reole, too."

It must have rained recently, because ankle-deep mud slimed the bottom of the trench. Two bodies lay face down in it. Their black uniforms smoldered around the holes chewed by shell fragments.

The bruises beneath Suilin's armor itched unbearably. "I wonder what my sister's doing," he added inconsequently.

"The Consies were just tacking the west bank down," Cooter said, his eyes on his multi-function display. "Nothin' serious."

"Nothin' that wasn't gonna run like rabbits when the shells hit—them as could," Gale interjected with a chuckle.

"All their heavy stuff this side of the river," the lieutenant continued, "that's at Kohang."

He shrugged. "Where we'll find it quick enough, I guess."

"Where's your sister?" Gale asked. The veteran gunner poked a knifepoint into the crust around the ejection port of his tribarrel. Jets of liquid nitrogen were supposed to cool and expel powergun rounds from the chambers after firing. A certain amount of the plastic matrix remained gaseous until it condensed on the outside of the receiver, narrowing the port.

Suilin unlatched his body armor and began rubbing the raw skin over his ribs. His fatigue shirt was sweaty, but the drenching in salt spray from the estuary seemed to have made the itch much worse.

"She's in Kohang," the reporter said. It was hard to remember what he'd said to whom about his background, about Suzette. "She's married to Governor Kung."

The past two days were a blur of gray and cyan. Maybe fatigue, maybe the drugs he was taking against the fatigue.

Maybe the way his life had been turned inside out, like the body of the Consie guerrilla his tribarrel had center punched. . . .

"Whoo-ie!" Gale chortled. "Well, if that's who she is, I sure hope she don't mind meetin' a few good men. Er a few hundred!"

The reporter went cold.

Cooter reached over and took Gale's jaw between a big thumb and forefinger. "Shut up, Windy," he said. "Just shut the fuck up, all right?"

"Sorry," muttered the wing gunner to Suilin. He brushed his mouth with the back of his hand. "Look, the place's still holdin', far as we know. We'll get there, no sweat."

He nodded to Cooter. "Anything on your box, El-tee?"

"Nothing yet. Junebug'll report in pretty quick, I guess."

The task force was moving fast in the open country between la Reole and Kohang further up the coast. A clump of farm buildings stood beneath an orchard-planted hillside two kilometers away.

Suilin found it odd to be able to see considerable distances with his normal eyesight. He felt as though he'd crewed *Flamethrower* all his life, but this was the first time he'd been aboard the combat car during daylight.

Almost daylight. The sun was still beneath the horizon. His fingertips massaged his ribs.

"You okay?" Gale asked unexpectedly.

"Huh?" Suilin said. He looked down at his bruises. "Oh, yeah. I—the armor, last night a bullet hit it."

He saw Gale's eyes widen in surprise a moment before he realized the cause. "Oh," he corrected. "I mean the night before. At Camp Progress. I lost track. . . ."

Cooter handed out ration bars. The reporter stared at his with loathing, remembering the taste of the previous one.

"Go ahead," Cooter encouraged. "You need the calories. The Wide-awakes, they'll keep you moving, but you need the fuel to burn anyhow."

Suilin bit down, trying to ignore the flavor. This bar seemed to have been compressed from muck at the bottom of the estuary.

The two tankers they'd rescued wanted to stay together, so Cooter had transferred them both to One-six. The vehicles of Task Force Ranson were fully crewed at the moment—over-crewed, in fact.

Dick Suilin had seen at Adako Beach how quickly a short burst could wipe out the crew of a combat car. Without the firepower of the two tanks lost at la Reole . . .

Funny to have another combat car directly ahead of *Flamethrower*. The only view of the task force the reporter'd had during most of the night was the stern of the tank which now lay at the bottom of the Santine.

"Will they raise her?" he asked. "The, that is, the tank that fell off the bridge?"

"Through the bloody bridge," Gale corrected.

"The hull's worth something," Cooter said.

His lips pursed in a moue. "Maybe the gun could be rebuilt to standard. But the really pricy stuff's the electronics, and that's all screwed for good 'n all. I figure the colonel, he'll combat-loss it and the other one both and try to squeeze a victory bonus outa your people to pay for 'em."

His eyes swept the horizon, looking for an enemy or a sign. "Lord knows we'll 've earned a bonus. If we win."

The display box beside Cooter's tribarrel clucked and spat.

"C'mon, El-tee," Gale demanded greedily. "What's she sayin'?"

"Give it a minute, will you?" the lieutenant said as he stared at his display. "It's a coded burst, right? And that takes a while."

Gale nodded to Suilin. "Tootsie's talkin' to the Old Man," the veteran explained. "Ain't meant for us to hear, but this close, we kin read anything she kin code."

He giggled. "The black box giveth and the black box taketh away."

"Bloody hell," Cooter muttered.

"Well, *c'mon!*"

"She told him we were across the Santine," Cooter said, still watching the display where holograms spelled words decoded by the vehicle's AI. "She told him about the casualties. Told him we were going ahead with the mission."

"Well, what did ya bloody expect?" Gale snorted. "Come this far and settle down to rest 'n refit?"

Cooter turned to face the other two men. He looked very worn. "Also she told Central," he went on, "that we were getting messages from First of the 4th Armored Brigade. They're ahead of us and they're requesting our positions so they can join up with us."

"Via," said Gale.

Dick Suilin blinked. "So we'll have a National armored battalion to support us entering Kohang?" he said, puzzled at the mercenaries' attitude. "I didn't realize there were any friendly units this near the city."

"Via," Gale repeated. He scowled at the tribarrel, picking at the ejection port with a cracked fingernail. "How many bloody tanks in a Yokel battalion?"

In the frozen moment before anybody else spoke, Dick Suilin remembered the truck he'd ripped apart near the Padma, a National Army vehicle filled with troops in National Army uniforms.

"I said it was First of the 4th," Cooter said. "I didn't say they were friendly."

★ ★ ★ ★

Warmonger had settled into a reed-choked draw. The other vehicles were invisible, but June Ranson's display indicated that all of them were in place and awaiting her orders.

Steam rising from la Reole behind them was golden in the light of sunrise.

Janacek watched her expectantly; Stolley scanned the sky past the reed bracts with a scowl of displeasure. He knew there wasn't a prayer that he'd be able to hit any incoming with his tribarrel, but he was determined to try.

Blue Three was the only task force vehicle in the open, poised 300 meters to the east on what passed for high ground in this coastal terrain. Its cupola gun quivered in air-defense mode.

Whether their sole remaining tank could provide *sufficient* defense depended on what came through the air at the task force while its leader held the vehicles grounded for a council of war.

Maybe nothing would come. Probably nothing would come.

"Booster," said Junebug Ranson. "Council display, all Tootsie units."

Her multi-function display hummed and clicked. Faces glowed in the thirty-centimeter cube, replacing the holographic map and location beads. She'd have done better to use the tank's big screens, but she couldn't risk leaving her command vehicle here.

They were within twenty kays of Kohang. Everything that had occurred since they left Camp Progress, the danger and the losses, was only a prelude to what would happen in the next few hours.

Faces—the entire fighting-compartment crews of the other four combat cars, and the tense, tight lipped visage of Wager in the turret of Blue Three—crowded the multi-function display.

For a moment, no one spoke; the crews were waiting for Ranson, and June Ranson's mind was extending into a universe of phosphor dots.

The image of Cooter's face brightened and swelled slightly to highlight it as the lieutenant said, "Junebug, we gotta figure these guys've gone over to the Consies. They left Camp Victory without orders, just before the general attack. Only question is, do we go around 'em or do we fight 'em?"

"We're tasked to get there, not to fight, ain't we?" said Tillman, blower captain of One-five. At the best of times, Tillman was a thin, sallow man. The past two days had sweated off weight he couldn't afford to lose.

"Look, just in case they are friendly . . ." said Chalkin. He looked sour, partly because he was crowded in the fighting compartment of One-six with Ortnahme and Simkins as well as the shot-up survivors of the car's original crew. "I wouldn't mind havin' fifty tanks alongside us when we hit Kohang, even if it's Yokels."

"Max of forty-four tanks," interjected Warrant Leader Ortnahme, looking at something off-screen low, probably his clenched knuckles. There were problems on One-six, *Daisy Belle*; not just the crowding, but a fat noncombatant with a lot of rank, dropped on a blower commanded by a mere senior trooper on transfer.

"There were forty-four at their bloody laager when the drone overflew 'em," Ortnahme continued, looking straight at the pickup in the car's multi-function display. "Some'll be dead lined, twenty percent given what passes fer Yokel maintenance."

His fingers rose into the tiny field-of-view, ticking off the third point: "Some more drop out on the route march to block us when they've finl'ly get the lead out. So, say thirty-five max, maybe thirty."

"And," said Cooter's voice in the enfolding electronic tendrils of June Ranson's mind, "there's no bloody way—"

"—that those bastards're friendly," Cooter snapped at the hologram display beside his tribarrel while Dick Suilin shivered on the ribbed plastic crates of ammunition lining the interior of the fighting compartment.

At the signal to halt in dispersed order for council, *Flamethrower* had forced its way into a thicket of knotbushes. Their gnarled branches sprang back to full four-meter height behind the vehicle, concealing the combat car on all sides and even covering it fairly well from above.

"Look, just 'cause they sat out the last couple days—" argued a voice that had spoken earlier, not one that the reporter recognized.

The net wasn't wide open, as Suilin first thought. The computer—the AI—controlling the discussion cut off whoever was talking the instant someone higher in the hierarchy began to speak.

"There was *no* sign from the recce flight that they'd been hit," Cooter boomed onward. "With all the Consies did the other night, there was *no* chance they'd 've ignored a tank battalion—except it'd gone over or it was about t' go over."

Suilin's face was turned slightly away from the display. There was probably a way to magnify the images through his helmet visor, but he didn't much care.

He felt awful, as though he were in the midst of a bad bout of flu. Despite his chills, his throat felt parched. He gestured toward the cooler on which Gale sat.

The veteran shook his head, then nodded in explanation toward the display.

"Later," he said in a husky whisper that presumably wouldn't carry to the pickup. He tossed Suilin another Wide-awake. "You're on the down side. No sweat. You'll get used t'it."

"Via, still wouldn't mind havin' the help," muttered a voice from the display. "*Some* cursed help."

The cone sent needles of delicious ice up the throat vein to which Suilin applied it. Gray fog cleared from his eyes. The holographic display sprang into focus, though the figures in it were featurelessly small.

He realized that Captain Ranson hadn't spoken during the discussion.

As though the jolt of stimulant in the reporter's bloodstream had unblocked the commander's tongue, the mercenary captain's cool—cold—voice said, "We are nearly in contact with a force of uncertain loyalty, estimated to be a battalion of thirty to thirty-five armored vehicles."

Tiny, toothed birds jumped and chittered through the branches of the knot-bushes, ignoring the iridium monster in their midst. Their wings were covered with pale fur, familiar to Suilin but probably exotic to his mercenary companions.

"If the battalion is allied with the Conservative Action Movement, it will threaten the rear of Task Force Ranson as the task force performs its mission of breaking through hostile forces encircling the Governmental Compound in Kohang."

The sense of glacial well-being reached Suilin's fingertips. His hands stopped shaking.

Probably *not* exotic. The Lord only knew how many worlds, how many life-forms, these scarred veterans had seen uncaring on their career of slaughter for money. . . .

"The loyalty of the battalion must first be ascertained. If hostile, the force must be engaged and neutralized before Task Force Ranson proceeds with its primary mission."

"Thirty bloody tanks," Cooter whispered.

"We will proceed as follows. First, I will inform the armored battalion that we have received heavy casualties and have taken refuge in the settlement of Kawana."

"Even bloody Yokel tanks. . . ."

"Blue three—"

Hans Wager's head jerked up. You can only stay scared for so long. Ranson's clop-clop mechanical delivery had bored him, so his attention had been on the holographic plan of a Yokel tank he'd called up on Screen Three.

"—will take a position north of Kawana, behind Chin Peng Rise."

"Roger, Tootsie Six," Wager said, suddenly afraid that he'd actually fallen asleep and missed some crucial part of the Operations Order.

"Set your sensors for maximum sensitivity," Ranson's voice continued without noticeable emotion. "You will supply the precise location and strength of the other force. In event the force proves hostile, you will be the blocking element to prevent them breaking out to the north."

"Roger, Tootsie Six," Wager repeated in a whisper.

They didn't operate with Yokel armor—the difference in speed was too great, and the mercenaries had a well-justified concern about the fire discipline of the local forces in general.

Still, Wager'd looked over Yokel tanks out of curiosity. Memories echoed in his mind when his eyes rested on the holographic image.

"We can expect the other force to continue their approach from due south," Ranson's bored, boring voice continued. "Tootsie Three, you'll command the eastern element. Proceed with your blower and One-six clockwise from Chin Peng Rise, around Kawana by Hull Creek and Raider Camp Creek. Stay out of sight. Wait at the head of Raider Camp Creek, a kilometer east of Sugar Knob to the south of Kawana."

Via, thirty of them. If it wasn't thirty-five.

Or forty-four, despite Blue Two's scorn of the Yokel's ability to keep their hardware operational.

Each tank weighed sixteen point eight tonnes. They were track-laying vehicles with five road-wheels per side and the drive sprocket forward. Steel/ceramic sandwich armor. Diesel engine on the right side, opposite the driver. A two-man turret with either a high-velocity 60mm automatic cannon or a 130mm howitzer.

Lightweight vehicles, designed for the particular needs of the National Army in a guerrilla war that might at any moment burst into pitched battles with a foe equipped by the Terran World Government.

Nothing Wager's panzer couldn't handle, one on one. Nothing a combat car couldn't handle, one on one.

Thirty. Or thirty-five. Or more.

"I will command the western element," Ranson said coolly. "Cars One-one, One-three, and One-five. We'll circle Kawana by Upper Creek and wait a kilometer west of Sugar Knob until the intentions of the other force become clear."

A shaped-charge round from the 130mm howitzer moved too fast for the close-in defense system to knock it down. A direct hit could penetrate the armor of a Slammers' tank.

The 60mm guns fired either high-explosive shells or armor-piercing shot. A single tungsten-carbide shot wouldn't penetrate Blue Three's hull or turret armor. Three hitting the same point might. Twelve on the same point *would* penetrate.

The clip-loaded 60mm cannon could cycle twelve rounds in twelve seconds.

"Blue Three," Ranson said, "if the other battalion is hostile, we will need *precise* data on enemy dispositions before we launch our counterattack. This may require that you move into the open so that your sensors are unmasked. Do you understand?"

"Roger, Tootsie Six."

Hans Wager's hands were wiping themselves slowly against his pants legs. The rhythmic, unconscious gesture dried his palms for less than the time it took for his arms to move back and start the process again.

"Blue Three—" still no emotion in the voice "—if you like, for this operation I can replace you and your driver with more experienced—"

"Negative!" Wager snarled. He hand-keyed his helmet to break out of the council net. "Tootsie Six, that's a negative. We'll do our job. We understand. Out."

"Roger, Blue Three," said the voice. "All Tootsie units, courses and phase lines are being downloaded into your AIs—now."

Wager's palms rubbed his thighs.

"Sarge?" whispered his intercom. "Thanks."

"Don't thank me, Holman," Wager said. "I think I just bought us both the farm."

Thirty or more guns aimed at them, and Blue Three wouldn't be able to reply until the combat cars had the data needed to target every one of the enemy tanks.

Yeah, he understood all right.

CHAPTER TWELVE

"D'ye got medics along?" the driver from Blue Three whined over the radio, a female voice in June Ranson's ears.

She sounded stunned and terrified, just as she was supposed to. The tank was the only vehicle of Task Force Ranson that would give a close-enough-to-correct reading to Yokel direction finders. . . .

"Via, we need medics. Via, we need help. This is ah, Tootsie Six, over."

A game, a test program for the officer commanding First of the 4th Armored. An electronic construct which was perfectly believable, like any good test program. The officer being tested would be judged on his reactions. . . .

"Booster," Ranson muttered. "Hostile Order of Battle."

She shouldn't have to speak. Electrons should flow from her nerve endings and race down the gold-foil channels of the artificial intelligence, then spring overhigh-frequency carrier waves to the sensorar ray of Blue Three. June Ranson should feel everything.

She should be the vehicles she commanded. . . .

"Tootsie Six, this is Delta three Mike four one," replied the voice that had been unfamiliar until it began whispering over the UHF Allied Common Channel an hour before, requesting Task Force Ranson's position. "We have doctors and medical supplies. We're ten kilometers from Kawana. We'll bring your medical help in half an hour, but you must stay where you are. Do you understand? Mike four one over."

The water of Upper Creek flared beneath *Warmonger* in a veil. The spray was iridescent where daggers of sunlight stabbed it through the low canopy. The two cars closely following *Warmonger* were hidden by the spray and the creek's wide loops.

Upper Creek drained the area south of Sugar Knob. The trees here had been cropped about ten years before so that their cellulose could be converted by bacteria to crude protein for animal feed. The second-growth trees that replaced the original forest were densely packed and had thin boles. They provided good cover, but they weren't obstacles for vehicles of the power and weight of combat cars.

Yokel tanks would find the conditions passable also, even if they left the trails worn by animals and the local populace.

"We can't go anywhere," Blue Three's driver whined. "We—"

Warmonger's artificial intelligence threw a print sidebar on the holographic condenser lens.

"—only got two cars left and they're shot t' bloody hell. We're right at the little store, where the road crosses the crik."

Willens, following the course Ranson and the AI set for him, nosed *Warmonger* against the north bank of the creek. The black, root-laced soil rose only a meter above the black, peat-rich water. The car snorted, then mounted to firm ground through a bending wall of saplings.

The distance between barren Chin Peng Rise and the thin trees of Sugar Knob was about a kilometer and a half. Ranson's western element followed a winding three-kay course to stay low and unnoticed while encircling the Yokels' expected deployment area. Cooter and the two-car eastern element had an even longer track to follow to their hide . . . but the Yokel tanks seemed to be giving them the time they needed.

Willens advanced twenty meters further, to give room to One-five and One-one behind him, then settled with his fans on idle.

Task Force Ranson didn't want to stumble into contact before they knew where all their targets were.

Blue Three's sensors had greater range and precision by an order of magnitude than those crammed into the combat cars, but the cars could process the data passed to them by the larger vehicle. The sidebar on Ranson's multi-function display listed call signs, isolated in the cross-talk overheard by the superb electronics of the tank pretending to be in Kawana while it waited behind Chin Peng Rise north of the tiny hamlet.

There were twenty-five individual call signs. The AI broke them down as three companies each consisting of three platoons—but no more than four tanks in any platoon (five would have been full strength). Some platoons were postulated from a single call sign.

Not all the Yokel tanks would be indulging in the loose chatter that laid them out for Task Force Ranson like a roast for the carving; but most of them would, most of them were surely identified. The red cross-hatching that overlay the relief map in the main field of the display was the AI's best estimate thus far of the armored battalion's dispositions.

Blue Three was the frame of the trap and the bait within it; but the five combat cars of west and east elements were the spring-loaded jaws that would snap the rat's neck.

And this rat, Yokel or Consie, was lying. It was clear that the leading elements of First of the 4th were already deploying onto the southern slope of Sugar Knob, half a kilometer from the store and shanties of Kawana rather than the ten kays their commander claimed.

In the next few seconds, the commander of the armored battalion would decide whether he wanted to meet allied mercenaries—or light the fuse that would certainly detonate in a battle more destructive than any a citizen of Prosperity could imagine. He was being tested. . . .

The two sharp green beads of Lieutenant Cooter's element settled into position.

She heard a whisper in the southern sky. *Incoming.*

"All right, Holman, move us hull-down," Hans Wager ordered as his driver whined, "They're shooting at us! They're shooting at us!" over the Allied Common Channel and the scream of the incoming salvo wrote its own exclamation point in four crashing impacts on the valley below.

The nameless tank lifted, scraped, and hopped forward—up and out of its stand-by hide to a position so near the crest of Chin Peng Rise that the turret and sensor arrays had a clear sight across Kawana to the slumping mass of Sugar Knob beyond.

The hamlet had never been prepossessing. It was less so now that the ill-aimed Consie salvo had shaken down several shacks. Raider Camp Creek roiled with the muddy aftermath of the shell that had landed on it, and the footbridge paralleling the ford had collapsed into the turbid current.

Men and women in the sugarbush fields dropped their tools to run for their homes. The sandy rows in which the bushes were planted would've given better protection than the board walls of the shanties.

That much came to Wager's eyes from the direct view of his main screen. Screen Three displayed the data his chuckling AI processed, a schematic vision of the terrain behind Sugar Knob and the unseen Yokel tanks showing themselves to Wager's sensors.

A sidebar on the main screen noted an incoming second salvo, ten rounds but very ragged—even for Yokel artillery.

The Yokel vehicles were diesel-powered, so Wager's tank couldn't locate them precisely from sparkcoil emissions; but their diesels had injector motors whose RF output could be pinpointed by the Slammers' sensors.

Without the added shielding of Chin Peng Rise to block Blue Three, the crosshatched blur south of Sugar Knob on Screen Three began to coalesce into bright red beads: Yokel tanks, located to within a few meters.

Their disposition explained why the second salvo was so scattered. The Consies were using the 130mm howitzers on ten of their tanks to supplement regular artillery firing from the vicinity of Kohang.

For indirect fire, these tanks were concentrated in a tight arc along Upper Creek. They'd run their bows up on the north bank in order to get more elevation for their howitzers than their turret mechanisms would permit.

The tank shells scattered around Kawana, detonating with white flashes and the hollow *whoomps* characteristic of shape-charge anti-tank warheads. Sand spewed in great harmless fountains.

The store where the unpaved road forded the creek flung its walls sideways at a direct hit. Half a body arced into the water and sank.

"Six, this is Blue Three!" Wager shouted. "Am I clear to shoot?"

Then, though Ranson could see it herself as easily as Wager could if the crazy bitch saw *anything*, "Six, there's ten tanks a kilometer south of the Knob, just off the road, but the rest of the bastards are moving onto the crest!"

The Yokels were moving into direct-fire positions covering Kawana . . . and which covered the tank on Chin Peng Rise with no more cover than the fuzz on a baby's ass.

The saplings on Sugar Knob shifted with the weight of black masses behind them, the dark-camouflaged bows of Consie tanks.

Two, three; seven tanks highlighted by Wager's AI. Their high-velocity 60mm cannons quested toward Kawana like the feelers of loathsome crustaceans. There were men in black uniforms riding on each turret.

If Wager fired, the plasma jolt from his powergun would blind and deafen the sensors on which the combat cars depended.

One of the long-barreled cannon suddenly lifted and turned. The tank commander had seen the gray gleam of the real enemy lurking behind Chin Peng Rise.

Red location beads were still appearing on Screen Three, the same view that was being remoted to the combat car AIs, but surely Ranson had enough data to—

"Tootsie Six!" Hans Wager cried, "Can you clear us?"

"Sarge, I'm backing—" Holman said.

"All Tootsie units," said the voice of Captain Ranson. "Take 'em."

The muzzle flash was a bright yellow blaze against the dark camouflage. The tungsten-carbide shot rang like a struck cymbal on the turret of Wager's nameless tank.

"Willens," said June Ranson, converting the holographic map on her display into a reality more concrete than the stems of young trees around her, "steer one-twenty degrees. West element, conform to my movements."

"Why we doin' this?" Stolley shouted, grabbing the captain's left arm and tugging to turn her.

Off to the left, only slightly muffled by intervening vegetation, the flat cracks of high-velocity guns sounded from the crest of Sugar Knob.

Ranson slipped her arm from the wing gunner's grip. "Thirty seconds to contact," her voice said.

Warmonger's artificial intelligence had given her a vector marker. Her eyes were on it, waiting for the vertical red line to merge with a target in her gunsights.

Stolley cursed and put his hands back on the grips of his tribarrel.

The gunfire from Sugar Knob doubled in intensity. *Warmonger* and the two cars accompanying it were headed away from the knob on a slanting course. As *Warmonger* switched direction, the AI fed another target vector to each gunner's helmet.

A wrist-thick sapling flicked Ranson's tribarrel to the side. Her hands realigned the weapon with the vector. They acted by reflex, unaided by the higher centers of her brain which slid beads of light in a glowing three-dimensional gameboard.

Her solution to the Yokel attack had been as simple and risky as Task Force Ranson's lack of resources required. She was using Slammers' electronics and speed to accomplish what their present gunpower and armor could not.

So, Candidate Ranson. You've decided to divide your force before attacking a superior concentration. Rather like Colonel Custer's plan at the Little Big Horn, wouldn't you say?

But there was no choice. The Yokels would deploy along the ridge. Only by hitting them simultaneously from behind on both flanks could her combat cars roll up six or seven times their number of hostile tanks.

So, Candidate; you're confident that the opposing commander won't keep a reserve? If he does, it's your force—forces, I should say— that will be outflanked.

The Yokels hadn't held back a reserve . . . but the ten tanks lobbing shells over the knob from a kilometer to the rear would *act* as a reserve—if they weren't eliminated first.

Guns fired from Sugar Knob a kilometer away, guns on the Yokel left flank that Ranson had decided to bypass only thirty seconds before—

Warmonger burst into a clearing gray with powdersmoke and dust kicked up by the ten stubby howitzers firing at high angles.

The Yokel tanks had their engines forward and their turrets mounted well back, over the fourth pair of roadwheels. With their hulls raised fifteen degrees by the stream bank, the vehicles bucked dangerously every time they fired their heavy weapons. The water of Upper Creek slapped between the recoiling tanks and its gravel bed.

The tanks were parked in the creek to either side of the road. Less than a three-meter hull width separated each vehicle from its neighbors. While the turret crews fed their guns, the tank drivers stood on both ends of the line of vehicles, mixing with a dozen guerrillas in black uniforms.

The dismounted men covered their ears with their palms and opened their mouths to equalize pressure from the muzzle blasts. When the three combat cars slid from the forest, their hands dropped but their mouths continued to gape like the jaws of gaffed fish.

Men spun and fell, shedding body parts, as Ranson's tribarrel lashed them. The group on the east side of the lined-up tanks had time to shout and run a few steps before *Warmonger* raced down Upper Creek as though the gravel bed were a highway, giving Ranson and Stolley shots at them also.

The Yokel tanks couldn't react fast enough to be an immediate danger, but a single Consie rifleman could clear *Warmonger*'s fighting compartment.

Could *have*. When the last black-clad guerrilla flopped at the edge of the treeline, Willens spun *Warmonger* in a cataclysm of spray and the three tribarrels blazed into the backs on the renegade tanks.

One-one and One-five had followed *Warmonger* into the stream, but they hadn't had to worry about the dismounted enemy. Two of the left-side tanks were already wrapped in sooty orange palls of burning diesel fuel. The turret blew off a third as main gun ammunition detonated in the hull.

Ranson centered her projection sight on a tank's back deck, just behind the turret ring. The target's slope gave her a perfect shot. Cyan bolts streamed through the holographic image of her sight, splashing huge craters in thin armor designed only to stop shell splinters.

In gunnery simulators, the screaming tank crew didn't try to abandon their vehicle a second or two after it was too late. Ranson's bolts punched into the interior of the tank. A blast of foul white smoke erupted from the turret hatches and the cavity ripped by the tribarrel.

The tank commander and the naked torso of his gunner flew several meters in the air. The tank began to burn sluggishly.

June Ranson's hands swung for another target, but there were no targets remaining here.

The tanks' thickest armor was frontal. Striking from above and behind, the tribarrels ripped them as easily as so many cans of sardines.

Cans of barbecued pork. The gunnery simulators didn't provide the odor of close action, either.

All the ammunition on a Yokel tank detonated simultaneously, pushing aside the nearest vehicles and flinging the turret roof fifty meters in the air in a column of smoke.

"Willens, steer three hundred degrees," Ranson heard/said. "West element, form on me."

Her eyes sought the multi-function display, while part of her mind wondered why she couldn't blend with Cooter's vehicles when she wanted to know their progress. . . .

Dick Suilin's ribs slammed hard against the edge of the fighting compartment as *Flamethrower* grounded heavily on its mad rush through the scrub forest. The reporter swore and wondered whether he'd be pissing blood in the morning, despite the clamshell armor that protected his kidney from the worst of the shock.

In the morning. He made a high-pitched sound somewhere between laughter and madness.

He'd fallen sideways because the only thing that he had to hang onto were the grips of his tribarrel. *That* was pointed over the left side, at ninety degrees to the combat car's direction of motion. The reporter swung back and forth as his weapon pivoted.

The blazing red-orange hairline on his visor demanded Suilin cover the left side. He horsed his gun in the proper direction again, wincing at the pain in his side, and tried to find a target in the whipping foliage.

There was no doubt where *Flamethrower*'s artificial intelligence wanted him to aim, though the rational part of the reporter's mind wondered why. They had—they were supposed to have—enveloped the enemy's right wing, so the first targets would be on the right side of *Flamethrower*. . . .

He supposed *Daisy Belle* was somewhere behind them. He supposed the other vehicles of the task force were somewhere also. He hadn't seen much of them. . . .

Dick Suilin supposed a lot of things; but all he knew was that his side hurt, his hands hurt from their grip on the automatic weapon, and that he really should've pissed in the minute while they waited for the go signal.

Flamethrower slid through a curtain of reeds. Two meters from the muzzle of Suilin's tribarrel, *that close*, was a tank with its hatches open, bogged in a swale. The soil was so damp that water gleamed in the ruts the treads had squeezed before being choked to a halt.

Right where the AI's vector had said it would be.

Suilin clamped his trigger so convulsively that he forgot for a moment that he was pointing a weapon. Two bolts splashed on the turret face, cyan and white, blazing steel, before several following rounds exploded stems and flattened further swathes in the reeds with blasts of steam and flying cellulose.

Flamethrower grunted past the tank's bow at the speed of a running horse. The reporter pivoted to follow the target with his gun, ignoring the way he thrust himself against the side armor just as the impact had done moments before.

His sights steadied where a ball mantlet joined the tank's slim cannon to the turret face. Panning like a photographer with a moving subject, Suilin kept the muzzles aligned as they spat cyan hell to within millimeters, bolt by bolt.

Suilin would have kept shooting, but the cannon barrel sagged and a sharp explosion lifted the turret a hand's breadth so that bright flame could flash momentarily all around the ring.

He didn't notice until they were past that there'd been a second tank on the other side of the swale, and that several men in National Army uniforms had been stringing tow cables between the vehicles. The second tank was burning fiercely. The crewmen were sprawled in the arc they'd managed to run before Gale's tribarrel searched them down.

Suilin thought the men were wearing black armbands, but he no longer really cared.

Dick Suilin heard the CRACK-CRACK-CRACK of automatic cannons upslope, the same timbre as machine guns firing but louder, much louder, despite the vegetation.

Shorty Rogers was running the valley south of Sugar Knob at a hellbent pace for the conditions. *Warmonger* cut to the right, bypassing some of the unseen tanks whose gunfire betrayed their presence.

Maybe the course was deliberate. Maybe *Daisy Belle* would take care of the other tanks. . . .

Suilin saw tank tracks slanting toward the crest an instant before he saw the tank itself, backing the way it had come. There was a guerrilla on the turret, hammering at the closed hatch. The Consie shouted something inaudible.

Suilin fired, aiming at the Consie rather than the tank. He missed both; his bolts sailed high to shatter trees on the crest.

That didn't matter. Cooter's helmet had given him the same target. The lieutenant's tribarrel focused on the hull where flowing script read *Queen of the South*. Paint blazed an instant before the armor collapsed and a fuel tank ruptured in a belch of flame.

Beyond *Queen of the South*, backing also, was a command vehicle with a high enclosed cab instead of a turret. Suilin caught only a glimpse of the vehicle before Gale's tribarrel punched through the thin vertical armor of the cab.

The rear door opened. Nothing came out except an arm flopping in its black sleeve.

They had almost reached the top of the knob. If *Daisy Belle* fired at them, the bolts would hit on Gale's side; but if *Flamethrower* was closing with the three cars in Captain Ranson's elements—

Dick Suilin aimed downhill because the glowing line directed him that way, but the artificial intelligence was using data now minutes old. The Consie tank was above them, backing around in the slender trees. It swung the long gun in its turret to cover the threat that bellowed toward it in a drumbeat of secondary explosions.

Suilin tried to point at the unexpected target. Cooter was firing as he swung his own weapon, but that tribarrel didn't bear either and the lash of cyan bolts across treeboles did nothing to disconcert the hostile gunner.

The cannon steadied on *Flamethrower*'s hull.

A 20cm bolt from Blue Three across the valley struck, and the whole stern of the light tank blew skyward.

The Yokel tank's shot was a white streak in the sky as it ricocheted from the face of Blue Three's turret.

Ragged blotches appeared on Wager's main screen as if the hologram were a mirror losing its silver backing. Booster spread the load of the damaged receptor heads among the remainder; the image cleared.

Hans Wager didn't see what was happening to his screen because he was bracing his head against it. He hadn't strapped himself into his seat, and Holman's attempt to back her hundred and seventy tonnes finally succeeded in a rush.

Wager wasn't complaining. His hatch was open and he could hear the *crack-crack* of two more hypersonic shots snapping overhead.

The Yokels' armor-piercing projectiles were only 43mm in diameter when they dropped their sabots at the gun's muzzle, but even here, a kilometer and a half away, they were travelling at 1800 meters per second. The shot that hit had smashed a dish-sized concavity from the face of Blue Three's armor.

"Holman!" Wager cried. "Open season! Get us hull-down again."

They grounded heavily. Wager thought of the strain the tank's huge weight must be putting on the skirts and wondered if they were going to take it. Still, Holman wasn't the first tank driver to get on-the-job training in a crisis.

Anyway, the skirts'd better take it.

Chin Peng Rise had been timbered within the past two years. None of the scrub that had regrown on its loose, rock-strewn soil was high enough to conceal Blue Three's skirts, but the rounded crest itself would protect the hull from guns firing from the wooded knob across the valley.

The thing was, Holman had to halt them in the right place: high enough to clear their main gun but still far enough down the back-slope that the hull was in cover.

Shells boomed among the shacks of Kawana. The residents wouldn't 've had any idea that two armies were maneuvering around them until the artillery started to land.

Innocent victims weren't Hans Wager's first concern right now. Via, it was their planet, their war, wasn't it?

His war too.

A plume of friable soil spewed from beneath the skirts as Holman fed power to her fans. Wager felt Blue Three twist as she lifted. *The silly bitch was losing control, letting 'em slide downhill instead of—*

"Holman!" he shouted. "Bring us up to firing level! They need us over—"

As Wager spoke the tank lifted—there'd been no downward motion, just the bow shifting. They climbed the 20° slope at a walking pace that brought a crisp view of Sugar Knob onto both the main and gunnery displays.

Shot and shells from Yokel cannon ripped the crest beside Blue Three, where the Slammers vehicle had lain hull-down before—and where they'd 've been now if Holman hadn't had sense enough to shift before she lifted them into sight again.

Wager could apologize later.

He'd locked his main and cupola guns on the same axis. His left hand rotated the turret clockwise with the gunnery screen's orange pipper hovering just above the projected crest of Sugar Knob. When the dark bulk of a Yokel tank slid into the sight picture, needlessly carated by the artificial intelligence, Wager thumbed his joystick control and laced the trees with cyan bolts from the tribarrel.

A bolt flashed white on the screen as it vaporized metal from the Yokel tank. Wager stamped on the pedal to fire his main gun.

Two more Yokel shots hit and glanced from Blue Three. Their impact was lost in the *crash* of the 20cm main gun firing.

Across the valley, the rear end of the Yokel tank jumped backward as the front became a ball of glowing gas.

Wager's main screen was highlighting at least a dozen targets, now. The Yokels had moved into positions overlooking Kawana so their direct fire could finish the tattered survivors of Task Force Ranson as soon as the artillery began to impact.

Some of the tank gunners were still focused on the innocent hamlet. Through the corner of his eye, Wager could see spouting tracks in the valley below as automatic cannons raked shacks and the figures running in terror among the sugarbushes they'd been tending.

Dirt blasted up in front of Blue Three an instant before the turret rang to a double hammerblow. Not all the Yokels were deceived as to their real enemy.

There wasn't time to sort 'em out, to separate the immediate dangers from the targets that might catch on in the next few seconds or minute. Hans Wager had to kill them all—

If he had time before they killed him.

Wager let the turret rotate at its own speed, coursing the further crest. He aimed with the cupola gun rather than the electronic pipper. During his years in combat cars, he'd gotten into the habit of hosing a tribarrel onto its target.

When things really drop in the pot, habit's the best straw to snatch.

Ignoring the shots that hit Blue Three and the shots that blasted grab-loads of dirt from the barren crest around them, Wager stroked his foot-trip again—

A tank exploded.

Again.

Too soon. The 20cm bolt ignited a swathe of forest beside the Yokel vehicle, but the tank's terrified crew was already bailing out. Wager's tribarrel spun their lifeless bodies into the blazing vegetation as his turret continued to traverse.

A huge pall of smoke leaped skyward from somewhere south of Sugar Knob. It mushroomed when the pillar of heated air could no longer support the mass of dirt, scrap metal, and pureed flesh it contained.

The ground-shock of the explosion rolled across Kawana in a ripple of dust.

Something hit Blue Three. Three-quarters of Wager's gunnery

screen went black for a moment. He rocked forward on his foot-trip. The main gun fired, shocking the sunlight and filling the turret with another blast of foul gases from the spent case.

The screen brightened again, though the display was noticeably fuzzier. Another of the tanks on Sugar Knob had become a fireball.

The Yokels were running, backing out of the firing positions on the hillcrest that made them targets for Wager's main gun. He didn't know how the combat cars were doing, but there were columns of smoke from behind the knob where his own fire couldn't reach.

The cars'd have their work cut out for them, playing hide 'n seek with the surviving Yokels in thick cover. At point-blank range, the first shot was likely to be the last of the engagement and the tanks' thick frontal armor would be a factor.

A target backed in a gout of black diesel exhaust as Wager's sight picture slid over it. He tripped his main gun anyway, knowing that he'd hit nothing but foliage. His turret continued to traverse, left to right.

The Yokel tank snarled forward again, through the trees the twenty-centimeter bolt had vainly withered. *That sonuvabitch hadn't run, he'd just ducked back to shoot safe—*

In the fraction of a second it took Hans Wager to realize that *this* target had to be hit, that he *had* to reverse the smooth motion of his turret, yellow light flashed three times from the muzzle of the Yokel's cannon.

Hot metal splashed Wager and the interior of the turret. The cupola blew off above him. The tribarrel's ammunition ripped a pencil of cyan upward as it burned in the loading tube.

The gunnery screen was dead, and the central half of the main screen pulsated with random phosphorescence. Motors whined as the turret began tracking counterclockwise across the landscape Wager could no longer see.

"*Blue Three, this is Tootsie Six—*"

Thousand one, thousand two—

"*—we had to bypass the east-flank hostiles. Cross the valley and help us soonest.*"

Wager trod his foot-trip. The gunnery screen cleared—somewhat—just in time to display the Yokel tank disintegrating with an explosion so violent that it snuffed the burning vegetation around the vehicle.

"Roger, Tootsie Six," Hans Wager responded. "Holman, move us—"

But Holman was already feeding power to her fans. You didn't have to tell her what her job was, not that one. . . .

Four more artillery shells burst in black plumes across the sandy furrows which Blue Three had to cross. The remains of Blue Three's cupola glowed white, and there was no hatch to button down over the man in the turret.

Hans Wager's throat burned from the gases which filled his compartment.

He didn't much care about that, either.

"Willens, bring us—" June Ranson began, breaking off as she saw the Yokel tank.

It was crashing through the woods twenty meters to *Warmonger*'s right, on an opposite and almost parallel course. The 60mm cannon was pointed straight ahead, but the black-clad guerrilla riding on the turret screamed something down the gunner's open hatch as he unlimbered his automatic rifle.

Janacek's tribarrel was on target first. Half the burst exploded bits of intervening vegetation uselessly, but the remaining bolts sawed the Consie's legs off at the knee before hammering the sloped side of the turret.

The outer facing of the armor burned; its ceramic cores palled inward, through the metallic backing. It filled the turret like the contents of a shotgun loaded with broken glass. Smoke puffed from the hatches.

The tank continued to grind its way forward for another thirty seconds while Janacek fired into the hull without effect. The target disintegrated with a shattering roar.

Ranson's multi-function display indicated that both the remaining blowers in her element were within fifty meters of *Warmonger*, but she couldn't see any sign of them.

She couldn't *feel* them. They were real only as beads of light; and the red beads of hostile tanks were no longer where Blue Three had plotted them before the Yokels began to retreat. . . .

A tank ground through the screening foliage like a snorting rhinoceros, bow on with its cannon lowered. June Ranson willed a burst through the muzzles of her tribarrel. . . .

Cyan bolts slashed and ripped at glowing steel.

Stolley swung forward. His bolts intersected and merged with the captain's. The cannon's slim barrel lifted without firing and hurled itself away from the crater bubbling in the gun mantle.

"No!" Ranson screamed at her left wing gunner. "Watch your own—"

Another Yokel tank appeared to the left, its gun questing.

"—side!"

Leaves lifted away from the cannon's flashing muzzle. The blasts merged with the high-explosive charges of the shells which burst on *Warmonger*'s side.

The combat car slewed to a halt. The holographic display went dead; Ranson's tribarrel swung dully without its usual power assist.

For the first time in—months?—June Ranson truly saw the world around her.

The Yokel tank was within ten meters. It fired another three-round burst—shot this time. The rounds punched through the fighting compartment in sparkling richness and ignited the ammunition in Janacek's tribarrel.

The gunner bellowed in pain as he staggered back. Ranson grabbed the bigger man and carried him with her over the side of the doomed vehicle. Leaf mould provided a thin cushion over the stony forest soil, but *Warmonger*'s bulk was between them and the next hammering blasts.

"Stolley," Janacek whispered. "Where's Stolley and Willens?"

June Ranson looked over her shoulder. Dunnage slung to *Warmonger*'s sides was ablaze. The thin, dangerous haze of electrical fires spurted out of the fan intakes and the holes shots had ripped in the hull. Where Janacek's tribarrel had been, there was a glowing cavity in the iridium armor.

Willens had jumped from his hatch and collapsed. There was no sign of Stolley.

Ranson rose in a crouch. Her legs felt wobbly. She must have hit them against the coaming as she leaped out of the fighting compartment. She staggered back toward *Warmonger*.

Shots rang against the armor. A chip of white-hot tungsten ripped through both sides to scorch her thighs.

She tried to call Stolley, but her voice was a croak inaudible even to her over the roar of the flames in *Warmonger*'s belly.

The handgrips on the armor were hot enough to sear layers from her hands as she climbed back into the fighting compartment.

Stolley lay crumpled against the bulkhead. He was still breathing, because she could see bubbles forming in the blood on his lips. She gripped his shoulders and lifted, twisting her body.

The synthetic fabric of her trousers was being burned into her flesh as she balanced. Janacek crawled toward them, though what help he could be . . .

Because her back was turned, June Ranson didn't see the tank's cannon rock back and forth as it fired, aiming low into *Warmonger*'s hull. She felt the impacts of armor-piercing shot ringing on iridium—

But only for an instant, because this burst fractured the car's fusion bottle.

Dick Suilin was looking over his shoulder toward the bow of *Flamethrower* when the center of his visor blacked. Through the corners of his eyes, the reporter saw foliage withering all around him in the heat of the plasma flare. His hands and the part of his neck not shielded by visor or breastplate prickled painfully.

The gout of stripped atoms lasted only a fraction of a second. *Warmonger*'s hull, empty as the shell of a fossil tortoise, continued to blaze white.

The Yokel tank, its cannon nodding for further prey, squealed past the wreckage.

Suilin's tribarrel was still pointed to cover the car's rear quadrant. Cooter's burst splashed upward from the tank's glacis plate, blasting collops from the sheath and ceramic core.

Before the tribarrel could penetrate the armor at its point of greatest thickness, the tank's 60mm gun cracked out a three-round clip. Dick Suilin's world went red with a crash that struck him like a falling anvil.

The impact knocked him forward. He couldn't hear anything. The fighting compartment was brighter, because cannon shells had blown away the splinter shield overhead. The sun streamed down past the bare poles of plasma-withered trees.

The ready light over his tribarrel's trigger no longer glowed green. Suilin rotated the switch the way Gale had demonstrated a lifetime earlier. The metal felt cool on his fingertips.

The cannon's muzzle began to recoil behind a soundless yellow flash. *Warmonger* shuddered as Suilin's thumbs pressed his butterfly trigger. Cyan bolts roiled the bottle-shaped flare of unburned powder, then carved the mantlet before the 60mm gun could cycle to battery and fire again.

Steel blazed, sucked inward, and blew apart like a bomb as the tank's ready ammunition detonated.

Suilin's tribarrel stopped firing. His thumbs were still locked on the trigger. A stream of congealed plastic drooled out of the ejection port. The molten cases had built up until they jammed the system.

The hull of the vehicle Dick Suilin had destroyed was burning brightly. Another tank crawled around it. The Consie on the second tank's turret was mouthing orders down the open hatch.

The long cannon swung toward *Flamethrower.*

Lieutenant Cooter rose to his hands and knees on the floor of the fighting compartment. His helmet was gone. There was a streak of blood across the sweat darkened blond of his hair. He shook himself like a bear surrounded by dogs.

Gale sprawled, halfway out of the fighting compartment. A high-explosive round had struck him between the shoulder blades. It was a tribute to the trooper's ceramic body armor that one arm was still attached to what remained of his torso.

Suilin unslung his grenade launcher, aimed at the tank thirty meters away, and squeezed off. He couldn't hear his weapon fire, but the butt thumped satisfyingly on his shoulder. His eye followed the missile on its flat arc to the face of the tank's swivelling turret.

The grenades were dual purpose. Their cases were made of wire notched to fragment, but they were wrapped around a miniature shaped charge that could piece light armor.

Armor lighter than the frontal protection of a tank. The guerrilla flung his arms up and toppled, his chest clawed to ruins by shrapnel, but the turret face was only pitted.

The tank moved forward as it had to do, so that as the turret rotated, the long gun would clear the burning wreckage of the sister vehicle.

Cooter dragged his body upright. He was still on his knees. The big man gripped the hull to either side of his tribarrel, blocking Suilin from any chance of using that weapon.

No time anyway. The reporter's grenades burst on the turret, white sparks that gouged the armor but didn't penetrate, couldn't penetrate.

Two hits, three—not a hand's breadth apart, remarkable rapid-fire shooting as the turret swung.

Suilin thought he could hear again, but the bitter crack of his grenades was lost in the howl of an oncoming storm. The ground shook and made the blasted trees shiver.

The last round in Suilin's clip flashed against the armor as vainly as the four ahead of it. The cannon's 60mm bore gaped toward *Flamethrower* like the gates of Hell.

Before the gun could fire, the great, gray bow of Blue Three rode downhill onto the rebel tank, scattering treeboles like matchwood.

The clang of impact seemed almost as loud to Dick Suilin as that of the shells ripping *Flamethrower* moments before. The Slammers' tank, ten times the weight of the Yokel vehicle, scarcely slowed as it slid its victim sideways across the scarred forest.

A tread broke and writhed upward like a snake in its death throes. The hull warped, starting seams and rupturing the cooling system and fuel tanks in a gout of steam, then fire.

Metal screamed louder than men could. Blue Three's skirts rode halfway up the shattered corpse of the rebel tank, fanning the flames into an encircling manacle. The Slammers driver twisted the hundred and seventy tonnes she controlled like a booted foot crushing an enemy's face into the gutter.

Cooter stood up. Shorty Rogers raised his head from the bow hatch, glanced around, and disappeared again. A moment later, *Flamethrower* shuddered as her fans spun up to speed.

Blue Three backed away from the crackling inferno to which it had reduced its victim. Nothing else moved in the forest.

Dick Suilin's fingers were reflexively loading a fresh clip into his grenade launcher.

CHAPTER THIRTEEN

Task Force Ranson, consisting of one tank and four combat cars under Junior Lieutenant Brian Cooter, was within seven kilometers of the outskirts of Kohang when it received word that Consie resistance had collapsed.

The Governmental Compound within the city was relieved a few minutes later by elements of the 12th and 23rd Infantry Brigades of the National Army.

CHAPTER FOURTEEN

Dick Suilin looked at Kohang with eyes different from those with which he'd viewed the fine old buildings around the park and Governmental Compound only days before.

The stone facades were bullet-pocked now, but Suilin had changed much more than the city had during the intervening hours.

"Good thing we didn't have to fight through these streets," he said.

His voice was a croak from breathing powergun residues. He didn't know whether he'd ever regain the honey-smooth delivery that had been his greatest asset in the life of his past.

Tents had sprouted around the wheeled command vehicles in the central park fronting the Compound. There was a line of tarpaulin-covered bodies beside the border of shattered trees, but for the most part, the National Army soldiers looked more quizzical than afraid.

"Yeah," said Albers, now manning the right wing gun. He spoke in a similar rasping whisper. "Narrow streets and every curst one a' those places built like a bunker. Woulda been a bitch."

"We'd've managed," said Cooter.

I doubt it, Suilin thought. *But we would have tried.*

The Compound's ornamental iron gates had been blown away early in the fighting. The makeshift barricade of burned-out cars which replaced them had already been pushed aside in the cleanup. Soldiers in clean fatigues bearing the collar flashes of the 23d Infantry stood aside as Task Force Ranson entered the courtyard.

Flamethrower settled wearily to the rubble-strewn cobblestones. The car gave a deep sigh as Rogers shut down its fans. The other vehicles were already parked within.

Blue Three listed to starboard since Kawana. The tank had brushed a stone gatepost to widen the Compound entrance, then dragged a sparking line across a courtyard-sized mosaic map of Southern District with all the major cities and terrain features described.

Flamethrower stank of burned plastic and blood. Gale's body was wrapped in his air-tight bedroll and slung to the skirts, but the part of him that had splashed over the interior of the fighting compartment didn't take long to rot in bright sunlight.

They took off their body armor. Suilin's fingers didn't want to bend. All three men were fumbling with their latches. Cooter gripped the edge of the hull armor and shivered.

"Blood and martyrs," he muttered tiredly. Then he said, "Tootsie One-five, this is Three. Take over here till I get back, Tillman. Colonel wants me to report t' Governor Kung."

Suilin heard the electronic click of an answer on a channel the AI didn't open to him. Surely assent. Nobody had the energy left to argue.

Cooter looked at the reporter. "You coming?" the mercenary asked.

Suilin shrugged. "Yeah," he said. "Yeah, sure. That's what I came for."

He didn't sound certain, even to himself.

"Albers," Cooter said as he climbed over the back of the combat-car. "See if you can help Tillman line up billets and rations, okay?"

Albers nodded minusculy. He was sitting on the beer cooler. He didn't look at the big lieutenant. Except for the slight lift of his chin, he didn't move.

Suilin slid down the last step and almost fell. His legs didn't want to support him. They seemed all right after a few steps.

"The Consies 're asking for a cease fire," Cooter announced as he and the reporter walked toward the entrance to the Governor's Palace, the middle building of those closing the Compound on three sides. "Not just here. Their Central Command announced it."

"From the enclaves," Suilin said, thinking aloud.

The soldiers at the entrance thirty meters away wore fatigues with the crossed-saber collar tabs of the Presidential Guard Force. They eyed the newcomers cautiously.

A buzzbomb had cratered the second floor of the Palace, directly above the entrance. Other than that, damage was limited to broken glass and bullet-pocks on the stone. The fighting hadn't been serious around here after all.

Dick Suilin now knew what buildings looked like when somebody really meant business.

"Will they get it?" he said aloud. "The cease fire, I mean."

Cooter shrugged. "I'm not a politician," he said.

Now that the reporter had taken off his clamshell armor, the sling holding his grenade launcher was too long. He adjusted the length.

The pink-faced captain commanding the guards blinked.

Cooter looked at his companion. "I'm not sure you'll need that in here," he said mildly.

"I'm not sure of anything," Dick Suilin replied without emotion. "Not anymore."

★ ★ ★ ★

"The hole in the skirt," said Warrant Leader Ortnahme in a judicious tone as he walked slowly toward Blue Three, "we can patch easy enough. . . ."

"Yes sir," said Tech 2 Simkins through tight lips.

When a Yokel tank blew up three meters from Simkins' side of *Daisy Belle*, he'd been spattered with blazing diesel fuel. Bandages now covered the Spray Seal which replaced the skin of the technician's left arm.

He wasn't hurting, exactly; nobody carrying Simkins' present load of analgesics in his veins could be said to be in pain. Still, the technician had to concentrate to keep his feet moving in the right order.

"The bloody rest of it, though . . ." Ortnahme murmured.

Hans Wager had managed to find a can of black paint and a brush somewhere. He was painting something on the tank's bow skirts. His driver, a woman Ortnahme couldn't put a bloody name to, watched with a drawn expression.

The pair of 'em looked like they'd sweated off five kilos in the last two days. Maybe they had.

The tungsten-carbide shot that holed the skirt must have been so close to the muzzle that its fins hadn't had time to stabilize it. The shot was still yawing when it struck, so it'd punched a long oval in the steel instead of a neat round hole.

Ortnahme estimated the shot's probable further course with his eyes and called, "Did ye lose a bloody fan when that hit you?"

Wager continued painting, attempting a precision which was far beyond his present ability.

The driver turned slowly toward the pair of maintenance personnel. She said, "Yeah, that's right. Number 3 Port went out. That was okay, but the air spilling through the hole here—" nodding toward the gaping oval "—that was bad."

She paused for memory before she added, "Can you fix it?"

"Sure,"the warrant leader said."As soon as they ship in a spare." He shook his head. "A whole bloody lotta spares."

Simpkins nodded without speaking.

"What, ah . . . are you doing?" Ortnahme asked.

Wager turned at last. "We're putting the name on our tank," he croaked.

Wager's vacant expression turned to utter malevolence. "She's ours and we can call her anything we bloody please!" he shouted hoarsely. "They're not takin' her and givin' us some clapped out old cow instead, d'ye hear? Not even the Old Man's gonna take her away from us!"

The warrant leader looked at the tank that had only been a call sign until now.

The turret had taken at least a dozen direct hits, most of them from armor-piercing shot. Ortnahme wondered if any part of the sensor array had survived.

One round had blasted a cavity in the stubby barrel of the main gun. It hadn't penetrated, but until the tube was replaced, firing the 20cm weapon would be as dangerous as juggling contact grenades.

Even a layman could see that the tribarrel's ammunition had chain-fired in its loading tube, vaporizing the weapon, the hatch, and the cupola itself. The warrant leader knew what a layman wouldn't: that when the bloody ammo went, it would've reamed its tubeway as wide as a cow's cunt, seriously weakening the turret forging itself. The whole bloody turret would have to be replaced before Ortnahme would certify *this* mother as fit for action.

Plus, of course, the fan nacelle. Pray Lord it was the only one gone when he and Simkins got underneath to look.

"No argument from me, snake," Henk Ortnahme said mildly. "I figure you guys earned the right to ride whatever you bloody well please."

Simkins had to keep moving for another half hour or so. Ortnahme nodded to the tankers, then walked on slowly with the technician's hand in his for guidance.

Behind them, Wager painted the last letter of *Nameless* on the skirt in straggling capitals.

Suzette, Lady Kung, wore neat fatigues and a look of irritation as she glanced over her shoulder toward the commotion by the door.

"Suzi!" Dick Suilin called, past the sergeant major who blocked him and Cooter from the dignitaries milling in the conference room.

His sister's expression shifted through blank amazement to a mixture of love and horror. "Dick!" she cried. "Dick! Oh good Lord!"

She darted toward Suilin with her arms spread, striding fast enough to make her lustrous hair stream back from her shoulderblades.

The sergeant major didn't know what was going on, but he knew enough to get out of the way of the governor's wife. He sprang to attention and repeated in a parade-ground voice what Cooter had told him: "Sir! The representatives of Task Force Ranson."

There were twenty-odd people in the room already, too many for the chairs around the map-strewn table. Most were officers of the National Army. A few civilian advisors looked up from the circle around Governor Kung.

Everyone was in fatigues, but several of the officers wore polished insignia and even medal ribbons.

Suzi hugged her brother fiercely, then gasped before she could suppress the reflex. Suilin had forgotten how he must smell. . . .

"Oh Dick," his sister said. "It's been hard for all of us."

The reporter patted her hand and let her step away.

He pretended that he hadn't seen the look of disgust flash across her face. Couldn't blame her. He'd lived two days in his clothes, stinking of fear every moment of the time . . . and that was before the shell hit Gale beside him.

Cooter walked toward the conference table, parting the clot of advisors with the shockwave of his presence.

Governor Kung shoved his chair back and stood. He looked like a startled hiker who'd met a bear on a narrow trail.

"Sir," Cooter said, halting a meter from the governor in a vain effort not to be physically threatening. "Colonel Hammer—"

"You're Ranson, then?" Kung said sharply, his tenor voice keyed higher than Suilin remembered having heard it before. "We were told you were going to relieve us. But I see you preferred to wait until General Halas had done the job!"

Dick Suilin moved up beside the mercenary. The edges of his vision were becoming gray, like the walls of a tunnel leading to the face of Governor Samuel Kung. Suilin's brother-in-law wasn't a handsome man, but his round, sturdy features projected unshakeable determination.

Cooter shook his head as if to clear it. "Sir," he said, "we got here as fast as we could. There was a lot of resis—"

"*My* troops met a lot of resistance, Captain," growled a military man—General Halas; Suilin had interviewed him a few weeks ago, during another life. "The difference is that we broke through and accomplished our mission!"

The tunnel of Dick Suilin's vision was growing red and beginning to pulse as his heart beat. Halas' voice came from somewhere outside the present universe.

"Sir," said Lieutenant Cooter, "with all respect—the Consies put the best they had in our way. When we broke that, broke *them*, the troops they had left in Kohang ran rather than face us."

"Nonsense!" snapped Kung. "General Halas and his troops from Camp Fortune kept up the pressure till the enemy ran. I don't know why we ever decided to hire mercenaries in the first place!"

"Don't you know why we hire mercenaries, Governor?" said Dick Suilin in a voice trembling like a fuel fire. "Don't you know?"

He stepped closer; felt the massive conference table against the front of his thighs, felt it slide away from his advance.

"Dick!" called Suzi, the word attenuated by the pounding walls of the tunnel.

"Because they fight, Governor!" Suilin shouted. "Because they win, while your rear-echelon pussies wait to be saved with their thumbs up their ass!"

Kung's face vanished. Suilin could see nothing but a core of flame.

"They saved you, you worthless bastards!" he screamed into the blinding darkness. "They saved us all!"

The reporter floated without volition or sight. "Reaction to the Wide-awakes," he heard someone, Cooter, murmur. "Had a pretty rough time. . . ."

A door closed, cutting off the babble of sounds. The air was cool, and someone was gently holding him upright.

"Suzi?" he said.

"You can't let 'em get t' you," said Cooter. His right arm was around Suilin's shoulders. His fingers carefully detached the grenade launcher from the reporter's grip. "It's okay."

They were back in the hallway outside the conference room. The walls were veneered with zebra-patterned marble, clean and cool.

"It's not okay!" screamed Dick Suilin. "You saved all their asses and they don't care!"

"They don't have t' like us, snake," said Lieutenant Cooter, meeting Suilin's eyes. "They just have t' make the payment schedule."

Suilin turned and bunched his fist. Cooter caught his arm before he could smash his knuckles on the stone wall.

"Take it easy, snake," said the mercenary. "It don't mean nothin'."

BRIDGE CROSSING

THE WARRIOR

PART I

The tribarrel in the cupola of *Warrior,* the tank guarding the northwest quadrant of Hill 541 North, snarled in automatic air-defense mode. The four Slammers in Lieutenant Lindgren's bunker froze.

Sergeant Samuel "Slick" Des Grieux, *Warrior*'s commander, winced. He was twenty-one standard years old, and a hardened veteran of two years in Hammer's Slammers. He kneaded his broad, powerful hands together to control his anger at being half a kay away from where he ought to have been: aboard his vehicle and fighting.

The incoming shell thudded harmlessly, detonated in the air.

Sergeant Broglie had counted out the time between the tribarrel's burst and the explosion. "Three seconds," he murmured.

The shell had been a safe kilometer away when it went off. The howl of its passage to an intersection with *Warrior*'s bolts echoed faintly through the night.

"Every five minutes," said Hawes, the fourth man in the bunker and by far the greenest. This was the first time Hawes had been under prolonged bombardment. The way he twitched every time a gun fired indicated how little he liked the experience. "I wish they'd—"

Lieutenant Lindgren's tank, *Queen City,* fired a five-round burst.

Cyan light shuddered through the bunker's dog leg entrance. A pair of shells, probably fired from the Republican batteries on Hill 661 to the northeast, crumped well short of their target.

"*Via*, Lieutenant!" Des Grieux said in a desperate voice. He stared at his hands, because he was afraid of what he might blurt if he looked straight at the young officer. "Look, I oughta be back on *Warrior*. Anything you gotta say, you can say over the commo, it's secure. And—"

He couldn't help it. His face came up. His voice grew as hard as his cold blue eyes, and he continued. "Besides, we're not here to talk. We oughta be kicking ass. That's what we're here for."

"We're here—" Lindgren began.

"We're the Federals' artillery defense, Slick," Broglie said, smiling at Des Grieux. Broglie didn't shout,but his voice flattened the lieutenant's words anyway. "*And* their backbone. We're doing our job, so no sweat, hey?"

"Our job . . ." said Des Grieux softly. *Warrior* fired three short bursts, blasting a salvo inbound from the Republicans on Hill 504. Des Grieux ignored the sound and its implications. " . . . is to fight. Not to hide in holes. Hey, Luke?"

Broglie was four centimeters shorter than Des Grieux and about that much broader across the shoulders. He wasn't afraid of Des Grieux . . . which interested Des Grieux because it was unusual, though it didn't bother him in the least.

Des Grieux wasn't afraid of anyone or anything.

"We're here to see that Hill 541 North holds out till the relieving force arrives," said Lindgren.

He'd taken Broglie's interruption as a chance to get his emotions under control. The lieutenant was almost as nervous as Hawes, but he was a Slammers officer and determined to act like one. "The AAD in the vehicles does that as well as we could sitting in the turrets, Slick," he continued, "and unit meetings are important to remind us that we're a platoon, not four separate tanks stuck off in West Bumfuck."

"North Bumfuck fiver-four-one," Broglie chuckled.Broglie's face held its quizzical smile, but the low sound of his laughter was drowned by incoming shells and the tanks' response to them. This was a sustained pounding from all three Republican gun positions: Hills 504 and 661 to the north, and Hill 541 South, ten kilometers southeast of the Federal base.

The Reps fired thirty or forty shells in less than a minute. Under the tribarrels' lash, the explosions merged into a drumming roar—punctuated by the sharp *crash* of the round that got through.

The bunker rocked. Dust drifted down from the sandbagged roof. Hawes rubbed his hollow eyes and pretended not to have heard the blast.

The sound of the salvoes died away. One of the Federal garrison screamed nearby. Des Grieux wasn't sure whether the man was wounded or simply broken by the constant hammering. The unanswered shelling got to him, too; but it made him want to go out and kill, not hide in a bunker and scream.

"Lieutenant," Des Grieux said in the same measured, deadly voice as before. "We oughta go out and nail the bastards. *That's* how we can save these Federal pussies."

"The relieving force—"Lindgren said.

"The relieving force hasn't gotten here in three weeks, so they aren't exactly burning up the road, now, are they?" Des Grieux said. "Look—"

"They'll get here," said Broglie. "They've got Major Howes and three of our companies with 'em, so they'll get here. And we'll wait it out, because that's what Colonel Hammer ordered us to do."

Lindgren opened his mouth to speak, but he closed it again and let the tank commanders argue the question. Des Grieux didn't even pretend to care what a newbie lieutenant thought. As for Broglie—

Sergeant Lucas Broglie was more polite, and Broglie appreciated the value of Lindgren's education from the Military Academy of Nieuw Friesland. But Broglie didn't much care what a newbie lieutenant thought, either.

"I didn't say we ought to bug out," Des Grieux said. His eyes were as open and empty as a cannon's bore. "I said we could *win* this instead of sitting on our butts."

Open and empty and deadly. . . .

"Four tanks can't take on twenty thousand Reps," Broglie said. His smile was an equivalent of Des Grieux's blank stare: the way Broglie's face formed itself when the mind beneath was under stress.

He swept an arc with his thumb. The bunker was too strait to allow him to make a full-arm gesture. "That's what they got out there. Twenty thousand of them."

The ground shook from another shell that got through the tribarrels' defensive web. Des Grieux was so concentrated on Broglie that his mind had tuned out the ripping bursts that normally would have focused him utterly.

"It's not just us 'n them," Des Grieux said. Lindgren and Hawes, sitting on ammunition boxes on opposite sides of the bunker, swivelled their heads from one veteran to the other like spectators at a tennis match. "There's five, six thousand Federals on this crap pile with us, and they can't like it much better than I do."

"They're not—" Lieutenant Lindgren began. Cyan light flickered through the bunker entrance. A Republican sniper, not one of the Slammers' weapons. The Reps had a few powerguns, and Hill 661 was high enough that a marksman could slant his bolts into the Federal position.

The *snap!* of the bolt impacting made Lindgren twitch. Des Grieux's lips drew back in a snarl, because if he'd been in his tank he just *might* have put paid to the bastard.

"Not line soldiers," the lieutenant concluded in an artificially calm tone.

"They'd fight if they had somebody to lead them," Des Grieux said. "*Via* , anything's better'n being wrapped up here and used for Rep target practice."

"They've got a leader," Broglie replied, "and it's General Wycherly, not us. For what he's worth."

Des Grieux grimaced as though he'd been kicked. Even Hawes snorted.

"I don't believe you appreciate the constraints that General Wycherly operates under," Lindgren said in a thin voice.

Lindgren knew how little his authority was worth to the veterans.

That, as well as a real awareness of the Federal commander's difficulties, injected a note of anger into his tone. "He's outnumbered three or four to one," he went on. "Ten to one, if you count just the real combat troops under his command. But he's holding his position as ordered. And that's just what we're going to help him do."

"We're pieces of a puzzle, Slick," said Broglie. He relaxed enough to rub his lips, massaging them out of the rictus into which the discussion had cramped them. "Wycherly's job is to keep from getting overrun; our job's to help him; and our people with the relieving force 're going to kick the cop outa the Reps if we just hold 'em a few days more."

Another incoming shell detonated a kilometer short of Hill 541 North. The Republicans knew they couldn't do serious physical damage so long as the position was guarded by the Slammers' tanks . . . but they knew as well the psychological effect the constant probing fire had on the defenders.

For an instant Broglie's hard smile was back. "Or not a puzzle," he added. "A gun. Every part has to do the right job, or the gun doesn't work."

"Okay, we had our unit meeting," Des Grieux said. He squeezed his hands together so fiercely that his fingers were dark with trapped blood between the first and second joints. "Now can I get back to my tank where I can maybe do some good?"

"The AAD does everything that can be done, Sergeant," Lindgren said. "That's what we need now. That and discipline."

Des Grieux stood up, though he had to bend forward to clear the bunker's low ceiling. "Having the computer fire my guns,"he said with icy clarity, "is like jacking off. With respect."

Lindgren grimaced. "All right," he said. "You're all dismissed."

In an attempt to soften the previous exchange, he added,"There shouldn't be more than a few days of this."

But Des Grieux, ignoring the incoming fire, was already out of the bunker.

A howitzer fired from the center of the Federal position. The night outside the bunker glowed with the bottle-shaped yellow flash.

There were fifteen tubes in the Federal batteries, but they were short of ammunition and rarely fired.

When they did, they invariably brought down a storm of Republican counterfire.

Des Grieux continued to walk steadily in the direction of *Warrior*; his tank, his home.

Not his reason for existence, though. Des Grieux existed to rip the enemy up one side and down the other. To do that he could use *Warrior*, or the pistol in his holster, or his teeth; whatever was available. Lieutenant Lindgren was robbing Des Grieux of his reason for existence. . . .

He heard the scream of the shell—one round, from the northwest. He waited for the sky-tearing sound of *Warrior*'s tribarrel firing a short burst of cyan plasma, copper nuclei stripped of their electron shells and ravening downrange to detonate or vaporize the shell.

Warrior didn't fire.

The Reps had launched a ground-hugging missile from the lower altitude of Hill 504. *Warrior* and the other Slammers' tanks couldn't engage the round because they were dug in behind the bunker line encircling the Federal positions. The incoming missile would not rise into the line-of-sight range of the powerguns until—

There was a scarlet streak from the horizon like a vector marker in the dark bowl of the sky. A titanic crash turned the sky orange and knocked Des Grieux down. Sandy red dust sucked up and rolled over, forming a doughnut that expanded across the barren hilltop.

Des Grieux got to his feet and resumed walking. The bastards couldn't make him run, and they couldn't make him bend over against the sleet of shell fragments which would rip him anyway— running or walking, cowering or standing upright like a man.

The Republicans fired a dozen ordinary rounds. Tank tribarrels splashed each of the shells a fraction of a second after they arched into view. The powerguns' snarling dazzle linked the Federal base for an instant to orange fireballs which faded into rags of smoke. There were no more ground-huggers.

An ordinary shell was no more complex than a hand grenade. Ground-hugging missiles required sophisticated electronics and a fairly complex propulsion system. There weren't many of them in the Rep stockpiles.

Ground-huggers would be as useless as ballistic projectiles *if* Lindgren used his platoon the way tanks should be used, as weapons that sought out the enemy instead of cowering turret-down in defilade.

Blood and Martyrs! What a way to fight a war.

The top of Hill 541 North was a barren moonscape. The bunkers were improvised by the troops themselves with shovels and sandbags. A month ago, the position had been merely the supply point for a string of Federal outposts. No one expected a siege.

But when the Republicans swept down in force, the outposts scrambled into their common center, 541N. Troops dug furiously as soon as they realized that there was no further retreat until Route 7 to the south was cleared from the outside.

If Route 7 was cleared. Task Force Howes, named for the CO of the Slammers 2nd Battalion, had promised a link-up within three days.

Every day for the past two weeks.

A sniper on Hill 661, twelve kilometers away, fired his powergun. The bolt snapped fifty meters from Des Grieux, fusing the sandy soil into a disk of glass which shattered instantly as it cooled.

Kuykendall, *Warrior*'s driver, should be in the tank turret. If Des Grieux had been manning the guns, the sniper would have had a hot time of it . . . but Des Grieux was walking back from a dickheaded meeting, and Kuykendall wasn't going to disobey orders to leave the tribarrel on Automatic Air Defense and not, under any circumstances, to fire the 20cm main gun since ammunition was scarce.

The garrison of Hill 541N, the Slammers included, had the supplies they started the siege with. Ground routes were blocked. Aerial resupply would be suicide because of the Rep air-defense arsenal on the encircling hills.

The sniper fired again. The bolt hit even farther away, but he was probably aiming at Des Grieux anyhow. Nothing else moved on this side of the encampment except swirls of wind-blown sand.

A shell fragment the size of a man's palm stuck up from the ground. It winked jaggedly in the blue light of the bolt.

Warrior was within a hundred meters. Des Grieux continued to walk deliberately.

The hilltop's soil blurred all the vehicles and installations into identical dinginess. The dirt was a red without life, the hue of old blood that had dried and flaked to powder.

The sniper gave up. A gun on 541S coughed a shell which Broglie's *Honey Girl* blew from the sky a moment later.

Every five minutes; but not regularly, and twice the Reps had banged out more than a thousand rounds in a day, some of which inevitably got through. . . .

"That you, Slick?" Kuykendall called from the *Warrior*'s cupola.

"Yeah, of course it's me," Des Grieux replied. He stepped onto a sandbag lip, then hopped down to *Warrior*'s back deck. His boots clanked.

The tanks were dug in along sloping ramps. Soil from the trenches filled sandbag walls rising above the vehicles' cupolas. Lieutenant Lindgren was afraid that powerguns from 661—and the Reps had multi-barreled calliopes to provide artillery defense—would rake the Slammers' tanks if the latter were visible.

Des Grieux figured the answer to *that* threat was to kick the Reps the hell off Hill 661. By now, though, he'd learned that the other Slammers were just going to sigh and look away when he made a suggestion that didn't involve waiting for somebody else to do the fighting.

Kuykendall slid down from the cupola into the fighting compartment. She was a petite woman, black-haired and a good enough driver. To Des Grieux, Kuykendall was a low-key irritation that he had to work around, like a burr in the mechanism that controlled his turret's rotation.

A driver was a necessary evil, because Des Grieux couldn't guide his tank and fight at the same time. Kuykendall took orders, but she had a personality of her own. She wasn't a mere extension of

Des Grieux's will, and that made her more of a problem than someone blander though less competent would have been.

Nothing he couldn't work around, though. There *was* nothing Des Grieux couldn't work around, if his superiors just gave him the chance to do his job. "Anything new?" Kuykendall asked.

Des Grieux stood on his seat so that he could look out over the sandbags toward Hill 661. "What'd you think?" he said. He switched the visual display on his helmet visor to infrared and cranked up the magnification.

The sniper had gone home. Nothing but ripples in the atmosphere and the cooler blue of trees transpiring water they sucked somehow from this Lord-blasted landscape.

Des Grieux climbed out of the hatch again. He shoved a sandbag off the top layer. *The bastard would be back, and when he was . . .*

He pushed away another sandbag. The bags were woven from a coarse synthetic that smelled like burning tar when it rubbed.

"We're not supposed to do that," Kuykendall said from the cupola. "A lucky shot could put the tribarrel out of action. That'd hurt us a lot worse than a hundred dead grunts does the Reps."

"They don't have a hundred powerguns," Des Grieux said without turning around. He pushed at the second-layer sandbag he'd uncovered but that layer was laid as headers. The bags to right and left resisted the friction on their long sides. "Anyway, it's worth something to me to give a few of those cocky bastards their lunch."

Hawes' *Susie Q* ripped the sky. Des Grieux dropped into a crouch, then rose again with a feeling of embarrassment. He knew that Kuykendall had seen him jump.

It wasn't flinching. If *Warrior*'s AAD sensed incoming from Hill 661, Des Grieux would either duck instantly—or have his head shot off by the tribarrel of his own tank. The fire-direction computer didn't care if there was a man in the way when it needed to do its job.

Des Grieux liked the computer's attitude.

He lifted and pushed, raising his triceps into stark ridges. Des Grieux was thin and from a distance looked frail. Close up, no one noticed anything but his eyes; and there was no weakness in them.

The sandbag slid away. The slot in *Warrior*'s protection gave Des Grieux a keyhole through which to rake Hill 661 with his tribarrel. He got back into the turret. Kuykendall dropped out of the way without further comment.

"You know . . ." Des Grieux said as he viewed the enemy positions in the tribarrel's holographic sight. *Warrior*'s sensors were several orders of magnitude better than those of the tankers' unaided helmets. "The Reps aren't much better at this than these Federal pussies we gotta nursemaid."

"How d'ye mean?" Kuykendall asked.

Her voice came over the intercom channel. She'd slipped back into the driver's compartment. Most drivers found the internal hatch too tight for use in anything less than a full buttoned-up emergency.

"They've got calliopes up there," Des Grieux explained as he scanned the bleak silence of Hill 661. The Republican positions were in defilade. Easy enough to arrange from their greater height.

"If it was me," Des Grieux continued, "I'd pick my time and roll'er up to direct fire positions. They'd kick the cop outa this place."

"They're not going to bet 3cm calliopes against tank main guns, Sarge," Kuykendall said carefully.

"They would if they had any balls," Des Grieux said. His voice was coldly judgmental, stating the only truth there was. He showed no anger toward those who were too stupid to see it. "Dug in like we are, they could blow away the cupolas and our sensor arrays before we even got the main guns to bear. A calliope's no joke, kid."

He laughed harshly. "Wish they'd try, though. I can hip-shoot a main gun if I have to."

"There's talk they're going to try t' overrun us before Task Force Howes relieves us," Kuykendall said with the guarded nonchalance she always assumed when talking to the tank commander.

Des Grieux's two years in the Slammers made him a veteran, but he was scarcely one of the longest-serving members of the regiment. His drive, his skill with weapons, and the phenomenal ruthlessness with which he accomplished any task set him gave Des Grieux a reputation beyond simple seniority.

"There's talk," Des Grieux said coldly. *Nothing moved on Hill 661.* "There's been talk. There's been talk Howes is going to get his thumbs out of his butt and relieve us, too."

The tribarrel roused, swung, and ignited the sky with a four-round burst of plasma. A shell from Hill 504 broke apart without detonating. The largest piece of casing was still a white glow when it tumbled out of sight in the valley below.

The sky flickered to the south as well, but at such a distance that the sounds faded to a low rumble. Task Force Howes still slugged it out with the Republicans who defended Route 7. Maybe they were going to get here within seventy-two hours. And maybe Hell was going to freeze over.

Des Grieux scanned Hill 661, and nothing moved.

The only thing Des Grieux knew in the instant he snapped awake from a sound sleep was that it was time to earn his pay.

Kuykendall looked down into the fighting compartment from the commander's seat. "Sarge?" she said. "I—" and broke off when she realized Des Grieux was already alert.

"Get up front 'n drive," Des Grieux ordered curtly. "It's happening."

"It's maybe nothing," the driver said, but she knew Des Grieux. As Kuykendall spoke, she swung her legs out of the cupola. Hopping from the cupola and past the main gun was the fastest way to the driver's hatch in the bow. The tank commander blocked the internal passage anyway as he climbed up to his seat.

The Automatic Air Defense plate on *Warrior's* control panel switched from yellow, standby, to red. The tribarrel rotated and fired. Des Grieux flicked the plate with his boot toe as he went past, disconnecting the computer-controlled defensive fire. He needed *Warrior's* weapons under his personal direction now that things were real.

When the siege began, Lieutenant Lindgren ordered that one member of each two-man tank crew be on watch in the cupola at every moment. What the tankers did off-duty, and where they slept, was their own business.

Most of the off-duty troops slept beneath their vehicles, entering the plenum chamber through the access plate in the steel skirts. The chambers were roomy and better protection than anything cobbled together by shovels and sandbags could be. The only problem was the awareness before sleep came that the tank above you weighed 170 tonnes . . . but tankers tended not to be people who thought in those terms.

Lindgren insisted on a bunker next to his vehicle. He was sure that he would go mad if his whole existence, on duty and off, was bounded by the steel and iridium shell of his tank.

Des Grieux went the other way around. He slept in the fighting compartment while his driver kept watch in the cupola above. The deck was steel pressed with grip rosettes. He couldn't stretch out. His meter-ninety of height had to twist between the three-screen control console and the armored tube which fed ammunition to the autoloading 20cm main gun.

Nobody called the fighting compartment a comfortable place to sleep; but then, nobody called Des Grieux sane, either.

A storm of Republican artillery fire screamed toward Hill 541N. Some of the shells would have gotten through even if Des Grieux had left *Warrior* in the defensive net. That was somebody else's problem. The Reps didn't have terminally guided munitions that would target the Slammers' tanks, so a shell that hit *Warrior* was the result of random chance.

You had to take chances in war; and anyway, *Warrior* oughta shrug off anything but a heavy-caliber armor-piercing round with no more than superficial damage.

Kuykendall switched her fans on and brought them up to speed fast with their blades cutting the airstream at minimum angle. *Warrior* trembled with what Des Grieux anthropomorphized as eagerness, transferring his own emotions to the mindless machine he commanded.

A Slammers' tank was a slope-sided iridium hull whose turret, smooth to avoid shot traps, held a 20cm powergun. The three-barreled automatic weapon in the cupola could operate independently or be locked to the same point of aim as the main gun. Eight intake ducts pierced the upper surface of the hull, feeding air down to drive fans in armored nacelles below.

At rest, the tanks sat on their steel skirts. When the vehicles were under way, they floated on a cushion of air pressurized by the fans. At full throttle, the power required to drive a tank was enormous, and the fusion bottle which provided that power filled the rear third of the hull.

The tanks were hideously expensive. Their electronics were so complex and sensitive that at least a small portion of every tank's suite was deadlined at any one time. The hulls and running gear were rugged, but the vehicles' own size and weight imposed stresses which required constant maintenance.

When they worked, and to the extent they worked, the Slammers' tanks were the most effective weapons in the human universe. As *Warrior* was about to prove to two divisions of Republican infantry. . . .

"Back her out!" Des Grieux ordered. If he'd thought about it, he would have sounded a general alarm because he *knew* this was a major attack, but he had other things on his mind besides worrying about people he wasn't planning to kill.

"Booster," Des Grieux said, switching on the artificial intelligence which controlled the tank's systems. "Enemy activity, one kay, now!"

Warrior shuddered as Kuykendall increased the fan bite. Sandy soil mushroomed from the trench walls and upward as the hull lifted and air leaked beneath *Warrior*'s skirts. Des Grieux's direct vision blurred in a gritty curtain, but the data his AI assembled from remote sensors was sharp and clear in the upper half of his helmet visor.

The ground fell away from the top of Hill 541 North in a 1:3 slope, and the tank positions were set well back from the edge of the defenses. Even when *Warrior* backed from her trench, Des Grieux would not be able to see the wire and minefields which the garrison had laid at mid-slope to stop an enemy assault.

Ideally, the tanks would have access to the Slammers' own remote sensors. Conditions were rarely ideal, and on Hill 541N they never even came close. Still, the Federals had emplaced almost a hundred seismic and acoustic sensors before the Republicans tightened the siege. Most of the sensors were in the wire, but they'd dropped a few in the swales surrounding the bill, a kilometer or so out from the hilltop.

Acoustic sensors gathered the sound of voices and equipment, while seismic probes noted the vibration feet and vehicles made in the soil. The information, flawed by the sensors' relative lack of sophistication and the haphazard way the units were emplaced, was transmitted to the hilltop for processing.

Des Grieux didn't know what the Feds did with the raw data, but *Warrior*'s AI turned it into a clear image of a major Republican attack.

There were two thrusts, directed against the east and the north-west quadrants of the Federal positions. The slope at those angles was slightly steeper than it was to the south, but the surface fell in a series of shallow steps that formed dead zones, out of the fire from hilltop bunkers.

A siren near the Federal command post wound up. Its wail was almost lost in the shriek of incoming.

The Reps had ten or a dozen shells in the air at any one time. The three tanks still working air defense slashed arcs across the sky. Powerguns detonated much of the incoming during its fifteen-second flight time, but every minute or so a round got through.

Most of the hits raised geysers of sand from the hilltop. Only occasionally did a bunker collapse or a shellburst scythe down troops running toward fighting positions in the forward trenches, but even misses shook the defenders' morale.

Booster thought the attack on the northwest quadrant was being made by a battalion of infantry, roughly 500 troops, behind a screen of sappers no more than a hundred strong. The eastern thrust was of comparable size, but even so it seemed a ludicrously small force to throw against a garrison of over 5,000 men.

That was only the initial assault; a larger force would get in its own way during the confusion of a night attack. Booster showed several additional battalions and a dozen light armored vehicles waiting in reserve among the yellow-brown scrub of the valleys where streams would run in the wet season.

As soon as the leading elements seized a segment of the outer bunker line in a classic infiltration assault, the Republican support troops would advance in good order and sweep across the hilltop. There was no way in hell that the Federal infantry, demoralized by weeks of unanswerable shelling, was going to stop the attack.

They didn't have to. Not while Des Grieux was here.

"Clear visor," Des Grieux said. He'd seen what the sensors gave him, and he didn't need the display anymore. He tugged the crash bar, dropping his seat into the fighting compartment and buttoning the hatch shut above him.

Warrior's three holographic screens cast their glow across conduits and the breech of the squat main gun.

"Driver, advance along marked vector."

Default on the left-hand screen was a topographic display. Des Grieux drew his finger across it in a curving arc, down from the hilltop in a roughly northwestward direction. The AI would echo the display in Kuykendall's compartment. A trackway, not precisely a road but good enough for the Rep vehicles and sure as *hell* good enough for *Warrior*, wound north from the swale in the direction of the Republican firebase on Hill 504.

"Gun it!" Des Grieux snarled. "Keep your foot on the throttle, bitch!"

It didn't occur to him that there was another way to give the order. All Des Grieux knew was that *Warrior* had to move as he desired, and the commander's will alone was not enough to direct the vehicle.

Kuykendall touched *Warrior* to the ground, rubbing off some of the backing inertia against the sand. She rotated the attitude control of the drive fans, angling the nacelles so that they thrust *Warrior* forward as well as lifting it again onto the air cushion.

The huge tank slid toward the edge of the encampment in front of a curling billow of dust. Size made the vehicle seem to accelerate slowly.

"Oyster Leader to Oyster Two," said Lieutenant Lindgren over the platoon's commo channel. "Hold your position. Break. Oyster four—" Hawes "—move up to support Oyster Two. Over."

The note of *Warrior*'s fans changed. Massive inertia would keep the vehicle gliding forward for a hundred meters, but the sound meant Kuykendall was obeying the platoon leader's orders.

"Driver!" Des Grieux shouted. "Roll it! *Now!*" Kuykendall adjusted her nacelles obediently. *Warrior* slid on momentum between a pair of bunkers as the fans swung to resume their forward thrust.

The Federal positions were dugouts covered by transportation pallets supported by a single layer of sandbags. Three or four additional sandbag layers supplied overhead protection, though a direct hit would crumple the strongest of them. The firing slits were so low that muzzle blasts kicked up sand to shroud the red flashes of their machine guns.

Warrior's sensors fed the main screen with a light-enhanced 120° arc to the front. The tank's AI added in a stereoscopic factor to aid depth perception which the human brain ordinarily supplied in part from variations in light intensity.

The screen provided Des Grieux with a clear window onto the Republican attack. A two-man buzzbomb team rose into firing position at the inner edge of the wire. Instead of launching their unguided rockets into the nearest bunkers, they had waited for the tank they expected.

Des Grieux expected them also. He stunned the night with a bolt from *Warrior*'s main gun.

Des Grieux used his central display for gunnery. It had two orange pippers, a 2cm ring and a 1cm dot for the main gun and tribarrel respectively. The sensor array mounted around *Warrior*'s cupola gave Des Grieux the direction in which to swing his weapon. As soon as his tank rose into a hull-down position that cleared the 20cm powergun, he toggled the foot-trip.

Because the tribarrel was mounted higher, Des Grieux could have killed the Reps a moment sooner with the automatic weapon, but he wanted the enemy's first awareness of *Warrior* to be the cataclysmic blast of the tank's main gun.

The cyan bolt struck one of the Rep team squarely and converted his body into a ball of vapor so hot that its glowing shockwave flung the other victim's torso and limbs away in separate trajectories. The secondary explosion of the anti-tank warheads was lost in the plasma charge's flashcrash.

Honking through its intakes, *Warrior* thundered down on the Republican attack.

Guns in dozens of Federal bunkers fired white tracers toward the perimeter of mines and wire. Heavy automatic weapons among the Republican support battalions answered with chains of glowing red balls.

The Federal artillerymen in the center of Hill 541 North began slamming out their remaining ammunition in the reasonable view that unless this attack was stopped, there was no need for conservation. Because of their hilltop location, the guns could not bear on the sappers. To reach even the Republican support troops, they had to lob their shells in high, inaccurate arcs. The pair of calliopes on Hill 661 burst many of the Federal rounds at the top of their trajectory.

Instead of becoming involved in firefights, the Rep sappers did an excellent job of pathclearing for the main assault force. A few of the sappers fell, but their uniforms of light-absorbent fabric made them difficult targets even now that Federal starshells popped to throw wavering illumination over the scene.

A miniature rocket dragged its train of explosive across the perimeter defenses. The line exploded with a yellow flash and a sound like a door slamming. Sand and wire flew to either side. Overpressure set off a dozen anti-personnel mines to speckle the night.

There were already a dozen similar gaps in the perimeter. An infiltration team had wormed through the defenses before the alarm went off. One of its members hurled a satchel charge into a bunker, collapsing it with a flash and a roar.

Warrior drove into the wire. Bullets, some of them fired from the Federal bunkers, pinged harmlessly on the iridium armor. A buzzbomb trailing sparks and white smoke snarled toward the tank's right flank. Five meters out, the automatic defense system along the top edge of *Warrior*'s skirts banged. Its spray of steel pellets ripped the buzzbomb and set off the warhead prematurely.

The tank rang like a bell when its defensive array fired, but the hollow *whoomp* of the shaped-charge warhead was lost in the battle's general clamor. Shards of buzzbomb casing knocked down a sapper. He thrashed through several spasms before he lay still.

Warrior passed the Federal minefield in a series of sprouting explosions and the spang of fragments which ricocheted from the skirts. The pressure of air within the tank's plenum chamber was high enough to detonate mines rigged to blow off a man's foot. They clanged harmlessly as a tocsin of the huge vehicle's passage.

The tank's bow slope snagged loops of concertina wire which stretched and writhed until it broke. Republican troops threw themselves down to avoid the unexpected whips of hooked steel. Men shouted curses, although the gap *Warrior* tore in the perimeter defenses was broad enough to pass a battalion in columns of sixteen.

Des Grieux ignored the sappers. They could cause confusion within the bunker line, but they were no threat to the ultimate existence of the Federal base. The assault battalion, and still more the thousands of Republican troops waiting in reserve, were another matter.

Warrior had two dual-capable gunnery joysticks. Most tank commanders used only one, selecting tribarrel or main gun with the thumbswitch. Des Grieux shot with both hands.

He'd pointed the main gun 30° to starboard in order to blast the team of tank killers. Now his left hand swung the cupola tribarrel a few degrees to port. He didn't change either setting again for the moment. Not even Des Grieux's degree of skill permitted him to aim two separate sights from a gun platform travelling at fifty kph and still accelerating.

But he could fire them, alternately or together, whenever *Warrior*'s forward motion slid the pippers over targets.

The tribarrel caught a squad moving up at a trot to exploit pathways the sappers had torn. The Republicans were so startled by the bellowing monster that they forgot to throw themselves down.

Three survivors turned and fired their rifles vainly as the tank roared past fifty meters away. The rest of the squad were dead, with the exception of the lieutenant leading them. He stood, shrilling insane parodies of signals on his whistle.

The tribarrel had blown off both his arms.

Des Grieux's right thumb fired the main gun at another ragged line of Republican infantry. The 20cm bolt gouged the earth ten meters short, but its energy sprayed the sandy soil across the troops as a shower of molten glass. One of the victims continued to pirouette in agony until white tracers from a Federal machine gun tore most of his chest away.

Fires lighted by the cyan bolts flared across the arid landscape.

Hawes in *Susie Q* tried to follow. His tribarrel slashed out a long burst. Sappers jumped and ran. Two of them stumbled into mines and upended in sprays of soil.

Susie Q eased forward at a walking pace. Hawes' driver was proceeding cautiously under circumstances where speed was the only hope of survival. Halfway to the wire, a buzzbomb passed in front of the tank. It was so badly aimed that the automatic defense system didn't trip.

Susie Q braked and began to turn. Hawes sprayed the slope wildly with his tribarrel. A stray bolt blew a trench across *Warrior*'s back deck.

A Rep sapper ran toward *Susie Q*'s blind side with a satchel charge in his hands. The automatic defense system blasted him when he was five yards away, but two more buzzbombs arced over his crumpled body.

The section of the ADS which had killed the sapper was out of service until its strip charge could be replaced. The rockets hit, one in the hull and the other in the center of *Susie Q*'s turret. Iridium reflected the warheads' white glare.

The tank grounded violently. The thick skirt crumpled as it bulldozed a ripple of soil. *Susie Q*'s status entry on *Warrior*'s right-hand display winked from solid blue to cross-hatched, indicating that an electrical fault had depowered several major systems.

Des Grieux ignored the readout. He had a battle to win.

Under other circumstances, Des Grieux would have turned to

port or starboard to sweep up one flank of the assault wave, but the Republican reserves were too strong. Turning broadside to their fire was a quick way to die. Winning—surviving—required him to keep the enemy off balance.

Warrior bucked over the irregular slope, but the guns were stabilized in both elevation and traverse. Des Grieux lowered the hollow pipper onto the swale half a kilometer away, where the Republican supports sheltered.

Several of the armored cars there raked the tank with their automatic cannon. Explosive bullets whanged loudly on the iridium.

Des Grieux set *Warrior*'s turret to rotate at one degree per second and stepped on the foot-trip. The main gun began to fire as quickly as the system could reload itself. Cyan hell broke loose among the packed reserves.

The energy liberated by a single 20cm bolt was so great that dry brush several meters away from each impact burst into flames. Infantrymen leaped to their feet, colliding in wild panic as they tried to escape the sudden fires.

An armored car took a direct hit. Its diesel fuel boomed outward in a huge fireball which engulfed the vehicles to either side. Crewmen baled out of one of the cars before it exploded. Their clothes were alight, and they collapsed a few steps from their vehicle.

The other car spouted plumes of multi-colored smoke. Marking grenades had ignited inside the turret hatch, broiling the commander as he tried to climb past them. Ammunition cooked off in a flurry of sparks and red tracers.

While *Warrior*'s main gun cycled its twenty-round ready magazine into part of the Republican reserves, Des Grieux aimed his tribarrel at specific targets to port. The tank's speed was seventy kph and still accelerating. When the bow slid over the slope's natural terracing, it spilled air from the plenum chamber. Each time, *Warrior*'s 170 tonnes slammed onto the skirts with the inevitability of night following day.

Though the tribarrel was stabilized, the crew was not. The impacts jounced Des Grieux against his seat restraints and blurred his vision.

It didn't matter. Under these circumstances, Des Grieux scarcely needed the sights. He *knew* when the pipper covered a clot of infantry or an armored car reversing violently to escape what the crew suddenly realized was a kill zone.

Two-cm bolts lacked the authority of *Warrior*'s main gun, but Des Grieux's short bursts cut with surgical precision. Men flew apart in cyan flashes. The thin steel hulls of armored cars blazed white for an instant before the fuel and ammunition inside caught fire as well. Secondary explosions lit the night as tribarrel bolts detonated cases of rocket and mortar warheads.

Warrior's drive fans howled triumphantly.

Behind the rampaging tank, Rep incoming flashed and thundered onto Hill 541 North. Only one tribarrel from the Federal encampment still engaged the shells.

Federal artillery continued to fire. A "friendly" round plunged down at a 70° angle and blew a ten-meter hole less than a tank's length ahead of *Warrior*. Kuykendall fought her controls, but the tank's speed was too high to dodge the obstacle completely. *Warrior* lurched heavily and rammed some of the crater's lip back to bury the swirling vapors of high explosive.

A score of Rep infantry lay flat with their hands pressing down their helmets as if to drive themselves deeper into the gritty soil. *Warrior* plowed through them. The tank's skirt was now here more than a centimeter off the ground. The victims smeared unnoticed beneath the tank's weight.

Warrior boomed out of the swale and proceeded up the curving track toward Hill 504.

The main gun had emptied its ready magazine. Despite the air conditioning, the air within *Warrior*'s fighting compartment was hot and bitter with the gray haze trembling from the thick 20cm disks which littered the turret basket. The disks were the plastic matrices that had held active atoms of the powergun charge in precise alignment. Despite the blast of liquid nitrogen that cleared the bore after each shot, the empties contained enormous residual heat.

Des Grieux jerked the charging lever, refilling the ready magazine from reserve storage deep in *Warrior*'s hull. The swale was blazing havoc behind them. Silhouetted against the glare of burning brush, fuel, and ammunition, Republican troops scattered like chickens from a fox.

Ten kilometers ahead of the tank, the horizon quivered with the muzzle flashes of Republican artillery.

"Now we'll get those bastards on 504!" Des Grieux shouted—

And knew, even as he roared his triumph, that if he tried to smash his way into the Republican firebase, he would die as surely and as vainly as the Rep reserves had died when *Warrior* ripped through the center of them

So long as Des Grieux was in the middle of a firefight, his brain had disconnected the stream of orders and messages rattling over the commo net. Now the volume of angry sound overwhelmed him: *"Oyster Two, report! Break! Oyster four, are you—"*

The voice was Broglie's rather than that of Lieutenant Lindgren. The Lord himself had nothing to say just now that Des Grieux had time to hear. Des Grieux switched off the commo at the main console.

"Booster," he ordered the artificial intelligence, "enemy defenses in marked area."

Des Grieux's right index finger drew a rough circle bounded by Hill 504 and *Warrior*'s present position on the topographic display. "Best esti—"

An all-terrain truck snorted into view on the main screen. Des Grieux twisted his left joystick violently but he couldn't swing the tribarrel to bear in the moment before the tank rushed by in a spray of sand. The truck's crew jumped from both sides of the cab, leaving their vehicle to careen through the night unattended. "—mate!"

Booster had very little hard data, but the AI didn't waste time as a human intelligence officer might have done in decrying the accuracy of the assessment it was about to provide. The computer's best estimate was the same as Des Grieux's own: *Warrior* didn't have a snowball's chance in Hell of reaching the firebase.

Only one of Hill 504's flanks, the west/southwest octave, had a slope suitable for heavy equipment—including ammunition vans and artillery prime movers, and assuredly including *Warrior*. There were at this moment—best estimate—anywhere from five hundred to a thousand Rep soldiers scattered along the route the tank would have to traverse.

The Reps were artillerymen, headquarters guards, and stragglers, not the crack battalions *Warrior* had gutted in her charge out of the Federal lines—

But these troops were prepared. The exploding chaos had warned them. They would fire from cover: rifle bullets to peck out sensors; buzzbombs whose shaped-charge warheads could and eventually *would* penetrate heavy armor; cannon lowered to slam their heavy shells directly into the belly plates *Warrior* exposed as the tank lurched to the top of Hill 504 by the only possible access. . . .

"Driver," Des Grieux ordered. His fingertip traced as a vagearc across the topo screen at ninety degrees to the initial course. "Follow the marked route."

"Sir, there's no road!" Kuykendall shrilled.

Even on the trail flattened by the feet of Republican assault battalions, the tank proceeded in a worm of sparks and dust as its skirts dragged. Booster's augmented night vision gave the driver an image almost as good as daytime view would have been, but nothing could be sufficient to provide a smooth ride at sixty-five kph over unimproved wilderness.

"Screw the bloody road!" ordered Des Grieux. "Move!"

They couldn't go forward, but they couldn't go back, either. The survivors of the Republican attack were between *Warrior* and whatever safety the Federal bunker line could provide. If the tank turned and tried to make an uphill run through that gauntlet, satchel charges would rip vents in the skirts. Crippled, *Warrior* would be a stationary target for buzzbombs and artillery fire.

Des Grieux couldn't give the Reps time to set up. So long as the tank kept moving, it was safe. With her fusion powerplant and drive fans rated at 12,000 hours between major overhauls, *Warrior* could cruise all the way around the planet, dodging enemies.

For the moment, Des Grieux just wanted to get out of the immediate kill zone.

Kuykendall tilted the nacelles closer to vertical. Their attitude reduced the forward thrust, but it also increased the skirts' clearance by a centimeter or two. That was necessary insurance against a quartz outcrop tearing a hole in the skirts.

Trees twenty meters tall grew in the swales, where the water table was highest. Vegetation on the slopes and ridges was limited to low, spike-leafed bushes. Kuykendall rode the slopes, where the brush was less of a problem but the tank wasn't outlined against the sky. Des Grieux didn't have to think about what Kuykendall was doing, which made her the best kind of driver. . . .

A tank running at full power was conspicuous under almost any circumstances, but the middle of a major battle was one of the exceptions. Neither Des Grieux's instincts nor *Warrior*'s sensor array caught any sign of close-in enemies.

By slanting northeast, Des Grieux put them in the dead ground between the axes of the Republican attack. He was well behind the immediately engaged forces and off the supply routes leading from the two northern firebases. If he ordered Kuykendall to turn due north now, *Warrior* would in ten minutes be in position to circle Hill 661 and then head south to link up with the relieving force.

It didn't occur to Des Grieux that they could run from the battle. He just needed a little time.

The night raved and roared. Brushfires flung sparks above the ridgelines where *Warrior* had gutted the right pincer of the attack. Ammunition cooked off when flames reached the bandoliers of the dead and screaming wounded.

Bullets and case fragments sang among the surviving Reps. Men shot back in panic, killing their fellows and drawing return fire from across the flame curtains.

The hollow chunking sound within *Warrior*'s guts stopped with a final clang. The green numeral 20 appeared on the lower right-hand corner of Des Grieux's main screen, the display he was using for gunnery. His ready magazine was full again. He could pulse the night with another salvo of 20cm bolts.

Soon.

When Des Grieux blasted the Rep supports with rapid fire, he'd robbed *Warrior*'s main gun of half the lifespan it would have had if the weapon were fired with time for the bore to cool between shots. If he cut loose with a similar burst, again there was a real chance the eroded barrel would fail, perhaps venting into the fighting compartment with catastrophic results.

That possibility had no effect on Des Grieux's plans for the next ten minutes. He would do what he had to do; and by God! His tools, human and otherwise, had better be up to the job.

The sky in the direction of Hill 661 quivered white with the almost-constant muzzle flashes. Shells, friction-heated to a red glow by the end of their arc into the Federal encampment, then flashed orange. Artillery rockets moved too slowly for the atmosphere to light their course, but the Reps put flare pots in the rockets' tails so that the gunners could correct their aim.

"Sarge?" said Kuykendall tightly. "Where we going?"

Des Grieux's index finger drew a circle on the topographic display.

"Oh, lord . . ." the driver whispered.

But she didn't slow or deviate from the course Des Grieux had set her.

Warrior proceeded at approximately forty kph; a little faster on downslopes, a little slower when the drive fans had to fight gravity, as they did most of the time now. That was fast running over rough, unfamiliar terrain. The tank's night-vision devices were excellent, but they couldn't see that the opposite side of a ridge dropped off instead of sloping, or the tank-sized gully beyond the bend in a swale.

Kuykendall was getting them to the objective surely, and that was soon enough for Des Grieux. Whether or not it would be in time for the Federals on Hill 541 North was somebody else's problem.

The Republicans' right-flank assault was in disarray, probably terminal disarray, but the units committed to the east slope of the Federal position were proceeding more or less as planned. At least one of the Slammers' tanks survived, because the night flared with three cyan blasts spaced a chronometer second apart.

Probably Broglie, who cut his turds to length. Everything

perfect, everything *as ordered*, and who was just about as good a gunner as Slick Des Grieux.

Just about meant *second best*.

Shells crashed down unhindered on 541N. Some of them certainly fell among the Rep assault forces because the attack was succeeding. Federal guns slammed out rapid fire with the muzzles lowered, slashing the Reps with canister at point-blank range. A huge explosion rocked the hilltop as an ammo dump went off, struck by incoming or detonated by the defenders as the Reps overran it.

Des Grieux hadn't bothered to cancel his earlier command: *Booster, enemy defenses in marked area.* When his fingertip circled Hill 661 to direct Kuykendall, the artificial intelligence tabulated that target as well.

Twenty artillery pieces, ranging from 2cm to a single stub-barreled 30cm howitzer which flung 400-kilogram shells at fifteen-minute intervals.

At least a dozen rails to launch 20cm bombardment rockets.

A pair of calliopes, powerguns with eight 2cm barrels fixed on a carriage. They were designed to sweep artillery shells out of the sky, but their high-intensity charges could chew through the bow slope of a tank in less than a minute.

Approximately a thousand men: gunners, command staff, and a company or two of infantry for close-in security in case Federals sortied from their camp in a kamikaze attack.

All of them packed onto a quarter-kilometer mesa, and not a soul expecting *Warrior* to hit them from behind. The Republicans thought of tanks as guns and armor; but tanks meant mobility, too, and Des Grieux *knew* every way a tank could crush an enemy.

Reflected muzzle blasts silvered the plume of dust behind *Warrior*. The onrushing tank would be obvious to anyone in the firebase who looked north—

But the show was southwest among the Federal positions, where the artillerymen dropped their shells and toward which the infantry detachment stared—imagining a fight at knifepoint, and thinking of how much better off they were than their fellows in the assault waves.

Warrior thrust through a band of stunted brush and at a flat angle onto a stabilized road, the logistics route serving the Republican firebase.

"S—" Kuykendall said.

"Yes!" Des Grieux shouted. "Goose it!" Kuykendall had started to adjust her nacelles even before she spoke, but vectored thrust wasn't sufficient to steer the tank onto a road twenty meters wide at the present speed. She deliberately let the skirts drop, using mechanical friction to brake *Warrior*'s violent side-slipping as the bow came around.

The tank tilted noticeably into the berm, its skirt plowed up on the high side of the turn. Rep engineers had treated the road surface with a plasticizer that cushioned the shock and even damped the blaze of sparks that Des Grieux had learned to expect when steel rubbed stone with the inertia of 170 tonnes behind it.

Kuykendall got her vehicle under control, adjusted fan bite and nacelle angle, and began accelerating up the 10° slope to the target. By the time *Warrior* reached the end of the straight, half-kilometer run, they were travelling at seventy kph.

Two Republican ammunition vans were parked just over the lip of Hill 661. There wasn't room for a tank to go between them.

Kuykendall went through anyway. The five-tonne vehicles flew in opposite directions. The ruptured fuel tank of one hurled a spray of blazing kerosene out at a 30° tangent to the tank's course.

The sound of impact would have been enormous, were it not lost in the greater crash of *Warrior*'s guns.

The tank's data banks stored the image of bolts from the calliopes. Booster gave Des Grieux a precise vector to where the weapons had been every time they fired. The Republican commander could have ordered the calliopes to move since Federal incoming disappeared as a threat, but that was a chance Des Grieux had to take.

He squeezed both tits as *Warrior* crested the mesa, firing along the preadjusted angles.

The night went cyan, then orange and cyan.

The calliopes were still in their calculated positions. The tribarrel raked the sheet-metal chassis of one. Ready ammunition ignited into a five-meter globe of plasma bright enough to burn out the retinas of anyone looking in the wrong direction without protective lenses.

There was a vehicle parked between the second calliope and the onrushing tank. It was the ammunition hauler feeding a battery of 15cm howitzers. It exploded with a blast so violent that the tank's bow lifted and Des Grieux slammed back in his seat. Shells and burning debris flew in all directions, setting off a second vehicle hundreds of meters away.

The shockwave spilled the air cushion from *Warrior*'s plenum chamber. The tank grounded hard, dangerously hard, but the skirts managed to stand the impact. Power returned to *Warrior*'s screens after a brief flicker, but the topographic display faded to amber monochrome which blurred the fine detail.

"S'okay . . ." Des Grieux wheezed, because the seat restraints had bruised him over the ribs when they kept him from pulping himself against the main screen. And it *was* all right, because the guns were all right and the controls were in his hands.

Buttoned up, the tank was a sealed system whose thick armor protected the crew from the blast's worst effects. The Reps, even those in bunkers, were less fortunate. The calliope which Des Grieux missed lay on its side fifty meters from its original location. Strips of flesh and uniforms, the remains of its crew, swathed the breech mechanisms.

"Booster," Des Grieux said, "mark movement," and his tribarrel swept the firebase.

The Republicans' guns were dug into shallow emplacements. Incoming wasn't the problem for them that it had been for the Federals, pecked at constantly from three directions.

The gunners on Hill 541 North hadn't had enough ammunition to try to overwhelm the Rep defenses. Besides, calliopes were *designed* for the job of slapping shells out of the sky. In that one specialized role, they performed far better than tank tribarrels.

Previous freedom from danger left the Republican guns hopelessly exposed now that a threat appeared, but Des Grieux had more important targets than mere masses of steel aimed in the wrong direction. There were men.

The AI marked moving objects white against a background of gray shades on the gunnery screen. *Warrior* wallowed forward again, not fully under control because both Kuykendall and the skirts had taken a severe shock. Des Grieux used that motion and his cupola's high-speed rotation to slide the solid pipper across the display. Every time the orange bead covered white, his thumb stroked the firing tit.

The calliopes had been the primary danger. Their multiple bolts could cripple the tank if their crews were good enough—and only a fool bets that an unknown opponent doesn't know his job.

With the calliopes out of the way, the remaining threat came from the men who could swarm over *Warrior* like driver ants bringing down a leopard. The things that still moved on Hill 661 were men, stumbling in confusion and the shock of the massive secondary explosions.

Des Grieux's cyan bolts ripped across them and flung bodies down with their uniforms afire. Artillerymen fleeing toward cover, officers popping out of bunkers to take charge of the situation, would-be rescuers running to drag friends out of the exploding cataclysm—

All moving, all targets, all dead before anyone on the mesa realized that there was a Slammers' tank in their midst, meting out destruction with the contemptuous ease of a weasel in a hen coop

Des Grieux didn't use his main gun; he didn't want to take time to replenish the ready magazine before he completed the final stage of his plan. Twice *Warrior*'s automatic defense system burped a sleet of steel balls into Reps who ran in the wrong direction, but there was no resistance.

Mobility, surprise, and overwhelming firepower. One tank, with a commander who knew that you didn't win battles by crouching in a hole while the other bastard shoots at you. . . .

A 20cm shell arced from an ammo dump. It clanged like the wrath of God on *Warrior*'s back deck. The projectile was unfuzed. It didn't explode.

Only *Warrior* and the flames now moved on top of Hill 661. Normally the Republican crews bunkered their ammunition supply carefully, but rapid fire in support of the attack meant ready rounds were stacked on flat ground or held in soft-skinned vehicles. A third munitions store went up, a bunker or a vehicle, you couldn't tell after the fireball mushroomed skyward.

The shockwave pushed *Warrior* sideways into a sandbagged command post. The walls collapsed at the impact. An arm stuck out of the doorway, but the tribarrel had severed the limb from the body moments before.

The tank steadied. Des Grieux pumped deliberate bursts into a pair of vans. One held 30cm ammunition, the other was packed with bombardment rockets. A white flash sent shells tumbling skyward and down. Rockets skittered across the mesa.

"Booster," said Des Grieux. "Topo blowup of six-six-one. Break. Driver—"

A large-scale plan of the mesa filled the left-hand display. *Warrior* was a blue dot, wandering across a ruin of wrecked equipment and demolished bunkers.

"—put us there—" Des Grieux stabbed a point on the south-western margin of the mesa. He had to reach across his body to do so, because his left hand was welded to the tribarrels controls "—and hold. Break. Booster—"

Kuykendall swung the tank. *Warrior* now rode nose down by a few degrees. The bow skirts were too crumpled to seal at the normal attitude.

"—give me maximum magnification on the main screen."

Debris from previous explosions still flapped above Hill 661 like bat-winged Death. A fuel store ignited. The pillar of flame expanded in slow motion by comparison with the previous ammunition fires.

Though the main screen was in high-magnification mode, the right-hand display—normally the commo screen, but De Grieux had shut off external commo—retained a 120° panorama of *Warrior*'s surroundings. Images shifted as the tank reversed through the ruin its guns had created. Air spilling beneath the skirts stirred the flames and made their ragged tips bow in obeisance.

A Rep with the green tabs of a Central Command officer on his epaulets knelt with his hands folded in prayer. He did not look up as

Warrior slid toward him, though vented air made his short-sleeved khaki uniform shudder.

Des Grieux touched his left joystick. The Rep was already too close to *Warrior* for the tribarrel to bear; and anyway . . .

And anyway, one spaced-out man was scarcely worth a bolt.

Warrior howled past the Rep officer. A crosswind rocked the tank minusculy from Kuykendall's intended line, so that the side skirt drifted within five meters of the man.

Sensors fired a section of the automatic defense system. Pellets blew the Republican backward, as loose-limbed as a rag doll.

Kuykendall ground the skirts to bring the tank to a safe halt at the edge of the mesa. *Warrior* lay across a zigzag trench, empty save for a sprawled corpse. The drive fans could stabilize a tank in still air, but shockwaves and currents rushing to feed flames whipped the top of Hill 661.

Des Grieux depressed the muzzle of his main gun slightly. On *Warrior*'s gunnery screen, the hollow pipper slid over a high-resolution view of Republican positions on Hill 504.

The mesa on which *Warrior* rested was 150 meters higher than the irregular hillock on which the Reps had placed their western firebase. The twelve kilometers separating the two peaks meant nothing to the tank's powerguns.

On Hill 504, a pair of bombardment rockets leapt from their launching tubes toward the Federal encampment. The holographic image was silent, but Des Grieux had been the target of too many similar rounds not to imagine the snarling roar of their passage. He centered his ring sight on the munitions truck bringing another twenty-four rounds to the launchers—

And toed the foot-trip.

Warrior rocked with the trained lightning of its main gun. The display blanked in a cataclysm: pure blue plasma; metal burning white hot; and red as tonnes of warheads and solid rocket fuel exploded simultaneously. The truck and everything within a hundred meters of it vanished.

Des Grieux shifted his sights to what he thought was the Republican command post. He was smiling.

He fired. Sandbags blew outward as shards of glass. There were explosives of some sort within the bunker, because a moment after the rubble settled, a secondary explosion blew the site into a crater.

Concussion from the first blast had stunned or killed the crew of the single calliope on Hill 504. The weapon was probably unserviceable, but Des Grieux's third bolt vaporized it anyway.

"I told you bastards . . ." the tanker muttered in a voice that would have frightened anyone who heard him.

Dust and smoke billowed out in a huge doughnut from where the truckload of rockets had been. The air-suspended particles masked the remaining positions on Hill 504. Guns and bunker sites vanished into the haze like ships sinking at anchor. The main screen provided a detailed vision of whorls and color variations within the general blur.

"Booster," Des Grieux said. "Feed me targets." *Warrior*'s turret was supported by superconducting magnetic bearings powered by the same fusion plant that drove the fans. The mechanism purred and adjusted two degrees to starboard, under control of the artificial intelligence recalling the terrain before it was concealed. The hollow pipper remained centered on the gunnery screen, but haze appeared to shift around it.

The circle pulsed. Des Grieux fired the 20cm gun. Even as the tank recoiled from the bolt's release, the AI rotated the weapon toward the next unseen victim.

"Booster!" Des Grieux snarled. His throat was raw with gunnery fumes and the human waste products of tension coursing through his system. "*Show* me the bloody—"

The pipper quivered again. Des Grieux fired by reflex. A flash and a mushroom of black smoke penetrated the gray curtain. "Targets!"

The main gun depressed minutely. To Des Grieux's amazement, a howitzer on Hill 504 banged a further shell toward the Federal positions. *Warrior*'s AI obediently supplied the image of the weapon to Des Grieux's display as it steadied beneath the orange circle.

A bubble of gaseous metal sent the howitzer barrel thirty meters into the air.

With only one calliope to protect them, the Reps on 504 had dug in somewhat better than their fellows on Hill 661. Despite that, there was still a suicidal amount of ready ammunition stacked around the fast-firing guns. The tank's data banks fed each dump to the gunnery screen.

Des Grieux continued to fire. The haze over the target area darkened, stirred occasionally by sullen red flames. A red 0 replaced the green numeral 1 on the lower right corner of the screen. The interior of the fighting compartment stank like the depths of Hell.

"I told you bastards . . ." Des Grieux repeated, though his throat was so swollen that he had to force the words out. "And I told that bastard Lindgren."

"Sarge?" Kuykendall said.

Des Grieux threw the charging lever to refill the ready magazine. Just as well if he didn't use the main gun until the bore was relined; but the status report gave it ten percent of its original thickness, a safe enough margin for a few bolts, and you did what you had to do. . . .

"Yeah," he said aloud. "Get us somewhere outa the way. In the morning we'll rejoin. Somebody."

Kuykendall adjusted the fans so that they bit into the air instead of slicing through it with minimum disruption. She'd kept the power up while *Warrior* was grounded. In an emergency, they could hop off the mesa with no more than a quick change of blade angle.

The smoke-shrouded ruin of Hill 661 was unlikely to spawn emergencies, but in the four hours remaining till dawn some Rep officer might muster a tank-killer team. No point in making trouble for yourself. There were hundreds of kilometers of arid scrub which would hide *Warrior* until the situation sorted itself out.

And there were no longer any targets around *here* worthy of *Warrior*'s guns. Of that, Des Grieux was quite certain.

Kuykendall elected to slide directly over the edge of the mesa instead of returning to the logistics route by which they had attacked. The immediate slope was severe, almost 1:3, but there were no dangerous obstacles and the terrain flattened within a hundred meters.

There were bound to be scores of Rep soldiers on the road, some of them seeking revenge. A large number might fly into a lethal panic if they saw *Warrior*'s gray bow loom through the darkness. A smoother ride to concealment wasn't worth the risk.

"Sarge?" asked Kuykendall. "What's going on back at 541 North?"

"How the hell would I know?" Des Grieux snarled. But he could know, if he wanted to. He reached to reconnect the commo buss . . . and withdrew his hand. He could adjust a screen, and he started to do that—manually, because his throat hurt as if he'd been swallowing battery acid.

Instead of carrying through with the motion, Des Grieux lifted the crash bar to open the hatch and raise his seat to cupola level. The breeze smelled so clean that it made him dizzy.

Kuykendall eased the tank toward the low ground west of Hill 661. With a swale to shelter them, they could drive north a couple kays and avoid the stragglers from the Republican disaster.

For it had been a disaster. The Federal artillery on Hill 541N was in action again, lobbing shells toward the Rep staging areas. Fighting still went on within the encampment, but an increasing volume of fire raked the eastern slope up which the Reps had carried their initial assault objectives.

The weapons which picked over the remnants of the Republican attacks were machine guns firing white tracers, standard Federal issue; and at least a dozen tribarreled powerguns. A platoon of Slammers' combat cars had entered the Federal encampment and was helping the defenders mop up. The relief force had finally arrived.

"In the morning . . ." Des Grieux muttered. He was as tired as he'd ever been in his life.

And he knew that he and his tank had just won a battle single-handedly.

Warrior proceeded slowly up the eastern slope of Hill 541 North. The brush had burned to blackened spikes. Ash swirled over the ground, disintegrating into a faint shimmer in the air.

Given the amount of damage to the landscape, there were surprisingly few bodies; but there were some. They sprawled, looking too small for their uniforms; and the flies had found them.

Half an hour before dawn, Des Grieux announced in clear, on both regimental and Federal frequencies, that *Warrior* was re-entering the encampment. The AI continued to transmit that message at short intervals, and Kuykendall held the big vehicle to a walking pace to appear as unthreatening as possible.

There was still a risk that somebody would open fire in panic. The tank was buttoned up against that possibility.

It was easier when everybody around you was an enemy. Then it was just a matter of who was quicker on the trigger. Des Grieux never minded playing *that* game.

"Alpha One-six to Oyster Two commander," said a cold, bored voice in Des Grieux's helmet. "Dismount and report to the CP as soon as you're through the minefields. Over."

"Oyster Two to One-six," Des Grieux replied. Alpha One-six was the call sign of Major Joachim Steuben, Colonel Hammer's bodyguard. Steuben had no business being here, "Roger, as soon as we've parked the tank. Over."

"Alpha One-six to Oyster Two commander," the cold voice said. "I'll provide your driver with ground guides for parking, Sergeant. I suggest that this time, you obey orders. One-six out."

Des Grieux swallowed. He wasn't afraid of Steuben, exactly; any more than he was afraid of a spider. But he didn't like spiders either.

"Driver," he said aloud. "Pull up when you get through the minefield. Somebody'll tell you where they want *Warrior* parked."

"You bet," said Kuykendall in a distant voice.

Federal troops drew back at the tank's approach. They'd been examining what remained of the perimeter defenses, and dragging bodies cautiously from the wire. There were thousands of unexploded mines scattered across the slope.

Nobody wanted to be the last casualty of a successful battle.

Successful because of what Des Grieux had done. Something about the Feds seemed odd. After a moment, Des Grieux realized that it was their uniforms. The fabric was green—not clean, exactly, but not completely stained by the sandy red soil of Hill 541 North either. These were troops from the relieving force.

A few men of the original garrison watched from the bunker line. It was funny to see that many troops in the open sunlight; not scuttling, not cowering from snipers and shellfire.

The bunkers were ruins. Sappers had grenaded them during the assault. When the Federals counterattacked, Reps sheltered in the captured positions until tribarrels and point-blank shellfire blew them out. The roofs had collapsed. Wisps of smoke still curled from among the ruptured sandbags.

A Slammers' combat car—unnamed, with fender number 116—squatted in an overwatch position on the bunker line. The three tribarrels were manned, covering the troops in the wire. Bullet scars dented the side of the fighting compartment. A bright swatch of Spray Seal covered the left wing gunner's shoulder.

A figure was painted on the car's bow slope, just in front of the driver's hatch: a realistically drawn white mouse with pink eyes, nose, and tail.

The White Mice—the troops of Alpha Company, Hammer's Regiment— weren't ordinary line soldiers.

Nobody ever said they couldn't fight but they, under their CO, Major Steuben, acted as Hammer's field police and in other internal security operations.

A dozen anti-personnel mines went off under *Warrior*'s skirts as the tank slid through the perimeter defenses. Kuykendall tried to follow a track Rep sappers blew the night before, but *Warrior* overhung the cleared area on both sides.

The surface-scattered mines were harmless, except to a man who stepped on one. Even so, after the third *bang!* one of the Feds watching from the bunker line put his hands over his face and began to cry uncontrollably.

Three troopers wearing Slammers khaki and commo helmets waited at the defensive perimeter. One of them was a woman. They carried submachine-guns in patrol slings that kept the muzzles forward and the grips close to their gunhands.

They'd been sitting on the hillside when Des Grieux first noticed them. They stood as *Warrior* approached.

"Driver," Des Grieux said, "you can pull up here."

"I figured to," Kuykendall replied without emotion. Dust puffed forward, then drifted downhill as she shifted nacelles to brake *Warrior*'s slow pace.

Des Grieux climbed from the turret and poised for a moment on the back deck. The artillery shell that bounced from *Warrior* on Hill 661 had dished in a patch of plating a meter wide. Number seven intake grating ought to be replaced as well. . . .

Des Grieux hopped to the ground. One of the White Mice sat on *Warrior*'s bow slope and gestured directions to the driver. The tank accelerated toward the encampment.

"Come on, Sunshine," said the female trooper. Her features were blank behind her reflective visor. "The Man wants to see you."

She jerked her thumb uphill.

Des Grieux fell in between the White Mice. His legs were unsteady. He hadn't wanted to eat anything with his throat feeling as though it had been reamed with a steel-bore brush.

"Am I under arrest?" he demanded.

"Major Steuben didn't say anything about that," the male escort replied. He chuckled.

"Naw," added the woman. "He just said that if you give us any crap, we should shoot you. And save him the trouble."

"Then we all know where we stand," said Des Grieux. Soreness and aches dissolved in his body's resumed production of adrenaline.

The encampment on Hill 541 North had always been a wasteland, so Des Grieux didn't expect to notice a change now.

He was wrong. It was much worse, and the forty-odd bodies laid in rows in their zipped-up sleeping bags were only part of it.

The smell overlaid the scene. Explosives had peculiar odors. They blended uneasily with ozone and high-temperature fusion products formed when bolts from the powerguns hit.

The main component of the stench was death. Bunkers had been blown closed, but the rubble of timber and sandbags didn't form a tight seal over the shredded flesh within. The morning sun was already hot. In a week or two, a lot of wives and parents were going to receive a coffin sealed over seventy kilos of sand.

That wasn't Des Grieux's problem, though; and without him, there would have been plenty more corpses swelling in Federal uniforms.

General Wycherly's command post had taken a direct hit from a heavy shell. A high-sided truck with multiple antennas parked beside the smoldering wreckage. Federal troops in clean uniforms stepped briskly in and out of the vehicle.

The real authorities on 541N wore Slammers khaki. Major Joachim Steuben was short, slim, and so fine-featured that he looked like a girl in a perfectly-tailored uniform among Sergeant Broglie and several Alpha Company officers. They looked up as Des Grieux approached.

Steuben's command group stood under a tarpaulin slung between a combat car and Lieutenant Lindgren's tank. The roof of Lindgren's bunker was broken-backed from the fighting, but his tank looked all right at first glance.

At a second look—

"*Via!*" Des Grieux said. "What happened to *Queen City*?"

There were telltale soot stains all around the tank's deck, and the turret rested slightly askew on its ring. *Queen City* was a corpse, as sure as any of the staring-eyed Reps out there in the wire.

The female escort sniffed. "Its luck ran out. Took a shell down the open hatch. All they gotta do now is jack up what's left and slide a new tank underneath."

"Dunno how anybody can ride those fat bastards," the other escort muttered. "They maneuver like blind whales."

"Glad you could rejoin us, Sergeant," Major Steuben said. He gave the data terminal in his left hand to a lieutenant beside him. His voice was lilting and as pretty as Steuben's appearance, but it cut through any thought Des Grieux had of snarling a response to the combat-car crewman beside him.

"Sir," Des Grieux muttered. The Slammers didn't salute. Salutes in a war zone targeted officers for possible snipers.

"Would you like to explain your actions during the battle last night, Sergeant?" the major asked.

Steuben stood arms akimbo. His pose accentuated the crisp tuck of his waist. The fall of the slim right hand almost concealed the pistol riding in a cut-out holster high on Steuben's right hip.

The pistol was engraved and inlaid with metal lozenges in a variety of colors. In all respects but its heavy 1cm bore, it looked as surely a girl's weapon as its owner looked like a girl.

Joachim Steuben's eyes focused on Des Grieux. There was not a trace of compassion in the eyes or the soul beneath them. Any weapon in Steuben's hands was Death.

"I was winning a battle," Des Grieux said as his eyes mirrored Steuben's blank, brown glare. "Sir. Since the relieving force was still sitting on its hands after three weeks."

Broglie slid his body between Des Grieux and the major. Broglie was fast, but Steuben's pistol was socketed in Broglie's ear before the tanker's motion was half complete.

"I think Sergeant Des Grieux and I can continue our discussion better without you in the way, Mister Broglie," Steuben said. He didn't move his eyes from Des Grieux.

The White Mice hadn't bothered to remove the pistol from the holster on Des Grieux's equipment belt. Now Des Grieux knew why. *Nobody could be that fast. . . .*

"Sir," Broglie rasped through a throat gone dry. "*Warrior* did destroy both the Rep firebases. That's what took the pressure off here at the end."

Broglie stepped back to where he'd been standing.

He looked straight ahead, not at either Des Grieux or the major.

"You've named your tank *Warrior*, Sergeant?" Steuben said. "Amusing. But right at the moment I'm not so much interested in what you did as I am in why you disobeyed orders to do it."

He reholstered his gorgeous handgun with a motion as precise and delicate as that of a bird preening its feathers.

"You got some people killed, you know," the major added. His voice sounded cheerful, or at least amused. "Your lieutenant and his driver, because nobody was dealing with the shells from Hill 504."

He smiled coquettishly at Des Grieux. "I won't blame you for the other one. Hawes, was it?"

"Hawes, sir," Broglie muttered.

"Since Hawes was stupid enough to leave his position also," Steuben went on. "And I don't care a great deal about Federal casualties, except as they affect the Regiment's contractual obligations."

The pause was deadly.

"Which, since we *have* won the battle for them, shouldn't be a problem."

"Sir," Des Grieux said, "they were wide open. It was the one chance we were going to have to pay the Reps back for the three weeks we sat and took it."

Major Steuben turned his head slowly and surveyed the battered Federal encampment. His tongue went *tsk, tsk, tsk* against his teeth.

Warrior was parked alongside Broglie's *Honey Girl* in the center of the hill. *Warrior*'s bow skirts had cracked as well as bending inward when 170 tonnes slammed down on them. Kuykendall had earned her pay, keeping the tank moving steadily despite the damage.

Des Grieux's gaze followed the major's. *Honey Girl* had been hit by at least three buzzbombs on this side. None of the sun-hot jets seemed to have penetrated the armor. Broglie had been in the thick of it, with the only functional tank remaining when the Reps blew their way through the bunker line. . . .

The Federal gun emplacements were nearby. The Fed gunners had easily been the best of the local troops. They'd hauled three howitzers up from the gun pits to meet the Republican assault with canister and short-fused high explosive.

That hadn't been enough. Buzzbombs and grenades had disabled the howitzers, and a long line of bodies lay beside the damaged hardware.

"You know, Sergeant?" Steuben resumed unexpectedly. "Colonel Hammer found the relief force's progress a bit leisurely for his taste also. So he sent me to take command . . . and a platoon of Alpha Company, you know. To encourage the others."

He giggled. It was a terrible sound, like gas bubbling through the throat of a distended corpse.

"We were about to take Hill 541 South," Steuben continued. "In twenty-four hours we would have relieved the position here with minimal casualties. The Reps knew that, so they made a desperation assault . . . which couldn't possibly have succeeded against a bunker line backed up by four of our tanks."

Joachim's eyes looked blankly through Des Grieux.

"That's why," the delicate little man said softly, "I really think I ought to kill you now, before you cause other trouble."

"Sir," said Broglie. "Slick cleared our left flank. That had to be done."

Major Steuben's eyes focused again, this time on Broglie. "Did it?" the major said. "Not from outside the prepared defenses, I think. And certainly not against orders from a superior officer, who was—"

The cold stare again at Des Grieux. No more emotion in the eyes than there would be in the muzzle of the pistol which might appear with magical speed in Joachim's hand.

"Who was, as I say," the major continued, "passing on *my* orders."

"But . . ." Des Grieux whispered. "I *won*."

"No," Steuben said in a crisply businesslike voice. Moods seemed to drift over the dapper officer's mind like clouds across the sun. "You ran, Sergeant. I had to make an emergency night advance with the only troops I could fully trust—"

He smiled with cold affection at the nearest of his White Mice.

"In order to prevent Hill 541 North from being overrun. And even then I would have failed, were it not for the actions of Mister Broglie."

"Broglie?" Des Grieux blurted in amazement.

"Oh, yes," Joachim said. "Oh, yes, Mister Broglie. He took charge here after the Federal CP was knocked out and Mister Lindgren was killed. He put *Susie Q*'s driver back into the turret of the damaged tank and used that to stabilize the left flank. Then he led the counterattack which held the Reps on the right flank until my platoon arrived to finish the business."

"I don't like night actions when local forces are involved, Sergeant," he added in a frigid voice. "It's dangerous because of the confusion. If my orders had been obeyed, there would have been no confusion."

Steuben glanced at Broglie. He smiled, much as he had done when he looked at his White Mice. "I'm particularly impressed by the way you controlled the commo net alone while fighting your vehicle, Mister Broglie," he said. "The locals might well have panicked when they lost normal communications along with their command post."

Broglie licked his lips. "It was okay," he said. "Booster did most of it. And it had to be done. *I* couldn't stop the bastards alone."

"Wait a minute," Des Grieux said. "Wait a bloody minute! *I* wasn't just sitting on my hands, you know. I was fighting!"

"Yes, Sergeant," Major Steuben said. "You were fighting like a fool, and it appears that you're still a fool. Which doesn't surprise me."

He smiled at Broglie. "The colonel will have to approve your field promotion to lieutenant, Mister Broglie," he said, "but I don't foresee any problems. Of course, you'll have a badly understrength platoon until replacements arrive."

Des Grieux swung a fist at Broglie. The White Mice had read the signs correctly. The male escort was already holding Des Grieux's right arm. The woman on the other side bent the tanker's left wrist back and up with the skill of long practice.

Joachim set the muzzle of his pistol against Des Grieux's right eye. The motion was so swift that the cold iridium circle touched the eyeball before reflex could blink the lid closed.

Des Grieux jerked his head back, but the pistol followed. Its touch was as light as that of a butterfly's wing.

"*Via,* sir," Broglie gasped. "*Don't.* Slick's the best tank commander in the regiment."

Steuben giggled again. "If you insist, Mister Broglie," he said. "After all, you won the battle for us here."

He holstered the pistol. A warrior's frustrated tears rushed out to fill Des Grieux's eyes. . . .

PART II

Xingha was the staging area for the troops on the Western Wing: a battalion of the Slammers and more than ten thousand of the local Han troops the mercenaries were supporting.

The city's dockyard district had a way to go before it adapted to the influx of soldiers, but it was doing its manful, womanly, childish, and indeed bestial—best to accommodate the sudden need. Soon the entertainment facilities would reach the universal standard to which war sinks those who support the fighters; in all places, in every time.

Sergeant Samuel Des Grieux had seen the pattern occur often during his seven years in the Slammers. He could describe the progression as easily as an ecologist charts the process by which lakes become marshes, then forests.

Des Grieux didn't care one way or the other. He drank what passed for beer; listened to a pair of Oriental women keen, *"Oh where ha you been, Laird Randall, me son?"* (Hammers Slammers came to the Han contract from seven months of civil war among the Scottish colonists of New Aberdeen); and wondered when he'd have a chance to swing his tank into action. It'd been a long time since he had a tank to command. . . .

"Hey, is there anybody here from Golf Company?" asked a trooper, obviously a veteran but wearing new-issue khaki. His hair was in a triple ponytail, according to whim or the custom of some planet unfamiliar to Des Grieux. The fellow was moving from one table to the next in the crowded cantina. Just now, he was with a group of H Company tankers next to Des Grieux, bending low and shouting to be heard over the music and general racket.

"Hey, lookit that," said Pesco, Des Grieux's new driver. He pointed to the flat, rear-projection screen in the corner opposite the singers. "That's Captain Broglie, isn't he? What's he doing on local video?"

"Who bloody cares?" Des Grieux said. He finished his beer and refilled his glass from the pitcher.

If you tried, you could hear Broglie's voice—though not that of the Han interviewer—over the ambient noise. Despite himself, Des Grieux found himself listening.

"Hey, Johnnie," chirped a woman in a red dress as she draped her arm around Des Grieux's shoulders. She squeezed her obviously padded bosom to his cheek.

She was possibly fourteen, probably younger. "Buy me a drink?"

"Out," said Des Grieux, stiff-arming the girl into the back of a man at the next table. Des Grieux stared at the video screen, getting cues from Broglie's lips to aid as he fitted together the shards of speech.

"No, on the contrary, the Hindis make very respectable troops," Broglie said. "And as for Baffin's Legion, they're one of the best units for hire. I don't mean the Legion's in our class, of course. . . ."

A fault in the video screen—or the transmission medium—gave the picture a green cast. It made Broglie look like a three-week-old corpse. Des Grieux's lips drew back in a smile.

Pesco followed the tank commander's stare. "You served under him before, didn't you?" he asked Des Grieux. "Captain Broglie, I mean. What's he like?"

Des Grieux slashed his hand across the air in brusque dismissal. "I never served under him," he said. "When he took over the platoon I was in, I transferred to . . . infantry, Delta Company. And then combat cars, India and Golf."

" . . . Baffin's tank destroyers are first class," Broglie's leprous image continued. "Very dangerous equipment."

"Yeah, but look," Pesco objected. "With him, under him, it don't matter. What's he like, Broglie? Does he know his stuff, or is he gonna get somebody killed?"

Near where the singers warbled, *"Mother, make my bed soon . . ."* a dozen troopers had wedged two of the round tables together and were buying drinks for Sergeant Kuykendall. Des Grieux had heard his former driver'd gotten a twelve-month appointment to the Military Academy on Nieuw Friesland, with a lieutenancy in the Slammers waiting when she completed the course.

He supposed that was okay. Kuykendall had combat experience,

o she'd be at least a cunt-hair better than green sods who'd never
)een on the wrong end of a gun muzzle.

Of course, she didn't have the experience Des Grieux himself
did. . . .

"For I'm sick at the heart, and I fain would lie down," the singers
chirped through fixed smiles.

"Slick?" Pesco pressed. "Sarge? What about the new CO?"

Des Grieux shrugged. "Broglie?" he said. "He's a bloody good
shot, I'll tell you that. Not real fast—not as fast as I am. But when he
presses the tit, he nails what he's going after."

"Either of you guys from Golf?" asked the veteran in new fatigues.
"I just got back from leave and I'm lookin' for my cousin, Tip Rasidi."

"We're Hotel Company, buddy," Pesco said. "Tanks. Why don't
you try the Adjutant?"

"Because the bloody Adjutant lost half his bloody records in the
transit," the stranger snapped, "and the orderly sergeant tells me to
bugger off until he's got his bloody office sorted out. So I figure I'll
check around till I find what's happened to Tip."

The stranger scraped his way over to the next table, rocking
Pesco forward in his chair. The driver grimaced sourly.

"I don't know if the Hindis are brave or not," said Captain
Broglie's image. "I suppose they're like everybody else, some braver
than others. What I do know is that their troops are highly disciplined,
and *that* causes me some concern."

"C'mon, what about him, then?" Pesco said. "Broglie."

"He'll do what he's told," Des Grieux said, staring at the video
screen. His voice was clear, but it came from far away. "He's smart
and he's got balls, I'll give him that. But he'd rather kiss the ass of
whoever's giving orders than get out and fight. He coulda been
really something, but instead . . ."

Sergeant Kuykendall got up from her table. She was wearing a
red headband with lettering stitched in black. The others at the table
shouted, "Speech! Speech!" as Kuykendall tried to say something.

"Yeah, but what's Broglie gonna be like as an officer?" Pesco
demanded. "He just transferred to Hotel, you know. He'd been on
the staff."

"Sure, courage is important," Broglie said on the screen. Though his words were mild enough, his tone harshly dismissed the interviewer's question. "But in modern warfare discipline is absolutely crucial. The Hindi regulars are quite well-disciplined, and I fear that's going to make up for some deficiencies in their equipment. As for Baffin's Legion—"

Kuykendall broke away from her companions. She came toward Des Grieux, stepping between tables with the care of some one who knows how much she's drunk. The letters on her headband read "SIR!"

"—they're first rate in equipment *and* unit discipline. The war on the Western Wing isn't going to be a walkover."

"Kid," said Des Grieux in a voice that grated up from deep within his soul, "I'll give you the first and last rule about officers. The more they keep outa your way and let you get on with the fighting, the better they are. And when things really drop in the pot, they're always too busy to get in your way. Don't worry about them."

" . . . from Golf Company?" trailed the stranger's voice through a fissure in the ambient noise.

Sergeant Kuykendall bent over the table. "Hello, Slick," she said in measured tones. "I'm glad to see you're back in tanks. I always thought you belonged with the panzers."

Des Grieux shrugged. He was still looking at the screen, though the interview had been replaced by a stern-faced plea to buy War Stamps and support the national effort.

"Tanks," Des Grieux said, "combat cars . . . I ran a jeep gun once. It don't really matter."

Pesco looked up at Kuykendall. "Hey, Sarge," he said to her. "Congrats on the appointment. Want a beer?"

"Just wanted to say hi to Slick," she said. "Me and him served with Captain Broglie way back to the dawn of time, y' know."

"Hey," Pesco said, his expression brightening. "You know Broglie, then? Looks to me he's gota lot of guts, telling'em like it is on the video when they must a been figuring on a puff piece, is all. Likely to piss off Hammer, don't you think?"

Kuykendall glanced at the screen, though it now showed only a desk and a newsreader who mumbled unintelligibly. "Oh," she said, "I don't know. I guess the colonel's smart enough to know that telling the truth now that the contract's signed isn't going to do any harm. May help things if we run into real trouble; and we might, Baffin's outfit's plenty bloody good."

She looked at Pesco, then Des Grieux, and back to Pesco. There were minute crow's feet around Kuykendall's eyes where the skin had been smooth when she drove for Des Grieux. "But Broglie's got guts, you bet."

Des Grieux shoved his chair backward. "If guts is what it takes to toady t' the brass, he's got 'em, you bet," he snarled as he rose.

He turned. "Hey, buddy!" he shouted. "You looking for Tip Rasidi?"

Voices stilled, though clattering glass, the video screen, and the singers' recorded background music continued at a high level.

The stranger straightened to face the summons. Des Grieux said, "Rasidi drove for me on Aberdeen. We took a main-gun hit and burnt out. There wasn't enough of Tip to ship home in a matchbox."

The stranger continued to stand. His expression did not change, but his eyes glazed over.

The girl in the red dress sat at the table where Des Grieux had pushed her, wedged in between a pair of female troopers. Des Grieux gripped the girl by the shoulder and lifted her. "Come on," he snarled. "We're going upstairs."

One of the seated troopers might have objected, but she saw Des Grieux's face and remained silent.

The girl's face was resigned. She knew what was coming, but by now she was used to it.

"The tow and the halter," sang the entertainers, "for to hang on on tree. . . ."

The gravel highway steepened by a couple degrees before the switchback. The Han driving the four-axle troop transport just ahead of Des Grieux's tank opened his exhaust cut-outs to coax more power from the diesel.

As the unmuffled exhaust rattled, several of the troops on the

truck bed stuck their weapons in the air and opened fire. A jol
threw one of the Han soldiers backward. His backpack laser slashed
a brilliant line across the truck's canvas awning.

The lieutenant in command of the troops leaned from the cab
and shouted angrily at his men, but they were laughing too hard to
take much notice. Somebody tossed an empty bottle over the side in
enough of a forward direction that the officer disappeared back
within the cab.

The awnings moldered to either side of the long, blackened
rent, but the treated fabric would not sustain a fire by itself.

The truck ground through the switchback, spewing gravel. Both
forward axles were steerable. The vehicle was a solid piece of equipment, well designed and manufactured. The local forces in this
contract were a cursed sight better equipped than most of those you
saw. Mostly the off-planet mercenaries stood out from the indig
troops like diamonds on a bed of mud.

Both sets of locals, these Han and their Hindi rivals. . . .

"Booster," Des Grieux muttered as he sat in the cupola of his
tank. "Hindi combat vehicles, schematics. Slow crawl. Out."

He manually set his commo helmet to echo the artificia
intelligence's feed onto the left side of the visor. Des Grieux's cold
right eye continued to scan the line of the convoy and the terraces
that they had passed farther down the valley.

A soldier tossed another empty bottle from the truck ahead
Because the truck was higher and the road had reversed direction a
the switchback, the brown glazed ceramics hattered on the turre
directly below Des Grieux. A line of heads turned from the truck's
rail, shouting apologies and amused warnings to the soldier farther
within the vehicle who'd thrown the bottle without looking first.

Des Grieux squeezed his tribarrel's grips, overriding its presen
Automatic Air Defense setting. He slid the holographic sight picture
across the startled Han faces, which disappeared as the men flung
themselves flat onto the truck bed.

Pesco shifted his four rear nacelles and pivoted the tank
around its bow, following the switchback. They swung in behind
the truck again. Des Grieux released the grips and let the tribarrel

hift back to its normal search attitude: muzzles forward, at a 45°
levation.

Des Grieux had only been joking. Had he been serious, he'd
have put the first round into the fuel tank beneath the truck's cab.
Only then would he rake his bolts along the men screaming as they
ried to jump from the inferno of blazing kerosene. He'd done that
often enough before.

The artificial intelligence rotated three-dimensional images of
Hindi armor onto the left side of the visor in obedience to Des
Grieux's command. The schematic of a tank as flat as a floor tile
ifted to display the balloon tires, four per axle, which supported its
weight. In particularly marshy spots—and the rice paddies on both
ides of the border area were muddy ponds for most of the year—
he tires could be covered with one-piece tracks to lower the ground
pressure still further.

The tank did not have a rotating turret. Its long, slim gun was
mounted along the vehicle's centerline. The weapon used combus-
ion-augmented plasma to drive armor-piercing shots at velocities
of several thousand meters per second.

Comparable Han vehicles mounted lasers in small turrets.
Neither technology was quite as effective as the powerguns of the
Slammers—and Baffin's Legion; but they would serve lethally, even
gainst armor as thick as that of Des Grieux's tank.

The AI began to display a Hindi armored personnel carrier, also
unning on large tires behind a thin shield of armor. Des Grieux
witched his helmet to direct vision. The images continued to
licker unwatched on the left-hand screen below in the fighting
ompartment. Adrenaline from the bottle incident left the mercenary
oo restless to pretend interest in mere holograms.

There were hundreds of vehicles behind Des Grieux's tank. The
onvoy snaked down and across the valley floor for as far as he could
ee without increasing his visor's magnification. Most of the column
was of Han manufacture: laser vehicles, troop transports, maintenance
ans. Huge, articulated supply trucks with powerplants at both ends of
he load; *they'd* be bitches to get up these ridges separating the fertile
alleys.

Des Grieux didn't care about the logistics vehicles, whethe indigenous or the Slammers' own. His business was with things tha shot, things that fought. If he had a weapon, the form it took didn' matter. A tank like the one he commanded now was best; but if De Grieux had been an infantryman with nothing but a semiautomati powergun, he'd have faced a tank and not worried about the disparit in equipment. So long as he had a chance to fight . . . .

The convoy contained a Han mechanized brigade, the Blac Banner Guards: the main indig striking force on the Western Wing The tanks of Hammer's H Company were spread at intervals alon, the order of march to provide air and artillery defense.

Out of sight of the convoy, two companies of combat cars an another of infantry screened the force's front and flanks. Hammer' air-cushion vehicles were much more nimble on the boggy lowland than the wheeled and track-laying equivalents with which the indig made do.

No doubt the locals would rather have built their own ACVs but the technology of miniaturized fusion powerplants was beyon the manufacturing capacity of any but the most sophisticated handfu of human worlds. Without individual fusion bottles, air-cushio vehicles lacked the range and weight of weapons and armor necessar for frontline combat units.

So they hired specialists, the Han and Hindis both. If one sid in a conflict mortgaged its future to hire off-planet talent, the othe side either matched the ante—or forfeited that future.

The rice on the terraces had a bluish tinge that Des Grieu didn't remember having seen before, though he'd fought on half dozen rice-growing worlds over the years. . . .

His eyes narrowed. An air-cushion jeep sped up the road from the back of the column. It passed trucks every time the grade surface widened and gunned directly up-slope at switchbacks to cu corners. Des Grieux thought he recognized the squat figure in th passenger seat.

He looked deliberately away.

Des Grieux's tank was nearing the last switchback before th crest. The vehicle ahead began to blat through open exhaust pipe again, though its engine note didn't change. Han trucks used hydraulic torque converters instead of geared transmissions, so their diesels always stayed within the powerband. Lousy troops, but good equipment. . . .

Des Grieux imagined the jeep passing his tank—spinning a little in the high-pressure air vented beneath the tank's skirts— sliding under the wheels of the Han truck and then, as *Captain* Broglie screamed, being reduced to a millimeter's thick streak as the tank overran the wreckage despite all Pesco did to avoid the obstacle.

Des Grieux caught himself. He was shaking. He didn't know what his face looked like, but he suddenly realized that the soldiers in the truck ahead had ducked for cover again.

The truck turned hard left and dropped down the other side of the ridge. Brakelights glowed. The disadvantage of a torque coverter was that it didn't permit compression braking. . . .

From the crest, Des Grieux could see three more ridgelines furrowing the horizon to the west. The last was in Hindi territory. Three centuries ago, this planet had been named Friendship and colonized by the Pan-Asian Cooperative Settlement Authority. The organizers' plans had worked out about as well as most notions that depended on the Brotherhood of Man.

More business for Hammer's Slammers. More chances for Slick Des Grieux to do what he did better than anybody else. . . .

Pesco pivoted the tank, changing its attitude to follow the road before sliding off the crest. As the huge vehicle paused, the jeep came up along the port side. Des Grieux expected the jeep to pass them. Instead, the passenger—Broglie, as Des Grieux had known from the first glimpse—gripped the mounting handholds welded to the tank's skirts and pulled himself aboard.

The jeep dropped back. For a moment, Des Grieux could see nothing of his new company commander except shoulders and the top of his head as Broglie found the steps behind their spring-loaded coverplates. If he slipped now—

Broglie lifted himself onto the tank's deck. Unless Pesco was using a panoramic display—which he shouldn't be, not when the road ahead was more than enough to occupy anybody driving a vehicle of the tank's bulk—he didn't know what was going on behind him. The driver would have kittens when he learned, since at least half the blame would land on him if something went wrong.

Des Grieux would have taken his share of the trouble willingly, just to see the red smear where *that* human being had been ground into the gravel.

Broglie braced one foot on a turret foothold and leaned toward the cupola. "Hello, Slick," he said. He shouted to be heard over the rush of air into the fan intakes. "Since we're going to be working together again, I figured I'd come and chat with you. Without going through the commo net and whoever might be listening in."

Des Grieux looked at his new company commander. The skin of Broglie's face was red. Des Grieux remembered that the other man never seemed to tan, just weathered. He looked older, too; but Via, they all did.

"I didn't know you were going to be here when I took the transfer to Hotel," Des Grieux blurted. He hadn't planned to say that; hadn't *planned* to say anything, but the words came out when he looked into Broglie's eyes and remembered how much he hated the man.

"Figured that," said Broglie, nodding. He looked toward the horizon, then added, "You belong in tanks, Slick. They're the greatest force multiplier there is. A man who can use weapons like you ought to have the best weapons."

It wasn't flattery; just cold truth, the way Des Grieux had admitted that Broglie was a dead shot. It occurred to Des Grieux that his personal feelings about Brogue were mutual and always had been.

He said nothing aloud. If the company commander had come to talk, the company commander could talk.

"What's your tank's name, Slick?" Broglie asked.

Des Grieux shrugged. "I didn't name her," he said. "The guy I replaced did. I don't care cop about her name."

"That's not what I asked," Broglie said. "Sergeant."

"Right," said Des Grieux. His eyes were straight ahead, toward the horizon in which the far wall of the valley rose. "The name's *Gangbuster. Gangbuster II*, since you care so much. Sir."

"Glad to be back in tanks?" Broglie asked. His voice was neutral, but it left no doubt that he expected answers, whether or not Des Grieux saw any point in giving them.

"Any place is fine," Des Grieux said, turning abruptly toward Broglie again. "Just so long as they let me do my job."

The anger in Des Grieux's tone surprised even him. He added more mildly, "Yeah, sure, I like tanks. And if you mean it's been five years—don't worry about it. I haven't forgotten where the controls are."

"I don't worry about you knowing how to handle any bloody weapon there is, Slick," Broglie said. They stared into one another's eyes, guarded but under control. "I might worry about the way you took orders, though."

Des Grieux swallowed. A billow of dust rose around *Gangbuster*'s bow skirts and drifted back as Pesco slowed to avoid running over the truck ahead.

Des Grieux let the grit settle behind them before he said, "Nobody has to worry about *me* doing my job, Captain."

"A soldier's job is to obey orders, Slick," Broglie said flatly. "The time when heroes put on their armor and went off to single combat, that ended four thousand years ago. D'ye understand me?"

Des Grieux fumbled within the hatch and brought up his water bottle. The refrigerated liquid washed dust from his mouth but left the sour taste of bile. He stared at the horizon. It rotated sideways as Pesco negotiated a switchback.

"Do you understand me, Slick?" Captain Broglie repeated.

"I understand," Des Grieux said.

"I'm glad to hear it," Broglie said.

Des Grieux felt the company commander step away from the turret and signal to the driver of his jeep. All Des Grieux could see was the red throb of the veins behind his own eyes.

Ten kilometers to the west, the Han and Hindi outpost lines slashed at one another in a crackling barely audible through the darkness.

"These are the calculated enemy positions," said Captain Broglie.

The portable projector spread a holographic panorama in red for Broglie and the three tank commanders of H Company, 2nd Platoon.

Ghosts of the coherent light glowed on the walls of the tent. The polarizing fabric gave the Slammers within privacy but allowed them to see and hear the world outside.

"And here's Baffin's Legion," Broglie continued.

A set of orange symbols appeared to the left, map west, of the red images. The Legion, a combined-arms force of battalion strength, made a relatively minor showing on the map, but none of the Slammers were deceived. Almost any mercenary unit was better than almost any local force; and Baffin's Legion was better than almost any other mercenaries. Almost.

"Remember," Broglie warned, "Baffin can move just as fast as we can. In fifteen minutes, he could be driving straight through the friendly lines."

A battery of the Slammers' rocket howitzers was attached to the Strike Force. The hogs chose this moment to send a single round apiece into the night. The white glare of their simultaneous muzzle flashes vanished as suddenly as it occurred, but after image from the shells' sustainer motors flickered purple and yellow across the retinas of anyone without eye protection who had been looking in the direction of those brilliant streaks.

"Are they shelling Morobad?" asked Platoon Sergeant Peres. Peres had been in command of 2nd Platoon ever since the former platoon leader vanished in an explosion on New Aberdeen that left a fifty-foot crater where his tank had been. She gestured toward the built-up area just west of the major canal that the map displayed. Morobad was the only community in the region that was more than mud houses and a central street.

Hundreds of Han soldiers started shooting as though the artillery signalled a major attack. Small arms, crew-served weapons, and even the soul-searing throb of heavy lasers ripped out from the perimeter. Flashes and the dull glow of self-sustaining brushfires marked the innocent targets downrange.

"Stupid bastards," Des Grieux muttered, his tone too flat to be sneering. "If they're shooting at anything, it's their own people."

"You got that right, Slick," Broglie agreed as he stared for a moment through the pervious walls of the tent. His face was bleak; not angry, but as determined as a storm cloud.

Han officers sped toward the sources of gunfire on three-wheeled scooters, crying orders and blowing oddly tuned whistles. Some of the shooting came from well within the camp.

A rifle bullet zinged through the air close enough to the Slammers' tent that the fabric echoed the ballistic crack. Medrassi, the veteran commander of *Dar es Salaam*—House of Peace—swore and hunched his head lower on his narrow shoulders.

"What we oughta do," Des Grieux said coldly, "is leave these dumb clucks here and handle the job ourself. That way there's only half the people around likely t' shoot us."

Cyan streaks quivered over the horizon to the west. The light wasn't impressive until you remembered it came from ten kilometers away. Shells burst in puffs of distant orange.

Broglie lifted his thumb toward the western horizon. "I think that's what they were after, Perry," he said to Sergeant Peres. "Just checking on how far forward Baffin's artillery defenses were."

"Calliopes?" Medrassi asked.

Firing from the Han positions slackened. In the relative silence, Des Grieux heard the *pop-pop-pop* of shells, half a minute after powergun bolts had detonated them.

"Baffin uses twin-barrel 3cm rigs," Broglie explained. "They're really light antitank guns converted to artillery defense. He's got about eight of them. They're slow firing, but they pack enough punch that a single bolt can do the job."

He smiled starkly. "And they still retain their anti-tank function, of course."

Des Grieux spit on the ground.

"The reason that we're not going to leave our brave allies parked here out of the way, Slick," Broglie continued, "is that we're going to need all the help we can get. Indigenous forces may include an entire armored brigade. The Hindis are tough opponents in their own right—don't judge them by the Han we're saddled with. And Baffin's

Legion by itself would be a pretty respectable opponent—even for a Slammers' battalion combat team."

"Great," Peres said, kneading savagely at the scar on the back of her left hand. "Let's do it the other way, then. We keep the hell outa the way while our indig buddies mix it with Baffin and get all this wild shooting outa their system."

"What we're going to do," Broglie said, taking charge of the discussion again, "is turn a sow's ear into a . . . nice synthetic purse, let's say. Second Platoon is going to do that."

He looked at his subordinates. "And I am, because I'm going to be with you tomorrow."

The holographic display responded to Broglie's gestures. Blue arrows labeled as units of the Black Banner Guards wedged their way across the map toward the Hindi lines. Four gray dots, individual Slammers tanks, advanced beyond the arrows like pearls on a velvet tray.

"The terrain is pretty much what we've seen in each of the valleys we crossed on the Han side of the boundary," Broglie said. "Dikes between one and two meters high. Some of them broad enough to carry a tank but *don't* count on it. Mostly the dikes are planted with hedges that give good cover, and Hindi troops are dug into the mud of the banks. At least Hindi troops—Baffin may be stiffening them."

"Morobad's not the same," Medrassi said through the hedge of his dark, gnarled fingers. "Fighting in a city's not the same as nothing. 'Cept maybe fighting in Hell."

"Don't worry," said Broglie dismissively. "Nobody's going anywhere near that far."

He looked at his tank commanders. "What the Strike Force is going to do, guys," he said. "You, me, and the Black Banner Guards . . . is move up—" blue arrows came in contact with the red symbols "—hit 'em—" the arrows flattened "—and retreat in good order, Lord willing and we all do our jobs."

"We'll do *our* jobs," Sergeant Peres grunted, "but where the hell's the rest of H Company?"

She raised her eyes from the horrid fascination of the

holographic display, where blue symbols retreated eastward across terrain markers and red bars formed into arrows to pursue. "Where the *hell* is the rest of the battalion, Echo, Foxtrot, and Golf?"

The blue arrows on the display had attacked ahead of the gray tank symbols. As the Han forces began to pull back, the tanks provided the bearing surface on which the advancing Hindis ground in an increasingly desperate attempt to reach their planetary enemies.

"Fair question," Broglie said, but he didn't cue the holographic display. Symbolic events proceeded at their own pace.

Outside the Slammers' shelter, a multi-barreled machine gun broke the near silence by firing skyward. Loops of mauve tracers rose until the marking mixture burned out two thousand meters above the camp. Han officers went off again in their furious charade of authority.

Des Grieux sneered at the lethal fireworks on the other side of the one-way fabric. The bullets would be invisible when they fell; but they were going to fall, in or bloody close to the Han lines. Broglie was a fool if he thought *this* lot was going to do the Slammers' fighting for them.

Red arrows forced their way forward over holographic rice paddies. The counterattack spread sideways as Han symbols accelerated their retreat. The gray pearls of the four tanks shifted back more quickly under threat of being overrun on both flanks. Orange arrows joined the red when the computer model estimated that Baffin would commit his far-more-mobile forces to exploit the Hindi victory.

"The rest of our people are here," Broglie said as lines and bars of gray light sprang into place to the north, south, and east of the enemy salient. "Waiting in low-observables mode until Baffin's got too much on his plate to worry about fine tuning his sensor data. Waiting to slam the door."

On either flank of the red-and-orange thrust was a four-tank platoon from H Company and a full company of combat cars. Gray arrows curving eastward indicated combat cars racing across rice paddies in columns of muddy froth, moving to rake the choke point just east of Morobad where enemy vehicles bunched as reinforcements collided with units attempting a panicked retreat.

The dug-in infantry of the Slammers' Echo Company blocked the Hindi eastward advance. On the holographic display, blue Han symbols halted their retreat, then moved again to attack their trapped opponents in concert with Hammer's infantry and the tanks of 2nd Platoon.

The display still showed 2nd to have four vehicles. Everybody in the shelter knew that rear-guard actions always meant casualties—and didn't always mean survivors.

Medrassi grunted into his hands.

"The hogs'll provide maximum effort when the time comes," Broglie said. "The locals have about thirty self-propelled guns, also, but their fire direction may leave something to be desired."

"It's not," Peres said, "going t' be a lot of fun. Until the rest of our people come in."

"The battle depends on 2nd Platoon," Broglie said flatly. "You're all highly experienced, and mostly your drivers are as well. Slick, how do you feel about your driver, Pesco? He's the new man."

Des Grieux shrugged. "He'll do," he said. Des Grieux was looking at nothing in particular through the side of the tent.

Broglie stared at Des Grieux for a moment without expression. Then he resumed, "Colonel Hammer put Major Chesney in command of this operation, but it's not going to work unless 2nd does its job. That's why I'm here with you. We've got to convince the Hindis—and particularly Baffin—that the attack is real and being heavily supported by the Slammers. After the locals pull back—"

He looked grimly at the display, though its image—enemy forces trapped in a pocket while artillery hammered them into surrender—was cheerful enough for Pollyanna.

"After the Han pull back," the captain continued softly, "it's up to us to keep the planned withdrawal from turning into a genuine rout. Echo can't hold by itself if Baffin's Legion slams into them full tilt . . . and if that happens—"

Broglie smiled the hard, accepting smile of a professional describing events which would occur literally over his own dead body.

"—then Baffin can choose which of our separated flanking forces he swallows up first, can't he?"

A Han laser slashed the empty darkness from the perimeter.

"Bloody marvelous," Peres murmured. "But I suppose if they knew what they was doing, they wouldn't need us t' do it for them."

Medrassi laughed. "Dream on," he said.

"Do you all understand our mission, then?" Broglie asked. "Sergeant Peres?"

"Yes sir," Peres said with a nod.

"Sergeant Medrassi?"

"Yeah, sure. I been in worse."

"Slick?"

Des Grieux stared at the wall of the shelter. His mind was bright with the rich, soul-devouring glare of a tank's main gun.

"Sergeant Des Grieux," Broglie said. His voice was no louder than it had been a moment before, but it cut like an edge of glass. "Do you understand the operation we will carry out tomorrow?"

Des Grieux looked at his commanding officer. "Chesney never came up with anything this cute," he said mildly. "This one was your baby? Sir."

"I had some input in the planning, that's right," Broglie said tonelessly. "Do you understand the operation, Slick?"

"I understand that it makes a real pretty picture, Cap'n Broglie," Des Grieux replied. "Tomorrow we'll see how it looks on the ground, won't we?"

Outside the shelter, machine gun fire etched the sky in pointless response.

The Han armored personnel carrier was supposed to be amphibious, but it paused for almost thirty seconds on the first dike. The wheels of the front two axles spun in the air; those of the rear pair churned in a suspension of mud and water with the lubricating properties of motor oil.

A Hindi anti-tank gun ripped the APC with a 50mm osmium penetrator. Half of the carrier's rear-mounted engine blew through the roof of the tilted vehicle with a *crash* much louder than the Mach 4 ballistic crack of the shot.

The driver hopped out of the forward hatch and fell down on the dike. His legs continued to piston as though he were running instead of thrashing in mud. Side-hatches opened a fraction of a second later and a handful of unhurt infantrymen flopped clear as well.

Inertia kept the APC's front wheels rotating for some seconds. A rainbow slick of diesel fuel covered the rice paddy behind the vehicle. It did not ignite.

Des Grieux smiled like a shark from his overwatch position on the first terrace east of the floodplain. He traversed his main gun a half degree. The Hindi antitank gun was a towed piece with optical sights. It had no electronic signature to give it away, and *Gangbuster II*'s magnetic anomaly detector was far too coarse a tool to provide targeting information at a range of nearly a kilometer.

When the weapon fired, though—

Des Grieux stroked his foot-trip and converted the anti-tank gun into a ball of saturated cyan light.

Han vehicles hosed the landscape with their weapons. Bullets from APC turrets and the secondary armament of laser-vehicles flashed as bright explosions among the foliage growing on dikes and made the mud bubble.

High-powered lasers raised clouds of steam wherever their pale beams struck, but they were not very effective. The lasers were line-of-sight weapons like the Slammers' powerguns. The gunners could hit nothing but the next hedge over while the firing vehicles sheltered behind dikes themselves.

The entire Han advance stopped when the Hindis fired their first gun.

Des Grieux had a standard 2cm Slammers carbine clipped to the side of his seat. Over his head, *Gangbuster*'s tribarrel pumped short bursts into the heavens in automatic air-defense mode. The sky, still a pale violet color in the west, was decorated with an appliqué of shell tracks and the bolts of powerguns which detonated the incoming.

Both sides' artillery fired furiously. Neither party had any success in breaking through the webs of opposing defenses, but there was no question of taking *Gangbuster II* out of AAD. The infantry carbine and the tank's main gun were the only means of slaughter under Des Grieux's personal control.

"Blue Two," Captain Broglie's voice ordered. "On command, advance one dike. Remaining elements look sharp."

Blue Two, *Dar es Salaam*, was on the southern edge of the advance, half a kilometer from *Gangbuster II*. Broglie's command tank, *Honey Girl*, was a similar distance to starboard of Des Grieux; and Blue One, Peres, backstopped the Han right flank a full kilometer north of *Gangbuster II*. The causeway carrying the main road to Morobad was the axis of the Strike Force advance.

The dikes turned the floodplain into a series of ribbons, each about a hundred meters wide. By advancing one at a time from their overwatch positions behind the Black Banner Guards, maybe the Slammers' tanks could get the Han force moving again. . . .

Though if instead the four tanks burst straight ahead in a hell-for-leather dash, they'd open up the Hindi lines like so many bullets through a can of beans.

"Blue Two, *go*."

Medrassi's tank lurched forward at maximum acceleration. The driver—Des Grieux didn't know his name; *her* name, maybe—had backed thirty meters in the terraced paddy to give himself a run before they hit the dike.

Water and bright green rice shoots, hand-planted only days before, spewed to either side as the fans compressed a cushion of air dense enough to float 170 tonnes. For a moment, *Dar es Salaam*'s track through the field was a barren expanse of wet clay; then muddy water slopped back to cover the sudden waste.

The tank didn't lift quite high enough to clear the dike, but the driver didn't intend to. The belly plates were the vehicle's thinnest armor. Hindi gunners, much less the Legion mercenaries, could penetrate even a Slammers' tank if it waved too much of its underside in the direction of the enemy.

Dar es Salaam's bow skirts rammed the top layer of the bank ahead of the tank. Fleshy-branched native osiers flailed desperately as they fell with the dike in which they had grown.

Honey Girl fired its main gun. Des Grieux didn't see Broglie's target but there *was* a target, because the bolt detonated an anti-tank gun's 400-liter bottle of liquid propellant in a huge yellow flash. The barrel of the Hindi weapon flew toward the Han lines. The bodies of the gun crew shed parts all around the hemispherical blast.

Des Grieux didn't have a target. That bastard Broglie was good, Lord knew.

A pair of Han laser-vehicles resumed the planned advance; or tried to, they'd bogged in the muck when they stopped. Spinning wheels threw brown undulations to either side but contributed nothing to the forward effort. The Han vehicles were supposed to be all-terrain, but they lacked the supplementary treads the Hindi tanks used. The paddies might have been too much for the balloon tires even if the heavy vehicles had kept moving.

Four APCs grunted into motion—drawn by *Dar es Salaam* and encouraged by the deadly 20cm powerguns on the mercenary tanks. The carriers found the going difficult also, but their lower ground pressure made them more mobile than the laser-vehicles were.

Thirty or more of the APCs joined the initial quartet. The advance, one or two vehicles revving into motion at a time, looked like individual drivers and officers making their own decisions irrespective of orders from above—but it had the effect of a planned leapfrog assault.

"Blue One," Broglie ordered. "On command, advance one dike. Remaining elements look sharp." Only buzzbombs and a few light crew-served weapons replied to the empty storm of Han fire. The Hindis kept their heads down and picked their targets.

Bullet impacts glittered on the glacis plate of an APC driving parallel to the causeway. The commander had been conning his vehicle with his head out of the cupola hatch. He ducked down immediately. The driver must have ducked also, even though he was using his periscopes. The APC ran halfway up the side of the causeway and overturned.

"Blue One, *go!*"

As Peres' driver kicked *Dixie Dyke* forward, Des Grieux's gunnery screen marked a target with a white carat. The barrel of a Hindi gun was rotating to bear when Peres' tank exposed its belly. Excellent camouflage concealed the motion from even the Slammers' high-resolution optics, but the magnetic anomaly detector noticed the shift against the previous electromagnetic background.

Gangbuster II's turret traversed four degrees to starboard on its magnetic gimbals. The cupola tribarrel snarled up at incoming artillery fire, but the only sound within the fighting compartments was the whine of the turret drive motors and the whistling intake of Des Grieux's breath as he prepared to kill a. . . .

The target vanished in the blue-white glare of *Honey Girl*'s bolt. Broglie had beaten Des Grieux to the shot again, and *fuck* that the target was in *Honey Girl*'s primary fire zone.

"Blue Three," Broglie ordered with his usual insouciant calm. "On command, advance two, I repeat two, dikes. Remaining elements, look sharp."

"Driver," Des Grieux ordered, "you heard the bastard."

Medrassi fired, but he didn't have a bloody target for a main-gun bolt, there *wasn't* one. A section of dike flash-baked and blew outward as ceramic shards, but Via! what did a couple Hindi infantry matter?

Des Grieux ordered, "Booster, echo main screen, left side of visor, out," and pulled up hard on the seat-control lever. The seat rose. Des Grieux's head slid out of the hatch just as the cupola rotated around him and the tribarrel spat three rounds into the western sky with an acrid stench from the ejected empties.

"Blue Three, *go!*"

"Goose it, driver!" Des Grieux said as he unclipped the shoulder weapon from his seat and felt *Gangbuster II* rise beneath him on the thrust of its eight drive fans to mount the dike.

The Han advance was proceeding in reasonable fashion, though at least a score of APCs hung back at the start point. Several laser-vehicles were moving also. The inaction of the rest was more likely the bog than cowardice, though cowardice was never an unreasonable guess when unblooded troops ran into their first firefight.

One laser-vehicle balanced on top of a dike. The fore and aft axles spun their tires in the air, while the grip of the central wheels was too poor to move them off the slick surface. Hindi skirmishers lobbed their buzzbombs at long range toward the teetering vehicle, but the anti-tank guns contemptuously ignored it to wait for a real threat.

To wait for the Slammers' tanks.

Des Grieux's eyes were four meters above the ground surface, higher than the tank's own sensors, when *Gangbuster II* humped itself over the dike. Through the clear half of his visor Des Grieux saw the movement, the glint of the plasma generator trunnion-mounted to an anti-tank gun, as it swung beneath its overhead protection.

The little joystick in the cupola was meant as a manual control for the defense array, but it was multi-function at need—and Des Grieux needed it. He rotated and depressed the main gun with his left hand as *Gangbuster II* started her fierce rush down the reverse side of the dike and the Hindi weapon traversed for the kill.

The pipper on the left side of Des Grieux's visor merged in a stereo image with the view of his right eye. He thumbed the firing tit with a fierce joy, knowing that *nobody* else was that good.

But Slick Des Grieux was. As the tank bellied down into the spray of her fans, a yellow fireball lifted across the distant fields. A direct hit, snap-shooting and on the move, but Des Grieux was the best!

Broglie fired also, from the other side of the empty road to Morobad. He must've got something also, because a secondary explosion followed the bolt, but the Hindis—strictly locals, no sign at all of the Legion—weren't done yet. A hypervelocity shot *spanged* from *Gangbuster*'s turret. Kinetic energy became heat with a flash almost as bright as that of a plasma bolt, rocking Des Grieux backward.

He turned toward the shot, pointing his short-barreled shoulder weapon as though it were a heavy pistol. The tank bottomed on the paddy, then bounced upward nearly a meter as water rushed in to fill the cavity, sealing the plenum chamber to maximum efficiency.

The Hindi weapon was dug in low; it had fired through a carefully cut aisle. Now the gunners waited to shoot again, hoping

for more of a target than Des Grieux's helmeted head bobbing over
the planted dikes between them. None of the three Slammers' tanks
providing the base of fire could bear on the anti-tank gun even now
that it had exposed itself by firing. *Gangbuster II*'s main gun was
masked by the vegetation, also, but Des Grieux's personal weapon
spat three times on successive bounces as the tank porpoised
forward. The gun's frontal camouflage flashed and burned when a
2cm bolt flicked it. Han officers, guided by the powergun, sent a
dozen ropes of tracer arcing toward the Hindi weapon from the
cupolas of their APCs. Hindi gunners splashed away from the beaten
zone, hampered by the mud and raked by the hail of explosive bullets.

The *peepeepeep* in Des Grieux's earphones warned him to
attend to the miniature carat on his visor: Threat Level I, a laser
rangefinder painting *Gangbuster II* from the hedge bordering the
causeway. No way to tell what weapon the rangefinder served, but
somebody thought it could kill a Slammers' tank. . . .

Des Grieux rotated the turret with the joystick, thrusting hard
as though his muscles rather than the geartrain were turning the
massive weight of iridium. "Driver, hard right!" he screamed,
because the traversing mechanism wasn't going to slew the main
gun fast enough by itself.

And maybe nothing was going to slew the main gun fast
enough.

Des Grieux shot twice with the carbine in his right hand. His
bolts splashed near the bottom of the hedge. One round blew glassy
fragments of mud in the air; the other carbonized a gap the size of a
pie plate at the edge of the interwoven stems of native shrub.

The laser emitter itself was two meters high in the foliage, but
that was only a bead connected to the observer's hiding place by a
coaxial optical fiber. The observer was probably *close* to the emitter,
though; and if the weapon itself was close to the observer, it would
simply pop up and make parallax corrections.

Soldiers liked things simple.

Pesco was trying to obey Des Grieux's order, but *Gangbuster II*
had enormous forward momentum and there was the dike they
were approaching to consider, also. A sheet of spray lifted to the

tank's port side as the driver dumped air beneath the left skirt. The edge of the right skirt dipped and cut yellow bottom clay to stain the roostertail sluicing back on that side.

Gangbuster II started to lift for the dike. That was almost certainly the Hindi aiming point, but Des Grieux had the sight picture he wanted, he *needed*—

Des Grieux tripped the main gun. Five meters of mud and vegetation exploded as the 20cm bolt slanted across the base of the hedge.

The jolt of sun-hot plasma certainly blinded the laser pickup. It probably incinerated the observer as well: no mud burrow could withstand the impact of a tank's main gun.

The causeway was gouged as if a giant shark had taken a bite out of it. The soil steamed. Fragments of hedge blazed and volleyed orange sparks for twenty meters from where the bolt hit.

The weapon the observer controlled, a rack of four hypervelocity rockets dug into the edge of the causeway ten meters west of the rangefinder, was not damaged by the bolt. The observer's dying reflex must have closed the firing circuit.

A section of causeway collapsed from the rockets' back blast. *Gangbuster II*'s automatic defense system fired too late to matter. The sleet of steel pellets disrupted the razor-sharp smoke trails, but the projectiles themselves were already past.

The exhaust tracks fanned out slightly from the launcher. One of the four rockets missed *Gangbuster*'s turret by little more than the patina on the iridium surface. The sound of their passage was a single, brittle *c-c-crack!*

Because *Gangbuster II* was turning in the last instant before the missiles fired—and because the main gun had blasted the observer into stripped atoms and steam before he could correct for the course change—the tank was undamaged, and Des Grieux was still alive to do what he did best.

It was time to do that now, whatever Broglie's orders said.

"Driver, steer for the road!" Des Grieux ordered. "Highball! We're gonna gut 'em like fish, all the way t' the town!"

"Via, we can't do that!" Pesco blurted. *Gangbuster II* dropped off the dike in a flurry of dirt, water, and vegetation diced by the fans. "Cap'n Broglie said—"

Des Grieux craned his body forward and aimed his carbine. He fired, dazzling the direct vision sensors built into the driver's hatch coaming. The bolt vaporized a tubful of water ahead of *Gangbuster II* and sent cyan quivers through a semicircle of the paddy.

"Drive, you son of a bitch!" Des Grieux shouted.

Pesco resumed steering to starboard, increasing the slant *Gangbuster II* had taken to bring the 20cm gun to bear. The gap that bolt had blown in the causeway's border steadied across the tank's bow slope.

A dozen Hindi machine guns in the dikes and causeway rang bullets off *Gangbuster II*'s armor. One round snapped the air close enough to Des Grieux's face to fluff his moustache. It reminded him that he was still head and shoulders out of the cupola.

He shoved down the crash bar and dumped himself back into the fighting compartment. The hatch clanged above him, shutting out the sound of bullets and *Gangbuster II*'s own tribarrel plucking incoming artillery from the air.

Des Grieux slapped the AAD plate to put the tribarrel under his personal control again.

All three of the tanks in overwatch fired within split seconds of one another. A column of flame and smoke mounted far to the north, suggesting fuel tanks rather than munitions were burning.

Of course, the victim might have been one of the Han vehicles.

The topographic display on *Gangbuster II*'s left-hand screen showed friendly units against a pattern of fields and hedges. The entire Han line was in motion, spurred by the mercenaries' leapfrog advance and the Han's own amateur enthusiasm for war.

They'd learn. At least, the survivors would learn.

"General push," Des Grieux said, directing the tank's artificial intelligence to route the following message so that everyone in the Strike Force—locals as well as mercenaries—could receive it. "All units, follow me to Morobad!"

His hand reached into the breaker box and disconnected *Gangbuster II* from incoming communications.

★ ★ ★ ★

The flooded rice paddies slowed the tank considerably. One hundred seventy tonnes were too much for even the eight powerful drive fans to lift directly. The vehicle floated on a cushion of air, but that high-pressure air required solid support, also.

The water and thin mud of the paddies spewed from the plenum chamber. *Gangbuster II* rode on the clay undersurface—but the liquid still created drag on the outside of the skirts as the tank drove through it. To make the speed Des Grieux knew it needed to survive, *Gangbuster II* had to have a smooth, hard surface beneath her skirts.

The causeway was such an obvious deathtrap that none of the Han vehicles had even attempted it—but the locals didn't have vehicles with the speed and armor of a Slammers tank.

And anyway, they didn't have Des Grieux's awareness of how important it was to keep the enemy off balance by punching fast as well as often.

Des Grieux latched the 2cm carbine back against his seat. The barrel, glowing from the half magazine the veteran had fired through it, softened the patch of cushion it touched. The stench intertwined with that oozing from the main gun empties on the floor of the turret basket.

Gangbuster II was now leading the Han advance instead of supporting it. Three Hindi soldiers got up and ran, left to right, across a dike two hundred meters west of the tank. All were bent over, their bodies tiger-striped by foliage. The trailing pair carried a long object between diem, a machine gun or rocket launcher.

Maybe the Hindis thought they were getting into a better position from which to fire at *Gangbuster II*. Des Grieux's tribarrel, *his* tribarrel again, sawed the men down in a tangle of flailing limbs and blue-white flashes.

Des Grieux didn't need to worry about indirect fire anymore, because the Hindi artillery wouldn't fire into friendly lines . . . and besides, *Gangbuster II* was moving too fast to be threatened by any but the most sophisticated terminally guided munitions. The locals didn't have anything of that quality in their arsenals.

Baffin's Legion *did* have tank-killing rounds that were up to the job. Still, the cargo shells which held two or three self-forging fragments—shaped by the very blasts that hurled them against the most vulnerable spots in a tank's armor—were expensive, even for mercenary units commanding Baffin's payscale, or Hammer's.

For the moment, the guns on both sides were flinging cheap rounds of HE Common at one another, knowing that counterfire would detonate the shells harmlessly in the air no matter what they were.

It'd take minutes—tens of seconds, at least—for Legion gunners to get terminally guided munitions up the spout. That would be plenty of time for the charge Des Grieux led to blast out the core of enemy resistance.

"Hang on!" Pesco cried as though Des Grieux couldn't see for himself that *Gangbuster II* was about to surge up onto the causeway.

A Hindi soldier stood transfixed, halfway out of a spider hole in the hedge on the other side of the road. His rifle was pointed forward, but he was too terrified to sight down it toward the tank's huge, terrible bow. Des Grieux cranked the tribarrel with his right joystick.

Gangbuster II rose in a slurp of mud as dark and fluid as chocolate cake dough. The Hindi disappeared, not into his hole but by jumping toward the paddies north of the causeway. A Han gunner, lucky or exceptionally skillful, caught the Hindi in mid-leap. A splotch of blood hung in the air for some seconds after the corpse hit the water.

An anti-tank shot struck the rear of *Gangbuster II*'s turret. The bustle rack tore away in a scatter of the tankers' personal belongings, many of them afire. Impact of the dense penetrator on comparably dense armor heated both incandescent, enveloping the clothes and paraphernalia in a haze of gaseous osmium and iridium.

The projectile had only a minuscule direct effect on the inertia of *Gangbuster*'s 170 tonnes, but the shock made Pesco's hand twitch on the control column. The tank lurched sideways. The lights in the fighting compartment darkened and stayed out, but the screens only flickered as the AI routed power through pathways undamaged when the jolting impact severed a number of conduits.

The second shot blew through the northern hedge a half-second later. Pesco was fighting for control. The projectile hit, but only a glancing blow this time. The shot ricocheted from high on the rear hull, leaving a crease a half-meter long glowing in the back deck.

Des Grieux spun the tribarrel because the cupola responded more quickly than the massive turret forging, but he didn't have a clear target—and the anti-tank gunner didn't need one.

Powergun bolts would dump all their energy on the first solid object they touched. It was pointless trying to shoot at a target well to the other side of dense vegetation. Heavy osmium shot, driven by a jolt of plasma generated in a chamber filled with liquid propellant, carried through the hedge with no significant degradation of its speed or stability.

Gangbuster II hesitated while Pesco swung the bow to port, following the causeway, and coarsened the fan pitch to regain the speed lost in climbing the embankment. The tank was almost stationary for the moment.

Hindi soldiers rose from spiderholes in the hedge and raised buzzbomb launchers. One of the rocketeers was a hundred meters ahead of *Gangbuster II*; the other was an equal distance behind, his position already enveloped by the Han advance.

Des Grieux's tribarrel was aimed directly to starboard, and even the main gun was twenty degrees wide of the man in front. The tanker's right hand strained against the joystick anyway. The Hindis fired simultaneously.

The third shot from the anti-tank gun punched in the starboard side of the tank's plenum chamber and exited to port in a white blaze of burning steel. Each hole was approximately the size of a human fist. Air roared out while *Gangbuster II* rang like a struck gong. The fan nacelles were undamaged, and the designers had overbuilt pressurization capacity enough to accept a certain amount of damage without losing speed or maneuverability.

The rocket from the man in the rear hit the hedge midway between launcher and the huge intended target. The buzzbomb's pop-out fins caught in the interlaced branches; the warhead did not go off.

The other buzzbomb was aimed well enough as to line, but the Hindi soldier flinched upward as he squeezed the ignition trigger. The rocket sailed over *Gang-buster II* in a flat arc and exploded in the dirt at the feet of the other Hindi. The body turned legless somersaults before flopping onto the causeway again.

Des Grieux and Broglie fired their 20cm guns together. The Hindi rocketeer and thirty meters of hedge behind him blazed as *Gangbuster II*'s bolt raked along it. Through the sudden gap, Des Grieux saw the cyan-hearted fireball into which Broglie's perfect shot converted the Hindi gun that had targeted the tank on the causeway.

"Go, driver!" Des Grieux shouted hoarsely, but Pesco didn't need the order. Either he understood that their survival lay in speed, or blind panic so possessed him that he had no mind for anything but accelerating down the hedged three-kilometer aisle.

The Black Banner Guards were charging at brigade strength. It was a bloody shambles. The Hindis might have run when they saw the snouts of hundreds of armored personnel carriers bellowing toward them—

But they hadn't. More than a score of anti-tank guns unmasked and began firing, now that the contest was clearly a slugging match and not a game of cat-and-mouse. It took less than a second to purge the chamber of a Hindi gun, inject another projectile and ten liters of liquid propellant, and convert a tungsten wire into plasma in the center of the fluid.

Each shot was sufficiently powerful to lance through four APCs together if they chanced to be lined up the wrong way. Broglie, Peres, and Medrassi ripped away at the luxuriance of targets as fast as they could, but the paddies were already littered with torn and blazing Han vehicles.

The heavy anti-tank weapons were only part of the problem. Hindi teams of three to six men crouched in holes dug into the sides of the dikes, then rose to volley buzzbombs into the oncoming vehicles at point-blank range. Some of the rockets missed, but the hollow *whoomp!* of a single warhead was enough to disable any but the luckiest APC.

For those targets which the first volley missed, additional buzzbombs followed within seconds.

The jet of fire from a shaped charge would rupture fuel cells behind an APC's thin armor. Diesel fuel atomized an instant before it burst into flame. Hindi machine gunners then shot the Han crews to dog-meat as they tried to abandon their burning vehicles.

Des Grieux *knew* that green locals always broke if you charged them. His mind hadn't fully metabolized the fact that these Hindis might not be particularly accurate with their weapons, but they sure as *blood* weren't running anywhere.

As for the Han, who'd already lost at least a quarter of their strength in an unanswered turkey shoot . . . well, Des Grieux had problems of his own. "Booster!" he said. "Clear vision!"

The images echoed onto the left side of his visor from *Gangbuster II*'s central screen vanished, leaving the screen itself sharp and at full size. Normally Des Grieux would have touched a finger to his helmet's mechanical controls, but this wasn't normal and both his hands were on the gunnery joysticks.

Gangbuster II was so broad that the tank's side skirts *brushed* one, then the other, hedge bordering the causeway. Morobad was a distant haze at the end of an aisle as straight as peasants with stakes and string could draw it. Des Grieux's right hand stroked the main gun counterclockwise to center its hollow pipper on the community. He didn't need or dare to increase the display's magnification to give him actual images.

A Hindi soldier aimed a buzzbomb out of the left-hand hedge. The man's mottled green uniform was so new that the creases were still sharp. His dark face was as fixed and calm as a wooden idol's.

Gangbuster II's sensors noted a human within five meters. They tripped the automatic defense system attached to a groove encircling the tank just above the skirts. A 50x150mm strip of high explosive fired, blowing its covering of steel polygons into the Hindi like the blast of a huge shotgun.

The Hindi and his rocket launcher, both riddled by shrapnel, hurtled backward. Leaves and branches stripped from the hedge danced in the air, hiding the carnage.

A second rocketeer leaned out of the hedge three steps beyond the first. The ADS didn't fire because the cell that bore on the new target had just been expended on his comrade. The Hindi launched his buzzbomb from so close that the standoff probe almost touched the tank's hull.

The distance was too short for the buzzbomb's fuse to arm. The missile struck *Gangbuster II*'s gun mantle and ricocheted upward instead of exploding. A bent fin made the buzzbomb twist in crazy corkscrews.

Now another explosive/shrapnel cell aligned. The automatic defense system went off, shredding the rocketeer's torso. Useless, except as revenge for the way the Hindi had made Des Grieux's heart skip a beat in terror—

But revenge had its uses.

Des Grieux put one, then another 20cm bolt into Morobad without bothering to choose specific targets—if there were any. All he was trying to do for the moment was shake up the town. Some of the Legion's anti-artillery weapons were emplaced in Morobad. If the other side kept its collective head, *Gangbuster II* was going to get a hot reception.

Deafening, dazzling bolts from a tank's main gun pretty well guaranteed that nobody in the impact zone would be thinking coolly.

That was all right, and Des Grieux's tank was all right so far, seventy kph and accelerating. *Gangbuster II* pressed a broad hollow down the causeway. The surface of dirt and rice-straw matting rippled up to either side under the tank's 170 tonnes, even though the weight was distributed as widely as possible by the air cushion.

The Han brigade that Des Grieux had led to attack was well and truly fucked.

Smoke bubbled from burning vehicles, veiling and clearing the paddies like successive sweeps of a bullfighters cape. Some APCs had been abandoned undamaged. Their crews cowered behind dikes while Hindi buzzbomb teams launched missile after missile at the vehicles.

The rocketeers weren't particularly skillful: buzzbombs were reasonably accurate to a kilometer, but bits were a toss-up for most of the Hindis at anything over 100 meters. Determination and plenty of reloads made up for deficiencies in skill.

Han gunfire was totally ineffective. The officer manning the cupola machine gun also had his vehicle itself to command. As the extent of the disaster became clear, finding a way to safety overwhelmed any desire to place fire on the Hindis concealed by earth and foliage.

The infantry in the APC cargo compartments had individual gunports, but the Lord himself couldn't have hit a target while looking through a view slit and shooting from the port beneath it. The APCs bucked and slipped on the slimy terrain. In the compartments, men jostled one another and breathed the hot, poisonous reek of powder smoke and fear. Their bullets and laser beams either vanished into the landscape or glanced from the sideplates of friendly vehicles.

Des Grieux hadn't a prayer of a target either. He was trapped within the strait confines of the hedges for the two minutes it would take *Gangbuster II* to travel the length of the causeway.

His tribarrel raked the margins of the road, bursts to the right and left a hundred meters ahead of the tank's bluff bow. Stems popped like gunfire as they burned. That might keep a few heads down, but it wasn't a sufficient use for the most powerful unit on the battlefield.

Des Grieux could order his driver into the paddies again, but off the road the tank would wallow like a pig. This time there would be Hindi rocketeers launching buzzbombs from all four sides. Des Grieux no longer thought the local enemy would panic because it was a shark they had in the barrel to shoot at.

By contrast, the remaining Slammers' tanks were having a field day with the targets Des Grieux and the Han had flushed for them. Tribarrels stabbed across a kilometer of paddies to splash cyan death across Hindis focused on nearby APCs. Straw-wrapped packets of buzzbombs exploded, three and four at a time, to blow gaps in the dikes.

The left-hand situation display in *Gangbuster*'s fighting

compartment suddenly lighted with over a hundred red carats. The tanks of a Hindi armored brigade, lying hidden on the east side of the canal which formed the eastern boundary of Morobad, had been given the order to advance. When the drivers lighted their gas turbine powerplants, *Gangbuster*'s sensors noted the electronic activity and located the targets crawling up onto prepared firing steps.

Morobad was less than a kilometer away. Hindi tanks maneuvered on both sides of the causeway to bring the guns fixed along the centerline of their hulls in line with *Gangbuster II*. The Hindi vehicles mounted combustion-augmented plasma weapons, like the anti-tank guns but more powerful because a tank chassis permitted a larger plasma generator than that practical on a piece of towed artillery.

Des Grieux's situation display showed the condition clearly. The visuals on his gunnery screen were the same as they'd been for the past minute and a half: unbroken hedgerows which would stop bolts from his powerguns as surely as thirty centimeters of iridium could.

A Hindi shot *cracked* left-to-right across the road, a tank's length behind *Gangbuster II*. Somebody'd gotten a little previous with his gunswitch, but the tank that had fired was still backing one track to slew its weapon across the Slammers' vehicle.

Des Grieux traversed his main gun, panning the target, and rocked the foot-trip twice. Instinct and the situation display at the corner of his eye guided him: the orange circle on the gunnery screen showed only foliage.

The first bolt flash-fired the wall of hedge. The second jet of cyan plasma crashed through the gap and made a direct hit on the Hindi tank.

The roiling orange fireball rose a hundred meters. The column of smoke an instant later mounted ten times as high before flattening into an anvil shape which dribbled trash back onto the paddies. The compression wave of the explosion flattened an expanding circle of new-planted rice. Rarefaction following the initial shock jerked the seedlings upright again.

A tank on the north side of the causeway slammed a shot into *Gangbuster II*'s bow. A hundred kilos of iridium armor and #2 fan nacelle turned into white-hot vapor which seared leaves on which it cooled.

Pesco shouted and briefly lost control of his vehicle. The tank's enormous inertia resisted turning and kept the skirts on the road despite a nasty shimmy because of the drop in fan pressure forward.

Des Grieux tried to traverse his main gun to bear on the new danger, but the turret had seventy-five degrees to swing clockwise after its systems braked the momentum of the opposite rotation. He wasn't going to make it in the half-second before the next Hindi shot transfixed *Gangbuster II*'s relatively thin side armor—

But he didn't have to, because Captain Broglie's command tank nailed the Hindi vehicle. Plates of massive steel armor flew in all directions even though the bolt failed to detonate the target's munitions.

Score one for Broglie, *the bastard*; and if he'd brought the rest of the platoon along with Des Grieux, maybe *Gangbuster II* wouldn't be swinging in the breeze right now.

Hindi tanks were firing all along the line. They ignored *Gangbuster II* because the tanks destroyed to the immediate north and south of the causeway blocked the aim of their fellows.

The Hindi CAP guns were useless except against armored vehicles—their solid projectiles had no area effect whatever. Against armor, they were neither quite as effective shot for shot, nor quite as quick-firing as the Slammers' 20cm guns.

They were effective enough, though, and there was a bloody swarm of them.

Broglie and his two overwatching companions hit half a dozen of the Hindi vehicles, destroying them instantly even though most of the cyan bolts struck the thickest part of the targets' frontal armor. Then the surviving Hindis got the range and volleyed their replies.

A shot hit the cupola above Broglie. Ammo burned in the feed tube of *Honey Girl*'s tribarrel. A blue-white finger poked skyward, momentarily dimming the rising sun. Des Grieux's display cross-hatched *Dixie Dyke* as well, indicating the north-flank tank had been damaged as Peres raked Hindi lines with both main gun and tribarrel. All three units jerked backward to turret-down positions as quickly as their drivers could cant their fans.

"Driver!" Des Grieux said as *Gangbuster II*, its front skirts dragging sparks from the stone road surface, crossed the canal bridge. "Turn us and we'll hit the bastards from behind. Booster, gimme a fucking city map!"

The cheap buildings of Morobad's canal district were ablaze. Some of the walls were plastered wattle-and-daub; other builders had hung painted sheetiron on scantlings of flimsy wood. Neither method could resist the two main-gun rounds Des Grieux snapped toward the town when *Gangbuster II* started its rush. The bolts had the effect of flares dropped into a tinder box.

The tank drove into a curtain of flame at ninety kph. There was something in the way, a wrecked vehicle or the corner of a building. *Gangbuster*'s skirts shunted it aside with no more commotion than the clang the automatic defense system made when it went off.

The tank's AI obediently replaced the topographic display on the left screen with a map of Morobad from *Gangbuster II*'s data banks. The streets were narrow and twisting, even the thoroughfare leading west from the causeway.

Two hundred meters from the canal was a market square bordered by religious and governmental buildings. That would give Pesco room to turn. When *Gangbuster II* roared out of the city again and took the turretless Hindi tanks in the rear, it'd be all she wrote.

The air cleared at street level. *Gangbuster II* scraped the brick facade of a three-story tenement which started to collapse on them. At least a score of Hindi soldiers opened fire with automatic weapons. Bullets ricocheted from the sloped iridium armor, scything down the shooters and their fellows. Cells of the automatic defense system fired, louder and more lethal still.

Haze closed in momentarily, but a telltale in the fighting compartment informed Des Grieux that Pesco had already switched to sonic imaging instead of using the electro-optical spectrum to drive. *Gangbuster II* swept into the market square, pulling whorls of smoke into the clear, sunlit air.

A six-tube battery of 170mm howitzers was set up in the square. Empty obturator disks and unneeded booster charges in white silk littered the cobblestones behind the weapons. The crew were desperately cranking their muzzles down to fire point-blank a *Gangbuster II*. Hindi infantry cut loose with small arms from al windows facing the square and from the triple tile overhangs of the large temple behind the walled courtyard to the south.

As Des Grieux squeezed both firing tits, a hundred-kilogran shell hit the turret. The round was a thin-cased HE, what the crev happened to have up the spout when they got warning of the tank' approach. The red flash destroyed thirty percent of *Gangbuster II'* forward sensors and rocked the tank severely, but the hatches wer sealed and the massive turret armor was never even threatened.

"Driv—" Des Grieux started to say as his hazy screens showe him Hindi gunners doubling up, flying apart, burning in puffs o vaporized steel as the powergun sights slid across the battery.

A legless Hindi battery captain jerked the lanyard of his las howitzer. The shell was a capped armor-piercing round. Even sc the round would not have penetrated *Gangbuster II'*s frontal armo if it had struck squarely. Instead, it hit Pesco's closed hatch edge-o and spalled the backing plate down through the driver's helmet an skull.

Pesco convulsed at the controls of *Gangbuster II*. The tanl skidded across the square, swapping ends several times. Th courtyard wall braked but did not stop the careening vehicle. De Grieux shouted curses, but words had no effect on the tank or it dead driver.

Gangbuster II slid bow-first into the stone-built temple. Block and tiles from the multiple roofs cascaded onto the tank and ove the courtyard beyond.

All *Gangbuster II'*s systems crashed at the massive overload.

Des Grieux knew nothing about that. Despite his shock harnes: his head slammed sideways into the map display so that he shu down an instant before his tank did.

Existence was a pulsing red blur until Des Grieux opened hi eyes. The pulsing continued every time his heart beat, but now h ould see real light: the tiny yellow beads of *Gangbuster II*'s standby llumination system.

The air in the fighting compartment was hot and foul. When he power went off, so did the air conditioning. The expended 0cm casings on the floor continued to radiate heat and complex ;ases.

Des Grieux reached for the reset switch to bring *Gangbuster II*'s ystems alive again. Movement brought blinding pain. The tank's hock harness had retracted when movement stopped, but the traps left tracks in the form of bruises and cracked ribs where they ad gripped Des Grieux to prevent worse.

His mouth tasted of blood, and there seemed to be a layer of round glass between his eyes and their lids.

"Blood and martyrs," Des Grieux whispered. The taste in his nouth came from his tongue, which had swollen to twice its normal ize because he had bitten it.

When the world ceased throbbing and his stomach settled gain, Des Grieux finished his movement to the reset switch. Pain ist meant you were alive. If you were alive, you could do for the astard who'd done *you.*

The snarl of powerguns dimly penetrated to the tank's interior. Neither of the indig forces had powerguns of their own. Either the lammers had entered Morobad, or Baffin had committed his egion to exploit the ratfuck the Black Banner Guards had made vhen they tried to follow *Gangbuster II*'s lead.

Des Grieux knew which alternative *he'd* put his money on.

Gangbuster II came to life crisply and fast. That was better than he man in her fighting compartment had managed.

"Booster," Des Grieux said. His injured tongue slurred his vords. "Order of Battle on Number One."

Screen #1, the left-hand unit, came up with the map of Morobad Des Grieux had ordered onto it before the crash and shutdown. The ew overlay showed Des Grieux just what he'd bloody expected, the range symbols of Legion vehicles streaming through the town and anning out when they crossed the canal.

This was no feint or stiffening force. Baffin was committing his

entire battalion-strength command to end the war here on th
Western Wing.

"Like bloody hell . . ." Des Grieux muttered. "Driver! Report!"
Nothing. "Pesco?"

Nothing. Des Grieux would have to crawl forward and see wha
the hell was going on; but first he checked the condition of his tank

Gangbuster II was fully operable. The tank was down one fan an
had five fist-sized holes in her skirts. Des Grieux had no recollectio
of several of those hits. Both guns were all right, and sixty percent c
the massively redundant sensor suite checked out as well.

The only problem was that, according to the echo-rangin
apparatus, the tank was covered by several meters of variegate
rubble: bricks, tiles, wooden beams, and the bodies of Hindi soldier
who'd been shooting from the temple roofs up to the momen
Gangbuster II brought the building's facade down on itself. All th
visual displays were blank because the pickups were buried.

Of course, if the Slammers' vehicle hadn't been so completel
concealed, Baffin's troops would have finished Des Grieux off b
reflex. Veteran mercenaries were generally men who'd survived b
never trusting a corpse until they'd put in a bayonet of their own.

A four-ship platoon of Baffin's tank destroyers slid eastwar
across the map of Morobad. They were air-cushion vehicles mountin
15cm power guns behind frontal armor almost as thick as that of th
Slammers' tanks. The main guns were in centerline mountings lik
those of the Hindi tanks—turrets were relatively heavy, and a
air-cushion vehicle could rotate easily in comparison to wheeled o
track-laying armor.

Companies of infantry preceded and followed the tan
destroyers in four air-cushion carriers apiece. Baffin carried hi
infantry in large, lightly armored vehicles; Hammer mounted his me
on one-man skimmers with their heavy weapons on air-cushio
jeeps. Either method worked well with good troops; and both o
these units were very good indeed.

Gangbuster II shone brightly on Des Grieux's display as a cross
hatched blue symbol, but the Legion troops advancing throug
Morobad showed no sign of awareness. Their screens would b

ned to the Han/Slammers defenses kilometers to the east . . . if
here were any Han troops left to thicken the line of cursing
lammers infantry and the survivors of 2nd Platoon.

Not all the Legion equipment in the square outside the collapsed
emple was moving. Des Grieux's #1 display marked four of Baffin's
cm twin guns, half the Legion's anti-artillery defenses, with neat
range symbols. The weapons were emplaced to either side of the
noroughfare. Support troops had hastily bulldozed the wreckage of
ne Hindi battery out of the way.

Ideally, artillery-defense guns should have a clear view to the
orizon on all sides. In practice, crews preferred to set up in defilade
where they were safe from hostile direct-fire weapons. Even so, the
uildings surrounding the market square reduced the defended area
o what seemed at first an unusually narrow cone.

Three command vehicles, armored air-cushion vans filled with
ommunications gear, were parked back-to-back in a trefoil at the
orthwest corner of the square. *That* was what the 3cm guns were
rotecting: Baffin in his advanced command post.

Des Grieux's muscles began to tremble with reaction. He no
onger felt the pain in his ribs; fresh adrenaline smoothed the
notted veins flowing to his brain. Baffin himself, a hundred and
fty meters from *Gangbuster II*'s main gun. . . .

"Pesco, you lazy bastard!" Des Grieux snarled, but he'd already
iven up on raising a response from his driver. He climbed out of his
eat and slid between the hull and the frame of the turret basket.

Thick 20cm disks littered the deck, the empty matrixes that
ad aligned the copper atoms which the powerguns released as
lasma. One disk blocked the small hatch separating the fighting
ompartment from the driver's compartment. Des Grieux tossed
ne empty angrily behind him. The polyurethane was hot and still
acky; it clung to his fingertips.

As soon as he opened the hatch, the smell told Des Grieux that
is driver was dead. Pesco had voided his bowels when the fragment
liced off the upper half of his skull. The liters of blood his heart
umped before the autonomic nervous system shut down had
lready begun to rot in the warm compartment.

Des Grieux swore. The hatch—the part of it that hadn't decapitate
Pesco—was jammed beyond opening by anything short of rear-echelo
maintenance. He didn't know what the *bloody* hell he was going t
do with the driver's body.

He released the seat latch so that the back flopped down. Th
remaining contents of Pesco's cranial cavity slopped over De
Grieux's hands. He rotated the seat forty-five degrees to its stop
then tilted the corpse sideways out onto the forward deck of th
compartment. There it blocked the foot pedals, but Des Grieu
wouldn't be able to use those anyway.

Des Grieux leaned over the bloody seat, set the blade angles a
zero incidence, and switched on the drive fans. All the necessar
controls were on the column; the duplicate nacelle-attitude control
on the foot pedals permitted a driver to do four things simultane
ously in an emergency—

But *Gangbuster II* didn't have a driver anymore.

Seven green lights and a red one marked the fan status scree
beneath the main driving display, but that was only half the story. De
Grieux knew the intake ducts were blocked as surely as *Gangbuster II*
hatches. That didn't matter at the moment, but it would as soon as h
rotated the pitch control and the fans started to suck wind.

No choice. Des Grieux could only hope that vibration as th
nacelles drew against the rubble above them would help to clear th
vehicle. Because that was what he needed to do first.

Des Grieux breathed deeply. He didn't really notice the smel
other things could get in his way, but not that. He adjusted th
nacelle angle to a balance between lift and thrust. He hoped he ha
the mixture right, but whatever he came up with would have to do

Des Grieux had been a lousy driver; he was far too heavy-hande
forcing the controls the way he forced himself.

For this particular job, a heavy hand was the only choice.

The fans hummed, running at full speed though the throttle
were at their idle setting. With the pitch at zero, the leading edges c
the blades knifed the air with minimal resistance. *Gangbuster I*
began to resonate with a bell-note deeper than usual because th
hull didn't hang free in the air.

Des Grieux sucked in another breath. His right hand drew the
linked throttles full on, while his left thumb adjusted the pitch to
sixty degrees. The tank wheezed and bucked like a choking lion. Des
Grieux scrambled backward out of the hatch.

The empties jounced on the floor with the violence of
Gangbuster II's attempts to draw air through choked intakes. Des
Grieux threw himself into his seat and grasped the gunnery joysticks.
The orange pippers glowed against a background of uniform gray
because the visual pickups were shrouded.

Des Grieux twisted the left joystick. Metal screeched as the turret
began to swing clockwise against its weight of rubble. Hot insulation
singed the atmosphere of the fighting compartment as the turret
drive motors overloaded.

Des Grieux twisted the control in the opposite direction. The
turret reversed a few centimeters. There was a squalling crash as the
mass of overburden shifted and slid away from *Gangbuster II*'s turret and deck. The tank bobbed like a diver surfacing through a sea
of rubble.

The fan blades bit the air for which they had been starving.
Uncontrolled, *Gangbuster II* lurched backward at an accelerating
pace.

Des Grieux shouted with glee as he rotated his turret and cupola
controls again. Now he had a sight picture and targets.

Gangbuster II had hit the temple facade nose on. Now it backed
through the hole it had torn in the wall, bucking over and plowing
through tiles and masonry from the building's upper stories.

The Hindis were using the temple's forecourt as a field hospital
for casualties from Des Grieux's initial attack. Medics and the
wounded who could move under their own power ran or crawled
from *Gangbuster II*'s bellowing reappearance.

Des Grieux ignored them. The gap his tank had smashed in the
courtyard wall showed a tone edge of his gunnery screen, and a pair
of Legion 3cm carriages were visible through it. The Legion guns
were firing upward at a 40° angle, snapping incoming shells from
the air as soon as they notched the horizon.

The tribarrel's solid sight indicator covered the Legion weapons an instant before the main gun swung on target. Brilliant cyan bolt raked the Legion crews and the receivers of their guns. A pannier of ammunition exploded with a flash like that of a miniature nova. I destroyed everything within a five-meter sphere, pavement included

Gangbuster II slewed across the courtyard in a scraping, sparking curve. The tank wasn't going to follow the track by which it had plunged in from the market square. The gap in the courtyard wall foreshortened into solidity as the damaged skirts slid the tank toward a point twenty meters west of its initial entry. The scream of wounded men in the vehicle's path were lost in the howl of steel on stone.

Des Grieux took his right hand from the joystick long enough to close the commo breaker. "Blue Three to Big Dog One-niner!" he shouted hoarsely to battalion fire control. "Get some arty on top of us! Get us—"

Gangbuster II struck the courtyard wall for the second time. The shock threw Des Grieux forward into his harness. Redoubled pain shrank objects momentarily to pinhead size in his vision, but he did not black out.

The tank's iridium hull armor smashed through the brickwork but the impact stripped off the already-damaged skirts. Momentum drove *Gangbuster II* partway into the market square. The vehicle halted there because half the plenum chamber was gone.

"—some firecracker rounds!" Des Grieux gasped to artillery control, demanding anti-personnel shells as his hands worked his joysticks.

Two of the 3cm pieces were undamaged. The crew of the gun nearest the ammunition blast was dead or writhing shrivelled on the pavement, but the gunners of the fourth piece were cranking down their twin muzzles to bear on the unexpected threat.

A bolt from *Gangbuster II*'s main gun struck the shield just below the stubby barrels of the artillery-defense weapon. The gun seemed to suck in, then flash outward as a ball of sunbright vapor.

A loader had turned to run when she saw death pointing down *Gangbuster II*'s 20cm bore. Gaseous metal enveloped all of the Legion soldier but her outflung hand. When the glowing ball condensed and vanished, the hand remained like a wax dummy on a framework of carbonized sticks.

Des Grieux's tribarrel raked the Legion command group. The plating of the vehicles' boxy sides was thick enough to turn about half the 2cm bolts—but at this short range, *only* half.

Gangbuster II's main gun continued to rotate on target. One of the three vans already sparkled with electrical shorts, while another puffed black smoke from the holes the powergun had blown across its flank.

"Blue Leader to Blue Three," Captain Broglie cried across the crackling, all-band static of powergun discharges. "Abandon your vehicle immediately! Anti-tank rounds are incoming on your location!"

"Screw you, Broglie!" Des Grieux screamed as his main gun slammed a bolt into the central command track, the one that was bow-on with its thicker frontal armor toward *Gangbuster II*'s tribarrel. The 20cm bolt blew out the vehicle's back and sides with a piston of vaporized metal which had been the glacis plate a microsecond earlier.

The Legion tank destroyer entering the square from the west snapped a bolt from its 15cm powergun into *Gangbuster II*'s turret. The tank rocked backward under the impact.

Des Grieux slammed into the seat. The screens and regular lighting went out, but the inner face of the turret armor glowed a sulphurous yellow.

Heat clawed at the skin of Des Grieux's face and hands. He started to draw in a breath. The air was fire, but he had to breathe anyway.

Gangbuster II's nacelles stopped bucking in the stripped plenum chamber when the power shut off. Now the tank shuddered with heat stresses.

Des Grieux punched the reset switch. A conduit across the turret burst with a green flash. The holographic displays quivered to life, then went blank.

A salvo of shells landed near enough to rock the tank with their *crump crump crump*-CRUMP! They were HE Common, not anti-tank.

The rounds had been in flight before the battery commander knew there was a hole blasted in the Legion's artillery defenses.

The seat controls were electrical; nothing happened when De Grieux tugged the bar. He reached up—his ribs hurt almost as much as his lungs did—and slid the cupola hatch open manually.

Buildings around the market square were burning. Smoke mingled with ozone from the powerguns, organic residues from propellant and explosives, and the varied stench of bodies ripped open as they died.

It was like a bath in cool water compared to the interior of the tank.

The iridium barrel of *Gangbuster II*'s main gun was shorter by eighty centimeters. That was what saved Des Grieux's life. At this range, the tank destroyer's bolt would have penetrated if it had struck the turret face directly.

The stick of shells that just landed had closed the boulevard entering the square from the west. The tank destroyer that hit *Gangbuster II* wriggled free of collapsed masonry fifty meters away. The vehicle was essentially undamaged, though shrapnel had pecked highlights from its light-absorbent camouflage paint, and the cupola machine gun hung askew.

Bodies, and the wreckage of equipment too twisted for its original shape to be discerned, littered the pavement of the square.

Des Grieux set the tribarrel's control to thermal self-powered operation. It wouldn't function well, but it was better than nothing.

The manual traverse wheel refused to turn; the 15cm bolt had welded the cupola ring to the turret. The elevating wheel spun, though lowering the triple muzzles as the tank destroyer's own forward motion slid it into Des Grieux's sight picture.

Cargo shells popped open high in the heavens. Des Grieux ignored the warning. He squeezed the butterfly triggers to rip the tank destroyer's skirts. Bolts which might not have penetrated the vehicle's heavy iridium hull armor tore fist-sized holes in the steel.

Des Grieux got off a dozen rounds before his tribarrel jammed. They were enough for the job. The tank destroyer vented its air

ushion through the gaps in the plenum chamber and grounded
vith a squealing crash.

Des Grieux bailed out of *Gangbuster II*, carrying his carbine. He
lid down the turret and hit the pavement on his feet, but his legs
vere too weak to support him. He sprawled on his face.

The anti-tank submunition, one of three drifting down from
he cargo shell by parachute, went off a hundred meters in the air.
The *whack!* of the blast knocked Des Grieux flat as he started to get
ip. The supersonic penetrator which the explosion forged from a
villet of depleted uranium had already punched through the thin
ipper hull of *Gangbuster II*.

Ammunition and everything else flammable within the tank
vhuffed out in a glare that seemed to shine through the armor. The
usion bottle did not fail. The turret settled again with a clang, askew
on its ring.

Secondary explosions to the east and further west within Morobad
marked other effects of the salvo, but none of the submunitions had
argeted the disabled tank destroyer. Des Grieux sat up and crossed
uis legs to provide a stable firing position. He wasn't ready to stand,
not quite yet. Heat from his tank's glowing hull washed across his
vack.

What sounded like screaming was probably steam escaping
from a ruptured boiler. Humans couldn't scream that loud. Des
Grieux knew.

He pointed his carbine.

The tank destroyer's forward hatch opened. The driver started
o get out. Des Grieux shot him in the face. The body fell backward.
ts feet were still within the hatch, but the arms flailed for a time.

The hull side-hatch—the tank destroyer had no turret—opened
a crack. Des Grieux covered the movement. Cloth—it wasn't white,
ust a gray uniform jacket, but the meaning was clear—fluttered
from the opening.

"We've surrendered!" a woman called from inside. "Don't
shoot!"

"Come on out, then," Des Grieux ordered. His voice was a
croak. He wasn't sure the vehicle crew could hear him, but a woman

wearing lieutenant's insignia extended her head and shoulders from the hatch.

Her face was expressionless. When she saw that Des Grieux did not fire, she climbed clear of the tank destroyer. A male commo tech followed her. If they had sidearms, they'd left them within the vehicle.

"We've all surrendered," she repeated.

"Baffin's surrendered?" Des Grieux asked. He had trouble hearing. He wanted to order his prisoners closer, but he couldn't stand up and he didn't want them looking down at him.

"Via, Colonel Baffin was *there,*" the lieutenant said, gesturing toward the three command vehicles.

The center unit that Des Grieux hit with his main gun was little more than bulged sidewalk above the running gear.

She shook her head to clear it of memories. "The Legion surrendered, that's what I mean," she said.

"We must've lost ten percent of our equipment from that one salvo of artillery. No point in just getting wasted by shells. There'll be other battles. . . ."

The lieutenant's voice trailed off as she considered the implications of her own words. The commo tech stared at her in cow-eyed incomprehension.

Des Grieux leaned against a slope of shattered brick. The corners were sharp.

That was good. Perhaps their jagged touch would prevent him from passing out before friendly troops arrived to collect his prisoners.

Regimental HQ was three command cars backed against a previously undamaged two-story school building. Flat cables snaked out of the vehicles, through windows and along corridors.

The combination wasn't perfect. Still, it provided Hammer's staff with their own data banks and secure commo, while permitting them some elbow room in the inevitable chaos at the end of a war— and a contract.

"Yeah, what is it?" demanded the orderly sergeant. The lobby was marked off by a low bamboo barrier. Three Han clerks sat at

lesks in the bullpen area, while the orderly sergeant relaxed at
he rear in the splendor of his computer console. Behind the
staff was a closed door marked headmaster in Hindi script and
adjutant/hammer's regiment in stenciled red.

Des Grieux withdrew the hand which he'd stretched toward the
throat of the Han clerk. "I'm looking for my bloody unit," he said,
"and this bloody wog—"

"C'mon, c'mon back," the orderly sergeant demanded with a
wave of his hand. "Been partying pretty hard?"

Des Grieux brushed a bamboo post and knocked it down as he
stepped into the bullpen. The local clerks jabbered and righted the
barrier.

"Wasn't a party," Des Grieux muttered. "I been in a POW camp
the past week."

The orderly sergeant blinked. "A *Han* POW camp," Des Grieux
amplified. "Our good wog buddies here—" he kicked out at the
chair of the nearest clerk; the boot missed, and Des Grieux almost
overbalanced "—picked me up when they swept Morobad. Baffin's
troops got paroled out within twenty-four hours, but *I* got stuck
with the Hindi prisoners 'cause nobody knew I was there."

The orderly sergeant's name tag read Hechinger. His nose wrinkled as Des Grieux approached. The Han diet of the POW camp differed enough from what the Hindi prisoners were used to that it
gave most of them the runs. Latrine facilities within the camp were
wherever you wanted to squat.

"Well, why didn't you tell them you were a friendly?"
Hechinger asked in puzzlement.

Des Grieux's hands trembled with anger. "Have you ever tried
to tell a wog *anything*?" he whispered. "Without a gun stuck down
their throat when you say it?"

He got a grip on himself and added, more calmly, "And don't
ask me for my ID bracelet. One of the guards lifted that first thing.
Thought the computer key was an emerald, I guess."

Hechinger sighed. "Mary, key data," he ordered the artificial
intelligence in his console. "Name?"

"Des Grieux, Samuel, Sergeant-Commander," the tanker said.

"H Company, 2nd Platoon, Platoon Sergeant Peres commanding. She *was* commanding, anyhow. She may've bought it last week."

The console hummed and projected data. Des Grieux, standing at the back of the unit, could see the holograms only as refraction in the air.

"One of our trucks was going by and I shouted to the driver," Des Grieux muttered, glaring at the clerks. The three of them hunched over their desks, pretending to be busy. "He didn't know me, but he knew I wasn't a wog. I could've been there forever."

"Well," said the orderly sergeant, "three days longer and you'd sure've been finding your own transport back to the Regiment. We're pulling out. Got a contract on Plessy. Seems the off-plane workers there're getting uppity and think they oughta have a share in the shipyard profits."

"Anyplace," Des Grieux said. "Just so long as I've got a gun and a target."

"Well, we got a bit of a problem here, trooper," Hechinger said as he frowned at his display. "Des Grieux, Sergeant-Commander, is listed as dead."

"I'm not bloody *dead*," Des Grieux snarled. "Blood'n Martyrs, ask Sergeant Peres."

"Lieutenant Peres, as she'll be when she comes off medical leave," the orderly sergeant said, "isn't a lotta help right now either. And if you're going to ask about—" he squinted at the characters on his display "—Sergeant-Commander Medrassi, he bought the farm."

Hechinger smirked. "Like you did, y'see? Look, don't worry, we'll—"

"Look, I just want to get back to my unit," Des Grieux said, hearing his voice rise and letting it. "Is Broglie around? *He* bloody knows me. I just saved his ass—again!"

The orderly sergeant glanced over his shoulder. "Captain Broglie we might be able to round up for you, trooper," he said carefully. He nodded back toward the Adjutant's office.

"Anyhow," Hechinger continued, "he was captain when he went in there. Don't be real surprised if he comes out with major's pips on his collar, though."

"That *bastard* . . ." Des Grieux whispered.

"Captain Broglie's very much the fair-haired boy just now, you know, buddy," Hechinger continued in his careful voice. "He stopped near a brigade of Hindi armor with one tank platoon. It was kitty-bar-the-door, all the way back to Xingha, if it hadn't been for him."

The office door opened. Sergeant Hechinger straightened at his console, face forward.

Des Grieux looked up expecting to see either the Adjutant or Broglie—

And met the eyes of Major Joachim Steuben, as cold and hard as beads of chert. Hammer's bodyguard looked as stiffly furious as Des Grieux had ever seen a man who was still under control.

Des Grieux didn't think that Steuben would recognize him. It had been years since the last time they were face to face. There was crinkled skin around the corners of the major's eyes, though his was still a pretty-boy's face if you didn't look closely; and Des Grieux just now looked like a scarecrow. . . .

Joachim was more than just a sociopathic killer, though the Lord knew he was *that*. He looked at the tanker and said, "Well, well, Des Grieux. Seeking our own level, are we?"

The way Joachim shot his hip could have been an affectation . . . but it also shifted the butt of his pistol a further centimeter clear of the tailored blouse of his uniform. Des Grieux met his eyes. Anyway, there was no place to run.

"Well, I understand your decision, Luke," said Colonel Hammer as he came out of the Adjutant's office with his hand on the arm of the much larger Broglie. The moonfaced Adjutant followed them, nodding to everything Hammer said. "But believe me, I regret it. Remember you've always got a bunk here if you change your mind."

Broglie wore no rank insignia at all.

Hechinger had to say *something* to avoid becoming part of the interchange between Steuben and Des Grieux. Nobody in his right mind—except maybe the colonel—wanted to be part of Joachim's interchanges, even as a spectator.

"Okay, Des Grieux," he said in a voice just above a whisper. "I'll cut you some temporary orders so's you can get chow and some kit."

Broglie heard the name. He glanced at Des Grieux. His face blanked and he said, in precisely neutral tones, "Hello, Slick. I didn't think you'd make it back from that one."

"Oh, you ought to show more warmth than *that*, Mister Broglie," Joachim drawled. He didn't look at Broglie and Hammer behind him. "After all, without Sergeant Des Grieux here to create that monumental screw-up, you wouldn't have been such a hero for straightening things out. Would you, now?"

"What d'ye mean screw-up?" Des Grieux said, *knowing* that Steuben was looking for an excuse to kill something. "*I'm* the one who blew the guts outa Baffin's Legion!"

"That's the man?" Hammer said, speaking to Broglie.

The colonel's eyes were gray. They had none of the undifferentiated hatred for the world that glared from Major Steuben's, but they were just as hard as the bodyguard's when they flicked over Des Grieux.

"Yes sir," Broglie murmured. "Joachim—Major Steuben? I'm not taking the job the Legion offered me out of any disrespect for the colonel. If you like, I'll promise that the Legion won't take any contracts against the Slammers so long as I'm in charge."

Joachim turned as delicately as a marionette whose feet dangle above the ground. "Oh, my . . ." he said, letting his left hand dangle on a theatrically limp wrist. "And a traitor's promise is *so* valuable!"

"I'm not—" said Broglie.

"Joachim!" said the colonel, stepping in front of Steuben— and between Steuben and Broglie, though that might have been an accident, if you believed Colonel Alois Hammer did things by accident. "Go to the club and have a drink. I'll join you there in half an hour."

Steuben grimaced as though he'd been kicked in the stomach. "Sir," he said. "I'm . . ."

"Go on," Hammer said gently, putting his hand on the shoulder of the dapper killer. "I'll meet you soonest. No problem, all right?"

"Sir," Steuben said, nodding agreement. He straightened and

strode out of the headquarters building. He looked like a perfect band-box soldier, except for his eyes. . . .

"And as for you, Luke," Hammer said as he faced around to Broglie again, "I won't have you talking nonsense. Your first duty is to your own troops. You'll take any bloody contract that meets your unit's terms and conditions . . . and I assure you, I'll do the same."

"Look, sir," Broglie said. He wouldn't meet Colonel Hammer's eyes. "I wouldn't feel right—"

"I said," Hammer snapped, "put a sock in it! Or stay with me—the Lord knows I'm going to have to replace Chesney anyway, after the lash-up he made when the wheels came off at Morobad."

Des Grieux was dizzy. The world had disconnected itself from him. He was surrounded by glassy surfaces which only seemed to speak and move in the semblance of people he had once known.

"Major Chesney—" Broglie began.

"Major Chesney had to be told twice," Hammer said, "first by you and then by *me,* a thousand kays away with 3d Operational Battalion, to set his flanking tank platoons to cover artillery defense for the center. You shouldn't have had to hold Chesney's hand while you were organizing Han troops into a real defense."

Broglie smiled. "Their laser-vehicles were mostly bogged," he said, "so they couldn't run. I just made sure they knew I'd shoot 'em faster than the Hindis could if they *tried* to run."

"Whatever works," said Hammer with an expression as cold as the hatred in Joachim's eyes a moment before.

The expression softened. "Listen to me, Luke," Hammer went on. "People are going to hire mercenaries so long as they're convinced mercenaries are a good investment. Having the Legion in first-rate hands like yours is good for all of us in this business. I'll miss you, but I gain from this, too."

Broglie stiffened. "Thank you, sir," he said.

"Listen!" Des Grieux shouted. "I'm the one who broke them for you! I killed Baffin."

"Oh, you killed a lot of people, Des Grieux," Colonel Hammer said in a deceptively mild voice. "And way too many of them were mine."

"Sir," said Broglie. "The disorganization in the Legion's rear really was Slick's doing. We pieced it together in post-battle analysis and—"

"Saved about ten minutes, didn't it, Broglie?" the colonel said "Before the flanking units closed on Morobad?"

Broglie smiled again, thinly. "That was ten minutes I was real glad to have, sir," he said.

Hammer stared up and down at Des Grieux. The colonel's expression did not change. "So, you think he's a good soldier, do you?" he asked softly.

"I think," said Broglie, "that . . . if he'd learn to obey orders, he'd be the best soldier I've ever seen."

"Fine, Mister Broglie," Hammer said. "I'll tell you what. . . ."

He continued to look at Des Grieux as if daring the tanker to move or speak again. Major Steuben was gone, but the White Mice at the outer doorway watched the discussion with their hands on the grips of their submachine guns.

"I'll let you have him, then," Hammer continued. "For Broglie's Legion."

Broglie grimaced and turned away. "No," he muttered. "Sorry, that wouldn't work out."

Hammer nodded crisply. "Hareway," he said to the Adjutant, "have Des Grieux here put in the lockup until we lift. Then demote him to trooper and put him to driving trucks for a while. *If* he cares to stay in the Slammers, as I rather hope he will not."

The lobby had a terrazzo floor. Hammer's boot-heels clacked on it as he strode off, arm and arm with Broglie. Their figures shrank in Des Grieux's eyesight, and he barely heard the orderly sergeant shout, "Watch it! He's fainting!"

PART III

The Slammers' lockup was a sixty-meter shipping container. The paired outer leaves were open, and the single inner door had been replaced by a grate. The facility was baking hot when the white sun of Meridienne cast its harsh shadows across the landscape. At night, when the clear air cooled enough to condense out the dew on which most of the local vegetation depended, the lockup became a shivering misery.

If the conditions in the lockup hadn't been naturally so wretched, Colonel Hammer would have used technology to make them worse. A comfortable detention facility would be counterproductive.

"Rise'n shine, trooper," called the jailor, a veteran of twenty-five named Daniels. "They want you there yesterday, like always."

Daniels' two prosthetic feet worked perfectly well—so long as they were daily retimed to match his neural outputs. He had the choice of moving to a high-technology world where the necessary electronics were available, or staying with the Slammers in a menial capacity. Since Daniels' only saleable skill—firing a tribarrel from a moving jeep—had no civilian application, he became one of the Regiment's jailors.

"Nobody's waiting for me," said Slick Des Grieux, lying on his back with his knees raised. He didn't open his eyes. "Nobody cares if I'm alive or dead. Not even me."

"C'mon," Daniels insisted as he inserted his microchip key in the lock. "Get moving or they'll be on *my* back."

He clashed the grate as best he could. It was formed of beryllium alloy, while the container itself had been extruded from high-density polymers. The combination made a tinny/dull rattle, not particularly arousing.

Des Grieux got to his feet with a smooth grace which belied his previous inertia. There was a 3cm pressure cut above his right temple, covered now with Spray Seal. His pale hair was cut so short that there had been no need to shave the injured portion before repairing it.

"What's going on, then?" Des Grieux asked. His tongue quivered against his lips as the first wisps of adrenaline began to dry his mouth. *There was going to be action. . . .*

"Sounds like it really dropped in the pot," said Daniels as he swung the grate outward. "Dunno how. *I* thought it was gonna be a walkover this time."

He nodded Des Grieux toward the climate-controlled container that he used for an office. "I wonder," Daniels added wistfully, "if it's bad enough they're gonna put support staff in the line . . . ?"

Des Grieux couldn't figure why he was getting out of the lockup five days early. The Hashemite Brotherhood controlled the northern half of Meridienne's single continent and claimed the whole of it. They'd been raiding into territory of the Sincanmo Federation to the south—pinpricks, but destructive ones. Unchecked vandalism had destabilized governments and economic systems more firmly based than anything the Sincanmos could claim.

In order to prevent the Sincanmos from carrying the fighting north, the Hashemites had hired off-planet mercenaries, the Thunderbolt Division, to guard their territory and deter the Sincanmos from escalating to all-out war with local forces. The situation had gone on for one and a half standard years, with the Hashemites chuckling over their cleverness.

The Thunderbolt Division was a good choice for the Hashemite purposes. It was a large organization which could be distributed in battalion-sized packets to stiffen local forces of enthusiastic irregulars; and the Thunderbolt Division was cheap, an absolute necessity. Meridienne was not a wealthy planet, and the Hashemites expected their "confrontation" to continue for five or more years before the Sincanmo Federation collapsed.

The Thunderbolt Division was cheap because it wasn't much good. Its equipment was low-tech, little better than what Meridienne's indigenous forces had bought for themselves. The mercenaries' main benefit to their employers was their experience. They *were* full-time, professional soldiers, not amateurs getting on-the-job training in their first war.

Then the Sincanmos met the threat head on: they hired Hammer's Slammers and prepared to smash every sign of organization in the northern half of the continent in a matter of weeks.

Des Grieux didn't see any reason the Sincanmo plan wouldn't work. Neither did Captain Garnaud, the commanding officer of Delta Company.

Normally line troops expected to serve disciplinary sentences after the fighting was over. In this case, Garnaud had decreed immediate active time for Des Grieux. D Company didn't need the veteran against the present threat, and Garnaud correctly believed that missing the possibility of seven days' action was a more effective punishment for Slick Des Grieux than a year's down-time restriction.

But now he was getting out early. . . .

Des Grieux followed Daniels into the close quarters of the jailor's office. The communications display was live with the angry holographic image of a senior lieutenant in battledress.

The face was a surprise. The officer was Katrina Grimsrud, the executive officer of H Company, rather than one of D Company's personnel. "Where the bloody hell have you been?" she snarled as soon as the jailor moved into pickup range of the display's cameras.

Daniels sat down at the desk crammed into the half of the container which didn't hold his bed and living quarters. His artificial feet splayed awkwardly at the sudden movement; they needed tuning or perhaps replacement.

"Sorry, sir," he muttered as he manipulated switches. His equipment was old and ill-mated, cast-offs from several different departments. Junk gravitated to this use on its way to the scrap pile. "Had to get the prisoner."

He adjusted the retinal camera. "Okay, Des Grieux," he said. "Look into this."

Des Grieux leaned his forehead against the padded frame. "What's going on?" he demanded.

Light flashed as the unit recorded his retinal pattern and matched it with the file in Central Records. Daniels' printer whined, rolling out hard copy. Des Grieux straightened, blinking as much from confusion as from the brief glare.

"Listen, Des Grieux," Lieutenant Grimsrud said. "We don't want any of your cop in this company. If you get cute, you're out. D'ye understand? Not busted, not in lockup: out!"

"I'm not *in* Hotel Company," Des Grieux snapped. He was confused. Besides, the adrenaline sparked by a chance of action had made him ready—as usual to fight anybody or anything, including a circle saw.

"You are now, Sarge," Daniels said as he handed Des Grieux the hard copy.

"Get over to the depot soonest,"Grimsrud ordered as Des Grieux stared at his orders. "Jailor, you've got transport, don't you? Carry him. We've got a replacement tank there with a newbie crew. Des Grieux's to take over as commander; the assigned commander'll drive."

Des Grieux frowned. He was transferred from Delta to Hotel, all right. It didn't matter a curse one way or the other; they were both tank companies.

Only . . . transfers didn't occur at finger-snap speed—but they did this time, with the facsimile signature of Colonel Hammer himself releasing Sergeant-Commander Samuel Des Grieux (retinal prints attached) from detention and transferring him to H Company.

"Look, sir," Daniels said, "it's not my job to dr—"

"It's bloody well your job if you *don't* get him to the depot ASAP, buddy!" Lieutenant Grimsrud said. "I can't spare the time or the man to send a driver back. D'ye understand?"

Des Grieux folded the orders into the right cargo pocket of his uniform. "I don't understand," he said to the holographic image. "Why such a flap over the Thunderbolt Division? We could put truck drivers in line and walk all over them."

"Too right," Grimsrud said forcefully. "Seems the towel-heads figured that out for themselves in time to hire Broglie's Legion. Colonel Hammer wants all the veterans he's got in line—and with you, that gives my 3d Platoon one, I say again *one*, trooper with more than two years in the Regiment. Get your ass over to our deployment area *soonest*."

Lieutenant Grimsrud cut the connection. Des Grieux stared in the direction of blank air no longer excited by coherent light. His whole body was trembling.

"Don't sound like she's lookin' for excuses," Daniels grumbled as he got to his feet. "C'mon, Sarge, it's ten keys to the depot from here."

Des Grieux whistled tunelessly as he followed the jailor to an air-cushion jeep as battered as the equipment in Daniels' office. His kit was still in D Company. He didn't care. He didn't care about anything at all, except for the chance fate offered him.

Daniels started the jeep. At least one drive fan badly needed balancing. "Hey, Sarge?" he said. "I never asked you—what was the fight about? The one that landed you here?"

"Some bastard called me a name," Des Grieux said. He braced himself against the tubular seat frame worn through the upholstery. The jeep lurched into motion.

Des Grieux's eyes were closed. His face looked like the blade of a hatchet. "He called me 'Pops,'" Des Grieux said. Memory of the incident pitched his voice an octave higher than normal. "So I hit him."

Daniels looked at the tanker, then frowned and looked away.

"Thirty-two standard years don't make me an old man," Slick Des Grieux added in an icy whisper.

A starship tested its maneuvering jets on the landing pad beside the depot's perimeter defenses. The high screech was so loud that the air seemed to ripple. Though the lips of Warrant Leader Farrell, the depot superintendent, continued to move for several seconds, Des Grieux hadn't the faintest notion of what the man was saying.

Des Grieux didn't much care, either. There was only one tank among the depot's lesser vehicles and stacked shipping containers. He stepped past Farrell and tested the spring-loaded cover of a step with his fingertip. It gave stiffly.

"Right," said Farrell. He held Des Grieux's transfer orders and, on a separate flimsy, the instructions which Central had downloaded directly to the depot. "Ah, here's the, ah, the previous crew."

Two troopers stood beside the depot superintendent. Both were young, but the taller, dark-haired one had a wary look in his eyes. The other man was blond, pale, and soft-seeming despite the obvious muscle bulging his khaki uniform.

Des Grieux gave them a cursory glance, then returned his attention to the important item: the vehicle he was about to command.

The tank was straight out of the factory in Hamburg on Terra.

Farrell's crew would have—should have done the initial checks, but the bearings would be stiff and the electronics weren't burned in yet

The tank didn't have a name, just a skirt number in red paint H271.

"Trooper Wartburg will move to driver," Farrell said. The dark-haired man acknowledged the statement by raising his chin a centimeter. "Trooper Flowers here was going to drive, but he'll go back to Logistics till we get another vehicle in."

Des Grieux climbed deliberately onto the deck of H271. The bustle rack behind the turret held personal gear in a pair of reused ammunition containers.

"You got any experience, Wartburg?" Des Grieux asked without looking back toward the men on the ground.

"Year and a half," the dark-haired man said. "Wing gunner on a combat car, then I drove for a while. This was going to be my first command."

Wartburg's tone was carefully precise. If he was disappointed to be kicked back to driver at the last instant, he kept the fact out of his voice.

Des Grieux slid the cupola hatch closed and open, ignoring the others again.

"One question, Sarge," Wartburg called. The irritation he had hidden before was now obvious. "Grimsrud told us a veteran'd be taking over the tank, but she didn't say who. You got a name?"

"Des Grieux," the veteran said. The tribarrel rotated on its ring, even with the power off. That was good, and a little surprising in a tank that hadn't yet been broken in. "Slick Des Grieux. You just do what I tell you and we'll get along fine."

Wartburg laughed brittlely. "The bloody hell I will," he said as he hopped up to the tank's deck himself.

Des Grieux turned in surprise. His eyes were flat and wide open. All he was sure of was that he'd need to pay more attention than he wanted to his new driver.

Wartburg said nothing further. He reached into the bustle rack and pulled out one of the cases, then tossed it to the ground.

The container crashed down and bounced before it fell flat.

Flowers jumped to avoid it. The dense plastic was designed to protect 3,000 disks of 2cm ammunition against anything short of a direct from another powergun. It withstood the abuse, and its hinged lid remained latched.

"What d'ye think you're doing?" Des Grieux demanded.

Wartburg threw down the other container. "I think I'm not doin' *any* bloody thing with you, Des Grieux," he said. He jumped to the ground.

"Wait a minute, Trooper!" said the outraged depot superintendent. "You've got your orders!"

He waggled the flimsies in his hand at Wartburg, though in fact neither of the documents directly mentioned that trooper.

Trooper Flowers looked from Wartburg to Des Grieux to Farrell—and back. His mouth was slightly open.

"Look, Warrant Leader," Wartburg said to Farrell. "I *heard* about this bastard. No way I'm riding with him. No way. You want me to resign from the Regiment, you got it. You wanna throw me in the lockup, that's your business."

He turned and glared at the man still on the deck of H271. "But I don't ride with Slick Des Grieux. If I ever get that hot to die, I'll eat my gun!"

"Screw you, buddy," Des Grieux said softly. He looked at the depot superintendent. "Okay, Mister Farrell, you get me a driver. That's your job. If you can't do that, then I'll drive and fight this mother both, if that's what it takes."

The three men on the ground began speaking to one another simultaneously in rasping, nervous voices. Des Grieux lowered himself through the cupola hatch.

H271's fighting compartment had the faintly medicinal odor of solvents still seeping from recently extruded plastics. Des Grieux touched control buttons, checking them for feel and placement. There were always production-line variations, even when two vehicles were ostensibly of the same model.

He heard the clunk of boot toes on the steps formed into H271's armor. Somebody was boarding the vehicle.

Des Grieux threw the main power switch. Gauges and displays

hummed to life. There was a line of distortion across Screen #3, but it faded after ten seconds or so. A tinge of ozone suggested arcing somewhere, probably in a microswitch. It would either clear itself or fail completely in the next hundred hours.

A hundred hours was a lifetime for a tank on the same planet as Colonel Luke Broglie. . . .

A head shadowed the light of the open hatch. Des Grieux looked up, into the face of Trooper Flowers.

"Sarge?" Flowers said. "Ah, I'm gonna drive for you. If that's all right?"

"Yeah, that's fine," said Des Grieux without expression. He turned to his displays again.

"Only, I've just drove trucks before, y'see," Flowers added.

"I don't care if you rolled hoops," Des Grieux said. "Get in and let's get moving."

"Ah—I'll get my gear," said Flowers. "I off loaded when they said I was back in Logistics."

"Booster," said Des Grieux, keying H271's artificial intelligence. "Course data on Screen One."

He watched the left-hand screen. He wasn't sure that the depot had gotten around to loading the course information into the tank's memory, but the route and topography came up properly. Des Grieux thought there was a momentary hesitation in the AI's response, but that might have been his own impatience.

The deck clanked as Flowers jumped directly to the ground in his haste. The way things were going, the kid probably slipped 'n broke his neck. . . .

The course to Base Camp Two and H Company was a blue line curving across three hundred kilometers of arid terrain. No roads, but no problems either. Gullies cut by the rare cloudbursts could be skirted or crossed.

Des Grieux spread his hands, closed his eyes, and rested his forehead against the cool surface of the main screen. Everything about H271 was smooth and cold. The tank functioned, but it didn't have a soul.

He shivered. He could remember when he had enough hair that

it wasn't bare scalp that touched the hologram display when he leaned forward like this.

Tank H271 was the right vehicle for Slick Des Grieux.

In the gully beside H271, twenty or so Sincanmo troops sang around a campfire to the music of strings and a double flute. There'd been drums, too. Lieutenant Kuykendall threatened to send a tank through the group if the drummer didn't toss his instrument into the fire *immediately.*

That was one order from the commander of Task Force Kuykendall that Des Grieux would have cheerfully obeyed. Not that he had anything against this particular group of indigs.

There were thirty or forty other campfires scattered among the gullies like opals on a multistrand necklace. With luck, the force's camouflage film concealed the firelight from the hostile outpost two kilometers away on the Notch. Silencing the drums, whose low-frequency beat carried forever in the cool desert air, was as much of a compromise as Kuykendall thought she could enforce.

The Sincanmos were a militia organized by extended families. Each family owned four to six vehicles which they armed with whatever the individuals fancied and could afford. Medium-powered lasers; post-mounted missile systems, both guided and hypervelocity; automatic weapons; even a few mortars, each of a different caliber. . . .

Logistics would have been a nightmare—if the Sincanmo Federation had *had* a formal logistics system. On the credit side, each band was highly motivated, extremely mobile, and packed a tremendous amount of firepower for its size.

The families made decisions by conclave. They took orders from their own Federation rather more often than they ignored those orders; but as for an off-planet mercenary—and a *female*—Kuykendall's authority depended on her own platoon of combat cars and the four H Company tanks attached to her for this operation.

Des Grieux chewed a ration bar in the cupola of his tank. The Sincanmos made their fire by soaking a bucket of sand in motor fuel and lighting it. The flames were low and red and quivered with frustrated anger, much like Des Grieux's thoughts. There was going to be a battle very soon. In days, maybe hours.

But not here. If Colonel Hammer had expected significant enemy forces to cross the Knifeblade Escarpment through the Notch, he wouldn't have sent Hotel Company's 3d Platoon with the blocking force. The platoon had been virtually reconstituted after a tough time on Mainstream during the previous contract. In a few years, some of these bloody newbies would be halfway decent soldiers. The ones who survived that long.

"Booster," Des Grieux muttered. "Ninety degree pan, half visor."

H271's artificial intelligence obediently threw a high-angle view of the terrain which Task Force Kuykendall guarded, onto the left side of Des Grieux's visor. The nameless sandstone butte behind the blocking force was useless as a defensive position in itself, because the only way for military equipment to get up or down its sheer faces was by crane. The mass of rock would confuse the enemy's passive sensors—at least the sensors of the Thunderbolt Division; Broglie's hardware certainly had the discrimination to pick out tanks, combat cars, and the Sincanmo 4x4s, even though the vehicles were defiladed and backed by a 500-meter curtain of stone.

The butte also provided a useful pole on which to hang the Slammers' remote sensors, transmitting their multispectral information down jam-free, undetectable fiber-optic cables. Des Grieux at ground level had as good a vantage point as that of the Hashemite outpost in the Notch; and because the image fed to the tanker's helmet was light enhanced and computer sharpened, Des Grieux *saw* infinitely more.

Not that there was any bloody thing to see. Gullies cut by the infrequent downpours meandered across the plain. They were shallow as well as direction-less, because the land didn't really drain. Rain sluiced from the buttes and the Escarpment flooded the whole landscape—and evaporated.

Winds had scoured away the topsoils to redeposit them thousands of kilometers away as loess. The clay substrates which remained were virtually impervious to water.

Seen from Des Grieux's high angle, the gullies were dark smears of gray-green vegetation against the lighter yellow-gray soil. Low shrubs with hard, waxy leaves grew every few meters along the gully floors, where they were protected from wind and sustained by the memory of moisture. The plants were scarcely noticeable at ground level, but they were the plain's only feature.

The butte was a dark mass at Des Grieux's back. In front of him, two kilometers to the south, was the Knifeblade Escarpment: a sheer wall of sandstone for a hundred kays east and west, except for the Notch carved by meltwater from a retreating glacier thirty millions of years in the past. A one in five slope led from the Notch to the plain below. It was barely negotiable by vehicles; but it *was* negotiable.

South of the Escarpment, the Hashemites and their mercenaries faced the Sincanmo main force—and Hammer's Slammers. Task Force Kuykendall was emplaced to prevent the enemy from skirting the Knifeblade to the north and falling on the Slammers' flank and rear.

The Hashemites themselves would never think of that maneuver; the Thunderbolt Division could not possibly carry out such a plan in the time available. But Broglie was smart enough, and his troops were good enough . . . if he were willing to split his already out-gunned force.

Alois Hammer wasn't willing to bet that Broglie wouldn't do what Hammer himself would do if the situation were desperate enough.

But neither did Hammer *expect* a real fight north of the Escarpment. All odds were that Task Force Kuykendall, two platoons of armor and 600-800 Sincanmo irregulars, would wait in bored silence while their fellows chewed on Hashemites until the Brotherhood surrendered unconditionally.

Thunder rumbled far beyond the distant horizon. In this climate, a storm was less likely than the Lord coming down to appoint Slick Des Grieux as master of the universe.

No, it was artillery promising imminent action. For other people.

The most recent bite of ration bar was a leaden mass in Des Grieux's mouth. He spat it into the darkness, then tossed the remainder of the bar away, also.

"Booster," he said. "Close-up of the Notch."

A view of flamelit rock replaced the panorama before the las' syllable was out of the tanker's mouth. The Hashemites were a' feckless and unconcerned as their planetary enemies; and unlike the Sincanmos, the Hashemites didn't have the Slammers' logistic personnel to dispense an acre of camouflage film which woulc conceal equipment, personnel, and campfires from—hostile eyes.

Of course, the Hashemites didn't think there were any hostil' eyes. They had stationed an outpost here to prevent the Sincanmo from using the Notch as a back door for attack, but the force was a nominal one of a few hundred indig troops with no leavening o' mercenaries. The real defenses were the centrally controlled mine' placed in an arc as much as a kilometer north of the Notch.

The outpost hadn't seen Task Force Kuykendall move into position in the dark hours this morning. In a few hours or days when the main battle ground to a conclusion, they would *still* b' ignorant of the enemy watching them from the north.

The troops of the outpost probably thanked their Lord that they were safely out of the action . . . and they were.

Des Grieux swore softly.

The outpost had a pair of heavy weapons, truck-mounted railguns capable of pecking a hole in tank armor in twenty seconds or so. De' Grieux wouldn't *give* them twenty seconds, of course, but while he dealt with the railguns, the remainder of the Hashemites woulc loose a barrage of missiles at H271. And then there were the mine' to cross. . . .

If the platoon's oilier three tanks were good for anything—i' one of the crews was good for anything—it'd be possible to pic' through the minefields with clearance charges, sonics, and ground penetrating radar. Trusting *this* lot of newbies to provide covering fire would be like trusting another trooper with your girl and your bottle for the evening.

Kuykendall's platoon was of veterans, but she had orders to keep a low profile unless the enemy sallied out. Kuykendall took orders real good. She'd do fine with Colonel Bloody Broglie. . . .

Hashemites drank and played a game with dice and marker'

round fuel-oil campfires on the Notch. The sensor pack high on he mesa gave Des Grieux a beautiful view of the enemy, but they vere beyond the line of-sight range of his guns.

A salvo of artillery ricocheting from the sandstone walls would rind the towel-heads to hamburger, but the shells would first have o get through the artillery defenses south of the Escarpment. Des Grieux remembered being told the first thing Broglie had done after aking command was to fit every armored vehicle in the Legion with tribarrel capable of automatic artillery defense.

Guns muttered far to the south. When Des Grieux listened very arefully, he could distinguish the hiss-*crack* reports of big-bore owerguns. Tanks and tank destroyers were beginning to mix it— wenty kilometers away.

Des Grieux shivered and cursed; and after a time, he began to ray to a personal God of Battles. . . .

"Sir?" said Trooper Flowers from the narrow duct joining his tation to H271's fighting compartment. The driver's shoulders vere a tight fit in the passage. "I'm ready to take my watch, sir. Do ou want me in the cupola, or . . . ?"

Des Grieux adjusted a vernier control on Screen #1, dimming the opographic display fractionally. "I'm not 'sir,'" he said. He didn't other to look toward Flowers through the cut-out sides of the turret asket. "And *I'll* worry about keeping watch till I tell you different."

He returned his attention to Screen #3 on the right side of the ighting compartment. It was live but blank in pearly lustrousness; Des Grieux was missing a necessary link in the feed he wanted to rrange.

"Ah, S-sergeant?" the driver said. The only light in the fighting ompartment was scatter from the holographic screens. Flowers' ace appeared to be slightly flushed. "Sergeant Des Grieux? What do ou want me to do?"

On the right—astern—edge of the topo screen, a company of lammers infantry supported by combat cars moved up the range f broken hills held by the Thunderbolt Division. The advance eemed slow, particularly because the map scale was shrunk to encompass a ten-kilometer battle area; but it was as certain and regular as a gear train.

If navigational data passed to the map display, then there *had* to be a route for—

"Sir?" said Flowers.

"Go play with yourself!" Des Grieux snarled. He glared angrily at his driver.

As Des Grieux's mind refocused to deal with the interruption, the answer to the main problem flashed before him. *The information he wanted wasn't passing on the command channels he'd been tapping out of the Regiment's rear echelon back in Sanga: it was in the machine-to-machine data links, untouched by human consciousness. . . .*

"Right," Des Grieux said mildly. "Look, just stick close to the tank, okay, kid? Do anything you please."

Flowers ducked away, surprised at the tank commanders sudden change of temper. His boots scuffled hollowly as he backed through the internal hatch to the driver's compartment.

"Booster," Des Grieux ordered the tank's artificial intelligence, "switch to Utility Feed One and synthesize on Screen Three."

The opalescent ready status on the right-hand screen dissolved into multicolored garbage. Whatever data was coming through UF didn't lend itself to visual presentation.

"Via!" Des Grieux snarled. "Utility Feed Two." He heard boots on H271's hull, but he ignored them because Screen #3 was abruptly live with what appeared to be a live-action view through the gunnery screen of another tank. The orange circle of the main-gun pipper steadied on a slab of rock kilometers away. There was no visible target—

Until the point of aim disintegrated in a gout of white-hot glass under the impact of the 20cm powergun of another tank. The ledge cracked from heat shock. Half of it slid away to the left in a single piece, while the remainder crumbled into gravel.

Iridium armor gleamed beneath the pipper. Des Grieux's boot trod reflexively on his foot-trip, but the safety interlock still disengaged his guns.

The real gunner, kilometers away, was only a fraction of a second slower. The image blurred with the recoil of the sending tank's main gun, and the target—a Legion tank destroyer—erupted at the heart of the cyan bolt.

"Sergeant Des Grieux?" said a voice from the open cupola latch. "I'm just checking how all my people are—good Lord!"

Des Grieux looked up. Lieutenant Carbury, 3d Platoon's commanding officer and almost as new to the business of war as Des Grieux's driver, stared at the images of Screen #3.

"What on earth is that?" Carbury begged/demanded as he turned to scramble backward into the fighting compartment of H271. "Is it happening now?"

"More or less," the veteran replied, deliberately vague. He pretended to ignore the lieutenant's intrusion by concentrating on the screen. His AI had switched the image feed to that from a gun camera on a combat car. Mortar rounds flashed in a series of white pulses from behind the hillcrest a hundred meters away.

The images were not full-spectrum transmissions. Each vehicle's artificial intelligence broadcast its positional and sensory data to the command vehicle of the unit to which it was attached. Part of the command vehicle's communications suite was responsible for routing necessary information—including sensory data stripped to digital shorthand to the central data banks at the Slammers' rear-area logistical headquarters.

The route was likely to be long and poor, because communications satellites were the first casualties of war. Here on Meridienne, the Regiment depended on a chain of laser transponders strung butte to butte along the line of march. When sandstorms disrupted the chain of coherent light, commo techs made do with signals bounced from whichever of Meridienne's moons were in a suitable location.

The signals did get through to the rear, though.

Des Grieux had set his tank's artificial intelligence to enter Central through Task Force Kuykendall's own long data link. The AI sorted out gunnery feeds, then synthesized the minimal squibs of information into three-dimensional holograms.

On Screen #3, fuel blazed from a vehicle struck by the probing mortar shells. A moment later a light truck accelerated up the forward slope of the next hill beyond. A dozen Hashemite irregulars clung to the truck. Their long robes flapped with the speed of their flight.

Des Grieux expected the camera through which he watched to record a stream of cyan bolts ripping the vehicle. Nothing happened. The Hashemite truck ducked over the crest to more distant cover again.

Three half-tracked APCs of the Thunderbolt Division grunted up the forward slope, following the Hashemite vehicle. Their steel-cleated treads sparked wildly on the stony surface.

The tribarrel through which Des Grieux watched and those of the combat car's two wing gunners poured a converging fire into the center APC. It exploded, flinging out the fiery bodies of Thunderbolt infantrymen. The rest of the combat car platoon concentrated on the other two carriers. Their thin armor collapsed with similar results.

Slammers infantry on one-man skimmers slid forward to consolidate the new position just as Des Grieux's AI cut to a new viewpoint.

"How do you *do* that?" asked Lieutenant Carbury as he stared at the vivid scenes.

The platoon leader was as slim as Des Grieux and considerably shorter, but the fighting compartment of a line tank had not been designed for two-person occupancy. Des Grieux could have provided a little more room by folding his seat against the bulkhead, but he pointedly failed to do so.

"Prob'ly the same way they showed you at the Academy," Des Grieux said. *They didn't teach cadets how to use a tank's artificial intelligence to break into Central, but Via! they were fully compatible systems.* "Sir."

The sound of real gunfire whispered through the night.

"Wow," said Carbury. He was sucking in his belly so that he could lean toward Screen #3 without pressing the veteran's shoulder. "Exactly what is it that's happening, Sergeant? They, ah, they aren't updating me very regularly."

Des Grieux rotated his chair counterclockwise. The back squeezed Carbury against the turret basket until the lieutenant managed to slip aside.

"It's all right there," Des Grieux said, pointing toward the map display on Screen #1. "He's got Broglie held on the left—" orange symbols toward the western edge of the display "—but that's just sniping, no *way* they're gonna push Broglie out of ground that rugged."

He gathered spit in his mouth, then swallowed it. "The bastard's good," the veteran muttered to himself. "I give him that."

"Right," said Carbury firmly in a conscious attempt to assert himself. Strategy *was* a major part of the syllabus of the Frisian Military Academy. "So instead he's putting pressure on the right flank where the terrain's easier—"

Not a lot easier, but at least the hills didn't channel tanks and combat cars into a handful of choke points.

"—and there's only the Thunderbolt Division to worry about." Carbury frowned. "Besides the Hashemites themselves, of course."

"*You* worry about the towel-heads," Des Grieux said acidly. He glared at the long arc of yellow symbols marking elements of the Thunderbolt Division.

Though the enemy's eastern flank was anchored on hills rising to join the Knifeblade Escarpment well beyond the limits of the display, the center of the long line stretched across terrain similar to that in which Task Force Kuykendall waited. Gullies; scattered shrubs; hard, windswept ground that rolled more gently than a calm sea.

Perfect country for a headlong armored assault.

"*That's* what he ought to do," Des Grieux said, more to himself than to the intruding officer. He formed three fingers of his left hand into a pitchfork and stabbed them upward past the line of yellow symbols.

On Screen #3 at the corner of his eye, an image flashed into a cyan dazzle as another main-gun bolt struck home.

"Umm," said Carbury judiciously. "It's not really that simple, Sergeant." His manicured index finger bobbed toward the left, then

the right edge of the display. "They'd be enfiladed by fire from th‹
Legion, and even the Thunderbolts have anti-tank weapons. Yo‹
wouldn't want to do that."

Des Grieux turned and stared up at the lieutenant. "Try me," h‹
said. The tone was unemotional, but Carbury's head jerked bac‹
from the impact of the veteran's eyes.

Screen #3 showed a distant landscape through the sights of ‹
combat-car tribarrel. The image expanded suddenly as the gunne‹
dialed up times forty magnification. The target was a—

Des Grieux's attention clicked instantly to the display. Free
from the veteran's glare, Carbury blinked and focused on the distar‹
scene also.

The target was a Thunderbolt calliope, shooting upward from ‹
pit that protected the eight-barreled weapon while it knocke‹
incoming artillery shells from the air. The high ground which th‹
combat car had gained gave its tribarrels a slanting view down at th‹
calliope four kilometers away.

The line-straight bolts from a powergun cared nothing fo‹
distance, so long as no solid object intervened. A five-round bur‹
from the viewpoint tribarrel raked the gun pit, reducing half th‹
joined barrels and the crew to ions.

That would have been enough, but the calliope was in actio‹
when the bolts struck it. One of the weapon's own high-intensit‹
3cm rounds discharged in a barrel which the Slammers' fire ha‹
already welded shut.

A blue-white explosion blew open the multiple breeches. Tha‹
was only the momentary prelude to the simultaneous detonatio‹
of the contents of an ammunition drum. Plasma scooped out th‹
sides of the gun pit and reflected pitilessly from rockfaces sever‹
kilometers away.

As if an echo, three more of the Thunderbolt Division's protectiv‹
calliopes exploded with equal fury.

The Slammers' toehold on the eastern hills wasn't the overtur‹
to further slogging advances on the same flank: it was a vantag‹
point from which to destroy at long range the artillery defenses ‹
the entire hostile center.

"Good *Lord*," Lieutenant Carbury gasped. He leaned forward in amazement for a closer view. Des Grieux shoved Carbury back with as little conscious volition.

H271's artificial intelligence switched its viewpoint to that of a jeep-mounted infantry tribarrel. Six red streaks fanned through the sky above the narrow wedge of vision, a full salvo from a battery of the Slammers' rocket artillery.

Powerguns fired from the hills to the west. Some of Broglie's defensive weapons had retargeted abruptly to help close the sudden gap in the center of the line. That was dangerous, though, since Hammer's other two batteries continued to pound the flanks of the enemy position.

Broglie's powerguns detonated two of the incoming shells into bright flashes and smears of ugly smoke. The help was too little, too late: the other four firecracker rounds popped open at preset altitudes and strewed their deadly cargo widely over the Thunderbolt lines.

For the moments that the anti-personnel bomblets took to fall, nothing seemed to happen. Then white light like burning magnesium erupted over four square kilometers. Hair-fine lengths of glass shrapnel sawed in all directions. The coverage was thin, but the blasts carved apart anyone within a meter of an individual bomblet.

Lieutenant Carbury jumped for the hatch, aiming his right boot at the back of the tank commander's seat but using Des Grieux's shoulder as a step instead. "Remote that feed to my tank *now*, Sergeant!" the lieutenant shouted as he pulled himself out of H271's cupola.

Des Grieux ignored Carbury and keyed his intercom. *Flowers had better be wearing his commo helmet.* "Driver!" the veteran snarled. "Get your ass aboard!"

On Screen #3, another salvo of anti-personnel shells howled down onto the Thunderbolt Division's reeling battalions.

Powerguns snapped and blasted at a succession of targets on H271's right-hand screen. For the past several minutes, the real excitement, even for Des Grieux, was on the map display on the other side of the fighting compartment.

The Hashemites and their mercenary allies were getting thei clocks cleaned.

The AI's interpretation of data from the battle area cross hatched all the units of the Thunderbolt Division which were sti on the plain. A few minutes of hammering with firecracke rounds had reduced the units by twenty percent of their strengt from casualties—

And to something closer to zero combat efficiency because c their total collapse of morale. The battle wasn't over yet, but it wa over for *those* men and women. They retreated northward in disorde some of them on foot without even their personal weapons. Thei only thought was to escape the killing zone of artillery and long range sniping from the Slammers' powerguns.

Half of the Thunderbolt Division remained as an effectiv fighting force on the high ground to the east—the original left-flan battalions and the troops which had retreated to their protectio under fire. Even those units were demoralized, but they would hol against anything except an all-out attack from the Slammers.

If the mercenary commander surrendered now, while his positio was tenable and his employers were still fighting, the Thunderbo Division would forfeit the performance bond it had posted with th Bonding Authority on Terra. That would end the division as a employable force—and shoot the career of its commander in th nape of the neck.

H271 quivered as its fans spun at idle. The tank was ready to g at a touch on the throttle and pitch controls. "Sarge?" Flowers aske over the intercom channel. "Are we gonna move out soon?"

"Kid," Des Grieux said as he watched holographic dots crawlin across holographic terrain, "when I want to hear your voice, I'll te you."

If he hadn't been so concentrated on the display, he would hav snarled the words.

The Thunderbolt Division's employers weren't exactly fighting but neither had they surrendered. The Hashemite Brotherhood wa no more of a monolith than were their Sincanmo enemies; an Hashemite troops were concentrated on the plains, where thei nobility seemed an advantage. Des Grieux suspected that the Hashemites *would* have surrendered by now if they'd had enough organization left to manage it.

Broglie's armored elements on what had been the Hashemite right flank, now cut off from friendly forces by the collapse of the center, formed a defensive hedgehog among the sandstone boulders. The terrain gave them an advantage that would translate into prohibitive casualties for anybody trying to drive them out—even the panzers of Colonel Hammer's tank companies. Broglie's Legion wasn't going anywhere.

But Broglie himself had.

Within thirty seconds of the time artillery defense had collapsed in the center of the Hashemite line, four tank destroyers sped from the Legion's strong point to reinforce the Thunderbolt infantry. There was no time to redeploy vehicles already in the line, and Broglie had no proper reserve. These tank destroyers were the Legion's Headquarters/Headquarters Platoon.

The move was as desperate as the situation itself. Des Grieux wasn't surprised to learn Broglie had figured the only possible way out of Colonel Hammer's trap, but it was amazing to see that Broglie had the balls to put himself on the line that way. Des Grieux figured that Broglie obeyed orders because he was too chicken not to. . . .

By using gullies and the rolling terrain, three of the low-slung vehicles managed to get into position. The single loss was a tank destroyer that paused to spike a combat car five kilometers away on the Slammers' right flank. A moment later, the Legion vehicle vanished under the impact of five nearly simultaneous 20cm bolts from Slammers' tanks.

Tribarrels on the roofs of the three surviving tank destroyers ripped effectively at incoming artillery, detonating the cargo shells before they strewed their bomblets over the landscape. The tank destroyers' 15cm main guns were a threat nothing, not even a bow-on tank, could afford to ignore. The leap-frog advance of Slammers' units toward the gap in the enemy center slowed to a lethal game of hide-and-seek.

But it was still too little, too late. The Hashemite and Thunderbolt Division troops were broken and streaming northward All the tank destroyers could do was act as a rear guard, like Horatiu and his two companions.

There was no bridge on their line of retreat, but the only practical route down from the Knifeblade Escarpment was through the Notch. Task Force Kuykendall and tank H271 had that passage sealed, as clever-ass *Colonel* Luke Broglie would learn within the next half hour.

Des Grieux began to chuckle hoarsely as he watched beads ooze across a background of coherent light. The sound that came from his throat blended well with the increasingly loud mutter of gunfire from south of the Escarpment.

"Shellfish Six to all Oyster and Clam elements," Des Grieux' helmet said.

Des Grieux had ignored the chatter which broke out among the Slammers' vehicles—the combat cars were code named Oyster; the tanks were Clam—as soon as Carbury gave the alarm. He couldn' ignore this summons, because it was the commander of Shellfish— Task Force Kuykendall—speaking over a unit priority channel.

"All blower captains to me at Golf Six-five ASAP. Acknowledge Over."

This was no bloody time to have all the senior people standing around in a gully, listening to some bitch with lieutenant's pips on her collar!

There were blips of static on Des Grieux's headset. Several commanders used the automatic response set on their consoles instead of replying—protesting—in person.

"Clam Six to Shellfish Six . . ." said Lieutenant Carbury nervously The tank-platoon commander was not only beneath Kuykendall in the chain of command, he was well aware that she was a ten-year veteran of the Slammers while he had yet to see action. "Suggest we link our vehicles for a virtual council, sir. Over."

"Negative,"Kuykendall snapped."I need to make a point to our employers and allies, here, Clam Six, and they're not in the holographic environment."

She paused,then added in a coldly neutral voice. "Break. This means you,too, Slick. Don't push your luck. Shellfish Six out."

Des Grieux cursed under his breath. After a moment, he slid his seat upward and climbed out of the tank. He'd grabbed a grenade launcher and a bandolier of ammunition at the depot; he carried them in his left hand.

He didn't acknowledge the summons.

Occasional flashes to the south threw the Knifeblade Escarpment into hazy relief, like a cloud bank lighted by a distant storm. Sometimes the wind sounded like human cries.

The gullies at the base of the butte twisted Task Force Kuykendall's position like the guts of a worm. Two combat cars and a tank were placed between H271 and Kuykendall's vehicle, *Firewalker*, in the rough center of the line. The gaps between the Slammers' units were filled by indigs in family battlegroups.

The restive Sincanmos had let their campfires burn down. The way through the gullies was marked by metal buckets glowing from residual heat. Men in bright, loose garments fingered their personal weapons and watched Des Grieux as he trudged past.

There was a group of fifty or more armed troops—all men except for Kuykendall and one of the tank commanders, and overwhelmingly indigs—gathered at *Firewalker* when Des Grieux arrived. Kuykendall had switched on the car's running lights with deep yellow filters in place to preserve the night vision of those illuminated.

"Glad you could make it, Slick," Kuykendall said. She perched on cargo slung to the side of her combat car. It was hard to make out Kuykendall's words over the burble of Sincanmo conversation because she spoke without electronic amplification. "I want all of you to hear what I just informed Chief Diabate."

The name of the senior Sincanmo leader in the task force brought a partial hush. Men turned to look at Diabate, white-bearded and more hawk-faced than most of his fellows. He wore a robe printed in an intricate pattern of black/russet/white, over which were slung a 2cm powergun and three silver-mounted knives in a sash.

"Colonel Hammer has ordered us back ten kays," Kuykendall continued. Two crewmen stood at *Firewalker*'s wing tribarrels, but the weapons were aimed toward the Notch. The air of the gathering was amazement, not violence. "So we're moving out in half an hour."

"Don't be bloody crazy!" Des Grieux shouted over the indignant babble. "You saw what's happening south of the wall."

He pointed the barrel of his grenade launcher toward the Escarpment. The bandolier swung heavily in the same hand. "Inside an hour, there'll be ten thousand people trying t' get through the Notch, and *we're* here t' shut the door in their face?"

Sincanmo elders shook their guns in the air and cried approval.

Kuykendall's sharp features pinched tighter. She muttered an order to *Firewalker*'s AI, then—regardless of the Hashemites in the Notch—blared through the combat car's external speakers, "*Listen* to me, gentlemen!"

Her voice echoed like angry thunder from the face of the butte. Shouting men blinked and looked at her.

"The colonel *wants* them to run away instead of fighting like cornered rats," Kuykendall went on, speaking normally but continuing to use amplification. "He wants a surrender, not a bloodbath."

"But—" Chief Diabate protested.

"What the colonel orders," Kuykendall said firmly, "I carry out. And I'm in charge of this task force, by order of your own council."

"We know the Hashemites!" Diabate said. This time, Kuykendall let him speak. "If they throw away their guns and flee now, they will find more guns later. Only if we kill them all can we be sure of peace. This is the time to kill them!"

"I've got my orders," Kuykendall said curtly, "and you've got yours. Slammers elements, saddle up. We move out in twenty . . . seven minutes."

Khaki-uniformed mercenaries turned away, shrugging at the slings and holsters of their personal weapons. Des Grieux did not move for a moment.

"I wanted you to see," Kuykendall continued to the shocked

Sincanmo elders. "*This* isn't a tribal council, this is war and *I'm* in charge. If you refuse to obey my orders, *you're* in breach of the contract, not me and Colonel Hammer."

Sincanmos shouted in anger and surprise. Des Grieux strode away from the crowd, muttering commands through his commo helmet to the artificial intelligence in H271. The AI obediently projected a view of the terrain still closer to the base of the mesa onto the left side of Des Grieux's visor.

Flowers waited with his torso out of the driver's hatch. "What's the word, Sarge?" he called as Des Grieux stepped around the back of a Sincanmo truck mounted with a cage launcher and a quartet of forty-kilo bombardment rockets.

"We're moving," Des Grieux said. He lifted himself to the deck of his tank. "There's a low spot twenty meters from the base of the butte. I'll give directions on your screen. Park us there."

He clambered up the turret side and thrust his legs through the hatch.

"Ah, Sarge?" Flowers called worriedly. His curved armor hid him from Des Grieux. "Should I take down the cammie film?"

Des Grieux switched to intercom. Screen #1 now showed the terrain in the immediate vicinity of H271. The site Des Grieux had picked was within two hundred meters of the tank's present location.

"It'll bloody come down when you bloody drive through it, won't it?" Des Grieux snarled. He slashed his finger across the topo map, marking the intended route with a glowing line that echoed on the driver's display. "Do it!"

The microns-thick camouflage film was strung, then jolted with high-frequency electricity which caused it to take an optical set in the pattern and colors of the ground underneath it. The film was polarized to pass light impinging on the upper surfaces but to block it from below. The covering was permeable to air as well, though it did impede ventilation somewhat.

H271's fans snorted at increased power, sucking the thin membrane against its stretchers. Sincanmo troops moved closer to their own vehicles, eyeing the 170-tonne tank with concern.

Flowers rotated H271 carefully in its own length, then drove slowly up the back slope of the gully. The nearest twenty-meter length of camouflage film bowed, then flew apart when the stresses exceeded its limits. Gritty soil puffed from beneath the tank's skirts.

"Clam Four, this is Clam Six," said Lieutenant Carbury over the 3d Platoon push. "What's going on there? Over."

Des Grieux closed the cupola hatch above him. This was going to be very tricky. Not placing the shot—he could do that at ten kays—but determining where the shot had to *be* placed.

H271 lurched as Flowers drove it down into a washout directly at the base of the mesa. Des Grieux let the tank settle as he searched the sandstone face through his gunnery screen.

"This where you want us, Sarge?" Flowers asked.

"Clam Four, this is Shellfish Six. Report! Over."

"Right," said Des Grieux over the intercom. "Shut her down. Is your hatch closed?"

The intake howl dimmed into the sighing note of fans winding down. Iridium clanged forward as Flowers slammed his hatch.

"Yes sir," he said.

Des Grieux fired his main gun. Cyan light filled the world.

The rockface cracked with a sound like the planetary mantle splitting. The shattered cliff slumped forward in chunks ranging in size from several tons to microscopic beads of glass. H271 rang and shuddered as the wave of rubble swept across it, sliding up against the turret.

"Clam Four to Clam Six," Des Grieux said. He didn't try to keep his voice free of the satisfaction he felt at the perfect execution of his plan. "I've had an accidental discharge of my main gun. No injuries but I'm afraid my tank can't be moved without mebbe a day's work by heavy equipment. Over."

"Slick," said Lieutenant Kuykendall, "you stupid son of a bitch."

She must have expected something like this, because she didn't bother raising her voice.

Kuykendall's right wing gunner worked over the Notch with his tribarrel as *Firewalker* idled at the base of the butte.

When H271 lighted the night with its main gun, the Hashemites guarding the Notch came to panicked alertness. During the ten minutes since, combat cars fired short bursts to keep enemy heads down while the Slammers pulled out.

This thirty-second slashing was different. The gunner's needless expenditure of ammunition was a way to let out his frustration—at what Des Grieux had done, or at the fact that the rest of the Slammers were running while Des Grieux and the indigs stayed to fight.

The troopers of Task Force Kuykendall were professional soldiers. If they'd been afraid of a fight, they would have found some other line of work.

Kuykendall squeezed the gunner's biceps, just beneath the shoulder flare of his body armor. The trooper's thumbs came off the butterfly trigger. The weapon's barrel-set continued to rotate for several seconds to aid in cooling. The white-hot iridium muzzles glowed a circle around their common axis.

Trooper Flowers lifted himself into *Firewalker*'s fighting compartment. His personal gear—in a dufflebag; Flowers was too junior to have snagged large-capacity ammo cans to hold his belongings—was slung to the vehicle's side. Combat cars made room for extra personnel more easily than Carbury's remaining tanks could.

Des Grieux braced his feet against the cupola coaming and used his leg muscles to shove at a block of sandstone the size of his torso. Thrust overcame friction. The slab slid across a layer of gravel, then toppled onto H271's back deck.

The upper surfaces were clear enough now that Des Grieux could rotate the turret.

Lieutenant Carbury's *Paper Doll* was an old tank, frequently repaired. An earlier commander had painted kill rings on the stubby barrel of the main gun. Holographic screens within the fighting compartment illuminated Carbury from below. His fresh, youthful face was out of place peering from the veteran vehicle.

"Sergeant Des Grieux," the lieutenant said. His voice was pitched too high for the tone of command he wished to project. "You're acting like a fool by staying here, and you're disobeying my direct orders."

Carbury spoke directly across the twenty meters between him self and tank H271 instead of using his commo helmet. The *hoosh* o lift fans idling almost washed his voice away. In another few sec onds, minutes at most, Des Grieux would be alone with fate.

The veteran brushed his palms against the front of his jumpsui He had to be careful not to rub his hands raw while moving rocks He'd need delicate control soon, with the opening range at two kays

"Sorry, sir," he called. "I figure the accident's my fault. It's m duty to stay with the tank since I'm the one who disabled it."

A combat car spat at the Notch. The Sincanmos, still unde their camouflage film, were keeping as quiet as cats in ambush whil the two platoons of armored vehicles maneuvered out of the gullies

The Sincanmos didn't take orders real well, but they were willing to do whatever was required for a chance to kill. Des Grieux felt momentary sympathy for the indigs, knowing what was about to happen.

But Via! if they hadn't been a bunch of stupid wogs, they'd have known, too.

They weren't his problem.

"Clam Six," said Lieutenant Kuykendall remotely, "this i Shellfish Six." She used radio, a frequency limited to the Slammer within the task force. "Are all your elements ready to move Over."

Carbury stiffened and touched the frequency key on the side o his commo helmet. "Clam Six to Six," he said. "Yes sir, all ready Over."

Instead of giving the order, Kuykendall turned to look at De Grieux. She raised the polarized shield of her visor. "Goodbye Slick," she called across the curtain of disturbed air. "I don't gues I'll be seeing you again."

Des Grieux stared at the woman who had been his driver decade before. They were twenty meters apart, but she still flinche minutely at his expression.

Des Grieux smiled. "Don't count on that, Lieutenant-sir," h said.

Kuykendall slapped her visor down and spoke a curt order

'an notes changed, the more lightly loaded rotors of the combat
ars rising in pitch faster than those of the tanks.

Moving in unison with a tank in the lead, the Slammers of
'ask Force Kuykendall howled off into the night. Their powerguns,
nain guns as well as tribarrels, lashed the Notch in an unmistakable
arewell gesture. The sharp *crack* of the bolts and the dazzling
ctinics reflected back and forth between the Escarpment and the
heer face of the mesa.

For Des Grieux, the huge vehicles had a beauty like that of
othing else in existence. They skated lightly over the soil, gathering
peed in imperceptible increments. Occasionally a skirt touched
own and sparked, steel against shards of quartz. Then they were
one around the mesa, leaving the sharpness of ozone and the
host-track of ionized air dissipating where a main gun had fired at
he Hashemites.

Des Grieux felt a sudden emptiness; but it was too late now to
hange, and anyway, it didn't matter. He slid down into H271 and
ried his gunnery controls again. Added weight resisted the turret
notors briefly, but this time it was only gravel and smaller particles
vhich could rearrange themselves easily.

The sight picture on H271's main screen rotated: off the blank
vall of the butte and across open desert, to the Notch that marred
he otherwise smooth profile of the Knifeblade Escarpment. Des
Grieux raised the magnification. Plus twenty; plus forty, and he
ould see movement as Hashemites crawled forward, over rocks
plit and glazed by blue-white bolts, to see why the punishing fire
ad ceased; plus eighty—

A Hashemite wearing a turban and a dark blue jellaba swept the
ight with the image-intensifying sight of his back-pack missile.

He found nothing. Des Grieux stared at the Hashemite's bearded
ace until the man put down his sight and called his fellows forward.
His optics were crude compared to those of H271, and the
Hashemite didn't know where to look.

Des Grieux smiled grimly and shut down all his tank's systems.
'rom now until he slammed home the main switch again, Des
Grieux would wait in a silent iridium coffin.

It wasn't his turn. Yet. He raised his head through the cupol
hatch and watched.

Because of the patient silence the Sincanmos had maintained
Des Grieux expected the next stage to occur in about half an hour
In fact, it was less than five minutes after the Slammers' armore
vehicles had noisily departed the scene before one of the outpost
switched the minefield controls to Self-destruct. Nearly a thousand
charges went off simultaneously, any one of them able to destroy
4x4 or cripple a tank.

An all-wheel drive truck laden with towel-heads lurched ove
the lip of the Notch and started for the plains below.

The locals on both sides were irregulars, but the Sincanmos i
ambush had something concrete to await. All the Hashemite guard
knew was that a disaster had occurred south of the Escarpment, an
that they had themselves been released from a danger unguesse
until the Slammers drove off through the night. *They* saw no reaso
to hold position, whatever their orders might be.

Three more trucks followed the first—a family battle grou
organized like those of the Sincanmos. One of the vehicles towed
railgun on a four-wheeled carriage. The slope was a steep twent
percent. The railgun threatened to swing ahead every time th
towing vehicle braked, but the last truck in the group held th
weapons barrel with a drag line to prevent upset.

The Sincanmos did not react.

A dozen more trucks grunted into sight. H271's sensors coul
have placed and identified the vehicles while they were still hidde
behind the lip of rock, but it didn't matter one way or the other t
Des Grieux. Better to keep still, concealed even from sensors fa
more sophisticated than those available to the indigs.

More trucks. They poured out of the Notch, three and fou
abreast, as many as the narrow opening would accept. Forty, sixty–
still more. The entire outpost was fleeing at its best speed.

The Hashemites must have argued violently. Should they go o
stay? Was the blocking force really gone, or did it lurk on the othe
side of the butte, waiting to swing back into sight spewing blue fire

But somebody was bound to run; and when that group seeme

n the verge of successful escape, the others would follow as surely
s day follows night.

There would be no day for most of this group of Hashemites.
Vhen their leading vehicles reached the bottom of the slope, the
incanmos opened up with a devastating volley.

The two-kilometer range was too great for sidearms to be
enerally effective, though Des Grieux saw a bolt from a semiau-
ɔmatic powergun—perhaps Chief Diabate's personal weapon—
ght up a truck cab. The vehicle went out of control and rolled
deways. Upholstery and the driver's garments were afire even
efore ammunition and fuel caught.

Mostly the ambush was work for the crew-served weapons. For
ıe Sincanmo gunners, it was practice with live pop-up targets. Dozens
f automatic cannon punched tracers into and through soft-skinned
ehicles, leaving flames and torn flesh behind them. Mortars fired,
ıixing high explosive and incendiary bombs. Truck-mounted
sers cycled with low-frequency growls, igniting paint, tires, and
loth before sliding across the rock to new targets.

A pair of perfectly aimed bombardment rockets landed within
ıe Notch itself, causing fires and secondary explosions among the
ıil end of the line of would-be escapees. The smooth, inclined
ırface of the Escarpment provided no concealment, no hope.
Iashemites stood or ran, but they died in either case.

Des Grieux smiled like a sickle blade and pulled the hatch
osed above him. He continued to watch through the vision blocks
f the cupola.

Truckloads of Sincanmo troops drove up out of their conceal-
ıent, heading for the loot and the writhing wounded scattered
elplessly on the slope.

Have fun while you can, wogs, Des Grieux thought. *Because you
on't see the morning either.*

Thirty-seven minutes after Chief Diabate sprang his ambush,
ncanmo troops in the Notch began firing southward. The shooters
ere the bands who'd penetrated farthest in their quest for loot and
ıroats to cut. Other bright-robed irregulars were picking over the

bodies and vehicles scattered along the slope. When the gun sounded, they looked up and began to jabber among themselves i search of a consensus.

Des Grieux watched through his vision blocks and waited H271's fighting compartment was warm and muggy with the environmental system shut down, but a cold sweat of anticipatio beaded the tanker's upper lip.

Half—apparently the junior half—of each Sincanmo battle grou waited under camouflage film in the gullies to provide a base of fir for the looters. The Sincanmos were not so much undisciplined a self-willed, and they had a great deal of experience in hit-and-ru guerrilla warfare.

The appearance of a well-prepared defense was deceptive, thougl The heavy weapons that were effective at a two-kilometer range ha expended much of their ammunition in the first engagement; an besides, the irregulars were about to find themselves out of the depth.

They were facing the first of the retreating Thunderbo Division troops. The Thunderbolts weren't much; but they wei professionals, and this lot had Luke Broglie with them. . . .

At first the Sincanmos in the Notch fired small arms at thei unseen targets; automatic rifles pecked the night with short burst Then somebody got an abandoned Hashemite railgun working. Th Notch lighted in quick pulses, the corona discharge from th weapon's generator. The *crack crack crack* of hyper-velocity slug echoed viciously.

A blue-white dazzle outlined the rock surfaces of the Notch. Legion tank destroyer kilometers away had put a 15cm bolt into th center of the captured outpost. Two seconds later the sound reache Des Grieux's ears, the glass-breaking *crash* as rock shattered unde unendurable heat stresses.

Three Sincanmo survivors scampered down the Escarpmen One man's robe smoldered and left a fine trail of smoke behind hin The men were on foot, because their trucks fed the orange-re flames lighting the Notch behind them.

The Sincanmo irregulars had gotten their first lesson. A sire n Chief Diabate's 8x8 armored car, halfway up the slope, wound owly from a groan to a wail. Exhaust blatted through open pipes as he indigs leaped aboard their vehicles and started the engines.

The first salvo howled from the Thunderbolt Division's nakeshift redoubt to the southeast. The shells burst with bright orange ashes in the empty plains, causing no casualties. The Sincanmos were ther in the gullies well north of the impact area or still on the slope, here the height of the Knifeblade Escarpment provided a wall against nells on simple ballistic trajectories.

Indig vehicles grunted downslope as members of their crews nrew themselves aboard. Another four-tube salvo of high explo- ves truck near where the previous rounds had landed. One shell mply dug itself into the hard soil without going off. Casing frag- nents rang against the side of a truck, but none of the vehicles owed or swerved.

The camouflage film fluttered as indigs in the gullies packed neir belongings. The trucks were both cargo haulers and weapons latforms for the battlegroups. When the Sincanmos expected action, ney cached non-essentials—food, water, tents, and bedding—beside ne vehicles, then tossed them aboard again when it was time to ave.

Another round streaked across the Escarpment from the outhwest. The Sincanmos ignored the shell because it didn't come vithin a kilometer of the ground at any point in its trajectory.

Broglie's Legion had a single six-gun battery, very well equipped s to weapons (self-propelled 210mm rocket howitzers) and the election of shells those hogs launched. The battery's first response o the new threat was a reconnaissance round which provided eal-time images through a laser link to Battery Fire Control.

Had Des Grieux powered up H271, his tribarrel in Automatic ir Defense mode could have slapped the spy shell down as soon as sailed over the Escarpment. It was no part of the veteran's plan to ive the tank's presence away so soon, however.

At least thirty guns from the Thunderbolt Division opened fire ccording to target data passed them by the Legion's fire control. purts of black smoke with orange hearts leaped like poplars among the Sincanmo positions, shredding camouflage film that had no deceived the Legion's recce package.

A truck blew up. Men were screaming. Vehicles racing bac from the slope to load cached necessities skidded uncertainly a their crews wondered whether or not to drive into the shellburst ahead of them.

The Legion's howitzers ripped out a perfect Battery Three three shells per gun launched within a total of ten seconds. The were firecracker rounds. The casings popped high in the air, loosin approximately 7,500 bomblets to drift down on the Sincanm forces.

For the most part, the Sincanmo looters under Chief Diabat didn't know what hit them. A blanket of white fire fell over th vehicles which milled across the plain for fear of Thunderbolt shell Thousands of bomblets exploded with a ripping sound that seeme to go on forever.

For those in the broad impact zone, it *was* forever. Smoke an dust lifted over the soil when the explosive light ceased. A doze Sincanmo vehicles were ablaze; more crashed and ignited in th following seconds. Only a handful of trucks were under consciou control, though run-while-flat tires let many of the vehicles caree across the landscape with their crews flayed to the bone by glas filament shrapnel.

Fuel and munitions exploded as the Thunderbolt Divisio continued to pound the gully positions. A pair of heavy caliber shel landed near H271, but they were overs—no cause for concern. Th indigs dying all across the plain provided a perfect stalking horse fo the tank in ambush.

Chief Diabate's armored car—the only vehicle in the Sincanm force with real armor—had come through the barrage unscathe It wallowed toward the eastern flank of the butte with its sire summoning survivors from the gullies to follow it to safet Sincanmo 4x4s lurched through the remnants of the camouflag film, abandoning their cached supplies to the needs of the momen

Sparks and rock fragments sprang up before and beside th armored car. Diabate's driver swerved, but not far enough: a secon

ree-round burst punched through the car's thin armor. A yellow
ash lifted the turret, but the vehicle continued to roll on inertia
ntil a larger explosion blew the remainder of the car and crew into
ieces no larger than a man's hand.

Leading elements of the Thunderbolt Division had reached the
otch. One of them was a fire-support vehicle, a burst-capable 90mm
un on a half-tracked chassis. The gun continued to fire, switching
om solid shot to high explosive as it picked its targets among the
eeing Sincanmo trucks. Other mercenary vehicles, primarily
mored personnel carriers with additional troops riding on their
oofs, crawled through the Notch and descended the slope littered by
e bodies of indigs locked in the embrace of death.

It was getting to be time. Des Grieux closed his main power
vitch.

H271's screens came alive and bathed the fighting compartment
ith their light. Des Grieux lifted his commo helmet, ran his fingers
rough his close-cropped hair, and lowered the helmet again. He
ok the twin joysticks of the gunnery controls in his hands.

"Booster," Des Grieux said to the tank's artificial intelligence.
On Screen One, gimme vehicles on a four-kay by one strip aligned
ith the main gun."

The topographic map of the main battle area flicked out and
turned as a narrow holographic slice centered on the Notch. The
PCs and other vehicles already north of the Knifeblade Escarpment
ere sharp symbols that crawled down the holographic slope
ward—unbeknownst to themselves—H271 waiting at the bottom of
e display.

The symbols of vehicles on the other side of the sandstone wall
ere hollow, indicating the AI had to extrapolate from untrustworthy
ata. The electronics, pumps, and even ignition systems of
hunderbolt and Hashemite trucks had individual radio-frequency
ectrum signatures which H271's sensor suite could read. Precise
cation and assignment was impossible at a four-kilometer range
yond an intervening mass of sandstone, however.

One vehicle was marked with orange precision: the Legion tank
estroyer which had huffed itself to within five hundred meters of

the Notch. The tank destroyer's tribarrel licked skyward frequentl to keep shells from decimating the retreating forces. The lines cyan fire, transposed onto the terrain map in the tank's data bas provided H271 with a precise location for the oncoming vehicl The other two tank destroyers were at the very top of the displa where they acted as rear guard against the Slammers.

They would come in good time. As for the closest of the three- it would have been nice to take out the tank destroyer with the fir bolt, the round that unmasked H271, but that wasn't necessar Waiting for the Legion vehicle to rise into range would mea sparing some of the half-tracks that drove off the slope an disappeared into swales concealed from the tank.

Des Grieux didn't intend to spare anything that moved th night.

The gunnery screen shrank in scale as it incorporated bot orange pippers, the solid dot that marked the tribarrels target—th leading APC, covered by the flowing robes of a score of Hashemit riding on top of it—and the main gun's hollow circle, centered at th turret/hill junction on the fire-support vehicle which still, from i vantage point in the Notch, covered the retreat.

Des Grieux fired both weapons together.

It took a dozen rounds from the tribarrel before the carrier ble up. By then, the screaming Hashemite riders were torches floppin over the rocks.

The main gun's 20cm bolt vaporized several square meters the fire-support vehicle's armor. Ammunition the Thunderbol hadn't expended on Sincanmo targets were sufficient to blow passing APC against the far wall of the Notch; the crumpled wreckag then slid forward, down the slope, shedding parts and flames.

Nothing remained of the fire-support vehicle except its axl and wheels, stripped of their tires.

Des Grieux left his main gun pointed as it was. He worked th tribarrel up the line of easy targets against the slanted rock, givin each half-track the number of cyan bolts required to detonate i fuel, its on-board ammunition, or both. Secondary explosio leaped onto the slope like the footprints of a fire giant.

Nothing more came through the Notch after the 20cm bolt pped it, but Screen #1 showed the Legion tank destroyer accelerat-ıg at its best speed to reach a firing position.

Des Grieux's face was terrible in its joy.

So long as H271 was shut down and covered by broken rock, it ʾas virtually undetectable. When Des Grieux opened fire, anybody ut a blind man could call artillery in on the tank's position. A umber of Thunderbolt Division personnel survived long enough ɔ do just that.

Four HE shells landed between ten and fifty meters of H271 as ʾes Grieux walked 2cm bolts across an open-topped supply truck ʾith armored sides. His sight picture vanished for a moment in the ɔouting explosions. A fifth round struck in a scatter of gravel well p the side of the mesa. It brought down a minor rockslide, but no gnificant chunks landed near the tank.

Des Grieux ignored the artillery because he didn't have any hoice. He'd ignited all eight of the supply truck's low-side tires ʾith the initial burst. When the debris of the shellbursts cleared, ιe vehicle was toppling sideways. Its cargo compartment was full of ʾounded troops who screamed as they went over.

Twenty or thirty shells landed within a dozen seconds. A few of ιe Thunderbolt gun crews had switched to armor piercing, but one of those rounds scored a direct hit on the tank. A heavy shell urst on H271's rock-covered back deck. The shock made all the isplays quiver. The air of the fighting compartment filled with dust ιaken from every minute crevice.

Screen #1 showed the Legion tank destroyer's orange symbol ntering the Notch from the south side. The heavy vehicle had ɔllided with several Thunderbolt Division APCs in its haste to ʾach a position from which it could fire at the Slammers' tank.

Des Grieux slapped the plate that set his tribarrel on Automatic ir Defense. He said in a sharp, clear voice, "Booster, sort incoming ʾom the southeast first," as his foot poised on the firing pedal for ιe main gun.

The 20cm weapon was already aligned. The eighty-times ιagnified tube of the tank destroyer's gun slid into the hollow

circle on Screen #2. More shells burst near H271, but not very nea
and the tribarrel was already snarling skyward at the anti-tan
rounds which the Legion battery hurled.

The tank destroyer's glacis plate filled Des Grieux's display. H
rocked forward on the foot-trip. The saturated blue streak punche
through the mantle of the 15cm weapon before the Legion gunne
could find his target.

The tank destroyer's ready magazine painted the Notch cya
Then the reserve ammunition storage went off and lifted the vehicle
armored carapace a meter in the air before dropping it back to th
ground.

The iridium shell glowed white. Nothing else remained of th
tank destroyer or its crew.

Des Grieux laughed with mad glee. "Have to do better 'n tha
Broglie!" he shouted as he slid his aiming point down the slope. H
fired every time the hollow pipper covered an undamaged vehicle.

There were seventeen 20cm rounds remaining in H271's read
magazine. Each bolt turned a lightly armored truck or APC into
fireball that bulged steel plates like the skin of a balloon. The last tw
half-tracks Des Grieux hit had already been abandoned by thei
crews.

Artillery fire slackened, though Des Grieux's tribarrel snarle
uninterruptedly skyward. A delay-fused armor-piercing shell struc
short of H271 and punched five meters through the hard soil befor
going off. The explosion lifted the tank a hand's breadth despite th
mass of rock overburden, but the vehicle sustained no damage.

Screen #1 showed a killing zone south of the Escarpment, wher
fleeing troops bunched and the Slammers maneuvered to cut ther
apart. Because the powerguns were deadly at any range so long a
they had a sight line, every knob of ground Hammer's troops too
cut a further swath through far-distant enemy positions.

When the Legion and Thunderbolt artillery directed its fir
toward Des Grieux, the cupola guns of the tanks were freed to kil
The process of collapse accelerated as tanks and combat cars too
the howitzer batteries themselves under direct fire.

Des Grieux waited. H271's fighting compartment was a stink

ng furnace. Empties from the rapidly fired main gun loosed a gray
aze into the atmosphere faster than the air conditioning could
bsorb it. The tank chuckled mechanically as it replenished the ready
nagazine from storage compartments deep in its armored core.

Fuel fires lighted the slope all the way to the Notch. Hashemite,
incanmo, and Thunderbolt vehicles—all wrecked and burning.
lames wove a dance of victory over a landscape in which nothing
lse moved.

Hundreds of terrified soldiers were still alive in the wasteland.
he survivors remained motionless. Incoming artillery fire had
eased, giving Des Grieux back the use of his tribarrel. He used it
nd H271's night vision equipment to probe at whim wherever a
ead raised.

Des Grieux waited as he watched Broglie's two tank destroyers.
They were no longer the rear guard for the Central Sector
efugees. The tank destroyers moved up to the Notch at a deliberate
ace which never exposed them to the guns of the panzers south of
he Knifeblade Escarpment. Always a cunning bastard, Broglie. . . .

Ammunition in a supply truck near the bottom of the slope
ooked off. The blast raised a mushroom-shaped cloud as high as
he top of the Escarpment. Two kilometers away, H271 shook.

The battle was going to be over very soon. The Thunderbolt
)ivision's horrendous butcher's bill gave its commander a legitimate
xcuse for surrendering whether his Hashemite employers did so or
ot. The bodies heaped on both sides of the Notch would ransom
he lives of their fellows.

It occurred to Des Grieux that he could probably drive H271
way, now. Incoming shells had done a day's work for excavating
quipment in freeing the tank from his deliberate rockfall.

There wasn't anyplace else in the universe that Des Grieux
vanted to be.

Screen #1 showed the tank destroyers pausing just south of the
Notch. A 15cm bolt stabbed across the intervening kilometers and
aporized a portion of the mesa's rim. Sonic echoes of the plasma
lischarge rumbled across the plain below.

Des Grieux blinked, then understood. When the Slammers i
Task Force Kuykendall moved out, they'd abandoned the sens
pack they'd placed on the butte. H271 wasn't connected to the pac
but Broglie didn't know that.

And trust that clever bastard not to miss a point before he mad
his move!

Des Grieux chuckled through a throat burned dry by ozone an
the other poisons he breathed. His hands rested lightly on the tw
joysticks. The pippers were already locked together, solid in circl
where they needed to be.

The left-hand tank destroyer backed, then began to accelerat
toward the Notch at high speed. The other Legion vehicle move
forward also, but at a relative crawl.

The right-hand tank destroyer had made the one-shot kill o
the tiny sensor pack two kilometers away.

It happened the way Des Grieux knew it would happen. Th
tank destroyer rushing through the left side of the Notch braked s
abruptly that its skirts rubbed off a shower of sparks against th
smooth rock. The other tank destroyer, Broglie's own vehicl
continued to accelerate. It burst into clear sight while H271's gunne
was supposed to be concentrating on the target ten meters to th
side.

But it was Des Grieux below, and Des Grieux's pippers fille
with the mass of iridium that slid into the sight picture. His tribar
rel and main gun fired in unison at the massive target.

The interior of H271 turned cyan, then white, and finally re
with heat like a hammer. The shockwave was not a sound but a blo
that slammed Des Grieux down in his seat.

The cupola was gone. Warning lights glowed across De
Grieux's console. Screen #3 switched automatically to a damage
assessment schematic. The tribarrel had vaporized, but the mai
gun was undamaged and the turret rotated normally the few mil
required to bring the hollow pipper onto its remaining target.

Luke Broglie was very good. He'd fired a fraction of a secon
early, but he must have known that he wouldn't get the additiona
instant he needed to center his sight squarely on the tank turret.

He must have known that he was meeting Slick Des Grieux for the last time.

Broglie's vehicle was a white glow at the edge of the Notch. The other crew should have bailed out of their tank destroyer and waited for the Hashemite surrender, but they tried to finish the job at which their colonel had failed.

Three 15cm bolts cut the night, two shots before the tank destroyer *had* a sight picture and the last round thirty meters wide of H271. Des Grieux penetrated the tank destroyer's thick glacis plate with his first bolt, then sent a second round through the hole to vaporize the wreckage in a pyre of its own munitions.

They should have known it was impossible to do what Luke Broglie couldn't manage. Nobody was as good as Broglie . . . except Slick Des Grieux.

Des Grieux could see both north and south of the Knifeblade scarpment from where he sat on top of the burned-out tank destroyer. Smudgy fires still burned over the sloping plain where the slammers' artillery and sharp-shooting powerguns had slashed the Hashemite center into retreat, then chaos.

Clots of surrendered enemies waited to be interned. Thunderbolt Division personnel rested under tarpaulins attached to their vehicles and a stake or two driven into the soil. The defeated mercenaries were not exactly lounging: there were many wounded among them, and every survivor from the punished battalions knew at least one friend who hadn't been so lucky.

But they would be exchanged back to their own command within hours or days. A mercenary's war ended when the fighting stopped.

The Hashemite survivors were another matter. They huddled in separate groups. Many of their trucks had been disabled by the rain of anti-personnel bomblets which the armor of the mercenary half-tracks had shrugged off. The Hashemites' personal weapons were piled ostentatiously at a slight distance from each gathering.

That wasn't necessarily going to help. Sincanmo irregulars were doing the heavy work of interning prisoners: searching, sorting, and gathering them into coffles of two hundred or so to be transferred to holding camps. The Slammers overseeing the process wouldn permit the Sincanmos to shoot their indig prisoners here in publi

What happened when converted cargo vans filled with Hashemit were driven ten kays or so into the desert was anybody's guess.

A gun jeep whined its way up the south face of the Escarpmen Victorious troops and prisoners watched the vehicle's progress. Th jeep's driver regarded them only as obstacles, and the passeng seated on the other side of the pintle-mounted tribarrel paid the no attention at all.

Des Grieux rolled bits of ivory between the ball of his thum and his left hand. He turned his face toward the north, where H27 sat in the far distance with a combat car and a heavy-lift vehic from the Slammers' maintenance battalion in attendance.

Des Grieux wasn't interested in the attempts to dig out H27 but he was unwilling to watch the jeep. Funny about it being a jee He'd expected at least a combat car; and Joachim Steuben presen not some faceless driver who wasn't even one of the White Mice.

The slope looked much steeper going down than it had when De Grieux was on the plain two kilometers away. By contrast, the tilte strata on the south side of the Escarpment rose very gently, thoug they were as sure a barrier as the north edge that provided the nam Knifeblade. There wasn't any way down from the Escarpment, excep through the Notch.

And no way down at all, when Slick Des Grieux waited belo with a tank and the unshakeable determination to kill everyone wh faced him.

They'd rigged a bucket on the maintenance vehicle's shearleg A dozen Hashemite prisoners shoveled rock from H271's back dec into the bucket.

Des Grieux snorted. *He* could have broken the tank free i minutes. If he'd had to, if there were someplace he needed to be wit a tank. While there was fighting going on, nothing mattered excep a weapon; and the Regiment's panzers were the greatest weapon that had ever existed.

When the fighting was over, nothing mattered at all.

The sun had risen high enough to punish, and the tan

destroyer's armor was a massive heat sink, retaining some of the fury which had devoured the vehicle. Nothing remained within the iridium shell except the fusion bottle, which hadn't ruptured when the tank destroyer's ammunition gang-fired.

The jeep was getting close. The angry sound of its fans changed every time the light vehicle had to jump or circle a large piece of debris. H271's main gun had seen to it that vehicle parts covered much of the surface of the Notch.

The heavy-lift vehicle had arrived at dawn with several hundred Sincanmos and a platoon of F Company combat cars—not Kuykendall; Des Grieux didn't know where Kuykendall had gone. Des Grieux turned H271 over to the maintenance crew and, for want of anything better to do, wandered into the gully where the blocking force had waited.

A 4x4 with two bombardment rockets in their launching cage was still parked beside H271's initial location. The Sincanmo crew sprawled nearby, riddled by shrapnel too fine to be visible under normal lighting. One of them lay across a lute with a hemispherical sound chamber.

Des Grieux lifted the driver out of his seat and laid him on the ground with the blood-speckled side of his face down. The truck was operable. Des Grieux drove it up the steep slope to the Notch, shifting to compound low every time he had to skirt another burned-out vehicle or windrow of bodies.

Troopers in the combat cars watched the tanker, but they didn't interfere.

The gun jeep stopped. Its fans whirred at a deepening note as they lost power. Des Grieux heard boots hit the soil. He turned, but Colonel Hammer had already gripped a handrail to haul himself up onto the tank destroyer.

"Feeling proud of yourself, Des Grieux?" the colonel asked grimly.

Hammer wore a cap instead of a commo helmet. There was a line of Spray Seal across his forehead, just above the pepper-and-salt eyebrows, where a helmet would have cut him if it were struck hard. His eyes were bloodshot and very cold.

"Not particularly," Des Grieux said. He wasn't feeling anythin at all.

The driver was just a driver, a Charlie Company infantryman He'd unclipped his carbine from the dash and pointed it vaguely i Des Grieux's direction, but he wasn't one of Joachim Steuben's fiel police.

Des Grieux had left his grenade launcher behind in H271. H was unarmed.

"They're trying to find Colonel Broglie," Hammer said. "Th Legion command council is, and I am."

"Then you're in luck," Des Grieux said.

He opened his left hand. Bones had burned to lime in the glar of the tank destroyer's ammunition, but teeth were more refractory Des Grieux had found three of them when he sifted the ashe within the tank destroyer's hull through his fingers.

Hammer pursed his lips and stared at the tanker. "You're sure? he said. Then, "Yeah, you would be."

"Nobody else was that good, Colonel," Des Grieux said softly His eyes were focused somewhere out beyond the moons' orbits.

Hammer refused to look down into Des Grieux's palm after th first brief glance. "You're out of here, you know," he snapped. "Ou of the Slammers for good, and off-planet *fast* if you know what' good for you. I told Joachim I'd handle this my own way, but that' not the kind of instruction you can count on him obeying."

"Right," Des Grieux said without emotion. He closed his hand again and resumed rubbing the teeth against his palm. "I'll do that.

"I ought to let Joachim finish you, you know?" Hammer said There was an edge in his voice, but also wonder at the tanker's fla affect. "You're too dangerous to leave alive, but I guess I owe some thing to a twelve-year veteran."

"I won't be joining another outfit, Colonel," Des Grieux said; statement, not a plea for the mercy Hammer had already granted "Not much point in it now."

Alois Hammer touched his tongue to his lips in order to have time to process what he had just heard. "You know, Des Grieux?" he said mildly. "I really don't know why I don't have you shot."

Des Grieux looked directly at his commanding officer again. Because we're the same, Colonel," he said. "You and me. Because here's nothing but war for either of us."

Hammer's face went white, then flushed except for the pink plotch of Spray Seal on his forehead. "You're a bloody fool, Des Grieux," he rasped, "and a bloody *liar*. I wanted to end this—" he gestured at the blackened wreckage of vehicles staggering all the way to the bottom of the slope "—by a quiet capitulation, not a bloodbath. Not like this!"

"You've got your way, Colonel," Des Grieux said. "I've got mine. Had mine. But it's all the same in the end."

He smiled, but there was only the memory of emotion behind his straight, yellowed teeth. "You haven't learned that yet. Have fun. Because when it's over, there isn't anything left."

Colonel Hammer pressed the Spray Seal with the back of his left hand, not quite rubbing it. He slid from the iridium carapace of the tank destroyer. "Come on, Des Grieux," he said. "I'll see that you get aboard a ship alive. You'll have your pension and discharge bonus."

Des Grieux followed the shorter man. The tanker walked stiffly, as though he were an infant still learning gross motor skills.

At the jeep, Hammer turned and said savagely, "And Via! Will you please throw those curst teeth away?"

Des Grieux slipped the calcined fragments into his breast pocket. "I need them," he said. "To remind me that I was the best.

"Some day," he added, "you'll know just what I mean, Colonel."

His smile was terrible to behold.

COMBAT CARS IN THE DESERT

COMBAT CAMP IN THE DESERT

THE DAY OF GLORY

The locals had turned down the music from the sound truck while the bigwigs from the capital were talking to the crowd, but it was still playing. "I heard that song before," Trooper Lahti said, frowning. "But that was back on Icky Nose, two years ago. Three!"

"Right," said Platoon Sergeant Buntz, wishing he'd checked the fit of his dress uniform before he put it on for this bloody rally. He'd gained weight during the month he'd been on medical profile for tearing up his leg. "You hear it a lot at this kinda deal. *La Marseillaise*. It goes all the way back to Earth."

This time it was just brass instruments, but Buntz' memory could fill in, "*Arise, children of the fatherland! The day of glory has arrived. . . .*" Though some places they changed the words a bit.

"Look at the heroes you'll be joining!" boomed the amplified voice of the blonde woman gesturing from the waist-high platform. She stood with other folks in uniform or dress clothes on what Buntz guessed in peacetime was the judges' stand at the county fair. "When you come back in a few months after crushing the rebels, the cowards who stayed behind will look at you the way you look at our allies, Hammer's Slammers!"

Buntz sucked in his gut by reflex, but he knew it didn't matter. For this recruitment rally he and his driver wore tailored uniforms with the seams edged in dark blue, but the yokels saw only the tank behind them. *Herod*, H42, was a veteran of three deployments and

more firefights than Buntz could remember without checking th
Fourth Platoon log.

The combat showed on *Herod*'s surface. The steel skirts enclosin
her plenum chamber were not only scarred from brush-busting bu
patched in several places where projectiles or energy weapons ha
penetrated. A two-meter section had been replaced on Icononzo
the result of a fifty-kilo directional mine. Otherwise the steel wa
dull red except where the rust had worn off.

Herod's hull and turret had taken even a worse beating; th
iridium armor there turned all the colors of the spectrum whe
heated. A line of rainbow dimples along the rear compartmen
showed where a fléchette gun—also on Icononzo—had waste
ammo, but it was on Humboldt that a glancing 15-cm powergu
bolt had flared a banner across the bow slope.

If the gunner from Greenwood's Archers had hit *Herod* squarely
the tank would've been for the salvage yard and Lahti's family bac
on Leminkainan would've been told that she'd been cremated an
interred where she fell.

Actually Lahti'd have been in the salvage yard too, since ther
wouldn't be any way to separate what was left of the driver from th
hull. You didn't tell families all the details. They wouldn't understand anyway.

"Look at our allies, my fellow citizens!" the woman called. Sh
was a news-reader from the capital station, Buntz'd been told. Th
satellites were down now, broadcast as well as surveillance, but he
face'd be familiar from before the war even here in the boonies
"Hammer's Slammers, the finest troops in the galaxy! And look a
the mighty vehicle they've brought to drive the northern rebels t
surrender or their graves. Join them! Join them or forever hang you
head when a child asks you, 'Grampa, what did you do in the war?'"

"They're not *really* joining the Regiment, are they, Top?" Lahti
said, frowning again. The stocky woman'd progressed from being a
fair driver to being a bloody good soldier. Buntz planned to give her
a tank of her own the next time he had an opening. She worried too
much, though, and about the wrong things.

"Right now they're just tripwires," Buntz said. "Afterwards

sure, we'll probably take some of 'em, after we've run 'em through newbie school."

He paused, then added, "The Feds've hired the Holy Brotherhood. They're light dragoons mostly, but they've got tank destroyers with 9-cm main guns. I don't guess we'll mop them up without somebody buying the farm."

He wouldn't say it aloud, even with none of the locals close enough to hear him, but he had to agree with Lahti that Placidus farmers didn't look like the most hopeful material. Part of the trouble was that they were wearing their fanciest clothes today. The feathers, ribbons, and reflecting bangles that passed for high fashion here in Quinta County would've made the toughest troopers in the Slammers look like a bunch of dimwits. It didn't help that half of 'em were barefoot, either.

The county governor, the only local on the platform, took the wireless microphone. "Good friends and neighbors!" he said, and stopped to wheeze. He was a fat man with a weather-beaten face, and his suit was even tighter than Buntz' dress uniform.

"I know we in Quinta County don't need to be bribed to do our duty," he resumed, "but our generous government is offering a lavish prepayment of wages to those of you who join the ranks of the militia today. And there's free drinks in the refreshment tents for all those who kiss the book!"

He made a broad gesture. Nearly too broad: he almost went off the edge of the crowded platform onto his nose. His friends and neighbors laughed. One young fellow in a three-cornered hat called, "Why don't *you* join, Jeppe? You can stop a bullet and save the life of somebody who's not bloody useless!"

"What do they mean,'kiss the book'?" Lahti asked. Then, wistfully, she added, "I don't suppose we could get a drink ourself?"

"We're on duty, Lahti," Buntz said. "And I guess they kiss the book because they can't write their names, a lot of them. You see that in this sorta place."

"*March, march!*" the sound truck played. "*Let impure blood water our furrows!*"

It was hotter'n Hell's hinges, what with the white sun overhead and its reflection from the tank behind them. The iridium'ɔ burn'em if they touched it when they boarded to drive back to H Company's laager seventy klicks away. At least they didn't have tɔ spend the night in this Godforsaken place. . . .

Buntz could use a drink too. There were booths all around thɛ field. Besides them, boys circulated through the crowd with kegs oɴ their backs and metal tumblers chained to their waists. It'd bɛ rotgut, but he'd been in the Slammers thirteen years. He guesseɔ he'd drunk worse and likely *much* worse than what was on offer iɴ Quinta County.

But not a drop till him and Lahti stopped being a poster tɔ recruit cannon fodder for the government paying for the Regiment'ɔ time. Being dry was just part of the job.

The Placidan regular officer with the microphone was talkinɡ about honor and what pushovers the rebels were going to be. Buntɑ didn't doubt that last part: if the Fed troops were anything like whaɂ he'd seen of the Government side, they were a joke for sure.

But the Holy Brotherhood was another thing entirely. Vehiclɛ for vehicle they couldn't slug it out with the Slammers, but they werɛ division-sized and bloody well trained.

Besides, they were all mounted on air-cushion vehicles. Thɛ Slammers won more of their battles by mobility than by firepower, but this time their enemy would move even faster than they did.

"Suppose he's ever been shot at?" Lahti said, her lip curling aɂ the guy who spoke. She snorted. "Maybe by his girlfriend, hey? Though dolled up like he is, he prob'ly has boyfriends."

Buntz grinned. "Don't let it get to you, Lahti," he said. "Listening to blowhards's a lot better business than having the Brotherhood shoot at us. Which is what we'll be doing in a couple weeks or I miss my bet."

While the Placidan officer was spouting off, a couple men had edged to the side of the platform to talk to the blonde newsreader. The blonde snatched the microphone back and cried, "Look here, my fellow citizens! Follow your patriotic neighbors Andreas and Adolpho deCastro as they kiss the book and drink deep to their glorious future!"

The officer yelped and tried to grab the microphone; the newsreader blocked him neatly with her hip, slamming him back. Buntz grinned: this was the blonde's court, but he guessed she'd also do better in a firefight than the officer would. Though he might beat her in a beauty contest. . . .

The blonde jumped from the platform, then put an arm around the waist of each local to waltz through the crowd to the table set up under *Herod*'s bow slope. The deCastros looked like brothers or anyway first cousins, big rangy lunks with red hair and moustaches that flared into their sideburns.

The newsreader must've switched off the microphone because none of her chatter to one man, then the other, was being broadcast. The folks on the platform weren't going to use the mike to upstage her, that was all.

"Rise and shine, Trooper Lahti," Buntz muttered out of the side of his mouth as he straightened. The Placidan clerk behind the table rose to his feet and twiddled the book before him. It was thick and bound in red leather, but what was inside was more than Buntz knew. Maybe it was blank.

"Who'll be the first?" the blonde said to the fellow on her right. She'd cut the mike on again. "Adolpho, you'll do it, won't you? You'll be the first to kiss the book, I know it!"

The presumed Adolpho stared at her like a bunny paralyzed in the headlights. His mouth opened slackly. *Bloody hell!* Buntz thought. *All it'll take is for him to start drooling!*

Instead the other fellow, Andreas, lunged forward and grabbed the book in both hands. He lifted it and planted a kiss right in the middle of the pebble-grain leather. Lowering it he boomed, "There, Dolph, you pussy! There's one man in the deCastro family, and the whole county knows it ain't you!"

"Why you—" Adolpho said, cocking back a fist with his face a thundercloud, but the blonde had already lifted the book from Andreas. She held it out to Adolpho.

"Here you go, Dolph, you fine boy!" she said. "Andreas, turn and take the salute of Captain Buntz of Hammer's Slammers, a hero from beyond the stars greeting a Placidan patriot!"

"What's that?" Andreas said. He turned to look over his shoulde

Buntz'd seen more intelligence in the eyes of a poodle, but wasn't his business to worry about that. He and Lahti together thre the fellow sharp salutes. The Slammers didn't go in for salutin much—and to salute in the field was a court-martial offense since fingered officers for any waiting sniper—but a lot of times yo needed some ceremony when you're dealing with the locals. Thi was just one of those times.

"An honor to serve with you, Trooper deCastro!" said Laht That was laying it on pretty thick, but you really couldn't overdo i a dog-and-pony show for the locals.

"You're a woman!" Andreas said. "They said they was takin women too, but I didn't believe it."

"That's right,Trooper," Buntz said briskly before his drive replied. He trusted Lahti—she wouldn't be driving *Herod* if h didn't—but there was no point in risking what might come ou when she was hot and dry and pretty well pissed off generally.

"Now," he continued, "I see the paymaster—" another bore clerk, a little back from the recorder "—waiting with a stack of piaster for you. Hey, and *then* there's free drinks in the refreshment car jus like they said."

The "refreshment car" was a cattle truck with slatted steel side that weren't going to budge if a new recruit decided he wanted to b somewhere else. A lot of steers had come to that realization over th years and it hadn't done 'em a bit of good. Two husky attendant waited in the doorway with false smiles, and there were two mor inside dispensing drinks: grain alcohol with a dash of sweet syru and likely an opiate besides. The truck would hold them, but bunch of repentant yokels crying and shaking the slats wouldn help lure their neighbors into the same trap.

Buntz saluted the other deCastro. The poor lug tried to salut back, but his arm seemed to have an extra joint in it somewhere Buntz managed not to laugh and even nodded in false approval. I was all part of the job, like he'd told Lahti; but the Lord's truth wa that he'd be less uncomfortable in a firefight. These poor stupi bastards!

The newsreader had given the mike back to the county governor. It was funny to hear the crew from the capital go on about honor and patriotism while the local kept hitting the pay advance and free liquor. Buntz figured *he* knew his neighbors.

Though the blonde knew them too, or anyway she knew men. Instead of climbing back onto the platform, she was circulating through the crowd. As Buntz watched she corralled a tall, stooped fellow who looked pale—the locals were generally red-faced from exposure, though many women carried parasols for this event—and a stocky teenager who was already glassy-eyed. It wouldn't take much to drink in the truck to put him the rest of the way under.

The blonde led the sickly fellow by the hand and the young drunk by the shirt collar, but the drunk was really stumbling along quick as he could to grope her. She didn't seem to notice, though when she'd delivered him to the recorder, she raised the book to his lips with one hand and used the other to straighten her blouse under a jumper that shone like polished silver.

They were starting to move, now, just like sheep in the chute to the slaughter yard. Buntz kept saluting, smiling, and saying things like, "Have a drink on me, soldier," and, "Say, that's a lot of money they pay you fellows, isn't it?"

Which it was in a way, especially since the inflation war'd bring—war *always* brought—to the Placidan piaster hadn't hit yet except in the capital. There was three months pay in the stack.

By tomorrow, though, most of the recruits would've lost the whole wad to the trained dice of somebody else in the barracks. They'd have to send home for money then; that or starve, unless the Placidan government fed its soldiers better than most of these boondock worlds did. Out in the field they could loot, of course, but right now they'd be kept behind razor ribbon so they didn't run off when they sobered up.

The clerks were trying to move them through as quick as they could, but the recruits themselves wanted to talk: to the recorder, to the paymaster, and especially to Buntz and Lahti. "Bless you, buddy!" Buntz said brightly to the nine-fingered man who wanted to tell him about the best way to start tomatoes. "Look, you have a

drink for me in the refreshment car and I'll come back and catch
you up with a couple more as soon as I've done with these other
fellows."

Holding the man's hand firmly in his left, Buntz patted him on
the shoulders firmly enough to thrust him toward the clerk with the
waiting stack of piasters. The advance was all in small bills to make
it look like more. At the current exchange rate three months pay
would come to about seventeen Frisian thalers, but it wouldn't be
half that in another couple weeks.

A pudgy little fellow with sad eyes joined the line. A woman
followed him, shrieking, "Alberto, are you out of your mind,
Alberto! Look at me!" She was no taller than the man but easily
twice as broad.

The woman grabbed him by the arm with both hands. He kept
his face turned away, his mouth in a vague smile and his eyes full of
anguish. "Alberto!"

The county governor was still talking about liquor and money,
but all the capital delegation except an elderly, badly overweight
union leader had gotten down from the platform and were moving
through the crowd. The girlishly pretty army officer touched the
screaming woman's shoulder and murmured something Buntz
couldn't catch in the racket around him.

The woman glanced up with a black expression, her right hand
rising with the fingers clawed. When she saw the handsome face so
close to hers, though, she looked stunned and let the officer back her
away.

Alberto kissed the book and scooted past the recorder without
a look behind him. He almost went by the pay table, but the clerk
caught him by the elbow and thrust the wad of piasters into his
hand. He kept on going to the cattle truck: to Alberto, those steel
slats were a fortress, not a prison.

A fight broke out in the crowd, two big men roaring as they
flailed at each other. They were both blind drunk, and they didn't
know how to fight anyway. In the morning they'd wake up with
nothing worse than hangovers from the booze that was the reason
they were fighting to begin with.

"I could take 'em both together," Lahti muttered disdainfully. She fancied herself as an expert in some martial art or another.

"Right," said Buntz. "And you could drive *Herod* through a nursery, too, but they'd both be a stupid waste of time unless you had to. Leave the posing for the amateurs, right?"

Buntz doubted he *could* handle the drunks barehanded, but of course he wouldn't try. There was a knife in his boot and a pistol in his right cargo pocket; the Slammers had been told not to wear their sidearms openly to this rally. Inside the turret hatch was a submachine gun, and by throwing a single switch he had control of *Herod*'s tribarrel and 20-cm main gun.

He grinned. If he said that to the recruits passing through the line, they'd think he was joking.

The grin faded. Pretty soon they were going to be facing the Brotherhood, who wouldn't be joking any more than Buntz was. The poor dumb bastards.

The county governor had talked himself out. He was drinking from a demijohn, resting the heavy earthenware on the cocked arm that held it to his lips.

His eyes looked haunted when they momentarily met those of Buntz. Buntz guessed the governor knew pretty well what he was sending his neighbors into. He was doing it anyway, probably because bucking the capital would've cost him his job and maybe more than that.

Buntz looked away. He had things on his conscience too; things that didn't go away when he took another drink, just blurred a little. He wouldn't want to be in the county governor's head after the war, though, especially at about three in the morning.

"*Against tyrants we are all soldiers,*" caroled the tune in the background. "*If our young heroes fall, the fatherland will raise new ones!*"

The union leader was describing the way the army of the legitimate government would follow the Slammers to scour the continent north of the Spine clean of the patches of corruption and revolt now breeding there. Buntz didn't know what Colonel Hammer's strategy would be, but he didn't guess they'd be pushing

into the forested highlands to fight a more numerous enemy. The
Brotherhood'd hand 'em their heads if they tried.

On the broad plains here in the south, though. . . . Well, *Herod*'s
main gun was lethal for as far as her optics reached, and that could
be hundreds of kilometers if you picked your location.

The delegation from the capital kept trying, but not even the
blonde news-reader was making headway now. They'd trolled up
thirty or so recruits, maybe thirty-five. Not a bad haul.

"Haven't saluted so much since I joined," Lahti grumbled, a
backhanded way of describing their success. "Well, like you say,
Top, that's the job today."

The boy kissing the book was maybe seventeen standard years
old—or not quite that. Buntz hadn't been a lot older when he joined,
but he'd had three cousins in the Regiment and he'd known he
wasn't getting into more than he could handle. Maybe this kid was
the same—the Army of Placidus wasn't going to work him like
Hammer's Slammers—but Buntz doubted the boy was going to like
however long it was he wore a uniform.

The last person in line was a woman: mid-thirties, no taller than
Lahti, and with a burn scar on the back of her left wrist. The record-
ing clerk started to hand her the book, then recoiled when he took a
look at her. "Madame!" he said.

"Hey, Hurtado!" a man said gleefully. "Look what your missus
is doing!"

"Guess she don't get enough dick at home, is that it?" another
man called from a liquor booth, his voice slurred.

"The proclamation said you were enlisting women too, didn't
it?" the woman demanded. "Because of the emergency?"

"Sophia!" cried a man stumbling to his feet from a circle of dice
players. He was almost bald, and his long, drooping moustaches
were too black for the color to be natural. Then, with his voice rising,
"Sophia, what are you doing?"

"Well, maybe in the capital," the recorder said nervously. "I
don't think—"

Hurtado grabbed the woman's arm. She shook him off without
looking at him.

"What don't you think, my man?" said the newsreader, slipping through what'd become a circle of spectators. "You don't think you should obey the directives of the Emergency Committee in a time of war, is that what you think?"

The handsome officer was just behind her. He'd opened his mouth to speak, but he shut it again as he heard the blonde's tone.

"Well, no," the clerk said. The paymaster watched with a grin, obviously glad that somebody else was making the call on this one. "I just—"

He swallowed whatever else he might've said and thrust the book into the woman's hands. She raised it; Hurtado grabbed her arm again and said, "Sophia, don't make a spectacle of yourself!"

The newsreader said, "Sir, you have no—"

Sophia bent to kiss the red cover, then turned and backhanded Hurtado across the mouth. He yelped and jumped back. Still holding the book down at her side, she advanced and slapped him again with a full swing of her free hand.

Buntz glanced at Lahti, just making sure she didn't take it into her head to get involved. She was relaxed, clearly enjoying the spectacle and unworried about where it was going to go next.

The Placidan officer stepped between the man and woman, looking uncomfortable. He probably felt pretty much the same as the recorder about women in the army, and maybe if the blonde hadn't been here he'd have said so. As it was, though—

"That will be enough, Señor Hurtado," he said. "Every family must do its part to eradicate the cancer of rebellion, you know."

Buntz grinned. The fellow ought to be glad that the blonde'd interfered, because otherwise there was a pretty fair chance that Lahti would've made the same points. Lahti wasn't one for words when she could *show* just how effective a woman could be in a fight.

"We about done here, Top?" she said, following Sophia with her eyes as she picked up her advance pay.

"We'll give it another fifteen minutes," Buntz said. "But yeah, I figure we're done."

"*Arise, children of the fatherland . . .*" played the sound truck.

★ ★ ★ ★

"It's gonna be a hot one," Lahti said, looking up at the sky abov *Herod*. The tank waited as silent as a great gray boulder wher Lahti'd nestled it into a gully on the reverse slope of a hill. The weren't overlooked from any point on the surface of Placidus—par ticularly from the higher ground to the north which was in rebe hands. Everything but the fusion bottle was shut down, and thic iridium armor shielded that.

"It'll be hot for somebody," Buntz agreed. He sat on the turre hatch; Lahti was below him at the top of the bow slope. They coul talk in normal voices this way instead of using their commo helmet: Only the most sophisticated devices could've picked up the low power intercom channel, but he and Lahti didn't need it.

He and Lahti didn't need to talk at all. They just had to wai them and the crew of *Hole Card*, Tank H47, fifty meters to the nort in a parallel gully.

The plan wouldn't have worked against satellites, but th Holy Brotherhood had swept those out of the sky the day the landed at New Carthage on the north coast, the Federation capita The Brotherhood commanders must've figured that a mutual lack c strategic reconnaissance gave the advantage to their speed an numbers. . . . and maybe they were right, but there were ways an ways.

Buntz grinned. And trust Colonel Hammer to find them.

"Hey Top?" Lahti said. "How long do we wait? If the Brotherhoo doesn't bite, I mean."

"We switch on the radios at local noon," Buntz said. "Likel they'll recall us then, but I'm just here to take orders."

That was a gentle reminder to Lahti, not that she was out of lin asking. With *Herod* shut down, she had nothing to see but the sky– white rather than really blue—and the sides of the gully.

Buntz had a 270° sweep of landscape centered on the Governmen firebase thirty klicks to the west. His external pickup was pinne to a tree on the ridge between *Herod* and *Hole Card*, feeding th helmet displays of both tank commanders through fiber-optic cable:

There were sensors that could *maybe* spot the pickup, but i wouldn't be easy and even then they'd have to be searching in thi

rection. The Brotherhood wasn't likely to be doing that when they
ad the Government battalion and five Slammers combat cars to
old their attention on the rolling grasslands below.

The Placidan troops were in a rough circle of a dozen bunkers
onnected by trenches. In the center of the encampment were
our 15-cm conventional howitzers aiming toward the Spine
om sandbagged revetments. The trenches were shallow and didn't
ave overhead cover; ammunition trucks were parked beside the
uns without even the slight protection of a layer of sandbags.

According to the briefing materials, the firebase also had two
alliopes whose task was to destroy incoming shells and missiles.
hose the Placidan government bought had eight barrels each,
rranged in superimposed rows of four.

Buntz couldn't see the weapons on his display. That meant
ey'd been dug in to be safe from direct fire, the only decision the
lacidan commander'd made that he approved of. Two calliopes
eren't nearly enough to protect a battalion against the kind of
repower a Brotherhood commando had available, though.

The combat cars of 3d Platoon, G Company, were laagered
alf a klick south of the Government firebase. The plains had
nough contour that the units were out of direct sight of one
nother. That wouldn't necessarily prevent Placidans from pointing
eir slugthrowers up in the air and raining projectiles down on
e Slammers, but at least it kept them from deliberately shooting
their mercenary allies.

Buntz' pickup careted movement on the foothills of the Spine to
e north. "Helmet," he said, enabling the voice-activated controls.
Center three-five-oh degrees, up sixteen."

The magnified image showed the snouts of three air-cushion
ehicles easing to the edge of the evergreen shrubs on the ridge
early twenty kilometers north of the Government firebase. One
as a large armored personnel carrier; it could carry fifteen fully
rmed troops plus its driver and a gunner in the cupola forward.
he APC's tribarrel was identical to the weapons on the Slammers'
ombat cars, a Gatling gun which fired jets of copper plasma at a
te of 500 rounds per minute.

The other two vehicles were tank destroyers. They used th
same chassis as the APC, but each carried a single 9-cm hig
intensity powergun in a fixed axial mount—the only way so light
vehicle could handle the big gun's recoil. At moderate range—up t
five klicks or so—a 9-cm bolt could penetrate *Herod*'s turret, an
it'd be effective against a combat car at *any* distance.

"Saddle up, trooper," Buntz said softly to Lahti as he droppe
down into the fighting compartment. "Don't crank her till I tell yo
but we're not going to have to wait till noon after all. They're takin
the bait."

The combat cars didn't have a direct view of the foothills, b
like Buntz they'd raised a sensor pickup; theirs was on a pole ma
extended from Lieutenant Rennie's command car. A siren woun
from the laager; then a trooper shot off a pair of red flare cluster
Rennie was warning the Government battalion—which couldn't k
expected to keep a proper radio watch—but Buntz knew th.
Platoon G3's main task was to hold the Brotherhood's attentio
Flares were a good way to do that.

The Government artillerymen ran to their howitzers fro
open-sided tents where they'd been dozing or throwing dice. Sever
automatic weapons began to fire from the bunkers. One was on th
western side of the compound and had no better target than th
waving grass. The guns shooting northward were pointed in the rigl
direction, but the slugs would fall about fifteen kilometers short.

The Brotherhood tank destroyers fired, one and then the othe
An ammunition truck in the compound blew up in an orange flasl
The explosion dismounted the nearest howitzer and scattered th
sandbag revetments of the other three, not that they'd been muc
use anyway. A column of yellow-brown dirt lifted, mushroomed
hundred meters in the air, and rained grit and pebbles down ont
the whole firebase.

The second 9-cm bolt lashed the crest of the rise which sheltere
the combat cars. Grass caught fire and glass fused from silica in th
soil sprayed in all directions. Buntz nodded approval. Th
Brotherhood gunner couldn't have expected to hit the cars, but h
was warning them to keep under cover.

Brotherhood APCs slid out of the shelter of the trees and onto
ne grasslands below. They moved in companies of four vehicles
nch, two east of the firebase and two more to the west. They
eren't advancing toward the Government position but instead
ere flanking it by more than five kilometers to either side.

The sound of the explosion reached *Herod*, dulled by distance.
little dirt shivered from the side of the swale. Twenty klicks is a
ell of a long way away, even for an ammo truck blowing up.

The tank destroyers fired again, saturated cyan flashes that
untz' display dimmed to save his eyes. Their target was out of his
resent magnified field of view, a mistake.

"Full field, Quadrant Four," Buntz said, and the lower left
rner of his visor showed the original 270° display. A bunker had
llapsed in a cloud of dust though without a noticeable secondary
plosion, and there was a new fire just north of the combat cars.
he cars' tribarrels wouldn't be effective against even the tank
stroyers' light armor at this range, but the enemy commander
asn't taking any chances. The Brotherhood was a good outfit, no
istake.

Eight more vehicles left the hills now that the advanced compa-
es had spread to screen them. Pairs of mortar carriers with pairs
APCs for security followed each flanking element. The range of
rotherhood automatic mortars was about ten klicks, depending on
hat shell they were firing. It wouldn't be any time before they were
position around the firebase.

Rennie's combat cars were moving southward, keeping under
ver. Running, if you wanted to call it that.

The Brotherhood APCs were amazingly fast, seventy kph
oss-country. They couldn't fight the combat cars head-on, but they
ouldn't try to. They obviously intended to surround the Slammers
atoon and disgorge their infantry in three-man buzzbomb teams.
nce the infantry got into position, and with the tank destroyers on
verwatch to limit the cars' movement, the Brotherhood could force
eutenant Rennie to surrender without a shot.

One of the Government howitzers fired. The guns could reach
e Brotherhood vehicles in the hills, but this round landed well

short. A red flash and a spurt of sooty black smoke indicated that th
bursting charge was TNT.

The gunners didn't get a chance to refine their aim. A 9-cm bc
struck the gun tube squarely at the trunnions, throwing the fro
half a dozen meters. The white blaze of burning steel ignite
hydraulic fluid in the compensator, the rubber tires, and the ha
and uniforms of the crew. A moment later propellant charg
stacked behind the gun went off in something between an explosic
and a very fierce fire.

Two howitzers were more or less undamaged, but their crev
had abandoned them. Another bunker collapsed—a third. Bun
hadn't noticed the second being hit, but a pall of dust was st
settling over it. Government soldiers started to leave the remainir
bunkers and huddle in the connecting trenches.

Flashes and spurts of white smoke at four points around th
firebase indicated that the mortars had opened fire simultaneousl
They were so far away that the bombardment seemed to be happer
ing in silence. That wasn't what Buntz was used to, which made hi
feel funny. Different generally meant bad to a soldier or anybo
else in a risky business.

The tank destroyers fired again. One bolt blew in the back of
bunker; the other ignited a stand of brushwood ahead of the comb
cars. That Brotherhood gunner was trying to keep Rennie of
balance, taking his attention off the real threat: the APCs and the
infantry, which in a matter of minutes would have the cars su
rounded.

Buntz figured it was time. "Lahti, fire'em up," he said. F
switched on his radios, then unplugged the lead from his helmet ar
let the coil of glass fiber spring back to the take-up reel on th
sensor. The hollow *stoonk-k-k* of the mortars launching final
reached him, an unmistakable sound even when the breeze sighir
through the tree branches almost smothered it.

The hatch cover swivelled closed over Buntz as *Herod*'s eig
drive fans spun. Lahti kept the blades in fine pitch to build spe
rapidly, slicing the air but not driving it yet.

"Lamplight elements, move to start position," Buntz ordere

1at was being a bit formal since the Lamplight call sign covered
1ly *Herod* and *Hole Card*, but you learned to do things by rote in
•mbat. A firefight's no place for thinking. You operated by habit
1d reflex; if those failed, the other fellow killed you.

The fan note deepened. *Herod* vibrated fiercely, spewing a sheet
' grit from beneath her skirts. She didn't move forward; it takes
ne for thrust to balance a tank's 170 tonnes.

A calliope—only one—ripped the sky with a jet of 2-cm bolts.
1e burst lasted only for an eyeblink, but a mortar shell detonated
 its touch. The gun was concealed, but Buntz knew the crew was
ewing it to bear on a second of the incoming rounds before it
nded.

They didn't succeed: proximity fuses exploded the three
maining shells a meter in the air. Fragments sleeted across the
•mpound. Because mortars are low pressure, their shell casings can
• much thinner than those of conventional artillery; that leaves room
r larger bursting charges. The blasts flattened all the structures
at'd survived the ammo truck blowing up. One of the shredded
nts ignited a few moments later.

Herod's fans finally bit deeply enough to start the tank climbing
） the end of the gully. Buntz had a panoramic view on his main
reen. He'd already careted all the Brotherhood vehicles either
hite—*Herod*'s targets—or orange, for *Hole Card*. That way both
nks wouldn't fire at the same vehicle and possibly allow another to
cape.

Buntz' smaller targeting display was locked on where the right-
1nd Brotherhood tank destroyer would appear when *Herod*
ached firing position. *Hole Card* would take the other tank
•stroyer, the only one visible to it because of a freakishly tall tree
owing from the grassland north of its position.

"*Top, I'm on!*" shouted Cabell in *Hole Card* on the unit
equency. As Cabell spoke, Buntz' orange pipper slid onto the
unded bow of a tank destroyer. The magnified image rocked as
e Brotherhood vehicle sent another plasma bolt into the
overnment encampment.

"Fire!" Buntz said, mashing the firing pedal with his boot.

Herod jolted backward from the recoil of the tiny thermonucle;
explosion; downrange, the tank destroyer vanished in a fireball.

Hole Card's target was gone also. Shrubbery was burning i
semicircles around the gutted wreckage, and a square meter of dec
plating twitched as it fell like a wounded goose. It could've com
from either Brotherhood vehicle, so complete was the destruction

There was a squeal as Cabell swung *Hole Card*'s turret to be;
on the plains below. Buntz twitched *Herod*'s main gun only a fe
mils to the left and triggered it again.

The APC in the foothills was probably the command vehic
overseeing the whole battle. The Brotherhood driver slammed int
reverse when the tank destroyers exploded to either side of him, b
he didn't have enough time to reach cover before *Herod*'s 20-c;
bolt caught the APC squarely. Even from twenty kilometers awa
the slug of ionized copper was devastating. The fires lit by th
burning vehicles merged into a blaze of gathering intensity.

Now for the real work. "Lahti, haul us forward a couple meter
get us onto the forward slope!" Buntz ordered. The main gun cou
depress only five degrees, so any Brotherhood vehicles that reache
the base of the rise the tanks were on would otherwise be in a dea
zone.

They shouldn't get that close, of course, but the APCs were ve
fast. Buntz hadn't made platoon sergeant by gambling when l
didn't need to.

The Brotherhood troops on the plains didn't realize—most
them, at least—that their support elements had been destroyed. Th
mortar crews had launched single rounds initially to test th
Placidan defenses. When those proved hopelessly meager, th
mortarmen followed up with a Battery Six, six rounds from eac
tube as quickly as the automatic loaders could cycle.

The calliope didn't make even a token effort to meet th
incoming catastrophe; the early blasts must've knocked it out. Th
twenty-four shells were launched on slightly different trajectories s
that all reached the target within a fraction of the same instan
Their explosions covered the interior of the compound as sudden
and completely as flame flashes across a pool of gasoline.

The lead APC in the western flanking element glared cyan; then
e bow plate and engine compartment tilted inward into the gap
porized by *Hole Card*'s main gun. As Lahti shifted *Herod*, Buntz
ttled his pipper on the nearest target of the eastern element, locked
e stabilizer, and rolled his foot forward on the firing pedal.

Recoil made *Herod* stagger as though she'd hit a boulder. The
rret was filling with a gray haze as the breech opened for fresh
unds. The bore purging system didn't get *quite* all of the break-
wn products of the matrix which held copper atoms in alignment.
lters kept the gases out of Buntz' lungs, but his eyes watered and
e skin on the back of his hands prickled.

He was used to it. He wouldn't have felt comfortable if it *hadn't*
ppened.

The lead company of the commando's eastern element was in
ne abreast, aligning the four APCs—three and a dissipating fireball
w—almost perfectly with *Herod*'s main gun. Buntz raised his
pper slightly, fired; raised it again as he slewed left to compensate
r the APCs' forward movement, fired; raised it again—

The driver of the final vehicle was going too fast to halt by
versing the drive fans to suck the APC to the ground; he'd have
nwheeled if he'd tried it. Instead he cocked his nacelles forward,
ping that he'd fall out of his predicted course. The APC's tribarrel
s firing in *Herod*'s general direction, though even if the cyan
eam had been carefully aimed the range was too great for 2-cm
lts to damage a tank.

As Buntz' pipper steadied, the sidepanels of the APC's passen-
r compartment flopped down and the infantry tried to abandon
e doomed vehicle. Buntz barely noticed the jolt of his main gun as
lashed out. Buzzbombs and grenades exploded in red speckles on
s plasma bolt's overwhelming glare. The back of the APC tumbled
rough the fiery remains of the vehicle's front half.

Half a dozen tribarrels were shooting at the tanks as the surviving
PCs dodged for cover. The same rolling terrain that'd protected
atoon G3 from the tank destroyers sheltered the Brotherhood
hicles also. Buntz threw a quick shot at an APC. *Too* quick: his
lt lifted a divot the size of a fuel drum from the face of a hillock

as his target slid behind it. Grass and topsoil burned a smok
orange.

The only Brotherhood vehicles still in sight were a mortar va
and the APC that'd provided its security. They'd both been assigne
to *Hole Card* originally, but seeings as all of *Herod*'s targets wei
either hidden or blazing wreckage—

Cabell got on the mortar first, so as its unfired shells erupted i
a fiery yellow mushroom Buntz put a bolt into the bow of the APC
The sidepanels were open and the tribarrel wasn't firing. Like as ne
the gunner and driver had joined the infantry in the relative safe
of the high grass.

The mortars hadn't fired on Rennie's platoon, knowing that th
combat cars would simply put their tribarrels in air-defense moc
and sweep the bombs from the sky. The only time mortar shel
might be useful would be if they distracted the cars from line-o
sight targets.

The Brotherhood commando had been well and truly hammere
but what remained was as dangerous as a wounded leopard. On
option was for Rennie to claim a victory and withdraw in compar
with the tanks. In the short term that made better economic sens
than sending armored vehicles against trained, well-equippe
infantry in heavy cover. In the longer term, though, that gave th
Slammers the reputation of a unit that was afraid to go for the thro
. . . which meant it wasn't an option at all.

"*Myrtle Six to Lamplight Six,*" said Lieutenant Rennie over th
command push. "*My cars are about to sweep the zone, west side firs
Don't you panzers get hasty for targets, all right? Over.*"

"Lamplight to Myrtle," Buntz replied. "Sir, hold your scree
and let me flush'em toward you while my Four-seven element keep
overwatch. You've got deployed infantry in your way, but if we ca
deal with their air defense—right?"

Finishing the commando wouldn't be safe either way, but it wa
better for a lone tank. Facing infantry in the high grass the comb
cars risked shooting one another up, whereas *Herod* had a reasonab
chance of bulling in and out without taking more than her armo
could absorb.

Smoke rose from a dozen grassfires on the plain, and the blaze
in the hills to the north was growing into what'd be considered a
disaster on a world at peace. A tiny part of Buntz' mind noted that
he hadn't been on a world at peace in the thirteen standard years
since he joined the Slammers, and he might never be on one again
until he retired. Or died.

He'd been raised to believe in the Way. Enough of the training
remained that he wasn't sure there was peace even in death for what
Sergeant Darren Lawrence Buntz had become. But that was for
another time, or probably no time at all.

While Buntz waited for Myrtle Six to reply, he echoed a real-time
feed from *Hole Card*'s on a section of his own main screen, then
pulled up a topographic map and overlaid it with the courses of all
the Brotherhood vehicles. On that he drew a course plot with a
sweep of his index finger.

"*Lamplight, this is Myrtle,*" Lieutenant Rennie said at last. The
five cars had formed into a loose wedge, poised to sweep north
through the Brotherhood anti-armor teams and the remaining
APCs. "*All right, Buntz, we'll be your anvil. Next time, though, we get
the fun part. Myrtle Six out.*"

"Four-seven, this is Four-two," Buntz said, using the channel
dedicated to Lamplight; that was the best way to inform without
repetition not only Sergeant Cabell but also the drivers of the two
tanks. "Four-two will proceed on the attached course."

He transmitted the plot he'd drawn while waiting for Rennie to
make up his mind. It was rough, but that was all Lahti needed—
he'd pick the detailed route by eyeball. As for Cabell, knowing the
course allowed him to anticipate where targets might appear.

"I'll nail them if they hold where they are, and you get 'em if
they try to run, Cabell," he said. "But you know, not too eager. Got
it over?"

"*Roger, Four-two,*" Cabell replied. "*Good hunting. Four-seven
out.*"

Lahti had already started *Herod* down the slope, using gravity to
accelerate; the fans did little more than lift the skirts off the ground.
Their speed quickly built up to forty kph.

Buntz frowned, doubtful about going so fast cross-country in tank. Lahti was managing it, though. *Herod* jounced over narrov rain-cut gullies and on hillock which the roots of shrubs ha cemented into masses a hand's breadth higher than the surroundin surface, but though Buntz jolted against his seat restraints th shocks weren't any worse than those of the main gun firing.

The fighting compartment displays gave Buntz a panoram view at any magnification he wanted. Despite that, he had an urg to roll the hatch back and ride with his head out. Like most of th other Slammers recruits, whatever planet they came from, he'd bee a country boy. It didn't feel right to shut himself up in a box whe he was heading for a fight.

It was what common sense as well as standing orders require though. Buntz did what he knew he should instead of what his hea wanted to do. When he'd been ten years younger, though, he regularly ridden into battle with his torso out of the hatch and h hands on the spade grips of the tribarrel instead of slewing an firing it with the joystick behind armor.

"*Boomer Three-niner-one, this is Myrtle Six,*" Lieutenant Renn said, using the operation's command channel to call the supportin battery. "*Request targeting round at point Alpha Tango one-thre five-eight. Over.*"

Herod tore through a belt of heavy brush in the dip between tw gradual rises. Ground water collected here, and there might be running stream during the wet season. The tank's skirts sheare gnarled stems, and bits that got into the fan nacelles were spraye out again as chips.

Hole Card fired. Buntz had been concentrating on the panoram screen, poised to react if the tank's AI careted movement. Now h glanced at his echo of Cabell's targeting display. The bolt missed, b a Brotherhood APC fluffed its fans to escape the fire spreading fror the scar which plasma'd licked through thirty meters of grass.

Cabell fired again. Maybe he'd even planned it this way, spendin the first round to startle his target into the path of the second. Th APC flew apart. There was no secondary explosion because th infantry had already dismounted, taking their munitions with them

A shell from the supporting rocket artillery screamed out of the southern sky. While the round was still a thousand meters in the air, a tribarrel fired from near the predicted point of impact. Plasma ruptured the shell, sending a spray of blue smoke through the air. It'd been a marking round, harmless unless you happened to be exactly where it hit.

Herod had just reached the top of another rise. The APC that'd destroyed the shell was behind a knoll seven kilometers away, but Buntz fired, Cabell fired, and two combat cars on the east end of Lennie's wedge thought they had a target also.

None of them hit the target, but Buntz got a momentary view of a Brotherhood soldier hopping into sight and vanishing again. He'd leaped from his cupola, well aware that it was only a matter of time—a matter of a short time—before the Slammers' concentrated fire hit the vehicle that'd been spared by such a narrow margin.

Lahti boosted her fans into the overload region to lift *Herod* another centimeter off the ground without letting their speed drop. The side-slopes were harsh going: the topsoil had weathered away, leaving rock exposed. Rain and wind deposited the silt at the bottom of the swales, so the Brotherhood troops waiting on the other side of the hill would expect *Herod* to come at them low.

Buntz'd angled his main gun to their left front, fully depressed. The cupola tribarrel was aimed up the hill *Herod* was circling. He saw the infantry on the crest rise with their buzzbombs shouldered. Before his thumb could squeeze the tribarrel's firing tit, his displays flickered and the hair on the back of his neck rose. The top of the hill erupted, struck squarely by a bolt from *Hole Card*'s main gun. Cabell's angle had given him an instant's advantage.

Twenty-odd kilometers of atmosphere had spread the plasma charge, but it was still effective against the infantry. There'd been at least six Brotherhood soldiers, but when the rainbow dazzle cleared, a single figure remained to stumble downhill. Its arms were raised and its hair and uniform were burning. The fireball of organic matter in the huge divot which the bolt blasted from the hilltop did most of the damage, but the troops' own grenades and buzzbombs had gone off also.

Cabell'd taken a chance when he aimed so close to *Herod* at lor range, but a battle's a risky place to be. Buntz wasn't complaining.

Herod rounded the knob, going too fast to hold its line when th outside of the curve was on a downslope. The tank, more massiv than big but big as well, skidded and jounced outward on the tur The four Brotherhood APCs sheltered on the reverse slope fire before *Herod* came into sight, willing to burn out their tribarrels fc the chance of getting off the first shot. The gunners knew that if the didn't cripple the blower tank instantly they were dead.

They were probably dead even if they did cripple the tank. The were well-trained professionals sacrificing themselves to give the fellows a chance to escape.

Two-cm bolts rang on *Herod*'s bow slope in a brilliant displa that blurred several of the tank's external pickups with a film c redeposited iridium. The Brotherhood commander hadn't had tim to form a defensive position; his vehicles were bunched to escape th tank snipers far to the west, not to meet one of those tanks at knif range. Three vehicles were at the bottom of the swale in a roug line-ahead; the last was higher on the slope.

Buntz fired his main gun when the pipper swung on—o *anything*, on any part of the APCs. His bolt hit the middle vehicle c the line; it swelled into a fiery bubble. The shockwave shoved th other vehicles away.

The high APC continued to hose *Herod* with plasma bolt hammering the hull and blasting three fat holes in the skirts.Tha tribarrel was the only one to hit the tank, probably because it gunner was aiming to avoid friendly vehicles.

Herod's main gun cycled, purging and cooling the bore witl a jet of liquid nitrogen. Buntz held his foot down on the trip screaming with frustration because his gun didn't fire, couldn' fire. He understood the delay, but it was maddening nonetheless

The upper half of the APC vanished in a roaring coruscation the explosion of *Herod*'s target had pushed it high enough that *Hol Card* could nail it. Cabell wouldn't have to pay for his drinks th next night he and Buntz were in a bar together.

Two blocks of *Herod*'s Automatic Defense Array went of

multaneously, making the hull chime like a gong. Each block lasted out hundreds of tungsten barrels the size of a finger joint. They ripped through long grass and Brotherhood infantry, several of them already firing powerguns.

A soldier stepped around the bow of an APC, his buzzbomb raised to launch. A third block detonated, shredding him from neck to knees. Pellets punched ragged holes through the light armor of the vehicle behind him.

Herod's main gun fired—*finally*, Buntz' imagination told him, but he knew the loading cycle was complete in less than two seconds. The rearmost APC collapsed in on itself like a thin wax model in a bonfire. The bow fragment tilted toward the rainbow inferno where the middle of the vehicle had been, its tribarrel momentarily spurting a cyan track skyward.

Lahti'd been fighting to hold *Herod* on a curving course. Now she deliberately straightened the rearmost pair of fan nacelles, knowing that without their counteracting side-thrust momentum would swing the stern out. The gunner in the surviving APC slammed three bolts into *Herod*'s turret at point-blank range; then the mass of the tank's starboard quarter swatted the light vehicle, crushing it and flinging the remains sideways like a can kicked by an armored boot.

Herod grounded hard, air screaming through the holes in her plenum chamber. "Get us outa here, Lahti!" Buntz ordered. "Go! Go! Go!"

Lahti was already tilting her fan nacelles to compensate for the damage. She poured on the coal again. Because they were still several meters above the floor of the swale, she was able to use gravity briefly to accelerate by sliding *Herod* toward the smoother terrain.

Buntz spun his cupola at maximum rate, knowing that scores of Brotherhood infantry remained somewhere in the grass behind them. A shower of buzzbombs could easily disable a tank. If *Herod*'s luck was really bad, well . . . the only thing good about a fusion bottle rupturing was that the crew wouldn't know what hit them.

The driver of an APC was climbing out of his cab, about a
that remained of the vehicle. Buntz didn't fire; he didn't eve
think of firing.

It could of been me. It could be me tomorrow.

Lahti maneuvered left, then right, following contours that
go unremarked on a map but which were the difference betwee
concealed and visible—between life and death—on this rollir
terrain. When *Herod* was clear of the immediate knot of enem
soldiers, she slowed to give herself time to diagnose the damage t
the plenum chamber.

Buntz checked his own readouts. Half the upper bank of senso
on the starboard side were out, not critical now but definitely
matter for replacement before the next operation.

The point-blank burst into the side of the turret was mor
serious. The bolts hadn't penetrated, but another hit in any of th
cavities just might. Base maintenance would probably patch th
damage for now, but Buntz wouldn't be a bit surprised if the turr
was swapped out while the Regiment was in transit to the ne>
contract deployment.

But not critical, not right at the moment. . . .

As Buntz took stock, a shell screamed up from the south. H
hadn't heard Lieutenant Rennie call for another round, but it wasn
likely that a tank commander in the middle of a firefight would've

Six or eight Brotherhood APCs remained undamaged, but th
time their tribarrels didn't engage the incoming shell. It burst
hundred meters up, throwing out a flag of blue smoke. It wa
simply a reminder of the sleet of antipersonnel bomblets tha
could follow.

A mortar fired, its *choonk!* a startling sound to a veteran at th
point in a battle. *Have they gone off their nuts?* Buntz thought. He se
his tribarrel to air-defense mode just in case.

Lahti twitched *Herod*'s course so that *Herod* didn't smash a stan
of bushes with brilliant pink blooms. She liked flowers, Buntz recalle
Sparing the bushes didn't mean much in the long run, of course.

Buntz grinned. His mouth was dry and his lips were so dry the
were cracking. *In the long run, everybody's dead. Screw the long rur*

The mortar bomb burst high above the tube that'd launched it. was a white flare cluster.

"*All personnel of the Flaming Sword Commando, cease fire!*" an nfamiliar voice ordered on what was formally the Interunit hannel. Familiarly it was the Surrender Push. When a signal ame in over that frequency, a red light pulsed on the receiving set f every mercenary in range. "*This is Captain el-Khalid, ranking fficer. Slammers personnel, the Flaming Sword Commando of the [oly Brotherhood surrenders on the usual terms. We request xchange and repatriation at the end of the conflict. Over.*"

"*All Myrtle and Lamplight units!*" Lieutenant Rennie called, also sing the Interunit Channel. "*This is Myrtle Six. Cease fire, I repeat, ease fire. Captain el-Khalid, please direct your troops to proceed to igh ground to await registration. Myrtle Six out.*"

"*Top, can we pull into that firebase while they get things sorted ut?*" Lahti asked over the intercom. "*I'll bet we got enough time to atch those holes. I don't want to crawl all the way back leaking air nd scraping our skirts.*"

"Right, good thinking," Buntz said. "And if there's not time, ve'll make time. Nothing's going to happen that can't wait another alf hour."

Herod carried a roll of structural plastic sheeting. Cut and glued o the inside of the plenum chamber, it'd seal the holes till base naintenance welded permanent patches in place. Unless the 3rotherhood had shot away all the duffle on the back deck, of ourse, in which case they'd borrow sheeting from another of the ehicles. It wouldn't be the first time Buntz'd had to replace his ersonal kit, either.

They were within two klicks of the Government firebase. Even if hey'd been farther, a bulldozed surface was a lot better to work on.)ut here you were likely to find you'd set down on brambles or a nest f stinging insects when you crawled into the plenum chamber.

As Lahti drove sedately toward the firebase, Buntz opened his natch and stuck his head out. He felt dizzy for a moment. That was eaction, he supposed, not the change from chemical residues to pen air.

Sometimes the breeze drifted a hot reminder of the battle pa
Buntz' face. The main gun had cooled to rainbow-patterned gra
but heat waves still shimmered above the barrel.

Lahti was idling up the resupply route into the firebase, a
unsurfaced track that meandered along the low ground. It'd ha
become a morass when it rained, but that didn't matter any longe

There was no wire or berm, just the circle of bunkers. Half
them were now collapsed. The Government troops had been pla
ing at war; to the Brotherhood as to the Slammers, killing was
business.

Lahti halted them between two undamaged bunkers at th
south entrance. Truck wheels had rutted the soil here. There wa
flatter ground within the encampment, but she didn't want to crus
the bodies in the way.

Buntz'd probably have ordered his driver to stop even if she'
had different ideas. Sure, they were just bodies; he'd seen his shar
and more of them since he'd enlisted. But they could patch *Hero*
where they were, so that's what they'd do.

Lahti was clambering out her hatch. Buntz made sure that th
Automatic Defense Array was shut off, then climbed onto the bac
deck. He was carrying the first aid kit, not that he expected t
accomplish much with it.

It bothered him that he and Lahti both were out of *Herod* i
case something happened, but nothing was going to happer
Anyway, the tribarrel was still in air-defense mode. He bent to cu
the ties holding the roll of sheeting.

"Hey Top?" Lahti called. Buntz looked at her over his shoulde
She was pointing to the nearest bodies. The Government troop
must've been running from the bunkers when the first mortar shell
scythed them down.

"Yeah, what you got?" Buntz said.

"These guys," Lahti said. "Remember the recruiting rally? Thi
is them, right?"

Buntz looked more carefully. "Yeah, you're right," he said.

That pair must be the deCastro brothers, one face-up and th
other facedown. They'd both lost their legs at mid-thigh. Bunt

ouldn't recall the name of the guy just behind them, but he was the
enpecked little fellow who'd been dodging his wife. Well, he'd
lodged her for good. And the woman with all her clothes blown off;
ot a mark on her except she was dead. The whole Quinta County
raft must've been assigned here.

He grimaced. They'd been responsible for a major victory over
he rebels, according to one way of thinking.

Buntz shoved the roll of sheeting to the ground. "Can you
andle this yourself, Lahti?" he said. He gestured with the first aid
it."I can't do a lot,but I'd like to try."

The driver shrugged. "Sure, Top," she said. "If you want to."

Recorded music was playing from one of the bunkers. Buntz'
nemory supplied the words: "*Arise, children of the fatherland! The
day of glory has arrived. . . .*"

AFTERWORD: WHAT'S FOR SALE

Samuel Johnson apparently meant (and lived by) his statement, "No man but a blockhead ever wrote, except for money." It disturbed Boswell a great deal to admit that, and of course the opinion isn't really defensible unless you define "blockhead" as, "Anybody who isn't Samuel Johnson." (I've read a lot of Dr. Johnson's writings. It's quite possible that he would've agreed with that definition.)

What most people mean when they quote Johnson is a different thing, though: "Money alone is a sufficient reason to write."

That statement is very easy to support. After all, people dig ditches because they'll be paid for doing so. People drive buses because they'll be paid for doing so. Why on Earth shouldn't people write books just because they'll get money when they turn the books in?

The funny thing is, I've never written simply for the money. (I *have* dug ditches, driven buses, mucked out a cow yard, and done any number of more unpleasant and less remunerative things than writing.)

Let me make explicit the limitations of that statement: I mean only the words themselves. I'm not implying I feel any sort of moral repugnance toward the practice of writing to order, nor am I suggesting that I'm superior as a man or as a writer to people who've made other decisions.

Furthermore, I am absolutely a commercial writer. I want my work to be read by the widest possible audience, and I want to get paid for that work. (Usually I do get paid, but I don't agree wit Johnson: I've donated both fiction and nonfiction to causes which believe in.)

It wasn't until I'd written an essay explaining why I continue to write when nobody would buy my fiction that it occurred to m to ask the opposite question: Why had I refused commissions t write things which were well within my skill set? The answer to th first was that I wrote as therapy, keeping myself between the ditch mentally after my return from Viet Nam. That realization gave me point from which to attack the puzzle.

A fact of life in publishing is that the people hired to writ media tie-ins, series novels, and similar projects, all have som stature. The only complete beginners involved are fans so heavil steeped in a fictional milieu (for example, Star Trek or Darkover that their specialized knowledge gives them status.

My first experience of this came at a convention in 1978, jus after I'd sold my first two books (but before they'd come out). Jir Baen, who as SF editor of Ace Books had bought *Hammer Slammers*, began chatting to me about a great new project: he' gotten the rights to *Armageddon 2419 A.D.* by Philip Franci Nowlan and had hired Spider Robinson to update it. Jim had the bought a case of beer for a pair of very successful writers and take notes while they noodled about the direction further Buck Roger novels should go. All that he needed now was a writer to turn thos plot notes into books.

I pretended I didn't know that I was being offered the job. I wa (I asked Jim many years later, just to be sure), and I knew that at th time.

It wasn't even that I was offended by the material. I'd read th title novella which formed the first half of the book (it wasn't for few years that I found the second half, *The Airlords of Han*) an was impressed by the way Nowlan had built on his presumptior that war in the twenty-fifth century would be along the lines o World War I.

But I didn't feel like writing Buck Rogers novels. It was really that simple. (Incidentally, the pay would've been even less than th

2,500 Jim had given me for *Hammer's Slammers*, but at the time I
idn't know that or care.)

Two years later Susan Allison, who'd taken Jim's place at Ace
hen he moved to Tor, called. War books were hot in 1980 and the
ublisher of Ace Books had told all his divisions to start war series.
Iammer's Slammers had been a success, so Susan asked me to write
Military SF series. She offered me full control over plot, characters,
nd everything else, so long as it was a series and it was Military SF.

This was a very good offer. I wasn't being requested to do
nything I wasn't perfectly willing to do; I'd have gotten full credit
nd royalties, and Ace would pay something in the order of $7,500
er book.

I thought about it, then said I'd write one novel to kick the
eries off. Ace could have the characters and setting for other writ-
rs to use, but I wouldn't be involved in the series after that first
ook. (It eventually came out from Tor as *The Forlorn Hope*.)

When I turned Jim down, I was a full-time attorney with a
easonable salary. In 1980, I was a bus driver earning $4.05 an hour
luring the 20-30 hours a week I worked. (My year of driving a bus
arned me a total of $6,100, including a couple months of summer
ayoff when unemployment—based on my previous job as an
ttorney—paid me more than I would've made if working.) I
referred to drive a bus rather than to write commissioned books
vhich would take me no more than six months apiece.

Looked at from the outside, that would appear to be an insane
lecision. In a manner of speaking, it *was* insane: I was finally getting
ny head up from Viet Nam. I did many things for other people;
vriting was the only thing I did for myself. I was separating the two
vith an irrational rigor. I didn't want to be tied to a series then, even
 series of my own creation. I would write what I felt like writing at
he time, and only that.

Since 1980 I've found that the time I spend writing solo novels
:onsistently earns me more money than the time I spend doing
nything else. During those years I've created shared universes and
written stories for shared universes owned by both myself and my
friends. I wrote a novel in a game-based universe, and I've written

over a dozen plot outlines for other writers to turn into novels o
which we share credit.

I did all those things because they seemed like good ideas at th
time. Sometimes they still seemed like good ideas afterward, an
sometimes I've shaken my head and wondered and how I manage
to get into something so stupid. That's life, after all.

Which is the point. Even in 1978 writing wasn't just a job to m
it was my life. And it still is.

Dave Drak
david-drake.cor

7/22/15